CRIME LORD SERIES

BOOKS 1-3

MIA KNIGHT

COPYRIGHT

CONTENT WARNING

This is a dark, mafia romance novel with content that may be upsetting to some readers. Please proceed with caution.

For a full list of triggers, visit my website:

https://miaknight.com/crime-lord-series-content-warning

CONTENTS

ONCE A CRIME LORD

CRIME LORD'S CAPTIVE

DEDICATION

To my dogs who put up with my odd hours, emotional outbursts and love me anyway.

1

"Do you have to go?" Morgan asked her boyfriend.

Jonathan grinned as he wrapped his arms around her. "Gonna miss me?"

"Yes." She couldn't shake the ball of dread in her stomach.

"I have to travel for work," he said as he stroked her back. "I haven't gone anywhere since you moved in, but I can't put it off any longer. Three months is a long time."

"I know."

He brushed a kiss over her mouth. "I love that you want me here, but I have to go. If we moved to the West Coast, I wouldn't need to travel as much."

Morgan's stomach jittered. "I like it here in Maine."

"Then we'll stay here."

He leaned down and gave her a deep kiss. She clutched handfuls of his jacket to prolong the moment. She didn't realize how much she depended on him until he announced his trip. It was just her luck that her boyfriend was an IT consultant who had to travel for work.

He pulled back, eyes warm. "At least I know you'll be here waiting for me."

She gave him a weak smile. "Yes, I'll be here. Hurry back to me."

He shouldered a laptop bag and pulled up the handle of his small suitcase. He opened the door and paused to look back at her. "You're going to be okay, right?"

He doesn't need this, she thought, and felt guilty for making him worry about her. "Yes," she said and tried to sound confident.

He blew her a kiss before he walked out of the apartment. She stared at the closed door for a long minute before she forced herself to get a move on. She could survive a week on her own. She was alone for two years before Jonathan entered her life. Travel was a necessity for him, so she had to learn to deal with his long absences.

Morgan went through her morning routine as the world slowly began to light up outside her window. She styled her long honey blond hair into a French twist and smoothed a hand over her conservative black skirt and white blouse. She surveyed herself in the mirror and was satisfied with her image. She looked competent and boring and did everything in her power not to draw attention to herself.

Her phone chimed, signaling it was time to leave for work. She grabbed her bag and gave the tidy apartment a cursory glance as she walked out the door. She walked two blocks to the bus stop just in time to see it pull up to the curb. She claimed the seat she always did and scanned the faces on the bus out of habit.

She tried to shake off her unease as she entered the bank and was greeted by her co-workers. *Just another day*, she reassured herself. She put her things in the break room and began her daily routine of setting up her desk and counting her money.

It was an uneventful day, which reassured her that she was overreacting. She was restless and on edge, but a call from Jonathan on her lunch break made her feel better. She had become so attached to him since they started dating a year ago. His easygoing personality was a balm to her uptight one. He made her feel safe and secure. She couldn't wait for him to come home. Before Jonathan entered her life, she had been a nervous wreck. Now, she felt a little more like her old self.

She left the bank at the end of the day, walking briskly as the sun set. She reached the bus stop precisely on time and leaped up the steps with a nod to the driver. Her normal seat was already taken so she settled for an aisle seat and tried to calm her nerves, which were taut now that night had fallen. Jonathan would be back in six days. No big deal.

She hopped off the bus and approached her building, climbing two flights before she reached her apartment. She knew her neighbors by sight but none by name, and that's the way she liked it. She glanced both ways as she unlocked her door and swiftly entered. She knocked the main light switch with her elbow, set her keys and purse on the stand beside the door, and froze.

A man sat on a stool in her kitchen. As she took a step back and slammed into the door, her mouth opened to shout, but the man shook his head in warning. The small gesture made the scream die in her throat. She stared at the man in the black business suit with an awful sense of doom growing in the pit of her stomach. He had merciless black eyes and a scar through his left brow.

"Lyla, come away from the door," Blade said.

Lyla. She hadn't heard that name for three years. Panic grabbed her by the throat. Her past couldn't be sitting in the apartment she shared with Jonathan.

"It's a good thing your boyfriend is away. I had orders to kill him," Blade said calmly.

She took two unsteady steps forward. "Jonathan has nothing to do with this."

Blade cocked his head to the side. "You think not?"

"I've been gone three years," she rasped. She thought she was safe.

"Yet here I am." He withdrew a phone from his pocket. He swiped his finger over the screen and jerked his head at her. "Come, Lyla, say hi to Gavin."

Nausea churned in her stomach as she watched Blade dial. She was torn between running or snatching the phone to break it into pieces. She did neither. Instead, she watched helplessly with her heart slamming against her ribs. Even though she knew running would be pointless, she reached for the door handle.

Blade's eyes narrowed into slits. "Don't, Lyla."

The threat in his voice made her freeze. She was well acquainted with Blade, Gavin's personal bodyguard. Blade was unflinchingly loyal to Gavin and would carry out any task, legal or illegal.

"Blade, please," she whispered.

He gave her an unreadable look before he focused on the phone in his hand. "She's here. Come, Lyla, Gavin wants to talk to you."

Blade turned the phone toward her. Gavin Pyre looked back at her from the screen. He hadn't changed. He wore a deep V-neck shirt that showed off his defined chest. He was otherworldly handsome with shoulder-length black hair and stunning amber eyes. The boyish charm he used to fool everyone into believing he wasn't dangerous was alarmingly absent.

"Lyla."

Her name rolled off his tongue. The sound of that deep voice, the one that haunted her dreams, made her take a step back in self-defense.

"You're more beautiful than I remember," he said softly.

She shook her head wildly. "Please, don't."

"Why, Lyla?"

She shuddered and whispered, "What do you want?" Gavin wouldn't send Blade to track her to Maine after three years for a friendly chat.

"I want to know why you ran from me."

She didn't answer. She couldn't. Three years did nothing to lessen the impact of his presence. She didn't realize she was moving until she hit the kitchen counter.

Blade followed her with the phone. She turned her face to the side to avoid eye contact with Gavin.

"Come back to me, Lyla."

"No," she choked and glanced at the screen in time to witness Gavin's expression smooth into unyielding lines. Dread morphed into full-blown terror as she witnessed the change. She knew how ruthless he could be.

"You might find this interesting," Gavin said coolly as he disappeared off the screen.

Against her will, she eased forward to get a better look while her mind tried to process what she was seeing. A man sat bound to a chair. His face was so swollen and disfigured that she wouldn't have been able to guess his identity, but she recognized the bloody crucifix around his neck. She clutched the countertop for balance as her head swam.

"What have you done to my father?" she whispered.

"He's been stealing from me," Gavin said as he strolled back into her line of sight.

He pulled a gun out of his waistband and pressed it to her father's temple. Her father came alive, bucking at the ropes, eyes rolling madly. She felt her world tilt sideways as she listened to her father's stifled screams through the gag.

"Gavin, no!" she cried as she took the phone from Blade, who let it go easily enough. She held the phone between shaking hands as she tried to stop him from pulling the trigger with her thoughts.

Gavin raised one brow. "You care if he lives, Lyla?"

"I have money," she said and tried to keep the phone steady as her hands shook like crazy.

"You have half a million?"

The bottom dropped out of her stomach. "Half a million?" Her father was a fool. She didn't have more than five thousand in her bank account, and that was because Jonathan didn't let her pay rent. Maybe she could get a loan—

"Your father knows the consequences of stealing from us," Gavin said.

Everyone knew not to fuck with the Pyres. The Pyre men weren't known for being merciful. They were hard, cruel, and calculating.

"What are you willing to do for him?" Gavin asked.

She broke out in a cold sweat. He knew what she would say.

"I'll do anything," she whispered.

"Blade will bring you to me."

"Gavin, I can't—"

"You want your father to live?"

She couldn't speak, so she nodded.

He lowered the gun and walked toward whoever held his phone. His face filled the screen. Her breath seized. The force of his personality reached through the phone and grabbed her by the throat.

"Didn't you miss me even a little bit, Lyla?"

She wanted to hurl the phone. His voice was soft and seductive, as if he wasn't blackmailing her and hadn't just held a gun to her father's head! As she silently glared at him, his expression darkened.

"Blade tells me your boyfriend is out of town. Count yourself lucky, or you would have come home to a bloody surprise." Before she could react, he continued, "Go with Blade. Don't give him any trouble. Come to me, Lyla, and I'll let your father live."

The screen went blank, and her legs gave out. She crumpled to the kitchen floor, hyperventilating.

"We don't have time for this," Blade said impatiently and hauled her up. "The jet is waiting."

"J-jet?" she wheezed, mind whirling.

"Pack what you need. You have ten minutes," Blade said curtly.

Her life just turned upside down, and he was giving her ten minutes? She ran to the bedroom and slammed the door. Three years, she'd been on the run. Three years, she planned every step only to end up caught. In a matter of minutes, Gavin crushed the normal life she'd built into tiny pieces. She wanted to believe that Gavin was lying about her father stealing half a million, but she knew better. Her father had a gambling problem, and Gavin didn't make idle threats. He would kill her father if she didn't go to him.

Blade pounded on the bedroom door. "Five minutes."

She wanted to curse, cry, and rage, but she didn't have the time for such a luxury. Blade was here to carry out Gavin's wishes, and he would do whatever it took to see it through. She snatched a handful of clothes off the hangers, and shoved them in a duffel before she grabbed a piece of notebook paper and began to write.

She didn't need a crystal ball to know that she would never see Jonathan again.

Jonathan,

I will never forget what you've done for me. You're an incredible man. I'm sorry for leaving like this. I hope you find a woman worthy of you.

Morgan

The pen shook in her hand. She stared at the name she'd scrawled. She had been Morgan for three years, but a new identity hadn't been enough to stay hidden. She hadn't told Jonathan she was on the run from Gavin Pyre. Morgan had a fictional background that didn't include a former relationship with the crime lord of Sin City.

"Open the door, or I'll break it down," Blade ordered.

She unlocked the door and barely avoided being hit when it slammed open and Blade charged in. He saw the note immediately. He read it, sneered, and tossed it on the bed.

"You're lucky I came instead of Gavin," he said.

Lyla said nothing as he grabbed her duffel.

"Anything else?" he asked.

She lifted her chin. "Is it true? Dad stole half a million?"

"Your dad's always been a dumb shit," he said and towed her toward the front door.

She dragged her feet to buy time, terrified to leave the safety of the apartment and the life she'd built for herself. "But half a million?"

"He's a greedy fuck."

She managed to wrench out of his hold and stood in the middle of the apartment, wringing her hands. "What does Gavin want with me?"

He surveyed her coldly. "What do you think?"

Her throat began to close. "He's going to kill me for running from him?"

"If he wanted you dead, I would have done it the moment you walked in."

That didn't reassure her. Maybe Gavin wanted to do the deed himself. "Why now? Why after all this time?"

"You'll have to ask him that." He opened the front door. "Let's go."

Her eyes brimmed with tears as she looked around the apartment that had become her short-lived haven. For three months, she allowed herself to believe in a happily ever after with a good man. What would Jonathan think when he discovered her note? The only way she could ensure her past didn't touch Jonathan was to leave without a trace. Jonathan was no match for Gavin Pyre.

She followed Blade out of the apartment and found a taxi waiting at the curb. Blade held the door open for her. She stopped, racking her brain for a way out of this, but ultimately, she had no choice but to get in. She and Blade sat side by side in silence. There was nothing to say to one another. Blade wouldn't reveal anything that would help her. She focused on keeping her roiling stomach under control.

The taxi dropped them off at a private airstrip where a sleek black and gold Pyre jet waited. Blade ushered her up the steps. A beaming flight attendant greeted them with warm cloths for their hands and champagne. She took the cloth before she collapsed into the nearest seat and closed her eyes. To be surrounded by such luxury would thrill most people, but she knew it was a gilded cage. A heavy pressure on her chest made it hard to draw in a normal breath. There were no other passengers on the jet aside from her and Blade. She tried to act as if she were sleeping, but knew she wasn't fooling him because she felt the impact of his stare.

She tried to wrap her mind around the fact she was heading back to Las Vegas and Gavin Pyre. Her body tingled with fear as she conjured up Gavin's face. Cold, beautiful, cruel. Once upon a time, she loved him with every fiber of her being. She would have done anything for him, and then he shattered her heart into pieces. Self-preservation made her run.

She turned her face toward the window to hide the tears. What did Gavin want from her? Why use her father to force her back to him? How would she pay off her father's debt? The thought filled her with mind-numbing terror.

LYLA WATCHED LAS VEGAS APPEAR, a city in the middle of the desert. She spotted several Pyre Casinos on The Strip, towers of gleaming black with a bold stripe of gold. Despite the fasten seat belt sign, Lyla lurched out of her seat and barely made it to the bathroom in time to vomit. The flight attendant handed her a miniature bottle of mouthwash, which she took gladly. Even after two ginger ales, her stomach rocked as if she were seasick. She hadn't been able to eat a thing.

Blade gave her an amused look, clearly enjoying her fear. He was in a better mood now that they were here. An unexpected storm in Chicago had delayed them. Blade had several terse conversations with Gavin, who was clearly displeased. She wished the delay had cost them days instead of hours, even though the suspense of not knowing what lay in wait consumed her. She hadn't been able to sleep and was now sick with exhaustion. She muttered prayers under her breath as the plane landed and taxied. When it came to a stop, she didn't loosen her death grip on the armrest. She held her breath as the jet door opened. She expected Gavin to barge in, but nothing happened. Blade impatiently unbuckled her seat belt, shuffled her forward, and ignored the flight attendant's appalled gaze. She was too tired to elbow him in the stomach for his rough handling.

She stumbled down the stairs and looked around, but Gavin was nowhere to be found. Her hands were clammy despite the warm wind that tugged hair out of her ruined French twist. Blade put her in the back seat of the private car waiting for them and sat up front with the driver. Because of the solid partition, she couldn't hear them, which put her on edge. Now what?

Las Vegas had changed little since she left. The stark desert landscape was a far cry from Maine's rocky coastline, lighthouses, forests, and lakes. They drove out of the city to a mansion surrounded by red mountains. This place was as familiar to her as her childhood home. Passing through an electronic gate into the inner courtyard, she eyed the armed guards patrolling the grounds. The car rounded the fountain in the drive and stopped.

Blade opened her door. She took his hand because she didn't want to fall on her face. Blessedly numb, she walked up the steps into the foyer and stopped. She took in the familiar white marble floors and open floor plan of Gavin's mansion. It was alarmingly quiet.

"He's at work," Blade said shortly. "You want something to eat?"

When she shook her head, he took her arm and led her upstairs.

"What about my father?" she asked.

"Gavin will talk to you about him."

"How do I know he's alive?"

"You don't," he said as he opened the door to a room and pushed her in. "I'm locking the door from the outside. If you need anything, use the phone on the nightstand."

Her tension rose to a screaming pitch as she surveyed the master bedroom. It hadn't changed since she'd picked out the sheets, drapes, and cream carpet. She and Gavin spent countless hours making love in this room.

"C-can I wait in another room?" *Anywhere* else.

"No."

He closed the door. She waited until his steps retreated down the hallway before she tried the door. Locked. She stared at the bed as if it would come to life and swallow her whole. The girl who once inhabited this house, this room, had been so naïve and trusting. She wasn't that girl, not any longer. She retreated to the window seat and looked out over the property.

Gavin's compound was ten minutes away from any sign of civilization. He was paranoid and liked his privacy. Even though she couldn't see it, she knew he had an Olympic size pool in the backyard and a monstrous garage that housed luxury cars. She knew a secret route to get out of the mansion in case of an attack, and the location of Gavin's safe house in New Mexico.

Tears slipped from her eyes. She was in Gavin's world again—a dangerous world swimming with violence, money, and sex. She wanted no part of it. Damn her father for putting her in this position.

She paced the room like a caged animal, taking in the walk-in closet, opulent bathroom, and familiar surroundings, which made her want to scream. She dug her nails into her arm, willing herself to wake from this nightmare. She had no idea how he interpreted her disappearance three years ago. She suspected he would make an effort to find her, but assumed he would have given up by now. Did he renew the search when he found out her father had embezzled money? Was she here to be punished?

Sick with worry and exhaustion, she settled on the window seat and wondered how long Gavin would make her wait. He knew the measures she had taken to remain hidden. She had a birth certificate, social security card, and driver's license declaring that her name was Morgan Lincoln. Her identification passed muster in five states. She traveled as far as possible from Nevada without leaving the country. She took low profile jobs and kept to herself until Jonathan. She didn't know how to protect herself from his friendliness and warmth. For a short time, she believed she could live a normal life. Now, she was back in hell, awaiting judgment. By now, Jonathan would know something was wrong. Would he come back early? Would he believe she left willingly? Who would leave a good man like him?

She stretched out on the window seat and dozed in the sunlight streaming through the window as a tear slipped from her eye.

2

Lyla lay against a warm chest. She looked up at Jonathan, who wore an unusually somber expression. They were in bed in their apartment. Sunlight poured through the window, but the apartment was curiously silent. She sat up and brushed a hand through his short-cropped hair. Something niggled at the back of her mind, but she pushed it away so she could focus on him.

"What's wrong?" she asked.

"Why didn't you tell me about him?" Jonathan asked.

She retracted her hand. She had no doubt who he was referring to. "How did you find out?"

"He called. He says he wants you back."

She tried to move off the bed, but Jonathan gathered her in his arms. She was surprised by his strength as he lay down and settled her beside him.

"Do you want to go back to him?" he asked gently.

"No!" she whispered, clutching fistfuls of his shirt. "Please don't make me."

"You want to stay with me?"

"Yes."

"Then we'll figure this out," he said.

She relaxed fractionally, willing herself to believe him. "We can?"

"I have connections," he said and brushed her hair back from her face. "I'll do anything for you."

Her heart swelled. Jonathan, her gentle knight. She was safe with him. Her hands went to his chest. She was so damn cold. Desperate to feel his hot skin against hers, she ripped the front of his shirt and heard buttons bounce across the floor.

"Lyla," he began, but she covered her mouth with his.

She had never been so hungry or desperate for touch and comfort. She tore off her clothes and plastered her naked chest to his. She moaned at the contact, even as he ripped her underwear. She felt the snap of fabric on her inner thighs and then cool air a moment before his fingers pressed into her. Even as his aggression made her hot, something about it struck her as odd, but she couldn't think past the inferno consuming them. She drank from his lips to wash away the taste of fear. His fingers burrowed into her channel, making her dizzy with need.

"I need you," she said as she trailed kisses over his face. "Don't let me go."

He suddenly pinned her beneath him. He spread her thighs and pressed the head of his cock over her slick lips.

"Do you want me, Lyla?" he rasped.

"More than anything," she said, reaching for him, needing him inside her. She needed him to claim her, to make her believe she was his and no one else's.

"Lyla," he moaned a second before he slid inside her.

She paused to savor the moment. Here, something was different as well, but she couldn't think when she was so full of him and his mouth devoured hers. He was dominant and animalistic, taking her as he never had before. Pleasure burst through her, eclipsing fear and replacing it with ecstasy.

"Do you belong to me?" he asked.

She tossed her head back as he sped up his thrusts. He was going deeper than he ever had, as if he could sense her desperation and need. Instead of his usual gentleness, there was an edge of violence to his lovemaking that made her wild.

"Lyla, promise me."

"Promise what?" She was having a hard time concentrating. Why did he want to talk now? She was so close—

He stopped moving. "Promise you won't leave me again."

"I never left you," she said and rocked against him, desperate for relief.

"You did," he growled.

Her breath stalled as a sliver of fear cut through the ecstasy. She tried to push away, but he kept her in place with heavy, deliberate thrusts that made her moan through clenched teeth.

"You'll never leave me again," he decreed.

She opened her mouth to argue, but the climax hit so hard and fast that she wasn't prepared for it. She let out a high-pitched scream as he pounded into her. Jonathan's face began to distort. Even as she reached up and raked her nails along Jonathan's back, she realized it was too broad and muscled. Confusion and panic clouded her mind. She blinked furiously as the orgasm faded and reality smacked her in the face.

She wasn't in her apartment in Maine with Jonathan. She was in Gavin's master suite in his home, and he was fucking her. Gavin's harsh breaths filled the room as he thrust into her, amber gaze spearing hers as he neared his climax. Through the dim light of a nearby lamp, she could see he was fully dressed in a gray suit, his shirt ripped down the front with his pants undone.

"No!" she screamed and tried to get away, but she was pinned beneath a solid body that definitely wasn't Jonathan's.

"I missed you so much."

As he brushed kisses over her face, she tried to avoid his mouth. His face darkened before he planted himself to the hilt.

"You're mine," he hissed.

She dreamed of escaping him, only to wake and find him fucking her. She began to shake uncontrollably as he hovered over her, not saying a word. The familiar scent of his cologne made her stomach lurch.

"How could you do this to me?" she whispered and then pounded his chest and screamed, "Get off me!"

"Lyla—"

"No, let me go!"

He flipped her onto her stomach and rested his full weight on her. She turned her head to the side so she could breathe and dug her nails into the rumpled sheets that smelled of them. Enraged and helpless, she beat at the mattress and tried to buck him off with no luck.

"Don't," he warned in a lethal voice.

"You raped me!" she seethed and tried to bite him.

"You wanted me," he said against her ear, causing her to shiver. "As soon as I put you in bed, you reached for me. You ripped my shirt and told me you needed me."

"I was dreaming, you asshole!" She didn't get wet for *him*; she was dreaming about Jonathan. That's why her body responded, right? She stiffened when his cock slid between her legs again.

"You recognize my touch even in sleep, baby girl."

"No!" She tried to dislodge him, but he controlled her easily. This couldn't be happening. "Please, Gavin."

His hands moved over her, just as they had in the dream. "Do you know how many times I dreamed of having you beneath me like this again?"

"You can't do this to me! Stop!" She sobbed as he moved inside her.

"I can do anything I want to you," he said, and brushed achingly light kisses along her wet cheek. "I own you, Lyla Dalton."

She buried her face in the sheets as he fucked her. Her body betrayed her, welcoming him and clutching at his cock. He groaned into her hair and moved faster.

"You won't escape me this time," he said, hands stroking her body, overloading her senses.

She shook her head, unable to speak as he came with a

triumphant shout that she was sure his security could hear. The moment he eased to the side, she rolled off the bed and ran to the en suite bathroom.

"Lyla—" he began, but she slammed the door.

She stepped into the shower and turned it on full blast. She scrubbed her body vigorously, trying to erase his touch and scent. How could her body respond to him? How had her dream merged seamlessly with reality so that she thought she was having sex with Jonathan instead of Gavin? She crumpled to the ground with her hands splayed on the floor as she wept. What did Gavin want from her? Was he trying to punish her? If he wanted to make her feel dirty and violated, he'd succeeded.

"Lyla."

She felt a draft as he opened the shower door. At any other time, she would have been mortified by the whimper that escaped, but she was too far gone to care. The impact of seeing him after all these years was like a punch in the gut. The young, slick boss in training was gone. His hair was longer than she remembered, and his body had a layer of muscle that made Jonathan look like a boy going through puberty. He crouched in front of her and brushed wet hair back from her face.

"Don't cry," he ordered roughly.

She stared into his beautiful eyes framed by dark lashes and had the suicidal urge to punch him.

His eyes narrowed. "Don't, baby girl."

She hated that he knew her so well, even after all this time. Was she that predictable? Had she learned nothing since she left him? Her mind skittered in a dozen directions as she tried to figure out how to handle him.

He picked her up with a show of effortless strength that scared her. He settled her on a seat built into the shower and squirted shampoo into his hands. Before she could get away, he began to massage it into her scalp. The familiar smell of her favorite shampoo startled, even as it soothed her. She sat like a broken doll as he bathed her. She felt as if she were in an alternate reality. This couldn't be real.

She couldn't be here with Gavin. She didn't have sex with him, and he couldn't be bathing her as if he had every right to. She retreated into her mind because she wasn't capable of digesting what was happening.

Gavin cleaned himself before he stepped out of the shower with her. He engulfed her in a soft cashmere robe and sat her in front of the vanity as he toweled her hair and brushed it. She was blessedly numb and didn't say a word. She examined him in the mirror as he tended to her. The man in the mirror was a far cry from the man she fell in love with. Back then, he had been arrogant and charming and possessed more power than one person should. Most people never witnessed the darkness in him since he was so good at disguising it. Now, it was on full display, as if he didn't bother wearing a mask these days. Although he was tending to her as efficiently as a maid, power emanated from him and kept her still and quiet before him. Once upon a time, she loved him without reservation, but she had been a fool. It took her four years to realize she was living a lie. Her emotions were a tangle of nostalgia, rage, fear, and betrayal. She loathed him, yet a small part of her still believed he was the man she'd fallen in love with. How could she love and hate him at the same time?

He seemed harder and colder than she remembered, and it scared her. He was so familiar yet... not. How much had he changed in three years? Even as she reminded herself that he had never been anything but gentle with her, she knew that could change in a heartbeat. She didn't realize she was crying again until he crouched in front of her. He cupped her face and brushed her tears away with his thumb. Piercing amber eyes moved over her face.

"Don't cry," he ordered.

"I don't know how to stop," she whispered and began to shake.

He gathered her in his arms and carried her into the bedroom. Panic infused her, and she began to struggle as he settled her on the bed.

"I'm not going to fuck you again," he said.

She took him at his word and curled into a ball on one side of the bed. There was an awful silence, and then arms pulled her back against a large body. She made a distressed sound and tried to get away, but her limbs were weak with exhaustion. She could feel his body heat through the robe, which reminded her of the dream and how she had ripped "Jonathan's" shirt, desperate to feel his skin against hers. Her eyes scanned the floor and stopped on the buttons scattered over the carpet. She moaned and covered her face with her hands. No wonder he fucked her. She'd practically begged him to do it. Guilt savaged her insides. She was in love with Jonathan, yet Gavin played her body as easily as if she'd never been with another man. She hated herself.

"I want to see my dad," she said. She wouldn't be able to rest until she saw that he was alive. Gavin was underhanded enough to use her father to bring her back and still kill him for embezzling half a million.

"Tomorrow."

"No." She rolled to face him. "I want to see him."

He stared at her for a long moment before he rose. "He's downstairs."

Her heart lightened a bit. She slipped out of bed and belted the cashmere robe, which was too large for her. Gavin pulled on a pair of jeans and a black T-shirt. She didn't comment as he put a gun in his waistband.

"Come," he said and opened the door.

She held her breath as she passed him. She stopped in her tracks when she saw movement at the end of the hallway. She flushed with mortification as Gavin ushered her forward. The guards were expressionless, but she knew they had heard their boss fucking her. She looked like the weak female they assumed she was. In this world, women were bought and sold to the highest bidder. And none was more powerful than Gavin. She tasted bile on her tongue as he led her down the staircase and to the basement, the only area in the house that had been off-limits to her.

Her damp palms slid along the iron railing as she walked down the steps that led into the basement. It was chilly down here, and the smell of blood was overwhelming. The basement had no windows, just endless concrete. Florescent lights revealed a figure in the middle of the room tied to a chair. Blood splattered the floor around him, and he wasn't moving.

She shoved past Gavin to reach her father. She clasped his face between trembling hands. His face was swollen, discolored, and grotesque. His nose had been broken, and his lips were ripped from being pummeled against his teeth. Unfocused, dark brown eyes opened.

"Dad?" she said urgently and snapped, "Gavin, untie him."

"Do it," Gavin said.

Blade appeared with a knife and cut the ropes. When her father tipped forward, she caught him and fell back on her ass as she took his full weight.

"He needs a doctor," she said as she held her limp father in her arms.

"No."

She glanced back at Gavin, who had his arms folded across his chest.

"The price for stealing is death. Healing naturally from his beating is small recompense for what he owes me." Gavin narrowed his eyes at her. "Don't look at me like that, Lyla. You know how our world works."

"*Your* world," she hissed.

"And you're back, so it's *our* world."

"I came back to pay his debt, not stay here permanently."

"You saved your father's life by coming back to me. I think it's fair to say a life for a life."

She went cold with fear. "Life?" Was he going to kill her? Torture her? Turn her into a prostitute?

"Lyla?" her father croaked.

"It's me, Dad."

Bloodshot brown eyes focused on her. "You shouldn't have left."

The venom in his voice battered at her.

"You ran off, leaving your mom and me to fend for ourselves, you selfish bitch..." he ranted, blood trickling out of his mouth and over her pristine robe.

Gavin appeared at her side and in one quick, ruthless shove, knocked her father out of her arms. Her father's head smacked the concrete. When she tried to go to him, Gavin jerked her against him.

"Your daughter is the only reason you're still breathing, Pat," he snapped.

She was sure her father was unconscious. The way his limbs were bent at unnatural angles made her stomach heave. She fought Gavin, but he easily controlled her. Her father moaned. She dug her nails into Gavin's arm, but he didn't budge.

"If she stayed, I wouldn't have had to borrow money from you..." her father garbled through a mouthful of blood.

"Borrow?" Gavin echoed in a dangerous voice.

"She used to give us half of the allowance you gave her every month." Her father's voice took on a whining note. "I've had a hard time paying the bills."

"You think I don't know how much money you gamble away every week?"

Gavin's rage was ice-cold and even more terrifying than she remembered. She wanted to tell her father to shut up, but he wouldn't listen to her. He never had.

"I thought if I could just make more money, I could hire my own investigator to find Lyla for you and—"

"Shut your mouth," Gavin said, and her father went silent. "The only person you care about is yourself. You never cared for Lyla. The only time you remember she exists is when you need money."

Gavin pushed Lyla behind him. She stumbled, and Blade steadied her. Gavin crouched and grabbed her father's face with one huge hand and squeezed.

"Gavin, no!"

Blade wrapped an arm around her waist to stop her from interfering. She was close to hyperventilating. She knew what Gavin was capable of.

"Don't you ever talk to Lyla like that again," Gavin said in a calm, even tone. "Even if your stupidity brought her back to me, deal or not, I'll end you."

Gavin released her father, who turned his head to the side and coughed up blood, which spread over the already stained floor. When Gavin turned, his expression darkened when it landed on them. Blade released her instantly. Gavin grasped her hand and when she tried to go to her father, he hauled her over his shoulder and carried her upstairs into his beautiful home that was untouched by the horror in the basement. He didn't stop until they were back in the master suite. He set her on her feet with a jarring thud.

"Your father is a piece of shit," he said as he took off her stained robe.

She didn't agree or disagree. He pulled her into the bathroom and washed her arms with warm water and took care of himself before he conjured up another cashmere robe and slipped her into it.

"You hungry?" he asked.

She shook her head. How could she eat after that? After Jonathan's gentle caring, her father's abrasive attitude felt like a slap in the face. Even sacrificing her life for his didn't inspire any warm emotions in him. Why had she expected her father to change in her absence? Wasn't distance supposed to make the heart grow fonder? That didn't apply to him. Even after all these years, she hadn't earned a crumb of his affection. Her father was a liar, gambler, thief... and her downfall.

"I have work to do," Gavin said abruptly.

Good, she thought. She needed to be alone.

"If you need anything, let me know." He pointed at a cell phone on the nightstand. "My number is speed dial one."

She nodded. When he moved toward her, she went rigid, but that didn't stop him from cupping her face and giving her a quick kiss. She didn't react. He rubbed his thumb over her bottom lip and searched her face. What the hell was he looking for?

"I wish the circumstances were different, and that you came back to me on your own, but I'm glad you're here," he said.

She didn't respond. He gave her another kiss before he walked toward the door. He opened it, paused, and looked back.

"No contact with anyone from your old life," he said, face hardening. "That's done now. You don't want anyone to get hurt, do you?"

How could he go from protector and lover to threatening her? She glared at him, but he didn't back down.

"You're back in my world, under my rules. You disobey, and I'll know. You got me?"

She nodded.

"I'll see you soon," he said and closed the door behind him.

She wanted to lay down, but she couldn't bear to sleep in a bed that smelled of their lovemaking. By fucking her, he severed her tie with Jonathan irrevocably. Did he do it deliberately? By staking his claim on her through ties of the flesh, he separated her from her old life and brought her back into his. There was no going back. She could feel it in her bones.

She stretched out on the window seat again and stared out at the moonlit grounds. There was a nagging ache between her legs. She covered her face with her hands and moaned in self-loathing. She was sacrificing her freedom for a father who greeted her after three years with disgust and scorn. She let out a long, shaky sigh. Even as she built a new life in Maine, a small part of her had always feared that coming back would be inevitable.

3

"LYLA."

A hand stroked her hair. The touch was so gentle that she smiled before she opened her eyes. But as she stared up at Gavin, her new reality snapped into place. The smile vanished from her lips as he brushed a finger down her cheek.

"This is the second time I've found you on the window seat. You got a problem with the bed?"

"No," she lied and sat up, fixing the robe that had come undone. She flushed under his regard, even though he was more familiar with her body than Jonathan.

"You must be hungry. The clothes you brought are old and tattered, so Blade got rid of them. Your old clothes are still in the closet." He gestured to the double doors. "Get dressed, come down to the kitchen, and we'll talk."

She slid off the window seat and winced as her stiff muscles protested. She didn't say a thing as she went to the closet and disappeared inside to escape his probing eyes. The closet was exactly as she had left it. One wall dedicated to outrageous heels while the other walls held racks of designer label clothes. These clothes belonged to a different person—someone who didn't have a care in the world. Back then, she didn't give a second thought to using Gavin's money or caring that she was glorified arm candy. That felt like a lifetime ago. She ran her hands over the fashionable, edgy garments and fought the urge to tear the closet apart. What would be the point? It wouldn't change her circumstances, and she had to find out Gavin's plans for her. Last night, he had said a life for a life. Surely, he didn't mean forever?

She chose one of the most conservative outfits—a long, skintight black skirt that had high slits on both sides and an electric blue crop top. She gave the wall of shoes a cursory glance before she selected a pair of strappy black heels. When she emerged from the closet, Gavin was gone. She took a deep breath and went into the bathroom to look for an extra toothbrush and paused. Last night, she'd been too distraught to examine the countertops. Now, she saw that, just like the closet, her perfumes, lotions, and makeup from her other life were here as well. She looked at herself in the mirror. She was pale, and her light blue eyes were bloodshot from exhaustion. She didn't feel like herself in the bright, revealing clothes. For three years, she tried to blend in, and now she felt exposed on so many levels. She reached for the makeup and sifted through the shimmery eye shadow, lip gloss, fake eyelashes, and playful lipstick shades. More reminders of the frivolous life she once had. She settled for mascara, Chapstick, and lotion.

When she left the bedroom, she half expected to see guards outside the door, but to her surprise, the hallway was empty. It made her skin prickle with alarm. Was Gavin planning to do something that he didn't want them to witness? For a moment, she thought of making a run for it. Her muscles tensed, and her heartbeat accelerated. The front door was so close... Common sense reasserted itself a moment before she heard footsteps and Gavin appeared.

"There you are. Come, breakfast is ready," he said.

Lyla took a deep breath before she started downstairs, her heels clicking on every step. Gavin's eyes moved over her, and he looked pleased. She averted her eyes as she passed him. An assortment of breakfast foods filled the marble island in the kitchen. Despite recent events, she was starving. She made a bowl of oatmeal with fresh cut strawberries, a bagel heavily smeared with cream cheese, and a plate of sausages. She carried her food to the table and ignored him when he sat beside her. She refused to let his stare unnerve her. He didn't eat, which either meant the food was poisoned or he had eaten earlier.

"Do you want more food?" he asked when she finished.

She shook her head.

"Look at me."

She clenched her teeth before she obeyed. Today he wore a blue shirt with the first two buttons undone and no tie beneath a black suit jacket. His carefully styled hair framed his attractive face, and he was freshly shaved.

"Do you want to see your mother?" he asked.

"You'd let me see her?" Was this a trick?

"Of course."

She searched his eyes. "Why?"

"I want you to be happy here."

"What?"

"Why do you look so surprised?"

She folded her hands on the table and braced herself. This was the moment of truth when she learned what her future looked like. She met his eyes and asked, "What am I doing here, Gavin?"

He frowned. "I want you here."

"For how long?" she asked, her heart threatening to beat out of her chest.

He didn't answer, and her palms dampened as anxiety slid through her veins. He watched her like a wolf daring its prey to make a move. One wrong step and he'd eat her.

"I can give you what money I have and make payments," she said.

"I don't need your money."

"Then, why?"

When he reached out and captured her chin in his hand, she resisted the impulse to jerk away. She was extremely vulnerable and at his mercy. She hated the feeling of helplessness that filled her, making her want to lash out.

"I can buy, bribe, or steal anything I want," he said.

It was true. Knowing the power he wielded kept her still and silent.

"Your dad stole a chunk of change he didn't earn and pissed it away. If he won, I would have charged him interest."

Which meant he'd known about her father stealing and allowed it to continue until he saw an opportunity to use her father's betrayal to his advantage.

"In the end, your father's stupidity and greed worked in my favor. I wanted you to come willingly—"

"I didn't," she snapped, and he tightened his hold.

"I have the manpower to have you watched day and night, but I need more insurance than that." He leaned forward until he was only inches away. "And I have yet to discover how you escaped me the first time. Do you want to enlighten me?"

"No." She would take it to her grave.

"No matter," he said as if he didn't care, but she knew better. "Your love for your worthless father gives me the insurance I need that you'll do what I say, when I say. Isn't that right, baby girl?" His thumb stroked over her lower lip.

She wanted to bite, but was too busy sifting through his statement. "And how am I supposed to pay off my dad's debt?"

"I told you."

He had? She frowned, and his eyes flashed.

"I want what we had."

She surged to her feet and clutched the back of the chair. "What did we have, Gavin?"

"A great life together."

She wanted to slap him. "I don't understand you! You have women begging to give you blowjobs. What do you need from me that you can't get from them?"

"There's no one like you."

She wanted to tear her hair out. She released the chair and began to wave her hands as she paced around the kitchen. "There are hundreds, no, *thousands* of women like me."

He said nothing, and she wondered if pride made him act impulsively. He didn't really want her. He wanted a submissive woman who doted on him. That wasn't her, not any longer.

"I want *you*, Lyla."

She shook her head. "You *had* me, Gavin. I wasn't enough for you." She gave him a sugary sweet smile while her blood began to boil. "Or did I imagine you having an orgy in the club?"

"I told you that was a mistake."

"And there were dozens of *mistakes* before I found out!" she shouted and turned away from him to regain her composure. How could she be so mad after all this time? She thought she had put it behind her, but seeing him in the flesh and having him say he wanted what they had made her chest burn.

"That's over."

"Yes, it is," she agreed and desperately tried to rein in her temper. Why were they even having this conversation? Oh, yeah, because he wanted things to go back to the way they'd been three years ago when she was a naïve fool. "I'm not the same person, Gavin. Whatever you think you'll get from me... I can't. Within a month, you'll be back to your old ways. Maybe I can pay off Dad's debt another way. Maybe I can—"

"No."

She turned as he rose and stilled when she saw his implacable expression.

"I took you for granted," he acknowledged as he rounded the table and closed the distance between them with deliberate steps. "I didn't want to change. I admit that. I liked having you in one section of my life and the business and girls in the other. I had it all, and then Min fucked up when he let you into the club without checking with Blade first."

"It would have been difficult for Min to check with Blade when he was getting sucked off by two women," she said and glared at him. "I can't believe you shot Min. It wasn't his fault!"

He shrugged as if it wasn't a big deal, and to him, it wasn't. He grew up in the cutthroat underworld. He learned to fight, fuck, and deal before he hit puberty. He wrapped a hand around the back of her neck and plastered her against him.

"I thought you'd been taken by one of my enemies. I thought you'd been killed." His eyes hardened. "How could you, Lyla?"

"I wanted out." Her heartbeat accelerated as his energy began to pulse in the surrounding air.

"I was tortured by thoughts of what my enemies did to you before they killed you. Three years of regret and then my investigator finds you in Maine with a different name, working as a bank teller." His eyes raked over her face. "And living with another man... a fucking nerd. You let another man touch you, make love to you? How could you do that to me?"

"You expect me to be faithful after you cheated on me?"

His eyes flashed with rage. He lifted her off her feet and shook her like a rag doll.

"What does he have that I don't, Lyla? You leave me for a man who makes fifty thousand a year? Who I could beat to a pulp?"

She struggled to get free, but he didn't seem to notice. His eyes blazed with fury, and his hands were moments away from crushing bone.

"Your life belongs to me. No other man is allowed to touch you."

She trembled in his grasp. "Gavin, you're hurting me."

"And you hurt me!" he shouted and shoved her away from him.

She staggered back and hit the glass door that led into the back-yard hard enough to make it bow and shudder in its frame. She shook like a leaf. She knew what Gavin was capable of. The night before she left him, she witnessed him kill a man with his bare hands. He was a savage beneath the polished veneer.

His ragged breathing filled the kitchen. She bowed her head and waited for him to come after her, to finish her off.

"Don't push me, Lyla. I'm so fucking angry with you. Look at me."

She was too afraid to raise her head. Suddenly, he was right in front of her, and once more, his hand shot out. She screamed as his hand closed around her throat. She wrapped both hands around his wrist and struggled to get away.

"When I tell you to do something, you do it!" he shouted in her face. She closed her eyes against the sight of him. "You don't leave me, Lyla. Do you understand me?"

She nodded because she couldn't speak.

"Open your eyes."

When she didn't obey, his hand tightened in warning. Her eyes popped open.

"Tell me you understand."

"I-I understand," she gasped as his hand threatened to cut off her airflow.

"Tell me you won't leave me."

A tear slipped down her cheek. "I w-won't leave you."

He grabbed her lower lip between his teeth. She moaned and tried to turn her face away, but he increased the pressure and bit. She tasted blood, and more tears slipped down her face. When he released her, a trickle of blood slipped down her chin. He glared at her as if he hated her and was debating whether she was worth the trouble. She held her breath.

"You belong to me," he stated without emotion, as if she was an inanimate object he was claiming ownership of. "You try to leave me again, I'll hunt you down and make you watch as I slaughter everyone you love. Then, I'll make you pay."

She couldn't conceal her horror. In the four years they were together, Gavin never touched her in anger. He had been so gentle with her, so caring. With everyone else, he was a beast, but he always reined it in around her. Now, it was on full display, and it made her tremble.

"Your place is by my side. You listen to me and follow my rules. You don't have the freedom you had last time. You check in with me for everything. You understand?" At her slow nod, he stepped back. "Go upstairs and fix your face. Then I'll take you to see your mom."

She lurched into motion, making a wide circle around him as she left the kitchen on unsteady legs. She walked upstairs and focused on putting one foot in front of the other. When she reached their bedroom, she closed the door and stood there for a long moment, mind racing. If she stayed, he would kill her. But there was nowhere to run where he couldn't find her. Even though he suspected his enemies had killed her, he hadn't called off the search. He meant every word he said in the kitchen. He would kill her family if she ran again. He didn't make idle threats.

She walked into the bathroom and stared at the blood and mascara smeared over her face. Her swollen lip was still seeping blood in a steady stream down her chin. Her arms ached where he grabbed her, and her neck began to darken with bruises. With shaking hands, she wet a washcloth and wiped her face.

The bedroom door slammed open. Moments later, Gavin appeared in the bathroom doorway. He leaned on the doorjamb and watched her with brooding eyes. She clutched the washcloth between shaking hands and waited for more punishment.

"You kill yourself, and I'll make your family wish they were dead, you got me?" he asked.

She gave a jerky nod.

"Hurry," he snapped.

She nodded again and finished wiping away the mascara. There was no chance of concealing her ravaged lip, and she had no idea what other things lay in wait for her. She didn't bother to reapply mascara. She turned, head bowed. He gripped her hand in his, and she swallowed hard to keep her breakfast down. He grabbed the cell phone she had yet to touch and slapped it in her hand.

"You keep this on you at all times," he said.

He led her downstairs and pulled her out of the house. No less than fifteen of his men were waiting for them. The men lounged on the steps and around the large fountain in the middle of the drive. She dropped her head to conceal her swollen lip as Gavin opened the passenger door of his silver BMW. She buckled herself in, clutched the phone between her hands, and stared straight ahead. Gavin spoke to Blade for several minutes before he climbed into the driver's seat. She leaned against the passenger door to gain more breathing room. The small space made her feel claustrophobic. Gavin sped off his property toward the automatic gates that opened at his approach. Neither of them said a word. When she couldn't stand it a second longer, she rolled down her window and took a deep breath to stop herself from vomiting in the expensive car. Gavin didn't object as he navigated the freeway.

The Strip didn't look as alluring in the daytime as it did at night. The Strip was Gavin's playground. She wanted to stay as far from it and him as possible. She wanted to believe this was a nightmare she would wake from.

When he drove up to her parents' house, of its own accord, her hand reached for the door handle. She was out of the vehicle before it stopped. She ran to the front door and raised her fist to knock, but it opened before she could. Her mother stood in the doorway. She leapt forward and embraced her mother before she got a look at her face.

"You're home," Mom whispered in her hair.

Her mother smelled of garlic and sesame oil. It stirred up bittersweet memories. Lyla held her tight, wishing she were a child again when everything was simple.

"Mrs. Dalton."

Gavin's voice broke through her hysteria. She stiffened in her mother's arms. Would he beat or slap her mother around to punish her further?

"Gavin, thank you for bringing my daughter home," Mom said, voice choked with emotion.

"No problem," he said. "How's your husband?"

So, her father was here, being tended by her mother. That was good news, but how dare he ask about her father's health as if he wasn't responsible for his state? She wanted to scream.

"I finished stitching him up a minute ago," Mom said pleasantly and patted Lyla on the back as if she were a newborn.

"I brought Lyla by to reconnect. You don't mind if I leave her here while I go to work?" he asked.

"Of course, not! I'm glad to have my baby back."

"Good. I need to speak to her before I go."

"Of course," Mom said and loosened her hold, but Lyla didn't let go. "Honey? Is something wrong?"

She didn't want to lose touch with her mother for a moment, but when a large hand touched the small of her back, she stiffened. Remembering the strength in that hand as it wrapped around her throat, she released her mother and whirled to face Gavin.

"Leave us," he said without looking at her mother.

"I'll be in the kitchen," Mom said.

Her mother's footsteps faded, leaving her to face Gavin in the foyer of her parent's humble home.

"You won't touch my mother," she said. She wasn't sure where this burst of defiance was coming from when she was emotionally and physically battered, but she knew one thing. She would die before he lay a finger on her mom.

"There's no reason to hurt your mother," he said.

But there was reason to hurt *her*?

"I have to go to work."

She nodded. Good. She needed time away from him to think.

"Blade will be outside along with several other guards. You're not allowed to leave here. I'll be back to pick you up."

She nodded again and took a step back. Before she could walk away, he grabbed her arm in the same place where she was already bruised. She hissed in pain. He instantly switched his grip to her elbow. He looked down at her discolored skin and brushed a thumb over it.

"I didn't mean to hurt you," he said quietly.

He cupped her chin and lifted her face. Gold eyes swirled with conflicting emotions. The maniac who attacked her in the kitchen was nowhere in sight. If she hadn't witnessed it for herself, she would have thought it was a hallucination. Right now, he was the cool businessman and appeared to have his emotions under control.

"You make me feel..." He shook his head. "*Everything*. You make me crazy."

She tried to ease away, but he tightened his hold.

"Be a good girl," he said and kissed her forehead before he released her.

She didn't bother to watch him leave. She turned on her heel and walked toward the kitchen. Her mother stood at the stove, stirring something in a pot. She wore white capris and a tight shirt that showed off her carefully maintained physique. Lyla was a mirror image of her mother. There was no sign of her father in her.

Mom turned. When she got a good look at Lyla, she dropped the wooden spoon, which skidded over the tiles.

"Lyla, what happened?"

Bile rose, and this time, she couldn't stop it. She ran to the nearest bathroom where she retched. Her mother held her hair and murmured soothingly as she gagged until nothing was left in her stomach. Mom mopped up her face with a warm rag and dabbed at her lip, which began to bleed again.

"Brush your teeth," Mom ordered as she handed Lyla an unused toothbrush.

When she finished, her mother led her back to the kitchen where she made peppermint tea. Mom set a steaming cup in front of her before reaching out to tap her clammy hand.

"Tell me everything," Mom said.

4

Lyla wrapped trembling hands around the hot mug. She was shaking too badly to pick it up, but was grateful for the soothing smell and warmth. She surveyed her mother's platinum blond hair cut into a chic bob that framed bright blue eyes. When she lived in Las Vegas, she rarely visited her mother after she moved in with Gavin. She had been too busy primping or partying.

"I'm sorry," Lyla whispered.

"For what?"

"I shouldn't have left."

"Why don't you tell me why you did," Mom prompted gently.

She rotated the cup between her hands. "Carmen and I went to Malibu, a girls' trip, but I missed Gavin and came back early to surprise him. I caught him having an orgy at a club."

Her mother showed no sign of surprise. Gavin was a Pyre, and this was Sin City, after all. The people of Las Vegas were as jaded as New Yorkers.

"I shouted at him, made a scene. I lost it." She had a vague recollection of smashing glasses and belting a prostitute across the face. "I drove home, and he met me there. He apologized and told me it would never happen again. I wanted to believe him, but I asked if this was the first time he cheated on me. It wasn't." She finally felt steady enough to sip tea. It coated her dry throat and warmed her from the inside out. "That week he bought me a new car, jewelry, more clothes. He told me we would go on a trip, just the two of us."

Her mother listened without saying a word. There was no condemnation or anger on her face, just calm expectancy.

"One night, Gavin said he had to do something before bed. I was suspicious, so I snuck past a guard and followed him to the basement. One of his guards was tied to a chair. Gavin beat the crap out of him and injected him with something to force him to stay awake. The guard was feeding information to the cops. Gavin questioned him and then beat him to death in front of his men. I left the next day."

She felt sick, so she drank the rest of the tea, hoping it would banish the awful taste in her mouth. She witnessed Gavin systematically rip a man apart. She hadn't been able to eat for a week after.

"I got a new identity and moved a lot, kept under the radar. I met a great guy in Maine."

When her voice broke, her mother reached out and squeezed her hand.

"We just moved in together. He's so good to me... I came back to my apartment and Blade was there. He showed me a live video of Dad. They said he stole half a million. Gavin told me if I didn't come back, he would..."

She didn't need to finish. Mom got to her feet while she stared into space. She had always known that Gavin was involved in shady shit. His father owned casinos, hotels, and clubs on and off The Strip. Parts of Gavin's job were legit and other parts weren't. She turned a blind eye to it until she watched that guard die a slow, painful death. She couldn't take her eyes off Gavin that night. She had seen him angry, but the detached, emotionless way he continued to beat the man chilled her to the core. He never raised his voice, never lost control. The way he dealt out punishment that night made her realize she couldn't live this way any longer. She couldn't get it out of her head that if she ever made Gavin that angry, he would do the same thing to her. The way he acted this morning confirmed her worst fears.

"Here." Mom set a sandwich in front of her. "It's only peanut butter. Your favorite." When Lyla made no move to touch it, she said, "You'll feel better."

Wanting to please her mother, she took a bite.

"I warned your father about stealing from the Pyres." Mom leaned against the counter and wrapped her arms around herself. "I knew it would cost him his life when they caught him, but he wouldn't stop. He's addicted to gambling, always has been, always will be. I knew when Gavin's men showed up what it meant." Tears sparkled in her eyes. "I never thought I'd see him again, and now you're both here."

She tried to respond to her mother's watery smile, but she couldn't.

"I know you don't want to be here, but I'm glad you came home. You saved your father's life."

Mom loved her father beyond all reason, the same way Lyla had once loved Gavin. Her father was brilliant with numbers and had never been able to stay away from gambling. When he hit a lucky streak, he'd shower her mother with gifts before he hit a bad one and everything went to hell. Her father struggled to keep a job because of his addiction. He became an accountant for Pyre Casinos when she was seventeen. While visiting her father at work, she met Manny Pyre, the CEO of Pyre Casinos and Gavin's father. She felt an instant connection with Manny. Despite her father's warnings, she dropped in on Manny throughout the summer and helped with minor administrative tasks. During her senior year, he hired her as a personal assistant. She shadowed his every move when she wasn't in school. Manny introduced her to Gavin, and the rest was history. Despite the fact Gavin was eight years older than she was, they began to date, much to her father's displeasure. It took her a year to realize something wasn't right with the business. Gavin never talked about it, but she wasn't stupid. Gavin moved her into his mansion, and she resigned from her job at Pyre Casinos to become a kept woman. She slipped her mother part of the allowance Gavin gave her when her father was on a bad streak. Life was good... until it wasn't.

She stared at her mother, who had yet to address the darker parts of her story. Although it had never been discussed, they knew the Pyre fortune had a dirty side. As an unspoken rule, it was never discussed.

"Gavin's going to kill me." The words burst out of her mouth before they materialized in her head.

Her mother waved a dismissive hand. "He won't."

She stared at her mother as she gestured to her injuries.

"What did you do?" Mom asked with a thread of accusation in her voice.

She surged to her feet and didn't notice the mug teeter off the table and shatter when it hit the ground. "What did *I* do?"

"Gavin loves you," Mom said in a consoling tone. "He wouldn't have hurt you unless you made him angry beyond reason."

"So, it's my fault I look like this?" she demanded. Her mother always stuck up for her father, and now, it seemed she was sticking up for Gavin, the man responsible for her father's nearly comatose state. "Did you *not* hear me say that he cheated on me and killed a guy with his bare hands?"

"He's a Pyre," Mom said, as if that dismissed Gavin's sins. "You should be grateful he still cares for you. You have to keep him happy, Lyla, for all our sakes."

"I should be grateful," she repeated dumbly. She should be grateful Gavin was so furious that she left three years ago that he wanted to punish her? Her world was caving in around her, and her mother was figuratively clapping her hands in delight. The feeling of homecoming and safety faded, and the nasty taste of betrayal filled her mouth.

"You didn't mention how you escaped," Mom said casually as she stirred the pot on the stove.

She went cold as her intuition pinged. Her mother would tell Gavin who helped her escape. She had no doubt Gavin would kill them.

"I have my own connections through the Pyres," she said mildly and got to her feet. "I want to rest."

"Of course, honey. Let me—"

"No, Mom, I got it," she said as she left the kitchen and started up the stairs. She went to her old bedroom and found it untouched. The room smelled musty, but she didn't care. She collapsed on the bed and heard her father yelling in pain from several doors down. She covered her ears with her hands, buried her face in her pillow, and screamed.

SHE MUST HAVE DOZED off because when she woke, someone was straddling her middle. As she lost her breath and transitioned from sleep to frightened wakefulness, the person grabbed her by the shoulders and shook her while screaming a torrent of profanities. She opened her eyes and tried to focus on her assailant as her head snapped back and forth. She reached out for leverage and encountered bare, silky skin. The person stopped shaking her and bounced on her tender tummy. She finally recognized the slim woman on top of her and couldn't hold back a delighted shriek. She wrapped her arms around her cousin and hugged her tight.

"Bitch, you roll back into town and forget to call me? What the fuck?" Carmen demanded, voice thick with tears.

"Got back yesterday," she said, voice muffled by Carmen's surgically enhanced bosom.

Her cousin released her and sat back on her thighs. Carmen wore a fire engine red dress that barely covered her ass with large cutouts on the sides. Her blond hair had fine streaks of fuchsia, and her face looked airbrushed, it was so perfect. Carmen's eyes flared as she took in her bruised throat, arms, and scabbed lip.

"What the fuck happened to you? Who hurt you?" Carmen leaped off the bed and didn't bother to brush her dress down to cover her girly bits. Carmen braced her legs apart like a superhero ready for takeoff, gold glitter hooker heels shining in the light. "I'll tell Vinny. He'll kill whoever did this to you."

"Vinny's going to kill his boss?" she asked sardonically and gingerly touched her swollen lip.

Carmen's eyes bugged comically wide. "*Gavin* did this?"

"Yeah."

"But Gavin loves you. He's been looking for you for years—"

"And he's pissed enough to beat the shit out of me," she said and brushed a hand over her tender throat.

Carmen flushed with rage. "What the fuck? What else did he do to you? I'll kill him myself!"

Carmen's overprotectiveness loosened something inside of her. Unlike everyone else, Carmen wasn't afraid of Gavin and was unrestrained and passionate. Her husband, Vinny, was Gavin's cousin. When they were younger, they double dated the Pyre men. That seemed like ages ago. Carmen was two years older than her and a Las Vegas native. Carmen showed her the ropes when her family moved from California when she was eight. They had been inseparable ever since. Carmen's father, an enforcer for the Pyre family, helped Lyla's father get the accounting job at a Pyre Casino when they hit a rough spot.

"I've missed you," she said simply.

Carmen's eyes filled with tears before she launched herself at Lyla, knocking the wind out of her.

"I'm here. It's going to be okay. I promise," Carmen whispered.

She clutched her. "I'm scared."

Carmen made a shushing sound and brushed her hair back like a mother would to comfort a young child. She took a deep, shuddering breath and took in Carmen's cotton candy scent.

"Do you know how he found you?" Carmen asked in a soundless whisper.

She shook her head. Carmen pulled back and clasped her face between her hands.

"We're going to get through this."

She didn't agree with Carmen's fervent reassurance. She felt as if she might shatter. She wanted to be anywhere but here. She felt unsafe, frightened, and desperate. She had nowhere to run, nowhere to hide, and no one to help her. No one fucked with the Pyre family. You screwed them; they destroyed you. Whatever you did to them, they paid back ten times over. They were the crime lords of Las Vegas. The Pyres had a stake in every sinful desire you could dream up, and the manpower and money to make anything happen. Why hadn't she realized she was playing with fire?

Carmen sat beside her on the bed and clasped her hand. "Tell me everything."

She kept her head down as she filled her cousin in about the past three years and ended with Jonathan.

"Gavin knows about this guy you were living with?" Carmen asked incredulously. At her nod, she asked, "And he's still alive?"

At her fearful look, Carmen quickly reassured her that Gavin probably wouldn't bother Jonathan as long as she didn't piss him off. She regained a little color in her face and told Carmen about her father's debt.

"Your father's always been a dumb ass," Carmen said.

In a quavering voice, she finished her story by explaining what occurred in the kitchen this morning. Carmen's baby blue eyes were alight with holy fire.

"He doesn't get to treat you like this!"

"He can do whatever he wants," she said with a shudder.

"Don't take this lying down."

"What do you mean?"

"Girl, you had him once."

"Yeah, me and a hundred other girls."

Carmen let out a disgusted sound. "You know what I mean. Gavin may have fucked around, but no man searches for their ex for three years unless he has feelings."

"Or an ego the size of Texas," she countered.

Carmen tapped her long, pointed acrylic nails together. "I don't believe that. I think he still loves you."

"*Love?*" she said, gesturing to her bruises. "Aside from the fact that he never said he loved me, he beat the crap out of my dad, and black-mailed me into coming back to him. That's fucked up, Carmen. This isn't a fucking romance novel."

"You have power."

"*Power?* Are you high?"

"He wants you. If Gavin wanted to kill you, he'd kill you. If he wanted to make you pay, he wouldn't bring you to his home, feed you, and then take you to your mother's house. Comprende?"

"Who knows why Gavin does what he does? He's losing it."

"Manny gave him the reins two years ago. Gavin doesn't take any shit. He's harder than Manny and ten times more ruthless. Vinny says he got worse after you left."

Lyla got up and paced her tiny bedroom. "Why? Gavin has a million girls to choose from. I'm nothing special."

Carmen wagged a finger. "Girl, everyone sees it but you."

"Sees what?"

Carmen braced her hands on Lyla's shoulders and gave her a small shake. "You're gorgeous."

"There are other girls more—"

"You're loyal, and you love with everything in you. You're strong. Strong enough to make it on your own without anyone's help. That probably pissed Gavin off the most." Carmen suddenly hooted and clapped her hands together. "Here he thought you'd been taken or would come back begging. Instead, he finds you after three years in Maine with another guy. Tell me that isn't funny."

"I have no idea what you're talking about."

"Well, I know and that's enough," Carmen said crisply. "You can work this to your advantage."

She tried to stomp on the trickle of hope. "Carmen—"

"Listen to me," Carmen snapped. "I'm older and wiser."

She took a deep breath. She was willing to try anything. "Okay. What do I do?"

"You make him crazy."

"Gavin *is* crazy."

"I mean, make him crazy for *you.*"

"But I don't want him crazy for me. I want him to forget I exist and let me go."

Carmen looked crushed. "But you just got back."

"Carmen, I left for a reason." Because her ex was a serial cheater and possible serial killer.

"I know, but what if Gavin's changed? Would you consider staying?"

"How the hell did you go from threatening to kill him to asking me to stay with him?"

"I don't want you to go." Carmen sounded like a petulant child. "I've missed you, bitch."

"I missed you too, but I'm a captive, *hello*."

"You're only a captive if you let yourself be. Captivate the captor," Carmen said with an exaggerated wink.

"What are you talking about?"

"Mama, use what the good Lord gave you." Carmen ran a hand between her legs, cupped her tits, and slapped her ass. "You look like a stripper and have the smarts to stay off his radar for three years. Use it to your advantage! Make Gavin your slave."

"He hates me, Carmen."

"It can't be all hate. He hasn't been the same since you left. Just try to get him to bed and see what happens."

Her hands clenched into fists. "Done that."

Carmen's eyes nearly bugged out of their sockets. "You fucked him?"

"He raped me."

"He raped you?"

"I was having a sex dream, and when I woke up, he was in me."

"A sex dream? About Jonathan? Is he, like, a *hot* IT consultant?"

"He's cute."

Carmen didn't look convinced. "You love him?"

She and Jonathan never discussed it, but, "Yes."

Carmen leaned in close and examined her suspiciously. "Like, *love him*, love him?"

"Yes," she said defiantly.

Carmen gave her a somber look. "Lyla, there's no escape this time. The moment you started dating Gavin, you became Pyre property."

"That was years ago!"

"Doesn't matter. It's obvious that Gavin will do everything in his power to make sure you stay put this time. Men like him don't let go of a good woman."

She made an impatient sound. Men like Gavin... Maybe she could get Gavin hooked on someone else, and she could pay off her father's debt another way besides as his sex slave... or whatever it was that he wanted from her. Invisible walls were closing in. The urge to run was an insistent drum beat in her mind.

She jumped when someone knocked on the bedroom door. Her mother appeared with the cell phone Gavin had given her in hand.

"It's Gavin. He wants to talk to you," Mom said.

Her heartbeat went into overdrive. Before she could figure out a way to avoid the call, Carmen snatched the phone from her mother's hand.

"Gavin, what the fuck did you do to my cousin?" Carmen demanded.

Fearing for Carmen's life, she lurched into action and tried to rip the phone out of her hand. Carmen shoved her away and continued to talk.

"Don't give me that shit, Gavin. If Manny sees her like this, he'll have a cow. What do you mean, it's none of my business? Of course, it is! She's my cousin." Carmen's heel tapped rapidly as she listened to Gavin's response. "No, I'm taking her out."

Carmen yanked the phone away from her ear. They could all hear Gavin shouting. She shook her head wildly while her mother wrung her hands.

"Carmen Pyre," Mom said and tried to take the phone from her.

Carmen held up one finger and gave her mother a threatening look before she put her hand over the phone and mouthed, "He needs to woo her back."

Lyla made a gagging sound.

Carmen put the phone back to her ear. "She needs some work

done. Hair, nails, the works. We're going to have a girls' day. You can see her after." Carmen listened for a moment, and her eyes flicked to Lyla. "Okay, fine. Here."

Carmen handed the phone over. She took it, afraid of what hell Carmen created and how dearly she would pay for it later. "Hello?"

"Lyla?" he bit out.

She closed her eyes against the sound of his voice and the memories of this morning. He wasn't the man she fell in love with. He wasn't a man she wanted to be around, ever. She learned to care for herself, to work for what she had. Now, she was reduced to a possession, a child who would be punished if she didn't please her master. She trembled with helpless rage. "Yes?"

A pause and then, "I should have known Vinny would tell Carmen you're back. Do you want to go with her?"

"Yes." She needed to get out of this house and away from her mother who worshipped the ground Gavin walked on. Carmen stood up for her when no one else dared. She would stick with her cousin as much as possible.

"Blade will shadow you," he said.

She said nothing.

"I'll come for you after work."

Again, she didn't reply. What was there to say? He called the shots, and she did as she was told. That's what he wanted, right? A submissive doll to dress, fuck, and control.

"Lyla?"

"Yes?"

He cursed and hung up. She wasn't sure what that meant and didn't care. "Let's go," she said to Carmen, who cheered.

"Lyla," Mom began.

She kissed her on the cheek as she passed. "I'll see you later, Mom."

She got out of the house as fast as possible and felt better once she was in the sun. She paused for a moment to brush off the effect Gavin's voice had on her, and saw Blade in the driver's seat of the SUV, ready to go. Gavin hadn't wasted time informing his security about their outing. Carmen put on a pair of pink sunglasses and jumped into a gold convertible. Her lips quirked at the ridiculous car. Of course, Carmen would have a gold car. She belted herself in and held on for dear life, since her cousin drove like a reckless demon.

"You don't know how happy I am that you're back," Carmen shouted over the sound of the wind and traffic. "I mean, I know you don't want to be here. You never liked the way they do business, and it sucks that you saw the worst of Gavin, but that's the way it is. This is home, and if you want, I know you can be happy here again. You were before you found out about the other girls. You have the power to make sure that doesn't happen again."

Had she ever been happy here? It was hard to remember since the events that caused her to leave overshadowed the good. She didn't want to think about rebuilding a life in Las Vegas with Gavin. She wanted to believe this was a fucking mistake that would go away. She would be set free and then... Then what? She would reinvent herself again. She couldn't go back to Maine, to Jonathan. Not after this. Fucking Gavin made her feel like a whore. Was it rape if she had an orgasm? Her body welcomed Gavin back as if the time between had never been. Apparently, her body didn't realize that they belonged to Jonathan now. Well, *used* to belong to Jonathan—

"Are you listening to me?" Carmen shouted and narrowly avoided rear-ending a Ferrari. When the driver honked, Carmen flipped the bird and resumed lecturing her about her new life. "Vinny adores me, and everyone knows it. I keep him topped up; you know what I mean? He's part of the underworld, but we're happy, girl."

"But I don't *want* Gavin!" she shouted back.

"You wanted him once, and if you can overlook some things, he'd make a solid man. He'd provide for you and protect the fuck out of you. He wouldn't take you for granted since you left him once already."

Carmen parked with a screech of tires in front of a salon. She linked her arm through Lyla's and walked in with Blade on their heels. The salon played hip-hop music shockingly loud. The stylists wore the craziest wigs and hairstyles she had ever seen. A large woman wearing a skintight dress and heels ran to them. She and Carmen exchanged air kisses before Carmen shoved her forward.

"This is my cousin, Lyla. She's with Gavin," Carmen said.

The hairdresser's eyes widened. "No shit?"

"No shit," Carmen said solemnly. "She needs the works. Don't cut her hair and no dye or he'll have my head." Carmen gestured to Blade and the two other guards at the entrance. "Her bodyguards. She should be in their sight at all times."

"No problem," the hairdresser said. "I'm gonna give you to one of my best. Keenan!"

A muscled black man in zebra tights and a sagging tank top stomped toward them with a sulky expression.

"Keenan, she's with Gavin Pyre and needs the works."

Keenan lit up as if he'd been offered a million dollars. He kissed her on the mouth and wrapped an arm around her. *"Girl!"*

"No kissing," Blade barked from the entrance, and the noise in the salon dimmed a bit.

Keenan blew Blade a kiss. "You got it, big boy."

"Trim, no dye," Keenan's boss ordered.

"You got it. Come, baby, and tell Keenan all about it." He ushered her into a private corner of the salon. "Let's condition that gorgeous hair. So, did Gavin rescue you from a rough customer?"

"Customer?" she echoed blankly.

"You're an escort, right? Gavin took you in?" Keenan gestured to her neck, lip, and arms. "Were you working for him and a customer got out of hand?"

Apparently, the salon catered to the Pyres and wasn't concerned how they made their money. The elite of Las Vegas were willing to get their hands dirty. Escorts, drug dealers, con men, strippers, and high rollers were the ones who rose to the top in this city.

She wasn't sure what to think about Keenan's conclusion. Did she look like an escort? Did Gavin take in a lot of girls? Her stomach clenched when she realized he didn't wear a condom last night. He could give her an STD. Thank God, she had an IUD. She got her first one in her teens before she and Gavin had sex for the first time. She should have been a slut after Gavin so she would be immune to him now. At least she had been Jonathan's, even if it was just for a short time.

"No, I'm not an escort," she said.

"Really? Stripper?"

She knew he wasn't trying to be insulting. "No. I've known Gavin since I was in high school."

Keenan looked like he might swoon. "*No.* You're high school sweethearts?"

Sweethearts? She didn't know how to explain what she and Gavin were and was relieved she didn't have to. Keenan spun a Romeo and Juliet tale in his mind. He drew his own conclusions and she didn't correct him. If only he knew how dark and twisted reality was.

With just a few sentences, she kept Keenan chattering excitedly about a range of topics, her least favorite being Gavin, who Keenan had a major crush on. Keenan talked about Gavin's nightclubs and strip bars. It brought up memories of the night she found Gavin cheating on her. It made her stomach turn even after all this time. Why the fuck did Gavin bring her back? He didn't want her, not really. If she meant so much to him, he wouldn't have fucked around on her. He seemed genuinely contrite after she confronted him at the club. He told her the women didn't mean anything to him and that he wouldn't do it again. She hadn't made up her mind whether she would give him a second chance or not when she witnessed him murder that guard in his basement. That was her tipping point. Gavin should have forgotten about her and moved on. Every year that passed, she became more confident that she was free of him, yet here she was.

Keenan chattered about his many lovers and their professions, which ranged from strippers to doctors, and interrupted himself to say, "I love your hair. I can't believe this is your natural color. Honey sunshine."

She smiled at the description. Keenan blow-dried her hair so it fell around her in shining waves. She couldn't deny that she felt like a million dollars. It felt good to let other people take care of her.

She gave Keenan air kisses and moved on to waxing. They waxed her bare (which was fine since she didn't have much hair anyway) and then started on her nails. Carmen chose a scarlet polish for her acrylic nails. Carmen chatted with everyone while she listened, not adding much to the conversation. Everyone was friendly and dressed with a seductive edge that reminded her she was no longer in Maine. A couple of days ago, she wouldn't have been mistaken for an escort. Her crop top and skirt made her appear nun-like compared to the salon workers.

She didn't know how to feel about her circumstances. Her emotions were a jumbled mess. Any moment now, she expected Gavin to burst through the door and beat the crap out of her in front of everyone. The hatred on his face this morning haunted her. Even if he decided to do something to her, no one would interfere when a Pyre was involved.

When they finished, she went to the front desk to pay.

"It's taken care of," Keenan said and gave her ass a smack on her way out.

Blade looked like he wanted to say something, but decided against it when Keenan fluttered his eyelashes at him. Carmen put the top up on her convertible so their hairstyles would keep.

"Where are we going?" she asked.

"My house. I told our cook to make something fabulous."

"But, what about Gavin?"

"If he wants to come, he'll come," Carmen said dismissively. "You look great, by the way."

"I feel better."

"Great. Now, we're going to get dressed up for dinner and figure out what to do with your life."

5

AN HOUR LATER, CARMEN PUT THE FINISHING TOUCHES ON LYLA'S makeup and stepped back. Lyla didn't look like Morgan Lincoln, a conservative bank teller. She looked like a sophisticated version of the Lyla Dalton who died three years ago. Carmen gave her the works with heavy eyeliner, fake eyelashes, lipstick, and enough concealer to take away the dark circles under her eyes. Carmen did an excellent job. She looked well rested and luminous. The dark shade of lipstick concealed the worst of her bitten lip, and the black long-sleeve dress with a high collar covered her bruises on her arms and throat. Carmen topped it all off with a diamond bracelet that could pay half of her father's debt. Despite the fact they were eating at Carmen's house, they were dressed for fine dining. Carmen believed in always looking her best and, of course, accessories.

"There's my heartbreaker cousin," Carmen said as she danced in her five-inch heels. "Gavin is gonna jizz his pants."

"I don't want him to want me," she protested.

"You're going to put Gavin in line. There's a reason they call us man-eaters. Men fear us."

Carmen posed in the mirror, showing off her legs and the indecently high slit on her eggplant dress before she turned and strutted toward Lyla, pouting her lips and making her eyes heavy-lidded. Carmen pressed a gentle kiss on her cheek and perched on her lap.

"You have to make him want you desperately," Carmen said in a throaty whisper that made Lyla's skin ripple with goose bumps. "You have to make yourself unattainable. You want him to work for your love and affection. Don't show fear or he won't respect you."

"He's not the same man," she said and then corrected herself. "Or maybe I never knew the real him."

"He's in there, Lyla. The good parts aren't gone, just buried. You can bring that out of him."

"How?" She didn't want Gavin's attention or desire, but if she had to deal with him, keeping him calm was her goal.

"That's the best part," Carmen said as she stood and grasped her hand. "You just be yourself."

"Myself?" She didn't know who she was anymore. She went from arm decoration to a mousy bank teller. Being invisible became her goal in life and now... Who was she? A desperate woman fighting for survival. It didn't matter that she was dripping in diamonds and looked as if she hadn't worked a day in her life. If anyone looked deep enough, they would see her fear. Her future depended on how well she could play her part. Maybe Keenan was right. With her looks and dress, she looked like a high-end escort. Could she play the part of an escort? That had been her role before. She had no choice but to put on the best performance of her life.

"Even though you're a hot piece of ass, Gavin loved you for *you*. He could have picked anyone since you've been gone, but I swear to you, I haven't seen him with one woman."

Before she could say she didn't give a shit if Carmen saw Gavin with five hundred women, there was a discreet knock. A maid entered with downcast eyes.

"A guest, Mrs. Pyre."

"Thank you. We're ready," Carmen said.

"Gavin?" she asked through stiff lips when the maid left.

"Probably. Are you ready?"

She glanced at her reflection and said goodbye to Morgan

Lincoln. Her eyes flashed with pain and longing as she thought of Jonathan and the simple life she left behind. What would Jonathan think if he saw her done up like a high-class hooker? She shoved self-loathing to the side. She would handle that later when she had time to wallow. Right now, she had a job to do.

They headed down the curved staircase. Carmen had decorated her home in bold colors and filled it with fine art, which included paintings, statues, and rare antiques. Carmen led her to the backyard, which had a beautiful infinity pool and a large dining table beneath a gazebo strung with white lights. A man got up from the table. Carmen and Lyla paused in mid-stride.

Manny Pyre, Gavin's father, wore a tailored black suit that wouldn't have been out of place on Wall Street. The top three buttons of his shirt were undone, giving him a rakish air. His shoulder-length white hair was combed into a slick ponytail at the base of his neck. Gold gleamed on his fingers and around his neck. Even at seventy, he was handsome. Despite losing some of his bulk, Manny still possessed the physique of a much younger man.

Her heart thumped rapidly. Even though she was glad to see her mom and Carmen, she'd been even more excited and terrified to see Manny. She had worked for Manny for a full year before Gavin asked her to be a kept woman. Manny was the father she never had, but what did he think of her leaving his son? Had he changed like Gavin? Did he loathe her? She swallowed hard as she suppressed the urge to run to him.

"Uncle Manny," Carmen said and rushed forward. "I didn't know you were coming!"

"Vinny told me my daughter came home," Manny said, without moving his eyes from Lyla.

She swallowed hard as emotion clogged her throat. From the very start, they had clicked. Manny called her his daughter when she and Gavin went on their first date. Back then, she worried that Manny's pushiness would turn Gavin off. To her surprise, Gavin didn't seem bothered by his father's interference, and he fell in line with his father's wishes. After she discovered he'd been cheating on her, she wondered if Gavin had dated her just to please his father.

"A drink, Uncle?" Carmen asked, sounding unusually nervous.

"No, I'm fine."

"I'll go check with the cook about the meal," Carmen said, and left them alone in the backyard.

She stared at Manny, the man she considered her father in every way but one.

"You don't have a welcome for me, baby girl?" Manny asked.

The pet name originated from Manny, and hearing it, she knew all was well between them. She wasn't aware of her feet moving, but she managed to pull back a moment before impact so she wouldn't topple the older man. She wrapped her arms around him, buried her face against his chest and lost herself in his musky scent. The smell filled her with nostalgia and bittersweet memories. From the very start, Manny saw something in her that no one else had and took the time to nurture her love of learning. She tried to wrap her mind around the fact that Manny ordered the hit on the man Gavin beat to death in the basement.

Manny drew back and cupped her face in one large paw. "Let me see you."

She tried to smile, but failed miserably. Tears coursed down her face as Manny examined her. His thumb brushed her bottom lip. She jerked, and he tipped her face up to the light. She knew the makeup didn't fool him.

"Lyla, what happened?" he asked gently enough, but she sensed danger in the air.

"N-nothing," she said and tried to draw back.

He clutched her arms to hold her in place. She wasn't able to stifle her painful cry, which she bit back immediately. She tried to draw away, but Manny manacled her wrist, and she froze, forcefully reminded that she didn't really know the Pyres. Manny patted her down as efficiently as a TSA agent. She couldn't contain her flinch when he located the bruises on her other arm and the ones on her neck. He smoothed her sleeves up and examined the black and blue marks before he tugged on the stretchy material of the high neck of her dress. When his hands fell away, she took a step back, unsure what to expect from him.

"Who did it?" he hissed.

Her mouth opened and closed soundlessly. "Manny, I—"

"Don't lie to me, Lyla."

For a moment, she wondered if she should fib despite the warning, but Manny possessed the same soul-searing gaze as his son. He was a human lie detector. Manny knew her better than her parents. Surely, he knew she wasn't here by choice... "Gavin."

Manny jerked as if she shot him. His incredulous expression made her flush with icy fear. Did he not believe her? Fuck, she should have lied. She reached out with placating hands as she tried to think of a way to fix it.

"I-It was nothing. It doesn't hurt. I'm fine. I bumped into—" she babbled.

He slashed a hand through the air, and she stopped. His face took on an ugly cast, and she began to shake. When Manny was pissed, heads rolled. Literally. She wasn't sure if his anger was aimed at her or Gavin. Either way, this wouldn't end well. If there was a choice between believing her or his son, she had no doubt who Manny would choose. She was on the precipice again, her life on the line. She was lightheaded with terror.

"Why are you here?" he asked, voice devoid of emotion.

Her heart shattered. She wrapped her arms around herself to ward off the sudden chill. Eyeing her painted toes, she whispered, "My dad embezzled. I'm here to pay his debt."

"How?" he bit out.

"I-I don't know."

"He beats you?"

"N-no."

"Don't lie to me."

She took another step back. Manny had never used that tone of voice with her before. How could so much change in so little time? How could she have considered Gavin and Manny to be family? They were capable of killing her without a second thought. She was a lamb in the lion's den. Once she walked into their lair, they would never set her free. She knew too much.

Voices echoed through the open doors that led to the backyard. Out of the corner of her eye, she saw Gavin, Carmen, and Vinny walk out of the house and come to a stop at the sight of her and Manny facing one another with her face covered in tears.

"Uncle Manny, what—?" Carmen began and would have run toward Lyla, but her husband pulled her back.

She had never felt so alone. Surrounded by people she once considered family, there was a possibility she would be beaten or killed by one of them. She huddled in on herself and wished she could disappear. When would this hell end?

"Dad?" Gavin asked.

"I see Lyla's back," Manny said tonelessly.

Gavin didn't answer. Manny closed the distance between himself and Lyla. Memories of the guard's brutal beating flashed in her mind, and she bit back a moan of fear. When Manny withdrew a gun from his suit and pointed it at her, she stared at him with shock and then numb defeat. Her biological father despised her. Her mother's loyalty was to her father, despite his gambling addiction. She was no one's first choice. She was disposable, replaceable, a pawn. She closed her eyes. She couldn't watch Manny pull the trigger. She hoped it would be quick. Her ears were ringing so she didn't hear the surrounding commotion, but she heard a gun blast and dropped to her knees with a scream. She hit the ground hard and waited for the pain, but it didn't come. Was she dead?

She opened her eyes. Gavin was several feet away, shouting at his father, who had the gun trained on him. Vinny had Carmen locked in his arms as she fought him to get to her.

"What the fuck? Are you insane?" Gavin shouted.

"Isn't this what you want?" Manny asked. "You want her frightened and down on her knees, right? You want to punish her for leaving you?"

Manny turned the gun back on her as she wrapped her arms

around her middle and bowed her head. Why prolong this? Was Manny toying with her for his own sick enjoyment?

"This is how you treat someone you hate," Manny instructed as if he were showing Gavin how to balance his checkbook.

"I don't hate her."

"Really?"

Manny knelt with effort and jerked her face up. He roughly wiped off her lipstick with his sleeve and ripped Carmen's dress to show her bruised arms and neck. She tried to get away from him, but his hand tightened on her in warning.

"Why is she here?" Manny hissed.

"She's here to pay her father's debt."

"How?"

"I haven't decided yet."

"You disappoint me, son."

There was a stark silence.

"This is how you treat my daughter?" he asked softly.

Gavin looked as if he'd been struck. He paled, and his eyes flicked back and forth between her and his father.

"This is how you treat someone *I* love?" Manny roared.

She whimpered, overloaded with terror. Manny dropped the gun and ignored her startled cry. He drew her into his arms and brushed gentle kisses over her face.

"I'm sorry, baby girl. I'm so sorry. I won't hurt you," he said and rose.

She stared at Manny, completely bewildered. She was close to passing out. Her heart beat a rapid tempo in her chest. Manny gently helped her up. When she sagged against him, he wrapped an arm around her waist.

"I gave you something precious, and you broke it," Manny said to his son. "What you don't care for and cherish, you lose. I would die for your mother, give everything I own for one more day with her, and you treat Lyla like this?"

"Dad—" Gavin began and reached for her.

Manny knocked his hand away as if Gavin were a child and not a man capable of killing with his bare hands. Carmen sucked in an audible breath.

Manny glared at his son. "You still have much to learn. I trusted you with Lyla, and she ran from you. Now that you have her back, you put bruises on her. The way to make a woman stay isn't by abusing her. It's by loving her so much that she can't imagine being without you." The silence stretched, and then Manny bellowed, "Ricardo!"

A Hispanic version of The Hulk appeared. Manny's bodyguard took in the scene and went straight to her. He acknowledged her with a gentle smile and picked up her quaking body.

"We're taking her home," Manny said.

She was too shaken to say a thing as Ricardo carried her out of Carmen's home and deposited her into a Rolls-Royce. Manny got into the back with her. She turned away and plastered herself against the door, wondering if her status went from bad to horrific. Manny tugged her toward him and tipped her against his chest. She trembled uncontrollably and moaned when he stroked her sweat soaked hair.

"I'm sorry I scared you. I promise I won't hurt you. I had to show him, to make him realize... Well, it doesn't matter now. It's over," Manny cooed.

"Y-you almost sh-shot..."

The car pulled out of Carmen's driveway. She wanted to leap out and make a mad dash, but her nerves were shot. She was wrecked. Too much happened in too little time. Everywhere she turned, doors shut in her face and fear yipped at her heels. Since her arrival in Las Vegas, it had been a roller coaster of uncertainty, dread, and terror. Gavin had changed beyond recognition, and it seemed, so had Manny. She loved these men, enough to look past the way they did business. She would have died for them, did anything they asked, and now she was being bandied between them like a stray puppy. She wished for Maine, sweet anonymity, and Jonathan. She felt as if she were tumbling headlong down the rabbit hole with no end in sight.

She must have dozed. When she came to, she was cradled in

Ricardo's arms, and she caught a glimpse of Manny's mansion. Although he wasn't in her line of sight, she heard Manny snapping out orders to the staff who were running in every direction. Ricardo set her on the edge of a heavenly bed, and a young woman wearing an old-fashioned maid's uniform bowed.

"My name is Juanita. The master wants you to bathe."

Lyla stared at her blankly. She was having a hard time concentrating.

"He says you might be a bit... upset. He thinks you're in shock," Juanita said gently and helped her into the bathroom and settled her on the edge of the tub before she began to fill it.

"I like tubs," she said. For some reason, this seemed important enough to say out loud.

Juanita gave her an encouraging look. "That's good. You should soak and relax."

She snorted. Relax when her life was spinning around so fast she couldn't get a hold of it? Juanita kept up a steady stream of mindless chatter as she helped her shrug off the ruined dress and expensive diamond bracelet she forgot she was wearing. She didn't have the energy to be self-conscious or worried. In the past two days, she had been blackmailed, fucked by her psycho ex, bit, threatened, pampered at a salon, and looked down the barrel of her adopted father's gun. She was so fucking *done*.

Voices sounded from the bedroom, and Juanita discreetly left to deal with it. She came back a minute later with a chagrined look on her face. "Master is very anxious."

Manny was anxious? He didn't seem anxious when he pulled a gun on her. Seriously, how the hell had she ever felt safe with the Pyres? She must have been brainwashed. The Pyre family was dangerous, unpredictable, and had their own set of rules. Manny held her at gunpoint and threatened to kill her. Why? She tried to figure out his motive, but couldn't process anything right now. She didn't even have the energy to wash, much less figure out how the Pyre mind worked. Juanita took over while her mind went on vacation. It required significant effort to scrub Carmen's makeup off, but they managed. Juanita had a prim nightgown ready for her. Whose nightgown was this? Did Manny have a girlfriend? This question seemed important for some reason.

Juanita asked if she was hungry, but she shook her head. Having her life threatened took care of her appetite for the foreseeable future. Juanita led her into a room she had occupied with Gavin a million years ago. The room was decorated in tasteful cream and gold. She sat on the edge of the bed after Juanita left.

Not even a minute later, the door opened, and Manny stood there, dressed in plaid pajamas and house slippers. He closed the door and approached slowly. She watched him with detached wariness. Now what? After taking care of her and making her feel safe, would he do something dastardly and turn on her again? That seemed to be the Pyre's MO so far.

Manny sat beside her and took her hand in his. Her skin prickled, but she didn't pull away.

"I'm so sorry," Manny said, and his voice sounded strained. "I was furious."

No shit, she thought. People with anger problems shouldn't carry guns for obvious reasons. Manny stroked his thumb over the back of her knuckles in a gesture that would have been comforting if she trusted him.

"I love my wife," he said.

It didn't matter that she had died over twenty years ago. She heard the ache in his voice. She had no doubt he mourned her every day. He squeezed her hand with surprising strength.

"Even though we had so little time together, she gave me Gavin and a lifetime of memories. No one can ever measure up to her, and I'm okay with that. I would rather have the real deal than a lukewarm imitation. Love is the most complex and rewarding emotion we can feel. I feel sorry for the poor bastards who never experience love or have it returned."

He brushed her hair back from her face. She knew he wanted her to look at him, so she mentally braced herself and turned her head. His eyes weren't filled with incandescent rage any longer. They were grief-stricken and imploring. It made her heart clench painfully because she loved him and hated to see that expression on his face.

"Lyla." He said her name like a prayer and kissed her hand. "I'm so sorry. I want you to know I would never hurt you. I love you as much as my son, and I want you to be happy. I just wish you could be happy with each other. That's always been my dream for you two."

A tear trickled down her cheek. She shook her head but said nothing. He kissed her hand once more and clasped it between his own.

"You came into my life at a time when I wasn't sure I could go on without her."

That penetrated her numb fog. She frowned.

"I felt that Gavin knew enough about the business to take over. He was reckless, but I figured he would learn from his mistakes. I went into the office on the weekend to take care of some odds and ends, and you peeked into my office." His mouth quirked. "You were waiting for your dad to finish work, and you asked if I needed help with something. No one dared to disturb me, and here you were, a slip of a girl, coming into my office and plopping down in a chair as if I was Santa Claus instead of the big bad wolf."

It was strange to think that that moment changed the course of her life. If she had kept to herself, she never would have gotten involved with the Pyres, and she wouldn't be here right now.

"I knew as soon as I met you that you were special."

His words were an echo of Carmen's. What the fuck was so special about her? No one, including herself, wanted to be where she was right now. If she was special, why did she have bruises on her body? If she was special, why were other people dictating her life? If she was special, why was she so afraid?

As if he sensed her internal distress, he turned her hand over and pressed a kiss on her palm.

"You're special," he reiterated and searched her eyes. "Your father did a number on you, that worthless asshole. The only good thing he did in his life was bring you into this world. If he weren't so selfish, he would realize that. Your mother isn't much better, that airhead."

He shook his head. She saw a flicker of anger, which he instantly controlled.

"The day you came into my office, you changed my life," he said solemnly. "I couldn't believe you were Pat's daughter, that he managed to create something so beautiful and pure. You have so much of my wife in you; originally, I suspected you were a reincarnation of her."

She stared at him. She wasn't sure how she felt about reincarnation, but she remembered being drawn to him, compelled even. As soon as they met, it felt as if they'd known each other all their lives. Manny felt like the safe haven she never had with her parents.

As she stared at him, she saw hope, loneliness, and a plea for understanding. Something inside her shifted. She leaned forward and rested her forehead against his. His tears fell silently. She wrapped her arms around him and tried to offer him a moment of respite from his grief.

"I wanted to tell you so many times, but I didn't know what you'd think. Now, I have to tell you or lose you like Gavin, and I can't allow that. I love you, baby girl," he whispered.

His words reverberated with truth and emotion. Her heart split in two. She mourned with him—for what he lost and what she had never experienced. She wasn't sure how long they stayed that way, embracing and comforting one another before he moved. He sat with his back against the pillows and pulled her down, so her head rested on his thigh. His hand sifted through her hair. She had never felt more loved and cherished than she did at that moment. There was nothing sexual in his touch; it was a simple human need for contact.

"Meeting you, it gave me life again and hope, not only for myself but for Gavin as well." When she stiffened, he made a cooing sound and stroked her hair and face until she relaxed again. "Since Gavin and I are so similar, I knew he would recognize in you what I did, and I was right. He's never committed to anyone the way he did to you. I knew he had other women on the side. I knew he would get rid of them once he made you his wife, but he kept putting it off, and then it was too late. I saw you once after you found out he cheated. Your light, it was gone. It had a profound effect on Gavin. I thought he would be able to change your mind, but before he could, you left."

Silent tears ran from the corners of her eyes, absorbed by his pajamas. It hadn't been an easy decision to leave.

"I knew within two weeks where you were."

She jerked and stared at him with wide eyes. He sniffed and wagged his pointer finger at her.

"Gavin still has a lot to learn, but I have my contacts."

"You knew and didn't tell him?"

"Gavin fucked up. I thought you deserved time to do what you wanted. I had a man check on you at least once a week in the beginning, and then once you got established, once a month. Once, Gavin's investigator got close to discovering where you were, so I derailed him with false information. That was quite fun."

She laughed weakly. How could she find anything funny after the hell she'd been through? But, miracle of miracles, she was. She also felt calm and safe, two things she shouldn't feel unless she was away from the Pyres. "Why did you do that?"

"Because you deserve to live your life. You were content, and Gavin fucked up. Sometimes, you only get one chance. I wanted him to learn that lesson."

She hesitated and then asked as gently as she could, "Are you going to let me leave?"

"No."

She closed her eyes as disappointment flared. She made a movement to get away from him, but his hand, gentle but firm, kept her in place.

"Let me tell you why."

She gave a curt nod and waited.

"Gavin changed when you left. He's relentless and merciless. That's why, when the investigator located you this time, I didn't interfere. Gavin needs you."

"Manny, I can't—" she began brokenly.

"The longer you've been away, the more remote he's become. I thought he might find someone else, but he never did, and he never stopped searching for you. He's using your father to keep you in line. I would do the same thing."

He smiled when she clucked her tongue in disgust.

"What I didn't expect was for him to take his frustration and anger out on you. I assumed he would woo you gently so he could persuade you to stay." His smile faded. "If I'd known what he would do, I never would have let him find you."

"What happens now?"

"Now we see how stupid he is. I threatened you." He paused to stroke her hair and pressed a kiss on her forehead to comfort her before he continued. "I wanted him to see how quickly you could be taken from him. You've been gone for three years. He should be kissing the ground you walk on, not scaring or hurting you. I gave you into his keeping, knowing that he needs light in his life to beat back the darkness. You humanize him, but if he's too far gone, I won't put you in his care. I'll get you out."

She felt giddy with relief. "You promise?"

He had a pained expression on his face. "Yes. As much as I'd like you to stay for myself because you make me happy, I know you deserve freedom."

"But not yet," she said sardonically.

He tapped her nose. "No. We're going to give Gavin one last chance."

"And if he fails?"

"Then I might have to kill my son."

6

The following day, she walked downstairs and was directed outside to the pool where Manny was eating lunch. He kept up a steady stream of chatter that reminded her why she enjoyed his company so much. He held her hands as he spoke to her. He treated her with care to erase last night's horror. No trace remained of the ruthless man she encountered. At times, she had flashbacks of Manny with the gun in his hand, and then remembered his admission that he had been contemplating suicide when she walked into his office all those years ago. Destiny. She pushed that to the back of her mind and enjoyed the moment.

He teased her about her not-so-delicate probing into the criminal side of the business before she left. She gave him a mock glare before they laughed. She saw movement out of the corner of her eye and saw Gavin standing nearby, watching them. Her smile disappeared. She would have pulled away from Manny if he didn't tighten his hold.

"Son," he acknowledged with a chill in his tone.

Gavin walked forward and stopped several feet away. "I want to talk to you."

Even as her hands clutched Manny's, he kissed her knuckles and rose. Father and son disappeared inside the house. She paced around the pool, twisting her hands together. She believed Manny. He wouldn't let her be around Gavin if he suspected his son wouldn't treat her right, but Gavin was a master manipulator and must be furious at his father for his interference. Or maybe Gavin wanted to wash his hands of her, and she would be free earlier than expected.

"Lyla."

She turned to find Gavin less than three feet from her. She couldn't stop herself from taking a reflexive step back and looking around for help. She wasn't happy to see that they were alone. Where was Manny?

"Lyla."

She took another step back when he took one forward. His hands twitched at his sides. Did he want to strangle her? Her heart began to race.

"I'm sorry," he said.

She blinked, sure she hadn't heard him right. "Excuse me?"

A muscle clenched in his jaw. "I'm sorry for putting my hands on you."

"Oh," she said, not sure how she was supposed to respond. "I'm okay."

He ran a hand through his hair, which was mussed and untidy. She scanned him and noticed his eyes were bloodshot and he looked exhausted. The fury and hatred he displayed toward her yesterday were absent, and he seemed more human.

"What Dad did last night..." He shook his head and then fixed her with an intense stare. "He knows how to make a statement."

"Yes, he does," she agreed.

"Do you want to be here?"

"Yes," she said hastily.

He didn't look pleased with her answer, but he didn't push. He clasped his hands behind his back and took a deep breath. "I know I haven't given you any reason to trust me, but the reason I brought you back was to re-establish our relationship."

So he blackmailed her to force her into a relationship that ended three years ago. Seriously, who could understand Gavin Pyre? "And if I don't want to go back to our old relationship?"

His expression hardened, and she saw him bite back whatever he wanted to say. His body was rigid with tension. "I want you to give me a chance."

"Why?"

"Why?" he echoed in a dangerous voice.

"Yes. Why?" She threw her hands up, confident in the knowledge that he couldn't touch her and wasn't able to kidnap her from Manny's house. Gavin was the only obstacle stopping her from going back to a normal life. She wanted to get to the bottom of why he was so fixated on her. There was no reason he couldn't find someone more compatible for him. He was good-looking, rich, and could be charming when he chose. Surely, a woman in Las Vegas existed who could give him what he needed. "I'm nobody. There must be someone you've met since I've been gone... or maybe someone from before?"

He'd been with a crapload of women. Although he tried to conceal it, she could feel his anger rising. Why?

"You're not a nobody. My father loves you like the daughter he never had. You make him happy," Gavin said.

"Is that why you think you need to be in a relationship with me? Because of him?"

"No."

He didn't elaborate, and she raised her brows. "Just, no?"

"Yeah."

She shook her head. "I don't understand you."

"Likewise." He stared at her as if she were a jigsaw puzzle. "I want to spend time with you. Come to dinner with me."

"No."

His eyes narrowed. "No?"

"Yes. My answer is no," she said firmly and prepared to run when he tensed.

"What if Carmen comes?"

She hesitated when she saw Manny watching from a lounge chair. She didn't want to go to dinner with him, but she wanted her life back, which meant spending time with Gavin and showing Manny they weren't meant for each other. Gavin wouldn't change for her. He was too far gone to be kind or considerate, and the sooner Manny saw that Gavin was a grenade waiting to self-destruct, the sooner he would send her on her way.

"Where?" she asked.

"My club, Lux."

"And Carmen will come?" she asked, needing to know there would be witnesses.

"And Vinny. Dad tells me he'll send Ricardo as well."

She relaxed, knowing that Ricardo would report everything to Manny. "Okay."

Gavin looked a tad suspicious, but he didn't push. He didn't know about her deal with Manny. If he knew that his lack of control would help her leave a second time, maybe he wouldn't be so keen to face her when she roused him to such anger. She knew stonewalling someone like Gavin was dangerous. He had been raised to take what he wanted, and her resistance went against everything he'd been taught. She was sure that tonight would put her one step closer to leaving Vegas behind.

"I'll see you tonight, then," he said.

"Yes."

"Can I send you something to wear?"

She hesitated and then shrugged since she didn't have anything at Manny's and Carmen's dress had been destroyed. "Okay."

He nodded and took a step forward, but stopped when she stiffened. His amber eyes flickered with some emotion before they became unreadable.

"I honestly regret that I hurt you. That was never my intention. I want this to work. It was never about the debt; it was just a means to get you here without fighting. You may not admit it, but this is your home, Lyla. It always will be."

She didn't deny it because it was partly true.

"I won't hurt you again; you have my word."

She wanted to believe him, but the kitchen incident was too fresh in her mind.

"I hurt you by having other women. You hurt me by leaving. We're even."

They weren't even, but she wasn't going to argue with him. She just wanted him to leave.

"I'll see you tonight, baby girl."

With that, he left. She watched him go before she walked over to Manny, who acted as if he was sleeping. She decided to do the same.

AT FOUR O'CLOCK, Carmen arrived. She looked great, as usual, but even her excellent makeup job couldn't hide her worry. Lyla rushed to her and hugged her tight.

"I'm fine," she said immediately.

"Are you really?"

"Yes."

"Holy shit, I hardly slept at all last night." Carmen waved at Manny who was talking on the phone at his desk.

She led Carmen upstairs and closed the bedroom door. "Gavin sent a dress." She gestured to the white sheath dress, which had a high neck and sleeves that ended at her elbow. The dress had an open back that packed the sensual punch all club clothes required. The dress looked demure in the front and scandalous from the back. It fit just right, which didn't surprise her. It arrived an hour ago with silver stilettos and a diamond necklace. She couldn't deny that she felt a pang of nostalgia, but she wasn't an idiot. Making sure Gavin failed to win her back was her goal. The sooner he failed, the sooner she could go back to a normal life where death didn't lurk around every corner.

Carmen started on her makeup as Lyla told her bits and pieces of what happened with Manny. She didn't tell Carmen about Manny's wife or the reincarnation part because it was too personal and

Carmen may not understand. But she explained Manny's agreement to let her go if she and Gavin couldn't reconcile.

"And Gavin doesn't know about this pact you have with Manny?" Carmen asked, aghast.

"He doesn't need to."

Carmen pursed her lips. "Girl, you should have seen him last night. He was a wreck."

She snorted. "You know who was a wreck? Me!"

Carmen waved a hand. "I know, but when Manny turned the gun on you, Gavin ran forward. Manny fired off a warning shot at him. I've never seen Gavin like that. He panicked. He may not show it, but he has deep feelings for—"

"Let's just finish up. I'm hungry," she said. Now that she had some measure of control over her life, she felt more like herself. She had an objective and wouldn't stop until it was completed. Gavin wasn't a part of her future.

Carmen gave her a judgmental look, but let the subject drop. It almost felt like old times as they got ready and strutted downstairs. Manny was there to admire and kiss their hands gallantly. They rode in the Rolls-Royce with Ricardo at the wheel. She tried to calm her nerves as they approached The Strip in all its colored glory. It had changed in the short number of years she was gone. New hotels replaced old ones, but the hyper, manic energy of those on the streets hadn't changed. People could be whoever they wanted here. They could pretend to be players, single, high rollers, or daredevils. As the slogan said, "What happens in Vegas, stays in Vegas." If only people didn't take it so literally...

They pulled up to a Pyre Casino. She took the hand that reached into the car to help her out and didn't realize who it belonged to until she was pulled against a hard body.

"You look great," Gavin said and gave her a quick kiss before he twined their hands together.

She gave an experimental yank and got nowhere.

"Lyla!"

She received a kiss on both cheeks from Vinny, who she thought of as a brother. He was even-tempered, which made him a good partner for both Gavin and Carmen. He was tall, dark, and handsome like Gavin, but his easy smile was genuine. She tried to get away to give Vinny a hug, but Gavin didn't let her go. A large group of employees milled around nervously, probably confused about the CEO and COO appearing to help someone out of a car.

"I've missed you," she said to Vinny with genuine regret and felt Gavin tense beside her. What the hell was his problem? He always had a quick temper, but now it was on a hair trigger. She looked around to make sure Ricardo was watching and found that he was.

"Let's eat," Vinny said and kissed Carmen before they went inside.

The casino was bustling with people. The familiar smells and sounds reminded her of a simpler time. When Manny hired her as his assistant, she walked through the casino with such pride, knowing she was a part of this. She took in the crowd and picked out the high rollers, gold diggers, tourists, and underage teens. As they neared the club, she heard the pump of music and saw the crowd waiting to get in. Gold ropes were cast aside as they approached, and they slipped into madness.

Lux was a new club with a massive dance floor and multiple bars to accommodate the crowds. Built like an amphitheater, it had five levels so everyone could see everything going on in the club. Strategically placed platforms highlighted professional dancers writhing in gold spotlights.

Gavin cut a path through the swarm. Despite the chaos, workers appeared to lead them to a large booth on the second tier. She scooted in and was disconcerted when Gavin sat beside her, so close that she was pressed against him. Ricardo slipped into the booth while Vinny sat on the end with Carmen on his lap. Workers in small leather skirts, tops, and hooker heels that lit up with each step brought trays of elegantly crafted appetizers and crazy-looking drinks that smoked.

She wanted to ask Gavin what she was drinking or eating, but she didn't want to engage him in conversation. She scooted farther into the booth so they weren't touching. The sheer number of people was staggering. It was like New Year's Eve in a club. After four drinks and clearing two plates of food, she felt flushed and restless. A steady parade of workers and VIPs stopped by to talk to Gavin. There was a wealth of respect there. He answered several phone calls and even responded to emails. He was a busy man, always had been. So why was he sitting with them in the middle of a club when he should be in an office?

As she looked over the dance floor, she focused on a man who walked on the fringes of the crowd. He wasn't dressed to impress. He wore jeans, a white shirt, and sneakers. He ignored the women who tried to get his attention. Even across the distance, she could see that he was hot. *Really* hot. He was tall, had a great body, and something about the way he moved reminded her of Gavin. As he approached, she saw that his eyes were a turquoise shade that stood out against his olive-toned skin. He had short-cropped hair and was clean-shaven. She straightened as he made his way toward them. Gavin's security stopped him before he reached their booth.

Vinny gave Gavin a nervous glance a moment before the stranger lashed out. Two guards dropped to their knees. Ricardo and Vinny withdrew guns, and more security rushed forward, but everyone halted when Gavin raised his hand. The man approached with an aggression that would have scared her if she cared about Gavin's well-being. When he stopped in front of Gavin, she saw that the collar of his shirt was soaked with sweat, as if he had jogged here. He was wound so tightly that she instinctively scooted as far back into the booth as she could.

"I want names," the man said, eyes trained on Gavin.

"What are you doing here, Eli?"

Eli leaned toward Gavin, a muscle clenching in his jaw. "You know."

When Eli's eyes flicked to her, her heart skipped a beat. He was hanging on by a thread. There was disdain in his eyes, but also a rage so potent that if Gavin weren't in front of her, she would have run like hell. When Gavin shifted, Eli's attention switched back to him.

"You should have set up a meeting, not approached me in public like this," Gavin said.

"My mom's in the hospital in a coma. You think I'm going to wait for you to set up a meeting?" The tendons on his neck stood out as he tried to rein in rampant emotions. "I want names, Gavin. I want them now."

"You think I know who did this to your mother?" Gavin asked in a voice that put her on edge.

Eli's tension increased. "Are you admitting there's something you don't know?"

"I didn't call the hit."

"But you know who did," Eli said, chest heaving as he tried to control his breathing. "Give me their names. Now."

"I'll take care of it."

Eli cocked his head to the side. "Did you not hear me, Pyre? They tried to kill my mother. She's not a part of this. This wasn't supposed to touch her."

Lyla's skin rippled with goose bumps.

"I got this, Stark."

"They're mine."

"You're a cop," Gavin reminded him.

"You think I'm going to leave this in your hands when this happened on your watch?" Eli hissed.

Gavin rose. Her heart nearly beat out of her chest. She knew Gavin was armed, dangerous, and fully capable of blowing someone's head off without a second thought. Vinny slipped Carmen into the booth and got between them.

Vinny placed a placating hand on Eli's chest. "Let Gavin take care of it."

Eli ignored Vinny and didn't move his eyes from Gavin. "Nothing happens without your say so."

"I don't handle low-level thugs," Gavin said.

"Every fucking crime should be on your radar. This is unacceptable, Pyre," Eli hissed.

"Don't tell me how to run my business," Gavin said, voice thick with menace. "We've been associates for many years. You know how I work; I know how you work. If anyone sees you here tonight, your testimony in court may not hold up. You're putting everything on the line."

"I don't give a fuck," Eli said through gritted teeth. "Give me their names."

"Grand, Frak," Gavin said.

Eli relaxed fractionally. He eased back from Gavin and glanced at Lyla again. She couldn't read his expression.

"We're done," Eli said and walked away.

Gavin's security moved out of Eli's way. Gavin sat and took a drink of water as calmly as if nothing out of the ordinary had happened. The look in Eli's eyes disturbed her. He would kill those men, cop or not. What other deals was Eli involved in?

"Let's dance!" Carmen shouted over the beat of the music.

She nodded. She didn't want to sit here and listen to Gavin's business. She eyed Gavin who was blocking her way and completely unaware of Carmen's suggestion... or her. Did he ask her to come tonight to ease his father's mind and make up for putting bruises on her? It only reinforced her suspicion that bringing her back to Las Vegas had everything to do with his pride and Manny's affection for her. Gavin didn't want her. He saw her as a possession that slipped through his fingers. Gavin respected and loved his father more than anyone in the world. How far would he go to make Manny happy? She glanced at Ricardo, who wore a deceptively uninterested expression. It was time to prove her point.

"Let me out," she said, and when Gavin ignored her, she placed a hand on his arm to get his attention.

His head snapped toward her. The intensity of his gaze startled her.

"I'm going to dance," she said. When he gave her a puzzled look, she was forced to lean toward him. "I want to dance with Carmen!"

He didn't move immediately. He scanned the dance floor and the surrounding tables before he stood. He held out a hand to help her out. She heard women at a nearby table grumble, jealous of Gavin's display of old-world charm. Of course, the dress covered her bruises. If only these women knew that beneath the gorgeous exterior, a killer lay in wait. When she and Carmen linked arms, Gavin gripped her hip to stop her.

"Stay in my sight," he said, lips brushing her ear.

She slipped away without saying a word, pushing thoughts of him away as she and Carmen walked onto the dance floor. Of course, Carmen didn't stop until they were in the middle of the crush. She panicked when people pressed in around her, but Carmen wrapped her close and squeezed.

"Feel it, Lyla!" she shouted. "Stop thinking and dance! We used to do this all the time, remember?"

She closed her eyes and forced herself to move. She and Carmen used to go to parties and clubs every night, but it felt like a lifetime ago. She didn't know how to move with the reckless abandon she once had.

Carmen hugged her from behind and moved to the beat. She smiled as Carmen's did ridiculous things with her hips that probably drove Vinny wild. She'd missed her cousin's free spirit. Carmen had her best interests at heart and had risked her life to get her out of Las Vegas and given her a considerable chunk of money to make her way in the world.

She opened her eyes. It took a minute for her to pinpoint Gavin through the blinking lights and sea of people. He was on his feet, leaning casually against the booth, talking on his phone. He looked good enough to be on the cover of a magazine. He was effortlessly masculine and gorgeous. No woman would pass him without a second glance. On impulse, she glanced around. She grabbed the arm of a woman two men were fighting over. The woman came willingly enough, and she found herself in a hot girl sandwich that made the men brush their hands over their crotches.

"You straight?" Lyla asked.

The stunning brunette tossed her hair and rubbed herself against Lyla's front. Carmen, never one to miss an opportunity, copped a feel of the woman's fake breasts and gave her a thumbs-up.

"Who's your doctor?" Carmen shouted.

She elbowed her cousin and leaned toward the brunette. "You see that guy?" She pointed at Gavin, who paced while he talked on the phone.

"Holy shit," the woman breathed.

"He's working too much," Lyla said with a pout. "You think you can get his attention, distract him?"

The brunette licked her lips before she turned to Lyla with a frown. "You his wife?"

"No. Trying to prove that he's still a cheater."

"Don't have to ask me twice," the brunette said and kissed Lyla on the lips before she made her way off the dance floor.

Some men chased after her, but the bombshell didn't give them a second glance. She was focused on her target.

"What the hell are you doing, Lyla?" Carmen demanded.

"Proving he hasn't changed," she said, and switched places with her cousin so she could watch the show over Carmen's shoulder. "He's a cheater and always will be. I need Ricardo to tell Manny we aren't meant for each other."

She and Carmen moved together in the middle of the bumping and grinding bodies and watched the brunette slowly make her way toward Gavin. Damn, the brunette was good. She leaned on the railing in front of the booth next to Gavin's, just far enough that if he were interested, he would have to turn his head.

"Get off the damn phone!" she bellowed.

"He's not interested, Lyla!" Carmen shouted gleefully.

"She's being too subtle... oh!"

Gavin finally caught sight of the brunette and looked her up and down. He hung up the phone and looked out over the dance floor. She whirled Carmen in the opposite direction. When she looked back, Gavin and the brunette were talking. Even while something sharp sliced through her stomach, she was grimly satisfied. Ricardo would report the encounter back to Manny. That was easy.

She danced until her feet ached, and her dress was soaked with sweat from the press of bodies.

"Drink?" she shouted at Carmen, who nodded.

She made her way to the bar and found herself face to pecs with a shirtless bartender. He grinned at her and made the muscles in his chest dance.

"What can I get for you, gorgeous?" he asked with a very white smile.

She pointed at some interesting looking drinks. "We'll try those!"

It wasn't until he was making the drinks that she realized she didn't have any money. She turned to see if she could get Carmen's attention, but that would be an impossible feat.

"I can get this for you."

She glanced at the man beside her. He had strange, angular features. He was the same height as her and had extremely narrow shoulders. The shirt tucked into his slacks brought attention to his tiny waist.

"Um, no, that's okay," she said uneasily.

"I insist."

Before she could say anything, he held out a fifty-dollar bill to the bartender. The bartender ignored him and took drink orders from two scantily clad women. When the man beside her flushed, she felt a flicker of sympathy.

"Thanks," she said. "What's your name?"

He couldn't hide his surprise. "Steven."

She held out a hand. "I'm Lyla."

His palms were damp with sweat. He quickly withdrew his hand, wiped it on his trousers, and then grasped her hand again to give it a vigorous, awkward shake. She stared at him for a moment before she burst into laughter. She put a hand on his arm when he tried to slink away.

"It's okay," she said, taking pity on him.

"I don't know how to talk to women," he muttered.

"I don't either," she said, deadpan.

Steven's thin lips twitched as if he wanted to smile, but didn't have much practice. He opened his mouth to speak but was rudely elbowed out of the way by another man who gave her a cocky grin.

The newcomer was lean, muscled, and well put together in a button-up shirt instead of thin cotton like most of the men in the club. He was attractive and stared straight into her eyes.

"Here you go," the bartender said, setting two smoking drinks on the bar.

Before Steven could extend his money, the newcomer handed a one-hundred-dollar bill to the bartender without moving his gaze from her.

She raised a brow. "I know the club is called Lux, but I think you're paying too much for my drinks."

He shrugged. "Money is no object, and I expect to be buying you drinks all night long. I'm Rafael."

"Oh, really?" The alcohol and environment gave her confidence a much-needed boost.

Rafael winked at her. "Yes. You're gorgeous. Is my brother bothering you?"

"Your brother?" she asked without comprehension before Steven stepped sideways to stand beside the much larger man.

There was no resemblance between them in looks or build.

"Steven makes people uneasy," the brother said with a careless wave at Steven who wore a blank expression. "He isn't wearing heels or his shoulder pads, so you might have mistaken him for a child."

"Um, no," she said and shot a look at Steven who didn't react to his brother's barbs.

"Your name?" the attractive brother asked.

"Lyla," she said without extending her hand.

"You're beautiful."

"You're not so bad yourself."

Rafael grinned roguishly. "I try. Are you here with someone?"

That brought her back to reality with an unpleasant jolt. "Yes."

"Pity," he said, and finally let his eyes roam over her. "You'll give me a call when you're free?"

When he reached into his pocket for his phone, she shook her head. "I don't have a phone, and I have to get going."

"You don't have a phone?"

She shrugged as she grabbed the drinks. "That's the honest truth." She spotted Carmen making her way to the restroom and smiled at Rafael. "Thank you for the drinks."

"Anytime," he said.

In the bathroom, she was mortified to find that her white dress was nearly see through. A moment later, she shrugged. She was more covered up than most of these women, and this was Vegas. Innumerable people touched her ass on the dance floor, so who cared if they got an eyeful of her body? She was sipping her drink when the brunette she sent to Gavin bustled into the bathroom and squealed.

"He's so *nice!*" she said as she rushed toward Lyla. "He offered me a job."

She choked on her drink. "What?"

"He said I have a good face and body. He asked if I want to be a hostess at one of his restaurants. You didn't tell me he's Gavin Pyre. Oh. My. God."

"Wait, he didn't hit on you?" she demanded.

The brunette gave a one shoulder shrug. "He said I was beautiful, but it was more like he was sizing me up. He asked if I had references and gave me the number of a restaurant manager. I have an interview tomorrow!" At Lyla's dumbfounded expression, the brunette said, "Maybe he's not a cheater anymore. Why would you want him to be? He seems like a great guy."

No, no, no! She glared at Carmen who was laughing her head off. She downed her drink and wished the brunette luck before she made her way back to the bar to order two more frothy drinks. Rafael and Steven were nowhere to be found.

"Are you trying to get drunk?" Carmen asked without judgment as she knocked back identical drinks. She believed that whatever pain Lyla went through tomorrow, that it was her job to go through it with her.

"Hunting for more women for Gavin," she said distractedly as she scanned the crowd. "Maybe he doesn't want a brunette. Maybe he wants an Asian chick. I saw him with a black girl that day..." She shook her head to banish the images. "She was pretty before I broke her nose. Anyway..."

Carmen mumbled under her breath as she followed her back to the dance floor. Lyla chose a handful of women Gavin wouldn't be able to turn down. Each woman was more than willing to test his control. Some were aggressive, while others played hard to get. One thing was certain. Each of them gained Gavin's attention for a time, but none of them stayed by his side. Some came back to her to report that he offered them a job or asked if they were trying to get back at an ex.

"What the hell? Is he the Santa Claus of jobs in Vegas?" she growled.

Carmen laughed hysterically. Lyla was talking to an exotic woman of Indian descent when a hand wrapped around her waist. She didn't need to look to know who it was.

"You have excellent taste in women," Gavin said in her ear, "but your parade is interrupting me from doing business."

She turned from the Indian woman who tugged down the neckline of her gown to give Gavin a better look at her cleavage. She turned in Gavin's arms in time to see him wink at the woman before he led her off the dance floor. He didn't go back to their booth; he led her behind the bar, into a small hallway off the kitchen. He backed her against the wall and stared down at her.

"What are you playing at?"

"Playing at?" She was drunk enough to give him a mystified expression even though she'd been caught red-handed.

"Are you interested in threesomes now?"

His question sobered her instantly. She dropped the act. "I don't do threesomes."

"Then why are you sending me all these women?"

"So you can pick one."

"For what?"

"For yourself!"

"I have you."

She stared at him, astounded by his bone headedness. "You don't have me, jackass!"

The predator in him rose and reflected in his eyes. "I will have you again, Lyla."

"You will never have me," she said, the drinks in her system making her reckless and not giving a crap about the consequences of pitting herself against Gavin Pyre. "You hurt me!" She slammed her hand against her racing heart and then over the bruises on her neck. "I don't trust you, and I never will."

Gavin said nothing. His face was expressionless.

"I want a normal life with a sweet guy," she said forlornly, her anger fading as suddenly as it swept through her. She stared up at him, imploring. "There must be someone else for you. These women want you, would do anything for you—"

"I don't want them."

She thumped his chest with her fist. "You're mad that I left you, that I was happy without you—"

He cupped her face and leaned down so their lips were centimeters apart. "You weren't happy without me."

"What?"

"You weren't happy without me," he stated with complete certainty. "You can't be happy without me."

"I was!" she insisted and shoved at him.

He lifted her, so they were at eye level. Servers rushed in and out of the revolving kitchen door, but no one paid them any mind, and they were too locked on one another to notice the pandemonium behind the scenes that made the club such a success. His finger traced the curve of her cheek and then her throat. When her breath hitched, his eyes glinted with triumph.

"If you were in love with that boring fuck you were living with, you wouldn't respond to me." He pressed against her, letting her know he was fully aroused. "You've been living a safe, boring life, baby girl. You missed this, missed me."

"No, I—" She bit back a moan as he rocked against her. "Stop it!"

"You're soaked for me, aren't you? Just like in your sleep. You want me, need me, Lyla. The moment I touch you, your body responds. It's still mine."

She was stunned. How had this backfired so badly? Her plan to incriminate Gavin crumbled as he turned the tables on her and showed her how susceptible she was. What the fuck? "Let me go."

"No."

He seemed content to keep her pinned against the wall with his cock nestled between her legs. She wriggled and froze when the bulge in his pants pressed against her clit. She hissed through her teeth and thumped his shoulder.

"Back off, Gavin!"

"So, you can send more women to me? I'm content right here," he said and squeezed her ass.

She bucked, and they both groaned. It took considerable effort to remember why she was holding him off and not indulging in the lust roiling through her. "You're doing this for Manny!"

"I'm giving myself a hard-on for my dad?"

"Don't get smart with me, Gavin! You're oversexed. We both know it. You don't know how to commit to one woman. You cheated on me the whole time we were together. One of those women," she jabbed her finger toward the club, "won't care that you fuck around. They won't say a thing. Just give them an unlimited credit card, and they'll do whatever you want. I'm not that girl, not anymore. The sooner we find you a girl, the sooner you get over your ego trip, and I can go back to—"

"You're not going anywhere," he interrupted and rocked himself against her core.

Her mouth fell open with a gasp.

"I've been looking for you for three years. You think now that I have you back, I'm going to fuck around again?"

"Why not? You did the first time. By the way," she prodded his rock-hard chest, "you didn't use a condom the other night."

He stilled. "You aren't on anything?"

"I have an IUD. I'm more worried about an STD."

Gavin looked murderous. "You think I'm that careless?"

"I don't know what you use when you fuck your whores," she said.

"I'm not fucking anyone."

She didn't believe him. They'd had sex almost every day when they were together, and he still had women on the side. Thinking of an abstinent Gavin was ludicrous. "So, you've been tested recently?"

"You're really trying to piss me off, aren't you?"

"By asking justifiable questions?" She sighed and shook her head, feeling weary all of a sudden. "If Manny hadn't thrown me at you, you wouldn't have noticed me. How many women did you have at that time?" He didn't answer, and her stomach twisted. She shoved against him. "I'm not interested in replaying our history, Gavin. Manny's not going to disown you if you let me go."

"Do you want to go home?" Ricardo appeared beside them. He didn't look surprised by their intimate position.

"Yes." She pushed at Gavin, but he didn't move. She met his glittering eyes. "Let me go, Gavin."

"For now," he said and released her, deliberately sliding her down his frame.

She hated her body's reaction to him. She was ashamed that her legs quaked a little when her feet touched the ground.

Gavin stepped back and then scowled. "Your dress is see-through!"

She shrugged. "You picked it. I thought that was the point. No one cares. It's Vegas."

"I fucking care," he snapped and slid out of his suit jacket and draped it over her.

She didn't want to be encased in his scent or heat. "I'm hot," she said as she tried to shrug off the jacket.

"You'll wear it to the car," he decreed.

She couldn't spend another second with him. He was such a bull-headed ass. Nothing she said made an impression on him. Besides the fact that their relationship had been based on Manny's approval and Gavin's infidelity, she had to remind herself about the guard who lost his life in the basement. Gavin was dangerous. She had to get away from him and his propensity for violence. She wanted a simple life. She wanted a man who loved her more than anything in the world. Once upon a time, she thought Gavin was that man. What a fucking reality check it had been to realize she was living a lie.

They made their way through the club. Gavin tucked her under his arm and ignored her attempts to get away from him.

"What about Carmen?" she shouted.

"She'll go home with Vinny."

He took her hand as they walked through the casino with Ricardo several paces behind them.

"Did you like the club?" Gavin asked.

Surprised by his attempt at civil conversation, she said, "Yes. The music is great, the bartenders are fast, and the people who get in look like they should be in a magazine."

His mouth curved. "Well said. It's the most successful nightclub on The Strip. You sent me a good array of girls tonight. I hope they come to work for me."

She rolled her eyes. "What positions did you offer them?"

"Front desk, dancers, bartender."

She was relieved to reach the hotel entrance. While Ricardo talked to the valet, Gavin turned her toward him with a grip on the jacket.

"You still want to be at my father's house?" he asked.

"Yes," she said emphatically.

"I'll send some of your clothes over."

"How gracious of you," she drawled, "since you threw away what I brought with me."

"It's an insult to your body to wear such shoddy clothes."

She glared at him. "Bank tellers don't have the budget to wear Armani or Prada."

"If you stayed with me, you wouldn't have to work at all."

"I don't mind working."

He surveyed her for a moment. "You could always work for me."

"No thanks," she said quickly.

"Come, Lyla," Ricardo called as the car pulled up.

When Ricardo ducked into the driver's seat, Gavin opened the back door. Before she could slip out of his jacket, he gripped the lapels and jerked her against him. His mouth covered hers before she had time to defend herself. His tongue stroked hers while his hands splayed on her bare back and caressed. She staggered back, breaking the kiss. He grinned and gave her one last chaste kiss before he tucked her into the back seat.

"Me wanting you has nothing to do with my father," he said as he buckled her in and deliberately brushed his hand over her breasts. "And if you think I've waited three years to let you leave me again, you're dead wrong."

With that threat hanging in the air, he stepped back and slammed the door. He strode into the hotel without looking back. She tried to steady her breathing and saw Ricardo watching her in the rearview mirror.

"He's an ass," she said.

"Yes, ma'am," Ricardo said with a grin.

7

The following morning, she descended the stairs wearing a fitted jersey dress that flirted around her ankles. Gavin had made good on his promise to deliver part of her old wardrobe.

Manny sat at the large dining table, surrounded by an assortment of breakfast foods. He set the newspaper aside; his face lighting up as if his day didn't start until she joined him. A streak of pain darted through her chest. She recognized the feeling. Love. Even as she tried to reassert common sense, Manny held his arms open as if she really was his daughter, and her eyes stung with tears as she fell into his embrace. His love washed away the fact she was being held here against her will.

"You slept well?" he asked when she drew away.

"Yes," she said as she sat beside him. "What are you up to today?"

"I thought I would go antique shopping. Interested?"

"Yes." Anything to distract her from her bizarre circumstances. She was a captive of the Pyre men who had different wants from her. Although she missed Jonathan and felt guilty for whatever pain her leaving caused, she couldn't deny she was enjoying her time with Manny. Her parents were too self-involved with each other to care what happened to her, so Manny was the closest thing she had to a parental figure. It just sucked that Manny was connected to Gavin.

"How did you like Lux?" he asked.

She gave him a similar answer to what she told Gavin the night before. Like Gavin, Manny seemed pleased.

"Ricardo tells me that you tried to find Gavin a replacement."

She paused in the middle of nibbling on a piece of bacon. While Manny's voice was mild, his eyes sparkled with mischief.

She lifted her chin defensively. "What of it?"

He smacked the table, making her jump.

"That's great!"

"It is?"

"The woman he wants doesn't want him and offers to help him find another. That's rich!" Manny howled with laughter.

She forked up hash browns. "I don't think it's funny."

"I do." He shook his head. "I know my son. What you did last night will only make him more determined to have you."

Her fork clattered to the table. "What? *Why?*"

"Lyla, you need to know something about men," he drawled, spreading his bejeweled hand over his chest. "We don't like being told no."

"I didn't tell him no. I'm letting him do whatever he wants. I want him to follow his natural instinct and leave me alone—" She had to stop because he was laughing hysterically. "Seriously, Manny, what's so funny?"

"Baby girl," he said, wiping tears from his eyes, "Gavin has been looking for you for three years."

"I know that."

"And why do you think he's done so?" he asked curiously.

"He's doing it for you," she accused.

He blinked. "Me?"

"He craves your approval. You practically demanded he marry me on our first date."

Manny cocked his head to the side. "And you think that Gavin would date a woman he didn't like because I told him to?"

"Yes," she said without hesitation.

"I told him to marry you many times."

"I know," she said.

"If he wanted my approval, why didn't he marry you to please me?"

"Because he doesn't want to tie himself to me *permanently*. He was just... indulging you."

"Gavin wants my approval, and he loves me," he conceded, "but Gavin wouldn't fuck one woman for four years to please me."

"He didn't fuck one woman; he fucked many," she said crisply.

He sobered and ran a hand down her hair, which hung loose around her shoulders. "That wrecked you, didn't it?"

She wasn't sure where the tears came from, but she valiantly shoved them back into the darkness where they belonged. "Finding out that it wasn't a one-time thing, that he'd been cheating from the beginning destroyed me. The only thing that makes sense is that he kept me for your sake. He had no intentions of marriage or really committing himself to me." She blew out a breath and was relieved to feel the tears recede. "I want a man who loves me more than anything, especially other women. Gavin made me feel like nothing." And he wouldn't get the chance to make her feel like that again.

Manny shook his head. "Boy screwed up."

"No, it was meant to be. It woke me up. I got to see the world a bit, and I found a great guy." She ignored his derisive look. "Jonathan's really sweet."

"I'm biased, mi amor."

"Of course, you are," she grumbled. "I just want normal, Manny."

"But you aren't normal."

She straightened in her chair. "Yes, I am."

"If you were normal, you wouldn't be here."

She didn't know how to challenge that statement, and didn't have the chance to since he rose.

"Eat, and we'll go shopping," he said and left her at the table, staring after him.

Of course, she was normal. If she hadn't gained Manny's attention as a teenager, her life would have been extremely ordinary. Maybe she would have followed her father into accounting or gotten married to some Joe Schmo and been a stay-at-home mom. She wasn't Carmen—adventurous and sexy with a personality that electrified the room. Everyone around her wasn't normal, which is why she clung to Jonathan. He was safe and ordinary. Gavin's words came back to haunt her. *If you were in love with that boring fuck you were living with, you wouldn't respond to me.* Of course, she loved Jonathan. The fact that she responded to Gavin was... It was...

"Ready, Lyla?"

Manny was dressed in jeans with a gold chain around his neck, a gold cane, and gold-framed sunglasses.

She got to her feet and grinned at him. "You look like a pimp."

"This is Vegas, baby girl; you have to dress with flair."

Ricardo had a Mercedes waiting for them in the driveway. When they got into the back seat, she wasn't surprised when Manny clasped her hand in his.

"Why did you retire?" she asked.

"I was too old for the bullshit." At her inquiring look, he shrugged. "I was losing my touch. They needed someone tougher at the helm. That wasn't me."

"And Gavin is tougher?" she asked carefully.

He squeezed her hand. "I made sure he would be. He needs to see the business through to the next generation."

Next generation? She ignored that and asked, "You're completely out of the business?"

"Yes. I don't know a thing," he said and waved a dismissive hand. "It's fantastic. True freedom."

That was what she wanted. She didn't want to wonder how many Gavin murdered, or if the man holding her hand with such care taught him to kill.

"Gavin is the CEO, Vinny the COO. They work well together. While they slave away all day, I do what I like."

"Which is?"

"Sometimes, I gamble for the hell of it. I went on a Mediterranean cruise and a safari. Whatever whim I have, I act on."

"Do you have any trips planned?"

He kissed her knuckles. "Not right now. If Gavin is a fool, you can choose a place you wish to visit."

If Gavin let her go, she would leave, not go on a vacation... But she didn't want Manny to go alone. She had to remind herself that she wanted away from Vegas and the Pyres.

Ricardo pulled up to a sketchy building where the man behind the counter greeted Manny by name and assumed she was his young mistress. Of course, the man wasn't stupid enough to say it out loud, but he didn't need to. The shopkeeper's poorly concealed jealousy made her edge closer to Manny. They browsed aimlessly, poring over knick-knacks or laughing over offensive paintings and statues they stumbled across. The day passed by pleasantly.

When they stopped for lunch on The Strip, she was relieved to see they weren't at a Pyre establishment. Manny led her into a dimly lit, quiet, and beautiful restaurant with nice views of the city. Despite the fact this wasn't one of their restaurants, the staff still fawned over Manny and called him by name. The Pyres were Las Vegas kingpins, and everyone knew them. Once they ordered drinks, she excused herself to go to the bathroom. She felt underdressed, but that couldn't be helped. She was on her way back to the table when someone called her name. She paused and saw Rafael and his brother, Steven, rise from a table. Rafael sauntered toward her while Steven ambled behind.

"Fancy meeting you here," she said.

"Yes." Rafael raised a brow. "You have no phone, but you seem to have no problem getting into exclusive places. It must be that pretty face."

"I have good friends," she said.

"I could be an even better friend," he said, spreading his arms wide and giving her a devilish grin. "And a more generous one."

He obviously thought she was someone's arm candy and could be bought. "Thanks for the offer," she said carelessly, "but I like the friends I have."

Rafael was about to say more when he looked past her. His eyes narrowed, and he reached for something in his jacket in a way that made her heart skip. She stepped back and collided with an unyielding body. A hand gripped her waist. She had no doubt who was holding her so possessively. What surprised her was the way Rafael's face morphed into cold fury. What the fuck?

"Stay away from Lyla," Gavin ordered.

Rafael's eyes flicked from Gavin back to her. "You've been holding out on me, beautiful. You didn't tell me who your *friend* is."

Gavin's grip tightened. "Keep your distance. She's mine."

Rafael's expression turned calculating. He went from flirtatious to menacing stranger in a millisecond.

"What if she doesn't want to stay away from me?" Rafael asked.

"She will," Gavin decreed. "I'll make sure of it."

Rafael inclined his head. "We'll see, Pyre."

The men at Rafael's table watched Gavin as if he were a ticking bomb. Maybe he was. Gavin ushered her past Rafael to their table.

"We're leaving," Gavin said shortly. "Rafael is here."

Manny rose without a word, and they left the restaurant. Gavin took Lyla's hand and squeezed a bit too tightly. She slapped his wrist, and when he looked down at her, she felt a chill. He looked murderous.

"What the—?" she began, but he shook his head and walked even faster.

He led her out of one casino and into the next, which he owned. He pointed at a restaurant.

"Dad, get us a table. I need to talk to Lyla," he said with poorly concealed fury.

Manny eyed Lyla briefly before he entered the restaurant and was greeted by servers who screamed and rushed to hug and kiss him in welcome. Gavin towed her in the opposite direction. It took her only a minute to figure out where they were going. She pulled back to slow him down, which resulted in him picking her up without breaking his stride.

"Let me go," she hissed and tried to smile reassuringly at the employees who goggled at the sight of their CEO toting a woman around. "You're making a scene."

"I'm trying *not* to make a scene," he hissed. "Shut up, Lyla."

She wanted to push, but decided against getting into a public knockdown, drag out fight in front of his employees. He strode into his office and locked the door. She knew from her time working for Manny that the executive offices in every casino were soundproof. That realization penetrated a moment too late.

"How do you know Rafael?" he bit out, body vibrating with tension.

"Who is he?"

"Lyla."

When his hands balled into fists, she took a step back.

"Tell me how you know him," he demanded.

"I met him last night."

He blinked. "What?"

"I met him at Lux."

"How the *fuck* did Rafael Vega get into my club?" he roared, veins in his neck popping.

The explosion propelled her backward. The back of her legs hit the couch, and she sat with a plop. She shrank into the cushions as he approached.

"So, you met him at Lux," he said, voice calm, but everything else about him pulsed with rage. "Where in Lux? What did he say?"

"He didn't say much. He bought me drinks." When he gaped at her, she said defensively, "I don't have money!"

He leaned down, fists depressing the cushions on either side of her. "Lyla, you don't let *anyone* buy you a drink, least of all Rafael Vega."

"Who is he, and why are you so pissed?"

"He's a sadistic fuck. He runs the prostitution ring in Las Vegas."

Her stomach lurched. The charming, cocky guy who bought her a drink last night ran a prostitution ring? Seriously, how the fuck did she attract men like that?

He caught her chin in his hand. "You don't *ever* talk to him."

"I don't want to," she said honestly.

That didn't seem to make any impact on his simmering rage.

"I can't leave you alone for a minute," he hissed. "Did he say anything else?"

"He asked for my number, but—"

"He *what?*"

He grabbed a paperweight and hurled it. Glass exploded, leaving a fist-sized hole in the wall. She got to her feet as he swept everything off his desk and onto the floor. Papers flew, his lamp shattered and pens flew like daggers.

"Gavin, stop!" When he reached for his computer, she rushed forward and grabbed his arms. "Gavin!"

At her touch, he froze. She could feel his muscles flexing beneath her fingertips. The force of his emotions was nearly physical. She felt battered by it, but didn't back away.

"Nothing happened," she said, hoping to get through to him. "He didn't even touch me."

For a moment, she wasn't sure he heard her, and then his mouth was on hers. He clasped her head still for his assault. Fear collided with lust and exploded inside her, sweeping away all rational thought.

"You're mine," he said when he drew back, gazing down at her with a hunger that should have made her run. "No one else's."

He gripped her hips and set her on his desk. Before she could figure out what he was doing, he brushed her dress up, spread her thighs, and ripped her thong.

"Gavin, what—?"

His tongue slipped into her vagina, and her mind went blank with shock. He dragged her to the edge of the desk and ate her as if his life depended on it. One hand pinned her thigh open while the other cupped her ass, drawing her tight to his intimate kiss. She couldn't think as pleasure ricocheted through her. His talented mouth suckled her clit. Before she could counteract the pleasure or get a hold on it, her climax, violent and unstoppable, blasted through her. She wrapped her legs around his head, body bowing as he slammed his fingers into her, eliciting mind-numbing pleasure so great, her mind shut down and her body took over. When it became too much, she yanked on his hair, trying to get his mouth to detach from her. He moaned but didn't budge. She could hear him swallow as he lapped up her juices.

"G-Gavin, please stop," she said hoarsely, shuddering.

Without moving his head, he pushed her, so she sprawled on her back in a boneless heap on the slick surface of his desk. He used his fingers this time, curling and stroking. The heat began to build again. She tried to kick him, but he pinned her wide. She had no defense as he teased her oversensitive nerves.

"I-I can't," she panted even as another climax punched through her.

She erupted, body jerking as he pulled the strings like the master he was. When rational thought returned, she found him standing over her, fingers still buried between her legs.

His eyes were ablaze with lust. "I didn't ask the first time. You say I raped you. Will you let me have you?"

It would feel damn good, but... "No."

His finger gave her clit a last swirl that made her gasp. He took his hand from between her legs and licked it. Her stomach clenched.

"This will tide me over until you ask me."

She forced herself to sit up even though she was trembling uncontrollably. "Ask you?"

"You will," he said as he walked into the bathroom and washed his hands and fixed his hair. He came back with a washcloth and efficiently cleaned her before he dragged her off the desk and gave her a deep kiss. "Dad's waiting."

Her mouth sagged open. Before she could get her wits together, he ushered her out the door and past his secretary.

"Have someone clean up my office. I made a mess," he said.

The hand on her waist tightened when she hissed at the double entendre. Her feet moved, but she didn't remember the trip through the casino back to the restaurant. Manny was in the middle of his meal when they walked in. He took one look at them and clapped his hands together.

"You are back together?" Manny shouted, drawing the attention of the other patrons and half the staff.

She wanted to disappear. "No, Manny."

He looked crestfallen.

"Soon," Gavin predicted as he guided her into a chair, kissed her cheek, and took the seat beside her.

"Progress is good," Manny said as he cut into his steak. "I ordered for all of us. Eat up. I'm sure you're both starving."

She let out an outraged gasp while Gavin chuckled. He went from The Hulk to a gentleman in the blink of an eye. What the fuck? He made her orgasm multiple times. No dream to blame this time. His expertise was undeniable, but if it had been any man between her legs, would she have responded the way she had?

"Eat," he said firmly.

When she glanced at him, he gestured to her pasta.

"It's our specialty. You'll like it."

He was acting as if the tantrum in his office never happened, as if the *three years* she was gone never happened.

"You're insane," she whispered.

He shrugged. "Where you're concerned, I don't act rationally."

That was the understatement of the century. Nothing was rational about Gavin. He blackmailed her into coming back to Las Vegas and wanted to resume a nonexistent relationship. He wasn't a homeless psycho or ugly bastard who had to pay for a mail-order bride. He could have *anyone*. Why fixate on her? And why oh, why did she go off like a geyser every time he touched her? This couldn't be happening.

"I can feed you," he said and reached for her fork.

She slapped his hand away. "I can feed myself."

"You need to keep your strength up," he said with a straight face.

"Fuck you, Gavin," she hissed.

"I can't wait."

Manny nearly choked on his steak from laughing so hard.

8

"No!" Lyla shouted.

Carmen put a hand on her hip. "What the hell is wrong with you?"

"I'm not going to another club with Gavin!"

"I'm going too."

"Big help you were last night when he pinned me against a wall!"

Carmen licked her lips. "You fucked in a hallway?"

She wanted to pull her hair out. "No!"

Carmen lost interest immediately. "Vinny will be there too. I haven't been to The Room yet. It's not crazy like Lux. It's a classier club."

"I'm not going."

"Don't be such a baby. I brought you a hot dress."

She gave the cute dress a cursory glance. "I'm not leaving this room."

"You wanna bet?"

Her heart sank. Carmen could be a bulldog when she wanted something. If she told her cousin that Gavin ate her out as if she were the elixir of life and gave her two mind-blowing orgasms, Carmen would be even more ruthless.

She had barely survived lunch. Gavin talked to his father as if the incident with Rafael and the interlude in his office had never happened. He was so calm and collected; she would've thought she imagined everything if her body didn't have aftershocks still coursing through her. Manny was gleeful and wouldn't listen when she told him not to get his hopes up. While she sat there and considered nailing her bedroom door shut, Carmen barged in and announced that they were going out again. Her life was seriously fucked.

Carmen forced her into the shower and made her look presentable while she tried to fortify her defenses. She had no idea where she stood with Gavin, and she had lost major ground with Manny today. He thought they had sex. Well, *she* had. Manny nearly danced into the house this afternoon. Her escape route was closing, and she needed it to reopen. Gavin was wise to her tricks and wouldn't respond to her attempts to find him a distraction. So, what tactic could she adopt to keep him at bay?

Even as they pulled up to another Pyre Casino and Gavin and Vinny appeared, she still wasn't sure how to handle him. Gavin helped her from the car and gave her a thorough kiss.

"I can still taste you," he said when he drew away.

Appalled, she elbowed him in the stomach and tried to walk into the casino without him. He laughed and caught up with her, dragging her beneath his arm.

"No one tastes like you, baby," he said.

"You'd know," she snapped.

"You really think I still want other women?"

"Nothing's changed."

He opened his mouth to respond, but the club bouncers inclining their heads respectfully distracted him.

"Mr. Pyre," they said, tones nearly reverent.

The Room was a high-end club with modern lounging furniture and blue lighting. A live band played bluesy, melancholy music that set the mood. Gavin guided her up the stairs, where behemoth-sized security manned the second floor. It looked out over the club with private alcoves and white pod chairs that two people could comfortably sleep in. Frosted white glass separated the top floor into private sections. She could see the silhouettes of the people next to them. Did people come here to fuck or watch other people get it on? Who wanted to have sex in a club? Gavin, of course. It turned her stomach, and when he tried to pull her down to share his pod chair, she resisted, but he wouldn't take no for an answer. He gave a firm yank, and when she plopped down beside him, he wrapped her close. Carmen and Vinny took another pod chair, while Ricardo took the last.

Scantily clad women swarmed around them, dropping artfully arranged appetizers on a tiny table in front of each pod. Even though she knew Carmen, Vinny, and Ricardo were nearby, they weren't able to talk to one another over the music. The pods were designed to encase each couple in a dome of privacy. This was too intimate for her peace of mind.

"Eat," Gavin said.

Because she wanted to calm her jittery stomach, she complied. The food was excellent, and the champagne mellowed her out. She watched the singer on stage perform, face rapt with emotion. Was that Ariel, Jonathan's favorite female singer and celebrity crush? She downed more champagne, but couldn't drown out the guilt and pain. How was he? She wished she could call him to apologize, to explain, but she couldn't. Her eyes burned.

"What are you thinking about?" Gavin asked, warm breath gusting over her cheek.

She refilled her glass and glanced sideways at Gavin, who looked devilishly handsome. She tried to put the events of this afternoon out of her mind, but it was impossible. How much of what Jonathan said during the dream had actually been Gavin? She licked her lip, which was nearly healed. That first night, Gavin took care of her, bathing and tending to her with soft kisses and gentle hands. The next morning, he morphed into a monster. Then he exploded over Rafael asking for her number and gave her orgasms? Who was he? *You humanize him*, Manny claimed. Gavin and Manny straddled the line between legal and illegal business and had no qualms about it. Gavin lived an unconventional, no-holds-barred life. It was no wonder he was part civilized, part barbarian.

"What do you want?" The question popped out of her mouth before she could stop it. The champagne loosened up her tongue and body, which slumped against him.

"I want many things," he said.

"And you always get what you want?"

"Until you, yes."

"What do you want from me? You can get what you want from anyone."

His hand splayed on her spine, branding her. She tried to twist away from him.

"Gavin—"

"I cheated on you because I hate the power you have over me."

She froze. The hand on her back increased its pressure ever so slightly before it relaxed again. She could feel his internal struggle. She shook her head, certain she didn't want to hear what he had to say.

"No, Gavin," she said and tried to push away.

"When Dad introduced us, I knew you were it for me. I didn't like it. I was too young to commit to one woman, so I fucked around because I could."

She let out an angry, disgusted sound and shoved against his chest. Man logic. Ego. She had no patience or interest in either.

"I thought no matter what I did, you would forgive me. I took your love for granted. When you found out, you changed. The way you looked at me... You wouldn't let me touch you, and no matter what I promised, you didn't believe me. You wouldn't let me fix it. I could feel you slipping through my fingers. I was going to propose, but you took off." He brushed a soft kiss on the corner of her mouth. "I know I drove you away. I was so fucking scared that someone had you and would..." He shook his head. "I figured that if you weren't being held against your will, you'd come back to me eventually." His eyes narrowed. "Then I found out no one took you, and you weren't just okay, you were doing fucking fine without me. I hated that. That you could live without me, that you had moved on. I hate it because I can't be without you."

Panic spread through her, a cold wave that made her skin erupt in goose bumps as he stared at her, resolve and something dangerous clear in his gaze.

"I'm going to do whatever it takes to make you love me again," he vowed.

She didn't want to be here, to be won over or seduced. She didn't want a man with a dark side, a hair-trigger temper, and a basement where he tortured and killed. She wanted a man who wouldn't hurt her emotionally or physically. She didn't want a man people feared. She wanted a man she could depend on. When would Gavin realize she wasn't a love-struck fool? That she couldn't give him what he wanted? She wasn't the girl for him.

"We're over, Gavin," she said, willing herself to believe it.

"We've never been over."

"Three years, Gavin. *Three*."

"That wasn't my choice. I don't care how much time passes. We're meant for each other."

She shook her head wildly, willing him to see, to understand. "I'm not what you want."

"You're exactly what I want."

"You don't know what you want!"

"Of course, I do."

She *hated* feeling like this—desperate, afraid, and fucking needy. When her eyes filled with tears, he groaned.

"Fuck, don't cry."

"I can't do this."

"You can. You can take it, Lyla."

"I have a life, Gavin. I was happy—"

"You weren't," he said in a near feral snarl.

"Stop saying that!"

His hands sank into her hair as he pulled her close. "Just as I know you were meant for me, you know it too. You feel it."

"No," she whispered and tried to shake her head, but his grip wouldn't allow it.

"No matter what you believe about me, Lyla, I care. I never stopped looking, never stopped wishing you were here with me. Does that sound like a man who doesn't know what he wants?"

"It sounds like an obsession. That means nothing."

"Obsession." He tasted the word and apparently approved of it because he nodded. "Yes."

There was a war taking place inside her. Heart and mind clashed. Was it better to live a safe life or live dangerously, straddling the line between love and hate and life and death?

"Whatever you need to be mine again, I'll do," he said.

"I don't trust you."

"I'll work on it. What else?"

Having his undivided attention unnerved her. He looked at her as if she mattered, as if his life depended on the words that fell from her lips. She averted her eyes and tried to regulate her breathing.

"What else, Lyla?" he insisted. "What do I have to do to get you back?"

Was she in an alternative universe? Was she actually contemplating giving him a chance? He wanted a list of rules? She would give him one. "Don't threaten me; don't threaten people I love."

He nodded.

"You don't hurt me *ever*."

"I won't."

She didn't believe him. His temper had gotten worse over the years, not better. "If this doesn't work out, you have to let me go. You can't expect anything I feel to be genuine if I'm a captive."

His fingers twitched. She could see that this last one went against his need to control, to dominate. Before, his alpha personality excited her. Now, she saw the damage it wrought, and it scared her. She wasn't a child who needed to be monitored. She was a full-grown woman who had been on her own for years and was fully capable of accomplishing what she set her mind to.

"How long?" he asked.

"Three months?"

"Give me three years."

"You have to be joking."

"I'm not," he said through clenched teeth. "You took away three years; you give me back three."

She shook her head at his logic. Psycho Pyres. "Six months."

"Two years."

"Eight months."

"One year."

Their negotiating was pointless since she already had a deal with Manny, but if that backfired, she needed another out. Could she last a year? She could hibernate in Manny's house when Gavin was too much to handle. A year in Vegas for real freedom where she didn't have to look over her shoulder? A year in Las Vegas with Carmen, her parents, Manny, and Gavin. Before she discovered Gavin's infidelity, she'd been happy here. She could spin this to her benefit and spend time with Manny and Carmen. She was giving Gavin a year, but that didn't mean she was spending a year with *him*. She was committing to staying *in Vegas* for a year.

"Final offer?" she asked, and he nodded. "Fine. One year."

He closed his eyes. When he opened them, they were unguarded and filled with joy. When was the last time she saw Gavin like this? When they first met? When Manny began to step back from the company, Gavin had changed. With more responsibility came less leisure time. It wasn't just the legitimate side of the business he had to tend to, either. At the thought of the man in the basement, her stomach clenched. It was a good thing she was staying with Manny. She didn't want to witness any more beatings or become Gavin's punching bag if he lost it. Distance was key when dealing with him.

She leaned forward and saw Carmen and Vinny making out in the other pod. "I want to dance!"

Carmen heard her because she broke her lip lock with her irritated husband and bustled over. She took Lyla's hand and led her downstairs. The music picked up when they stepped on the dance floor. She gave herself up to the beat. Life was too complicated to plan, and it would do whatever it felt like anyway. She had no control over anything. She was so fucking tired of being on the run, of trying to anticipate bad shit. She let it all go and danced her troubles away.

Large hands splayed on her abdomen and pulled her back against a broad body. She kept her eyes closed as they moved. Songs changed, but the hands didn't leave her. At some point, she turned to face him and realized what a big mistake that was. His cock pressed against her belly and she saw that his face looked carnal in the blue lights from above. She hated that she responded to the desire on his face. How could she want him, even after all the things he'd done? Ashamed, she turned to Carmen, who was dry humping Vinny.

"I'm done. I want to go home," she said.

"I'll take you," Gavin said.

"I rode with—"

"I know."

He pulled her off the dance floor and jerked his head at Ricardo. They walked out of the club and past the line of people still waiting to get in. They were both soaked with sweat. She was tired. She wanted to take a shower and crash in Manny's guest bedroom, away from Gavin. His energy buzzed around her. People felt the force of his personality and got out of the way. Gavin had been groomed to lead, protect, and succeed. A woman who belonged to a man like him had to stand toe to toe with him and be able to take the heat. She wasn't that woman.

The Rolls-Royce was waiting for them. Ricardo got behind the wheel, and when Gavin helped her in, she let out a relieved breath until he rounded the car and got in on the other side.

She gaped at him. "What the hell are you doing?"

"Seeing you home. That's what you do after a date."

A date? Oh, fuck no. "And how are you going to get home?"

"Blade can pick me up from Dad's house."

She relaxed fractionally and belted herself in. She wanted away from him, but of course, he wouldn't go until he was ready.

"Tell me about the life you built without me."

Her head whipped around. "What?"

"Tell me why you want to return to that life." His eyes flashed in warning. "Don't bring up that fuck. We both know you don't have feelings for him."

"I love—"

He clamped a hand over her mouth. "What did I say?"

She glared mutinously at him. She loved Jonathan, didn't she? Then why had the ache of leaving him gone from a relentless pain to a distant pang within a matter of days?

"Don't test my control where he's concerned. He should never have touched what was mine. Be grateful I've had you since you arrived and that allows him to continue living his pathetic life."

When he dropped his hand, she stared at him.

"You really are obsessed."

"I claimed you at eighteen."

"You claimed me when I was too young and stupid to know any different!"

He snorted. "You're an old soul, Lyla, and wise beyond your years. You knew what you were getting into with me."

She hated that he was right. She suspected a dark side to Gavin and his business, but she chose not to focus on that and put her head in the sand.

"I didn't know everything," she mumbled.

"I can protect you from that shit. It's not an issue."

"Not an issue?" she repeated incredulously and thought of Eli and his mother who was now in the hospital.

"There are safeguards in place to make sure the Pyre Casinos continue even if the other side of the business is questioned."

"You have enough money from the casinos. Why bother with the illegal stuff?"

"If we don't run the underworld, someone else will, and there would be another asshole to deal with. It's easier to run it all."

"I don't want to be a part of that, Gavin."

"You aren't," he said, voice clipped and impatient.

"I am."

"How so? You don't know what I do."

"I do." The words were out of her mouth before she could stop them.

"Explain."

She stared at him, mouth dry. She couldn't retract her words, and didn't have a hope in hell of distracting him. Gavin's eyes pierced her in the dim light. Something dark unfurled between them. She saw suspicion and then comprehension in his eyes a moment before they went expressionless.

"I always wondered why you left when you did. You didn't run because of the girls, did you?" he murmured.

She reached behind her for the door handle. She could taste violence in the air. The taut silence and the way he watched her made her heart skip with fear. This was the man capable of strangling her, the one who terrified her. This was the man she fled from.

"You saw what happened in the basement, didn't you?"

His flat voice scared the crap out of her.

"Gavin—"

"Answer me."

The car stopped, and she bolted. She ran into the mansion and heard Manny call her name as she streaked past the living room, but she didn't stop. She couldn't. Fear had her by the throat. She ran into the guest bedroom and bolted the door. She wrung her hands before her eyes fell on a dresser. She pushed and heaved with all her might until it was in front of the door as an extra barricade. When that was done, she escaped into the bathroom and locked that door, too. Nothing would stop Gavin. She knew that, but she wouldn't make it easy on him. What would he do now that she knew his secret? She was a liability. Oh, fuck. Oh, *fuck*. How could she be so fucking stupid to let that slip? He was too sharp not to figure out that her timing was suspicious.

She searched the bathroom for a weapon, but nothing would protect her from a gun or fists trained by UFC fighters. She sat on the lip of the tub and waited for the door to be kicked in or the roar of a chainsaw, but there was nothing. She paced and when she couldn't stand the suspense, got down on her stomach and looked beneath the door into the bedroom. The dresser was still in place.

She waited for what felt like hours. Her anxiety didn't wane. She decided to take a shower, wrapped herself in a robe, and waited. No sound. No entreaty from Manny to open the door, and no forceful entry. What did that mean? She didn't have the energy to figure it out. She made a nest of towels on the ground, curled into a ball, and waited for whatever came next.

SHE WOKE SLOWLY, warm and content. She stretched beneath the covers and yawned as she opened her eyes. Morning light filtered through the window of Manny's guest bedroom. Something niggled at the back of her mind, but she was too groggy to concentrate. She sat up in bed and froze when she saw Gavin sitting in a chair.

She stilled as memories of last night flooded back. Her eyes went to the door. The dresser was back in its original position against the wall. She was in bed instead of on the bathroom floor where she fell asleep. What the fuck? How—?

"How much did you see?"

His voice was rough and raspy. He wore the same suit from last night, which meant he never left. He looked dangerous with a five o'clock shadow and bright amber eyes.

She opened and closed her mouth, but couldn't find her voice.

"How much did you see, Lyla?"

She swallowed hard and gripped handfuls of the bedsheet before she admitted, "Everything."

The air in the room thickened. She didn't notice him make any movement, but she sensed his body tighten in preparation. Her flight instinct urged her to run, but she knew it was useless. Nothing would stop him from getting to her.

"Why did you go to the basement?" he asked.

There was no use in trying to cover up the truth now. "I didn't trust you after the orgy. I thought you might be..."

"You thought I would cheat on you in our home? Even after I said I wouldn't?"

A muscle jumped in his jaw. He leaned forward, bracing his elbows on his knees.

"You heard why he was there?"

She was glad her stomach was empty, so she wouldn't embarrass herself and vomit. She could see the guard's face in her mind, clear as day. Could she have stopped Gavin, or would she be dead and buried along with that man three years ago?

"I did what I had to," he said.

She couldn't look at him. Before she witnessed the brutality in the basement, she ignored what the Pyres did in the dark because she could. When she saw what Gavin was capable of, his infidelity seemed trifling. She didn't want to be around someone who could do that to another human being. She left, disillusioned and chilled to the core.

"So, you left because of what you saw in the basement, not the women," he said.

"I left because of both. I don't want to be a part of this life, Gavin." Her voice broke, and she looked down at her trembling hands.

"You shouldn't have seen what you did."

She lifted her head. "But I did. Now what?"

His silence made her heart race. In a sudden burst of anger that startled them both, she erupted from the bed. She rearranged the robe to cover her adequately and fisted her hands at her sides as she faced him.

"I know what you do for work, Gavin, and I can't stand it," she said, voice shaking. "His face haunts me. I can hear his pleas in my sleep. You didn't stop. You *tortured* him." She had to stop as bile rose in her throat.

"I needed to know if he was telling the truth."

She slashed her hand through the air. "Slicing his throat would have been better than what you did."

"You don't understand—"

"And I don't want to!" she screeched.

He flinched, but showed no other outward reaction to her outburst. She could feel herself splintering into pieces. Watching the man she loved torture someone to death destroyed her. When she left Las Vegas, she was a shadow of her former self.

Her emotions were a tangled mess. This man incited so much in her—fear, lust, confusion, and love. She hated that even after all this time, she cared for him. She loved Gavin with every particle of her being and had never been the same since. He stole her innocence in more ways than one. He branded her soul. No matter what she did, she couldn't exorcise him. She clung to Jonathan because he was Gavin's polar opposite. Did she really love Jonathan? She was grateful he took her in, but what she felt for him paled in comparison to what Gavin roused in her.

"You don't have to do this," she whispered.

He said nothing.

"You have more money than you could possibly spend in your lifetime. Why risk the Pyre Empire over another revenue with so much risk?" Her eyes filled with tears. "How do you think I feel, knowing that the food I eat and the clothes I wear were bought through blood and murder? Why do you think I left everything behind? I would rather work forty hours a week to earn just enough to survive and have a clear conscience than—"

"Don't, Lyla. That blood's on my hands, not yours."

"And that makes it better?" she challenged.

He looked so remote. She hated it. She took her life in her hands and walked toward him. His eyes tracked her every move and went heavy-lidded when she knelt in front of him. Moving slowly, she reached out and grabbed his hands. She cradled them in hers and looked up.

"You don't have to have blood on your hands, Gavin."

"You have no idea what's at stake."

"*Your life* is at stake. What if they catch you? You could go to prison!"

"That won't happen."

She dropped his hands and rose. There was no reasoning with

him. "You're so arrogant and pigheaded." She paced away and then turned back. "I don't understand you, Gavin. I loved you. I gave you everything only to find out you cheated the whole time. Not only that, but you have this other life you don't tell me about that forces you to do things you shouldn't have to do. You can't tell me it doesn't haunt you. Is that where the other women come in? Is that where *I* come in?" She paused, but there was no answer. "What else aren't you telling me? What else am I too stupid or young or naïve to know about? What we had, Gavin, it wasn't a relationship. It was a role, one any woman can fill."

She wrapped her arms around herself. His eyes were trained on her, monitoring every nuance of her expression.

"I want out," she whispered.

"No."

"I never told a soul, and I won't!"

He ran his hands through his hair. "God, you're a piece of work."

"And you aren't? You're hot, cold, hot..." Her voice faded away when their eyes locked. A shaft of heat burst in her belly and spread low. "Fuck! I hate you!"

"Is that why you don't want my hands on you? Because of what you saw me do?"

"You were so cold." She shivered and tried to shake away the awful memories. "You can turn your emotions on and off. That's why you were able to cheat on me and come home with a clear conscience. It's why you're good at doing the illegal side of the business." She tapped her chest, trying to get him to understand her. "That's not me."

No response, no flicker of emotion in his eyes.

"I told you, this isn't going to work," she said, voice low

"It will if you let me take care of it."

"By controlling what I do, where I go?"

"It's the only way I know to keep you safe."

"If you weren't doing whatever the fuck you're doing on the side, you wouldn't need to keep me safe! Don't you see that?"

"This is what my family has always done."

"And traditions are meant to be broken," she spat.

"I never let that shit touch you, not then and not now."

"Look what happened with Rafael... You can't stop it from touching me."

"You won't see him again."

She shook her head. "You can't control that."

"Yes, I can."

"By keeping me imprisoned?"

"By putting a man on you to keep you safe."

"Now we're back to square one. If you weren't in the business, I wouldn't need a bodyguard. I can't live this way." She shook her head. "I *won't*."

He got to his feet. She couldn't stop her quick retreat and noticed his jaw lock.

"You think I'm a monster."

His voice was devoid of emotion.

"It doesn't matter what I think," she murmured.

He stared at her for a long minute before he walked out the door. She stared after him, not sure what just happened. She felt as if she had just avoided an execution. She was breathing hard, and her palms were damp with sweat. Her cell phone rang on the nightstand. She glanced at the screen and picked it up with a sigh of relief.

"Carmen."

"Hey, girl. I'm heading to the mall. Want to keep me company?"

She could tell from the whooshing sound in the background that Carmen probably had the top down on her convertible. "Yes!"

"Be there in five."

She dashed into the bathroom and made herself look decent before she rushed downstairs where she found Manny pacing.

"Baby girl, we need to talk." Manny looked troubled. "Gavin just left. What did you say to him?"

Too much, too little. She shrugged. "We're not meant to be, Manny. I think he's beginning to see it."

"I'm sorry you saw what happened in Gavin's basement." Manny ran a hand through his hair. "It was business."

She had no doubt that Manny did atrocious things during his time as ruler of the underworld. How was she supposed to feel about these men she cared for? How did she reconcile the men she knew with the ruthless dictators who did what had to be done in the crime world? "I know it's business, Manny; I just don't want to be around it."

"He can shield you from it—"

"Manny," she said and squeezed his hand, "this type of stuff isn't for me."

"We're not asking you to deal with it. You were never supposed to see... Gavin, the look on his face when he left..." He stared at her imploringly. "You have to fix it."

She ignored the stab in her belly. She was well on her way to making Gavin realize that they weren't meant for each other. Letting him believe she thought he was a monster got her a gigantic step closer to freedom. She averted her eyes from Manny because she couldn't stand to see him in distress.

She squeezed his hand as a car horn honked. "I love you, Manny, but I'm not the one for him."

"But you are," Manny insisted. "I know it!"

The honk came again. "I'm going out with Carmen. I'll be back," she said and kissed him on the cheek. How could she explain that she couldn't condone the things they did? She didn't see things in shades of gray like them. They justified murders by putting it under the label of business. She wasn't that open-minded and didn't want to be. Her time away from Las Vegas had solidified her beliefs. It was better to live a clean, uneventful, possibly boring life than to live on the edge.

She rushed out the front door, desperate for fresh air and time away from the Pyres. Sure enough, Carmen's convertible top was down. Carmen's hair should have been windblown, but her hair was done in a slick, kick ass braid. She slid into the passenger seat, and they were off.

"Anything exciting happen last night?" Carmen hollered.

"No!" she shouted back. She wasn't in the mood to discuss Gavin. "What are we shopping for?"

"Don't know yet."

Carmen sped toward the city and kicked on the radio, which spat out old school tunes. She sang along in an effort to forget Gavin's expression as he walked away from her. Why the hell did she feel so guilty? She was being honest. She didn't want to live that way. It would kill her slowly but surely. The people of Las Vegas had questionable morals. When you grew up in a city of illusions and sin, it was easy to justify almost everything. But murder? No. Gavin was too volatile. She couldn't handle him. He wasn't meant for her. She just had to convince Manny of that.

She and Carmen shopped hand in hand. She was distinctly aware of the fact that she had no money and wondered how she could access her bank accounts but shrugged it off. It wasn't worth looking into, not when her life was so out of sorts. Plus, she had a sneaking suspicion that Gavin took care of it.

Carmen loved beautiful and well-made things. She took pictures of what she wanted and sent them to Vinny in a not so subtle hint even though she could whip out a credit card and pay for it herself. Carmen loved presents.

"You're happy," she commented, examining her cousin who modeled lingerie in a mirror.

"Of course," Carmen said without hesitation. "Vinny loves me, I get to do what I want, and you're back."

"Temporarily."

Carmen snorted. "Girl, don't think I didn't see the way Gavin looked at you last night. Stop fooling yourself. The man is gone over you. You could ask him for anything and get it in a snap."

"He's in temporary lust with me," she corrected.

Carmen turned to face her, and Lyla had to admit her body looked fantastic.

"Lyla Dalton, you need to get your head out of your ass."

She blinked. "Excuse me?"

"Gavin Pyre can have anyone he wants. Capisce?"

"Yes," she agreed.

"Then why would he look for you for three years and take time away from work to dance with you last night? He's been taking you to *his* clubs, so everyone will know your face and give you whatever you want. I'm gonna tell you something, cousin, and I don't care if you believe me or not. I haven't seen Gavin with anyone since you left. I know that doesn't mean a lot to you, but he could have replaced you, and he didn't. You are the only woman he claimed, the only one he lived with. That's huge. I know you don't trust him, but if you talk to him, like *really* talk to him, you might be surprised what he's willing to do to get you to stay."

She didn't tell her cousin she already committed to a year in Las Vegas. There was no sense in getting her hopes up. If she had done as much damage this morning as Manny implied, her one-year commitment might be void.

"I'll wait outside," she said.

Carmen gave an impatient huff, which she ignored. She made her way out of the shop bustling with Playboy bunny type women, strippers, and male oglers. The mall was teeming with people. She narrowly avoided a collision with a reckless senior in a wheelchair and headed to the restrooms, texting Carmen as she went.

She used the facilities and was in the middle of wiping her hands with a paper towel when the door burst open. She looked up and caught a fleeting glimpse of two Hispanic men before they were on her. She tried to scream, but one of them covered her mouth with a cloth soaked in something. She couldn't breathe. She fought against her attacker, but her head was spinning, and then everything went black.

9

Her head throbbed and her body ached as if she had the flu. She tried to sit up and discovered that her hands and feet were bound, and she had a strip of duct tape over her mouth. A sheer red cloth covered her eyes, and she lay on a dirty, lumpy mattress in a concrete room with one window. Unadulterated panic filled her as she remembered the attack in the mall bathroom. Who were these men and why had they taken her? She held up her bound hands and saw a plastic tie cutting into her skin. There would be no getting out of this. She looked around the barren room and focused on a small window high up on the wall. Even if she managed to get to her feet, she wasn't tall enough to see outside.

She heard the echo of voices a moment before the door slammed open. The Hispanic men who attacked her in the bathroom stood there. One of them swaggered in with a cocky grin while the other hung back, expressionless. They were dressed in basketball jerseys and low-riding shorts that showed off their underwear. They couldn't be older than twenty-five. Punks. Wannabe gangsters. The fact that they didn't bother to conceal their faces made her stomach curdle with anxiety.

"Had a nice nap?" the one who entered the room asked. "I was hoping you were still asleep so I could wake you up the way I wanted."

He gave her a lecherous smile that made her shuffle backward until she hit the wall. Her useless hands twitched in front of her as she waited for him to make a move.

"You don't look like Pyre's type," he said.

Even though she suspected that Gavin had something to do with this, the confirmation made her body go icy with fear. Oh, fuck.

The cocky bastard sat on the edge of the bed. Without hesitation, he reached out and squeezed her breast through the thin material of her dress. She screamed through the tape and tried to knock his hand away with her bound hands. He stretched out beside her and dragged her on top of him. His hands went under her dress, clutched her bare ass and mashed their crotches together. He moaned and bucked, bouncing her on top of him like a depraved animal as his hot breath fanned over her face.

She struggled, but couldn't do anything with her hands being held over her head and her legs bound together. This couldn't be happening. He dry humped her while his partner watched from the doorway. She shrieked into the tape as the man beneath her thrust faster. The thin material of his pants stopped him from full penetration.

"Hurry the fuck up," the other man said, leaning against the doorjamb.

"You like that, bitch?" the man beneath her panted.

She screamed profanities as he went faster, pumping his hips so hard she knew her thighs would bruise. She looked away as he came in his pants, grunting and then going completely lax beneath her. Afraid of puking with tape over her mouth, she rolled away and landed on the dirty concrete. She used her elbows to push herself into a sitting position and looked at the man standing by the doorway, watching her with blank eyes. Beyond him, she saw they were in what looked like an abandoned warehouse. Where the fuck were they? Were they still in Vegas? It was easier to focus on useless questions rather than the man on the bed behind her. She felt as if spiders were crawling over her skin. She fought the plastic tie around her wrists, even though she knew it was pointless.

"Fuck, I needed that," the man on the bed said and pulled a phone out of his pocket and dialed.

They all listened to the phone ring as he put it on speaker. She closed her eyes and tried to control the urge to hurl.

"Who the fuck is this?"

Gavin's voice on the other end of the phone made her head snap up. Painful relief burst in her chest.

"You don't need to know who it is. All you need to know is I have your girl," the man on the bed said and winked at her.

"Let me talk to her," Gavin ordered.

The man on the bed rolled with a squeak of rusty springs. He gripped her face and ripped the strip of tape off her mouth. Her face burned, but she didn't make a sound. Did she still have lips?

"Lyla?" Gavin snarled.

"Gavin—" she said through throbbing lips.

The man shoved her carelessly. Her back hit the wall hard, and she moaned. She looked up as he stood over her, the wet spot on his pants obvious.

"Got your attention, Pyre? Your chick is a great lay."

"You touch her, even one finger, I'll murder you with my bare hands," Gavin said, voice so chilling that her captor stared at the phone for a second before he walked over to his partner and handed the phone over.

"We want ten million. Cash," the remote captor said.

"Drop off?" Gavin asked without missing a beat.

"Reno. Ten o'clock. I'll text the address."

"Who's your boss?"

Gavin sounded calm, but she knew when his voice went icy like that, heads rolled.

"We don't have a boss," the hotheaded pervert snapped, taking the phone back from his emotionless counterpart. "*We're* our own boss."

"You made a mistake, taking something of mine," Gavin said. "You're walking dead men."

"You have many enemies," the quiet man said. "What did you think would happen once you revealed a weakness?"

"I want to speak to her again," Gavin ordered.

"She can hear you," the stupid captor said in a singsong voice.

"Lyla, I'm coming for you."

The line went dead before she could respond. She couldn't stop shaking. Gavin would come for her; she had no doubt about it. These men, these despicable, perverted bastards were walking corpses, and for the first time in her life, she understood that some people shouldn't live. The captor, the one who used her like an inanimate object with no feelings, caught her attention when he brushed his hand over his crotch again. She forced herself to look at him. She poured all the loathing she could into her eyes. She should stay as compliant as possible, but fury pumped through her veins.

"Fuck."

Her heart skipped when she saw that the pervert had another hard on.

"One more time," he said and started forward.

"No." His partner pulled him back. "I shouldn't have let you do it even once. If Pyre thinks you fucked her, he might give us less money."

These men didn't know who they were dealing with. They had no idea how possessive Gavin was. Touching her with one finger was too much. What these men did—kidnapping and using her as a sex doll —bought them a first-class ticket to a slow and painful death.

The disgusting captor slipped his hands into his pants and pumped his cock, eyes focused on her face. "I won't touch her. I'll just come on her face."

"No."

"Come on. I know you want her too."

She gagged as he ran a hand over his partner's crotch, obviously trying to arouse him. The impassive man didn't push his partner's hand away. He stood there, letting the other man stroke his dick through his pants. When the horny pervert dropped to his knees and pulled the man's pants down, she pressed against the wall, wishing it would absorb her. She tried to block out the sounds of what was happening behind her. Oh, God. She heard quickening breaths, moans, and then a grunt of relief.

"Can I have her now?" the eager one asked.

"No."

"*What?* I just sucked you off."

"I'll give you a twenty later."

The door slammed on the pervert's whines. She vomited and then scooted into the opposite corner of the room. This couldn't be happening. She jumped at every little sound, praying they wouldn't come back. These men were animals. They didn't look at her as a human being, but something to be used and tossed away like trash. They would fuck her and slit her throat without blinking an eye. They were too young to be so cruel and inhumane.

She closed her eyes and willed Gavin to find her. If she was in Vegas and they were sending him to Reno... Gavin was smart, ruthless, and had countless resources at his fingertips. He would find her. She had to believe that or go mad.

***

SHE WOKE when a hand clamped over her mouth. It was dark. The only light in the room came from a cell phone propped against the wall, which blinded her. As her eyes adjusted, her heart nearly leapt out of her chest when she saw a pair of desperate, depraved eyes staring back at her. The pervert was back. Even as her mind snapped into full wakefulness, he slapped a fresh strip of duct tape over her mouth.

"He stepped out for some cigarettes. We don't have much time," he panted and ripped her dress from neck to belly button.

She bucked and slammed her bound wrists against his chest. The force of it knocked him on his ass. She tried to get to her feet, but with her ankles bound, she toppled back to the floor.

"Stupid bitch. You think you're too good for me, huh?"

He rolled her onto her back and finished ripping her dress in half. She went cold with terror as he grabbed his phone and raised the light so he could see her body, clad only in underwear.

"Fuck, your skin is so pretty. If I had my knife, I'd mark you so every man who fucked you would know I was the first to brand you."

Tears leaked out of the corner of her eyes. Her body trembled in revulsion. He appeared even younger in the harsh light, yet the expression in his eyes was an ancient evil that had no place in a human.

"The world is divided into two types of men," the pervert said as he slid a grubby, dirty hand over her breasts, down her quivering stomach, and then beneath her thong. "Men who ask, and men who take." On the last word, he shoved his fingers into her dry core.

Her head kicked back at the pain. Her head hit the concrete so hard she saw stars. The pervert jammed his fingers into her body unmercifully, completely immune to her cries and body's rejection of the intrusion.

"Come on, get wet for me, slut," he said and picked up the pace. "We don't have time."

She cried out as his dirty fingernails jabbed into the wall of her vagina. What the fuck was he doing? Apparently, he only fucked sex dolls because he didn't seem to know that no woman would respond to this. If she wasn't gagged, she would have told him this while she ripped his balls off. She had never been so furious and terrified in her life. Despite her throbbing head and the hopeless situation, she struck out with her bound hands and managed to claw his face. He screeched and dropped the phone, throwing the room into complete darkness.

"You *bitch!*"

The blow came out of nowhere. Her head collided with the floor, and everything went black.

SOMEONE WAS SCREAMING, and the sound of agony pierced through the pain. Her eyes opened. Dim orange light filtered through the small window high up on the wall. Something warm and sticky covered her. A flurry of movement to her left caught her attention. Even as she tried to remember where she was, she heard an awful gurgling sound, and the screams abruptly stopped. She saw a faint light nearby. Pervert's phone. The light was smothered by the floor and something else...

As memory returned, she reached for the phone. The darkness and awful silence made panic dig into her belly. She raised the phone, which was wet and sticky, and aimed the light in the direction of where that awful screaming had been coming from.

A large man crouched over a mangled thing she didn't realize was a body until she registered that the floor was covered in red. She let out a choked sound, and the man turned his head and looked at her. At first, she didn't recognize the murderous savage as Gavin with his face streaked with blood. His teeth were bared in a snarl, eyes feral and eclipsed by hatred. The phone fell from her hands and lay face down in its owner's blood. The prism of light exposed a gory room out of a horror movie.

"Lyla."

She didn't recognize his voice. It sounded hoarse, as if he'd gargled with glass.

"Lyla, are you—?"

She ripped the tape off her mouth and retched. Even after she emptied everything out of her stomach, she continued to dry heave. Hands skimmed down her back, and then a soaked jacket fell around her. She didn't realize how cold she was until his animal heat engulfed her. When he lifted her into his arms, she buried her face against his slick chest. Voices echoed around them.

"Holy fuck! Lyla?"

She recognized Vinny's voice, but couldn't look up and tell him she was all right because she wasn't sure. Gavin spoke, and she recognized Blade's voice as well. There was a flurry of activity around her, but she blocked it out. Gavin ducked, and then a car door slammed. He cut the ties on her wrists and ankles. Her limbs were numb from being in one position for so long. She wasn't aware she was crying until Gavin spoke.

"Shh, Lyla, you're safe," he said gruffly.

She grabbed fistfuls of his ruined suit and shook her head. Her body hurt, but what scared her the most was the throbbing between her legs. How far did the pervert go before Gavin arrived? How many times did he fuck her? What did he do to her? A sob escaped and then another until she was crying, as she'd never cried before in her life. She pounded Gavin's chest with her fists until she was exhausted. He didn't say a word.

When the car stopped, he carried her outside. The cold night air made her very aware of the fact that Gavin's jacket concealed her nakedness. The tattered strips of her dress clung to her bloody legs. She hiccupped against Gavin's chest and fought the need to vomit again. She felt so dirty, so violated. Gavin hurried somewhere, never easing his hold on her, never letting her feel for one moment that she was alone.

More voices, hushed and concerned, and then the sound of running water. She heard a hollow echo as he stepped into a shower stall. He let her feet touch the tiles. She hissed as feeling returned to her arms and legs with a vengeance. Her limbs quaked, unable to handle her weight. When he tried to tug the jacket off, she yelled unintelligibly, desperate to hold on to anything that would cover her. With an arm around her waist to hold her up, he stripped off his clothes.

The warm water bounced off them and tinged the glass stall with red droplets. She gagged. Gavin turned her sideways so she could puke, but he didn't let her go. He shampooed her hair. She couldn't look at him. Her mind was locked in a blank state she didn't try to fight. He carried her from the shower to the bathtub, which was filled with steaming water, and climbed in with her. He wrapped her close and rested his forehead against the back of her head. The heat didn't penetrate, and the bright lights in the bathroom made her feel exposed after the darkness in that hellhole. She couldn't stop shaking.

"I'm sorry. I'm sorry, Lyla. Can you forgive me?" he whispered.

Tears slid down her face. She hugged the jacket to her and pushed at the hands around her waist. She needed to be alone. His arms tightened for a moment before they fell away. They sat like that until she scooted forward so they weren't touching. He left the tub. The water level dropped, and she sank deeper into the water. She heard the rustle of clothes and then dropped her head forward when the bathroom door closed.

She wasn't sure how long she sat there when the door opened again. A woman she had never seen before knelt beside the tub. She had long white hair twisted into a French twist and smiled kindly at her.

"Lyla, I'm a doctor. I want to take a look at you," she said.

"I-I'm fine," she replied through chattering teeth.

"I was told you went through something traumatic this evening. I know you're cold. Mr. Pyre gave me pajamas for you." She held up a pair of sweatpants and an oversized sweater. "You can have these."

She wanted the clothes, but didn't want to leave the safety of the tub.

"That jacket is stained. You want to wear something clean, don't you?"

She shuddered and nodded.

"Are you in pain?" the doctor continued.

She nodded, staring straight ahead. Her head throbbed, and she felt seasick, stomach pitching and rolling even though she was completely still.

"I can give you something for the pain, but I want to examine you first."

Silent tears slipped down her cheeks. A gentle, cool hand brushed over her hair.

"I can help you, Lyla."

She swallowed hard and slowly released her death grip on the jacket. She parted it and began to sob. The doctor spoke soothingly as she allowed the jacket sink to the bottom of the tub. She slipped the tiny strips of her dress off her shoulder and that too pooled around her.

"Can you stand?" the doctor asked.

She gripped the side of the tub and pushed. It took a moment for her legs to steady, for her head to stop spinning. The doctor immediately wrapped her in a robe, which she buried her face in. The doctor helped her out of the tub and sat in front of the vanity.

"I'm going to give you a quick exam, okay? Then we can get you into your clothes," the doctor said.

She nodded and got a glimpse of herself in the mirror. Her face was bloodless and her eyes were glossed with horror. She looked away and felt faint when the doctor brushed her hand over her head.

"You have several bumps on your head."

The doctor's calm, clinical tone kept her from losing her mind. The doctor knelt in front of her and slowly opened the robe.

"I just want to make sure you're okay. We don't want any scratches or cuts to get infected."

Remembering the pervert's dirty hands in her, she jolted. The doctor spoke quickly and firmly, stroking her rigid back.

"We want to make sure there are no repercussions, yes?"

She nodded and opened the robe. The doctor's hands moved quickly and efficiently over her. A steady stream of tears slipped down her face.

"Are you on birth control?"

"IUD." Thank God.

"I want to check you down there. Can you handle that?"

She nodded. The doctor positioned her on the bench seat and with her eyes closed, felt the doctor prod, pause.

"You're bleeding. Are you on your period right now?"

She shook her head wildly.

"Your IUD isn't in the right place. I'm going to take it out and examine you more thoroughly, okay? Tell me if I'm hurting you."

She trembled like a plucked bow. "I can't... I can't get pregnant, right?" Her whole body hurt. Her mind was a dizzy whirlwind of fear and pain. The doctor reported that there was a tear in her vagina. That fucker's fingernails. "H-He was dirty. He was rough. I-I—"

"Let me clean you up and swab you to see if anything was transmitted."

She wanted to scream and fight. Instead, she lay there and let the doctor finish her examination. The doctor cleaned the cuts on her wrists and ankles and wrapped them with bandages before she helped her into her pajamas.

"You have a concussion, vaginal lacerations, and bruises. I'm prescribing painkillers. You need a lot of bed rest."

"C-can you tell how many times he—?" she asked, stumbling over her words.

"You're bruised, bleeding and tender, but I don't see semen. I'll let you know the test results. But just in case, I've brought you a morning after pill to take."

She held out a hand and downed it even though her mouth was dry as dust.

"I'll be back in a few days. I'm only a phone call away." The doctor hesitated and then said, "If you need to speak to someone, I know plenty of great counselors."

When the doctor helped her into the bedroom, she realized she was at Gavin's house instead of Manny's. The doctor helped her to bed and handed her painkillers. She took those too, but this time drank from a water bottle on the nightstand. She pulled the covers up to her chin and tried to get warm. The doctor left, dimming the lights as she left. She lay there, tossing and turning. Her body hurt, her insides hurt, and every time she closed her eyes, she saw that fucker's face. She needed someone beside her, someone who would beat back the memories battering her. She needed her monster. He came for her and destroyed that twisted human being. Suddenly pissed, she staggered to the bedroom door and flung it open.

Blade stood in the hallway. His eyes flicked over her, but his expression was unreadable.

"Lyla?" he asked cautiously.

"Where's Gavin? I want Gavin," she said through chattering teeth. "He's—"

"Get him for me." He hesitated, and she screamed, *"Now!"*

Blade backed away with his hands up and ran. If she weren't so shaken, his turnabout in attitude would have amused her. Instead, she struggled to keep herself from falling apart as she stood there, waiting. Male voices echoed down the hallway and then she heard the sound of running footsteps. Gavin stopped in front of her, hollow-eyed and wary. She hesitated only a second before she launched herself at him. Gavin caught her as she wrapped her arms and legs around him.

"You can't leave me," she babbled.

"Lyla—"

"You can't!" she shouted and buried her face against his neck, trying to absorb his heat, his scent. "You can't leave me like this."

A tremor passed through him as he walked to the bed and got in with her clinging to him. He lay on his back and pulled the covers over them. She tucked her head under his chin and lay over his big, strong body. *I'm safe, I'm safe,* she chanted in her head and willed herself to believe it.

"You stay with me," she ordered.

"I won't go anywhere," he promised.

She closed her eyes and let his presence wash away the horror. Her shaky breaths filled the room. His hands moved over her gently, as if she were made of glass. Her tears soaked his shirt. Neither of them said a thing.

SHE WOKE WITH A SCREAM.

"Shh, baby girl, I'm here."

She wept into Gavin's chest as he held her. She wasn't sure if hours or minutes passed. She dozed fitfully and took turns demanding he not touch her and then plastering herself against him. Gavin obeyed whatever dictate she issued. He didn't leave the bed. He fed her bland foods so she could take more painkillers and forced her to drink water. He held her hair when she barfed it all up and filled the bathtub when she couldn't stop shaking. He carried her back to bed, blocked out the sunlight, and slid in beside her. No one disturbed them, and neither spoke.

10

She woke on her side, facing Gavin. She wasn't sure how many days had passed since they locked themselves in his master bedroom. He was asleep with his hand gripping hers, their only skin contact. It was the first time she woke without lashing out or trying to defend herself from a dead man. Her body was still sore, but she felt better. Although she had been in bed for days, she was exhausted. Her mind and body were weighted down with the knowledge of what lurked outside these walls. She had been touched by pure evil. Her mind desperately tried to punch through to fresh air, but her heart cowered in the dark, trying to piece itself together.

She slipped her hand from his. He shifted and reached for her, brow furrowing. She hesitated a moment before she ran a hand down his face. He relaxed instantly as if he recognized her touch and settled into deeper sleep. He had dark circles under his eyes and hadn't shaved in days. He looked dark and dangerous even in sleep. Instead of making her back away, it made her want to burrow against him. Gavin kept his word. He killed the pervert with his bare hands.

She went into the bathroom and filled the tub. She'd taken more baths in the past couple of days than she would in one year. She tossed in salts and oils before she slipped in. She sat with her arms wrapped around her legs and let the heat penetrate her aching body. It was hard to think of anything but what happened in the warehouse. She couldn't get her captors' faces out of her mind, couldn't think past the pervert's attack. She was grateful she didn't remember... but what did Gavin see? She moaned and buried her face against her knees. It felt like a lifetime that she had been back in Las Vegas. In less than two weeks, she had irrevocably changed. There was no way to backtrack or deviate from the path laid out in front of her. She was on a bullet train, and there was no getting off.

The door opened and Gavin appeared. He sat beside the tub, watching her. She didn't meet his eyes. She couldn't. There were things she wanted to say, things she wanted to know, but she wasn't sure she could handle it.

"The doctor will be here in an hour," he said.

With the test results. She clenched her teeth and nodded. It was better to know what the pervert did to her.

"Do you want to see Carmen?"

She shook her head. Carmen was dramatic and over the top. She couldn't handle that right now. She could barely handle her emotions, much less someone else's.

"Do you want me here when the doctor comes?"

He looked tired, but his eyes were focused and lethal. He was still on edge. So was she.

"Do you want to be?" she asked.

"Yes."

"That's fine with me." After rescuing and caring for her, his presence was a welcome buffer between her and reality.

They sat in silence until there was a knock on the bedroom door. When Gavin went to answer it, she got out of the tub and slipped into a robe. The same doctor from the night of the assault was in the bedroom and wasted no time.

"There was no trace of STD, semen, or anything else," the doctor said.

Something within her loosened. For the first time in days, she felt as if she could take a full breath.

"You're looking better. Let's look at your tear." The doctor gave Gavin a long, direct look, but when he didn't move, and Lyla didn't object, she snapped on her gloves and got to work. "It looks good. You're not spotting?"

"No."

"Great."

The doctor checked the wounds on her wrists and ankles and approved of Gavin's dressings before she prodded Lyla's concussion. She still felt like she might pass out, so the doctor prescribed more rest and painkillers. The doctor asked if she wanted to speak to a counselor, and when Lyla declined, she handed her a business card in case she changed her mind. When the doctor left, Lyla changed into yoga pants and Gavin's sweater that stopped at mid-thigh.

"I want to go outside," she said.

Gavin didn't object. He opened the bedroom door, and they came face to face with Blade. Knowing he witnessed her being carried out of the warehouse and likely heard her outbursts over the past couple of days, she didn't meet his gaze. She walked downstairs, through the kitchen, and thrust open the door that led into the backyard. She stepped onto heated tiles and tipped her face up to the sun. She didn't have to look around to accustom herself to her surroundings. An Olympic-sized pool occupied most of the yard. In the middle of the pool was a sunken cabana with oversized pillows and cushions. She crossed on oversized stones that led to the sitting area. The sound of the waterfall cascading into the other end of the pool soothed her. Gavin settled nearby, never taking his eyes from her.

"What did you see?" she asked.

He jerked as if she slapped him. "Don't ask me that."

"I am," she said, their beautiful surrounding at odds with the topic they were dancing around.

"You're recovering. You don't need—"

"Tell me."

He rose and turned his back to her, but not before she saw his murderous expression.

"He was on top of you, dick out. I didn't know if he was finishing, beginning..." He let out a growl and ran his hands through his hair. "You weren't moving. I fucking lost it. I didn't even look at you; I just wanted to kill."

"Come."

He turned, movements stiff as he walked to her. When she tugged on his wrist, he fell to his knees in front of her. His eyes focused on a target over her shoulder that no one could see. She could taste the violence and rage bottled up inside him. She clasped his face between her hands and kissed the corner of his mouth. He didn't relax, didn't look at her.

"I'm fine."

"Are you?" he asked, voice gritty and rough.

She wrapped her arms around his neck and leaned into him, needing and giving comfort.

"I don't know," she whispered. Less than a day in that hellhole changed her. How long would it take to feel normal? To feel safe? When would she feel clean or close her eyes and dream of something other than human monsters?

She rested her chin on his shoulder, but his hands stayed fisted on the cushions on either side of her. She thought back to that night and tightened her hold on him, needing reassurance even though she saw what he was capable of.

"Maybe he didn't have a chance to fuck me," she whispered.

"That's what I have to believe," Gavin bit out.

She nuzzled him even though he felt like a block of stone. "Thank you."

"For what?"

"For coming for me, for taking care of me." She cursed the tears that rose. At least their position meant she could talk freely without being pinned by his searing gaze. "I've been difficult, and I kept you from work—"

He jerked back, forcing her to loosen her hold on him.

"I promised that it wouldn't touch you," he said harshly.

For a moment, he looked crazed. Then he dropped his head to hide his expression. The cushions shifted beneath her as he strangled them. He was a bomb waiting to detonate. He wouldn't lash out at her, she knew, but the rage emanating from him turned her stomach.

"He's dead," she reminded him.

He raised his head. The look on his face made her uneasy.

"You saw what I did," he said.

"Yes." Even though his brutality terrified her, she would sleep better knowing that the pervert was dead. He didn't deserve to live.

"You still think I'm a monster?" he asked gruffly.

She clasped his face. "You're *my* monster."

He shuddered and wrapped his arms around her waist, his head on her breasts. "Can you forgive me?"

"Yes." She didn't need to think about it. He was swimming in guilt, tortured by the kidnapping. Her hands sifted through his hair in an effort to dim the awful energy engulfing him. "How did you find me?"

"Carmen called us when she couldn't find you. Stupid bastards didn't get rid of your phone until they were downtown. I had men searching the area when they called. I kept them on the phone to track them. It still took a couple of hours. Too long. We haven't found his partner yet."

She went rigid. "He went to get cigarettes."

"I'll get him."

The bloodthirsty eagerness in his voice distracted her from the memory of the dead eyes of the captor who hadn't touched her but scared her just as much. "You're going after him?"

"Him and everyone associated with them."

His flat tone sent chills down her spine. He wasn't really with her; he was planning murder and revenge. She splayed her hand over his heart. "So they kidnap me, you kill them, and then what? When does it end?"

"It ends when they're all dead."

He still wouldn't look at her, wouldn't let her touch penetrate. Her hands dropped from him. It always came back to this part of his life. Even though she was glad that the pervert was dead, Gavin had paid a price. They both had. Interacting with people like her captors chipped away at

Gavin's soul and pulled him deeper into their world. She saw him in action, face dripping with blood and no trace of humanity in his eyes— just blind rage. Knowing the filth he dealt with, she couldn't stomach it.

She beat back the pain and asked, "When am I going back to your dad's house?"

His eyes snapped to her. "What?"

"I agreed to stay for a year, but I can't be around you, not when you're involved in this."

Silence. She pushed against his chest, but he didn't move.

"I told you I couldn't live like this. They went for me because they think I mean something to you. They'll come after me again. They'll kill me next time. I can't—"

"Baby—"

She shoved his hand away. "No, Gavin. I want out."

His hands moved to her hips and gripped. "Out?"

She ignored the bite in his words. She had to put as much distance between them as possible. The bond between them was incredibly tight, especially after being kidnapped. She needed to break it off now while she could. She couldn't reach him. No one could. He would go on a killing spree, and she couldn't talk him out of it.

"I think we both know I can't..." She waved a hand at herself and then the house where she forced him to hibernate with her. "I can't," she repeated. "I'm better. Y-You helped, staying with me. I'm grateful—"

"Lyla—"

She shook her head and hated that she still had a store of tears in her. "I can't be around you when you're doing this shit. I can't go through this again." Her throat tightened. They left the warehouse covered in someone's blood, and she still hadn't washed it all away in her mind. Gavin wouldn't be satisfied with the death of the other captor. How many would he kill before the rage dissipated? Before he felt that justice had been served? How many would die, and what toll would it take on his soul? Every kill pushed him further into the dark, further from emotion and anything normal. "You won't give it up, and I—"

"I give it up, you stay with me."

She wasn't sure she heard him right. "What?"

His eyes bored into hers. "I let go of that side of the business, you stay with me. Permanently."

She was stunned speechless.

"That's why you left me the first time; why you want to leave me now?"

She shook her head to clear the buzzing in her ears. "You'd give it up?" She couldn't keep the skepticism out of her tone.

"Yes."

The man before her was a dangerous predator. The businessman was the civilized part of him. The ruthless killer surfaced when he dealt with people like the pervert. There were two sides to Gavin's nature—both lethal and both a part of him. How could he get rid of the darkness that was so much a part of his personality? Where would the aggression go? Was he capable of giving up his need for revenge? Of letting go and allowing others to step up and handle it? Ceding control wasn't in his DNA.

"Tell me what you're thinking," he ordered.

"*Can* you give it up?"

"I need to find someone to take my place, but it's possible."

"Who?"

"Lyla," he said impatiently, "answer my question."

"Why can't you quit that shit for yourself?"

"Because I don't care what happens to me."

Her head snapped back. "What do you mean?"

He tightened his hold on her. "Yes or no, Lyla."

"If I say no, you continue doing this on the side?"

"Yes."

The force of his personality battered at her. He was too much for her to handle. "Gavin, you're so angry—"

"Yes, I'm fucking angry!" He wrapped his arms around her when she tried to move away. "No, you don't run when I'm pissed. You go toe to toe with me like you did in my office and when you took my hands in yours. You've seen the worst in me, and you wanted me to hold you after that fucker—" He cupped her face between rough, shaking palms. "I did you wrong. I made you cry and showed you parts of my world you should have never seen. I can't take it back, but I can try to make it right this time. You have to give me a chance, a real one. No holding back, no hiding in my dad's house. Before, you were handed to me on a fucking platter. I didn't have to work for your love; you took me whole. You were tailor-made for me, fucking spoiled me. Then you left. I won't take you for granted, ever."

Her hands twisted in his shirt as her mind whirled.

"What little I feel revolves around you. Haven't felt a fucking thing since you left. I brought you back, and I keep fucking it up. I feel too much for you." Brooding eyes traced her features. "I learned to control my emotions at a young age. I learned what to let in and what to keep out. I saw what Mom's death did to my dad. I didn't want to be at someone's mercy like that, so I held you at arm's length. I thought I had you under control, that I hadn't let you in. It wasn't until you left that I realized you were already in. The woman meant for me, gone without a trace." His eyes burned with a fevered light. "You can't leave me, Lyla."

"Gavin," she whispered.

He kissed her tears away and ran his hands down her sides as if reassuring himself that she was here with him.

"When I held you in the tub, you pulled away. Fucking killed me. I thought after what you saw, you wouldn't let me touch you ever again. Then you demanded I stay with you, hold you."

He rested his forehead on hers, amber eyes staring into hers with a desperation that made her heart ache.

"I won't let you go this time. Whatever you want, I'll give. You want me to quit; I'll do it. But I quit the business, you stay with me."

"W-what if—?"

"No ifs. Yes or no." When she hesitated, his face hardened. "I have you for a year. If you think I'm going to let you hide in my dad's house, think again. I'm not letting you out of my sight. I'll do everything in my power to make sure you want to stay another year, and then another. You try to leave; I'm coming with you. I won't leave you alone. I can't."

They were both surprised by her watery chuckle. She framed his face with her hands. Gavin Pyre was a scary bastard. He was fire and ice in a gorgeous package she wasn't sure she could handle, but it looked like she had no choice.

"You're so romantic," she said and kissed him.

He drew her closer, so she was on the edge of her seat. She could taste his need and the sharp edge of danger that was so much a part of him. When she drew back, hungry eyes searched hers.

"When you say permanently, you mean..."

"No running, no time limit. You stay here, not with my dad."

She chewed her bottom lip. "I don't know if I can give you what you want."

He laughed and wrapped himself around her. There was a dark edge to it, but it was still a sound of humor.

"Baby, you make me happy just by being."

A warm ray of hope lit her soul, and she hugged him to her. "I'll stay."

He didn't move or speak for a long minute. Locked in their own world, it was just the two of them. When he pulled back, he smiled at her. Joy made him look ten years younger. He pressed a gentle kiss to her lips and unwrapped himself from her.

"Are you good?" he asked.

"Yes."

"I have work to do," he said and rose.

"What?"

"The sooner I get rid of the title, the sooner we can move on."

"Oh. Do you know who you're going to pass it off to?"

"Don't worry about it. We'll get that other fucker. He isn't allowed to live."

She didn't bother to contest that. She would feel better knowing that demon in human flesh was dead. "But you won't...?"

"No. I'll get someone else to make the hit. You okay if I go to the office?"

She would rather not be alone, but knew he had to work and get this other stuff tied up. She nodded.

He cupped her chin in his hand and brushed his thumb over her bottom lip as he considered her. "You want to see my dad?"

Her eyes filled with tears, and she nodded.

"Come, I'll drop you off before I go to work."

Twenty minutes later, Gavin donned a tailored suit, while she opted to stay as she was in her oversized sweater and yoga pants. He drove his car while Blade and another group of men followed.

"I won't stay past eight," he said as he grabbed her hand and placed it on his thigh.

She glanced at his intimidating face as his fingers threaded through hers.

"Blade and several others will stay with you. My dad will be insulted if I leave more than five of my men on his turf. He has his own security."

She nodded.

"You want me to come and get you, you call me. You have your new phone?"

"Yes." She had a small bag with a change of clothes, painkillers, and a new phone he handed her on their way out the door.

"It'll take me some time to put things in order."

"I know, Gavin."

The Pyres had been running the underworld for generations. There was a niggle of doubt in her mind that he could get out, but she pushed it away. He didn't make false promises.

His thumb stroked her absently as he drove. She stared at his possessive hold and thought of the deal she had made. Permanent. No future of independence, no Jonathan. She closed her eyes and said goodbye to the man who had been there for her when she needed him. Jonathan deserved more than what she could give him. She had given her love to Gavin Pyre before she was old enough to understand the consequences. She committed willingly this time, knowing what he was capable of and witnessing the stain on his soul. She sensed a yearning in him and something else... Need? He was capable of unspeakable cruelty and incredible gentleness. He was complicated, possessive, calculating, and *hers*. He was her monster, and she loved the hell out of him—always had, always would. The experience with her captors knocked down all barriers between them. On impulse, she raised his hand and kissed his raw, bruised knuckles.

"What are you doing?" he asked hoarsely.

"Loving you."

His fingers flexed around hers. The look he shot her made her stomach jitter. She cradled his hand in both of hers and placed it on her lap.

"You won't regret it," he said gruffly.

She relaxed and closed her eyes. When Gavin pulled up to Manny's house, they saw him standing on the steps. He rushed to her door and shouted in Spanish as he pulled her into his arms. Manny pulled back to look at her, crushed her against him, and then pulled back once more to make sure she was whole. Gavin replied in Spanish, the words spoken too rapidly for her to catch. Manny stiffened. She looked up and saw his dumbfounded expression. Gavin pulled her away from his father and ushered her into the house. Manny came after them, still speaking in his native tongue. Father and son faced off. When Gavin took a threatening step toward his father, she stepped between them.

"What's going on?" she asked.

"Nothing," Gavin said shortly and tipped her face up for a kiss. "Call me if you need me."

She nodded, and he walked out of the house without another word to his father. She stared at Manny, who looked flustered and disturbed.

"What is it?" she asked.

Manny shook himself and hugged her again. "You want him to give it up."

She could tell from his tone of voice that he didn't approve. She stiffened and drew back. "Yes, I do."

Manny sighed and ran a hand through his hair. "I understand. I do, but…"

"But what?" she demanded. "He could be killed. Don't you care how doing that side of the business affects him… and me?"

"Of course, I care, baby girl, but we have contracts and deals."

She crossed her arms, seeing Manny in a new light. Gavin agreed to give it up for her, but apparently, Manny wasn't so eager. Her belly clenched. "What happened to me isn't more important than your deals and contracts?"

Manny drew back as if she struck him.

"I was almost raped, Manny," she said, voice thin and jagged. "He touched me. That doesn't matter to you?"

"Lyla."

He reached for her, but she stepped back.

"I love you," she stated, "and I love Gavin, but I don't like what you do for a living. I don't like that you take chances with your lives, your souls. You think I can heal Gavin, but you have to stop sending him into the dark where the other monsters are. You don't know what —" She wrapped her arms around herself and fought the urge to vomit as she remembered Gavin covered in blood. "The price is too high. It's not worth it."

Manny stared at her for a long minute before he said, "I've done many things. Things I'll never tell a living soul. At the time, they were necessary measures that had to be taken. Somebody needs to rule the underworld, and I groomed Gavin to take that position. He's damn good at it." When she opened her mouth, he held up a hand and allowed, "Maybe *too* good. Gavin has built himself a reputation that keeps everyone in line. If he steps back, no matter who replaces him, they'll have problems."

"Yet his reputation didn't protect me," she said quietly.

"A strike like this has never happened before. It was suicide. Someone who was testing the waters contracted those men. We need to send a message back, a bloody one that will send ripples through the underworld."

Manny didn't look like a seventy-year-old man; he looked like a ruthless general, which reminded her of Gavin. That intensity in his personality would never fade, never yield to anyone. It was still thriving in his father, who went antique shopping and had retired from the business.

"So Gavin won't be able to get out of it?" she asked, stomach rocking.

His expression softened. "He'll find a way."

"But you think it's a mistake?"

"He's the best man for the job, but I see why he's stepping down. You have a profound effect on him, and this is your requirement to move forward." He nodded. "If this is what you want, I wouldn't hesitate to tell him to do so. It was just the shock. I wasn't prepared for it." He gave her a small smile. "I hear you're moving out?"

She tried to smile, but was still troubled. "Yes, but Manny—"

He waved his hands. "Don't worry. I shouldn't have said anything. Don't be upset with me."

"I'm not," she said, even though she was.

"Come, we'll watch movies," he declared and led her into his ostentatious living room.

"Manny—"

He clasped her face. "Everything will be okay. Gavin will make sure of it."

11

When Manny asked what she wanted to watch, she asked for *Die Hard*. The choice surprised Manny, but he didn't question it. Juanita brought a steady stream of food until Lyla begged her to stop.

It took a long time to relax, but eventually, Manny convinced her to stretch out on the couch. After a slew of action movies, Manny popped in *The Godfather*. With her head on his lap, she watched the movie unfold. It was his favorite, no surprise there. Even while she saw parallels between the movie and the Pyre men, she found it amusing that Manny could imitate Vito Corleone perfectly. He could quote the entire movie word for word. Manny cussed people out while he played with her hair.

She dozed and woke when she felt herself being lifted. She tensed and then relaxed when she realized that she was in Gavin's arms. He spoke to Manny in Spanish. Manny's tone was a lot softer than it had been earlier in the day. Gavin carried her to his car and deposited her in the passenger seat. She belted herself in and turned toward him as he got in.

"Okay?" he asked.

Sleepy and relaxed, she nodded. "Get a lot done?"

"Yes, but I have to go in tomorrow." A pause. "Are you okay with that?"

"Yes." He had an empire to run, and she had to learn how to live, knowing what type of evil was out there.

"I'll ask Carmen to keep you company. You up for that?"

"Yeah." She felt steadier. She deliberately brought up the image of the pervert. Her heart began to race, and her hands felt clammy. She reached for Gavin. He took her hand, laced their fingers together, and she could breathe again. She would fight this. It would be okay. She wouldn't let psychos, perverts, and murderers stop her from living her life.

"Are you okay?" he asked.

"Trying to be."

He squeezed her hand. "You will be. Just give it time."

"Is everything okay with you and Manny?"

"Just a difference of opinion. We're fine. Did you have a good time with him?"

"Yes. I love your dad."

His hand tightened on hers, but he said nothing else. They drove home in silence. One of the guards opened her door when the car stopped. She nodded to him and went inside.

"I'll meet you in our room. I need to take care of some things," he said.

She nodded as he went into his office and closed the door. She went upstairs and checked the closet, bathroom, and under the bed before she stripped and got into the shower. It was the longest she'd gone without bathing herself. She saw that as a small victory. The feeling of being filthy was all in her mind, but that didn't stop her from scrubbing her skin so hard that she was bright red when she stepped out of the shower. She claimed another oversized sweater and had just finished slathering on lotion when Gavin walked into the bathroom. He kissed her cheek and stripped. She watched in the mirror and saw his cock standing at attention. He ignored his body and stepped into the shower, washing briskly. Although she felt a tingle of response between her legs, she walked away. She couldn't. She wasn't ready.

She got into bed and curled on her side, staring out of the window at the stars. Gavin came out of the bathroom in a pair of boxers and nothing else. His shower was too quick to get himself off. He tossed his cell phone on the nightstand and brought his laptop to bed. She relaxed and listened to him type. She buried her face in her pillow, drew in his scent, and let sleep take her.

"LYLA."

She moaned into her pillow.

"Come on, baby. Wake up."

Large hands flipped her over. She hung onto the pillow so it covered her face. Gavin chuckled and with one swift jerk, sent the pillow flying.

She glared at him balefully. "What?"

"There's my girl," he crooned and brushed kisses over her face. "You slept through the night."

She blinked. Another victory. She didn't dream at all. Dressed for the office, Gavin smelled delicious.

"I have to go. Carmen should be here any minute. I thought I'd give you a warning," he said.

"Thanks."

"You're okay?" he asked, brushing a gentle hand over her body.

She rested her hands on his chest and found herself thinking about his erection last night. He usually woke up hard. Did he get off this morning? She was annoyed with herself for obsessing about his dick. Didn't she have more pressing things to worry about besides his masturbating schedule? *He wouldn't cheat on you after what happened,* she told herself. But what if she couldn't... Gavin had needs, and she might not be able to—

"Lyla?"

"What?"

"You're okay?" he repeated.

"Uh-huh."

He gave her an odd look before he kissed her forehead. "I'll have my phone on me at all times. Do you need anything?"

"No."

"I'll see you tonight."

He grabbed his phone and laptop and walked out of the room. She lay there for several minutes, letting her mind drift, before she showered. This time, she didn't scrub herself hard enough to bleed. Another victory. She took the time to braid her hair and put on a little makeup. For some reason, it was painful to look at her reflection. She settled on jeans, and because she felt too exposed, pulled on a slouchy jacket.

When she walked downstairs, she found Blade standing guard. She averted her eyes until he called her name. When she looked up, he came forward.

"I want you to feel safe," he said gruffly.

She considered this and muttered, "Thanks."

"What happened the other day will never happen again. No one will ever touch you. Not on my watch."

"I'm okay, Blade."

He clasped his hands behind him and spread his legs in a military stance. "I'll protect you with my life."

This was a far cry from the man who laughed at her nerves when he picked her up in Maine. "Thanks."

He gave a curt nod and then said, "You make the boss happy."

The front door burst open, saving her from having to respond. Blade drew his gun before he turned. Carmen stood in the doorway, tears streaming down her face. She didn't notice Blade or the gun in his hand. She let out a scream that could shatter glass and hurled herself at Lyla. She cried as if her heart were breaking.

"Carmen?"

"It's all my fault!" Carmen wailed. "If I hadn't tried on those crotchless panties, I would have been there!"

Blade shook his head as he holstered his weapon and walked away while she ran a hand down Carmen's back.

"We would have both been kidnapped," Lyla said, holding her cousin tightly.

"At least you wouldn't have been alone, and I could have helped kill those bastards!" Carmen howled.

Because her body was still sore, she led Carmen to the sofa. Carmen went willingly enough, but she didn't release her and listed dozens of ways she would have defended her.

"Carmen, I'm fine."

Carmen drew away, makeup streaming down her face. *"Are you?"*

Her eyes burned with tears, but she took a deep, fortifying breath and gave a small nod. "Yes."

Carmen clasped their hands together. "Tell me everything."

Her heart skipped a beat. She hadn't told anyone what happened. No one asked and even a day ago, she wouldn't have been able to. But she had to get it off her chest. She took a deep breath and told Carmen about her hours in hell. She faltered when she talked about what the pervert did. Seeing the horror on Carmen's face made her feel guilty and relieved at the same time.

"Go on," Carmen said, squeezing her trembling hands.

She brushed away the tears and continued. She told Carmen about Gavin's rescue, how he stayed by her side all these days, and about the test results from the doctor. She felt better now that it wasn't festering in her chest. Carmen raged enough for them both. They went through half a box of Kleenex before Lyla felt a very basic urge.

"I'm hungry."

Carmen snapped to attention. "Yes. You need to eat. I'll cook."

"You cook?" she asked as Carmen led her to the kitchen.

"Is pouring milk in cereal cooking?"

She cracked a smile as she sat at the dining table and Carmen rummaged through the fridge.

"We're in luck. These breakfast burritos just need to be heated. Thank God."

Carmen set the oven before making coffee. She sat, grabbed Lyla's hand, and teared up again.

"God, I'm so sorry—"

"Carmen, I'm okay."

"How can you be? You were kidnapped, nearly raped... or raped. We don't know." Carmen's eyes flared. "I'm glad that fucking pervert is dead. Gavin should have shoved a rusty spike through his asshole and let him suffer for days until the Devil came to drag him down to hell where he belongs."

She blinked. "Wow. Gross."

"What about the other fucker?"

"Gavin's looking for him."

"Good. I want to know when he's dead."

Carmen fetched her purse and pulled out a hand mirror with her name spelled on the rim in rhinestones. She repaired her makeup and squirted a fresh layer of perfume on her chest. When the bell dinged, Carmen jumped up to put the burritos in the oven. Lyla drank her coffee and tried to recover from the draining talk.

"You're here instead of Manny's," Carmen observed belatedly.

"Yes. Gavin stayed in bed with me for days. Whatever I needed, he was there."

Carmen clasped her hands over her heart. "I'm glad."

"Yes." She turned the cup between her hands. "You know why I left the first time, and now this... I can't live like this, knowing what he does, risking himself. You don't know what he looked like that night. He's so distant. Nothing can reach him. He goes cold and shuts off. It scares me."

"That's what he needs to do, Lyla."

"He said he would give it up if I stay with him permanently."

Carmen jerked in surprise. "What?"

"He says he'll walk away."

Carmen held both hands up like a traffic cop. "You're *staying*?"

"If he gives it up."

"Which he will since he's in love with you." Carmen erupted from her seat and did an energetic twerk, interrupted by the oven buzzer.

Still shaking her ass, Carmen pulled the burritos out of the oven and made them both a plate. She slapped the plate in front of Lyla, kissed her on the mouth, and did a shimmy. "Yaaaaaasss! Go, Gavin, go Gavin. You can do it; you can do it. You're a badass, yes, yes! Get yo' girl! Woohoo!" Carmen plopped down in her seat and forked up a mouthful of burrito, eyes shining. "I am so happy!"

"No kidding," she said with a smile.

"This is unbelievable. Who knew this kidnapping business would have a good outcome?"

"Not me."

"So, you forgave him for... before?"

"Yes." They ate in silence before she blurted, "Manny's worried."

"Why?"

"He says Gavin's reputation keeps everyone in line, and if he leaves..."

Carmen shrugged. "Don't worry about it. That's Gavin's business."

She tried to put it out of her mind. Carmen noticed her preoccupation and smacked her arm.

"Lyla, stop worrying."

"Easy for you to say."

"Yes, it is because I trust Vinny to take care of me. Maybe after Gavin gives it up, you'll feel the same, and you guys can go back to the way you were before."

"The way we were?"

"Yes. We do whatever we want and love the hell out of our men when they come home to us."

Before, she was a kept woman. She couldn't deny that not having to worry about bills would be nice, but would staying at home make her stir-crazy?

"Girl, I can hear your wheels turning. You're a worrier, always have been. You're always thinking ten steps ahead and biting your nails about things that may never happen. It comes from your parents. You had to step up when things with your dad went sour so you got a job in high school when you shouldn't have been worrying about such things."

She cocked her head. "Have you been taking psychology classes?"

"Just because I'm hot doesn't mean I can't be smart too," Carmen said absently as she rearranged her nipples in her top.

"I guess. What are we doing today?"

"We aren't going anywhere. You and I are going to talk, eat, cry, and laugh. Nothing else."

Carmen was as good as her word. The day passed in a blur of emotion. They migrated from the house to the pool where Carmen persuaded her to get rid of the jacket. She wasn't sure why she was so self-conscious of her body, but Carmen distracted her so she didn't dwell on it. Carmen was exhausting, entertaining, and supportive. When Lyla took a nap, Carmen cuddled with her in bed, arms holding her tight. It wasn't as comforting as Gavin's hold, but she was grateful nonetheless.

They ordered pizza and watched chick flicks while they French braided one another's hair. Gavin's cook arrived and asked if she had any food preferences, and explained that she delivered meals once a week. She showed Lyla the instructions for the meatloaf for dinner and left.

When Vinny arrived at sunset, Carmen launched herself at him as if she hadn't seen him in years. They shared a deep kiss before he set her down. His eyes were cautious when they shifted to Lyla. Thanks to Carmen, she felt almost normal. She smiled and allowed him to give her a long, tight hug.

"Lyla," Vinny began and said nothing else.

"I'm okay."

He drew back. "Anything you need, you let us know."

"Thanks."

"Gavin said maybe another hour, and he'll come home."

"Is everything okay?"

He rubbed a hand down her arm. "Yes. He's just catching up. Gavin's never spent more than a day away from the office. He needs to learn how to delegate."

"Oh." And she kept him away for days.

"This is a good thing, Lyla," Vinny said. "Work was his life. Now he has a reason to change."

"So, you'll have more responsibility?"

Vinny laughed. "Yes, and I'm looking forward to it. Gavin's changing a lot of things. Promoting, firing, and putting people through their paces."

"Why?"

"I think he wants more time away from the office." Vinny wagged his brows suggestively, and she laughed.

She put the meatloaf in, and they sat at the dining table, drinking wine while it cooked. She was disappointed when Gavin didn't arrive in time for dinner, but Carmen and Vinny were excellent company. They were meant for one another. They finished each other's sentences, and even though they'd been together since their teens, their love hadn't waned. Lyla felt a hollow pang in her chest watching them. They were so open and in sync with one another. She and Gavin were... She wasn't sure. They had a volatile relationship that was still a work in progress.

Gavin arrived as Carmen and Vinny were on their way out. It was past nine o'clock, and she took note of the hard look Gavin and Vinny exchanged before he made his way to her.

"Sorry I'm late," he said and gave her a long, deep kiss. "You taste good."

"It's meatloaf."

"Damn, that sounds good." Gavin kissed Carmen on the cheek. "Thanks for keeping Lyla company."

"No problem, and thanks for keeping her here permanently." Carmen winked at them before she dashed to Vinny's revving car.

"Had a good day?" he asked as they walked inside.

"Yes. I'm glad she came." She hadn't known that she needed girl time. "How was work?"

"Busy."

She made him a plate of meatloaf and a glass of wine and sat with him as he ate. She sensed something was wrong, but didn't press.

Instead, she told him about her day and waited until he finished eating.

"What is it, Gavin?"

"The second kidnapper is dead," he said without inflection, and drained his wine.

She let out a long breath. "How?"

"Gunshot to the temple."

"You?"

He gave her a very direct look. "No. Eli."

"Eli? The angry cop from the club?"

Gavin drained his wine. "Your captor was present the night Eli's mother was attacked. Eli got to him before one of my men could."

She waited for him to continue. He drank another glass of wine and held the delicate stem between his fingers. She sensed his attempt to smother his emotions, but they filled the room. She could taste his temper, though nothing showed on his face.

"Someone's testing me," he said quietly.

A chill ran up her spine. He turned the glass slowly between his fingers, not looking at her.

"I've made some progress by shifting things over to another care-taker, but it'll take time."

"Okay."

"I'm rearranging things so I can spend time away from the office." He focused on her. "I thought we could go on a trip somewhere. Get away."

When they were together before, they rarely traveled. Their lives revolved around The Strip. He was always working. *He's trying to change*, she thought and smiled. "That sounds wonderful."

"Good. I'm trying to make my schedule more flexible."

"That's great."

He surveyed her. "You look good."

"I feel better."

He nodded and rose. "I'm exhausted."

She put everything in the sink, and they went upstairs. She hesi-tated when he stripped. Gavin turned to her and gently slipped her out of her clothes before he shuffled her into the shower. She allowed him to wash her hair since he liked to do it. He was hard again. She turned from him to wash the suds out of her hair. Because he was with her, she didn't scrub her skin. She rinsed and stepped out before him. She donned another sexless garment and slipped into bed before he emerged. Her teeth clenched as he got in on his side. This time, he didn't bring his laptop to bed. He settled her against him and sighed. Within minutes, she heard his breathing even out. It took a long time for her to go to sleep.

THE NEXT DAY, Carmen arrived with junk food and a stripper workout video. They danced on the dining room chairs. She lost her inhibitions when she saw Carmen dancing as if her life depended on it. They celebrated the workout by eating brownies and then taking a dip in the pool. She wondered if Carmen noticed her awkwardness with her body yesterday and was trying to get her to reclaim her sexuality. If that was her intention, it was working.

Gavin came home at a more reasonable hour, but he seemed preoccupied and excused himself during dinner to take a call. He never came back to the table. Carmen kissed her goodbye when Vinny swung by to pick her up.

She paused by Gavin's closed office doors and couldn't hear anything since it was soundproofed. Was he having trouble turning the underworld over to someone else? She worried about it as she showered. She took her time, but Gavin didn't appear. She got into bed and waited. Still, he didn't show. She closed her eyes as she snuggled under the covers. She needed to sleep alone eventually. Gavin wouldn't always be there to tuck her in. She wasn't a child. Lyla forced herself to take deep breaths and eventually yawned. Using the deep breathing method, she lulled herself into an uneasy doze.

SHE DREAMED OF THE PERVERT. He held her down and laughed as she did everything in her power to get him off her. She breathed through her nose since there was a strip of tape over her mouth and tried not to hyperventilate. He grabbed her face between his hands and squeezed cruelly.

"I'm going to ruin you so Pyre won't want you anymore." He kissed her over the tape. "He can have anyone he wants. Why would he want you? Women beg to be with him. You've been nothing but trouble. He'll tire of you and give you back to me."

There was the sound of clothes tearing. His hand quested down her stomach, between her legs, and shoved in.

SHE WOKE WITH A SCREAM, sitting up and clawing at someone who wasn't there. Gavin ran out of the bathroom with a towel in his hands, body dripping.

"Are you okay? Bad dream?" he asked, coming toward her.

She wrapped her arms around him, forcing him to sit on the bed. She rested her forehead, covered in cold sweat, against his chest. She was trembling and could still feel that hand moving down her body, into her.

"Touch me," she said.

He stiffened. "What?"

She grabbed his hand and slipped it beneath the sweater and placed it on her stomach where the pervert's hand had been in the dream. She relaxed instantly. She wouldn't mistake Gavin's large hand for the pervert's grubby, clammy paws. She shuddered. Gavin tried to pull his hand away.

"No, I need—" she began and stopped, realizing how crazy she was acting. "I'm sorry, I—"

"Don't apologize," he said and kissed her. "What else do you need?"

She searched the hard planes of his face. He still had water droplets on his eyelashes, and he was naked. His body was strong and unapologetically masculine. As she stared into his amber eyes, she had a vivid memory of what happened in his office. Her body tingled. She clung to the memory of Gavin going down on her rather than the recent dream, which chilled her.

"I need you," she said and moved his hand from her stomach to the apex of her thighs.

His eyes didn't waver from hers. "You really want this?"

She nodded emphatically. She needed to exorcise the pervert from her mind and body.

His hand moved, and she forced herself to spread her thighs. When his fingers stroked her, she clenched her teeth, and he stopped.

"You're not ready," he said and withdrew his hand.

She wrapped her arms around herself. "You don't want...?" She couldn't finish the sentence. Maybe he didn't want her after the pervert—

He lunged forward and kissed her. His tongue swept in and claimed her. She clutched him as relief swept through her in a heady wave. She could taste his hunger, his need. It called forth her own. She pressed against him, desperate to feel. His hands moved over her, rough and seeking. His mouth fused with hers, demanding everything she had to give.

When she was aching for him, he broke away. She let out an irritated sound and saw his brilliant smile. He dragged her to the edge of the bed so her legs dangled over the side. When he went on his knees, her breathing became shallow with excitement.

"Eating you out in my office was a mistake," he said.

She paused as she lifted her hips so he could pull off her sweatpants. "Mistake?"

He tossed the pants and draped her thighs over his shoulders. "*Big* mistake."

She was confused by the way he stared at her vagina as if it was gold and his contradictory words. "What are you talking about?"

"At work, all I think about is your pussy. I've been hard and aching at my desk for two days," he growled and leaned down to lick her.

She hissed, and he moaned.

"Fuck, watching you come for me, having you give in to me made me so fucking happy." He spread her lips and stabbed his tongue into her. "You're about to do it again."

Her back arched, and she grabbed his hair and tugged. "Oh, my God."

"Say my name," he mumbled.

"Gavin."

"Louder."

His tongue hit her clit, and she clamped her thighs around his head. "Fuck!"

"My name," he insisted. "Let everyone know who you belong to."

"G-Gavin?"

"I'm not a question, baby. I'm the answer to everything."

How could he make her laugh at a time like this? She moaned and then screeched when he sucked on her clit, toying with her and making her crazy. She was close to an orgasm when his mouth disappeared. She started to protest and sucked in a breath when he thrust inside her. He leaned down to kiss her, sharing her taste.

"You taste that? That's ambrosia. My ambrosia," he said against her lips and planted himself deep. "My Lyla. Mine."

"Yes," she whispered.

He moved slowly, letting her body adjust to him, and watched her face closely.

"Okay?" he asked with a pained expression.

"Mmm," she said and felt him twitch inside her.

"Can you take it hard? Do I need to go slow?"

His words tumbled over one another. She smiled and wrapped her thighs around him, in no doubt what he wanted.

"Ride me hard."

She saw his eyes glaze a moment before he gripped her hips and fucked her. It was hard and glorious. The light from the bathroom shone over them. She watched his hunger for her erupt. She climaxed first, legs convulsing. He came a minute later, hands dragging her as close as possible before pouring himself into her. His top half collapsed on top of her while his legs stayed solidly planted on the ground.

"Thank you," he whispered into her hair.

"For what?"

He raised his head. "For trusting me that much."

Her eyes burned with tears. "I wouldn't have made it without you. You make me feel clean again."

"If that's the case, you're about to be the cleanest person on the planet."

In a show of effortless strength, he lifted her limp body in his arms, rounded the bed, and lay on his back with her sprawled over him without once losing contact with her. His hands slid beneath her sweater and stroked her back.

"I needed that," he said and let out a long breath. "The first night you were back, the moment I touched you, you wrapped your arms around me. I knew you were asleep, but I was starved and not about to turn you down." Hungry eyes scanned her face. "How can you be better than I remember?"

"It was good for you?" she asked.

His brows shot up. "You have doubts?"

Fuck. Her insecurities were showing. It was hard to imagine satisfying a man like Gavin. She hadn't been able to before, and now she was a fucking mess. "Just checking."

He smiled as if she was funny and played with her hair. He didn't insist that she take off the sweater. She felt more comfortable with it on for some reason.

"Is everything okay at work?" she asked, stroking her hand over his chest.

"Nothing important."

That was a lie. If it weren't important, he wouldn't have left during dinner and locked himself in his office. She glanced at the clock and saw that it was three in the morning. He'd been working for hours.

"It has to do with you letting go of the underworld, doesn't it?"

"Seriously, baby, don't worry about it."

"But you're still following through?"

He tensed. "I said I would."

"But you're having trouble turning it over to someone else?"

He sighed. "Nothing in business is simple, and dealing with something like this takes time and care."

She accepted that explanation and relaxed, very aware of the fact that he was still penetrating her. "What do you want me to do?"

"What do you mean?"

"You're working all day, and I'm here. Maybe I can help."

He squeezed her ass. "Knowing you're at home waiting for me is helping. I need to know you're safe."

"I'm used to working. I can get a job—"

He kissed her and tipped them both to the side. He pulled her thigh over his hip and moved slowly in and out of her. She forgot what they were talking about as the chemistry between them rekindled. He moved leisurely while he savored her mouth. Time passed, and when she couldn't take the playful lovemaking anymore, she shoved him onto his back and straddled him. He laughed and then groaned.

"Are you trying to make me crazy?" she snapped as she rocked on top of him.

"It's what you deserve for running from me," he said through gritted teeth.

"Is this a game to you?" she asked, enjoying the burn in her thighs as she raised and lowered herself on his thick cock.

His eyes glinted. "I don't play games when it comes to you."

"So, what are you doing?" she panted.

He sat up and sank both hands in her hair. He took her mouth hungrily, tilting her head sideway for better access. She lost her rhythm and sank her nails into his chest. When he pulled back, allowing her to breathe, they stared at one another.

"I want you desperate for me."

He flipped her onto her back and held one thigh high as he thrust in. When she screamed, he gave her a feral smile.

"I want you bound to me so tightly you can't imagine life without me."

He pounded hard, demanding her compliance and need. She reared up and bit his shoulder as she climaxed.

"Marking me, baby girl?" he asked, voice filled with amusement. "That's a good start."

He waited until she calmed before he began to move again, holding off his climax to make her mindless. Her skin was so fevered that she ripped off the sweater. She cupped the back of his neck.

"Fucking finish me," she commanded.

"Who do you belong to?"

"You."

"Who?" he demanded, dropping the easygoing façade. "Who do you belong to?"

"Gavin."

"Say it. Say you belong to me."

"I belong to you."

"For how long?"

"Forever."

His eyes glinted as he slammed into her. He bounced her on the bed, letting their momentum cause him to penetrate deeper than he had before. She was breathless and delirious with lust. She kissed, bit, and sucked what she could reach of him. She came again and he finally joined her, shouting her name and planting himself deep. He raised his head and looked down at her, golden eyes staring straight into her soul.

"Whatever it takes to have you with me, I'll do. Never doubt it."

12

Lyla woke alone. She moaned because she was definitely feeling the effects of her night with Gavin. It was nearly noon, and she was tangled in bedsheets. She hadn't felt him leave the bed or get ready for work. She must have been dead to the world. How much sleep did he get? She worried about him as she showered. He was dealing with the scum of the earth. He needed to be on his toes. She didn't want him going out there half-cocked. Once she dressed, she searched the bedroom for her phone, but couldn't find it. Annoyed, she went into the kitchen and made herself a bowl of cereal. She spied the phone on the counter and texted him. *Did you sleep at all?*

He replied a minute later. *Enough.*

She rolled her eyes and texted him back. *You need to sleep more.*

Worried about me, baby girl?

Stupid man. Of course, she did. *Yes.*

"That's good to know."

She shrieked and whirled, milk and cereal splashing over the floor. Gavin walked into the kitchen wearing sweatpants and nothing else.

"I thought you went to work!" she snapped and grabbed the roll of paper towels.

"After you let me have you again?" He wrapped an arm around her, lifting her clear of the mess and plopping her on the marble island. "I'm not leaving unless I have to."

"But what about—?" She lost her train of thought when he unbuttoned her blouse and licked her nipple through her sheer bra. "W-What are you doing?"

"Making up for lost time." He grinned when she gripped his hair. "You don't want me to go, do you, baby?"

"I..." She couldn't align her thoughts. They scattered in every direction.

"I have to take care of something tonight, but today, I'm spending my day in you."

He was as good as his word. He ate her out and then fucked her on the marble island. When she tried to clean up the mess, he carried her into his office where he sat her on his lap and ordered her to ride him. Watching his eyes go blind with lust was something she quickly became addicted to. The first time they were together, they had sex daily, but it hadn't been so intense, consuming, and insatiable. He couldn't keep his hands off her and spent most of the day stroking every inch of her he could reach. She had never seen him like this. Before, there had always been a cool distance. Now, he looked at her as if she were his savior.

They shut out the outside world and spent the day making love, eating, and just being. Feelings she thought were long gone rose up as he napped with his head on her lap. It was like having a lion sprawled over you—strong, wild, and capable of anything. This man, this terrifying, unstable being was hers. Always had been, always would be. He claimed her the moment they clapped eyes on each other. Confident, mature, and powerful, he controlled every aspect of their relationship. She had never been completely sure of him, and seeing him eating out one woman while another fucked him and two others licked and kissed his body destroyed her. The man he became in the intervening years was nothing she could prepare herself for. He was more forbidding, passionate, volatile, and dangerous than she ever imagined.

Now, here they were. He seemed perfectly content to spend the day with her, but she knew it wouldn't last. He was a natural leader. The craving to acquire spurred him on. He was naturally restless. She had no idea what her life would be like tomorrow, in a week, or one year, but she committed herself to him. Permanently. Her hands twitched nervously as she touched his hair. Would this sudden need for her wane with time? Would he crave the dark violence she was asking him to give up? She shook away worries she didn't know the answers to and forced herself to concentrate on what was on TV.

He got up at seven and ate her out again before he showered. She warmed up the leftover meatloaf, and they ate together before he left.

"Are you going to be okay?" he asked.

"Yes."

"Call me if you need me. If you have bad dreams, I want to know about it."

She nodded and gave him a kiss before he headed out the door. This felt so domesticated, almost normal, aside from the fact he was leaving at nearly ten o'clock at night. She didn't have to ask to know he was dealing with the illegal side of his business.

She showered and was in the middle of cleaning herself when a thought struck fear into her heart. She wasn't on birth control. She always had an IUD, so pregnancy wasn't a worry she ever contemplated, but because of the pervert, it was gone.

She stumbled out of the shower and found the doctor's business card. She dialed while she tracked wet footprints over the carpet. The doctor was alarmed at first, but Lyla reassured her that everything was fine. When she asked for another IUD, the doctor said she was out of town and wouldn't be back until next week. She swallowed her disappointment and scheduled an appointment. She thought of going to another doctor or Planned Parenthood, but she had no insurance, no ID. Her only choice was to wait until Gavin's private doctor returned. She didn't even have money to buy the morning after pill.

She and Gavin had never discussed children. Ever. She didn't even know if he liked children. They were together for years, and he never spoke of marriage, so children were completely out of the question. Did she want children? Deep down, she did. She wanted the white picket fence, and she wanted to be a stay-at-home mother. It was a dream that had briefly seen the light of day with Jonathan, but *Gavin*? She had extremely light periods to the point where she barely noticed them. She had no way of knowing where she was in her cycle. She sat on the edge of the bed and put her head between her legs because she felt close to passing out.

Gavin said he was going to propose after she discovered his infidelity. Would she have said yes? She had no idea. Even as she imagined a child, a son, that looked like Gavin, her stomach rocked with terror and elation. No. Her life was unstable, and her relationship with Gavin, even more so. He wanted her now, but long term? She wanted to believe he really did care for her, but she couldn't be certain. She had agreed to stay because her heart wouldn't let her say no. Gavin was an enigma. There was nothing special about her. She was ordinary in every way. The only difference between her and other women was her relationship with Manny. She still suspected his father was a factor Gavin wouldn't admit to.

When she could think clearly, she realized that the bedsheets were soaked through. She stripped the bed and finished her shower. She found another set of sheets and remade the bed. She stomped on towels to absorb the water she had tracked around the room and went to the kitchen to do the dishes and sterilize the countertops and floor. When that was finished, she searched for a vacuum.

"What are you doing?"

She jumped and whirled to find Blade standing in the living room with his gun at his side. She turned off the vacuum and gestured vaguely.

"I'm just... cleaning."

"It's one in the morning."

"Oh." She searched for a plausible explanation and decided on, "I can't settle."

Blade holstered his weapon. "You want me to call Gavin?"

"No!" When his expression turned suspicious, she waved her hand. "I mean, I-I'm fine. Just keeping busy."

"He'd want to know."

"It's not an issue. I'll go to sleep now," she said and began to roll up the cord.

"You want a sleeping pill?"

She should have done that hours ago. "Yes, please."

Blade fetched her sleeping pills. She popped one in her mouth and was aware of his scrutiny.

"I'm fine. Really. I don't want to bother him," she said quietly.

"Anything to do with you isn't bothering him," he returned.

She gave him a strained smile and climbed the stairs. She slid between the fresh sheets and was glad the pill worked quickly.

DESPITE THE PILLS, she woke around six. The first thing on her mind was the risk of pregnancy. She felt like she had a hangover. She crept downstairs and peeked in Gavin's office, but he wasn't home. She made herself a cup of coffee and paused during her first sip. Pregnant women weren't supposed to drink coffee, right? Fuck. She rushed upstairs to get her phone. She paced the room as she dialed.

"Hello?" a cautious voice answered.

"Mom?"

"Lyla?"

Her mom was a notoriously early riser. She'd been counting on that. Some things never changed.

"Whatcha doing today?" she asked, trying to sound normal.

"Grocery shopping. Baking."

"Can I come with you?" She needed to get out of the house and didn't want to chance letting something slip to Carmen or Manny. They would be ecstatic. Logically, the chances of getting pregnant were slim. It would be a miracle if she got pregnant after two days of unprotected sex, but it was a possibility.

"Of course. How have you been, honey? Is this your new number?"

"Yes. Let me get ready, and I'll be over."

A pause and then, "With Gavin?"

"No. Just me." She grimaced. "Maybe Blade."

"I don't know how your father's going to feel about that."

"Blade will stay outside," she said as she went into the closet and paired a dress with a jacket and gladiator style sandals.

"Okay. I'll see you soon."

She put on enough makeup to hide the dark circles under her eyes and hurried downstairs. When she opened the front door, she came face to chest with Blade. His eyes narrowed suspiciously.

"I'm going to see my mom," she said.

His brows arched. "Why?"

A valid question since she left her parents' house in a hurry last time. But her mother was her mother. "Because." When he didn't budge, she said, "You don't have to come with me. I can drive myself."

"Not likely. Does Gavin know?"

She'd been hoping to avoid that. "I would rather not bother him. He must be really busy if he hasn't come home yet."

"Call him."

It was part dare, part demand. She could see that he wouldn't budge without Gavin's consent. She clenched her teeth as she pulled the phone out of her pocket and found his name under contacts. She turned away from Blade and paced to the fountain as the phone rang.

"You're up early," Gavin said.

"Yes." She paused, mind going blank with nerves before she said in a rush, "I want to see my mom."

A short pause. "I'm going to be finished in a couple of hours. I was hoping to be home before noon to spend time with you."

"I'll be back before then. I just need to talk to her."

"Okay."

She swallowed hard. "Thanks. See you later."

"Call me if you need anything."

"You're okay?" she asked belatedly.

He chuckled. "Of course."

"Okay. Just checking."

"Bye, baby girl."

When she turned, she saw Blade on his phone. She crossed her arms, wondering if Blade called Gavin to make sure she had been talking to him or whether Gavin was making arrangements. Honestly, it didn't matter. When Blade opened the back door of an SUV, she climbed in and was surprised when he climbed in beside her. Two guards sat up front. No one spoke, and the tension got on her nerves. She leaned against the window and watched them approach the city.

"I want a donut," she said absently.

"What kind?" Blade asked.

"Maple."

The driver pulled up to a Dunkin' Donuts. She was mildly amused when Blade put in his donut preference, as did the guard in the passenger seat. She felt marginally better when he came back with two dozen warm donuts. She snatched a chocolate and maple donut before anyone else could claim theirs and finished both before they pulled up to her parents' house. When she threw open the door to get out, Blade put a restraining hand on her arm.

"Let us check it out first," he said and jerked his head at the two guards who climbed out.

When the guards gave the all clear, she slipped out and walked into the house, which had already been searched by the driver. Her mother appeared serene, but Lyla saw the unease and fear beneath the façade. She shooed the guys out before she hugged her mother.

"Hi, Mom."

"You look great! Gavin must be doing something right." She wore an overly bright smile, and then worry crept into her expression. "You're keeping him happy, right?"

With all that happened recently, it was easy to forget that her father's half a million-dollar debt brought her here in the first place. She and Gavin hadn't talked about the debt since the night at the club. Another touchy subject she didn't want to bring up. Half a million was a lot of money, money she didn't have. Her temples throbbed with tension.

"Gavin's fine."

"And you're with him?" Mom asked hopefully.

"Yes."

She blew out a breath. "Good. Why don't you go see your father while I get my things together?"

A not so subtle hint that she had daughterly duties to attend to. She went upstairs and knocked on her parents' open bedroom door. Her father's left arm and both legs were in casts. His face still looked mangled. After witnessing what Gavin did to the pervert, she knew her father got off easy. He lifted his head and sneered at her. She half hoped he'd tell her to take a hike.

"If it isn't Princess Lyla," he drawled. "Come to see your boyfriend's handiwork?"

She gritted her teeth and walked forward, so he wouldn't get a neck cramp. "No. Came to go shopping with Mom." His nose had been broken and not reset well. It was off center.

"You know how long I gotta stay like this?" he demanded as if she'd done this to him. "Three months!"

She said nothing.

"I feel like a fucking handicap."

Still, she said nothing.

Mean brown eyes narrowed on her. "Enjoy living the high life, princess?"

The sarcasm and jealousy in his voice made her want to back away, but she stood her ground. He never wanted her with Gavin, not because of his family business, but because Gavin took her from her father's control. She had done everything in her power to make her father love her; she even went as far as getting a job and giving him a portion of her paycheck to gamble away. That stopped once she got involved with the Pyres. Manny showered her with affection she didn't have to work for, and her father's approval became less important. Her father resented the Pyre's power and money.

"I'm okay," she said. Her parents knew nothing about the kidnapping, and honestly, she didn't know if they'd care.

"I bet you are," her father grunted. "You think about anyone but yourself?"

She blinked. "Excuse me?"

"I don't have a fucking job, and your mother's never worked!" he bellowed, face red with rage. "You ever think how we're going to buy food if I'm bedridden and don't have a job?" When she just stared at him, he mumbled, "Selfish fucking whore."

"Don't talk to me like that," she snapped.

"Why not? You waltz in and out of this family as if we're nothing to you. You don't give a shit what's going on in our lives."

She opened her mouth to shout, but heard Mom calling her name. She slammed the door on her father's stream of insults and stomped downstairs.

"Everything all right, honey?" Mom asked.

She bit back all the angry words that wouldn't make a difference to her mother and nodded.

"Let's go, then."

When they walked outside, her mother came to a stop when Blade gestured toward the SUV.

"I have a car," Mom said, gesturing to an old Honda. "I have some errands to run."

"We don't mind," Blade said.

"Come, Mom," she said and took her mother's hand.

One of the guards moved into the last row of seats so she and her mother could sit together. Blade took shotgun, and they were off. Her mother was clearly uncomfortable giving the driver instructions. Lyla climbed out of the car when they reached the bank and watched as her mother stuck first one and then another card into the ATM machine with a pinched, worried expression. Gut clenched, she accessed her account in Maine through her phone, and wasn't surprised to find that it had been closed.

She dialed Gavin's number as her mother tried the first card again.

"Hey, baby girl," he said.

She took a deep breath. "My money in my account, the five thousand, you have it?"

"Yes."

Why the hell did she think seeing her mother would make her feel better? It made her realize how fucked up her life was. Gavin had all the power, and she had nothing. She tried to tread carefully. "Is the five thousand a down payment?"

"Down payment for what?"

"Dad's debt." She paced as she watched her mother slap the screen of the ATM, as if that would change what she was seeing. "I-I know five thousand is nothing but—"

"What's going on?" His voice was clipped.

"I need some money," she said.

Dead silence on the other end. Her heart began to pound, and she tightened her grip on the phone.

"I can get a job to pay you back." Still no response. Her eyes stung with tears of desperation. "I know I owe you for Dad's debt, and we haven't talked about how I'm going to—"

"Blade has a credit card. We'll discuss this later," Gavin said and hung up.

She swallowed hard as she pocketed the phone. Her mother hurried back to the car without cash. Lyla sat silently as they stopped at the post office and then a store. Her mother chose a ghetto grocery store where people sold tamales and black-market DVDs out of the trunks of their cars. Blade and the other guards had their hands in their jackets, clearly on edge. As her mother grabbed a wagon, she sidled up to Blade.

"Gavin said you have a credit card we can use?" she asked in a low undertone.

"He texted me. I have the card," Blade confirmed.

She nodded and rushed to keep up with her mother who seemed to be trying to get away from them. "Mom, get whatever you need."

Her mother wouldn't look at her. "I just came for a few things."

"Gavin will pay for it," she said, stomach tight with nerves.

Her mother flushed with embarrassment. "We're okay."

"No, you're not, and you might as well get what you can while we're here."

"Really?" Mom asked, hopeful but wary.

"Yes. I don't know when you'll have another chance."

Her mother took Lyla at her word and filled her basket. She grabbed a package of condoms because it couldn't hurt and distracted her mother when they were rung up. Blade didn't blink as he handed the credit card over. Her mother was in a better mood as they loaded up the groceries and headed back to the house. Blade and the other guards carried the groceries inside. Her mother filled the empty fridge with food, and it comforted her even though she had to deal with Gavin. Her mother insisted on making lunch for them. The guards were allowed to sit in the living room while she watched her mother put away ingredients and start the preparations for her homemade fried chicken.

Under normal circumstances, she would have been eager to taste her mother's cooking, but not knowing how Gavin would react to this latest incident made her queasy.

"What's this?"

She looked up and saw her mom holding the box of condoms. She held out her hand, but her mother didn't hand them over.

"What *is* this, Lyla?" she asked as if Lyla was fifteen-years-old.

She raised her brows. "Condoms. You put them on dicks to save yourself from an STD or getting pregnant."

"Yes, but why would you need these? You're with Gavin, right?"

"Yes."

Her mother's face turned sympathetic. "Is he still cheating on you?"

Arrow through the fucking heart. She was stunned by the pain that simple question caused.

"They're men, honey," her mother said, patting her cold hand. "But if they take care of you and come home to you, who cares?"

She cared. She cared too fucking much.

"You might want to take out your IUD if you want to hook him," Mom continued as she dipped chicken in battered eggs.

"Hook him?" she echoed.

"He's a ladies' man. He might move on and then where will we all be? You have to have insurance."

A child as insurance... She rose from her seat. "I have to go to the bathroom."

She walked out before her mother could say anything else and passed Blade who had been standing just outside the kitchen. She ran upstairs and sat on the closed toilet lid, hands over her face. When her phone rang, she jolted and reluctantly pulled it out of her pocket. When she saw Gavin's name, she considered ignoring it, but he paid for her parents' groceries, and he might want to discuss how she could pay him back.

"Hi," she said.

"I'm home. I want you here."

Her hand tightened on the phone. "Mom's making fried chicken."

"I'm calling Blade. He's bringing you to me."

He hung up, and she sat there, wondering what the fuck was wrong with her life. It didn't take two minutes for Blade to knock on the door.

"Lyla? We have to go," he said.

"A minute."

He knocked again. "He's pissed. We don't have a minute."

Oh, fuck. She rose and opened the door.

Blade gave her a sharp look. "Are you okay?"

"Fine." She walked past him and ignored her father's curses when he caught sight of her. He fell silent when Blade stopped in the doorway.

"What are you doing in my house?" her father roared.

"Gavin told you what he'd do if he heard you talk to Lyla like that," Blade said quietly. "I hear you insult her again, I'll finish the job he started."

She stopped by the kitchen to kiss her mother on the cheek.

"But the chicken!" Mom protested.

"Enjoy it," she said and put the condoms in her pocket.

"Remember what I said, Lyla!" she called.

She rushed out of there as fast as she could and got into the SUV, feeling worse than she had this morning. How could she have forgotten that her parents had no income? Yes, it was her father's fault, but how would they survive? She wouldn't let them live on the street. She could get a job and help until Dad was on his feet again.

"You shouldn't let your father talk to you like that," Blade said.

"I don't let him, he just does."

"Gavin won't stand for it."

Gavin might cuss her out himself when she saw him.

"You have no idea what you mean to him," Blade said impatiently.

She glanced at the guards in the front seat who could hear every word and huddled against the door, wishing Blade would shut up and leave her alone.

"I heard what your mom said about hooking Gavin and him cheating on you again," Blade said.

"Will you shut up?" she snapped, finally losing her temper. What was going on in her head was bad enough. She didn't need everyone voicing their opinions. "I'm not going to trap him, so you don't need to report that to him! God!" What would Gavin think if he heard what her mother said?

"You're different from the others," Blade said.

So there were still others... She blinked back tears. "Blade, please, shut up."

Her mind raced. She would never be able to repay the five hundred thousand her father stole. She possessed nothing of value that she could exchange for even a fraction of the cost. Not only had Gavin paid for groceries, but she also had to ask him for a loan until she could get a job.

When the SUV pulled up to Gavin's compound, she had to force herself to move. She put her hands in her pockets and walked slowly toward the door. She felt as if she were walking toward a firing squad. Her fingers closed around the pack of condoms as she entered. She closed the door and stood there, listening. She jumped when Blade came in behind her.

"You're supposed to stay outside," she said.

"I have to give my report."

When he tried to step around her, she blocked his way. "What report? About me?"

"Yes."

"What is there to report?" she demanded. "Nothing happened."

Blade walked around her. In a desperate move, she leaped on his back to stop him.

"Please don't tell him," she whispered, mortified.

"Tell me what?"

She froze as Gavin came out of his office. She could feel his energy, and it didn't bode well for her. His eyes were bloodshot from lack of sleep, and he looked ill-tempered. Blade shrugged her off as if she were a flea. She dropped behind him and waited for the explosion.

"We need to talk," Blade said.

She bit back another plea as he walked into the office. Gavin beckoned her with one finger. Slowly, she went to him and wasn't prepared for the hand that shot out to cup her face. She couldn't stop her reflexive jerk backward. His eyes began to blaze.

"We're back to this?" he hissed.

She said nothing.

"Don't go anywhere," Gavin snapped before he slammed the office door.

13

She sat on the couch for what seemed like an eternity, hands clasped between her knees. She would tell Gavin that she had no intention of trying to trap him with a baby. She had proof! She scheduled an appointment with the doctor last night. As for her parents... that was harder. Why would he give money to help someone who stole from him?

Blade came out of the office. She didn't look at him as he walked outside, closing the front door with a quiet click. Tattletale. She needed to remember that fact in the future.

"Lyla, come here."

Gavin didn't yell. That was a good sign, right? She rose and tried to conceal her nerves as she walked into his office. He sat behind the desk in the office chair she rode him in yesterday. That felt like a lifetime ago. She didn't have the courage to look him in the eye. She could feel his anger pulsing in the air. She clasped trembling hands together and waited.

"Blade had a lot to say."

Loudmouthed, traitor bastard.

"Do you really think I'd cheat on you?"

She ignored the painful wrench in her chest. "Not right now—" she blurted and stumbled back when he erupted from his chair.

"Not right now?"

"I mean, I meant—"

"Jesus Christ, are you fucking serious?"

"I don't think you're cheating," she said, trying to sound firm, but it sounded unintentionally tentative.

He stared at her. She couldn't read him, but she felt something building and tried to head it off.

"I-I believe you're happy with me," she said, and when he didn't comment, her confidence took a nosedive. How could he be happy with someone with such a fucked-up family? "Or satisfied." Still no response. "I-I know I don't have any right to ask for anything. Thank you for paying for the groceries today. I would have used my money, but..." But he had it. "Dad's bedridden for a couple of months, and Mom's never worked. I need to help them, at least until he's well enough to find a job."

"Why would anyone hire a thief as an accountant?"

She blinked. "You'd stop him from trying to get another job?"

"I'm not going to give him a fucking reference."

Of course, he wouldn't. Would her father *never* get another job? She twisted her hands together. "I can get a job, pay you back for the groceries and—"

"No."

She stopped talking, but he didn't elaborate. She raised her eyes and was caught by his predator stare.

"You aren't going to work," he decreed.

"But I need to help. They're my parents."

"Then you ask me for money."

"You'd give me money to pay their bills?"

A muscle twitched near his left eye. "Yes."

She felt awful, even though he could afford it. "Thank you. You don't have to do that."

"I think you're confused about something."

She tensed.

"You think I don't care about you."

She frowned. "I know you care."

"Do you? Because I've been trying to show you that I'm all in, and you're backing away like I'm going to hit you."

"I'm sorry." After all he'd done for her, he didn't need this crap.

"Come here."

She hesitated for a second before she rounded the desk. She stopped a foot away from him.

"Look at me."

She looked up as he framed her face. His touch was gentle even though his features were stiff and cut into brutal, unyielding lines.

"If I want pussy, I can get it," he said.

She jerked, and his hold on her firmed. "I know."

"I don't want other women," he continued, eyes boring into hers. "They don't know me, don't give a fuck about me. I know the difference between a slut and a real woman."

His thumb brushed over her bottom lip as he considered her. Her heart pounded in her ears.

"You're right."

When he didn't continue, she prompted, "About what?"

"Back then, the things I did for business still bothered me. It kept me up at night. I didn't want it to touch you, so I used other women. I poured that shit into them. They welcomed it, craved it."

When she tried to twist away, his hand dropped from her face to her arm. He hauled her close.

"Now I don't need the other women. I don't feel anything when I do what I have to."

She said nothing.

"Three years without you, you think I'd be dumb enough to fuck it up again?"

"I think you need more," she whispered.

"More what?"

"More than I have to give. Right now, you think I'm enough, but eventually—"

He clapped a hand over her mouth and stared at her as if he'd never seen her before. "For the rest of my life, you'll be enough."

His eyes were hungry, desperate pools that wanted to swallow her.

"I never told you I loved you, did I?"

Her heart stopped.

"I never told you that I would die for you, that I adore everything about you. I can't get enough of you. I never will." His voice was strong and sure. "I'm fucking greedy when it comes to you. I don't want anything between us, even my dad, and that's fucked up. But I don't care. I want you to need me, and you don't. You can live without me. You did it for years."

He jerked away and paced, hands running through his hair, breathing hard. She watched him, torn between backing away or going to him. She did neither and stayed where she was.

"I hate that you went on without me, that you *could*." Veins popped out on his neck. "You let another man touch you, turned to him for—" He broke off and sent everything on his desk flying. "I forced you to run from me. I know that. Living without you was my punishment, and I suffered, Lyla."

He whirled back to her, his movements jerky and uncontrolled.

"I love you."

It sounded like a threat.

"And I will never let you go, never turn to another woman. You're everything I need."

Tears poured down her face.

"I have men watching you. I call them constantly because I need to know you're still here. I don't care if it makes me look weak. I need to know you're waiting for me. I'm identical to my father in one aspect. When we love, we do it once and forever. I'll never let you go. I recognize what you are, what place you have in my life. I can feel you slipping through my fingers. I won't allow it." He spread his arms wide. "You want to hook me, baby? Take me. Anything, everything. Show me you want *something* from me and aren't waiting to run when my back is turned. I know I don't deserve you, that most people only get one shot at love. If they blow it, that's it. I forced you to give me a second and third shot. I'll keep asking you for chances because we will never be over."

Her heart thundered in her ears as she drank in every word.

"You're not part of our world. That's why Dad and I were drawn to you. Innocence, loyalty, purity, and love. You remind me of my mom. You have her spirit. She kept my dad grounded. I lost it when you left. Suddenly, I looked forward to doling out punishments, to sowing fear into the slums. I had nothing to lose, nothing to go home to, and then I found you."

His eyes flashed with a rage so potent that goose bumps rose on her arms.

"I haven't had a weakness for them to exploit until now. Your kidnapping was a test to see how I'd react. Their orders were to grab you, ask for a ransom, and see how quickly I'd get the money together. You weren't supposed to be touched. Someone's fucking with me, and everything in me wants to retaliate, but I have to pass that duty onto someone else. I can be content with those worthless fucks' deaths because I have you. My future flows through you, so I'll pay the price, whatever it is, to have you."

She reached for him, and he came toward her, a wild rush of man, power, and need. He kissed her hard, punishing and cherishing at the same time. His hands roamed over her, digging into flesh, clutching at her clothes. With an angry growl, he set her on the desk. She grabbed his shoulders for balance as he lifted her dress and spread her legs. She had only a moment's warning before his cock sank into her. She moaned into his mouth as he slid slowly but inexorably into her. He didn't stop until he sheathed himself completely. When he yanked her jacket off, the box of condoms fell out of her pocket and bounced on the desk. He pulled back from the kiss to yank her dress straps down and spotted them.

"No," he growled as her dress pooled around her waist and he unsnapped her bra.

"No?" she gasped as he sucked on her pulse and pulled her tight against him.

"No condoms, no IUD." He raised his head. "You should take your mom's advice. Hook me, Lyla."

"A baby?" she breathed, mind whirling.

"We're going all the way this time. My ring on your finger, my baby planted in your belly. No half measures. You agreed, baby girl."

"When did I agree to that?" she demanded and bit back a moan.

He gripped her hair as he powered into her, hard strokes that left her gasping for more.

"You agreed to stay with me. Permanently. I won't stop until I have you bound to me in every possible way."

"But I didn't know..." She let out a short scream and convulsed around him as she climaxed.

He held back as he watched her come apart for him. When she was weak and trembling in his arms, he began to move again.

"You're trying to kill me," she moaned, grimacing against the nearly painful aftershocks.

"No, I'm greedy," he corrected as he lifted her thighs so he could go deeper. He bared his teeth as he thrust. "If you're pregnant, I'd be fucking ecstatic. That loyalty you have toward your parents, I want it. I *need* it."

"You have it."

"No." He bit her bottom lip and tugged, but didn't break the skin as he had in the kitchen. "I don't have your loyalty yet, but I will. You're still unsure of me. We'll move past that."

His hands moved to her clit. She jumped and tried to pull his hand away.

"I can't!" she groaned, head tucked under his chin.

"You will," he decreed. "Come with me, baby girl."

He knew just how much pressure to use. She erupted again, and this time, he came with her, driving himself as deep as possible and then slumped over her, head resting on her chest as she sprawled on his desk. They stayed that way for a while before he disengaged and carried her upstairs. They settled in bed facing one another. That awful tension shimmering in the air around him had dissipated.

She stroked his cheek and watched his eyes close as if her touch brought him unspeakable joy. Her throat clogged with tears. "I love you, Gavin. Too much."

His eyes snapped opened. "You can never love me too much."

"It scares the hell out of me."

He clasped her face. "Say it."

"I love you."

"Again."

"I love you."

"You'll marry me?"

She bit her lip, and he grinned.

"You love me; you marry me."

"I do love you, but marriage..."

"Is inevitable. I already talked to a wedding planner."

She tried to rise, but he kept her lying beside him. "Wedding planner? Are you insane?"

His smile had an edge to it. "The day you agreed to stay, I talked to him. He's over the top. He's handled some prestigious weddings. You can meet with him, go over details."

"Details for a wedding," she said numbly. "You don't ask for much, do you?"

"We wasted years. I'm not wasting another month."

"*Month?*"

"Didn't I tell you, baby girl? We're getting married in a few weeks."

She held up a hand as her stomach pitched as if she were on a roller coaster. "Gavin, we can't—"

"Of course, we can. We'll have the wedding at one of our hotels, invitations are being made, and anyone will jump at the chance to make your dress."

"This is too fast!" she exploded, thumping his shoulder with her fist. "Within two weeks, you show up and turn my life upside down. I've been blackmailed, pushed around, seduced, kidnapped, and now ordered to marry you! When is it going to stop?"

"When you're mine," he said firmly. "I should have the other side of the business wrapped up by then, and I'm not wasting any more time. I'm tying up loose ends, so we have time to build a life, a family." His eyes searched hers. "Do you want that with me?"

"Holy shit, I'm not ready for this."

"You will be. I'll make sure of it."

"What about my parents?"

"Give them whatever you want. My money is your money. I'll get you a credit card and put you on my bank accounts."

He had given her an allowance before, but this gave her even more freedom. His trust and generosity stunned her. "Really?"

He flopped on his back and fit her into the curve of his shoulder. "You want them to pay for not being good parents, so be it. Let them be homeless. You want them to be millionaires; I don't give a fuck. I don't respect them. You're you despite their influence. They have no idea how special you are. If they had treated you right, I would have rewarded them. Instead, I watched your father skim hundreds, thousands, and then hundreds of thousands. I'm not going to lie and tell you that I didn't enjoy beating the hell out of him."

"Why did you allow him to steal from you?" It was a question that had bothered her from the start. Five hundred thousand was a lot of money. Gavin wasn't the type to miss something like that.

"Your family is your biggest weakness. When I found you, I'd need a way to hold you here, keep you indebted to me. I let him dig himself a hole and waited to use him for my benefit."

"What if you never found me?"

"I would've found you, Lyla, sooner or later." He shut his eyes and wrapped her close. "Stay with me while I sleep."

"Okay."

She stared out the window at the brilliant blue sky and wondered if she would ever have a simple life. Probably not. Not when she was about to marry Gavin Pyre. She never imagined that he had marriage on his mind, but he always managed to surprise her. His expression, even in sleep, was fierce and foreboding. He loved her. She loved him. They were complete opposites, yet somehow, they fit together. She said a silent prayer before she dozed off.

SHE WOKE ALONE, which pissed her off. She had always been a light sleeper, but now it seemed that she slept like the dead. It was dark outside, which meant she had been out for a while. She decided to shower and was in the process of shampooing when her hair snagged on something. She yelped and slowly jiggled her hair until it came loose. She lifted her left hand and froze. A beautiful diamond ring winked seductively at her. She held her hand up to the spray and stared at a pale blue diamond set on a thin band decorated with white diamonds. It took her breath away.

"Gavin?" Her voice was weak.

Her hand began to shake. Of course, she remembered talking about marriage, but the ring made it painfully real. She washed the suds out of her hair, wrapped herself in a robe and ran downstairs. She found Gavin in his office on the phone. He quickly ended the call when she flapped her hand in his face.

"You don't like it?" he asked warily.

"When did you buy this?" she demanded.

"Over three years ago."

She was so shocked; she took a step backward. "You bought this *before*?"

"Yes, I've been waiting to give it to you for a long time. You like it?"

Her eyes filled with tears. "I love it," she managed before she launched herself at him. She wrapped herself around him and hugged him tightly. "Are you sure you want to—?"

"Yes."

She kissed him and pulled back. "We need to tell your dad."

He grinned. "He might faint."

"We need to tell him tomorrow... and Carmen. Oh, God." Just the thought of their reactions made her chest tighten with anxiety.

"Don't worry about it. They'll be happy for us," he said.

"I know, but you said you wanted the wedding by the end of the month? How is that going to happen?"

"Money," he said carelessly, and kissed the palm of her hand. "I hope you know what kind of wedding you want."

"What do you mean?"

"You know, colors, theme, that kind of thing."

She nibbled on her bottom lip. "We can't elope?"

He burst out laughing. The lighthearted sound took away most of her anxiety. She liked seeing him carefree and happy. He was usually so grim and serious.

"Aside from the fact that Dad would kill us, I want the big wedding."

"Why?" If it were up to her, she would have a backyard wedding. She didn't want to be on display, in the papers, gossiped about. Gavin was high-profile enough to garner media attention, which she hated.

"I'm only getting married once, and we have the resources to make our union legendary. Plus, I want our business associates to attend."

"How many guests are we talking about?" she asked warily.

"I don't know. My assistant gave some numbers to Armand, the wedding planner. You have an appointment to meet him by the end of the week."

"Pushy."

"*Very* pushy," he agreed and tasted her lips. "By the end of the month, you'll be Lyla Pyre." His eyes glinted with hunger. "You ready for that, baby girl?"

"No."

"Too bad." He softened his words by kissing her again. "I have to take care of some business, and then we can eat dinner. The cook is making something. Ten minutes."

She unwrapped herself from him and hurried out of the office. She finished her shower and then paced the room as she dialed Carmen, who picked up on the fourth ring.

"Hey, girl," Carmen puffed.

She paused. "Did I catch you at a bad time?"

"No."

"Why do you sound as if you've been working out?"

"I've been working out with Vinny in bed," Carmen cackled.

TMI. She took a deep breath and blurted, "I'm getting married."

Utter silence and then a weak, "No."

"Yes."

A bit louder, "No."

"Yes."

"*No!*"

"Yes," she repeated.

"Fuck, yeah!" Carmen screamed. "Vinny, they're doing it. Not fucking, getting married! Yeah! No. I don't know. Let me ask her." Carmen's voice was frantic with excitement. "When are you getting married?"

"He wants to get married by the end of the month."

"What? How are you going to do that?"

"A wedding planner. Armand?"

"You got *Armand*? Oh. My. God. This is insane. I'm so excited! Are you happy?"

"Yes." Terrified, but happy. "I don't know what I'm going to do."

"Obviously, you have to figure out what kind of wedding you want. I want to see the ring! Send me a picture."

She wrung her hands. "I want to elope."

"You can't elope," Carmen said sharply.

"I know. Gavin won't let us."

"Thank God for that. Okay, we need to get you a dress, and do you know what kind of flowers—?"

"I have no idea."

"I'm the maid of honor, right?"

"Of course."

"Better be. And Vinny's best man?"

"I think so."

"Better be," Carmen said again. "I'm going on Pinterest right now. We should shop for wedding dresses tomorrow, so you have an idea of what you want. I'll send you ideas."

The line went dead. She wanted to call Manny, but this wasn't something she wanted to tell him over the phone, and they should tell him together.

She went to the kitchen and saw that the cook prepared salmon and an amazing salad with wine and candles. The cook chatted with her before she left for the night. Lyla was pouring wine when Gavin came in.

"This is nice," she said.

"We just got engaged. We should celebrate," he said and kissed her long and deep.

"You keep that up; we won't eat," she said.

"Fine with me," he said, drawing her closer.

"I'm hungry," she said and pushed him into his seat.

Gavin went easily enough. They fixed their plates while she stared at her ring.

"Carmen wants to look at wedding dresses tomorrow," she said.

He nodded. "Good."

"I have to visit my parents," she mused, thinking about their financial problems and her upcoming wedding. She hesitated and then said, "I don't want my dad to walk me down the aisle. I want Manny to do it."

"Dad would be honored," he said.

Her phone chimed. She picked it up and saw Carmen's text, demanding to see the ring. She took a picture and sent it.

"Why the blue diamond?" she asked.

"Your eyes."

She looked up. "My eyes?"

"The diamond is the same color as your eyes. I knew you wouldn't wear something over the top, but I wanted the ring to be unique."

"It is," she said and when the phone chimed, she told him, "Carmen agrees. Is Vinny going to be your best man?"

"Of course. He's like my brother. Why?"

"Just making sure before Carmen confronts you." She examined the man she had agreed to shackle herself to. "You're going to be fine with one side of the business and not the other?"

"I'm training someone to take over. He already knows parts of the business, but certain contacts need to be handled directly."

"Who's taking over?"

"It's better that you don't know."

Yes. The less she knew about it, the better, but, "Why are you so involved? I mean, you play the same role with your casinos as you do with the underworld, right? You're at the top and usually don't get involved in the day-to-day operations. Don't you have, like, a manager or something?"

"I have men I trust under me, but my name is what gives us credibility and strength. I get involved when it goes bad. In this case, I need to introduce the new crime lord, and that has to be done in person."

That was a part of their lives that would soon be a thing of the past. Gavin loved her enough to give it up. The strength of his feelings scared and thrilled her. She would never be able to handle him, but she was okay with that. He was his own person and a force to be reckoned with. She tried to imagine a baby cradled in his arms and felt her throat tighten with emotion. God. Gavin Pyre, a father...

"What are you thinking about?" he asked.

"You want to be a father?"

"Yes. My mom had a hard pregnancy, so she only had me. I always wanted a big family. You?"

"I wished I had a sister or older brother, but I had Carmen, and she was enough. For that matter, we're both only children."

"I'm up for the challenge of a big family if you are."

She tried to imagine kids running around the mansion and smiled. "I'm up for it." He reached for her, and she tutted and scooted backward. "We're eating dinner!"

"We'll eat after," he decreed and hauled her into his arms.

14

Manny punched his fist in the air and danced around the dining room after Gavin announced their impending nuptials. Manny kissed his son on both cheeks before he wrapped Lyla in a hug and rocked her from side to side. When he set her down, he clasped her face.

"Thank you," he whispered.

The tears rose unexpectedly and spilled over. "W-Will you walk me down the aisle?"

Manny staggered back as if her words mortally wounded him. "Walk you down the aisle?"

"My dad is..." She shrugged. It was no secret that her father cared little for her. "I want you to do it if you don't mind."

Manny took a deep breath. "It would be my honor."

She hugged him tight. "I'm so happy."

"This is all I wanted for both of you," Manny said solemnly.

"I'm going to look for a dress today. Carmen's coming with me."

"When's the wedding?" Manny asked.

"By the end of the month," Gavin said.

Manny didn't look surprised. He nodded and clapped his hands together. "We have much to do. Let me know what I can do to help. Anything you need, it'll be done."

They left shortly after, hand in hand. Gavin drove with one hand on her thigh.

"I'm glad we told him in person," she said.

"Yes."

"And he's going to walk me down the aisle."

"Did you have doubts that he would?" Gavin glanced sideways at her. "You're his daughter in every way but blood."

"You never know how people will react. I'm just relieved he agreed."

"I've never seen my dad react to anyone the way he does to you except my mother." He stroked her thigh with his thumb. "You're good for both of us."

She felt a pang in her chest but said nothing as they pulled up to Carmen's mansion. Her cousin rushed out, screaming and reaching for the door before Gavin came to a stop. She hauled Lyla out so she could see the ring.

"I knew this was going to happen!" Carmen crowed, bouncing on her stilettos.

"I'm glad we proved you right," Gavin said dryly as he got out of the car.

Vinny came down the steps and gave Gavin a manly handshake and clap on the back before he came to Lyla. He wrapped her close and whispered in her ear, "He loves you, you know?"

She pulled back and smiled up at him. "I know."

Vinny nodded and kissed her before he looked at Gavin. "We'll leave these two together, huh?"

Gavin leaned down to kiss her. She wasn't prepared for the carnal kiss or the way his fingers dug into her hips. When he pulled away, she searched his eyes.

"You okay?" she asked.

"Get whatever dress you want. Money's not a factor."

"I hear ya!" Carmen chirped.

"You feel okay?" he asked, and she nodded. "You need anything, call me."

"Okay."

"A month, Lyla. That's all I'm willing to wait," he warned.

"I'm not contesting it," she said.

"Good." He looked at Carmen. "Take care of her."

Carmen tossed her hair. "Of course."

"Blade will shadow you," Gavin said, gesturing to the SUV.

"Okay."

"Don't let your parents give you any shit," he said in a more businesslike tone. "You don't owe them anything."

She nodded.

He gave her another hard kiss before he ducked into his car. Vinny took the passenger seat.

Carmen linked their arms together and led her to the gold convertible. "I love seeing Gavin like this."

"Like what?"

"Desperate."

"Desperate?" she echoed, offended on his behalf. "He isn't desperate."

"Any man who gives his fiancée only a month to tie the knot is worried the woman will change her mind."

"I won't."

Carmen gave her a sidelong look. "Good. Because you'd have to deal with Gavin *and* me." Carmen peeled out of the driveway, forcing Blade's tires to squeal as he tried to keep up. "So we have an appointment with a legendary dressmaker. I talked to Armand, and he recommended her. Do you know what type of dress you want?"

"White?"

Carmen gave her a disgusted look. "Girl, you're lucky you have me."

SHE WAVED at Carmen before she trudged up the steps to Gavin's home. She was numb with exhaustion. Wedding details swirled around her head. Between Carmen's boundless enthusiasm and the no-nonsense dressmaker, she had no idea what she wanted. She tried on countless dresses until they all began to blur together. This was Vegas. The dressmaker was extravagant with her creations. When Lyla described a traditional and simple dress, the designer and Carmen wore identical appalled expressions. Tomorrow they had a follow-up appointment and she was dreading it. She showered and dressed in the most comfortable pajamas she owned. She went downstairs, warmed up a meal, and curled up on the couch to call Gavin.

"Are you sure we can't elope?" she asked when he answered.

"Yes. Are you home?"

"Yes. Carmen dropped me off. I'm eating dinner and then going to bed. When are you coming home?"

"I'm not sure."

"I went to see my parents. I told my mom we're engaged, and you're going to take care of their bills."

"You're taking care of it. I couldn't care less."

"I know, but the money is coming from you."

"Lyla, it's your money."

"Okay, well, she didn't like that Manny would walk me down the aisle but—"

"It isn't up to her."

"Yes, I know, and I told her that," she soothed. "Everything's fine. Are you all right?"

"Yes. Hearing from you made me feel better." A pause and then, "Tell me you love me."

She didn't hesitate. "I love you."

"Even though you know what I'm capable of?"

A chill skipped down her spine. "Is something wrong?"

"No, I just need to hear you say it doesn't matter."

"I love you no matter what." No response. "Come home to me, Gavin."

"I will. Once I get this squared away, you won't be able to get rid of me. Dream of me, baby."

"I will."

She finished her meal and stared into space, thinking of the strange conversation and their upcoming wedding. It was clear that Gavin was pushing the new crime lord hard. She wouldn't be able to rest until he left the underworld completely.

She climbed into bed and stared up at the ceiling as she marveled at how much her life changed in such a short time. She thought of Jonathan with a distant sense of regret. Now that she was back with Gavin, it was clear that what she gave Jonathan was a watered-down version of love. He deserved better.

She didn't like being in bed by herself. She cursed the fact that Gavin's business kept him out at all hours of the night. Who was the new crime lord? What was Gavin doing tonight that made him uneasy enough to seek reassurance from her? She buried her face in the pillow and fisted her hands. Images of the pervert and his partner flashed into her mind, quickly followed by the memory of Gavin covered in the pervert's blood. She relaxed instantly. Gavin would do whatever he had to, and he would come back to her. Nothing would stop him.

"Lyla."

A hard shake jolted her awake. She opened her eyes and saw Gavin standing beside the bed. She opened her mouth to ask what was going on and saw something smeared on the side of his face, neck, and suit. She shot out of bed as her mind registered that he was covered in dried blood.

"What happened? You're hurt!"

"It's not my blood," he said tonelessly. "Get dressed."

"What? Whose blood is it?"

"Vinny. He's dead."

She went cold. "Dead?"

"Get dressed. We need to see Carmen."

"Vinny's dead?" she repeated and shook her head. "No, I just saw him!" This morning, Vinny kissed her on the cheek and said Gavin loved her.

"We don't have time, Lyla. We have to get to Carmen."

"Carmen? Oh my God," she whispered. How would Carmen react when she found out that her husband was dead?

"Hurry. Get dressed."

She changed out of her pajamas, mind whirling. Vinny dead? She'd known Vinny for nearly a decade. She considered him to be a brother. She braced her hand against the wall as the full impact of his loss slammed into her. Her eyes flooded with tears. Male voices shouted outside, reminding her that she didn't have time to grieve. She had to get to Carmen.

She grabbed a clean shirt for Gavin and ran downstairs. He was on the phone, rapping out orders in Spanish. When he saw her, he slammed the front door open and pulled her outside. Men and cars were everywhere. Guns were displayed openly. The buzz of fury emanating from the men made her feel as if she walked into a war zone. Blade beckoned her to an SUV. She slid into the back seat, shaking hands clasped on her lap. Gavin got in beside her and continued to talk on his phone in a clear, precise tone that was far too calm.

When he hung up, he shrugged off his stained suit jacket and the shirt beneath. He reached for a water bottle and wiped his cheek and neck. The stench of blood made her stomach lurch. He slipped into the clean shirt. She couldn't stand the suspense any longer.

"What happened?"

"Vinny went to a meet and the contact decided to test him. Vinny wasn't expecting it. He was shot three times in the chest. Five of my men died."

She covered her mouth, unable to comprehend what he was saying. "The contact decided to test Vinny? Why?"

"They're like wild dogs. They sensed he wasn't strong enough." Gavin's voice began to shred as his emotions came through. "I rushed down there, but he was already dead. The contact took the shipment, the money, everything. I never should have let him go alone." Gavin slammed his fist into the back of the seat. The guard in the passenger seat rocked forward from the blow. *"Fuck!"*

Something clicked in her brain. "Vinny was the new crime lord?" she asked in numb horror.

"He wanted it. The money, the power..." Gavin shook his head. "I thought I could train him, teach him the ropes. I—"

As his voice faded, she reached out and placed a hand on his thigh. His body was tight and coiled, ready to strike. She resisted the urge to draw away. This was Gavin. He wouldn't hurt her. He didn't acknowledge her touch, but he didn't push her away either. She fought back tears. Vinny wasn't strong enough to take on men like the pervert and his partner. Vinny was cheerful and easygoing. He didn't possess the predatory instincts that had been beaten into Gavin from birth.

When they pulled up to Carmen's home, she couldn't move. Did Carmen know that Vinny had agreed to take Gavin's place in the underworld?

Gavin grasped her hand and pulled her out of the SUV. Security nodded to them and backed away as he rang the doorbell. Her heart pounded as they heard footsteps, and then Carmen opened the door. She clearly hadn't gone to sleep, despite the early morning hour. Her inquiring look shifted when she saw Gavin standing there. Her cousin's eyes locked on his face, and then she backed up, shaking her head wildly.

Gavin reached for her. "I'm sorry, Carmen—"

"No!" Carmen screamed. "No! Don't say it."

"I'll find who did this and—"

Carmen leaped forward and beat her fists against Gavin's chest. "You *promised* me!"

Her shrill scream chilled Lyla to the bone. She hauled her cousin backward just as Carmen hit Gavin across the face. Carmen ripped herself out of her hold and grabbed the closest thing to her—a priceless vase, and hurled it at the wall. Rainbow shards rained down around Carmen, but she didn't pause. Lyla watched with her hands over her mouth as Carmen systematically destroyed her art collection, even beating a metal statue with an iron poker until it was a misshapen blob.

"Blade," Gavin bit out.

Blade walked forward with something in his hand.

"What is that?" Lyla asked.

"A sedative," Gavin said a moment before Blade stuck a syringe in Carmen's neck.

Carmen whirled and tried to hit Blade with the poker. Blade efficiently disarmed Carmen. The momentum he used to rip the poker from her grasp made Carmen hit the ground hard. Lyla knelt beside her cousin who was breathing hard, eyes dilated with shock and grief.

"He can't be gone," Carmen whispered. "I can't live without him."

She stroked Carmen's hair back from her face. "I'm so sorry."

Carmen's eyes fluttered shut. Blade waited a few moments before he picked her up. Lyla led the way to Carmen's room and turned back the covers. Blade set her on the bed.

Lyla glared at him. "You carry sedatives on you?"

"I'm always prepared," he said as he walked out of the room.

She wet a washcloth and wiped Carmen's tear streaked face before she climbed in bed with her. She hugged her cousin who trembled uncontrollably. Carmen let out a keening sound that ripped her heart to shreds. Lyla murmured soothingly into her hair. Vinny was the closest thing Gavin had to a brother and best friend. They had been raised together. Her heart pounded with dread and fear. What would Gavin do?

When Carmen finally succumbed to the sedative, she went downstairs and found Gavin on the phone. Carmen's inconsolable rage and grief left her feeling raw and terrified for Gavin. She wrapped her arms around herself and waited for him to get off the phone. She could taste violence in the air, and it turned her stomach. The sun rose, revealing the destruction Carmen wrought in her museum-like home.

"How is she?" Gavin asked when he turned to her.

"Not good."

"I'll avenge Vinny."

She had a vivid image of Gavin crouched over the pervert's body —savage and devoid of all humanity. She reached for him. "Gavin."

He stepped away from her. She stilled with her hands suspended in midair. His eyes were a burning copper that revealed nothing. Gavin was morphing into the man she ran from, the man she didn't want him to be.

"This won't stop," she said.

"It will once I make them pay. They'll beg for death before I give it to them."

"Gavin, when does it end?"

"When they end."

She licked dry lips. "You're supposed to be letting this go, not going deeper into it."

"My cousin died," he said quietly.

"Yes."

"It's my fault he's dead."

She shook her head. "No, Gavin."

"He wasn't cold enough to blow their heads off for insulting him. He was too soft. I fucking knew that, but I was so desperate to be with you that I allowed you to cloud my better judgment."

She accepted the blame and the verbal blow. Vinny's death was on her as well. "So you're saying you're the only one who can do this?"

Gavin said nothing. He didn't have to. He would keep the crime lord mantle and turn back into the monster he had to be.

"So we're back to where we started," she whispered, heart splintering.

"You want more people to die?" he hissed.

"What if it's you next?" she shot back. "What if it's someone else you love?"

"I won't give them the chance."

"Gavin—"

"They'll pay. They all will."

She reached for him, and once more, he avoided her. "What are you doing?"

He stared at her, a mixture of need and rage spiking across his features before he turned away. "I don't have time for you. I have to fix this fuck up."

"By killing more people."

He stopped, then turned. "By doing what I have to."

"So you're not going to let go of the business?"

"And have someone else die in my place? No."

She felt a slashing pain in her chest. "You promised, Gavin."

"What do you expect me to do?"

"Let it go. Vinny's death should convince you that it's not worth it."

"Grow up, Lyla. If I ignore this, they'll never stop."

"They kidnapped me, and now they killed Vinny. Someone's gunning for you, Gavin! Can't you see that?" she shouted. Seeing Carmen's breakdown felt like a preview of what she was in for if Gavin died.

"Let them come," he hissed.

"I love you!" Tears filled her eyes and spilled over. "You said nothing else matters but us."

"Look where that's brought us!" he roared.

The force of his shout made her take a step back. She clasped her shaking hands together. "So, you're breaking your promise to me." He was ten feet away, but it might as well have been miles. There was no trace of softness in him, no trace of the man she agreed to marry.

"I have to." With that, he walked out the door.

She heard the screech of tires and the murmur of male voices outside. She wanted to rage and scream. Instead, she found a broom and dustpan and began to clean with silent tears slipping down her face. She mourned Vinny, the only brother she'd ever known and partner for her cousin and Gavin, the people she loved the most. What now?

The front door opened and Carmen's parents stepped into the house. Lyla dropped the broom and ran to them. Her burly uncle wrapped her close. She spent most of her time at Aunt Isabel and

Uncle Louie's house as a teenager. They treated her like a second daughter.

"Lyla," Uncle Louie murmured as she began to sob, the events of the past hours overwhelming her.

"Where is she?" Aunt Isabel asked.

Lyla pulled it together and took a deep breath. "She's upstairs. They had to sedate her." She gestured to the ruined paintings, statues, and shattered glass.

Aunt Isabel put a hand over her heart. "My poor girl."

"S-she's devastated."

"Did Gavin get the fuckers?" Uncle Louie demanded.

He was a sweet man, which made it easy to forget that he had been Manny's enforcer once upon a time.

"I-I don't know," she said.

"He will," Uncle Louie said with a curt nod.

"I don't know how long she's going to be out," Lyla said, rubbing her throbbing forehead, and then headed into the kitchen. "You should see her. I'll make coffee."

Carmen's parents went upstairs while she made a much-needed pot of coffee. The doorbell rang. She heard murmured voices but focused on starting breakfast instead of seeing who it was.

"Baby girl."

She turned and saw Manny. The tears came again, and she went to him. He rubbed her back as he held her tight.

"He won't stop," she whispered.

"Let Gavin work out his rage," Manny said.

"By killing people?" she asked, pulling back to see his face.

Manny looked as if he aged since she saw him yesterday. "It's what we know."

She shook her head. "He blames me for Vinny's death, for influencing his decision to pass the crime lord title off to someone else."

Manny sighed. "He's in pain, Lyla. Give him time."

She let out a long breath. "Sit. I'm going to make breakfast."

"Where's Carmen?"

"Asleep. Blade sedated her."

"Carmen's a passionate woman. If she was trained like Gavin, she would be hunting right alongside him."

She shuddered because she knew it was true. Aunt Isabel and Uncle Louie entered the kitchen and greeted Manny respectfully. They made small talk, but they fell into a weighted silence as they all wondered if Gavin had found Vinny's killer yet.

THE NEXT FEW days passed in a roller coaster of emotions. She spent every waking moment with Carmen. She let her cousin rage, reminisce, and grieve. She forced Carmen to eat and bathed her after outbursts that left Carmen weak as a baby. Through Aunt Isabel's gentle suggestions, Carmen was able to plan a funeral, but it left them all exhausted. By the end of the week, Lyla was bone-weary and heartsick. There was no word from Gavin, which increased her anxiety and stress, but she pushed that away and focused on Carmen. She slept at her cousin's house and even wore her clothes.

The night before the funeral, neither of them slept. They lay side by side in bed, staring up at the ceiling. She couldn't believe how the course of their lives could change so drastically in so little time. Vinny's murder haunted her. How could one human being do that to another? In retrospect, it was now glaringly obvious that Vinny would be Gavin's choice for crime lord since he trusted so few. If she'd known that Vinny would take over, would she have put a stop to it?

"How could God do this to me?" Carmen whispered.

"Things happen," she said, focusing on Carmen instead of her dark thoughts. "Did you know that Vinny had agreed to take over that side of the business?"

"Yes, I knew, but..."

Carmen began to cry. Lyla squeezed her hand.

"I never thought something like this would happen. He said he could handle it, and I trusted him to be careful, to come home to me."

"I'm sorry, Carmen," she whispered, heart heavy with guilt.

"It's not your fault."

"Gavin's not going to give it up after this," she said quietly. "He doesn't want anyone else to get hurt."

Carmen turned her head on the pillow to look at her. "What are you going to do?"

"I don't know. He hasn't called me in a week. He's gone cold."

"Maybe after he finds who did this to Vinny, he'll come back to you."

"We'll see," Lyla said doubtfully. "They kidnap me and then kill Vinny. What next?"

CARMEN DECIDED to keep Vinny's funeral small, but that was nearly impossible because of the Pyres connections in the city. Carmen wore a black dress, veil, and red hooker heels. Lyla stood by her side as they greeted everyone. Uncle Louie and Aunt Isabel stood in the receiving line with them. It wasn't a secret how Vinny died, which created an underlying tension in the church that turned her stomach.

Lyla's heart felt as if it was breaking. A week ago, Vinny was alive, and now they were at his funeral. A week ago, she tried on wedding gowns, and now she was wearing unrelieved black. She looked up as someone made a path through the crowd. Her heart lightened when she saw Gavin. He was alive... and pissed. He hadn't called or stopped by Carmen's house. A part of her wanted to think he was staying away because he didn't want to intrude on Carmen's grief and believed he was to blame, but the wrathful look he directed at her made her heart shrivel into a ball. Clearly, he still blamed her for Vinny's death.

"Gavin?" Uncle Louie demanded.

"I got him," Gavin said.

There were cheers and satisfied grunts from the crowd, and the dark energy in the room dissipated slightly. As everyone took their seats, Gavin went up to the podium and began to lead the service, while Lyla sat between Carmen and Manny. The family got up to tell stories and honor Vinny's life. *Such a waste*, she thought and examined Gavin who stood off to the side as a childhood friend told a story about him and Vinny when they were kids. Gavin looked as remote as ever. He didn't look at her. She called the wedding planner and dressmaker to let them know about the tragedy. She was shocked to hear that Gavin had already postponed the wedding until further notice. What did that mean? She twisted the blue diamond ring on her finger.

After the funeral, they congregated at Carmen's where everyone could eat, talk, and decompress. She didn't stray from her cousin's side. Carmen had a few outbursts, but she quickly got herself under control. It was dark before she was able to look for Gavin in the crowd. She found him in the backyard, staring at nothing. He didn't acknowledge her presence.

"So, you got whoever did this to Vinny?" she asked.

"Yes."

"Just him?"

"I needed to make a statement."

"So, you killed more than one person?"

He said nothing.

"I called Armand. He said we're postponing the wedding," she said gently. She wasn't opposed to it, but he should have told her himself.

"I have to take back the reins for both businesses. I don't have time to get married right now."

His dismissive tone raked her raw. She ignored the pain and asked, "What do you want, Gavin?"

"Control."

"Of?"

"Everything. And until I get it, I'm not going to stop."

"Does that apply to me as well?" she asked.

He eyed her impassively. "I won't allow you to sway my decisions anymore."

She beat back the anger. "Meaning you're going to stay in the business and risk all our lives?"

"*No one* will cross me now."

She shook her head. "There will always be someone who wants to challenge you. You're in more danger than ever. Within a week, I was kidnapped, and Vinny murdered. You don't think that means something?"

"It means I should never have let myself be distracted by you!"

She stepped back from the force of his shout. In the house, the remaining guests quieted. He panted as he tried to reel in his emotions, but he was unraveling in front of her. Guilt and rage ripped across his features.

"Just leave me be, Lyla," he said and walked away.

She walked into the house and began to clean up along with the staff they hired. She couldn't stop moving. If she did, she'd break down. When the last guest left, she and Carmen collapsed in her bed.

"It's over," Carmen whispered.

"Yes," Lyla agreed.

"What did Gavin say?"

She swallowed hard. "He postponed the wedding indefinitely and told me that he wouldn't allow me to sway his decisions anymore."

"Dumb fuck," Carmen said and wrapped her close. "What are you going to do?"

"I don't know. He blames me for Vinny's death."

"It's no one's fault but the man who pulled the trigger," Carmen said and let out a long sigh. "I'm not going to lie. I'm glad that Gavin killed him."

"I know." She slept better knowing that the pervert and his partner were dead too, but the price Gavin paid was dear. He morphed from a man looking forward to his future back to a man who thought he had nothing to lose. All hope, excitement, and love extinguished. Hate and rage took precedence over everything, including her. Where did they stand now? Another curveball in her life, another bump in their relationship. Did she bide her time until Gavin calmed down and try to coax him out of the darkness? Or should she cut her losses and leave? She couldn't leave, not when her cousin needed her. Plus, she wasn't capable of making any decisions right now, not when grief weighed her down.

"I know I've been difficult. I'm glad you're here," Carmen said.

"Of course." Silently, she added, *It's the least I can do.*

"You and Gavin will figure it out."

She let out a long breath and tried to suppress the urge to cry. She'd shed too many tears in the past week. She drifted into uneasy sleep with Carmen reaching for a husband who would never sleep beside her again.

15

The next day, Carmen urged Lyla to do something for herself. Although she was wan and thinner than she had been a week ago, Carmen looked steady. Blade drove her back to Gavin's where she showered and changed. The house seemed as cold and empty as she felt. There was no sign that Gavin had been sleeping in their bed. She paced for a half hour before she asked Blade to take her to Manny's. She found him sitting by the pool. When he opened his arms to her, she fell into his embrace.

"You've been taking care of Carmen?" he asked.

She nodded.

"That's good. How are you doing?"

She took the chair beside him. "I don't know."

He patted her arm. "You two will get through this. Gavin's preoccupied at the moment."

"Preoccupied?" she repeated with a snort. "He hates me."

"It's not your fault."

"And it's not his either!"

"I know." Manny scrubbed a hand down his face, looking older than his years. "I can come out of retirement and—"

"No, Manny."

"Gavin still has a future—"

"And you do too," she insisted.

"I'm tougher than I look."

"Neither of you should be doing this. Gavin should be running the casinos, not killing people for revenge. You should be enjoying your retirement, not contemplating going back to a life of crime."

"I don't want this to affect your relationship with Gavin."

"That's up to him."

Manny took both of her hands in his. "Don't give up on him. He needs you."

"He's losing himself to these people. I want *him*, not all this crap that comes with his job."

There was a soft popping sound. She turned her head and saw Ricardo topple sideways. Before she could comprehend what she was seeing, men in white masks and black suits glided into the backyard. She couldn't catch her breath to scream as Manny rose and pushed her behind him.

"What do you want?" Manny asked.

Two men grabbed Manny by the arms and dragged him into the house. They didn't touch Lyla, but with a jerk of their guns, indicated that she follow Manny inside. Mind a blank canvas, she obeyed and stopped stock-still beside Ricardo who had been shot in the head. Manny was thrown to the ground in the middle of a circle of men dressed in identical suits and masks. There was an ominous silence on the grounds. Where were Blade and the rest of Manny's security? They couldn't *all* be dead, right? She opened her mouth to scream, but a soft voice caught her attention.

"I've heard stories about you, mighty crime lord."

Manny faced a masked man who had a gentle, pleasant voice that didn't belong to a killer.

"You look harmless, but I know what you're capable of."

"Who are you?" Manny asked.

The man gave a mocking bow. "The new crime lord, of course."

"What do you want?" Manny asked as he braced himself on his hands and knees.

"I want your crown," the leader said, pacing around Manny with his hands clasped behind his back. "Gavin Pyre needs to be taken down a peg. Killing his cousin was just the beginning. It's a bonus to find his little fiancée here. Now I get to kill two birds with one stone."

Lyla raked her mind for a way out of this, but her mind was alarmingly blank.

"But I think some payback is in order first."

The leader's leg flashed out, and Manny's head snapped back. He fell backward, his head colliding with the marble floor with a horrible smacking sound. She screamed and tried to go to him, but a man grabbed her arm in a bone-crushing grip. When she fought him, he shoved her to her knees and held her at gunpoint.

"I'm doing the unthinkable—scaling an all-out attack on the Pyres. No one thought it was possible, but here we are."

When the monster spread his arms wide, his men chuckled. She felt faint with panic. This couldn't be happening. The leader stomped his foot on Manny's chest. She heard bones break as Manny gasped and tried to get away.

"No!" she screamed, past the point of caring that a gun was being pointed at her.

Her captor used his fist to stun her into silence. The impact made her ears ring and her vision blurred. She blinked hastily, unable to rip her eyes from Manny, who was being beaten to death. Other men joined their leader and broke every bone in Manny's body. She fought her captor until he slammed her on the ground and sat on top of her. She couldn't breathe. The leader with the sweet voice used the butt of his gun to crush Manny's face as if he wasn't a human being but a clay sculpture that needed to be remade. Bone crunched, and the horrible sound of Manny's screams faded into an ominous silence.

"Please, I'll do anything! Please stop," she yelled, fingernails clawing the floor as terror eclipsed all rational thought. "Take me instead."

The monster paused in his torture to look at her. "Don't worry. We haven't forgotten about you."

"He's old. He can't take this," she whispered.

"Do you know what this man has done?"

When he jerked Manny's head back, it flopped lifelessly. She shrieked and reached for him, even though she knew the gesture was useless.

"Please, please." She was past pride or fear. She needed to get to Manny to reassure herself that the man she considered her father was still breathing.

"This man has killed more innocents than a serial killer. The Pyre family doesn't care who gets in their way. They don't kill, they *obliterate*. Power hungry, arrogant... They forget they're human and can bleed."

The monster dropped Manny, who fell to the floor and didn't move. When he raised his booted foot, the scream she released was filled with all the horror and helpless rage she possessed. She struggled with all her might, but couldn't get free. Manny lay like a broken puppet. His limbs were bent at odd angles. The monster standing above him pulled out a gun and fired. Manny's body jerked. Blood splattered the man's pants and pooled beneath his feet.

As she retched, the man sitting on top of her rose. Blood stained shoes came into her line of sight. A black leather glove smeared with red reached out and gripped her hair. A vicious tug forced her head back. She stared up at the mask that concealed the murderer's face and channeled her hatred into her stare.

"You're so beautiful," the man said and brushed his gloved thumb over her lips.

The tang of Manny's blood seeped into her mouth, and she gagged. The man clucked his tongue.

"It's a shame you had to see that," he crooned, stroking back her hair while she trembled in shock. He pressed his lips to her ear. "You're at the wrong place at the wrong time, baby."

She stared into the slits of his mask at fathomless black eyes. The man shoved her so she sprawled on her back. When the monster withdrew a shiny blade from his pocket, she tried to flee, but a man pinned her wrists above her head while the monster straddled her hips. Light glinted off the knife in his hands. She stared at the blade, knowing her time was up. This is where she died.

"You fucker—" she began before pain ripped through her abdomen.

She didn't have enough breath to scream. Another stab and then another as the monster slashed with great zeal. She writhed, pleaded, threatened, all to no avail as her face was splattered with her blood. Her body was on fire and just when she thought she couldn't take another second, the monster grabbed her face and kissed her through the mask before he buried the knife in her chest. The arms pinning her down disappeared, freeing her hands, which automatically went to the hilt of the knife as the monster got to his feet, looking down at her. The lightest touch made her consider repositioning the blade to end her agony. She curled on her side into a ball, knowing there was no surviving this.

Suddenly, there were shouts, scrambling feet, and then gunshots. This mattered little to her. As her vision darkened with black spots, she focused on Manny. She didn't register the fact that bodies were dropping around her. Her entire being was focused on getting to him. The blood spurting from her wounds helped her slide across the floor with more ease. When she reached Manny's broken hand, she dropped her face onto it.

"Dad, I'm here." If there was a spark of life in him, she hoped he heard her. She kissed his palm and whispered, "I'll see you on the other side."

16

Lyla swam through a sea of pain. She wanted the suffering to stop, so she embraced dark, fathomless oblivion.

———

Every inch of her body hurt. Opening her eyes to a blast of light made her feel as if nails were being drilled into her skill. She closed her eyes and drifted until something soft brushed against the back of her hand, distracting her from the mind-numbing agony. She braced herself before she opened her eyes and focused on the shadow at the periphery of her vision. A person sobbed at her bedside with such fervor that Lyla fought against the blanket of lethargy and confusion. It took considerable effort to move her fingers. She let out a strangled cry that made the blonde head rise. Bright blue eyes awash with tears stared at her. Carmen. Lyla shifted and immediately went rigid as thousands of razorblades dug into her skin. She wanted to scream, but she had no voice.

"You're awake, you're awake," Carmen babbled and ran to the door and shouted, "She's awake!"

A slew of people congregated around her bed. Crisp, direct words were said, but she couldn't make sense of them. A doctor shone a light in her eyes and tried to adjust her, which made her grunt urgently.

"Thank God," Carmen whispered and shoved a nurse aside to take Lyla's hand. "I can't lose you too. I just can't. Vinny, Manny—"

Memories of the men in masks, Manny's prolonged torture, and then being stabbed... Rage ripped through her. She tried to lever her body off the pillows. The monitors went crazy, and the medical personnel began to shout. Lyla collapsed as her head swam. She was dimly aware of Carmen's death grip as darkness consumed her.

WHEN SHE OPENED HER EYES, it took a moment to register the man at her bedside. Dressed in a black suit, Gavin seemed out of place in this sterile setting. As if he sensed her regard, he lifted his head. They stared at one another. Gavin looked untouched by recent events. He was cool, calm, collected. It made her lightheaded with fury as memories of Manny savaged her mind.

"I know you're angry with me," he said.

Her lower lip trembled. She compressed her lips to stop the telltale action, but tears spilled over anyway. Anyone could get angry over stubbing their toe. What she felt toward Gavin wasn't mere anger. The taste of betrayal on her tongue was like acid, eating away at her insides. She wanted to strike him, beat him with her fists until he was bruised and bloody. She would never get those images of Manny out of her head. If her body wasn't so broken, she would have launched herself at him. Instead, she was forced to lay there with him inches away. She could smell his cologne but couldn't feel his body heat, and she was so cold. She should be dead. What was she doing here? She didn't want to be on this planet. It had too much hate on it, too much suffering. She wanted to be with Manny, not here with his son who was so closed off; she wouldn't know he was human if he didn't blink and breathe.

"Blade was shot. He's in critical condition, but he regained consciousness long enough to send me an alert. I got there in time to save you, but not Dad. I didn't get all of them. They're still on the run. Can you give me any information? Do you know what the leader looks like? Who they work for?"

She was lying in a hospital bed, unable to move, and he was asking about the monster who did this. He didn't ask about his father or her wounds. She wanted to scream. Instead, she turned her face in the other direction and wept for the man who would never be her father-in-law and for the son he left behind who was a hollow shell of a human being.

"Lyla, I need information," he said without inflection.

After Vinny's death, she told Gavin to let it be. He didn't, and this was the result. His father paid the ultimate price and she... She would never be the same. Witnessing such cruelty, she couldn't imagine ever feeling normal again. Gavin broke his word. Therefore, she wasn't obligated to honor hers.

"I don't have a lot of time," he continued, "I'm a suspect in several murders, but they don't have enough evidence. They're looking into my businesses and trying to pin me with money laundering. I'm going to be tied up with lawyers and cops. I need to know who they were."

What more did he need to know? These men were from the criminal underworld and had a personal vendetta against the Pyres.

"Lyla."

He touched her arm. That made her whip her head around, which made her feel sick. Despite the blast of pain, she managed to say, "*Don't* touch me."

Her voice was a bare whisper, but it was there. Her chest felt as if it was being carved all over again.

Gavin's soulless amber eyes didn't so much as flicker with emotion. "I need information."

"This was payback. He's the new crime lord. Vinny was just the beginning," she rasped.

There was a charged silence and then, "Anything else?"

"No," she said in a broken whisper.

The door burst open. She smelled cotton candy before she saw Carmen. She looked like a ray of sunshine in Lyla's otherwise bleak world. She used the last of her strength to hold up her hand. Carmen rushed over with tears coursing down her cheeks.

"You're awake," Carmen said fervently and pressed her face against Lyla's palm. "You can't leave me, Lyla. You *can't.*"

Gavin rose. Carmen shot him a frosty look as he walked out, back ramrod straight.

"You were in a coma. I was scared you wouldn't wake up." Carmen swallowed hard and brushed away tears, which were instantly replaced by fresh ones. "But you're awake now. You're going to be okay."

It wouldn't be okay. It would *never* be okay. Lyla closed her eyes as tears slipped down her cheeks. She felt as if she were going to shatter.

"I don't know what the fuck is wrong with Gavin. This is the first time he's come to the hospital. I don't know where he's been. Cops are all over the place," Carmen hissed.

Would they find enough evidence to convict Gavin for multiple murders? He had more than enough blood on his hands to be put away for life. She didn't have to ask Carmen to know there had been a bloodbath following Manny's death. If Gavin had been remote before, he was completely gone now. Lyla brushed her hand over Carmen's and got her instant attention.

"We need to go," she said.

Carmen didn't need her to elaborate. All she asked was, "Are you sure?"

Tears spilled down her cheeks. "He broke his promise. I'm free."

"Gavin's men are outside your door."

"You know how to get around them."

"You really want to do this?"

"Please," Lyla croaked.

Carmen nodded decisively and shouldered a gold rhinestone purse. "Let me see what I can do."

Carmen shimmied out the door, hooker heels clacking. Lyla had no doubt that Carmen would be able to get her out a second time. She used her thumb to slide the engagement ring off her finger. It clinked when it hit the floor and disappeared from sight. She felt as if a weight had been lifted from her shoulders. She was done.

RECAPTURED BY THE CRIME LORD

DEDICATION

To the authors who nourished my love for stories and taught me from a young age how to dream.

1

LYLA

Lyla Dalton strolled along a creek in Montana, willing the tranquility of her surroundings to ease her troubled mind. She didn't sleep much. No place, no matter how isolated or beautiful, made her feel safe. Most days, she felt like a walking zombie—no thoughts or emotion penetrated the thick layer of white noise that shielded her from the outside world. Other times, she felt so much she couldn't stand it.

Once upon a time, she and her cousin, Carmen, led privileged lives with men who loved them. That life shattered when Carmen's husband and Lyla's future father-in-law were murdered. She had been mutilated by the same killer, who was interrupted before he could finish her off.

Eight stab wounds and three slashes over six inches in length marred her abdomen. The raised edges of her scars brushed against the thin material of her shirt. Witnessing merciless criminals break every bone in Manny's body made her ill. She couldn't forget the sound of Manny's screams being abruptly cut off as he drowned in his blood.

She stopped on the trail and put her hands on her knees as she waited for the nausea to pass. Following the tragedies, she and her cousin took off while her ex-fiancé, Gavin Pyre, faced money laundering and murder charges. Carmen bought an RV, and they went on the road. They periodically stayed in motels or rented cabins when they needed a break from the close confines of the RV. They paid for everything with cash, so there was no trail. If they felt the urge to move on, they did so. They lived cautiously, avoiding big cities and populated areas. On the rare occasions when Lyla was forced to interact with others, her composure creaked under the strain of trying to appear normal.

She settled on a flat-topped rock along the creek and tipped her face up to the sky. Montana was beautiful and had been their home for about a week. She wished the warmth from the sun would touch her cold soul, which had holes in it that would never heal. Despite the fact they had been on the road for a year and a half, she still felt as fragile as she'd been the day Manny was murdered. Knowing people in the world were capable of that level of brutality kept her up at night.

Carmen told her that Gavin went to jail for money laundering, the only charge they were able to pin on him, since they didn't have enough evidence to convict him of murder. She didn't ask how long he would be in jail. She didn't care. When she woke in the hospital, Gavin didn't ask about Manny's murder or her well-being. All he wanted was information on the men he was hunting. Since the men involved in Manny's murder wore masks, she wasn't useful to him, and she hadn't seen him again. Gavin blamed her for Vinny's death and had been distant and remote while she lay in a hospital bed, held together with stitches and staples. She focused on getting better and left the moment she could. Carmen distracted his men, so they could make their getaway. Slowly, her body mended, but not her spirit.

After the sun heated her skin, she started back to the cabin. Since she skipped physiotherapy, she made a point to be as active as possible and spent a lot of time exploring her surroundings. Branches snapped beneath her sneakers. Her eyes swept the forest for bears, rattlesnakes, coyotes, or cougars. She carried a pistol to defend herself against wildlife and any man who thought two women traveling alone would be fair game. Carmen taught her how to use a gun, and she had become a decent shot, but hadn't had the opportunity to put her new skills to the test.

She left the path as she made her way back to the rented cabin and heard voices up ahead. She cleared the trees and took in the bizarre scene. A small army of SUVs and men were in the clearing. For a second, she thought they were police officers until she registered that they were in suits, not uniforms.

A large man prowled through the crowd. The other suits gave way to him. Even across the distance, she sensed the air crackling around him. Fear shot through her along with a healthy dose of adrenaline. Even as her legs tensed to run, the man stopped in his tracks and turned. Her finely honed survival instinct kicked in. She whirled and ran back along the path as fast as she could. Between the burble of the creek and her heart beat, she couldn't hear anyone behind her, but she didn't stop. Her mind was a blank slate of fear and denial. He couldn't be here.

There was no warning. One moment she was running headlong down the path, and the next she was falling as something crashed into her from behind. As they tumbled, she fought tooth and nail. He spoke, but she couldn't hear over the ringing in her ears. She reached for her gun, but he disarmed her without effort and pinned her hands over her head. He sat on her stomach, taking her breath away. She stared up at Gavin Pyre, the man she'd run from twice in her lifetime. He had an angular face, slick black hair, and blazing amber eyes. His gray suit was now covered in dead leaves, twigs, and dirt.

"Stop," he hissed.

She panted beneath him, unable to find her voice. How did he find them? What was he doing here? What did he want? He didn't look like he just got out of jail. He looked as pristine and polished as always.

He tucked her pistol into the back of his trousers and hauled her up. Before she had time to register that he was really here and touching her as if he had every right to, he began to march her back along the path to the cabins. Rage gave her the extra strength she needed to break away. Her mind screamed at her to get as far away from him as possible.

She left the path and began to zigzag through the forest. She didn't gain more than a dozen paces before Gavin caught up to her. When he swung her around, she went for his face with her nails. He dodged and twisted one hand behind her back, but she wasn't deterred. She balled her fist and clipped his jaw before he restrained her other hand. She glared up at him, chest pumping, daring him to retaliate.

A muscle clenched in his jaw. "Don't."

"I hate you!" she shouted and struggled to no avail. "Why are you here?"

"Because you are."

She lunged at him, hoping to unbalance him, so she could make another run for it. He made an impatient sound and shoved her forward with her hands locked behind her. She had to focus on her footing or fall flat on her face.

When they walked into the clearing, the suits fell silent. Under their scrutiny, sanity reasserted itself, and she looked at Gavin. Ice blue eyes clashed with gold for a beat before he released her, only to grab her forearm to make sure she followed him into the cabin. She came to a dead stop when she found Gavin's head of security standing over her cousin with a gun. Carmen, once the arm candy of one of the wealthiest men in Las Vegas, was unrecognizable. She chopped off her long blonde locks and wore jeans and hiking boots instead of cutout dresses and hooker heels.

"What the fuck are you doing, Blade?" Lyla demanded and tried to go to her cousin, but Gavin held her back.

"Lyla, long time no see," Blade said pleasantly.

"I assume Carmen's the one who helped you escape the first time," Gavin said.

She didn't answer. What difference did it make?

"I've been searching for you two for six months. If it wasn't for your beauty, you would have gone unnoticed and remained untraceable," Gavin said and gestured to someone outside.

An older gentleman walked into the cabin with a Bible clasped to his chest. He was sweating profusely and eyed Gavin and Blade as if they were savages. Gavin turned to her with a placid expression that was completely at odds with the grip he had on her and the fury glittering in his eyes.

"How much do you care for your cousin?"

She stiffened. "What are you talking about?"

"You wouldn't want anything to happen to her, would you?" he asked with soft menace.

"What are you...?"

Her voice trailed off as he reached into his pocket and pulled out the blue diamond engagement ring she slipped off her finger in the hospital room. Seeing the ring after all this time felt like a slap in the face. He stopped her automatic retreat and leaned down so their faces were less than an inch apart.

"Fight me, and she'll pay," he promised.

This was a nightmare. Gavin couldn't be here in Montana with her old engagement ring, threatening to end Carmen's life.

"Do you want me to hurt her?" Gavin pushed.

"*No!*"

"Then do as I say."

He let out an angry growl when she clenched her hand into a fist. He forced her hand to unfurl, and despite her attempts to evade, slipped the ring on her finger before he turned to the man with the Bible.

"Begin," Gavin ordered.

The stranger avoided her gaze as he began to speak.

"We are gathered here today to witness the union of Gavin Pyre and Lyla Dalton."

"No!" she shouted as her knees buckled.

Gavin wrapped an arm around her waist and hauled her against him. When Carmen opened her mouth to protest, Blade clucked his tongue to discourage her and pressed the gun to her temple.

"Lyla, don't do this. He can't make you," Carmen spat.

"Keep going," Gavin barked at the pastor who was clearly terrified before he leaned into her and whispered, "You want Carmen to walk out of this cabin breathing, then you agree with everything he says."

"How can you threaten, Carmen? She lost her husband!" She glared up at him. "You remember Vinny?"

His implacable expression didn't soften. "Twice now Carmen's taken you from me. I should kill her for all this wasted time."

"She has nothing to do with our relationship, and you wouldn't hurt her."

"Want to put it to the test?"

No, she didn't want to test him. Gavin didn't bluff, and his bone-crushing grip suggested he wasn't in a teasing mood. "Why are you doing this?"

"Gavin Pyre, in taking Lyla Dalton to be your wife, do you promise to honor, love, and cherish her in sickness and in health, in poverty and in wealth, in hardship and in blessing, until death do you part?" the pastor asked in a quavering voice.

"I do," he said.

"And Lyla Dalton, in taking Gavin Pyre to be your husband..."

When she shook her head, Gavin turned to her and clasped her face between his hands to stop the motion.

"We've wasted too much time," he said roughly.

Her eyes burned with tears. "Every night, I hear your father screaming. I can't get it out of my head. I won't go back to that life."

His expression hardened. "You gave yourself to me. There's no out for either of us."

"I made my choice," she said, gesturing around her at the cabin. "I choose to live without you."

"Not acceptable," he bit out.

"Lyla Dalton, do you take Gavin Pyre to be your husband?" the pastor asked tentatively, clearly dreading her answer.

Gavin gripped the back of her neck. "Say yes."

"No—" she began, but Gavin covered her mouth with his.

She was too stunned to defend herself against the sensual assault. His tongue swept into her mouth, reclaiming her as his, a claim he revoked the moment he stepped back into the criminal underworld. She dug her nails into his chest, desperate for air and space. Gavin was overwhelming—always had been, always would be. She could feel how tense he was, a coiled spring ready to erupt. He was a law unto himself. When he pulled back, her lips tingled.

"Say yes and I won't punish Carmen for taking you from me," he said in a low voice only she could hear. "No one comes between us."

"*You* let business come between us."

"Say yes," he ordered, so close that all she could see were his burning gold eyes, demanding her compliance.

"Clearly," Carmen said sarcastically, "she doesn't want him."

"Blade," Gavin snapped.

In one swift movement, Blade twisted Carmen's arm behind her back, causing her to cry out before he shoved her toward the front door with the muzzle of his gun pressed against the back of her neck.

"What are you going to do to her?" Lyla shrieked.

"Say I do, or I swear to God, you'll never see her again," Gavin growled.

Lyla stared at him in horror. "What's wrong with you?"

"Say it now, goddammit!"

"I do," she said quickly, heart thundering in her chest.

Blade stopped in the doorway and looked back at her. His wink made her vision bleed to red.

"By the power vested in me, I now pronounce you married," the pastor said and wiped the sweat out of his eyes.

"Where's the marriage license?" Gavin asked.

The pastor presented the piece of paper and offered a pen, which Gavin handed to her. She signed, eyes on Carmen, who looked as if hell warmed over. If looks could kill, Gavin and Blade would be dead. Blade signed as the witness and escorted Carmen outside.

"Where is he taking her?" she demanded. "You promised you wouldn't—"

"He's taking her to her mother," Gavin said shortly as he pushed a diamond wedding band on her finger. It fit snugly against the blue diamond engagement ring. Before her bemused eyes, he pulled out a gold wedding band and placed it on his left ring finger.

In the span of thirty minutes, Gavin Pyre once again turned her life upside down. Without another word, he led her out of the cabin. He placed her in the back seat of an SUV and climbed in next to her. She sat there in shock, staring straight ahead.

"Where are we going?" she asked.

"Home."

Even though she had been expecting that answer, she shut her eyes against the flood of tears. Las Vegas, where she didn't feel safe, and her nightmares took place in real life. Just the thought of going back made her tremble with panic.

"I can't," she whispered.

"You will."

"Why?"

He didn't answer.

"I can't take this," she whispered. "How many times do I have to tell you? I want no part of your life. I hate you."

"Stop."

"No! You show up, tackle me, threaten to hurt my cousin, and force me to marry you. Who the hell do you think you are?"

He turned toward her. If she could run, she would have. Gavin had always been scary, but there was a quality to him now that made him seem even more menacing.

"I'm your husband," he said in a soft voice that sent chills up her spine. "Don't forget it."

When she tried to scoot away, he anchored her to his side. It didn't take long to reach a small, private airstrip. Her stomach plummeted when she saw the Pyre private jet, the same one that had collected her from Maine almost two years ago. He led her on board.

She was relieved to see Carmen there, unhurt. She broke away from Gavin and ran to her cousin, who hugged her tight.

"Girl, are you okay?" Carmen whispered.

She didn't answer. She wasn't sure how she felt. Being legally bound to Gavin wasn't 'okay,' and Carmen knew it. A hand twisted in the back of her shirt and inexorably pulled until she was out of her cousin's embrace. She landed against a rock-hard chest. Muscular arms wrapped her close.

"You have some nerve," Carmen began, hands on hips. "You have no idea what she's been through because of you!"

"I'll let you live out of respect for Vinny," Gavin said, icy voice easily cutting through Carmen's outraged one.

Carmen paled, and when Lyla looked up, she could see why. Something that looked very close to hatred pulsed in Gavin's eyes.

"You must've been grief stricken and temporarily insane to remove Lyla from my protection to go driving around the United States with my father's killer on the loose," Gavin said. "Don't mistake my leniency toward you for forgiveness. I'm sending you to your mother. Your father passed two months ago."

Carmen staggered back, clearly stunned. Uncle Louie died? It was another shock on top of too many.

"He had a heart attack. You'll stay with your mom. I sold your house and put a freeze on what's left of your money, so you don't do anything stupid. You need money for something, you need to go through me," he said in a clipped voice.

"That's *my* money!" Carmen shouted.

"Not anymore."

In contrast, Gavin's voice was whisper quiet and way more effective.

"You've shown that you're reckless and thoughtless. Until I'm satisfied, you won't have access to your money or Lyla."

"You smug bastard! You have no idea what she's been through," Carmen said as she flushed with rage. "Have you seen her scars? Have you heard her screaming at night? Were you there to hold her when she cried? Do you know what happened the day your father died? No, you don't. I wish I didn't, but I do. You broke your promise and left her alone in a hospital bed when she needed you. You went off to chase those fuckers, so I took your place. She asked me to get her out, so I did. You think she would have been safe with your expensive security detail?" Carmen sneered. "If she was so safe, your father would still be alive, and she wouldn't be scarred for life."

Lyla felt his body go rigid a moment before his fist flashed out. Blade deflected his punch before it connected with Carmen's face. The air around them went electric as Gavin went apeshit and launched himself at her cousin. Guards went flying and blood sprayed the luxurious carpet as Gavin's security team tried to restrain him. Flight attendants screamed and ran off the jet. She caught a glimpse of Gavin's face, contorted with blind rage. It made her clammy with fear. Security couldn't hold him back, so they tackled him. He disappeared beneath a pile of men. Blade knelt beside him, trying to talk sense into him.

When Gavin resurfaced, everyone watched him like a ticking bomb. Although his expression was once again impassive, no one trusted his control. Several men stood in front of Carmen with their hands on their weapons. He ignored all this and scanned the crowd until his eyes fixed on Lyla. When he moved toward her, she backed up, but there was nowhere to run. He caught her up in his arms, walked to the back of the jet, and locked them in a private room. Even as he dumped her on the bed and came down on top of her, she heard the engine rev. He tucked his head under her chin and settled on top of her.

"Get off me!" she shouted and pounded his shoulders, but he didn't budge. "You could've killed her."

No response.

"You're out of control."

"Going to jail will do that to you," he said, lips moving against her skin as he spoke.

She hesitated before she asked, "How long were you in?"

"A year. I've been out for six months, looking for you."

"You didn't have to. I'm fine," she said.

"So what Carmen said isn't true?"

She didn't answer. She heard the low murmur of voices on the other side of the door, but no one interrupted them as the jet gained speed and lifted off. Gavin showed no signs of moving, so she blocked him out and stared at the ceiling. It took nearly half an hour for her to process everything that happened, but two points stood out among the rest. One, she was now married to Gavin Pyre. Two, she was going back to where it all began.

2

GAVIN

Gavin crossed the clearing. He couldn't believe they were in Montana. If he weren't grasping at straws, he would have thought the tip that brought them here was a mistake. It never occurred to him that Carmen would be able to live in an RV. She was high maintenance, materialistic, and the furthest thing from a Girl Scout. Lyla, on the other hand, he could imagine on the road. She had always wanted a simple life.

The tip paid off. Carmen was here, but where was Lyla? Carmen claimed Lyla had gone to town, but he didn't believe her. She took Lyla from him not once but twice. He barely refrained from snapping her neck. He spent sleepless nights in jail, being tortured by visions of Lyla being murdered in one hundred different ways. *Where was she?*

He was halfway across the clearing when the back of his neck prickled. He turned, looked past the ranks of men, and saw a slight woman with a trucker's hat pulled low over her face. That didn't disguise the exquisite face, generous mouth, and ice blue eyes. Even across the distance, he sensed her panic. He opened his mouth to call out to her, but didn't bother when she turned and ran.

He shoved through his men and took off after her. Adrenaline shot through his system. He had been looking for her for six months.

He wasn't about to let her out of his sight. She was fast, but he was faster. She kept to the trail, which made it easier for him. He gained on her, eyes never leaving the golden ponytail streaming behind her like a cape.

When he was close enough, he lunged and wrapped his arms around her. He took the brunt of the fall before he rolled and pinned her beneath him. He wanted to see her face and look into her eyes, but Lyla was fighting him like a wild animal.

"Stop, Lyla!" he ordered, which made no impact whatsoever.

Her eyes were blind with fear. He saw a flash of silver and knocked the gun out of her hand. At least Carmen had the brains to teach her how to defend herself. He rested his weight on her abdomen and pinned her hands over her head. The impact she had on his senses was devastating. He couldn't decide whether to strangle or make love to her. She was thinner than he remembered, and the sheer terror in her eyes gutted him.

"Stop," he hissed.

He was close to losing it. If they stayed out here any longer, he would bury himself in her to make sure this wasn't a dream. He hauled her up, eyes averted, and started back toward the cabin. Lyla twisted out of his hold and began to dodge through the trees. Fear made him move faster than he had in his life. He swung her around and wasn't quick enough to avoid the blow. The force of the punch surprised him. It jerked his head to the side and made him realize how much she changed. The woman looking back at him had nothing to lose. She was capable of anything.

"I hate you!" she shouted as she struggled. "Why are you here?"

"Because you are."

The last time he saw her in the hospital, he'd been a prick. Worse than a prick, but that couldn't be helped. He'd been working day and night to find the culprit who murdered his father and tried to kill her. He couldn't afford to sit by her hospital bed while the cops were breathing down his neck. The way she looked at him that day haunted him. He would make it up to her, but first, he had other things to see to.

He marched her back to the cabin, pushing her at a merciless pace; his need to bind her to him a drum beat in his blood. He was acting crazy and didn't care. She was alive, and he wouldn't let go until she was legally his. When they entered the cabin, he was grimly satisfied to find Blade holding Carmen at gunpoint. Lyla stopped in her tracks. He was glad she grasped the situation so quickly.

"What the fuck are you doing, Blade?" Lyla asked as she tried to go toward the traitor.

"I assume Carmen's the one who helped you escape the first time," he said, and didn't wait for an answer. "I've been searching for you two for six months. If it wasn't for your beauty, you would have gone unnoticed and remained untraceable." The trucker who tipped them off went into great detail about Carmen and Lyla's attributes. He allowed the trucker to live with the memory of them, since he would never lay eyes on them again.

He caught a whiff of Lyla's scent. He shook his head to keep himself focused. He would indulge later. Now, they had shit to settle. He gestured to the pastor and mentally braced as he looked down at Lyla. "How much do you care for your cousin?"

Ice blue eyes widened. "What are you talking about?"

"You wouldn't want anything to happen to her, would you?" he asked as he pulled out the engagement ring she left behind. He saw recognition and rage rip across her face before she tried to get away as if he were holding a poisonous snake. He could feel the combined distress of both women, but he couldn't back down. Not now.

"Fight me, and she'll pay," he promised.

She looked at him as if he was a monster, and even as that sent a shaft of pain through his chest, he continued with his plan. "Do you want me to hurt her?"

"*No!*"

"Then do as I say."

He had to make a conscious effort not to hurt her as he struggled to get the ring on her finger. When he succeeded, he clasped their hands together and ignored her twitching fingers. He ordered the pastor to get on with it and caught Lyla before she hit the floor. He wanted to strangle Carmen when she said Lyla had a choice. She didn't. Neither of them did, they just didn't know it yet. Lyla saying Vinny's name caused a bone deep pain, a clawing guilt that chewed at him day in, day out.

The pastor prompted him for those two words that would bind Lyla to him. He didn't hesitate. "I do."

The predator in him lunged to the surface when Lyla refused to take him as her husband. He tried to rein in his wrath as he turned to her and framed her face between his hands to stop her from shaking her head. She would have him. He would make sure of it, but...

"We've wasted too much time," he said, and felt his insides twist when her eyes filled with tears.

"Every night, I hear your father screaming. I can't get it out of my head. I won't go back to that life."

He had to beat back the murderous haze. He focused on her for all he was worth. He couldn't lose it, not when he was so close to his goal. "You gave yourself to me. There's no out for either of us."

"I made my choice. I choose to live without you."

"Not acceptable." Didn't she understand that?

"Lyla Dalton, do you take Gavin Pyre to be your husband?" the pastor prompted.

All he needed was two words. She would give them to him. He gripped the back of her neck and applied pressure. "Say yes."

"No—" she began, and he lost it.

He covered her mouth with his and swept his tongue into her mouth, reclaiming her. Her nails dug into his chest, but he didn't release her. She tasted the same—sweet with a hint of rebellion. When he pulled back, he was pleased to see that her lips were swollen, and she looked stunned.

"Say yes, and I won't punish Carmen for taking you from me. No one comes between us." Didn't she know that? Not that fucking IT guy she met in Maine, not Carmen, not her parents. No one.

"*You* let business come between us."

He ignored that. "Say yes."

"Clearly, she doesn't want him," Carmen said.

His temper roared to life. If he weren't holding Lyla, he would have put his hands on her worthless cousin.

"Blade," he bit out and took note of Lyla's instant panic. If he was a decent human being, he wouldn't take away her free will and blackmail her into marrying him. He wasn't a decent human being. "Say I do, or I swear to God, you'll never see her again."

"What's wrong with you?" she whispered.

He wanted her fucking agreement. If he had brought her asshole father, he could have filled him with bullets, which would make Lyla agree faster and satisfy his bloodthirsty mood.

"Say it now, goddammit," he said through clenched teeth, dimly aware of the fact that Carmen was nearly out of the cabin. Five, four, three...

"I do," Lyla said swiftly.

While she signed the marriage license, he slid his father's wedding ring onto his finger. That's where it would stay until the day he died, just like his father. In the back of the SUV, he tried to calm himself with the knowledge that she was here and legally bound to him. The savage creature inside him bared its teeth when Lyla ran to Carmen once they boarded the jet. He twisted his hand in the back of her shirt and pulled her against him.

"You have some nerve," Carmen began, hands on hips. "You have no idea what she's been through because of you!"

"I'll let you live out of respect for Vinny," he said, hoping she would shut the fuck up, so he could keep himself under control. "You must've been grief stricken and temporarily insane to remove Lyla from my protection to go driving around the United States with my father's killer on the loose. Don't mistake my leniency toward you for forgiveness. I'm sending you to your mother. Your father passed two months ago."

He should have felt bad for revealing that her father died in such an abrupt manner, but he didn't. His killer instinct urged him to eradicate anyone who got between him and Lyla. Every word out of Carmen's mouth fanned the icy rage in his belly. The only thing that kept him sane was Lyla's body pressed against his.

"You smug bastard! You have no idea what she's been through. Have you seen her scars? Have you heard her screaming at night? Were you there to hold her when she cried? Do you know what happened the day your father died? No, you don't. I wish I didn't know, but I do. You broke your promise and left her alone in a hospital bed when she needed you. You went off to chase those fuckers, so I took your place. She asked me to get her out, so I did. You think she would have been safe with your expensive security detail? If she was so safe, your father would still be alive, and she wouldn't be scarred for life."

He could still hear the echo of gunfire as he stepped into his father's mansion that day. Men were everywhere. His gaze landed on two bodies on the floor, covered in blood. Neither moved. Even as his mind refused to believe what he was seeing, he knew it was Lyla and his father. The memory fired his blood, triggering every aggressive instinct he possessed. Annihilating the masked men who weren't fast enough to escape his wrath did nothing to assuage his need for blood. Nothing would until the man who murdered his father and Vinny stopped breathing. They couldn't exist on the same planet.

He wasn't aware that he moved until the smell of fresh blood stung the air. The feel of his fists connecting with flesh made him hungry for more. It wasn't until he was buried beneath a pile of sweaty men that he could think rationally. Fuck. He lunged at Carmen, and his men had to step in. Lyla wouldn't forgive this.

"Get the fuck off me," he ordered.

No one moved until Blade reinforced the order. Everyone knew he was off his rocker. Fuck. He rose and searched the jet for his wife. Covered in dirt and milky pale, she stared at him as if he was the devil incarnate. Maybe he was, but she was stuck with him. He ignored his throbbing fists, hauled her into his arms, and walked into the room in the back of the jet. Lyla gasped when he dumped her on the bed and splayed his revved-up body over hers.

He drank in the feel of her. She was alive and trembling. He rehearsed what he would say when he found her again—apologies, threats, and promises—but his carefully crafted speeches were scrambled in his mind. How could he have forgotten that she made him feel like a fucking caveman? Where she was concerned, he wanted to control, devour, and possess. Lyla Pyre was his.

He tried to eradicate the lethal fury pumping through him. He could have broken Carmen's jaw or worse. He wrapped himself around Lyla, wanting to be absorbed by her. Carmen's accusations butchered his already mangled conscience. He wasn't completely sane. Had he ever been? Maybe not. After witnessing what those savages did to his father and Lyla, he wasn't sure he ever would be. The need to hunt, to kill, was a compulsion he couldn't get rid of. He lay on top of Lyla, hoping her presence would calm him the fuck down. He inhaled her scent—soap, the outdoors, and fear. He had things to say to her. He should cradle her on his lap and beg for forgiveness, but he couldn't move or speak. He couldn't accept she was here after another disappearing act. Never again. She would never get away from him again. He would make sure of it this time. He fucked up too many times to count, but he wouldn't let her give up on him. If there was a woman in the world who could save him, it was the one he just made his wife.

His hands moved up and down her sides, reacquainting her with his touch. He heard the hitch in her breathing and ignored her struggles to get free. He couldn't look into her eyes, not after seeing his reflection. He would remake himself, be the man his father and Lyla believed he could be. He would do whatever it took to make her happy, but right now, he couldn't do anything but let his flesh imprint on hers.

"Get off me! You could've killed her."

He could have. It didn't even register in his mind that he was going to strike. He reacted without thinking. He wasn't going to admit that to her.

"You're out of control."

"Going to jail will do that to you." Being caged when he should have been hunting for the new crime lord drove him insane. Not knowing where Lyla was caused him to use the walls of his cell as a punching bag.

"How long were you in?"

"A year. I've been out for six months, looking for you."

"You didn't have to. I'm fine."

Fine after watching his father be tortured to death and being stabbed multiple times? There were shadows in her eyes that would never fade. "So what Carmen said isn't true?"

She didn't answer. He was fine with that. He had her where he wanted her. Her scent lulled him as nothing else in the world could. He was in danger of drifting off when she spoke.

"Gavin, let me up."

"I need this." How could he tell her that her presence was the only thing keeping him in one piece?

"I can't do this," she whispered.

"You can." She had to.

"You can't just show up and take over," she said as she slapped his shoulders.

He didn't bother to contradict her since that's exactly what he'd done and would continue to do without mercy. At eighteen, she claimed him. It didn't matter what happened in the intervening years. What was left of his soul craved her. She had loved him once. She would again.

"What do you want from me?" she asked.

"Everything you promised me."

She strained beneath him, but had no hope of jostling him. He weighed twice what she did, and was solid muscle.

"You broke your promise to me!"

He had, and it ate at him. If he had listened to her, his father would still be alive, and she wouldn't have run from him again. "Everything's going to be different this time around," he said against the smooth skin of her throat.

"It doesn't feel like it. You blackmailed me into marrying you, and now you're holding me down."

"When we get home, I swear it'll be different." He couldn't talk here. He wanted to be in their home, in their bed when he spilled his guts. Knowing that everyone was on the other side of the door made him feel crowded and crazed.

He only gave a shit about three people on this planet, and two of them had been murdered on his watch. He watched the life drain out of the man who shot Vinny, only to find out that he was a pawn of the new crime lord. He dreamed of ways to torture the man who had murdered his father. Some called him a psychopath. Maybe he was. He didn't have a wide range of emotions unless it involved the small circle of those he loved. With Vinny and his father gone, Lyla was his only anchor. He couldn't function without her. He hoped she was ready to take him on because she was the only one who could.

3

LYLA

SHE SPENT THE TWO-HOUR FLIGHT FROM MONTANA TO NEVADA IN BED with Gavin, but neither of them slept. Every word out of his mouth sounded as if it pained him. Her struggles and complaints made no difference, so she stayed prone, wondering why God hated her so much. When the plane landed, Gavin didn't move until Blade knocked on the door.

"She's gone," Blade said.

"Who's gone?" she demanded, knowing full well he was referring to Carmen. "Where did she go?"

"To her mother." Gavin sat up and paused as if he needed to get his bearings.

"Are you on something?" It would explain his psycho behavior.

"I wish," he muttered and rose. "Let's go."

She stretched and didn't flinch when he took her hand. After having him lay on top of her for nearly two hours, handholding was nothing. He led her off the jet and into the dry desert heat. Las Vegas. She couldn't escape Sin City; it kept calling her back.

Gavin led her to the waiting SUV and climbed in the back with her. He wore sunglasses, so she couldn't read his expression. She had no idea what was going on in his head. If they crossed paths again, she expected him to grovel at her feet or be the remote killer he'd been when she left Las Vegas. The man who forced her into marriage was neither. Something was brewing beneath the surface, and she didn't want to find out what it was.

When they reached his compound, she stepped out of the SUV but made no move to enter. He propelled her inside. She gave their surroundings a cursory glance. Nothing had changed. Had she expected it to? Being here made her want to weep with frustration and rage.

"Shower," he said and led her upstairs.

When he pulled her into the bathroom, she yanked her hand away and crossed her arms. She wanted a shower, but she wasn't going to take one with *him*.

"We're not going to shower together," she snapped.

He opened his mouth to argue and then hesitated. "I guess it wouldn't be a good idea. We need to talk."

"Yes, we do," she agreed.

Abruptly, he stripped out of his ruined suit. She turned away, but not before she caught a glimpse of his incredible body in the mirror. He was even more muscular than before. He looked more like a boxer than the CEO of Pyre Casinos. *Was* he still the CEO? He went to jail, and Vinny's death left an opening for COO, so where did that leave the company? How did Gavin get out of the murder charges? Apparently, he was still wealthy since he had security, the jet, and the mansion. Questions she refused to think about for the past year and a half bubbled to the surface. She didn't think about Gavin because it hurt too fucking much. Now, there was no way to avoid him.

Being with Gavin was like riding a roller coaster—unexpected turns, drops, and rolls. She wasn't sure whether to hang on, raise her hands in the air, or let go. Her personality demanded she let go, and she had—*twice*. But he refused to release her completely, which is why she was back in this opulent bathroom with a priceless blue diamond on her finger. He shocked her out of her sleepwalking state and roused her emotions. She wanted to go back to a half-life where she wasn't living or dead. No bumps in the road, no drama, and no Gavin Pyre. She didn't want friction. Gavin was a stick of dynamite.

She left the bathroom and went to the walk-in closet. Once again, she was struck by the fact that nothing had changed. He was a stubborn bastard. She left him twice, but he still kept her clothes and shoes. Most men would have gone on a rampage and tossed her shit out. Not Gavin. What would Manny say about that? He would probably puff his chest out and beam with pride.

The stabbing pain in her chest made her keel over. Living a half-life also meant she didn't have to think about Manny. The only thing she pondered on the road was the next destination. She refused to let herself think about Vegas or the Pyres. Now all she could think about was the father she lost. She didn't realize she was sobbing until wet arms wrapped around her. She broke free and whirled to find Gavin with a towel around his waist, water streaming everywhere. For the first time that day, she really looked at him. He may have bulked up, but there was a stark quality to his muscles, as if he was working out more than he was eating. As she looked past his implacable expression, she saw something starved and feral lurking in his eyes. It was focused on her.

"What's wrong?" he asked.

"What's wrong?"

She grabbed a two-thousand-dollar shoe and hurled it at him. He ducked to the side. The shoe whistled past and cartwheeled across the bedroom floor.

"What the fuck do you want from me, Gavin? Why am I here? I don't have anything else to give you!" She pounded her chest with a shaking fist. "I don't have anything left! Vengeance was more important to you than me, than your father, than *life*. You blamed me for Vinny's death, for *influencing* your choice. You threw me away like I always knew you would. I knew I would never be enough for you. You need the darkness. In that world, you're judge, jury, and executioner. That's fine for you, but me? *No*."

She ran her hands through her tangled hair and paced in a small circle. After being tackled, married, and brought back to her past life, she was beginning to unravel.

"I never wanted to be a part of your world. I know what I can handle, and what you do, I *can't*." Her chest burned as she glared at him through her tears. "Do you know what it feels like to be helpless? Truly helpless? I do."

When he reached for her, she backed away, walking deeper into the closet filled with expensive clothes and sassy heels from another lifetime. Nothing mattered anymore. She didn't care what she looked like or what she wore. All that mattered was that she got through one day and then the next without giving in to the urge to slit her wrists.

How many times had she wondered if Carmen would be better off without her? The world wouldn't miss Lyla Dalton. She wasn't the CEO of a big corporation or an integral part of her family. Her parents barely noticed her existence, and she would be easily replaced at any job she qualified for. But she couldn't do that to Carmen. Her cousin had left everything for her. She suspected Carmen had needed the time-out as well. Now, life threw a curveball, and she was back with Gavin. Why? He didn't need her. She would rather live a half-life where she had no feelings than with a man she couldn't trust and put her through hell. Again.

She couldn't look at Gavin and not think of his father. Manny and Gavin Pyre, the crime lords of Las Vegas, were the great loves of her life; the first people who saw something special in her. She would never know what drew her to these dangerous men, but they changed her life forever. Gavin Pyre was a law unto himself and would do whatever he thought was necessary. Case in point, she was back in Vegas with his ring on her finger.

"I can still hear your father screaming," she whispered and swallowed her own howl of grief. "I watched everything. I screamed until I had no voice."

"You have to know I would do anything in my power to take it back," he said.

She grasped handfuls of her hair. "I told you to stop, and you wouldn't!"

He said nothing. He just stood there like a gladiator from centuries past.

"What's the point?" she demanded, striding up to him and jabbing him in the chest. "Why make me your wife? Because that's what your father would have wanted?"

He shook his head.

"What, Gavin?" she shouted as she pounded his flesh with her fists. "You're not done with me yet? You want to punish me for Vinny's death? For not dying when I was stabbed? You can't hurt me more than I already do! I have nothing left!"

He wrapped her close. She scored his skin with her nails as she tried to get away.

"I'm not going to hurt you."

"Seeing you hurts me, having you touch me hurts," she sobbed. "*You* hurt me. You left me."

"I won't leave you again," he said into her hair, holding her desperately close.

"I'll never believe a word you say. I should have died that day with Manny."

He jerked her chin up. "Don't say that."

She shoved at him and got nowhere. "What do you want from me?"

"We can make it, Lyla."

"I don't want to make it with you. You broke me!"

He lifted her into his arms and hissed when she bit his shoulder. He cursed and carried her into the bathroom. When she tasted the unmistakable tang of blood, it shocked her so much that she didn't react when he began to undress her. It wasn't until her chest was bare, and his hands stopped, that she realized he was staring at her scarred abdomen. She whirled away and crossed her arms over her chest. White, raised scars and long gashes made her look like Frankenstein. Even Carmen winced when she caught a glimpse of her disfigured body. She hadn't looked at herself in a mirror since the attack.

She couldn't stand the silence behind her. Of course, he knew about her wounds, but seeing them was a different story. His body was a work of art, unblemished and powerful. Hers looked as battered as she felt. She would never be able to wear a dress or V-neck shirt without horrifying people. Her body was a walking testament to the evil that walked this earth.

"Get out," she whispered.

"Lyla—"

"Get *out*, Gavin!"

He hesitated before he walked out of the bathroom, quietly shutting the door behind him. She stripped off her remaining clothes and sank into the hot bath he had prepared. When the wounds were fresh, the smallest droplet of hot water made her feel as if she were being stabbed again. Even now, she moved cautiously as the hot water touched her scars, but there was no pain. The sweet aroma of the bath salts and the size of the luxurious tub felt wrong after being on the road for so long. She stiffened when the door opened.

"Clothes," he said and set something on the vanity before he left again.

She rested her forehead on her knees. Their talk wasn't over, not by a long shot, and she felt so incredibly weary. His abrupt reappearance made her feel as if she'd aged ten years. She turned her back to the mirror as she dressed in the nightgown Gavin produced. It was cut low enough to show the beginning of the ragged scar between her breasts and the wound centimeters from her heart that should have killed her. She fussed with the nightgown before she brushed her hair. She wondered if there was a way to avoid Gavin, and then scoffed. He refused to be left behind or ignored.

She walked into the bedroom and found him sitting on the edge of the bed, waiting for her in sweatpants and nothing else. She wished he would wear a shirt, and then realized she should be grateful he was wearing something. His eyes moved over her and then focused on her chest. Did her scars disgust him? Why the fuck did she care?

"I'm tired," she said.

His eyes flicked up to hers.

"I'll take one of the guest bedrooms." She started for the door and was brought up short when he stepped in front of her.

"You sleep here."

"Are you going to sleep somewhere else?" she asked pointedly.

"No."

"I'm not sleeping with you, Gavin."

"We're married."

"Don't you *dare* throw that in my face!" she exploded, stomping her feet and waving her hands wildly. "We're as married as your father is alive."

He rocked back as if she shoved him. "It's legal, Lyla."

"I'm not married until I feel married."

"We can rectify that."

She pointed her finger in his face. *"Don't."*

"I'm not going to force you to have sex with me. I just need to be near you."

"Why?"

He stared at her, his expression a mixture of exasperation and anger. "I need to know you're with me." When she said nothing, his hands fisted at his sides. "I haven't had a decent night of sleep since Dad died. I need to hear you breathing. I need to touch you. Not sexually, if that's what you want."

"No sex," she growled.

Out of habit, she took the side of the bed closest to the window. As she sank into the mattress, she suppressed a sigh of pleasure. It really was the little things in life...

He climbed onto the opposite side of the bed. He didn't touch her, but she felt his body heat. How was she supposed to sleep beside her ex, who was now her husband? She stared blindly ahead for a long time before her eyes fluttered shut.

4

LYLA

She opened her eyes and froze. She was lying on her side facing Gavin with her arm tossed over his middle, tucked against him as if they slept together every night. Apparently, her body forgot she wasn't with him anymore. She spied the blue diamond ring on her finger and bared her teeth in a silent snarl. So, what if she was 'technically' married to him. That didn't mean anything.

She took a minute to examine him. She had no idea what drove him to do the things he did. He blamed her for Vinny's death, refused to leave the criminal world for her, and was an emotionless bastard when she woke in the hospital. Why look for her after he got out of jail? Why force her into marriage? Even though he denied it, she knew it had something to do with Manny. Maybe he felt guilty that she got hurt...? No. If he felt guilty, he wouldn't have threatened to kill Carmen to get her to marry him. The Pyre mind was a complex, tangled web she had no hope of comprehending.

Although he was asleep, his features weren't relaxed. He was tense, as if he were ready to react at any second. Her hand twitched on his chest before she slowly began to pull away. His eyes snapped open, and she stilled. Alert amber eyes moved over her face, and then he relaxed.

"Okay?" he asked.

He was asking if she was okay *now*? She needed him to ask that when she felt as if she died with his father. She needed him to ask that when he saw her in Montana. He didn't even ask how she was; he just demanded that she marry him.

She pounded his chest with her fist and found small satisfaction in his grunt of surprise before she rolled out of bed and went into the bathroom. She locked the door and took care of business before she waltzed out. He sat up in bed, and when she walked toward the door, he jumped up.

"Where are you going?"

"I'm hungry," she said shortly.

She was happy to see that Blade and the other security weren't patrolling the hallway. Having them hover after being on the road with Carmen would suffocate her. Dealing with Gavin was more than she wanted to handle. She opened the fridge, which was usually filled with pre-made meals, and wasn't disappointed. She made herself a bowl of yogurt, fruit, and granola and dug in. Gavin appeared as she finished. She ignored him and went back to the fridge. She popped some waffles in the toaster and slathered them with peanut butter and honey and felt semi-human again.

He leaned against the counter with a cup of coffee and said nothing. She knew he was waiting for her to make the first move, which irritated the hell out of her. He pushed and shoved when he felt like it, and now he was acting like a patient gentleman, allowing her to set the pace this morning. Asshole.

"I want to talk to Carmen," she said.

He waved a hand at the landline. She ground her teeth as she punched in the numbers for her cousin's prepaid phone. Carmen picked up on the second ring.

"Lyla?"

"It's me. Are you okay?"

"Yes. You?"

She hesitated and then said, "Yes," a bit grudgingly.

"Really?" Carmen asked, obviously picking up on her tone.

"Yes." Aside from manhandling her and nearly punching Carmen, Gavin hadn't made any threatening moves toward her. The last time she arrived at Gavin's mansion, he roughed her up and scared the crap out of her. But she didn't sense rage in him this morning. Of course, that could change in a nanosecond. "Are you with your mom?"

"Yes. And he was telling the truth. My dad's gone."

Her heart clenched with regret and sadness. Uncle Louie, a former enforcer for Manny, was a good man who had been there for Lyla in her younger years. "I'm so sorry, Carmen. When's the funeral?"

"In a couple of days."

Silence on both ends of the phone.

"Are you sure you're okay?" Carmen asked.

She sighed. "I should be asking you that. Yes, I'm fine. I'll call you later. Are you going to keep this phone?"

"Yes. You left yours behind, didn't you?"

"Yes, but you can call me here."

"Okay. I love you. You need me, call me."

"Same. Love you."

She hung up and turned to Gavin, who hadn't moved. His wedding ring caught her eye.

"Your father's ring," she said and swallowed hard.

"Yes."

She took a deep breath, braced her feet apart, and looked him in the eye. "What am I doing here?"

"I told you."

She glared at him. "You said you wanted everything I promised."

"Yes."

"There were conditions," she reminded him in case he forgot. "You broke your end of the deal."

"I did," he acknowledged.

"So, you can renege on your end, and I can't? Fuck you!"

"Vinny was murdered. What did you expect me to do?"

"I knew you would go after them." It seemed ludicrous to be

talking about this almost two years later, but he wouldn't leave it alone, so they would have this out once and for all. "I knew you would avenge Vinny, but you turned back into the man I ran from!" She tried to keep her voice even, but suppressed emotions were rising, refusing to be contained a second longer. "You blamed me for Vinny's death! Do you think I would have asked you to give up the title of crime lord if I knew Vinny would die?"

"It wasn't your fault. I apologize."

His calm delivery made her see red. She grabbed a mug and hurled it at his head. He sidestepped, and it smashed into the wall.

"You apologize? That's it? You think you can blame me for someone's death, apologize, and that makes it okay? People don't function like that, Gavin!"

He made no reply. Instead, he sipped his coffee and watched her with unreadable amber eyes.

"I don't want to be here," she said.

"I know."

"Yet you force me to be. Why? How many times do we have to do this before you realize this isn't going to work?"

"As many times as it takes. I fucked up. I might in the future, but I'll keep bringing you back. We're meant to be, Lyla."

She stared at him. "Are you crazy?"

"Some think so."

"I can't do this again," she whispered, and was ashamed of her tears. She shook her head. "I can't."

"Lyla," he began as he started around the island.

"No!" she shouted and held her hand up like a traffic cop. "Just... no. I learn from my mistakes. I won't let you do this to me again."

"After Dad's murder..." He sighed and ran a hand through his hair before he leaned back against the counter and crossed his arms over his chest. "I couldn't find out who was behind the attack. The trail was cold, and the cops knew something big went down. They were trying to get their hands on a body to pin me for first-degree murder, but they couldn't find one. They got me for money laundering instead. I let go of the underworld completely. I was going to tell you before I went to jail, but you were gone."

She shook her head. "The damage is done, Gavin."

His muscles flexed as he tensed. "I know."

"You know? That's all you have to say?" she demanded, slapping her hands on the marble island. *They tortured him.* She felt as if her heart were breaking all over again. "I watched them kill him." The awful memories, never far from the surface, made her body erupt with goose bumps.

"I'm sorry."

"Stop saying that!"

"What do you want me to say?"

"Nothing. Just like you did in the hospital."

His eyes had an unnatural sheen to them. "If I had known the price of avenging Vinny, I wouldn't have done it."

"I told you what would happen! They'll never stop, even if you say you're out." Something in his eyes told her that he agreed, but he didn't say it out loud. "What's done is done."

"I can't change our past, but I can damn well try to make it up to you."

"So that's why you brought me back? Because you feel guilty?" she asked in a dead voice.

"I feel guilty as hell." His eyes flicked to her chest and then back to her eyes. "You're mine to protect, and twice you were harmed. There won't be a third time."

"If you let me live my own life, there's no reason for them to come after me."

He said nothing for a beat and then, "I can't do that."

"Do what?"

"Let you live without me. I lashed out at you when Vinny died because I've never felt pain like that in my life. I knew he wasn't ready. *I* killed him, and I have to live with that. I also have to live with Dad's death." An agonized expression twisted his features. "I think about it every day, every hour. Knowing his killer is still out there..." The veins in his neck popped as he tried to contain his rage. "I want—no, I *need* to kill him."

After what she witnessed, she couldn't agree more. The man who killed Manny was a sadist. Because of him, she would never be the same.

"But I can't," Gavin continued. "Maybe it's a good thing I went to jail. It forced me to stop obsessing, to think about my future..."

His unwavering stare made her heart skip with anxiety.

"You're my future."

Her hand crept up to her throat.

"You nearly died. You should have. Your injuries..." He shook himself as if he couldn't handle the images in his mind. "I never prayed in my life until that day, and I think God had mercy on me. I can live without my cousin, I can live without my dad, but I can't live without you."

The spark of warmth in her belly scared her. No. She couldn't let him in because he was a smooth talker.

"I know you hate me. You have every right to. I forced you into a life you didn't want. Even if you can't forgive me, I don't want to live without you. I need you here." He set his mug down with enough force to jolt her before he paced away. He kept his back to her as he admitted, "If I had an ounce of mercy in me, I'd let you live a normal life, but I can't leave you alone." He turned back to her, jaw tight, hands fisted at his sides. "I know you're angry, and you'll never forget what happened. Neither will I. Make me pay for it."

"What?"

He spread his hands wide. "Do your worst, Lyla."

"You married me to punish you?" He'd officially lost his mind.

"I brought you back because my life is worthless without you. I married you because I need you bound to me. You anchor me. After the hit on you and Dad, I lost it. I went on a fucking rampage. I killed..." He touched his temples as if he went lightheaded for a moment before he shook himself and continued, "I need you to keep me from losing my shit. I need to see you, smell you, touch you. Your presence keeps me from going black."

"I can't do anything for you."

"You can. Yesterday with Carmen, I fucked up again. I can't rein it in. I'm a fucking bomb waiting to go off. That's why I took you in the room on the jet. You calm me the fuck down. I can take anything if you're with me. I just... need you."

She didn't know what to say.

"I'm messed up," he said unapologetically, "and I don't give a shit about most of the world, but you... you humanize me. I need you with me. I'll take whatever you give me."

"I have nothing left to give," she whispered.

"Just you being here, it's enough."

She shook her head. "This is crazy."

"Yes."

"I can't—"

"You don't have to do anything."

"You really think that after all we've been through that we can go back to the way it was?"

"No. We'll never go back to that. We both have scars from that day. We've both changed, but we're still us at the core. I know what I need. What do you need, Lyla?"

"I need to be alone."

"Not going to allow that. What else?"

She wanted to throw something, but she was shaking too badly to have decent aim. "I don't want drama."

"I'm planning to be pretty boring. I'm still CEO of Pyre Casinos. I can do that job in my sleep. I gave up my title as crime lord when I went to jail, and I haven't picked up the mantle since I got out."

He looked as calm as could be, as if his psycho tackling episode yesterday never happened. "You really are crazy."

He inclined his head. "I know."

"Who's the crime lord?"

"Don't know, don't care."

She didn't believe he was completely out of the underworld, but she didn't want to discuss it. "You forced me to marry you."

"Yes."

"And now you expect me to sleep in the same bed as you, punish you, and live an ordinary life with you?"

"Is that a problem?"

"You're impossible! I don't want you, and I don't want to be here!"

"I know, but you aren't going anywhere."

"So, I'm a captive again?"

"For now. For your own safety."

She wanted to rip her hair out. "I was fine on my own!"

"No, you weren't." He held up a hand when she hauled in a breath to rage. "Yesterday, your eyes were blank, your skin was pale, and you didn't eat. Today, you ate enough for the both of us, your cheeks are flushed, and you look like you might commit murder. You're waking up, Lyla. What you did this past year wasn't living."

"The last time I tried to live life to the fullest, I nearly died," she said bluntly.

"This time, you'll flourish."

"I don't believe it."

"You will in time."

"I hate you."

She stalked out of the kitchen and went upstairs. She couldn't bear to go back to the bed they slept in. The guest bedroom was clean and dusted. She flopped on the bed, folded her hands on her stomach and closed her eyes as a migraine snuck up on her. She breathed deeply and tried to organize her chaotic thoughts. When she felt the mattress dip, she shot up to a sitting position.

"What do you think you're doing?" she shouted.

"Lying down with you," he said as he settled beside her.

"This is my space."

"Your space is my space."

"No, it isn't."

He copied her, hands folded on his middle, and closed his eyes.

"Don't you need to go to work? You're the CEO."

"I'm on my honeymoon."

Her head throbbed painfully. She dropped on the pillow and flung her arm over her eyes. "You're an asshole."

"Janice has been working overtime since news of Dad's murder hit the news and I went to jail. She's been waiting for something good to report. When I told her I was getting married, she nearly burst into tears."

"Who's Janice?"

"My PR person."

"And she bought your story that a woman who ran from you twice would happily accept your proposal after you got out of jail?" she asked scathingly.

"She didn't ask for specifics."

"Go away. You're giving me a migraine."

"I heard that sex cures headaches and migraines."

"You touch me, I'll murder you."

"Let me know if I can do anything to help," he said solicitously.

"Leaving me the fuck alone to live the life I choose would be nice."

"I can't do that. I haven't found a way to let you live without me. I don't intend to, either. Whatever you want, whatever you need, I'm here."

She turned away from him and tried to escape from his words.

LYLA WOKE in the afternoon and wasn't pleased to find Gavin still beside her. She ignored him as she slipped out of bed and went into the master bathroom to shower. She put on the most sexless pajamas she owned before she went to the kitchen where she warmed up spaghetti and meatballs. She sat on the counter and called Carmen, who answered immediately and told her all was well on her end. Gavin entered the kitchen, freshly showered. She tried to keep Carmen on the phone, but knew she had to let her cousin tend to Aunt Isabel, who was sobbing in the background. She reluctantly hung up and continued to ignore Gavin, who warmed up his own meal and watched her in silence.

It took less than ten minutes for his unwavering regard to make her retreat to the backyard. He riled her so easily. She clung to the mundane because being in Gavin's vicinity, regardless of whether he was the crime lord or not, wouldn't be an easy life. His adamant claim on her would flatter most women, but she was terrified. His love bordered on obsession. He would never let her go. She would never be free of Gavin Pyre, so what did that mean for her future?

The backyard was cast in orange light. She sat on a lounge chair near the waterfall that cascaded into the Olympic sized pool and closed her eyes. She was so damn tired. It had been almost two years, and she hadn't recovered from Manny's murder. Gavin was right in one sense. The life she and Carmen indulged in wasn't living. It was existing. There was no joy or wonder in their travels. They were on the run and doing everything in their power to avoid the real world. Gavin put a stop to that, and now he wanted to resume the life they would have had if Vinny and Manny hadn't been murdered. Was that even possible? Gavin was more volatile than ever, though he hadn't had a fit since they arrived at his home. He wasn't giving her the space she needed, but he also wasn't forcing his touch on her. He was hovering, as if he really did need to be close to her. The fog of depression and hopelessness she existed in was beginning to lift.

She stiffened when the lounge chair beside her creaked. Freaking Gavin. She didn't have to open her eyes to confirm that he had, once again, interrupted her solitude. Her nose told her that he chose chicken Marsala for dinner. She wanted to ask him what he thought marrying her would accomplish, but she already knew the answer. He believed she could put his life on track to some kind of normal. How could she accomplish that when *she* didn't feel normal? She had been diced into pieces. Carmen attempted to glue her back together, but any moment now, she would fall apart again, and she wasn't sure he was up to the task of putting her back together.

She let out a long breath and tried to ignore the tightness in her chest. Manny was the father she never had. He loved her unconditionally, as much as he had his own son. She would never be able to run to him for advice, never lay her head on his lap and have his hands sift through her hair. It was probably selfish of her to want him here for her sake. He was with his wife, the woman he loved more than life itself. He was in a better place, and they had to clean up their messy lives on their own. Manny had been able to slap sense into Gavin when he was going off the rails, but now that authority figure in their lives was gone forever. How did people move on after losing someone they loved?

"Dad left you half of his assets."

Her eyes popped open. "What?"

"You own a considerable chunk of Pyre Casinos."

She didn't know how to process that, and then narrowed her eyes. "And since you married me?"

"*We* own a considerable chunk of Pyre Casinos."

She snorted. She wasn't concerned about money or power, so it meant little to her, but the fact that Manny put her in his will warmed her heart.

"Dad left me his journals." He ate slowly, staring out at nothing as he considered his words. "I've been reading them since I got out of jail. Some of the entries are revelations and thoughts, but a lot of them are addressed to me." He turned and looked at her. "He knew where you were the first time you left."

Manny had told her so, but she was wary of Gavin's reaction. Manny went so far as to give Gavin's investigator false leads to give her more time.

"He wrote a lot about you," he said and shook his head. "Between the two of us, you never had a chance."

Her mouth curved the slightest bit. It was true. Manny hired her as an assistant within two weeks of meeting her. She worked with him after school and on weekends during her senior year. When she met Gavin, their chemistry had been undeniable. Gavin claimed her before she had a chance to go off to college and meet anyone else.

"He thought you possessed a part of my mom's spirit, and that's why we both fell hard for you."

The faint smile fell from her lips. She couldn't explain her connection to the Pyres. It was bizarre that she would have such a strong connection to people so different from her. They were the crime lords of Las Vegas and ran casinos. She grew up in a middle-class family with a father who had a gambling addiction. They had nothing in common, yet she loved them beyond rational thought.

"Dad told you about it. You never said anything to me," he said.

"It was between him and I."

"Maybe so, but you should have told me."

"That your father believed I had a piece of your mother's soul? Even *I* don't know how I feel about it."

"But you didn't push him away once you knew. It meant a lot to him."

She swallowed hard. "I know. He meant the world to me."

He touched her hair. The brush of his fingers was so light that she thought she imagined it at first. Then her hair shifted as he ran his fingers through the wavy mass. Her first instinct was to jerk away, but the motion reminded her so much of Manny that she stayed put.

"He wrote that he wanted to commit suicide before he met you. You gave him hope."

A tear trickled down her cheek. "Don't."

"You give me hope too."

"You both expect too much from me."

"I don't think so. You survived our worst. You're still you despite our influence. You're stronger than you think."

"I don't feel strong."

"Neither do I."

She snorted. "But you are."

"There's strong and then there's strong," he said with a shrug. "You have inner strength. I don't. That's why you're able to live without me. I can't function not knowing where you are, without having you with me. I'm like my dad, I guess."

She rested her cheek on her knees as she regarded him. Gavin had a dominant, alpha personality. A keen business sense paired with lethal physical attributes ensured that no one fucked with him. His wealth gave him the power to do anything he wanted. To hear him admit that he wasn't strong was ludicrous. He could kill with his bare hands, and he thought of himself as weak?

"What else did you read?" she asked.

"He talked a lot about Mom. How he felt about her, how he suffered without her. He talked about life, and how I need to focus on you because you're all that matters."

"I figured he had something to do with this," she said quietly, and wriggled her left hand, so the blue diamond shimmered.

"I had men looking for you before I cracked open his journal." He paused while she digested that and continued, "What he wrote was confirmation for me. No matter what's happened in the past, we're supposed to be together. That's the only way we're going to get through this life intact."

She wanted to argue, but she didn't have the energy. He continued to play with the ends of her hair as the sky darkened and night fell around them. The underwater lights from the pool illuminated their faces as they stared at one another.

"I fucked up so many times," Gavin said and stroked a gentle finger down her cheek. "Can you forgive me?"

"I don't know," she said honestly. "I wasn't surprised that you went after Vinny's killers. I even understand why you blame me for his death."

"Vinny's death is on me. I shouldn't have put that on you."

"Vinny's death is on the man who pulled the trigger," she corrected, and when he looked as if he wanted to interrupt, she lifted her finger. "Vinny accepted the position. You didn't force it on him, right?"

"No."

"Then let it go, Gavin."

"Have you?"

"After watching Carmen suffer every day, it's damn hard to convince myself all of this isn't my fault. She doesn't blame me, which makes me feel even worse. She doesn't blame you, either."

He didn't reply.

She looked away, since it was easier to talk without facing his dissecting gaze head on. While they were on the road, she wondered what she would say to him. Now that she had her opportunity, the words were lost in a maelstrom of emotion. He suffered because of Vinny and Manny's deaths. She could see that for herself. His need to be around her, to touch her, was genuine. After everything, he needed comfort, but she wasn't sure she could give it to him. She was broken and bleeding herself. They were two broken and lost souls.

"Do you miss the dark stuff?" she asked.

"No."

"You haven't had to do anything for the criminal side of the business?"

"No. Everyone knows I'm out."

"But you still have Blade and the other security?"

"Dad and Vinny's killer is on the loose. I'm not taking chances."

"Are you hunting for him?"

"No trace of him. There's nothing to hunt."

"He might come for me to finish the job." She sensed his energy tinge the air with violence.

"I'd love to get my hands on him."

She snatched her hair from his hands and got to her feet. She stood beside his lounge chair and glared at him. "I'm not taking that chance again, Gavin! I won't!"

"I won't either." He stared at her pensively. "Carmen taught you to shoot?"

She blinked. "Yes. What does that have to do with anything?"

"It doesn't hurt to be prepared. Tomorrow we'll go to a shooting range, see how good of a shot you are."

"You're going to let me have a gun?"

"Whatever it takes for you to feel safe. I have guns stashed everywhere. I'll show you. You remember how to get out of the house if there's an attack?"

She nodded. He had a wine cellar with a secret door that led into the red mountains.

"I've added extra security. Blade will be with you at all times. I don't want you going anywhere without a security detail. I prefer you don't leave the house without me."

She didn't tell him that she didn't *want* to go anywhere without him. Despite the way she felt about him, she knew he would die for her.

"That doesn't mean you're a prisoner. Our marriage is real; our life together is real. I want you to do what you want. If you want to go on a trip, I'll arrange time off from work. If you want to buy a new wardrobe or see your parents, you can. But Lyla..." He gave her a very direct and predatory look. "Don't run from me again. We can work this out."

"Work what out?" she snapped.

"Our relationship."

"We don't have a relationship."

"The ring on your finger says differently."

"Oh, this?" she asked sarcastically.

He was off the lounge chair and in her face before she could pull the damn thing off her finger. He clasped her hand between his and dipped his head, so their faces were less than six inches apart.

"Don't take it off."

His angry tone made her eyes narrow.

"You forced me to marry you."

"Yes, I did. You've taken off on me too many times. You need to get this, Lyla. You're stuck with me. Legally."

"I had my reasons for *taking off*." She yanked her hand from his. "You've hurt me more than anyone else. I don't know how I feel about you. Every instinct I possess tells me I can't afford to be with you again. My heart can't take it. You flip-flop between the ruthless crime lord and the man who says he can't live without me. Which man are you?"

"Both."

"That's what scares me," she said quietly. "You can't separate one from the other, and I never know when the other is going to take over."

"I'm not a crime lord any longer. The only man I am is the CEO of Pyre Casinos, but more importantly, I'm your husband."

She could feel his will pressing on her. It made her tip her chin up defiantly. She looked evil right in the eye. Gavin Pyre wouldn't intimidate her, even if he was a murderer.

"Before Vinny died, you and I made promises to one another. I admit it. I lost it when he was murdered, and I took it out on you. I refused to leave the underworld after Vinny's death because it would make me look weak. I needed to put them in line. I thought they wouldn't retaliate, but it backfired. I left you in the hospital fighting for your life and unleashed hell in the underworld. I worked out my demons, but it wasn't enough. When I surfaced, the cops were waiting. Thank God my men are loyal to me. They covered my tracks. Not one crumb of evidence was found. You woke from your coma. I wasn't completely sane, so Blade sedated me, so I could talk to you. That's why I was such a bastard that day. I focused on my objective and ignored what you went through because I couldn't handle it."

He cupped the back of her neck and squeezed. When she tried to shrug off his hold, he pressed his lips against her temple.

"I need this," he whispered, and the pain in his voice made her freeze. "I've needed to say this for so long."

She closed her eyes as he cradled the back of her head. His other hand swept up and down her back as she trembled. His touch, his scent, roused her emotions to a fevered pitch. She was torn between throwing herself into his arms or punching him in the face. Instead, she stood there with her eyes closed, trying to keep herself from reacting to anything he said.

"I can't begin to understand what you went through that day," he murmured, warm breath feathering over her face. "I don't blame you for running from me. I don't blame you for hating me. After I walked into the house and I saw you and Dad on the floor, covered in blood, not moving... I don't remember anything after that. I blocked it from my mind. You don't have that luxury. I'm so fucking sorry."

Her head dropped and landed on his shoulder. Tears slipped down her cheeks. She fisted her hands in his shirt to stop herself from screaming.

"I wasn't there for you when you needed me. I don't know what you went through. I can't imagine, and I don't want to. I know the extent of Dad's injuries and yours." His hand swept over her as if reassuring himself that she was whole. "Your survival is a miracle, and I'm not going to waste it. Whatever you need, I'll give."

She couldn't hold back a keening sob. He wrapped her tight against him as she began to shake uncontrollably.

"I made promises to you that I've broken. I'm remaking them now. I love you. I want children with you. I want to spend the rest of my life with you." When she tried to push away, he made shushing sounds and rubbed her back soothingly. "I want to make you happy. I want you to teach me how to laugh again, how to feel without going off the deep end. I need you to let me take care of you. I need to see you heal, so I know I haven't destroyed the most important person in the world to me. I need you to give me hope."

She shook her head against his chest.

"I love you, Lyla. I'm fucked up, and you always seem to pay the price. Not this time. I'm out of the business and walking a straight line to you. Only you can get me through this. Blade's been sedating me since I got out of jail, so I stop breaking things... and people. I can act normal for a few hours at work before I have to leave or get sedated again. I need you to ground me. You don't need to love me back; you don't even need to like me. I just... need."

She sniffled against his shirt. "I don't know if I can do this."

"You don't need to do anything. Just be with me."

She felt as if she hadn't slept in days. "I'm so tired."

He didn't hesitate. He picked her up in his arms and carried her into the house. He took her upstairs to the master bedroom. She buried her face in the pillow and wept, great gasping sobs that racked her whole body. A warm, hard body wrapped around her.

"You're not alone," he said into her hair. "I'm here. We're going to get through this."

5

GAVIN

He grasped her hand as they walked onto the gun range. Although she stiffened, she didn't jerk away. He held her while she cried her heart out last night. The sound of her sobs followed him into sleep. This morning, her eyes were swollen and lifeless, but she didn't protest when he asked if she wanted to go to the gun range. Now that she mentioned it, he was eager for her to be armed and ready. It would make both of them feel better.

He had to admit that her wardrobe was lacking the necessary clothing for a visit to the range. She drew stares from men and women. She wore large sunglasses to cover bloodshot eyes, a sleeveless turtleneck, and short shorts with thigh-high gladiator sandals. It was warm out, so the turtleneck should be a last resort, but she didn't want to show her scars. The glimpse he had of her chest and abdomen had made him sick with rage. He had to resist the urge to pull her clothes off, so he could see everything. When she allowed him to touch her, he'd show her in no uncertain terms how he felt about her scars.

He stood back to watch her shoot and felt himself get hard as she braced herself and took aim. Clearly, Carmen was a better marksman than he gave her credit for. Lyla had nearly perfect form, and her aim was better than he could have hoped.

"How did I do?" she asked when she took off her ear protectors.

"Excellent." He kissed her and ignored her startled expression. He wouldn't stop pushing until she was completely his... and maybe not even then. "I'll have Blade bring you to the range a couple of times a week to keep you fresh. He can even teach you to spar if you feel up to it."

She nodded. He put his arm around her and stared down a man who was gawking at her. She was oblivious to the attention, which is the only reason he was able to keep his shit together. If she ever looked at another man, he wasn't sure what he would do. Just the thought of that geeky IT guy made him want to kill. It crossed his mind when she went on the run that she might have gone back to him. If he wasn't so pissed at Carmen, he would have thanked her for keeping Lyla away from that bastard.

He helped her into the back of the SUV and didn't apologize when he rested his hand on her thigh. She tried to shift away, but he tightened his hold. When she glared at him, he held her gaze. He didn't lie or exaggerate. He needed touch to anchor him. Blade had a syringe filled with a sedative, just in case he went off the rails. If he didn't have so much respect for his second in command, he would have shot Blade the first time he was drugged.

"Where are we going?" she asked.

"We're going to get you new clothes, and then we'll get you a gun."

"I don't need clothes."

"If you want to go to the gun range, you need jeans and sneakers, not heels."

She made a face. He resisted the urge to stroke her thigh. That would be pushing it. Touching her at all was pushing it, but he couldn't help it. He wanted to think he made progress with her last night. Mere words wouldn't make everything okay, but they didn't hurt. He would do everything in his power to make her happy.

When they arrived at the mall, Blade and the other men fanned out, so they didn't crowd her. He paused by the directory, unsure where to go. Lyla sighed and tugged him in the direction of a boutique. When a bubbly sales associate approached her, he relaxed. He wanted Lyla to feel comfortable. If her existing wardrobe didn't work, they would throw it away and start over.

He stopped the sales associate as she bustled around. "She needs everything—shoes, underwear, jeans, skirts, dresses, the works."

She looked him up and down and winked. "You got it, big boy."

He frowned as the sales associate walked away with Lyla.

Blade came up beside him. "All good?"

He ran a hand through his hair. No. It wasn't 'all good.' It may never be 'all good,' but he could hope. "As good as can be under the circumstances."

"You're keeping your shit together."

"She lets me touch her. That's enough for now," he said and started forward when he lost track of her. "Where is she?"

"Dressing room," Blade said.

He tried to ignore his anxiety as he checked his phone and replied to Marcus, the new COO of Pyre Casinos. Marcus was a young, intelligent bastard who kept things running better than he and Vinny ever had. He appointed Marcus right before he went to jail. Marcus could have taken advantage of his absence, but instead maintained everything to perfection. Upon his release, Marcus began to suggest plans to expand the Pyre Empire. Occupied with Lyla and keeping his mind off a murderous rampage, he was grateful for Marcus's eagerness to take on the bulk of his workload. Marcus had been on his radar ever since he interned at Pyre Casinos. Marcus didn't have a privileged background, and his hunger to prove himself honed a keen business sense that Gavin used to his advantage.

When he couldn't stand it any longer, he went into the dressing room, which had five rooms and three large mirrors against one wall. Only one door was closed.

"Lyla?" he called.

"Yes?"

He rubbed a hand over his sweaty face and hid shaking hands in his pockets. He had to keep it together. "Are you finding what you need?" he asked lamely.

A pause and then, "Yes."

Feeling like an idiot, he sat because his legs were weak. He couldn't stand being away from her. He had her back for two fucking days. His worry was justified, wasn't it? She had been butchered and then disappeared for a year and a half. That wannabe fucking crime lord was still breathing, and Lyla didn't want to be here. Of course, he was on edge. It would take time for them to trust one another, and he wouldn't take chances with her.

The sales associate came in with armfuls of clothes and paused when she saw him.

"Miss me?" she asked cheekily.

"Missed my wife," he said and jerked his head at the closed door.

"Aw! Honey, this one is a keeper!"

Lyla opened the door and gave him an inscrutable look. The sales associate eagerly displayed the dresses and outfits.

"I don't want anything low cut," Lyla said, voice quiet but firm.

"No?" the sales associate asked, bewildered. "Your body is banging."

"I have," Lyla paused and glanced at Gavin before she finished, "scars on my chest."

The sales associate looked startled and then sympathetic. "Okay. Well, let me see what else I can find." She grabbed more than half of the outfits and left.

Lyla and Gavin stared at one another. He wanted to go to her but knew this wasn't the time or place.

"You can model for me if you want," he said, trying to sound upbeat even as a bubble of rage began to creep up his throat. When he found the fucking coward who attacked his father and Lyla, he would make them suffer a thousand times over for what they did to his family.

Lyla bared her teeth and closed the door in his face. He relaxed on the sofa and answered emails and returned some calls, while the sales associate ran in and out of the dressing room with clothes. Lyla didn't model anything for him, but he was satisfied that she wasn't throwing a fit about his proximity.

They went to three more stores. It amused him that, unlike her old wardrobe, she was going for comfort rather than fashion. She did accept several dresses, but her choices were practical and not aimed toward seduction. He didn't bother to tell her it didn't matter what she wore. He was painfully aroused, whether she wore lingerie or sweatpants. Although his eyes moved over her body often, he was drawn to her face. The way her eyes lit up when she liked something, her pursed lips when she was making a decision, and the smile that didn't come often enough. He was to blame for that.

Blade and the men were relieved to make their way out of the mall and perked up when they went to a gun shop. Lyla didn't go for something girly and cute. She chose a stainless steel semi-automatic pistol that was light, small, and powerful. He approved and watched as she tried out her choice in the store's gun range. After unloading the bullets into a target, she turned to him and nodded. She had changed since Dad's death. She had become solemn and wary. He believed her light was still there, just buried. He kissed her and took care of the purchase.

When they got back to the car, he gave directions to a trusted establishment. He put his arm around Lyla as they walked into the restaurant. The hostess recognized him and directed Blade and his other security to tables that flanked the one he and Lyla sat at. Before they opened their menus, the owner appeared in his chef's uniform. Gavin rose and hugged him.

"You good?" Carlo asked.

He nodded and gestured to Lyla. "This is my wife, Lyla."

When she rose, Carlo engulfed her in a hug. Gavin would have been jealous to see her in another man's arms if it wasn't for her startled expression.

"I wasn't invited to the wedding?" Carlo demanded.

"Shotgun wedding," he said with a shrug.

Carlo winked at Lyla. "I understand. I had to get my woman pregnant before she'd marry me."

Lyla's eyes bugged.

Carlo sobered and regarded both of them solemnly. "My condolences to your family. Your father was a good man."

Gavin's stomach tightened with his constant companion, rage. "He was."

"Did you catch the bastard who did it?"

It burned him to say, "Not yet."

Carlo looked at Lyla. "The Pyres are good people, which makes you good people. We protect our own."

She nodded but shot Gavin a puzzled look before Carlo clapped his hands together.

"I will send you dishes that will make your mouth water. Just you wait," Carlo declared and noticed Blade and the others. "I will send *plenty* of dishes. Let me get to it."

Carlo disappeared as quickly as he appeared. Lyla sat and raised her brows. He enjoyed seeing her curiosity. Every day she seemed a little more animated and a little less like a woman who had survived hell.

"Dad helped Carlo's family open this restaurant. They've done well and expanded to other cities," he explained.

A server appeared with champagne bottles and poured glasses for all three tables. Lyla sipped and nodded, clearly pleased with the taste.

"Did he really get his girlfriend pregnant, so she would marry him?"

His lips twitched. "Yes."

"Why wouldn't she marry him?"

"She doesn't believe in marriage. Hardcore feminist."

"And getting pregnant changed her mind?"

"When she had the baby, her feminist ways went out the window. She demanded his help because she couldn't do it on her own, but Carlo wouldn't unless she married him." He chuckled at Lyla's dumbfounded expression. "And they lived happily ever after. Carlo has five kids. His wife is extremely trapped."

"He did it purposely?"

He didn't answer, which made her snort. When a plate of appetizers appeared, he felt a flood of warmth when she reached for it without waiting for him. She was hungry. Good. She ate most of the dish before realizing he hadn't eaten a thing.

"Try it. It's great," she said and moved the plate toward him.

He took one to appease her before he pushed the dish back. He chewed and didn't taste a thing. "Finish it."

She shrugged and cleaned up the first appetizer as two more were brought to their table. She didn't try to initiate conversation, which never bothered him before, but now he was unsure of her. He didn't know what she was thinking or feeling. Lyla was an introvert and all in her head, which scared the crap out of him.

"You liked being on the road?" he asked because he needed to know.

Ice blue eyes clashed with his. His belly clenched. That face. That was all it took for him to fall for her. Lyla was innocent but confident enough to challenge him from the beginning. She knew her worth and left when she caught him cheating on her. She didn't care about money or status, which made her the best and worst because he couldn't bribe her. Nothing mattered except who he was as a person, and most of the time, he didn't like the reflection of himself in her eyes.

"Being on the road gave us the escape we needed," she said.

Even though he didn't like it, he understood. "Did you have trouble on the road?"

"There was an incident with some truck drivers at a pit stop, but Carmen pulled out her gun and that put an end to it. That's when she taught me how to shoot. We had a bear visit us once when we were asleep. He rocked the RV. That was memorable." She finished her first glass of champagne and gave the server a small nod of thanks when it was refilled. "We broke down on the freeway once."

"What happened?"

"Flat tire." She raised her brow. "Do you know how eager men are to help a couple of blondes in short shorts?"

His hands fisted. He could damn well imagine men pulling on the side of the road to help Lyla and Carmen. Both of them were stunning. Together, they were trouble. Lyla was ice; Carmen was fire. They were opposites that complemented one another. He had been jealous of their close bond on more than one occasion, but having Carmen take Lyla from him when he didn't know the location of his father's killer made her an enemy in his book.

She watched him steadily. She knew he was a jealous, possessive bastard. Was she teasing or punishing him?

"We handled life on the road well," she finished.

He didn't like that answer. He didn't want her to be able to live without him, and she knew it. "Well, now you can have a normal life."

"Normal?" she echoed as if she didn't know the definition of the word.

He didn't blame her. His life was anything but normal and because of him, hers went haywire. "Well, our kind of normal. As mundane as you want it to be."

The main course of perfectly prepared steaks was placed in front of them. Once again, he felt a surge of pleasure when she cut into her food with gusto.

"How are my parents?" she asked without looking at him.

"Still receiving the allowance you granted them." He hesitated and then said, "It's very modest."

"Even when my dad was making good money, my mom cut coupons. Plus, my dad doesn't need extra money to gamble. I know exactly how much they need to survive." She looked up from her steak. "And my father doesn't deserve even that. Thank you."

"My pleasure." And it was. He couldn't care less about her father, but whatever made him look less like a monster, he would do. Gladly. "Do you want to see them?" He knew for a fact that she hadn't contacted her parents. He monitored them closely and discovered they were just as clueless to Lyla's whereabouts. Like his father, Gavin couldn't believe how little her parents cared for their only child.

"I expect I'll see them at the funeral since Mom is Aunt Isabel's cousin," she said.

He didn't want her near Carmen, but he wouldn't stop her from attending her uncle's funeral. "When is it?"

"Day after tomorrow. Starts at noon and there's a get-together at Aunt Isabel's house afterward."

"I'll go with you."

She didn't argue. The steak nearly melted on his tongue. They ate in silence. When she finished, she sat back and folded her hands over her stomach.

"I need a nap," she said.

She was sleeping a lot. Not that he minded, since he had become an insomniac. Having her home allowed him to sleep longer than three hours at a stretch.

He signaled to Blade before he grabbed her hand. They went into the kitchen to thank Carlo. It was late afternoon when they drove home. She staggered into the house and collapsed on the couch. When he offered to carry her upstairs, she gave him a long look and turned on the TV. She stretched out on the sofa and cuddled into a pillow as she flipped through the channels. His men placed her shopping bags in the foyer. The maid would put her clothes away tomorrow.

He settled on the sofa and watched her out of the corner of his eye. She didn't look as if she wanted to bolt, but then again, he wasn't the best at reading her. He retrieved his laptop and worked while she relaxed and eventually drifted to sleep.

He wanted to touch and stroke, but he wouldn't jeopardize the progress he made. He wanted her more than anything in the world, but he couldn't rush this. He had to be patient, a virtue he didn't possess. At least she was here with him. In Montana, he had bullied and coerced her. Now, he would woo his wife into spending a lifetime with him and giving him all the things he needed from her. If she knew the depth of his obsession, she would run. He had to keep it in check. She already thought the worst of him, and he gave her good cause. What good he possessed, he hoped it would be enough for her because he couldn't let her go.

6

LYLA

They pulled up to a humble church bursting at the seams with people. She wore a new sleeveless dress with a high neck collar and black pumps. She was glad that Gavin had insisted on a new wardrobe, though she would never tell him so. Her old wardrobe was for arm candy—a woman who showed off her assets at every opportunity and didn't have a care in the world. She felt decades older than the woman who had once worn expensive labels with such carelessness.

She wasn't surprised when he grabbed her hand as they walked toward the church. Over the past two days, he was never far from her. She would have called it stalking if she didn't see that the only time he was completely relaxed was when he was touching her. They slept in the same bed, and though she always fell asleep on her side, she woke in his arms. Neither of them said much. She mulled over the things he said and gauged his actions. He seemed content to work on his laptop and be as close as possible without making any sexual moves, which made her feel safe yet frustrated. She wasn't ready, but her body seemed to disagree. When he came for her in Montana, he had been the merciless crime lord. Since they had arrived in Las Vegas, he was affectionate, honest, considerate, and eager to please. He was the Gavin she always knew he could be.

Over the past couple of days, she realized one thing. He took their marriage seriously, never mind that he forced her into it. There was no out this time. He wouldn't allow it. She had no idea what he envisioned for their future, but he was determined to make this work.

When they entered the church, people turned to look at their entourage and quickly averted their eyes. The chatter dimmed and people made way for them. For the first time, she wondered what the media reported about Gavin's extracurricular activities and the hits on his family members. She had no clue if her presence at Manny's murder had been noted or concealed by Gavin and his team, so she could recover in peace.

When her mother, Beatrice, spotted them, she rushed forward to give her a tight hug. Lyla felt absolutely nothing and noticed that Gavin didn't step back or offer his hand or cheek to her mother, who gave him a bright smile.

"I heard you got married!" Mom gushed.

"Yes." Gavin didn't elaborate.

"Finally," Mom said playfully, and grasped Lyla's left hand to examine the ring. Her mouth fell open. "It's gorgeous!"

"I want to give my condolences to Aunt Isabel," Lyla said, aware that all eyes were on them, and her mother was making a scene.

"Oh, of course, dear," Mom chirped and stepped aside.

Her mother didn't ask where she'd been for the past year and a half or if she was happily married. Her mother wanted to believe in the happily ever after fantasy because she lived off Gavin's good will. Lyla tried to brush away her bitchy thoughts as she hugged Aunt Isabel, who looked skeletal and wan. The last time she'd been in this church was for Vinny's funeral. Carmen and her mother had become widows far too early in life.

"He was the best uncle," Lyla whispered in her aunt's ear.

She had fond memories of sleepovers at their house. Aunt Isabel and Uncle Louie were down to earth, practical, and loving. Her heart ached for simpler times.

"He was." Aunt Isabel cupped her chin and gave her a watery smile. "He loved you and Carmen so much."

She blinked back tears. So much loss in so little time. When she stepped back, her heart warmed when Gavin embraced her aunt. She turned to Carmen, who practically collapsed in her arms. She held her cousin and could feel the faint tremble running through her body.

"Are you okay?" she whispered.

"I'll be glad when this is over," Carmen said hoarsely. "You're coming to the house after, right?"

"Of course." She kissed Carmen's cheek and gave her another squeeze before she released her.

She was surprised to see Gavin was still speaking to Aunt Isabel, who looked shell-shocked.

"Thank you," Aunt Isabel breathed.

Gavin turned, and though his eyes hardened when they landed on Carmen, he inclined his head respectfully. "I'm sorry for your loss."

Carmen said nothing. He led Lyla to the front pew, while Blade and the other guards stood on the sidelines, guarding the exits. They didn't stand out as much in this crowd, since their black suits blended in with the other attendees. She spotted her father before she took her seat. The last time she saw him, he had been bedridden from Gavin's beating. She hoped he wasn't stupid enough to say or do anything today. Gavin wouldn't stand for it, and neither would she. Watching a sadist beat Manny to death changed her. Manny had been her father in every way but blood. She was honored to have him in her life and wouldn't take any bullshit from her biological father. Not anymore.

Gavin sat on her left. He placed his arm on the back of the pew and drew her against him. "You okay?"

She let out a shuddering breath. "I don't think I can take another funeral."

He clasped the back of her neck and massaged gently.

She looked up. "What did you do about your dad?"

His jaw clenched. She felt awful for bringing it up, but she had to know.

"He didn't have a funeral. I couldn't with his killer on the loose. His ashes are at the house."

"They are? Where?"

"In my office." His eyes raked her face. "Is that fucked up?"

She shook her head. "No. I'm glad he's still with us."

She thought she saw a glimmer of wetness in his eyes before he leaned down and kissed her. It was over before she could react.

Carmen took the seat on her right and twined their hands together as the pastor took the stage. She squeezed to comfort her cousin as friends and relatives began to share amusing and touching stories about Uncle Louie.

"I have to go up. Will you come with me?" Carmen whispered.

She hesitated a moment before she said, "Okay."

They rose, hand in hand, and walked to the podium. She felt clammy and cold as she looked out over the church. They had been anonymous wanderers for over a year, and now they were back in the public eye, the focus of intense scrutiny. If it weren't for Carmen, she would have walked offstage. Could people see beneath the carefully applied makeup to the broken being she was inside?

Carmen's stifled sob refocused her attention. Carmen gave her a pleading look. Her cousin had done so much for her. Now, it was time to forget her personal shit and step up. She approached the mic. Her eyes fell on Gavin in the front row, watching her with steady amber eyes. The force of his personality made most people edge away, but she absorbed his strength.

"Uncle Louie was a great man," she said, and was proud that her voice didn't shake. "He convinced my parents to leave California and come to Sin City, where he guaranteed that we'd fit in."

Carmen let out a broken laugh, and she managed a small smile.

"He was right." Her eyes moved to her parents and then Aunt Isabel, who had a hand over her mouth as she wept. "He welcomed me in as if I were his daughter and made Vegas feel like home. I'll never forget him." Another father figure lost. A lance of pain struck her heart, and she wanted to cry and rage. "He raised one of the best women in the world." Lyla raised Carmen's hand in hers. "My cousin lost her father and husband, but she's still here."

A smattering of claps filled the church.

"Our lives are better because he was in it. That's how we go on, by remembering the good times."

Aunt Isabel gave her a watery smile and blew her a kiss. She stepped back, and Carmen took the mic. Her voice was shaky but strong.

"My father was a good man. He taught me to love with all my heart and to support and protect our family." Carmen looked at her mother. "We're going to get through this, Mom. Thank you all so much for coming here today to celebrate his life with us. He's in a better place now. That's what matters."

Hums of agreement rang through the church as they took their seats. Carmen's uncle closed the funeral with an acoustic guitar playing in the background. They said death came in threes. Lyla closed her eyes and prayed this would be the last one for a long time. She wouldn't be able to handle the death of another person so close to her.

"I'll see you at the house," Carmen said when they rose at the end.

Lyla kissed her cheek and nodded. Gavin pulled her out a side door. Blade pulled the SUV around, and they were off before anyone could waylay them.

"That was a good speech," Gavin said.

She let out a long breath. "He deserved it."

"Yes, he did. He liked Vinny."

"Who didn't? What did you say to Aunt Isabel?"

"I'll cover the cost of the funeral and whatever else she needs help with."

"What?"

He glanced at her. "She's family."

"*My* family."

"She's Vinny's mother-in-law. He isn't here to help, but I am."

His generosity surprised and touched her. Who was this man?

They reached the house as Carmen and her mother pulled up. Carmen gave Gavin a frosty look before they went inside and prepared for their guests. Gavin and the men stayed out of the way as Carmen talked to the caterer. Lyla reluctantly filled in as hostess and greeted people at the door before ushering them into the backyard where everything was set up. She chatted with distant relatives from her mother's side. No one asked about her life with Gavin. They seemed to realize it was best they didn't know.

Seeing familiar faces should have evoked feelings of warmth and safety, but she felt anxious and weary instead. Making polite chitchat was something she used to do so effortlessly, but now, she wanted to go into a dark room and shut the door. Smiling took more effort than it should, and she had a raging headache. After mingling for an hour, she made her way to the house for solitude and came face to face with her father, Pat Dalton.

"You got nothing to say to me?" he asked.

She crossed her arms over her chest. "Am I supposed to go out of my way to say hi to you?"

Her tone, derisive and sharp, caught him off guard. She'd never spoken to him like this in her life, and it felt damn good. He always treated her like dirt, but no longer. She sacrificed herself to save his ass after he stole half a million from Gavin. Her father's gambling addiction made him reckless and stupid. Gavin had every right to end her father's life for embezzling. Pat's punishment was broken bones, a tap on the cheek for his sins. She shouldn't be surprised that her parents ignored the rumors swirling around Manny's death and her lengthy disappearance. All her father could think about was himself. Typical.

"You can't talk to me like that," he snapped.

"I can talk to you however I want," she said crisply. "Get out of my way."

"We have to talk."

"About?" she asked suspiciously.

"That shit allowance you have us on. It's too small."

Of course, he wanted to discuss money. That's the only time he remembered she existed. When she was in high school, he had a string of bad luck, that led to her getting a job at Pyre Casinos to help with the mortgage. And when Gavin gave her an allowance, a considerable portion of it went to her parents, who were perpetually short. All these years later, Gavin was still paying their bills, since no one would hire an accountant with a tarnished reputation, and it still wasn't enough for her greedy, ungrateful father.

"You shouldn't have an allowance at all," she said and turned away.

He whirled her back to face him. "Don't walk away from me, you selfish bitch."

She jerked away and when he reached for her again, she hit him. Her hand tingled from the impact, but she didn't shake away the pain. She endured mindless agony when she was carved open. This was nothing.

She faced off with her father and sensed someone approaching. She had no doubt who it was when she felt the force of his fury.

"Don't touch me," she hissed at her father.

Gavin gripped her waist and squeezed. Her father took a step back, his righteous fury dialing down a bit, but still evident.

"I need more money," her father said.

"For what?" she asked, wondering what bullshit answer he was going to come up with this time.

"The bills are going up," he said lamely.

"Maybe you should downsize and move into an apartment," she suggested.

His eyes flicked to her ring. "You're swimming in money and can't give your father an extra thousand? You worthless whore."

Gavin lunged, but she stepped in front of him, so he couldn't get at Pat. Gavin tried to push her to the side, but she clung to him.

"You just lost your allowance," she said, and Gavin stilled.

"What?" her father shouted.

"You stole half a million and gambled it away. Then Gavin gives you an allowance to survive, and you're still not satisfied. You insult me and treat me like I'm nothing. Well, from now on, we are nothing.

You never acted like a father, so my duty is done. Find a way to get a job and survive. If Mom needs a place to stay, she has one. You? No. I'm done."

She pushed against Gavin, who allowed her to lead him in the opposite direction. Of course, their argument had attracted some attention, but once she made eye contact, people turned away and resumed talking.

"I'm your father!"

She closed her eyes at her father's furious bellow. He was a glutton for punishment. Gavin's body was tight against hers. She knew he wanted to pummel her father, or worse. She took a deep breath and turned to see Pat was red in the face and dripping with sweat as if he'd run a marathon.

"You're not my father. My father was murdered nearly two years ago," she said loud enough for everyone to hear.

Gavin's arm around her flexed.

"Manny Pyre?" Her father scoffed. "He got what he deserved."

She wasn't aware that she moved. One moment, there was a good fifteen feet between them, and the next, she was in his face. Her fist flashed out and rammed into his mouth. He stumbled back and fell to the ground, cursing. She stood over him with her fists clenched, shaking like crazy.

"Don't you ever talk about Manny like that!" she raged.

Pat sneered at her. "What did you do, Lyla? Fuck father and son?"

She dropped on top of her father and used one hand to grab a fistful of his shirt and used the other to belt him across the face. There was a sickening crack as his nose broke and blood dribbled down his face.

"Both of them are better men than you will ever be! They would do anything for me. What have you done except cause me grief? You care for no one but yourself," she screamed and drew her fist back again. Before she could land the hit, she was lifted off him. Even as Gavin carried her away, she kicked and caught Pat on the temple. "If I ever hear you insult my family again, you'd better hope I'm not armed, you son of a bitch! You're lucky I didn't let them finish you off, you worthless piece of crap!"

She cursed as Gavin walked through the house. She didn't stop shouting until she was tossed into the back of an SUV and pinned to the seat.

"Holy fuck!" Gavin tucked his head under her chin and began to laugh.

"That was the shit," Blade said as the SUV pulled away from the curb.

"Why did you stop me?" she screamed and bucked beneath Gavin, bloodlust clouding all rational thought. "I sacrificed everything for him! I could rip him apart. Why didn't you kill him when you had the chance? If I ever see him again, I... *Why the fuck are you laughing?*"

"Oh, baby, that just made my day," Gavin said and raised his head. He had a broad grin on his face, and his eyes were shining with delight. "I enjoyed beating his ass, but watching you do it was ten times better. Then you jumped on him and kept going."

He leaned down and kissed her. Rage morphed into something carnal as his tongue slipped into her mouth. Her fingers dug into the back of his suit and her legs wrapped around him. He sensed the change. The kiss deepened and became more seductive. His tongue stroked hers while one hand began to knead her breast. She bit his lip and wrenched her mouth away.

She looked toward Blade and the guard riding shotgun. The radio was blasting, and they were staring straight ahead, but... Gavin gripped her chin and turned her face back to him.

"You want me?" he asked in a low, growly voice that made her instantly wet. When she hesitated, his hold tightened fractionally. "Do you?"

"Have I ever stopped?" she snapped.

Gavin followed a code that made even the most hardened criminals blanch, but he loved her. She was so fucking tired of feeling dead inside, of wondering what her fate was. She was tired of being a means to an end. Gavin looked at her as if she were his world and beckoned her out of the darkness and into the light. No matter how much she wanted to suppress her emotions, they were at full mast right now.

Gavin folded one of the seats down. She stared, bemused, as he crawled in the back of the SUV and beckoned. His eyes were blind with need. He didn't give a fuck, and currently, neither did she. After she crawled in the back, he flipped the seat up. He dragged her beneath him and ran his hand up her thigh. She let her legs fall open. He hissed when his fingers slipped easily into her. She was soaked. She wasn't sure if it was the adrenaline or Gavin. Death pressed in around them. She needed affirmation that she was alive and that someone would care if she was gone.

She reached for his zipper and jerked it down. He was going commando. His fully erect cock fell into her hand. She gripped and gave him one long stroke. He jerked her hand away and positioned himself between her legs.

"I'm not going to last. It's been too fucking long," he said through clenched teeth.

He latched his mouth on hers and entered her with a hard thrust, going in to the hilt. She gasped and dug her fingers into his suit as he ground himself against her. There was no give on the floor. She moaned into his mouth as the radio, playing hard rock, blasted even louder. He grabbed fistfuls of her hair as he pounded into her. She wrapped her legs around his waist and sent her hands questing over him, seeking skin. She yanked his shirt from his slacks, shoved her hands beneath the fabric and dug her nails into his muscled back. Gavin sped up his thrusts. Her eyes flew open as she climaxed, breaking their kiss to bury her face in his chest as her body convulsed.

"Look at me," he commanded.

She opened blurry eyes and saw him above her, face drawn with unquenchable hunger. She was dimly aware of the car rocking from side to side as Blade made turns. She glimpsed buildings through the long windows on either side of them.

"I love you," he said.

"I know," she said and bucked as he planted himself deep.

"I'll love you until the day I die."

She dragged his mouth to hers for a desperate kiss, fingers exploring as much of him as she could reach. He shuddered and braced his hands on either side of her as he quickened his pace. She watched his eyes burn to gold as he flooded her with his seed. He kept thrusting until he had nothing left and then collapsed on top of her. She wrapped her arms around him, panting.

"I won't fuck up this time," he vowed.

"Shh." She cradled his face and kissed him.

He moaned into her mouth and kissed her back. Her body buzzed with endorphins. She should have been exhausted and sated, but she was hungry for more. He rolled until she was splayed over him. She moved on him, ignoring her aches and how sensitive her body was. Gavin bared his teeth at her, but didn't stop her from doing what she wanted to him.

She sat up and realized they were on the freeway. There were cars on either side of them, and if the windows weren't tinted, truck drivers would have seen a show. Instead, the only ones who knew what was going on were the other men in the car. Blade had his shades on, so she wasn't sure if he was staring at her in the rearview mirror or straight ahead. She moved on Gavin and was urged onward by the adoration on his face. He quickly grew hard again, more than ready to meet her needs. He was completely open to her, his emotions on full display, and it spurred her on. His hands flexed on her as she bounced and then tipped forward, hands braced on either side of his head as he thrust upwards.

When he reared up and latched onto her shoulder, her vision blurred as pain and pleasure collided. Her nails scrabbled over the trunk as he fucked her like he was possessed. When she collapsed on top of him, spent, it took him much longer to reach that pinnacle. When he finished, she was boneless. Her neck and shoulder throbbed. She would bear evidence of his marks for days, but she didn't care.

"We're almost there, boss," Blade called.

Gavin lapped at her neck. "You okay?"

"Mmm." The part of her that cared what others thought urged her to make herself presentable, but she didn't. It didn't matter how others perceived them. She had to live in the moment and embrace her feelings. That was what made her human.

"If Blade saw anything, I'll kill him," he said against her neck.

She laughed.

"It's not funny," he growled.

Gavin looked ravished, delectable, and dangerous.

"Maybe if we didn't fuck in a car with him, then he wouldn't see anything," she murmured and brushed kisses over his face.

He closed his eyes and tightened his hold on her, sinking that much deeper inside her. His cock twitched to life.

"We're almost home," she said and toppled to the side with a loud thump. She giggled as he forced himself into his pants. She felt blissfully unconcerned as they pulled up in front of the mansion, and Gavin fussed with her clothes. Blade stopped the car and flipped up the back door of the SUV to let them out. Gavin hauled her into his arms as the rest of his security parked in the driveway. She waved at Blade, who was grinning like a maniac, as Gavin carried her inside and slammed the front door. He pressed her up against it and kissed her long and hard.

"I love you," he said fervently.

"I love you, too."

His arms tightened to the point of pain, and his expression turned fierce.

"Don't tell me you love me unless you mean it."

She brushed her nose with his. "You hurt me, but I can't stop loving you."

He dropped his head on her shoulder. "Thank you, thank you God." He raised his head and looked her straight in the eye. "I swear, baby girl, I won't let you down this time."

"I know you won't." He was different, and so was she. Death separated them twice. She wasn't going to run a third time. This time, she would fight. She would fight for Manny because it was his dying wish that she and Gavin be together. Gavin was no longer a part of the underworld, and she chose to live.

"We're going to spend the rest of the day in bed," he decreed.

That sounded great to her. He carried her upstairs. When he leaned down to undo her shoes, she noticed that her dress had splashes of her father's blood and her hand was swollen. She flexed it and winced.

"Want me to call a doctor?" he asked, cradling her hand.

"No, I think I'm okay," she said and noticed that he had blood on him as well. She must have gotten it on him when they were fucking.

"Come on," he said, helping her stand and pulling down her zipper.

The dress began to fall before she remembered her scars. She clutched the dress to her front and bit her lip as cold, hard reality seeped back. He made love to her without seeing...

"What is it?" he asked.

"I... It isn't pretty. You may not want to see—"

He gently pried her hands from the dress and let it fall. She closed her eyes as she was left standing in her underwear, her scars on full display. Even she could barely stand them. Gavin was used to beautiful things, and she definitely wasn't. Her chest was a representation of how she felt inside—disfigured and ugly. The silence stretched. She started to turn, but he fell to his knees, wrapped his arms around her and pressed his face against her stomach.

"Gavin—"

"I don't care about the scars," he said, and she stilled. "I'm so fucking happy you're here with me."

He pressed his lips to the horizontal scar across her lower abdomen and traced the raised line with his tongue. Goose bumps raced over her skin as she watched him, stupefied, as he laved her scars with his tongue. Beauty out of ashes, she thought. When he bent his head, she saw the dried blood on his neck, and it dimmed her lust. She didn't want a reminder of her father to intrude on their time together.

"Let's shower," she said.

He kissed her belly and rose. She stood under the spray and let him wash her hair, a habit from their past. She enjoyed the feel of his hands in her hair and returned the favor. He sat on the bench and moaned as her fingers moved over him. He really did have a fantastic body. When she finished, he toweled her dry.

"I can't believe we consummated our marriage in the back of an SUV," he muttered.

She flushed a little, wondering how much Blade had seen or heard. She didn't have time to ponder this because Gavin picked her up and tossed her on the bed. She bounced and watched him prowl toward her. Her breath caught as he lay beside her and traced her scars. This was their history. There was no way to forget it. Fury, sadness, and guilt crossed his face.

"It's okay, Gavin," she said quietly.

He splayed his hand on her stomach. "Can you get pregnant?"

Her heart skipped. "What?"

"I want kids. We can adopt, but... do you know if you can carry children?"

"I-I don't know. I didn't ask," she stammered, completely bowled over by this. A week ago, she had a hard time getting through each day, and now Gavin was asking about children. Holy crap. Talk about life moving onward. She left a funeral and might have created a new life. She wasn't on any type of birth control. She sat up and ran her hands through her tangled, damp hair.

"We'll go to a doctor," he said. "We should know if something was damaged, or if we need to take extra precautions."

"Mmm," she said distractedly, tugging at a big knot in her hair. "Let me brush my hair."

She ran to the bathroom, grabbed her brush, and attacked her hair. She couldn't stand to look at her body, so she grabbed a robe and put that on before she resumed taming the beast. Since she was in the bathroom, she brushed her teeth and was gargling mouthwash when Gavin leaned against the doorjamb. She spit out the green liquid and because she needed something else to do, began to slather lotion on her body.

"You want some?" she asked Gavin.

"No."

She was in the process of deciding whether to French braid her hair when he spoke.

"You don't want kids?"

Her eyes flicked to his in the mirror. He was stark naked and, apparently, fine with it. Well, why wouldn't he be? He could be Brad Pitt's stunt double in Troy. She played with the ends of her hair before she turned to face him. She loved the brutal, unapologetic lines of his face and the hungry look in his eyes whenever he focused on her. Gavin Pyre was a lot of man, and he was hers legally and emotionally.

"It's taken everything I have to get through each day, and now you're talking about kids."

"You don't want one."

She tapped her fingers on her thigh and imagined a little boy in Gavin's image or a little girl with her father's eyes, and her knees went weak. "I do. I just... I didn't realize that was on the table."

"Everything's on the table." He pulled her against him and kissed her. "I told you, I want everything that we promised each other before."

"And you want kids?"

"We don't have to have them right now, but I want to know whether it's possible or not. I'm not getting any younger, and I'm out of the underworld."

"You want kids," she said and blew out a long breath. Holy shit. She was married, and her husband wanted kids. Most women would be jumping for joy, but she felt as if she'd been slapped across the face. This was a gigantic step. They had just slept together for the first time in almost two years, and the first thing on his mind was kids. For some reason, she thought of Carlo and how he got his girlfriend pregnant to marry her. She considered Gavin, wondering if he had an ulterior motive.

"You don't have to get pregnant tomorrow," he said with an easy smile she didn't trust. "I just want you to think about it."

If she didn't want to get pregnant, she needed to see a doctor for birth control. There were dozens of reasons not to get pregnant, but she didn't want to think about them now. She wrapped her arms around his neck, and he carried her back to bed. He tore off her robe, and they slid under the covers.

He pulled her against him and buried his nose in her hair. "Dad would have been so proud of you."

"Manny tried to protect me that day and my dad…" She closed her eyes and fought the tears that were always so fucking close to the surface. "My dad couldn't care less about me. He's a selfish bastard that doesn't deserve your money or my concern. I'm done."

"I'm glad." His hand cupped her breast, as if memorizing the texture and weight. "You defended me."

She looked at up when she heard the strange note in his voice. "Of course, I did."

"You've run from me twice."

"For good reason."

"Yet you defend me in front of your family."

"You did what you've done out of loyalty, duty, and love, which makes you ten times the man my father is. He cares for no one but himself."

He stared at her for a long moment. "So, you forgive me?"

"You'd kill yourself before letting harm come to Manny or me," she said solemnly. "Maybe the hit would have come even if you didn't go after Vinny's killer. We'll never know. I understand why you didn't want to let go of the underworld. I don't like it, but I get it. But you're out now, right?"

"Yes."

"Then we don't need to discuss it."

He kissed her long and deep and positioned himself between her thighs. "I love you."

He lifted her thigh and slid inside her. She moaned.

"I've been dreaming about making love to you for almost two years. I've wanted to apologize, to touch you. I didn't know if you would ever let me in again." He moved gently as his eyes opened and drilled into hers. "I won't take you for granted."

"You'd better not," she said breathlessly.

"You won't run from me again," he stated.

"No."

"Promise me, Lyla."

She wrapped a hand around his neck and pulled him down for a kiss. "You'd find me if I ran away."

He shook his head. "No, baby, I need the words."

"I won't run," she vowed.

"Give me a chance. I'll make you happy."

"I'll make sure of it," she said.

7

LYLA

"I DON'T HAVE TO GO TO WORK TODAY," GAVIN SAID.

She went on tiptoes and kissed him. "You have to go back some-time, and Marcus has been calling you a couple of times a day."

"He can figure it out."

"Gavin." She clasped his face between her hands. "Go. I'm going to have a girls' day with Carmen and Aunt Isabel. I'll be back before you get home."

"I'd rather you stay here."

"I need to apologize for causing a scene at the funeral in person."

"Take your phone and don't leave Blade's sight," he ordered.

"I know. Maybe he should get a pedicure with us," she teased.

She felt extremely lighthearted and carefree. Last night, Carmen accused her of being in a sex coma. Perhaps she was right. Gavin spent the past three days making up for lost time. He was an insa-tiable beast, and she loved it. He worshipped her to the point of exhaustion, but the real world was calling, and they both needed to answer.

"I don't care if he gets a pedicure as long as he's armed," he said.

"I'll be fine." When he hesitated, she took pity on him. She wrapped her arms around his waist. "Do you want me to call you?"

"Every hour."

"Every hour? Isn't that a bit much?"

"After losing you twice and with a killer on the loose? I don't think so."

"Aren't you going to be busy today? You don't want me inter-rupting—"

"That's precisely what I want you to do. It's the only way I'll be able to get anything done."

"Okay," she conceded. "Once an hour. Be expecting eight phone calls."

"Looking forward to it." He kissed her deeply and then met her eyes. "Be here when I get home."

"I will be."

He gave her another kiss before he strode toward his Aston Martin. The guards got out of his way. When he opened the driver's door, he eyed Lyla over the roof of the car. He pointed at her before he got in and peeled out of the driveway.

Blade walked up to her with a grin. "So, you got him to go back to work. That's good."

She raised a brow. "He had to go back sometime."

"I thought he would go back in a month or two." Blade shrugged. "What are you up to today?"

"I'm going to have a girls' day with Carmen and her mom. I'll leave in an hour?"

"We're ready when you are."

She nodded and rushed upstairs. Gavin's staff was coming in today. He had given them strict orders to stay away since he brought her back. The mansion was in dire straits, thanks to their activities.

She took the time to put on makeup and do something with her hair. They were going to get the works today—hair, nails, wax. She proposed it as a way to spend time together and get their minds off Uncle Louie's death. Carmen grudgingly accepted. She was armed with an unlimited credit card from Gavin.

She examined the thigh-length gray ruffle wrap dress. She gave an experimental twirl in front of the mirror and realized she was smiling. It was remarkable how much could change in so little time. A week ago, she was contemplating whether her life was worth living. Now, she was married and looking forward to her future. Gavin scheduled an appointment with a gynecologist who had been horrified when she took in Lyla's scarred abdomen. The doctor requested her hospital records and verified that no vital organs had been damaged. She should be able to get pregnant, but they would monitor her closely to make sure everything progressed normally. Despite this reassurance, she requested oral contraception. Gavin didn't comment, but his expressionless face said it all.

She was halfway down the stairs when her phone rang. She fetched it out of her purse and shook her head when she saw the name on the screen.

"Hello," she said.

"It's been an hour," Gavin said.

"I haven't even left the house yet."

"We agreed, every hour."

"I'm surprised you didn't insist we video chat," she said as she made her way to the foyer.

A pause and then, "That would be even better."

"Gavin, I'm walking out the door. I'll call you in an hour."

"Tell me," he said.

She knew what he wanted. He demanded she say it several times a day. "I love you."

"I love you too, baby girl."

She walked down the steps and climbed into the back of the SUV. She had to resist the urge to look in the trunk to see if there was any sign of their consummation. She would never be able to ride in this SUV without remembering their hot sex session. She texted Carmen that she was on her way and got an unpleasant reply—her mother was at Aunt Isabel's house. She ignored the knots in her stomach. She hadn't changed her mind about taking away her parents' allowance. It wasn't Gavin's duty to support them. Her father had embezzled, and if he couldn't get a job as an accountant, he had to find another career. How many times had he dragged Lyla and her mother down with him? He would never change. Her connection to the Pyres made her father feel entitled to more money, as if Gavin owed him a dowry or something.

Blade helped her out when they parked in Aunt Isabel's driveway. She walked up to the front door with three guards. The door was answered by Carmen, who looked annoyed. She reached out and dragged Lyla into a tight hug.

"You're really okay?" Carmen asked.

"Yes. Are you ready to go?"

Carmen gave her a put-upon look. "Your mother's been here since six, crying and carrying on."

Lyla straightened her shoulders. "Where is she?"

Carmen led her into the kitchen, while the guards stayed in the living room. Her mother sat at a small dining table. She looked awful with puffy eyes, unbrushed hair, and a pile of used tissues in front of her. When she spotted Lyla, she rushed over.

"Lyla, Daddy told me you took away our money. How are we going to live?" Mom wailed.

"He needs to find a job."

"But you know it's going to be difficult for him after the misunderstanding at Pyre Casinos."

Lyla cocked her head to the side. "Misunderstanding? It wasn't a misunderstanding, Mom, he stole half a million."

Her mother held up both hands. "I know, honey, but—"

"He's a liar and a gambling addict," Lyla said succinctly, shocking her mother into silence. "I asked Gavin to let you two live off a generous allowance. He didn't have to do that. He never asked Dad to repay anything he stole. At the funeral, Dad insulted me and the Pyres. He has no respect for anyone, so why should I have respect for him? You and Dad need to figure it out."

Mom's mouth dropped open. Lyla's calm delivery had clearly stunned her.

"But what if he can't get another job?"

"That's his problem. If you need a place to stay, you're always welcome, but Dad isn't."

"He's your father, Lyla."

"Calling me a slut and a whore doesn't make me feel charitable toward him, especially when I gave up everything to save his ass when he embezzled."

"He can be callous sometimes, but—"

"No, Mom, I'm done." Lyla looked at Aunt Isabel, who was clearly fascinated by the conversation. "Hi, Aunty, are you ready?"

"You can't do this to us!" Mom burst out. "You have a responsibility to take care of us."

"When you can't take care of yourselves, I will, out of duty," Lyla said dispassionately. "But right now, if he can run his mouth as easily as he does, he can channel that into making a living."

"You've changed," Mom said accusingly.

"Yes, I have."

"I don't know what you've become, but you aren't the daughter I raised."

Lyla stared at her. "You haven't asked where I've been for the past year and a half."

"What?"

"You haven't asked how I am, where I've been, if I'm happy. Parents who cared would ask." She waited for her mother to say something, but when nothing happened, she said, "Let's go, Aunt Isabel."

She walked out of the house and was joined in the back of the SUV by Aunt Isabel and Carmen. Aunt Isabel took her hand and squeezed.

"Your parents care in their own way," she said.

Lyla gave her a weak smile. "That's not relevant. How are you?"

"Getting by. I haven't been good company."

"It'll take time," Lyla said and then, "I'm sorry about what happened between me and my dad. I shouldn't have—"

"I heard what he said. If you hadn't done something, Gavin would have, and he had every right to," Aunt Isabel said. "If Louie heard your father, he would have whooped his ass too."

"I don't know what came over me."

"Years of pent-up frustration, probably. Pat never treated you right, and you've always been so sweet."

Carmen snickered. "That was spectacular. He's been begging for it for years. Dad would have been proud."

They chatted on the way to the salon. Carmen air kissed the cheek of the owner, and Lyla did the same. It seemed like a lifetime since they had been here last. The hairdressers were clucking over the state of their hair when her phone rang again. She picked up as she leaned toward a large, lit up mirror.

"Hi," she said.

"You're frying my nerves here," Gavin growled.

"Sorry. We just got to the salon." She fluffed her hair. "You think I'll look cute with pink hair?"

"Come again?"

"Pink hair? Short hair?"

"Don't dye your hair. It's gorgeous, and I like it the way it is. Blade said your mom was at the house. Trouble?"

"No. I took care of it."

"Are you okay?"

"Yes."

"Call me in an hour. I love you."

"I love you too."

They hung up, and she set the alarm on her phone. A hairdresser with bulging breasts barely contained by her apron dragged her fingers through Lyla's hair.

"What can I do for you, darling?"

"I'm going to be boring. Just trim and condition, please," Lyla said.

"Are you certain? I can do great things with your hair."

"My... husband likes it as is," she said, stumbling over the h word.

"I can see why," the hairdresser said, and held her hair up to the light. "Women would kill for this shade."

Aunt Isabel dyed her silver hair an auburn shade and paired the color with a short cut that wouldn't take much time to style. Lyla was flabbergasted when Carmen dyed her blonde hair black. The stark color against her pale skin and blue eyes was a startling contrast that changed her whole demeanor. During her blow dry, Blade came over with the phone. She apologized to Gavin and tried to convince him that she set the alarm, but didn't hear it. He wasn't pleased. When they went to get their mani and pedis, Carmen chose pointed maroon nails that went with her biker chick vibe. Lyla went with modest rose-colored nails, while Aunt Isabel got a French tip.

"How are you?" she asked Carmen.

"I'm fine."

"Carmen."

"What?"

Lyla took in Carmen's drastic new look and saw beneath the nonchalant attitude to the pain beneath. "What are your plans?"

"Can't make any without money," Carmen said archly, reminding her that Gavin had frozen her accounts.

"Right. I'll talk to him about that."

"Did you know Mr. Important wants to pay for Dad's funeral?" Carmen asked with a curled lip.

She tried to hold on to her temper. She left the house this morning with a great attitude, but it was deteriorating rapidly. She wished she asked Gavin to stay home and hibernate for another day in their love nest.

"He wants to help," she said.

"If he gave me my money, I could pay for it myself."

"I know. Just let Gavin pay for it, and I swear, I'll talk to him about your money tonight."

"So, you forgave him for everything?"

"Everything?" she echoed.

The woman doing her manicure tugged on her fingers, which were trying to ball into a fist.

Carmen's eyes dipped to her chest. "You left him for a reason."

"I did," she said, striving for calm. "He hurt me; I hurt him. We've both made mistakes, but I still love him."

"Just because you love each other doesn't mean you're meant to be together. You must have some reservations. I mean, he hasn't changed. He forced you to marry him."

"Yes," she said and blew out a breath. "He won't allow any distance between us."

"His love is toxic."

"Carmen," she snapped and glared at her cousin. "I love you. Please, just, don't. I know what I'm doing." She didn't know how to explain the need in Gavin's eyes, the way he held her almost desperately close. She owed Carmen so much, yet she couldn't let her cousin derail her relationship with Gavin.

They finished their manicures in silence while Aunt Isabel's manicurist told raunchy jokes. Lyla felt like a million dollars by the time they left the salon. She called Gavin on their way to a restaurant.

"Hey, you," she said.

"Hey. What color is your hair?"

"Still blonde."

"Good. Length?"

"Long enough."

"Lyla?"

"Yes?"

"I miss you."

"I miss you too. Can you call in tomorrow?"

"Yes."

He didn't hesitate. She'd had a hell of a day so far. She'd need a day or two to recover.

"Is Marcus going to hate me?" she asked.

"Doesn't matter."

"It does, Gavin. I know you need to work. No, you should go in tomorrow. I'm just going to sleep all day."

"And I can keep you company."

Even while that appealed to her, she said, "How about you go in for a half day, so I don't feel so selfish?"

"Deal. Where are you now?"

"We're going to have a late lunch."

"Okay. Love you."

"Love you too."

They had a pleasant lunch. Aunt Isabel had color in her cheeks, and although she had an unexpected breakdown during the meal, she was in good spirits. Lyla couldn't take her eyes off Carmen, who was drawing just as much attention with black hair as she had as a blonde. She looked edgy and dangerous. Was she doing it purposely? Lyla didn't know what to make of her transformation. Carmen rolled her eyes when she excused herself to call Gavin. By the time they arrived back at Aunt Isabel's house, she was satisfied but exhausted. She hugged Aunt Isabel and told her if she needed anything, to call her. She wasn't surprised when Carmen saw her to the door.

"I can see you're happy," Carmen said and shrugged. "I'm scared for you."

"I know."

Carmen swallowed hard. "I miss Vinny and my dad."

She hugged her. "I know. I miss them too."

"I can't lose you too."

"You won't."

"You can't guarantee that."

"Gavin won't let anyone touch me. You know that, right?"

Carmen sighed. "I went from my childhood home to Vinny, and now I'm back to square one. What am I supposed to do with my life?"

"You can do whatever you want, but I hope you stay in Vegas with me."

"After being on the road, it's nice to be in one place and have space," Carmen said as she drew back and wiped her wet cheeks.

"Definitely." She braced her hands on her cousin's shoulders. "I'm going to talk to Gavin about your money. I want to be involved in whatever you do next. If you guys need anything, I'm here, okay?"

Carmen nodded. "I'm glad you finally stood up to your parents. Manny's death changed you for the better."

Why did it always take a tragedy to invoke change?

"I don't know what goes on with you and Gavin, and I don't want to. I know he loves you. He always has and, apparently, always will." Carmen's eyes filled with tears. "The way he watched you at the funeral... it's the way my dad looked at my mom, the way Vinny looked at me, but Gavin... He's an entirely different ball game. He doesn't have the sweetness that Vinny did. Gavin can be ruthless and cruel, and you've never been a match for him." Carmen leaned back and considered her. "Maybe now you are."

"I hope so." She hesitated before she asked, "After all that's happened, do you think we can have normal lives?"

"You, perhaps. If Gavin keeps his nose clean, and he keeps worshipping the ground you walk on." Carmen fluffed her black tresses. "Me? I don't know."

"Why not?"

Carmen's lower lip trembled before she controlled it. "I loved Vinny with everything in me. Who's lucky enough to love like that twice in a lifetime? It might kill me."

For the first time in a long time, she thought of Jonathan, the gentle IT consultant who had coaxed her into a relationship. Her affection for him couldn't be compared to what she shared with Gavin. It was like trying to compare a kitten to a tiger. No, she couldn't imagine having what she had with Gavin with another man.

"I'm here for you," she said.

Carmen nodded and hugged her again. "I love you."

"I don't know what I would have done without you. I owe you everything."

"It was my pleasure," Carmen said with a watery smile and bowed.

"You're crazy, you know that?" She laughed as Carmen sashayed away.

When they reached home, she went upstairs and drew a bath. She moaned as she climbed into the tub and closed her eyes. She understood Carmen's worry. Most would think she was a glutton for punishment, but no one saw Gavin the way she did. He was rough around the edges—animalistic, merciless, and savage. But there was also gentleness in him and a craving for touch and love—her touch, her love. Aunt Isabel and Carmen couldn't hide the crippling pain of losing their men.

She didn't have to ask to know neither woman regretted their time with their husbands. They would take the pain and live with it for the rest of their lives, knowing it was a small price to pay for the memories.

"Baby?"

She opened tear-drenched eyes and blinked up at Gavin. A sob escaped. He crouched down and kissed her. She gripped his wrists and then twisted her hand in his shirt, dragging him down, so she could feel him against her. Gavin lost his clothes, climbed in the tub, and hovered over her.

"Tell me you won't leave me," she said.

He pulled back. "What?"

"Vinny, Uncle Louie, and Manny. They didn't intend to die. I can't lose you too. You can't die."

"I'm not going to die."

"They might come for you and—"

"Lyla, I'm not going anywhere."

"You promise?"

"I promise."

"Make me believe."

His mouth covered hers. He sat and pulled her astride him.

"I need," she said, reaching down to position him.

He gripped both sides of the bathtub, eyes alight with excitement. "Take me."

She moved on his cock, absorbing the feel of him inside her. He was hers to touch and explore. She didn't know how to explain the need for comfort after being with Carmen and Aunt Isabel. Their grief was etched on them for all time. She required the connection with Gavin, the reassurance she wasn't alone. Her man was here, and she would fight to keep him.

"I love you," she said as she moved on him. "I always have."

His hungry, starved gaze watched her every move.

"I can run, but my heart and mind always knew you would come for me."

"Always," he said through gritted teeth, muscles flexing.

"I don't want a marriage like everyone else. I want a marriage that suits us."

He gave a jerky nod. She rode him harder, splashing water heedlessly over the sides. His eyes went blind a moment before he gripped her hips and shoved himself all the way inside her. She screamed and climaxed a moment before he did. Gavin rested his face in the hollow of her neck as she panted. His hands moved lazily over her.

"You have to know something about me," he said.

She tried to move back to see his face, but she was too exhausted. "What?"

"I won't give you up."

She chuckled. "You do whatever you have to keep that promise."

"I will." His hands moved over her. "Did you have a good day?"

"Yes and no. You?"

"Same."

"Are you hungry?"

"Yeah."

"Give me a minute, and I'll remember how to walk."

He rose and set her on the vanity bench to towel her dry. They dressed in robes and went downstairs where a delicious roast was waiting for them. They made their plates and sat at the table. She told him about her mother and her day with Carmen and Aunt Isabel. He reciprocated with Marcus's ideas for Pyre Casinos and how he was becoming an excellent asset and partner. She was pleased. Maybe they could have a normal life after murder and mayhem.

They retired to the couch, where Gavin propped her feet on his lap and gave her a massage. She tipped her head back and moaned. When she opened her eyes, she saw that his eyes were trained on her gaping robe. She ignored the fire in her belly and said, "You need to release the hold on Carmen's money."

His hands stilled.

"You have no right to control her money. Vinny wouldn't like it either. She needs the freedom to do what she wants, especially after losing her dad and husband."

He had a strange look on his face. She wriggled her toes impatiently.

"What are her plans?" he asked.

"I don't know, and it's none of our business."

"I want to know what her plans are before I give her the money."

"Why?" she asked, and then her intuition pinged. "You don't want to give her the money because you think we'll run again?"

A muscle clenched in his cheek. "I told you, I'm not taking chances with you."

"What the hell was that in the tub? I just committed myself to you ten times over! You can't punish Carmen for the choices I make. I asked her to get me out, and she did. She's my cousin and saw me get diced up by a psycho. Of course, she's going to do whatever I ask of her. She loves me."

"I'm not going to give her money, so she can cause trouble."

"Believe it or not, Carmen respects us. Besides that, how many times have I promised to stay?" She spread her arms wide. "I'm here, Gavin."

"Because I forced you."

His words stung. She withdrew her feet from his lap and sat up. "So, you don't trust me."

"I don't want her to tempt you."

"I promised you I wouldn't run."

His eyes were hot with conflicting emotions.

"I'm not playing you. I'm here, and I'm not going anywhere."

"Give me a guarantee," he said.

"I have nothing to offer but my word! You either trust me or you don't. I have to trust you won't cheat on me or decide to go back to the underworld."

"Low blow, Lyla."

"I'm not interested in sugarcoating anything, Gavin. It's too late for that. We have to trust each other."

She walked toward the staircase, but didn't get far. On the first stair, he hauled her backward.

"Don't walk away from me," he growled in her ear.

"Don't be such a jackass!" she countered as he carried her back to the couch and tossed her on it. She bounced on the plush cushions and grunted when he came down on top of her. "You can't control everyone."

"I can try."

She huffed. "You can't do that to Carmen. It's not fair."

His hands sank into her hair and gripped. "I just got you back. I don't want Carmen distracting you or making you wonder if you're better off with her again."

"You have to trust me. Do you?"

His expression was tormented. "I want to."

"But you don't."

His hand cupped her nape and squeezed. "I want all of you."

"You have me."

He parted her robe, uncovering her abdomen. His hand splayed over her scarred stomach.

"Are you sure of me?" he asked.

She was, right? As the silence stretched, his fingers twitched.

"If you trust me, why'd you ask for birth control?"

She tried to shove him off her, but he didn't budge. "That's my choice, Gavin!"

"Why do you want to prevent pregnancy?"

"We shouldn't rush into having kids. We have plenty of issues to work through first."

"Like?"

"Like what kind of life we're going to have in a month! You just went back to work today. I had to call you every hour. That's not normal, Gavin."

"You know why I'm doing it."

"I get it, but you can't tell a kid to do that. Or maybe you want to homeschool it because you can't stand to have the kid be away from you? You can't make a kid a prisoner, Gavin."

His eyes narrowed. "You feel like a prisoner?"

"At first, yes, but I want to be your captive so..."

"So, what are we talking about?"

"We're talking about your need for control. I don't know if you're going to ease up in a few weeks or never."

"Dad's killer is still on the loose."

"Yet I can get a full night's sleep without worrying about that, and I'm the one who looked into his eyes." She shuddered. "We can't let him stop us from doing what we want. We need to live. That's what Manny would have wanted for us."

"And living means trying for a baby," he said implacably.

Her stomach iced over. "I would rather not bring anyone into our situation unless it's stable."

"Meaning I'm not?"

"Neither of us are. I could slip into depression tomorrow, and so could you. We don't know how this marriage is going to work or how the underworld is going to handle you being out of the game. There are so many variables."

"As you said, we can't live our lives based on other people's agenda. We need to do what we want regardless of those factors. In my mind, our life goes like this: I wake up with you, make love to you, and go to work. You do whatever you want during the day. I come home; I want you here. We eat, shower, and fuck. I fall asleep with you wrapped around me. That's what I plan for us. What about you?"

She didn't know what to say. He stroked her stomach, and when his eyes met hers, she caught her breath at the hunger there.

"When I was in jail, I had a dream that we had a daughter who looked exactly like you. I walked in the front door, and this little girl ran to me. I picked her up. She was so small and full of life. She covered my face with kisses and told me I needed to help her make cookies. Her name was Nora."

"Your mother's name?" Her heart wrenched at the image he painted in her mind.

"Yes. She was so real. I know exactly what she was wearing, the smell of her hair, the weight of her against my chest. Even now, I have feelings for her, and she doesn't exist."

Her eyes filled with tears. This man knew how to rip her heart out. She heard the yearning in his voice and ached to give him what he wanted. "You're killing me here."

"I love you," he said fiercely. "No one will ever love you like I do."

He was telling the truth. It wasn't possible for any man to love her more than Gavin Pyre did.

"Our kids will be my redemption, my way to make up for all the shit I've done. In my mind, we need kids to move forward, or we're going to keep sliding backward. Nora was..." He shook his head, and she saw his eyes glint with tears. "Beautiful. Pure. I need that in my life."

"No pressure on me," she said faintly.

"You don't need to worry about it. It'll happen," he said with complete confidence.

"How do you know?"

"The same way I knew you were meant for me the moment I met you, the way I know God spared you because I couldn't live without you. This is why we're here... to create good out of the hell we've been through."

She thumped him on the shoulder. "How do you do this to me?"

"Do what?"

"Wreck me, convince me to believe in the impossible."

"It's a gift." He searched her face. "You understand why I want to try?"

"Yes."

"Are we going to?"

She tossed a hand over her face, seeing the image he created so vividly in her mind. A little girl who pressed kisses over Gavin's face, demanding he make cookies with her. Everything in her yearned to give that to him and herself. A child... "Yes."

He kissed her hard. "Thank you."

"Are you going to give Carmen her money?"

"Yes," he said as he spread her robe wide and positioned himself between her legs. He lifted her thighs on his shoulders and slid his tongue over her. "I missed your taste."

She locked her ankles around his back and clutched the couch cushions.

"Are you on the pill?" he asked, voice muffled as he talked against her.

"No."

"Good."

He sat up and positioned himself between her legs. The slide of his cock made her insides quiver and burn as she stretched. She shivered beneath him as he slid in all the way. He shuddered as if he couldn't handle the sensation and pumped his hips.

"If we have a girl, can we name her after my mom?"

As if she would deny him after hearing his dream. "Of course," she panted.

He kissed her, smearing her taste on her lips. She whimpered as he ground into her.

"Thank you," he whispered.

"You do know we may not have a girl or even get pregnant?"

"We will," he said firmly. "And we will have a girl."

Knowing she wasn't protected and that he was trying to get her pregnant made her hot. Really hot. "Fuck me, Gavin."

He gave her a feral smile. "Don't mind if I do."

He didn't hold back. He fucked her as if his life depended on it, as if this were the last time he would have sex in his life. He fucked her so hard that she screamed and clawed his chest. She begged him to stop and then begged for more. He didn't let up until she convulsed around him. He came seconds later, planting himself as deep as possible and filling her with him.

8

GAVIN

Lyla was getting restless. She didn't say so, but he noticed, and it made him uneasy. It had been four months since he brought her back from Montana. He gave Carmen access to her money, and to his relief, she made no drastic moves and continued to live with her mother. Lyla spent three days a week with Carmen and Aunt Isabel, either hanging out at their house or going out to do girl things. Carmen joined Lyla at the gun range. Blade reported that their skills were progressing quickly.

He was able to pull back on his need to have Lyla call him every hour when she was out of the house, but he couldn't resist checking the cameras when she was home. If she knew how much he watched her, she would freak, but he couldn't help it. He needed constant access to her to get anything done. He was back to working sixty hours a week, and it felt good. At times, he reached for the phone to call Vinny before he remembered he wasn't there.

The rumors surrounding the money laundering charges and his father's murder made their casino a notorious hotspot, and they were raking in stupid cash. Marcus made improvements in the clubs and subtle updates to the casino that made all the difference in the world. For the first time in his life, he was able to think about something else besides business, and that something was his wife.

He knew a psychologist would have a field day with him. His love was an obsession, but that was nothing new. Lyla had captivated him from the start. He resented her hold on him until she left, making him realize how worthless his life was without her. Now, he held nothing back. He claimed her every chance he had to reinforce their bond, to ensure she knew he loved her. The need to shower her with gifts was wasted on her, since she wanted nothing. The first three months were rocky, with both of them waking from nightmares in a cold sweat. Lyla had bouts of depression that kept her in bed for days at a time. He didn't mind staying home to care for her. Marcus didn't question his absences from work. Every day that he loved her out of the darkness, she bloomed, and when she smiled at him with her eyes shining, he could barely breathe. He felt drunk on her, addicted to her smiles and laughter and love. He steeped himself in her, and it kept his demons at bay.

The cops were monitoring him, but for the first time in his life, he was clean as a whistle. He put out lures to see if the underworld would reveal the new crime lord's identity, but nothing came back. Not a whisper, which made him sick with worry. There were always rats in the underworld, greedy fuckers who would sell their children for money. What made this new crime lord untouchable, and why was everyone more afraid of this fucker than him? The unanswered questions tortured him, making him all the more protective of Lyla, who, thankfully, didn't seem to mind the suffocating blanket of security he insisted on. He didn't sleep as much as he should. He spent most nights holding her against him and plotting the murder of the faceless man who dared challenge him.

He accessed the security cameras around the house. Although half of her week was taken up, Lyla spent most days cleaning (even though they had a maid), swimming, or pacing. She spent a lot of time in his office, where his father's ashes were. He didn't intrude on their time together.

He asked if she wanted to go on a trip, but she declined. He was running out of things to distract her. She didn't complain, but he sensed her growing agitation. She was recovering physically and mentally from the trauma, and with that came more energy, which she didn't have an outlet for. He was trying his damnedest to get her pregnant, not only to make his dream of having a daughter a reality, but to bind her more tightly to him. Lyla was softhearted, caring, and loving. A child would flourish under her care. He couldn't wait to have her pregnant with his child. It would be a girl. God wouldn't give him such a dream unless he would make it come true.

He scowled as he clicked through the cameras and couldn't find his wife. She hadn't told him she had plans today. Maybe Carmen came by for a last-minute excursion? He called her cell. No answer. He called Blade, only to have the call go to voicemail. A fine layer of sweat covered his body as panic sank in. He got to his feet and was about to call another member of his wife's personal security when his secretary buzzed him. He was about to tell her to fuck off, but before he could do so, the door opened.

Lyla walked in, dressed in a skirt that showed off her legs, a deep orange blouse, and a trench coat.

"Why the fuck didn't you answer my call?" Didn't she know how much she meant to him? Didn't she know he would fucking lose it if she disappeared?

She closed the door and walked toward him. "Gavin, I was two minutes away from your office. I came to surprise you. Do you want to eat lunch?"

"You don't fucking ignore my calls, got it?"

She crossed her arms and frowned at him. "What's wrong with you?"

"Neither you nor Blade answered. What am I supposed to think? You never told me you were going anywhere."

"That's what a surprise is," she said slowly.

"I don't fucking like surprises."

"Apparently."

He closed the distance between them, buried his shaking hands in her hair, and kissed her. She had no idea what he was capable of, no idea the control he had to exert to keep himself from sliding into destruct mode. The violence he once channeled into the underworld, he released in the boxing ring with UFC fighters. When he could, he lost the business suit and trained. The physical exertion made his rage manageable, but it kept coming back. Lyla was the only person on the planet that made him feel normal. The moment he was away from her, he was restless, savage, less human.

She kissed him back, and it fired up his blood. He placed her on the desk and thrust two fingers into her. She gripped his shirt and moaned into his mouth. He growled in satisfaction when he found her soaked for him.

"Did you come for this?" he asked, pulling back, so he could see her face.

"I was going to let you have me after lunch," she said and spread her thighs wide, showing him her black lace underwear.

"I'll have you then, too," he decided on the spot as he unzipped his pants and slid inside her. Lyla belonged to him. Every inch, every breath. He was her master and slave. He shivered as she closed around him. Every morning, every night, he took her. He couldn't get enough. No other woman could do this to him. The others had been cheap imitations of sex, but this—this was heaven on earth. Their souls spoke to one another in the aftermath, and every time he claimed her, he renewed their vows.

"I've been missing you," she said, framing his face with her small hands.

"Good," he grunted as he sank in to the hilt. "I want you to miss me every second I'm not with you."

"Did you miss me?"

He didn't know how to tell her what she meant to him without scaring the shit out of her. "Always."

She moved his shirt aside to suck on his neck. "I like distracting you at work and getting you all hot and bothered."

"Anytime," he said, and looked down at the delectable angel on his desk being impaled by his rock-hard cock. "This should be a part of my schedule."

"You'll get tired of it."

He nipped her bottom lip. "I assure you, I will never get tired of you. Ever."

Lyla smiled, and he couldn't help himself. He began to thrust hard, deep, and fast. After the fucking scare she gave him, he couldn't go slow. He gorged on her, and she writhed against him.

"Fuck me, Gavin. Take me," she panted.

"Fucking tell me who you belong to," he ground out.

"You."

He gripped her hair and tilted her head back, so he could bite the base of her neck. "I need to plant a baby in you."

"Do it."

He bit her neck as he pumped into her. God, he wanted nothing more than to see her pregnant, her body becoming full and lush with the continuation of life. He thought it would calm him somewhat, knowing his daughter was on the way, but it hadn't happened yet. On the other hand, he had no problem seeing to it that Lyla was properly filled with cum every chance he got.

He pinched her clit, and she convulsed around him. He jerked her to the edge of the desk as he came, grinding into her and pouring all he had inside her. He tipped her head back and loved the glazed, sated look on her face.

"Tell me you love me," he demanded.

"I love you."

He kissed her because he couldn't get enough. Lyla didn't stop him, even though her lips were swollen and bruised by the time he felt sane.

"Have I ruined you?" he asked, pulling away, so he could scan her clothes.

"Completely," she said with a wicked grin, and he smiled back. "But I seem to be presentable."

She pushed him away and went to the bathroom to clean up while he watched.

"You told Blade not to answer his phone," he guessed as his mind flashed back to his earlier panic.

"Yes." She turned and wagged her finger at him. "Don't punish him for that."

"He doesn't take orders from you."

When she stiffened, he inwardly cursed. Her silver blue eyes flashed with anger, replacing her satisfied look.

"Excuse me?" she asked in a dangerous voice.

"Your safety is—"

"Not in question," she said crisply. "We were a few yards from your office, or else I would have allowed him to pick up your call."

"I don't care how close you are. He isn't allowed to ignore me."

"Gavin, nothing happened."

"I need to know where you are at all times. I need your head of security to pick up his fucking phone."

"Blade managed to call you even though he'd been shot five times," Lyla snapped. "You think he wouldn't call you if my life was in danger?"

If he wanted her to visit him again, he had to put this shit to the side. Nothing happened and she wanted to surprise him. He shouldn't bitch. For now.

"Come here," he said, holding his hand out to her.

"No."

He shook his head and went to her. She knocked his hand away, showing him that her sparring sessions with Blade were working. She was becoming quite the little fighter, and it aroused him. He never believed that the young innocent he claimed at eighteen would morph into the woman she was today.

He put his hand around her nape and hauled her close. She glared mutinously up at him.

"Thank you for the surprise. I enjoyed it," he said.

She snorted.

"I won't punish Blade, but I don't want you countering my instructions, especially when I nearly had a heart attack when neither of you answered."

"Fine. I'll let him tell you a white lie next time."

He didn't like that either, but he didn't want to argue about it. "Let's eat."

She mumbled something under her breath and then caught sight of his computer screen, which had live feeds of the bedroom, living room, and pool.

"You watch me?" she asked.

He raked his mind for an acceptable answer. "I check on you every now and then."

"And you didn't think to mention it?"

"No."

She shook her head. "You are unbelievable."

"Lyla—"

"No."

She walked out of the office. Blade and a team of six were waiting for them. Blade met his glare head-on. They would have words later, but he wouldn't punish him since the result had been pleasurable, and it was his fault for leaving the live security feed on his computer. He wanted to haul her back into the office, but she was fuming and might make a scene if he did. God, this woman was going to kill him.

Marcus approached, eyes focused on Lyla. Gavin wanted to throw his hands up in frustration. He thought he had control over things, and now his day was being royally fucked.

"I heard a rumor you were here," Marcus said as he took Lyla's hand. "I'm glad we finally got to meet."

"And you are?" she asked.

"This is Marcus, my COO," Gavin said grudgingly.

Lyla and Marcus were sizing each other up, and it struck him that they were around the same age, unlike him, who was almost ten years older. Lyla's fair beauty complemented Marcus's All-American good looks. His hands balled into fists as the silence stretched.

"Gavin told me a lot about you," she said finally. "I hear you're doing great things for the company."

"Yes, and I'm glad you're doing well enough for him to come back to work," Marcus said.

She nodded and glanced at Gavin before she said, "You should join us for lunch."

Before Gavin could decline for him, Marcus accepted.

"My pleasure."

His chest locked as Marcus offered his arm. She took it without hesitation, leaving Gavin behind as they walked away.

Blade placed a hand on his heaving chest. "Cool it, Gavin."

He shrugged Blade off and went after his COO and wife. It wasn't rational that he was jealous of her being able to converse with another man. He claimed her before anyone had a chance to, and had always been aware of that fact. Seeing her with Marcus made him lightheaded with fury. Just when he was about to pound his fist into his partner's face, he registered what she was saying.

Lyla had worked as his father's personal assistant for a little over a year. He assumed she did filing, scheduling, and phone calls. He was struck speechless by the managerial tasks his father issued to her and the depth of her involvement in company projects that had since become a reality. Her knowledge of the company shocked him. Marcus began to pick her brain while he walked mutely beside them. Her face lit up as Marcus bounced ideas off her. He was torn between pride at her insight and irritation that he hadn't thought to ask for her opinion. Why didn't he talk to her more about work? It was obvious Lyla was intelligent and knowledgeable, thanks to his father.

Marcus led them into one of the five restaurants in the casino and acknowledged the hostess before he chose a booth in the quietest corner possible during the lunch rush. He was hard-pressed not to grab Marcus by the collar and fling him when he scooted into the booth after his wife. To compound his sins, Marcus turned toward her, elbow on the table as she spoke. Blade nudged him in the side, a warning to keep his head before taking a seat at another table.

The server interrupted Lyla and Marcus's conversation. Gavin ordered whiskey to drown out the rage fizzing in his veins. Lyla gave him an odd look before Marcus claimed her attention again. Marcus was a relentless businessman—keen, ruthless, and sharp. He respected the hell out of Marcus, but currently, he wanted to kill him.

"What are you doing this Friday?" Marcus asked.

His temper went black. "Are you asking my wife out?"

"Well, yes," Marcus said with a shrug. "She should be at the opening of our new nightclub, Incognito."

"My wife doesn't go out," he said through gritted teeth.

"Why...? Oh." Marcus's expression sobered. "Forgive me. I understand. You wouldn't be comfortable going out after—"

"Actually, I would love to go," Lyla said. "What time should I be there? Are you going to pick me up?"

"Fuck that." He reached across the table to grab Marcus when a woman tapped him on the shoulder.

"Scoot in. I need to talk to you both about the press release for Incognito," Janice said.

He scooted to the middle of the booth, so he could yank Lyla away from Marcus. He clamped a hand on her thigh and glared at Marcus, who gave him a puzzled look, as if he couldn't figure out why he was so steamed.

"Have we met?" Janice asked Lyla.

"This is my wife," he said.

Janice's mouth sagged. She reviewed Lyla and beamed. "Are you coming to the opening of Incognito? Your face will photograph great and next to Gavin, you'll look stunning! This will be great publicity."

"That's precisely what I was thinking," Marcus said. "She used to be Manny Pyre's personal assistant, you know."

"No, I didn't," Janice said and stopped the server to order herself a meal. "That's fascinating."

His staff were looking at Lyla as if she were Mother Teresa. Janice had a hell of a time trying to polish his tarnished image, not that he cared. Marcus did, and it was obvious they wanted to use Lyla to make him do appearances and shit.

"I found you. Yay!" Alice, the Community Outreach Coordinator, sat beside Janice. "Are you discussing what's going to happen on Friday? I know we're scheduled for a meeting tomorrow, but if we're all here... Oh, hi. Sorry, have we met?"

"This is Lyla, Gavin's wife," Janice explained. "She used to work with Manny Pyre."

"Is that right? Which projects were you involved in?" Alice asked.

He wanted to bang his head on the table. Everyone ignored him and focused on his wife. He should have expected this. With the way Lyla stayed out of the public eye and the rumors surrounding the day his father was killed, it was only natural for them to be curious about her. Add Lyla's beauty, age, and obvious intelligence and everyone was hooked on her. Lyla outlined the projects she'd been involved in and noticed Janice and Alice exchange looks.

Lunch was served. He firmly turned the conversation back to Janice's plans for Incognito's opening. He had planned to stop by to make sure all was well, but now it looked like he'd be there all night. Lyla listened attentively and even clarified some key points that made Janice blink in surprise.

"Are you looking for a job?" Marcus asked bluntly.

Lyla flushed. "Actually—"

"No," he snapped.

Lyla turned to him. "Excuse me?"

"You're not getting a job."

Lyla turned back to their fascinated audience. "I'll get back to you on that."

He wanted to strangle Marcus, who slapped his hand on the table and roared with laughter. He wanted to haul Lyla out of the restaurant and cart her back to his office, where he would show her who was the boss. Instead, he was forced to sit there and act as if his blood wasn't boiling. Lyla seemed completely at ease, eating and chatting with his staff as if they were old friends.

"I'd like to help you with outreach," Lyla said to Alice, who looked excited until she glanced at his face.

By the time lunch was over, he could barely contain himself. Marcus kissed Lyla's hand and took off at a trot, talking to his secretary on his phone as he went. Janice and Alice shook Lyla's hand and said they would see her on Friday before they took off.

"I'm taking her home," he said to Blade.

She looked up as he clamped a hand on her waist. "What? Why?"

He didn't say a thing as he led her through the casino. They took the elevator down to the parking garage. She gave him a strange look before she got into the Aston Martin. He revved the engine and liked the sound of the car's squealing tires as he drove into traffic.

"Is there a reason you're driving me home?"

"We need to talk," he said, flexing his hands on the wheel.

"About?"

"Do you find Marcus attractive?"

She turned toward him. "Are you fucking serious?"

"You let him touch you, and you were hanging on every word he said." Yeah, he sounded like a possessive bastard, but he couldn't help it. He couldn't stand seeing another man touch her or enjoy her company. It made him homicidal, thinking that she might have chemistry with another man. He wouldn't allow it.

"I still have your cum inside me," she said.

The unexpected comment made him glance at her. She looked furious, gorgeous, and all his.

"You really think I would cheat on you?" she demanded, voice rising in the small space.

"Don't test me, Lyla."

"You're an idiot!"

"I'm an idiot for noticing your fascination with each other?"

"If you weren't such a blind prick, you would've noticed that our fascination wasn't for each other but a mutual caring for your company. I came by today because I've been going stir-crazy. I've been on the road for over a year. In Maine, I had a full-time job. It's all well and good to go out with Carmen and Aunt Isabel, but I need something to get my mind off the past."

"I don't want you to get a job."

"Why?"

He didn't know how to put into words how he felt because everything he wanted to say was downright selfish.

"Why?" she persisted and jabbed him in the arm. "Because you want me at your beck and call?"

"I don't want you to have to quit a job when you get pregnant." That sounded like the least selfish thing to say.

"And if I never get pregnant?"

His hands tightened on the wheel. "Lyla, I run a company. When I come home, I want you there. I don't want you working a different schedule from me where we never get to see each other, and you're exhausted."

"But I need to do something, and I love your company. If we never dated, I would still be working there."

"Dad taught you a lot in a short amount of time." That much was obvious.

"Yes. I want to go to the opening of Incognito. Have there been other parties you've turned down because you think I don't want to go?"

"Yes and no. I'd rather be at home with you."

"I think it'll be good for us to go out. I'll have Carmen come too."

He ground his teeth. Not only would he have to keep an eye on Lyla, but he also had to watch out for Carmen, and she was unpredictable.

"If you won't let me work, then I'll volunteer for outreach with Alice."

That was something he couldn't object to. If he tried to stop her, she might accept a job from Marcus, and that couldn't happen. "That will make Janice happy. I believe Alice has a project every month, but you don't need to attend every one."

She returned to her earlier question. "Do you really think I would cheat on you?"

She hadn't done anything to deserve his accusation. He was the one who had been unfaithful. He feared she would find someone kind, gentle, and normal. He honestly didn't know what she saw in him. "No, I know you wouldn't."

"Then why accuse me of that?"

He was going to sound like an asshole. There was no getting around that. "I'm jealous."

"I know," she said.

He let out a long breath. "I've always had you to myself. I like it like that. Marcus is closer to your age and you two hit it off so easily... I don't like seeing any man close to you."

When she didn't respond, his heart began to pound. Had he just eradicated four months of relationship building with foolish words?

"I'm sorry," he said as he exited the freeway. "I'm fucked up. When it comes to you, my emotions are all over the place. I'm still trying to adjust to having you here. I want you to be happy, but I also want to be the center of your world. I know that's messed up, but it's how I am."

He glanced at her, but the fall of her hair concealed her expression.

"Lyla?"

No answer.

"I'm going to try to rein it in. If you would like to volunteer with outreach, that's fine."

Still no response.

"If you need more things to keep you busy, you can work with me." He floored the gas pedal, so they could get home faster, and he could see just how badly he was fucking this up. "I haven't been trying to hide you away; I've been trying to give you time to recover. Me too. It's not easy going into work and acting like everything's okay. Sometimes I pick up the phone before I realize Vinny's not going to pick up on the other end. Knowing I can't call my dad is even worse. The only bright spot in my life is you, and I need access to you all the time. That makes me greedy and selfish. I don't want to share you with anyone. I want your whole focus on me when I come home. But I realize you do need more, and I'm going to have to adjust to that. Yes, I watch you on the home security cameras. Not because I think you're doing something wrong. I need to see for myself that you're okay. Knowing the man who murdered Dad and hurt you is still out there will always make me paranoid."

He turned into the driveway of their home and turned to her.

"Look at me," he said.

She turned her silver blue eyes on him, and his stomach clenched with want.

"I'm sorry."

She shook her head.

"What?"

"I like the way Marcus, Alice, and Janice looked at me today. They didn't see me as a victim or in recovery. They just saw me for me, and that felt good. It made me feel normal. Marcus liked my ideas, and Alice was ecstatic that I wanted to help her with outreach. I need to be needed too, Gavin."

"I understand that." She required a life outside of him. At least she would be working for Pyre Casinos. He should be thankful for that.

"I think Marcus is hot."

His desire to make amends flew out the window. *"What?"*

She grinned mischievously. "I can admire his looks without being interested in him sexually."

"No, you can't." He reached for her and hauled her over the console. "You're not allowed to think that any man is remotely attractive. I can't take it."

"I belong to you, Gavin."

That didn't reassure him.

"I won't leave you, and I think you're the hottest man I've ever seen. I love you." She pressed a chaste kiss on his lips. "Now, go back to work, and when you come home, you'll make it up to me."

His heart was in his throat as she got out of the car and sashayed slowly to the front door.

9

LYLA

"Stop, Gavin."

"I don't like this," he said for the eighth time in an hour.

Lyla eyed her possessive husband, who looked outstanding in a tux. He freaked out when he saw what she was wearing—a crisscross black halter dress with a row of diamonds low on her back and stilettos. She and Carmen had their hair done at the salon, and then Carmen did her makeup. She enjoyed Gavin's stupefied look when she posed for him. He made love to her twice and begged her to change into another dress, but she held firm. She had to repair both her makeup and hair while he changed.

He'd been moody ever since she had lunch with Marcus, Janice, and Alice, but he didn't object when Alice asked if she would be interested in volunteering at a local dog shelter. She told Carmen about it, and she was down to help. She understood Gavin's need for control, but she wouldn't let it dictate her life. She needed something to keep her occupied. Being able to help others through the Pyre Foundation seemed like a win-win.

"I don't want you out of my sight," he said.

"I know."

"Blade and the others will be there as well."

She didn't complain, since his concern for her safety wasn't unfounded. She had been kidnapped and attacked by a killer who carved her up like a turkey on Thanksgiving. He wouldn't allow it to happen again. This event was giving Manny's killer an opening if he wanted to finish the job. She almost backed out, but stubbornness forced her to attend. She couldn't hide forever, and this was good publicity for the casino and Gavin's image. There were more pros than cons, so, despite his bitching, here they were.

She took his hand. "It's going to be fine."

He didn't answer, but he squeezed her hand. She looked out at the colorful Strip as the SUV crawled through traffic. It was Friday night in Las Vegas, and The Strip was pumping with people looking for a good time.

The SUV pulled up to one of the Pyre Casinos. Gavin opened the door and helped her out. Janice prepped her for the press coverage, but she underestimated the noise and size of the crowd. Reporters called out their names and begged for pictures. Janice appeared out of nowhere and told them where to stand to be photographed. She had attended many of these in her younger days, but she and Gavin had both changed since then. Her anxiety skyrocketed, and her palms became damp with sweat. She instantly regretted coming and felt exposed and uncomfortable.

"I love you."

She looked up at Gavin as the click of cameras echoed around them. "What?"

"I love you," he said as if his staff, the press, and a ridiculous number of people begging to explore a new Pyre nightclub didn't surround them.

"I love you too," she said.

He raised her hand to his lips and kissed her palm. The paparazzi went nuts, and she was nearly blinded by camera flashes.

"Dad would be proud of you for forcing me to come out for this," he said.

She smiled up at him. "He loved these events."

He grunted. "He thrived on the energy. I used to. Things are different now."

She placed her hand on his chest and smiled for the cameras, so they could move on. "Yes, we've changed. We don't have to attend every opening, but we should go occasionally."

"Great, amazing!" Janice said and ushered them into the club. "Thank you for bringing him, Lyla," she said in a low undertone before she addressed Gavin. "We have Ricky Mars and his band playing for three hours, and two other hot artists going on after him. We have ten celebrities, one at each VIP table. Athletes, singers, movie stars. We only have room for about a quarter of the people waiting outside, but there's always tomorrow night. We're giving masks at the door. This is Incognito, after all."

"Are we going for kinky?" Gavin asked.

"It's an added layer of mystery to keep the libido going. The celebrities are going to wear their masks unless they're taking pictures, of course. Please stay at least two hours. Looks like we'll be wrapping this up around five."

"In the morning?" Lyla asked.

Janice winked. "If I'm lucky. I have a table reserved for you, but you should circulate. Gavin, there are plenty of heavy hitters here tonight. I know Marcus has a list of people he wants you to meet, so you might want to hook up with him to discuss. I've got to go. Enjoy, and here are your masks."

Lyla took her mask, which was made of elaborate black lace with diamonds framing her eyes. Gavin had a black mask that was very Phantom of the Opera. It covered his eyes and half of his face. She froze when he donned the mask. Even though she knew it was him, she felt a chill as she was forcefully reminded of the mask Manny's murderer wore.

"Here." He took the strip of lace from her nerveless fingers and tied the ribbon in the back of her head to secure it. "I'm getting too old for this shit, but we'll do it to make Janice happy."

She shook herself as Gavin led her through the nightclub, which had a very different vibe to it than Lux or The Room. Incognito had two levels. From the second level, she could see the whole club. Sweeping staircases gave the club a Renaissance flair. The seductive crimson light invited one to indulge in dark fantasies. The furniture was unrelieved black, as were the walls. Large mirrors on the walls reflected the light and projected images of people writhing on the dance floor. The undercurrent of sexuality in this club ensured it would be a success. The bartenders and servers wore leather and lace uniforms and masks that enhanced their features. The staff was amped and ready to go.

"What do you think?" Gavin asked.

"There will be a lot of sex in this club," she said wryly.

He laughed. "If they have the stamp from the club, they get a discount on a room in the hotel. Let's hope people want a full one-night stand instead of a quickie."

"This is Sin City."

"You have to love it," he said and put an arm around her as he led her down the staircase.

The staff inclined their heads to them as a woman wearing head to toe leather escorted them to their private table, which was already occupied. It took her a moment to recognize Carmen in her skintight leather pants, sky-high heels, and a lace bustier that bared two inches of her flat, toned stomach. Her white lace mask had ruby-colored stones highlighting her electric blue eyes. Gavin stopped and cursed under his breath. Lyla rushed to Carmen and threw her arms around her.

"You look great!"

"You too," Carmen said and gave her ass a sharp smack.

"Carmen," Gavin acknowledged in a terse voice.

Carmen gave him an equally frosty look. "Gavin."

"Don't get into trouble tonight."

Carmen stiffened and put her hands on her hips. "Excuse me?"

"You look like—"

She clapped her hand over Gavin's mouth. "You look hot, and you're going to cause a commotion. He's nervous."

Carmen flipped her hair and adjusted her boobs in her top. "He should be."

Gavin yanked her hand from his mouth. "I just want to get through tonight without drama. Got me?"

"I'm not making any promises," Carmen said.

"Gavin?" Marcus joined their group, wearing a dashing cape and scarlet shirt with his tux. He wore a red mask identical to Gavin's. He kissed her on the cheek. "You look great." His eyes moved to Carmen. "I don't think we've met."

"This is Vinny's widow, Carmen," Gavin said.

Marcus took Carmen's hand and kissed her knuckles. "My condolences."

Carmen gave Gavin a steely look before she focused on Marcus. "Thank you. And you are?"

"Marcus. I'm the new COO."

Carmen's lips pursed, and she withdrew her hand. "Vinny's replacement. Nice to meet you. You finished Incognito. It looks great."

"I'd like to talk to you, if you don't mind."

Gavin stiffened, but she kept her gaze on Carmen, who looked surprised.

"I'm here to have fun and keep Lyla company. I would rather not discuss my husband," Carmen said.

"We don't have to discuss him. We can discuss something else," Marcus said.

"Can I talk to you?" Gavin asked brusquely.

"Sure." Marcus nodded to Carmen. "I'll look for you later."

As Gavin led Marcus away, Carmen voiced what Lyla was thinking.

"For what?"

"Marcus is blunt and a bit strange, but I like him," she said in his defense.

"But why would he want to talk to me? As Gavin said, I'm just a widow," Carmen said bitterly. "As if that's all I am, a dead man's wife. Jesus, I'm a person, damn it."

"You know Gavin has no tact," she said consolingly.

"And no manners."

"Let's get a drink," she said and led the way to the bar.

Carmen took care of ordering drinks and was in the middle of asking the bartender where she got her boob job when Lyla heard someone call her name. She turned to see the community outreach coordinator, Alice, wearing a satin monstrosity that looked like it was from an 80s prom.

She gave Alice a hug and turned to Carmen and the bartender, squeezing each other's boobs. She cleared her throat, and when that didn't get Carmen's attention, she gave her cousin a solid kick in the butt.

"Carmen, this is Alice, the community outreach coordinator. Alice, this is my cousin, Carmen. She's coming with us to the dog shelter next week to volunteer."

"Nice to meet you." Carmen looked Alice up and down and was clearly disturbed by her appearance. "You work for Pyre Casinos?"

"Yes. I just moved from Utah," Alice said uneasily.

"Mormon?" Carmen asked.

"No. Why?"

"Just wondering."

Lyla gave Carmen a quelling glance before she turned back to Alice. "I'm really looking forward to volunteering. I like dogs. I've always wanted one, but my parents wouldn't let me have one."

"And now?" Alice asked.

"Now?" she repeated blankly.

"Since the recession, hundreds of dogs have been abandoned. Each shelter is filled to the max," Alice said. "If you've always wanted a dog, now's the time to get one."

"Does Gavin even like dogs?" Carmen asked as she handed her a pink drink.

"No idea."

"Oh, gosh, um, maybe adopting a dog isn't the best idea," Alice said, wringing her hands.

"How long have you been working at Pyre Casinos?" Carmen asked.

"A year. My position was created after..." Alice flushed and looked away.

"After Gavin went to jail and my husband and Manny Pyre were murdered?" Carmen asked.

"Oh, my gosh, I'm so sorry," Alice said and pressed a hand to her chest.

"It's okay, Alice," she said and squeezed her hand. "I'm glad your position was created. I think it's wonderful that the Pyre Foundation is giving back to the community."

"Yes," Alice said, clearly relieved. "Mr. Pyre has given me free rein, really. I'm so excited that I get to make a difference through his generosity."

She liked Alice's earnest, down to earth personality. There were far too few of her type in Las Vegas, the land of sex, money, and superficiality. Carmen wore a pensive expression as she eyed Alice.

"Here come the masses," she said as the VIPs came down the staircase with their entourages and a swarm of paparazzi.

"Kody Singer's here?" Carmen snapped.

"The movie star?" Alice asked, going on tiptoe to get a better look.

"He'd better keep his distance," Carmen said.

"Why?" Alice asked.

"He used to drunk call me all the time, that asshole. It used to piss Vinny off."

Alice's mouth sagged open. "You used to date...?"

"He was a weeklong fling when Vinny and I were on a break," Carmen said with a one-shoulder shrug.

"She broke his heart," she told Alice. "Kody is a pretty nice guy for an actor." Carmen let out a rude snort. "Come on, Carmen, he was really romantic."

"He doesn't know how to take no for an answer," Carmen said sourly and spotted the next celeb. "Douchebag in the house! Carter Raymond is here. Seriously, when's the last time he even played football? What a fucking showoff."

"You know him personally?" Alice asked.

"When your husband is the COO of Pyre Casinos, you go to plenty of events. You meet people," Carmen said offhandedly.

"You stay around long enough, you'll know celebrities personally," Lyla said, recognizing Jennifer Kingsley, an actress who thought she was God's gift to the world. Yes, Janice invited some big shot VIPs who would draw a massive crowd.

"Me? Celebrities?" Alice let out a nervous giggle-snort. "I don't think so."

Carmen signaled to the bartender for another drink. "If you get celebrities involved in your community projects, it would be great publicity."

"I'm having a hard time recruiting volunteers, much less a celebrity."

Carmen downed another drink. "I'll see what I can do."

"W-what?" Alice asked, but Carmen had already disappeared into the crowd.

"Come, let's go to our table," Lyla said.

"Table?"

"Janice reserved a table for us," she said and took her hand.

"I don't think I'm invited. That's for Mr. Pyre and—"

"And I'm his wife, and I say you're invited," she said and began to pull her through the crowd.

The music was pumping, and there was an electric buzz in the air. She noticed Janice flitting through the crowd, no doubt making sure the photographers got enough shots. Halfway across the dance floor, Blade appeared out of nowhere and cleared a path. She gripped the back of his jacket and refused to release Alice, who came up with a dozen excuses why she shouldn't be at her boss's table.

"Hi, who are you?" Alice asked Blade when he helped her into the booth.

"I'm Lyla's bodyguard."

"Bodyguard?" Alice echoed, eyes wide. "Are you in danger because of... before?"

"Gavin's cautious," she said, and looked out over the club. "Will you look at that?"

The dance floor was at full capacity. People were dancing on the staircases and any place there was room. It was like a flash mob of exotic people. Drinks were flowing, and the compulsive beat urged people to move. A seductive haze hung in the air.

"I prefer my work to this," Alice said nervously. "This is the first club I've been to in my life. I don't even know what I'm supposed to do."

"Do?" Lyla asked without taking her eyes off the dancers.

"I'm supposed to get a drink and... what?"

"Dance," Lyla said.

"Where? There's no room."

"There's always room to dance," Lyla said and winked at her. "Clubs are a fantasy, a place where people can forget their woes and flirt with a sexy stranger."

Alice eyed her uncertainly. "I don't see the appeal."

She grinned. "Some people don't, but people come to Vegas to indulge in their fantasies. Come."

Impulsively, she reached for Alice's hand and pulled her out of the booth. Blade sighed but led them to the dance floor and stood nearby like a statue. She pulled Alice back against her and felt the other woman go rigid. Had Alice never danced or partied in her life? Everyone had to let go sometime. That was why she was here, after all. She came out tonight, so her brain could shut off, and she could just be.

"Listen to the beat," she said and moved her hips.

Alice tried to copy, but her movements were stiff and awkward. Carmen appeared with a hot man wrapped around her. His hands moved greedily over her body. She felt a shaft of pain course through her at seeing Carmen with a stranger. It was inevitable that Carmen would move on, but it felt so wrong. Lyla buried her face in Alice's hair, so she didn't have to witness Carmen losing herself in another man to drown out her grief.

She glanced around at the constantly shifting crowd. A man stood on the sideline, watching the dancers. He stood mostly in shadow, but the intensity emanating from him snagged her attention before she registered who he was. Eli Stark approached Gavin when they were at Lux. Unlike the first time she saw him, Eli was dressed all in sleek black. He worked hand in hand with Gavin before some thugs beat his mother into a coma. Eli retaliated, even though he was a cop. Was he still on the police force? As if he sensed her regard, he turned his head and met her gaze through the throng. She wasn't sure whether Eli was a good or bad guy, and wasn't willing to take any chances. She caught Blade's eye. He immediately muscled his way toward her.

"Eli," she shouted.

Blade searched the crowd. "Where?"

"He's—" She pointed, but felt a chill when she saw he was gone. "He was right there."

"And he saw you?" Blade demanded.

"Yes. We made eye contact." She released Alice, who was now moving to the beat on her own. "Is he good?"

Blade sneered. "Eli went off the rails after his mom was attacked. He quit the force, went on a bloody rampage, and disappeared off the grid."

Her heart skipped a beat. "You mean no one's seen him until now?"

"Gavin has unfinished business with Eli, but we thought he'd been killed while he was chasing down the gang members who targeted his mother."

"Why did they attack his mom?"

"He was scheduled to testify in court against a powerful drug lord. Gavin didn't hear about the hit on his mother until it was too late."

She searched the dancers, but it was impossible to find anyone in the crush. She edged closer to Blade. "So...?"

Blade brushed a hand over his weapon. "So, we keep our eyes open. I'll let Gavin know."

She was distracted by thoughts of Eli when Marcus appeared at her side, eyes narrowed on Carmen and her horny companion. He walked up to Carmen and her partner, who stopped their bump and grind. Carmen's mouth dropped open, and the man backed away with his hands up. Marcus tried to pull Carmen off the dance floor, but she shoved him away. Carmen pulled Alice into the crowd, leaving Marcus behind, looking irritated.

Hard hands circled Lyla's waist. She jumped as Gavin pulled her back against him.

"I've been looking for you," Gavin said in her ear. "I want to show you the private rooms."

Blade tapped his arm. Gavin leaned toward him and Blade conveyed his information. Gavin's reaction was immediate. His eyes narrowed to slits and his gaze swept the crowd before he carried her off the dance floor. He led her to a room manned by two security guards. Gavin waved a key card over the lock and pulled her into a dimly lit room while Blade waited outside. The room had a stripper pole, a black loveseat, and a floor-to-ceiling window that looked out at the club. It took her a moment to realize she was looking through one of the large mirrors mounted on the wall.

"Can they see us?" she asked.

Couples were making out, drinking, and laughing at tables on the other side of the glass. She could see the dance floor from here. The music penetrated the walls and kept her blood pumping.

"There are about ten of these hidden rooms. Each one is different," Gavin said. "Are you okay?"

"Because of Eli?"

"Yes."

"I'm a little creeped, but I don't think he was looking for me."

"What makes you say that?"

"He was searching the crowd. He felt me looking at him, and then I called Blade."

"He used to grease the wheels in the police department for me. He's always been dependable, but now he's a loose cannon. I don't know his agenda."

"We shouldn't worry about it. We should just enjoy tonight."

She saw the hunger in his eyes and knew they were going to use this room for what it had been designed for. She gave him a small shove. He sat on the couch and tried to draw her on his lap, but she sauntered toward the stripper pole. She stepped onto the platform and ran her hand down the pole. Gavin was as still as a mannequin and barely breathing.

"Carmen and I have taken plenty of classes, but I don't think you've ever seen me on a stripper pole, have you?" she asked.

He cleared his throat. "No."

"Hmm." She stroked the pole slowly and then walked around it, dragging her stilettos and shifting her hips seductively. She did a slow spin, feet completely off the ground, letting her body weight swing her around the pole before she stopped in front of him, legs spread wide, the slit in her dress riding high on her hip. She dropped into a split and rocked her body forward, arching her back.

"Jesus Christ!" he shouted and shot up from the couch.

"You're supposed to watch, not touch," she chastised as her gaze went past him to the people less than six feet away, completely unaware of what she was doing on the other side of the mirror.

"If you think I can watch you dance without touching you, you're out of your mind," he growled.

"Sit, Gavin, and let me dance for you."

A sultry beat slipped through the walls. Gavin didn't go back to the couch. He stood less than two feet away, hungry eyes fixed on her. His crotch was tented. He was hanging on by a thread, but he was keeping his distance, which meant she could push a little more before he broke.

She stood in front of the pole, hands above her head, and slowly, very slowly sank down. She could hear his ragged breathing over the music, and watched as his hand went to his crotch and gripped. The tendons on his neck stood out starkly. He wasn't going to last much longer. Taking pity on him, she went on her hands and knees and stuck her butt out as she rose. He cursed and grabbed her.

She laughed as he positioned her on her knees on the couch, facing the club. She felt cold air caress her ass as he lifted her dress, and then his fingers slid into her. She moaned and then clapped her hand over her mouth as a man leaned toward the mirror to fix his hair. He was a foot away, staring right at her, and Gavin was about to fuck her. She tried to wriggle away.

"He can't see you," Gavin said in her ear as he slid inside her in one firm push that sheathed him to the hilt.

"B-but, I can't!" she said, scandalized as a woman joined the man. She panted like a bitch in heat. "Oh, my God, Gavin!"

"People get off on this shit, fucking in public," Gavin said, slipping his hand into her dress and squeezing her breast. "I wouldn't mind fucking you in front of an audience. I want everyone to know you belong to me. Only I ever get to fuck you."

"I thought that was what the ring was for." She squirmed beneath him, not caring about the congregation of girls in front of her who were putting on lip-gloss and fixing their tits. As he thrust slowly, torturously, she began to lose all inhibitions. Who cared if only a mirror separated her from hundreds of people? Her man was making love to her. Nothing else mattered.

"The ring isn't enough. Nothing is," he said as he sped up his thrusts. "I can't stand having people look at you, having you smile at others. I want it all for myself."

"You're the one who's in me," she said as he collared her throat.

"I'm the only one, *ever*."

She touched herself as Gavin brought it home. She braced a hand on the fogged-up glass as she panted and writhed against it before she went limp. A young woman came up to the glass and checked out her ass before she winked at herself and disappeared into the crowd.

"I needed my fix," Gavin said as he pulled out and trailed kisses down her spine. "This damn dress."

She shuddered and sat back on her heels, trembling. "Do you think this will ever ease up?"

"No." He nuzzled her face and kissed her long and sweet. "Maybe if we have a couple of kids, I'll have to rein it in..."

"You're kid crazy," she said and shook her head.

"Have you taken a pregnancy test?"

"I had my period recently."

He zipped himself up. "I'd better up my game."

"You up it anymore, I won't be able to walk."

He drew her to her feet and kissed her. "I love you, Lyla Pyre."

She let out a shaky breath. "I believe you."

"Good." He smacked her ass. "Now that you forced me to come to this, first we circulate, then we're going home to spend all weekend in bed."

Lyla ignored the guards' lecherous grins and Blade's smirk when they walked out. She went to the mirror to make sure she looked presentable and that no one could see inside. She was lazy-eyed, lipstick smeared and hair mussed, but otherwise perfectly presentable for a nightclub. Her eyes glittered through the slits in the mask.

They circulated to the VIP tables where Gavin caught up with acquaintances, asked about their accommodations, and got feedback on the club. Some celebrities asked outright about Manny and his murder. Gavin told the truth—that whoever did it hadn't been apprehended. He introduced her as his wife. People looked at them curiously or with a knowing smirk, as if they knew that they had just fucked. Gavin's hands were constantly moving over her ass, bare back, or belly. Kody Singer was the only one stupid enough to try to draw her away from Gavin, who had him in a headlock before Kody could say two words to her.

"Don't touch my wife," Gavin hissed.

There were flashes from the paparazzi as they honed in on the commotion. When Gavin showed no signs of releasing Kody, Lyla punched him in the shoulder.

"I know him, Gavin!" she shouted.

He turned to her, wrenching poor Kody's neck. "How the fuck do you know him?"

She heard Kody choking and punched him again. "He used to date Carmen. Let him go!"

He released Kody as Janice appeared. Janice looked from the gagging movie star to the paparazzi and then Gavin, who was as composed as ever.

"What happened?" Janice demanded as she tried to shoo away the paparazzi.

"Misunderstanding," Gavin said and clapped Kody on the back. "You're okay, right?"

Kody wore a terrified expression until he noticed the paparazzi. He was an A-list movie star for a reason. His face smoothed into a world-class smile, and the paparazzi lowered their cameras, clearly disappointed. As soon as Janice succeeded in moving the paparazzi along, Kody jerked away from Gavin as though he were a serial killer. Lyla tried to make amends, but Kody backed away as if she had a contagious disease.

"He's my husband," Lyla told Kody in an apologetic tone.

"We're leaving," Gavin announced and dragged her out of the club.

"God, you're such a psycho," she grumbled while Blade followed, chuckling. "You can't kill someone for talking to me."

"Did that asshole not see my hands on you? My ring on your finger?" he growled.

"He wanted to talk to me about Carmen."

Gavin boosted her into the back of the SUV and got in beside her.

"First Marcus and now that asshole. What the fuck? Carmen just lost her husband. Maybe it's the way she's dressed," he said sourly.

"What about Marcus? He's interested in her?"

"I don't know what he is. I asked him to lay off, and he told me to butt out of it."

"He told you that?" *Go, Marcus*, she thought.

Gavin ran a hand through his hair. "The freaking world is tilting sideways. Shit."

10

LYLA

"You're so beautiful."

A man in a black suit and white mask hovered over her. He brushed his gloved thumb, slick with some warm liquid, over her lips. The iron tang of blood touched her tongue. She tried to spit it out, but the man clamped a hand over her mouth. She gagged as Manny's blood slid down her throat. Fathomless black eyes stared at her through the slits in the mask.

"It's a shame I have to do this to you. You're at the wrong place at the wrong time, baby."

She saw the glint of metal out of the corner of her eye and knew what was coming. No matter how hard she fought, she couldn't defend herself. Pain ripped through her abdomen as the knife sliced through skin and muscle. She felt a gush of blood, and then her attacker slashed down again and again and again. There was no reprieve.

Lyla screamed and sat up in bed, fingers curled into claws as she tried to gouge out the eyes of the crime lord. She stared at her surroundings through a haze of tears before she realized she wasn't in Manny's mansion but the master suite of her home with Gavin. She rocked back and forth, trying to banish the vivid memories of the attack and the taste of Manny's blood. She was shaking uncontrollably and covered in a layer of cold sweat. The memories came without warning, slamming into her with such force that she curled into a protective ball.

She was grateful that Gavin was already gone for the day. A text from Carmen drew her out of the past and into the present. Today, she was supposed to help Alice at the dog shelter. She didn't want to leave the house, but Gavin would know something was wrong if she didn't go. She forced herself to dress, put on makeup, and go downstairs.

"Lyla," Blade said and gestured to the waiting SUV.

"I want to drive myself," she said, glad for the shield of sunglasses. Her eyes were still a little swollen. Blade would have reported that small detail to Gavin.

Blade hesitated and then, "Security-wise, this is the safer choice."

She held up the keys to Gavin's Aston Martin. "Can you have one of the guys bring the car around?"

"Lyla..."

"Blade, not today," she said shortly.

Blade tossed the keys to one of the men and pulled out his phone. She scowled as he spoke to Gavin.

"Lyla wants to drive herself," Blade said without preamble, and then extended the phone to her.

She snatched it from him and snapped, "I'm driving myself."

"Why?" Gavin asked.

"Because I want to."

"It's safer to—"

"I need some space today, Gavin," she said, and her voice shook.

"What's wrong?"

"Nothing. I just want to drive myself."

Gavin didn't say anything for a moment, and then said, "Give the phone back to Blade."

She did as she was told and hurried to the Aston Martin. The guard blinked when she got behind the wheel. Blade rushed to an SUV and got into the driver's seat. She blew out a breath. Gavin wasn't going to push the issue, thank God.

Two SUVs flanked her as she made her way to Aunt Isabel's house. After she parked in the driveway, she went in and chatted with her aunt before Carmen came downstairs in Ugg's, ripped designer jeans, and a crop top.

"Why are you driving yourself?" Carmen asked when they walked outside.

"Because I feel like it," she said shortly.

Carmen's brows went up. "What's up with you?"

"Bad dreams." She rolled her shoulders to relieve the itch between her shoulder blades.

"Are you fighting with Gavin?"

"No."

"Is it because he was a prick at Incognito?"

She glanced at Carmen as she backed out of the driveway. "A prick?"

"Gavin's tiff with Kody was in the papers."

"That's your fault," she said sourly. "I think Kody wanted to ask me about you. Gavin got pissed when he tried to pull me to the side."

"I'm telling you, Kody's an idiot."

"What about you?"

Carmen laughed. "Alice turned out to be good company after five shots."

"What? You didn't corrupt her, did you?"

"Just a little. I took care of her after she puked her guts out. Alice couldn't go in to work the next day and vowed never to party with me again. Can we get coffee?"

She navigated through the neighborhood and rolled her eyes when Blade changed lanes, nearly running someone off the road.

"Poor Alice. What kind of coffee do you want?" she asked as she pulled up to a Starbucks drive-through.

"Get me a triple tall latte and a maple scone. What do you want?"

"Nothing."

"Are you sick?"

"No." She sucked in a fortifying breath and shoved down the tears just beneath the surface. "I'm just bitchy, and nothing tastes good."

Carmen hummed happily as she drank coffee and nibbled on her scone. Lyla followed the GPS instructions to the dog shelter and found a bus of casino workers with Alice and a photographer. Everyone wore bright orange T-shirts with the Pyre Casino logo. Alice clapped her hands in delight when she caught sight of Lyla and gave Carmen a frosty smile before she introduced them to the other volunteers. A low murmur of surprise rumbled through the crowd when Alice introduced her as Gavin's wife. Blade and the other guards joined the group and were forced to wear matching T-shirts. Alice gave a rundown of tasks they were going to do, which included baths, cleaning kennels, and walking the dogs.

"This place looks like a prison," Carmen muttered under her breath.

Lyla agreed as a staff member led them through the building. Her heart wrenched as dogs pressed against their cages, yipping and crying out for attention. She stopped and pressed her hands against a gate. A large gray pit bull went up on its hind legs and licked her hand.

"Hi, boy," she whispered. "You're gorgeous."

"Gavin might get a new bed buddy," Carmen said with a wicked grin.

She forced herself to walk away from the pit bull named Beau and finished the tour of the dog shelter. She opted to walk the dogs while Carmen decided to help at the bathing station. The first dog she took out of a cage was a small Yorkie that barked at the other dogs as he pranced by. She actually found the walking path soothing, but the Yorkie didn't have the stamina to make it halfway along the trail. She carried the dog back to the kennel and made a mark on the dog's sheet to let the other staff know she had walked him. She walked and walked, but didn't seem to be getting anywhere. There were too many dogs and not enough volunteers. It warmed her heart to see Blade cleaning the kennels. He didn't have to participate, but did so because he was a good guy. That made her feel like a bitch since she threw a fit this morning and made his job difficult.

Hours passed. When everyone else took a break to eat lunch, she made her way over to Beau. She talked to the pit bull until he calmed down. She scratched him behind the ears and smiled when he closed his eyes in delight. She opened the kennel, and even though Beau pulled at his leash, he eased up once they were outside. He sniffed the air and hopped around playfully before he fell into step beside her.

She could relate to Beau's joy at being out of his cage. She was slowly learning how to live again. These abandoned dogs hoped someone would take them home. They needed a second chance, like her. Flashbacks hit her at the strangest times. She could be swimming or watching TV, and all of a sudden, she would be covered in cold sweat, unable to breathe as she remembered being stabbed or the sound of Manny's tortured screams. Carmen reassured her that the panic attacks were normal, considering all she'd been through. She didn't want to tell Gavin because there was nothing he could do, and he had his own demons to battle.

She glanced down at Beau and wondered what his story was. Had he been abused, or had his family decided they couldn't take care of him? Maybe he'd been found on the side of the road? Beau trotted along, marking shrubs and trees as they went. No matter what happened in his past, it wasn't stopping him from enjoying the moment. She tipped her head up to the sun, took a deep breath, and everything went black.

SOMETHING wet and slimy slid over her face. She turned her face away and moaned. She heard a scream, and then the sound of someone running over gravel. She shielded her eyes against the sunlight and blinked at Beau, who stood over her, tongue lolling. She grimaced when she caught a whiff of his doggy breath.

"Oh, my God! What happened? Did the dog attack you? Mr. Pyre is going to kill me!" Alice shouted as she grabbed Beau's leash and pulled him away from Lyla, who lay flat on her back on the walking path.

"He didn't attack me. I think I passed out," she said and put a hand to her forehead as she sat up. She dropped her face between her knees and tried to think straight.

"Did you take a break?" Alice asked.

"No."

"Oh my God, I overworked the CEO's wife," Alice said, wringing her hands.

"No, I'm fine. I'm just not feeling like myself today. I wanted to walk Beau before I got a drink."

"Phil! Phil! Come over here. She fainted!" Alice said, bouncing up and down in well-used sneakers.

An attractive man wearing worn jeans and a gray T-shirt ambled over. He pet the dog before he hunkered down beside her. Phil fixed her with an unsettling, piercing look.

"How ya feeling?"

"Crappy," she admitted.

"This heat isn't helping," he said and hauled her up.

She swayed on her feet and tried to blink away the black spots marring her vision. Phil tightened his hold.

"Come, let's get you in the air conditioning," he said and helped her inside.

Alice followed with Beau, who nudged the back of Lyla's leg as if he were worried about her. Alice led Beau back to his kennel. She silently promised Beau that she'd come back and give him a decent walk. It wasn't his fault that she fainted on the path. Shit. How long would it be before he saw daylight?

Phil led her to an office not much bigger than a closet, with pictures of dogs and cats covering the walls. He uncapped a water bottle and handed it to her. She took a healthy gulp.

"Here."

Phil held out a handful of Wheat Thins. Under normal circumstances, she wouldn't take crackers from his questionably clean hands, but she was desperate. She nodded in thanks, and once she began to munch, instantly began to feel better. Phil gave her that direct look again.

"What?" she asked defensively.

"People don't just pass out. It's not that hot."

"I know. I've been feeling strange all day."

Phil cocked his head to the side. "Are you pregnant?"

Even as her body went cold with shock, she shook her head. "No."

"How do you know?"

She glared at him. "Why do you want to know?"

"I don't want you to sue me."

"What?"

"I run this place. Volunteers passing out aren't good advertisement."

"Oh. Well, I'm fine now." But she didn't get up because her legs were still trembling.

"Maybe you should go to the hospital."

"No."

"I insist. If you're not pregnant, it could be something else. You don't want to take chances. Plus, you look like shit."

Before she could respond to that, Carmen appeared in the doorway. Her cousin looked as if she'd been in a wet T-shirt contest. Her crop top was nearly transparent, her jeans were covered in fur, and her Ugg's squelched with each step. Phil perked up.

"I heard you fainted," Carmen said. "Are you sick?"

"I'm not sick; I just feel queasy," she said and gave Phil a dirty look.

"Who are you?" Carmen asked, getting right to the point.

"I'm Phil, a vet."

Carmen raised a brow. "And you're examining Lyla?"

Apparently, Carmen thought this was hilarious because she grinned. Phil's head kicked back as if Carmen's beauty had the power to physically move him. She didn't know whether to be amused or irritated.

"In your professional opinion, what's wrong with her? You think she has fleas, or she's in heat?" Carmen asked with mock seriousness.

"I assumed she was pregnant, but she says it's not possible," Phil said.

Carmen's head whipped toward Lyla. "Pregnant?"

"I'm not," she said.

"What? How do you know? Are you on something?"

Lyla gave Phil a pointed look, but he didn't budge. He seemed to be transfixed by the exotic creature in his shitty office.

She wiped her clammy brow. "I had my period recently."

Carmen looked at Phil. "She can still spot if she's pregnant, right?"

Phil blinked. "I really don't know much about human women who are breeding."

"Right," she drawled and forced herself up. "I think I'm done for the day. I'll come back to walk Beau and the others another time."

"Thanks, Doc." Carmen winked at Phil before she followed Lyla into the hallway. "Are you sure you're not pregnant?"

"Positive."

Carmen didn't say anything as Blade jogged up to them. He stopped, and they got a whiff of a very distinct poop smell. They both took a step back.

"What happened? Alice said you fainted," Blade said.

"I'm fine." She bounced to show that she was fine, and instantly regretted it when another wave of nausea hit her. "You know, I think I really need something to eat."

"Let me get you a bologna sandwich."

She blanched. "No, I need something..." She waved her hand. "Light and fresh."

"Like what?"

"Some noodle salad or something," she said, knowing she sounded nuts but not caring. She wanted some light, fluffy meal from the deli section of a supermarket. She didn't know exactly what she wanted but...

"Okay," Blade said and pulled out his phone. "I have to call Gavin."

"Why? Nothing happened!"

"Do you want me to die?" Blade asked as he dialed.

"I'm—" She ground her teeth and then snatched Blade's phone before he could speak.

"Blade? What is it?" Gavin asked brusquely on the other end.

"Hey, baby," she said and slapped Blade's hand away.

"Lyla?"

"Yeah, something happened at the dog shelter and Blade's overreacting," she said and ignored Blade's glare.

"What happened?"

She grimaced. Gavin sounded calm, but she knew better. "I'm just not feeling well, that's all. I'm fine, though. We're leaving now."

"Are you sick? Should I call the doctor?"

"No, I'm fine. Too much sun."

"You're going home?"

"Yes. We'll pick up something to eat first."

"Okay. I'll see you tonight."

"Okay. Love you," she said and hung up. She handed the phone back to Blade. "I'm fine."

He shook his head but didn't push it. She apologized to Alice, who told her to get some rest. Her first "job" and she passed out within a couple of hours. What the hell? If Gavin heard that she fainted, he would see it as a sign that she shouldn't volunteer, which was bullshit. Maybe she shouldn't have volunteered after her episode this morning.

Blade wouldn't let her drive, which was probably a good thing. He gave the Aston Martin keys to one of the guards, who would stay to finish their tasks. Carmen was unusually quiet as they climbed into the SUV. Lyla belted herself in, leaned back, and closed her eyes. She told Blade which supermarket to go to and rolled down the windows since they were all pretty smelly.

"Before I ruined everything, how did bath time go?" Lyla asked.

"I don't think some of those dogs have ever had baths. They fought me like crazy, but they looked fab afterward. One of the dogs howled when I tried to blow dry him. I want to go back. There's so much to do."

"I'm sure Phil will enjoy that," she said and patted Blade's shoulder. "Thanks for helping."

Blade didn't reply. He parked, and they walked into the store. Carmen grabbed a hand basket and disappeared, while Lyla went to the deli and found a pasta salad. She grabbed fresh bread and some spreads, while Blade grabbed something for himself. Carmen insisted on paying for everything.

Lyla grabbed one of three shopping bags. "What did you buy?"

"Odds and ends. I'll eat at your place, and one of the guys can take me home later," Carmen said.

She was too busy eating her salad and ripping off a chunk of bread to care. Carmen handed her chilled green tea. She was a bit taken aback, but enjoyed the cool refreshment. They carried everything into the house and ate at the table.

"Come on, you have to finish your drink," Carmen said. "You're dehydrated."

She finished the drink, so her cousin would stop fussing. Carmen chatted about the different dogs and their needs. She was happy that Carmen enjoyed herself and also wanted to return. She agreed, with Beau on her mind. Pit bulls had such a bad rep, but Beau was a sweetheart. While Blade and Carmen chatted, she went upstairs to pee. She was startled when someone pounded on the door.

"What are you doing?" Carmen shouted.

Lyla stared at the door. "Um, I'm using the bathroom."

"Number one or number two?"

Seriously? "Why do you care?"

"Because I have to pee too."

"Go to another bathroom!"

"Why? You said you're doing number one. Just don't flush."

"What?"

"You're wasting water, and we live in the desert!" Carmen slapped her hand on the door for emphasis. "We need to conserve as much water as possible!"

Used to Carmen's outbursts and eccentricities, she opened the door to her cousin, who clapped her on the back like a bro and shut the door in her face. She went downstairs and found the cook in the kitchen.

"How are you today, Mrs. Pyre?" she asked.

"I'm okay," she said and backed away at the smell of steamed broccoli.

"Is something wrong?"

She waved a hand in front of her face. "I don't know."

The cook stared at her. "You like broccoli, right?"

"I do normally, but... maybe I'm coming down with some kind of weird bug."

"A bug," the cook repeated carefully. "You know I can prepare anything you want. In the past, Mr. Pyre preferred that I make meals at home and deliver, but I'm not opposed to coming here if you want to request something special."

"Oh, no, I'm fine. I'm sure it'll pass."

A bloodcurdling scream rang out from the top of the stairs. She bolted upstairs with Blade on her heels. She ran to the master bathroom and found Carmen on the floor, holding something to her chest with her head bowed, rocking back and forth. What the hell? Wondering if her cousin was having a grieving episode, she got down on her knees and gave her a hug.

"Are you hurt?"

Carmen shook her head. Blade closed the door to give them privacy.

"What's going on?" she asked.

Carmen mumbled something incoherent.

"What is it? You're scaring me."

Carmen raised her tear-streaked face. The broad grin on her face startled Lyla.

"You're pregnant," Carmen said.

Her arms fell away. "What? What are you talking about?"

"I did a pregnancy test using the pee you left in the toilet."

It took a moment for her to register what Carmen was saying.

When it penetrated, she fell back on her ass. Her cousin held up a white wand with the word 'pregnant' on it. Lyla snatched the test and shook it as if it were an eight-ball and the words would change.

"I can't be. I just had my period two weeks ago."

"I looked it up on my phone. Initially, you can still spot when you're pregnant."

She couldn't describe the feelings rushing through her. She leaped to her feet and jabbed the wand at her cousin. "You had no right to do this!"

Carmen stared at her. "Don't you want to know?"

She paced around the bathroom, blindsided by the news. She was still trying to overcome panic attacks, bad dreams, and depression, and now she was pregnant? She stopped and shook her head. "I want to take another test."

Carmen got to her feet, watching her cautiously. "Lyla, you can't fake this kind of stuff."

"B-but I'm not ready," she stammered.

Carmen held up both hands. "Wait, do you want to be pregnant?"

"Yes. No. Not right now."

"But you haven't been on birth control. You must have known this was a possibility."

She ignored that. "You bought a test at the store?"

"Yes."

"Do you have another one?"

"Yes. Can you pee again?"

"That's why you gave me that green tea, isn't it?"

Carmen nodded.

She didn't have to pee, so she tossed the wand in the trash and hurried downstairs with Carmen on her heels. Blade was nowhere to be found, which was a good thing, considering she wouldn't be able to hide that something was wrong. She downed two bottles of water while Carmen pulled a bouquet out of her shopping bag and arranged the flowers on the dining table.

Lyla couldn't stay still. She went outside to get some fresh air and paced around the pool, arms wrapped around herself. She couldn't be pregnant, could she? Yes, she hadn't taken the pills, which left her open to pregnancy, but they had been married less than four months. What were the chances that Gavin had super sperm? Oh, God, he would be ecstatic. She covered her face with both hands. Gavin Pyre, former crime lord, CEO of Pyre Casinos, husband, and maybe baby daddy. Pregnant... She felt a surge of protectiveness, joy, and terror when she thought about the being that could be growing in her tummy.

When she was ready for the next test, she rushed into the house, interrupting Carmen and the cook, who were deep in conversation. The second pregnancy test was on the vanity. Lyla was trying to read the directions when Carmen barged in.

"Here."

Carmen took the wand out of the box, uncapped it, and rushed her over to the toilet. "You have to pee on here," she instructed.

Carmen obviously wasn't going anywhere, and Lyla was feeling strangely vulnerable, so she didn't say anything. After she peed on the stick, Carmen recapped it and set it on the counter.

"Now we wait."

She sat on the edge of the tub and clasped her hands together. "Oh, my God."

Carmen sat beside her. "Aren't you excited?"

"I don't know. I knew this was a possibility, but I never thought I would get pregnant." She couldn't take her eyes off the innocent looking wand that would change her life.

"Have you talked about kids?"

"Yes. He wants them badly."

"Well, he's older than you are."

"Yes." She hesitated and then confided, "When he was in jail, he had a dream about a little girl named Nora. He said the dream was so real he could smell her, feel her weight against his chest. She gave him hope."

"Nora," Carmen said quietly. "I like it. His mother's name, right?"

She nodded. "I wanted to go on birth control, but after he told that story, I couldn't. I didn't want to take that away from him. He believes our kids will be his redemption."

"You might be making his dreams come true, but what about yours?"

"It's too late now, isn't it?" she asked with a hollow laugh, gesturing to the pregnancy test.

"You have choices, Lyla."

"Like what?"

Carmen pinched her. "You know how I feel about Gavin."

"Actually, I'm not sure what you think about him anymore."

Carmen straightened her shoulders. "I didn't really know Gavin when you started dating him. I just liked the fact we were cousins dating cousins. I thought that was cool. I knew Gavin loved you, and Vinny loved me. In my mind, that's all we needed. I didn't care what they did on the side, as long as they came home to us. I had no idea Gavin would cheat on you. I felt just as betrayed as you did. I trusted Gavin to take care of you, to love you as your father never had, and he failed. Then he killed that man in your basement, and you begged me to help you leave. Helping you escape, knowing I may never see you again, was one of the hardest things I ever had to do." Carmen let out a ragged breath. "Gavin never stopped looking for you. I didn't know if you were better off without him. I'm not going to lie. When he brought you back, I would do almost anything to make you stay. I'm glad that Manny got involved. You've always had a strong connection with him, almost as strong as your connection with Gavin."

She brushed away tears. Manny would never see his grandchild. Her child never knowing its paternal grandfather made her heart ache with grief, bitterness, and anger. Life was so unfair... and his killer was still out there. She shivered.

"Manny made Gavin see reason, and Gavin began to treat you like the queen you are. Then Vinny died."

Carmen's voice was flat and emotionless. She put an arm around her cousin to comfort her.

"Everything started to fall apart. Manny was murdered, and I almost lost you again." Carmen sniffled. "I'm glad you asked me to get you out of Vegas. It's what I was planning for myself, and I was glad to have a partner, even though I suspected Gavin would look for you. I was right." Carmen let out a watery laugh. "God, he is one stubborn son of a bitch."

Some of her anxiety slipped away. If they could get through the murders of their loved ones, they could handle this.

"When he came for you in Montana, I couldn't read him, and that scared the crap out of me. I didn't know if he would punish you for leaving. When he forced you to marry him, I was even more alarmed. In the jet, he nearly hit me." When she opened her mouth, Carmen patted her hand. "I know Gavin's been through the wringer, and he carries a lot of guilt on his shoulders. We're all scarred by what happened, and Gavin doesn't know how to deal with losing his father and best friend. I get it. We're women, and we have each other. Gavin? He only has you. When I saw you at the funeral, I knew."

"Knew what?"

"That he had let you in all the way. His shields were down. He wasn't a coldblooded robot; he was just... Gavin. You make him human. He needs you." Carmen let out a choked sob and leaned forward, hands over her chest. "It's the way Vinny needed me. I miss him so much."

She rested her head on her cousin's shoulder. They cried together, their sobs echoing in the bathroom.

"I'm happy for you, even though I think he's a shithead." Carmen helped her to her feet and clasped their hands together. "Life moves on, which means we have to as well. I'm so happy for you. I'm going to be here for you every step of the way. Everything will be fine. You know that, right?"

She nodded, too overcome to speak.

"Are you ready?" Carmen asked.

She took a deep breath, walked to the vanity, and peered down at the wand.

Pregnant.

Her head spun. "Oh, my God."

Carmen squealed. "I'm going to be an aunty!"

"And I'm going to be a mom," she said, and felt her world tilt sideways.

Carmen pushed her on a bench and clapped her hands together. "Okay, so I already talked to your cook. She's going to come daily to prepare meals, since you're sensitive to certain foods right now. She's preparing something extra special for tonight."

"What? Why?"

"You have to tell Gavin, right?"

She took a deep breath. "Yes."

"How do you want to tell him?"

"What do you mean?"

Carmen fetched her phone. "On the ride home, I went on YouTube and there are all these ways women have told their husbands they're pregnant. Here, watch this one; it's so *cute!*"

She watched a woman send her husband on a scavenger hunt. Carmen proceeded to show her at least eight videos of women telling their husbands they were pregnant in creative ways. Instead of being inspired, it made her feel more nervous.

"Can't I just tell him?"

Carmen's face dropped. "Well, yeah, but this is your first. Don't you want it to be extra special?"

"I can't imagine telling Gavin to get a bun out of the oven or giving him a crossword that he has to figure out. That's just not us."

"Okay." Carmen pocketed her phone, clearly disappointed, but then she lit up again. "Oh, my gosh. You will not believe what I found at the store! It's going to be perfect!"

Carmen ran out of the bathroom. She listened to the sound of her thundering downstairs while she stared at the positive pregnancy test. Her life would never be the same. Carmen came back with a pink onesie in her hands that said, "Daddy's Princess." Lyla clapped a hand over her chest because it felt as if her heart was breaking.

"They didn't have a boy outfit, so I guess this is meant to be."

"It's perfect," she choked out and hugged her cousin. "What would I do without you?"

"You'll never have to know."

"Will you be her godmother?"

Carmen burst into tears.

WHEN GAVIN WALKED through the front door, she was relieved. Carmen had been going crazy on Pinterest for hours. Lyla was so wound up that she wanted to blurt it out the second she saw him. Instead, she ran and threw herself into his arms.

Gavin gave her a deep kiss. "You all right, baby girl?"

"I am now."

He looked past her and noticed Carmen. "What happened to you?"

"This is what you look like after you give ten dogs a bath," Carmen said with a hand on her hip.

"How's your mother?" he asked.

Surprised and pleased he was trying to be social and considerate, she patted his chest.

"She cleans a lot," Carmen said with a shrug, "but her friends signed her up for salsa classes, so she's been going out more."

"Have you made any plans?"

"Like?"

"If you want to buy a house, or if you're going to stay here?"

Carmen glanced at Lyla with a mischievous twinkle in her eye. "I'm not planning to leave anytime soon."

He relaxed slightly. "The RV is in a safe place. I didn't get rid of it."

"Good to know," Carmen said and eyed him. "What are your plans?"

"Excuse me?"

"What's your plan for the future?"

"To keep Lyla happy and safe."

Lyla glanced between the two people she loved most and wanted to shake her head. They glared at one another as if they were adversaries.

"Bye, Carmen!" she said deliberately.

Carmen sniffed. "One of your guys is taking me home. Lyla, call me later."

She waved and looked up at Gavin. "You want to shower before we eat?"

"Yeah." He cupped her face. "You sure you're okay?"

"Yes." How would he react to her news? He made it clear that he wanted her pregnant, but how would he be after he realized he was successful? Her enthusiasm dimmed as old insecurities crept in.

"I'll be quick," he said and kissed her. He paused and dropped his nose to her neck and inhaled. "You smell good."

"Pomegranate body wash."

"Yum."

He slapped her ass and went upstairs. She paced and chewed her nails. She felt as if there was a balloon expanding in her chest. It kept growing until she couldn't breathe properly. She grabbed her wine glass, which held sparkling apple cider. She imagined it was wine and downed it in one gulp. The dining table was set with the flowers Carmen bought and candles. Because she had to do something, she prepared their plates. When Gavin appeared, he took in the table setting.

"What's the occasion?" he asked.

"Your cook wanted to do something nice for us," she said, and made a concentrated effort not to look at the gift bag on the chair.

He fingered the petals of a flower. "Nice."

They sat, and he immediately dug into the meal. She examined him furtively. He wasn't the same man she fell in love with as a teenager. At eighteen, how could she have prepared herself for a life with him? They had their highs and lows, and now, here they were, expectant parents. She tried to imagine Gavin holding a baby. The image tugged at her heartstrings. He was such an alpha. If he loved their baby as much as he loved her, their daughter would never want to leave home. *It might not be a girl*, she reminded herself.

"How was the dog shelter?" he asked.

"Um, it was great," she said and forced herself to eat. "I want to volunteer there regularly. Carmen does too. She bathed dogs, and I took them out of their kennels and walked them on this path. There was this cute pit bull, Beau, that I walked—"

"A what?"

She frowned. "A pitbull."

"Pit bulls are one of the most aggressive breeds in the world."

"He's not aggressive. He's a sweetheart. When I fainted, he just stayed with me until someone found me—" She broke off when he dropped his fork. "What?"

"Did you just say you fainted?" he asked in a quiet, icy voice.

Oh, shit. "I felt a little dizzy, and I had a spell, but I'm fine now."

"Why the fuck didn't Blade take you to the hospital?"

He looked murderous. Things were spinning out of control, as usual. She splayed a hand on his chest, which was hard as a rock.

"Gavin, I'm fine."

"Will you stop saying that? People don't pass out if they're fine. And you were walking a pit bull that could have mauled—"

"Gavin!" She braced her hands on his shoulders. "Nothing happened."

"Something sure as fuck did happen. You lied to me," he growled.

"But I'm fine now." She jumped with her hands in the air. "See? I'm fine."

"But you fainted."

"I didn't eat. I was stupid, and it's not Blade's fault. He tried to tell you, but I took his phone. I'm sorry."

"You realize you hold my sanity in your hands?" Amber eyes probed hers. "Take care, baby girl."

"I will," she said and leaned into him. She didn't want to tell him about the baby when he was pissed off. She needed him calm. God, he was going to be an absolute pain in the ass when he found out she was pregnant.

"You're not allowed to walk any dog over ten pounds," he snapped.

She sighed. "I'm telling you, this pit bull was adorable. When I passed out, he stayed right by my side."

He ran a hand down his face.

"*What*, Gavin?"

"He could have killed you!"

"Don't be dramatic," she chided as she sat on his lap and draped an arm around his neck. "I know how to deal with beasts." She wagged her eyebrows at him, but he wasn't amused.

His hand squeezed her hip. "Lyla, I don't know how to tell you this."

"What?"

He wrapped an arm around her waist and squeezed. "Nothing can happen to you."

She softened. "Nothing will."

His hand went to her chest and unerringly found the stab wound inches from her heart. "I've had too many close calls. I want to chain you to the bed with a twenty-four-hour guard, but you won't let me, and you need to live your life. I get that, and I'm trying and..." He turned her, so she straddled his lap and laid his head on her chest. "You're making this damn hard."

She ran her hands through his hair. "I'm fine."

"You have to be."

He tipped his head back. When she brushed kisses over his face, he closed his eyes, clearly reveling in her love. She wondered if this was how Manny had been with his wife. They stayed like that for long minutes, just holding one another. Slowly, his tension eased. Their meal was forgotten as they took comfort in one another. When he was relaxed and content, she knew it was time.

"I have something for you," she said.

"What?" he asked without opening his eyes.

"Keep your eyes closed. Let me get it."

She scooted off his lap. Her heart began to speed up as she stared at him in the candlelight. He was devilishly handsome. He hadn't lost an ounce of the muscle he gained in jail. She loved him—always had and always would. He owned her, heart and soul, and it went both ways.

Carmen wanted her to announce her pregnancy with rose petals, balloons, or a new lingerie set. That wasn't them. The big society wedding never happened, and that was fine with her. So much of his life was in the spotlight. These moments were special and poignant. In her eyes, the simpler, the better, and Carmen had conceded reluctantly. She took a deep breath and placed the gift bag on his lap. He opened his eyes and looked at the bag and then her.

"What's this?"

She could feel the tears crawling up her throat. She waved a hand. "Just look inside."

He sat up, peered into the bag, and pulled out the small outfit. He frowned, and when he held it up with both hands, the onesie unfolded, showing the message on the front. He didn't react for a moment, and then he erupted from his seat. Any semblance of relaxation vanished. The air crackled around him with manic energy.

"Are you pregnant?"

She nodded and pulled the positive pregnancy test from her pocket and held it out to him. "I took two. They're both positive."

He took the pregnancy test and looked from the white stick to the onesie and back again. His ecstatic expression was too much for her. Tears trickled down her cheeks. He tossed everything on the table and hauled her into his arms.

"Thank God. Thank you, thank you," he said into her hair.

"You're happy?" she mumbled into his chest.

"This is the best day of my life." He tilted her chin up and raked her face with assessing eyes. "Are you happy?"

"I'm scared," she whispered.

"And happy?"

"Yes."

He closed his eyes, but not before she saw a glimmer of wet. He kissed her, his tongue caressing and claiming, before he released her. She stared as he backed up and punched his fist in the air.

"I'm going to be a dad!"

He rushed toward the front door and opened it. She caught a glimpse of Blade's alarmed expression before Gavin shouted the news for his security team to hear. Blade smiled and clapped him on the back. After a round of congratulations, Gavin came back in and rushed toward her. He unbuttoned her shirt and splayed his hands over her still flat stomach.

"Okay, tell me everything," he ordered.

She told him about her sensitive stomach and how Carmen tricked her into taking the pregnancy test. Gavin laughed uproariously.

"Thank God for Carmen," he said. "So, you don't know how far along, nothing?"

"No, I have an appointment tomorrow with an obstetrician."

"I'm coming."

"Yes, I want you there." She was terrified. How did single mothers do this? She would demand that Gavin be there every step of the way.

"Nora's coming," he said, running his hands over her scarred abdomen.

"We don't know if it's a girl."

"Then we keep trying until we do." He caught her up in his arms. "Holy shit, I'm happy."

He carried her to the couch and set her on the cushions before he dragged off her shorts and underwear and then his own pants. His cock lay flat against his belly, he was so turned on. He crouched over her, rubbing his dick against her entrance as he kissed her breathless. His hands moved over her, rough and possessive.

"I can't wait," he muttered as he slid inside her. He shuddered and looked down at her like the warrior he was. "You belong to me, Lyla Pyre."

"Every inch," she reassured him.

"Every breath." He brushed his thumb over her bottom lip. "Every moan." He slid out so only the tip of him was inside her, and then thrust back in, slow and easy. She caught her breath, and he grinned. "Every smile. Mine."

"And I own you," she declared, wrapping her legs around his waist and forcing him deeper. "You're going to be with me every step of the way. I'm not doing this alone."

"I'm going to be there for everything." He ran his hands down her sides. "You're going to be beautiful pregnant. I know it."

She grimaced. "From what I read today, it's not going to be pretty."

"I'm game, baby."

"I want a dog," she blurted.

He paused. "What?"

"If we have kids, I want a dog. I've always wanted one, but my dad wouldn't let me."

"Then get one," he said carelessly, and leaned down to taste her neck. "God, you smell good."

She felt a frisson of excitement and arched her back.

"You're asking for it," he growled.

"Yes, I am," she said in a deliberately breathy voice as she trailed her hand between them and cupped his balls. "Are you going to give it to me?"

His eyes went blind with animal lust. He sat up and forced her legs to unwind from around him. He draped her legs over his shoulders and fucked her hard. She dug her nails into the cushion beneath her as pleasure ripped through her. He powered into her with short, hard thrusts that shoved her toward climax.

"Come on, baby girl, I want to feel you come."

A wicked finger applied pressure to her clit, and she came with a scream.

"I want my men to hear you," he said as he kept up his rhythm. "Who owns you, Lyla?"

"You do," she panted.

"Yes." He pulled out and wrapped a fist around his cock as he came on her belly. "You're mine."

"I know."

"And this baby binds you to me," he said, massaging his semen into her skin. "You'll never be able to escape me now."

"You have to be the most primitive man on the planet."

"Most men are like me, but they suffocate their beast beneath a layer of politeness and civility. I don't bother."

11

GAVIN

Lyla was trying to kill him. He paced around his office and resisted the urge to go home and spank his wife's rebellious ass. She adopted that fucking pit bull! She had no fear or sense of self-preservation. Blade reassured him that the pit bull acted like a cocker spaniel around his wife, following her everywhere and not showing any signs of aggression, but hell! For the past month, she had visited the animal shelter three times a week. She never mentioned the pit bull, so he assumed she listened to him and walked Chihuahuas or some other yappy dog she could easily control. Instead, his wife befriended the most aggressive breed in the shelter. That shouldn't surprise him. Against all the odds, she was with him, a fucking murderer, and he worshipped the ground she walked on. If she decided to shine her light on anything, it would blossom as he had. She had been drawn to this dog from the start, so he wouldn't be able to banish it without his wife raising hell. Fuck! Didn't she understand how much she meant to him?

He slammed his fist against the glass wall of his office and glared out at the red mountains surrounding Las Vegas. Since Lyla announced her pregnancy, he'd become a fucking savage. He was overprotective, oversexed, and overbearing. Carmen informed him that he was acting like a psycho. The beast he usually kept chained in the deep recesses of his mind prowled on the surface, waiting for another disaster to strike. He was ecstatic about Lyla and the baby. He'd never been so fucking happy, but he was so vulnerable. Everyone knew how he felt about his wife. He couldn't hide it and didn't want to. He was waiting for another attack and couldn't stand the suspense. He'd done too much shit in the underworld for those fuckers to allow him to live out a normal life. The men who lived in the underworld lived shit lives, where paranoia and a lack of empathy kept them alive. They wouldn't let him get away scot-free.

Lyla was four months pregnant, and he could barely contain himself. This weekend was the gender reveal party. He was ninety-nine percent certain the baby was a girl. He prayed every night that Nora would be here soon. Having a girl would be confirmation from God that he was forgiven for his sins. Nora would be his absolution, his redemption. Until then, he was a condemned man.

In jail, he contemplated suicide. Pyre Casinos would've continued without him, and Lyla would have moved on. Everyone connected to him was in danger, and he deserved to die for the shit he allowed to happen to those under his protection. A wave of exhaustion had forced him into an uneasy sleep, and that night, he dreamed of Nora. Since then, he focused on getting Lyla back and trying to repair what was left of their souls. The feel of Nora's little arms going around him was something he had to experience in this lifetime.

He worked out in the boxing ring every day and ate as much as an athlete training for the Olympics. He made sure Lyla went to the gun range and that he practiced as well. He trained for an attack he knew would come. And when it came, he would hit back so hard, no one would dare touch what was his. Those bastards weren't allowed to touch something so elegant and pure. Lyla and the baby were his to protect, and he would do so with his dying breath. Whatever it cost to keep his family, he would pay.

A cursory knock sounded on his door before Marcus entered. He had a stack of papers in his hand, and he was on the phone. Gavin turned to glare at him as Marcus finished the call.

"Something wrong?" Marcus asked.

"My wife adopted a pit bull," he growled.

Marcus grinned. "From the shelter?"

Know-it-all bastard. "Yes."

Marcus shrugged. "Your wife isn't stupid. She knows what she's doing."

"I know that," he spat. "What do you want?"

"Are you inviting me to the baby gender reveal?"

"How the fuck do you know all this shit?"

"I have my sources," Marcus said. "So, am I invited?"

"You want to go to a gender reveal party?"

"It's your baby gender reveal party, not some stranger's. Plus, I love your wife—"

"No."

Marcus never failed to push his buttons. He didn't care that there was no sexual attraction between Lyla and Marcus. He didn't like the way Marcus made her laugh or that she allowed him to put a brotherly arm around her. Marcus enjoyed her company, and he couldn't stand it, not when he was so on edge. Hearing Marcus say he loved his wife, even jokingly, made his blood pressure rise.

"Fine. I think she's a goddess," Marcus amended.

He crossed his arms. "Not even that."

"God, you're a possessive son of a bitch."

"Yes, I am." He wouldn't apologize for it. Lyla was his.

"Whatever, man. What do you bring to a gender reveal party?"

"How the hell do I know?"

"Do you want a boy or girl?"

"Girl."

Marcus blinked. "Why? So, you can beat the crap out of any man who tries to date her?"

His stomach clenched. He had been so focused on the image of a little girl that he never considered what would happen when she grew up. Dating? Fuck no.

"Since you want a girl, I'm going Team Boy." Marcus waved the papers. "I need your signature, big guy."

He forced himself to sit when he wanted to pummel someone. "What is it?"

"Contract renewals and my research on building another tower." Marcus set the stack down with a flourish.

Marcus wanted to build another tower that would cater to homeowners. He didn't want to cater to anyone, but Marcus was convinced it would be a great investment for high rollers.

"I'll read your report, but I'm not making any promises," he said as he signed the contracts after a cursory glance.

Vinny had been more laid-back. Marcus wasn't born into the role and was hungry to keep Pyre Casinos at the forefront. He collected business contacts as if they were going out of style and wanted to be involved in everything from housekeeping standards to the safety of the pole dancers in the clubs. Marcus was on top of everything, including his boss. He had no idea how Marcus had time to monitor his activities when his schedule was jam-packed. Nosy young bastard. On the other hand, he admired Marcus's innovation, drive, and fearlessness. Marcus had done more to advance Pyre Casinos than he had in five years. After he took over the position of crime lord, it became Vinny's job to run Pyre Casinos smoothly.

"When are you going to the boxing ring on Monday?" Marcus asked.

He shouldn't be surprised that Marcus knew he boxed every day. His secretary kept a two-hour window open, so he could train. If no one was available to train in the ring, he went to the gym.

"I have meetings in the afternoon, so I'll work out at ten. Why?"

"I'll join you."

He hid a wolfish grin. Getting Marcus in the ring might be fun. "I'm looking forward to it. Now, get out of my office."

"See you at the party tomorrow. What time does it start?"

"Noon. Do you know where I live?"

"Of course."

Marcus snatched the signed papers and exited with a spring in his step. Promoting Marcus was one of the best decisions he ever made, but the damn kid was getting on his nerves. He paced as he read Marcus's proposal and snorted in disgust before he tossed it on his desk. He logged onto his computer and ignored Marcus's email asking what he thought of his business plan. The proposal was ambitious and brilliant, but he wouldn't tell Marcus that. No, he would let the young bastard quake in his shoes and make him think it was a no-go. There were investors waiting for his go-ahead, but he would make them wait.

He made some phone calls and walked through the casino with his head of security. He greeted a high roller who occupied the presidential suite for a month and dropped a cool half a million daily. Then he went to the bar to have drinks with an old business acquaintance named Harmon, who straddled the line between legal and illegal.

"Still no word on the identity of the new crime lord," Harmon said as he sipped Scotch.

"How can that be?" He resisted the urge to smash the delicate crystal glass. "Since when are there such loyal fucks in the underworld?"

"You know there's only one thing that keeps people quiet."

Fear.

"I want to know who he is. I don't care what it costs," Gavin said.

He wouldn't rest until the man who murdered his father and Vinny was dead. The specter that haunted his every waking moment would die. He couldn't live in the same world with that fucker lurking in the shadows. He wouldn't give up until the specter's blood coated his hands.

He went back to his office, but dissatisfaction ate at his gut. Whoever this guy was, he had everyone by the balls. Why? Was he a dirty cop, politician, or richer than him? Unease made him short-tempered and clipped during the rest of his meetings. When he couldn't take the confines of his office a second longer, he left the casino. On impulse, he requested the escort of a branch of his security that dealt with the underworld. When he drove out of the casino, he looked in his rearview mirror and saw five SUVs filled with his most lethal men. He couldn't twiddle his thumbs any longer. There was one man who had always been hungry for power, and Gavin knew where he worked.

He parked in front of Vega & Sons, the most successful attorney's office in Las Vegas. He armed himself and walked into the building with five men flanking him, while the others waited outside. The workers quieted immediately when they caught sight of him. Every local knew his face. He bypassed the stammering secretary on his way to the executive offices and entered Paul Vega's sanctuary. The old man was on the phone, but hastily put it down when he entered.

"Gavin," Paul said, running a hand over what little hair he had left. "To what do I owe this honor?"

"Don't fuck with me," he said, and didn't stop until he stood beside Paul. He didn't trust the fucker behind his desk. He was sure that Paul had a gun stashed somewhere. "I want Rafael."

Paul's expression didn't change. "What?"

His temper snapped. He grabbed fistfuls of Paul's shirt and hauled him out of the chair. "You know why."

"Gavin, I don't—"

Gavin withdrew his gun and shoved it under Paul's chin. "Rafael's always wanted the title. He always pushed the limits by coming to my clubs and trying to bribe my men. How many times has he toed the line? How many times did you cover for him?"

"You think he killed Manny?"

His finger tightened on the trigger. "Does he have an alibi?"

"Yes."

"What is it?" he hissed.

"He's dead."

"What?"

"Rafael was murdered a couple of days before Manny." Paul sounded weary instead of frightened.

Gavin released him and watched Paul sink into his chair, looking very much like an old man rather than his father's rival. "Where was he murdered?"

"At his home."

"You know who it was?"

Paul rubbed a shaking hand over his face. "No." The hand lowered, and the eyes that looked up at him were filled with fire. "I was planning a hit on you when I heard Manny and your girl were attacked."

"Who's the new crime lord?"

"Fuck if I know. No one's saying shit."

"You think it's the same killer?"

Paul glared at him. "Rafael was so disfigured I had to identify by his tattoos. I heard Manny got the same treatment, and your girl got gutted."

"Fucker likes knives," he said in an even tone, but the need to retaliate burned a hole in his chest. "I talked to Harmon today. I've put out a fuck load of money, but no one's talking."

"They will eventually," Paul said, as he lit a cigarette. "I heard you're married."

He tensed. Even though he and Paul had a common enemy, he didn't trust him. Bad blood flowed between their families. Despite the Vega's money, connections to the police, and under-the-table deals with criminals, they hadn't been able to dethrone the Pyres. Paul and his son Rafael took it personally. They had clashed and spilled blood more than once.

Paul blew out smoke. "Heard the gal's a looker. Rafael had a lot to say about her."

The memory of Rafael and Lyla talking in that restaurant riled his beast. "If Rafael wasn't already dead, I'd shoot him."

Paul shook his head. "You Pyres are something else. You get so fired up about your women."

It wasn't a secret that Paul Vega had no respect for females. The word was he treated his prostitutes like cattle. According to his father, Paul impregnated countless prostitutes until he got the sons he wanted.

"Stay away from my family."

Paul blew smoke out of his nostrils. "You have nothing I want, Pyre. Not anymore. Now, get out of my office."

He flicked the cigarette from Paul's lips and grabbed him by the throat. Paul's eyes bulged as he applied pressure. He enjoyed the feel of Paul's vocal cords squishing beneath his fingertips. It had been too long since he dealt out a punishment. He leaned in close and stared into the old man's panicked eyes.

"I may not be the crime lord anymore, Vega, but you know what I'm capable of, don't you?" Even though Paul nodded vigorously, he didn't release him. "I could break your neck so easily. Don't test me."

When the old man was purple, he let him go. Paul fell to his hands and knees, retching and gasping for air. Gavin stood over him and debated whether to shoot Paul for the hell of it when the door opened behind him. He turned as a skeletal man rushed in. Since his men wouldn't let just anyone into the office, Gavin examined the newcomer and realized it was Paul's younger son.

Gavin gestured to Paul, who was gasping like a fish out of water on the floor. "I was just getting reacquainted with your father."

The son said nothing, but his eyes flicked from Paul to Gavin and back again. He didn't say a word, which was wise, since one punch would crumple this guy. He was reed thin and had a dainty air about him that neither his father nor brother possessed. It wasn't surprising that this brother held no resemblance to Rafael, since they probably had different mothers. To Gavin's knowledge, this nerdy brother wasn't involved in the criminal underworld, but was a damn good lawyer.

"What's your name?" he asked into the loaded silence.

The son swallowed hard. "Steven."

"Your father tells me your brother was murdered."

Steven gave him a jerky nod but said nothing. He clasped his hands in front of him. Gavin noted that he was trembling. He hoped Steven had enough dignity not to wet himself.

"You have any leads?"

Steven opened and closed his mouth without uttering a word.

"Spit it out," he said impatiently.

"E-eli Stark."

Everything in him froze. "Eli?"

Steven's eyes fixed on something behind him. It was all the

warning he needed. He dodged to the side just as Paul fired his gun. Steven let out a high-pitched scream as the bullet meant for Gavin nicked his arm. He whirled and shot Paul in the wrist. Paul shouted blasphemies as he dropped his gun and clutched his injured arm. Gavin stalked forward and shot his father's nemesis in the shoulder at point-blank range. Paul fell out of his chair and twitched on the ground. He shot him in the thigh for good measure and didn't bother to shut him up since the office was soundproof.

The hair on his nape rose in warning. Gavin turned and was mildly surprised to see Steven fumbling with a gun. It took him only a split second to aim. One bullet shattered Steven's kneecap. He squealed like a pig and crumpled to the ground, hands hovering over his useless leg. Gavin reloaded his gun and debated whether Steven needed more punishment and if he should let Paul bleed out.

He crouched beside Paul. He welcomed Paul's loathing, and the flicker of fear in his otherwise soulless eyes.

"You don't want me to visit you again, do you, Paul?"

Paul bared his teeth. "No."

"Then you'll let me know what you find out about this crime lord, won't you?"

"He killed Rafael!"

"And I'll make sure he dies nice and slow, you got me?"

Even though he was in acute agony, Paul nodded, giving Gavin the right to avenge their loved ones. He rose and strolled over to Steven, who wasn't taking the pain well. Tears streamed down his face, and he was pleading for Gavin to call 911. When Gavin placed his foot on Steven's shattered knee, he shut up immediately.

"You got off easy today." He exerted enough pressure to make Steven's eyes roll in their sockets. "You ever pull a gun on me again, it'll be the last thing you ever do. You understand me?"

Steven nodded fervently. Gavin lifted his foot and allowed Steven to believe that was the end of his punishment for thirty seconds before he belted the lawyer across the face. A sharp crack filled the office as he dislocated Steven's jaw. Steven collapsed against the wall and then slid to the floor.

"Be a good boy and stick to what you know," he advised. "I'll be in touch if I need a good lawyer."

He rose and opened the door to find his men talking loudly, drowning out the sound of the Vega's moans. He closed the door and walked out of the building, discontentment eating at his gut. His men dispersed once they were in the parking lot.

He drove home, his temper nowhere near assuaged by the encounter with the Vega's. The new crime lord couldn't be Eli Stark, could it? Lyla saw Eli at Incognito. Did that mean something? Had Eli known they would be there? Was he gunning for her? The savage beating Raphael and his father endured didn't fit with what he knew of Eli's past work, but anyone could change.

He made it home in record time and wasn't pleased when he heard a deep bark when he walked through the front door. Lyla ran toward him, her delighted face doing crazy things to his insides. She hurled herself at him. She had to stop doing that at some point, but he fucking loved it. He wrapped his arms around her and drank from her mouth. He needed her more than he needed food or water. She was everything to him. Her silver blue eyes were alight with happiness, and his worries fell away as he lost himself in her.

Pregnancy suited her. She had bouts of nausea, but they didn't last long. Much to his delight, her pregnancy was now obvious. Her slim build made her stomach painfully obvious, and her breasts were swelling and extremely sensitive. She seemed to be shining from the inside out. It made his heart ache.

"How was your day?" she asked, linking her hands behind his neck.

"Fine," he said and looked down at a gray, muscled beast.

Dark assessing eyes met his. The dog sniffed his bloody shoes. He tightened his hold on his wife, keeping her airborne and away from the predator watching him so closely. He wanted to lock Lyla in a room and get the damn thing out of his house. Why the fuck did he assume she would pick a poodle or something? Fuck. Lyla never did what he expected.

"You see Beau?" she asked and fought to get out of his arms.

He didn't release her. "Can't miss him."

She caught his tone and gave him an exasperated look. "Gavin, he's a gentle soul. I see him three times a week. He's really great. I couldn't leave him there. He cries when I leave. It broke my heart."

He gritted his teeth. Another male who had a piece of her heart. He released her reluctantly but kept his hand fisted in the back of her shirt as she leaned down and scratched the beast under the chin. The dog closed his eyes in ecstasy.

"You're such a sweet boy, aren't you? You're happy here, huh?" she cooed before she turned to him. "Come on, dinner's ready."

He slipped off his shoes but kept his hand on his gun. She walked into the kitchen with the dog happily trotting behind her.

"Enjoy the peace and quiet," she advised as she dug into her chicken. "Tomorrow will be chaos. Carmen says she'll be here with the party planner at seven."

"I'll be in my office."

He had no interest in the decorations and games and shit. He just wanted to know the sex of the baby. It was Carmen's idea to do the gender reveal party, and when Lyla agreed, he decided to indulge her. The doctor informed the baker making the cake what the sex of the baby was. If he had known which bakery was making the cake, he would have called because he couldn't stand the suspense. Tomorrow he would know what he was having—Nora or a boy. He thought of Marcus's remark about Nora dating and scowled.

"What is it?" Lyla asked.

"Fucking Marcus." He loathed the small smile that curved her mouth. If Marcus was stupid enough to show up at the boxing ring, he might show him his lethal right hook.

"What about him?" she asked.

"He invited himself to the party."

"He wants to come? Oh, my gosh. I didn't think about giving him an invitation. He's a man."

"He's a weird bastard." He eyed the dog that looked blissed to be near Lyla's painted pink toenails. "I don't even know how he knew about it."

"Maybe Alice or Janice told him."

He wasn't sure how he felt about Lyla befriending his staff, but the damage was done. Alice and Janice became Lyla's fans when she forced him to attend the Incognito opening and volunteered at the dog shelter. They were becoming quite chummy with Carmen, as well, which could only be a recipe for disaster, but he knew better than to interfere with Lyla's attempts to socialize. At least she was still in his realm, which meant he possessed a modicum of control.

"They'll be here tomorrow?" he asked.

"Yes. Janice and Carmen have been driving the party planner crazy. Some of the volunteers I met at the dog shelter are coming too."

He didn't care who came as long as Lyla was happy, and he found out the sex of the baby. On that thought, he smoothed his hands over the loose button-up shirt she wore. "How is she?" He would assume the baby was a girl until it was confirmed otherwise.

"She's active today." Lyla waved her hands. "It feels like a weird flutter in my tummy."

"I can't wait for her to kick." He glanced at the dog, who was doing a good impression of a furry rug. The dog was obviously house-trained and comfortable with Lyla. "Do you know the dog's story? Where he came from? Why was he turned in?"

"His name is Beau," she said primly, which made him want to bite her. "I don't know how he came to be there, but he was at the shelter for about a year. He seems uneasy with males, so only women walk him."

"And out of all the dogs, he's the one you wanted?" Beau looked like a freaking tank. If the dog used his teeth and muscle, he could easily take down a full-grown man. "You say he doesn't like men?"

"He shies away from them. I think some asshole must have done something to him. I hope Beau fought back."

She rubbed her foot over the dog's head. He suppressed a snort when the dog's tail began to wag. While Lyla discussed plans for tomorrow, he ate and let the sound of her voice chase away his frustration and rage. Pregnancy had the desired effect—Lyla looked to the future with excitement and no small amount of trepidation. He loved the way she clung to him and demanded things from him. Before, she'd been too wary to ask for anything. Now, she called whenever she wanted to, and it eased something inside him. She was settling into married life. He wanted to believe that things could go on as they were, but the grim reality of the past whispered in his ear whenever he wanted to believe in a happily ever after. He didn't deserve Lyla and the miracle in her womb, but he would keep taking everything she had to give.

When he finished his meal, Lyla continued to talk as they headed upstairs. He wasn't pleased when the dog followed. When he entered their bedroom, Lyla pointed at a giant pillow on the floor on her side of the bed. The dog glanced at him before he obeyed, spinning twice on the bed before he lay down with his head on his paws, not taking his eyes off Lyla. Apparently, she couldn't resist the sad puppy dog look. She went on her knees beside the huge dog, making Gavin want to train his gun on it, just in case. She whispered to the dog and kissed him on the head before she went into the bathroom. Lyla stripped, and he admired the view before he followed her into the shower. Having his hands on her made the savage beast in his head retreat.

When they toweled off, he nixed the nightgown in favor of feeling her bare skin against his. They climbed into bed. She baby talked to the dog again, and he realized the dog was here to stay because she was besotted.

"Thank you for letting me have Beau," she said, tossing an arm over his chest and snuggling close.

"If I'd known you were going to bring home a sixty-pound beast, I would have laid down more conditions."

"He's a good dog."

"We'll see."

He suppressed a grin when she nibbled on his neck. He liked her bite.

"I love you," she said.

He would never tire of hearing that. It was a gift from God he could never repay. This woman had been created for him, and he would do everything in his power to ensure she left this world knowing she had been loved.

"I love you too much," he said.

Her dark chuckle made him hard.

"You can't love me too much."

"I do," he said, dragging her on top of him. He catalogued every precious inch of her exquisite face. If she had the height, she could have been a supermodel, but she didn't use her looks to get what she wanted. She looked beneath the surface, as so few people did. "You don't know what I'd do to keep you safe."

When she searched his face, he held his breath. She, more than anyone else, knew how dark and twisted he was. She'd left him twice because of it, and he wouldn't survive a third time.

"I know what you'd do," she said quietly and brushed his hair back. "I just hope you don't have to do it."

If he had a tail, it would have wagged. He craved her touch. He didn't care where she touched him or why. He wanted her hands on him all the time. It took effort to focus on her words.

"I might have to," he said.

Spectacular blue eyes narrowed. "Why?"

"Because he's still out there."

"But he's been quiet."

"For how long?"

She gripped his hair. He liked the streak of pain.

"You don't go looking for him, you understand me?" she hissed.

He caressed her ass and reached down to position his cock between her legs. Before she could wriggle away, he gripped her ass, so he could go deep.

"Gavin, stop trying to distract me," she huffed.

He sank his hand into her damp hair and rocked her on him as he forced her lips to his. She tried to resist, but he wouldn't allow her to pull away.

Her nails sank into his chest. "I can't lose you."

"You won't."

The coward who claimed the title of crime lord went after a man in his seventies, a woman, and Rafael Vega. Rafael was mostly talk and usually high or drunk. His security did the dirty work, unlike Gavin. The crime lord was a fucking coward. There was no doubt in his mind that he would win in a battle against him. Sheer rage trumped the specter's petty personal agenda.

"You promised not to go back to the underworld," she said.

"I'm not. I'm trying to draw him out of it."

"So you can kill him?"

"Of course," he breathed as he planted himself deep. "He'll come back. If not today, then tomorrow or the next day. I need to know who he is."

"I don't like this."

He hated hearing the worry and fear in her voice. She had survived that fucker, but still had nightmares, though they had grown less frequent. The specter haunted his every waking thought, but that was his cross to bear, not hers.

"Don't worry about it, baby girl. I got this," he said as he sucked on her pink nipples.

She gasped and arched, causing his cock to jerk. He began to move faster, desperate to feel her convulse around him with her silken limbs holding him hostage. There was no sweeter way to go to sleep than with his wife's vagina milking his dick for every last drop of sperm.

"Gavin."

He could see she wanted to discuss the specter, that she wouldn't let it go. He rolled her beneath him and crouched over her as he fucked her. Her lips parted, and her eyes went blind with need.

"I put this in you," he said, rubbing his hands over her belly. "You both are mine. Nothing will take you from me."

"But Gavin—"

"No." He kissed her long and slow. He loved her taste, her scent, everything about her. "He needs to die."

IF HE DIDN'T WANT to know the sex of his child so badly, he would have run like hell. There was an explosion of pink and blue in his home. Glitter banners hung on the walls, balloons covered his ceiling, and everyone wore a bow or bow tie to show which team they were on.

Lyla wore a bow in her hair and a bright pink shirt, clearly declaring herself Team Girl. He allowed Janice to pin a pink bow to his shirt because he sure as fuck wasn't going to pin it in his hair. There were pink and blue cupcakes, napkins, utensils, straws, the works. The men migrated outside while the women chattered inside and played guessing games.

"Hey, boss. You look at the proposal yet?"

Marcus approached wearing a blue shirt and blue bow tie beneath his chin.

"Is that why you decided to come? To bother me?" he asked.

"I knew you wouldn't give me an answer yesterday. So, what do you think?"

"I think it's going to be a tight fit."

"You read it?"

"Most of it."

He sipped on his pink drink and nearly spit it out when he realized it was pink lemonade. Shit. He put the glass on a passing waiter's tray and snatched a small plate of finger foods while trying not to grimace. This wasn't his scene. He would feel like an idiot if he weren't looking forward to cutting the three-tier cake that would reveal the baby's sex.

"You have feedback for me?" Marcus bounced on his toes. "I can take it."

He gave him a cool look. "I'll let you know if I have any questions."

Marcus looked crestfallen. If Gavin had a heart, he would have felt a flicker of remorse. He spotted Lyla's mother and scanned the crowd for her father, but didn't see him. His sources told him that Pat Dalton got a job at a gas station. Lyla's parents were barely making ends meet, but that wasn't his problem or hers.

Carmen ran toward them. "Come on, it's time!"

He didn't need to be told twice. He shouldered his way through the crowd. The cake was white and decorated with baby shit like bottles, booties, stuffed animals, and blue and pink dots. Lyla's eyes lit up when she saw him. She handed him the knife.

"This is it," she said.

He felt a buzz of adrenaline as he asked her where he should cut. He was dimly aware of camera flashes, Lyla squeezing his arm, and the sound of his heartbeat. He poised the knife above the smooth frosting, closed his eyes for a bare second, and said a silent prayer before he cut. He raised the blade, but he couldn't see a speck of cake on it.

"Cut again!" Carmen screamed impatiently.

Hand shaking, he sank the knife home again and lifted a thin slice of cake. His body went numb.

"It's a girl!"

12

LYLA

SHE TRIED TO KEEP UP WITH ALICE'S FAST, ENERGETIC PACE. IT WAS A daily struggle not to give in to the urge to wear sweatpants and laze around the house. Finding clothes that fit was a bitch. She had complained to Carmen, who took her on a shopping spree two days ago. Gavin put his foot down about her going to the dog shelter, and she had to admit he was right. She wouldn't be able to handle the bigger dogs if they decided to yank her along the path, and she couldn't lean over to pick up poop, so... yeah. She had to be content with Beau, who she took to the gun range and everywhere else possible. He didn't even need a leash. He never left her side, and when she indulged in an afternoon nap, he climbed into bed with her. Of course, she didn't tell Gavin, since he still referred to Beau as "dog."

"You were great with the kids yesterday," Alice said enthusiastically.

"They were adorable, but a handful."

Although she enjoyed the trip to the school where the volunteers from Pyre Casinos painted, cleaned, and played with the students, she was exhausted. The number of volunteers had tripled in the past months, and Alice was ecstatic.

"The students require better computers, and did you see those desks? They were ancient. The music room had plastic flutes and a beat-up guitar. I wish..." Alice trailed off.

"What?"

"I just want more for the kids, you know? They're satisfied with what they have, but they deserve better."

"I agree. Why don't you ask Gavin for more money to get the kids what they need?"

They passed a poker table full of smokers and women wearing strong perfume. She coughed and waved her hand in front of her face to dispel the noxious odor. Her super smelling nose seemed to get more sensitive by the month. She didn't feel nauseated, but she still had odd cravings. Last night, Gavin watched her eat a cucumber dipped in chocolate with poorly concealed disgust.

"I can't do that," Alice said, twisting her hands together. "I mean, they just created this position, and Mr. Pyre's already put a considerable amount of money in my budget."

"It doesn't hurt to ask," she said as they walked through the employee hallway. Cocktail waitresses, card dealers, spa attendants, security, and other workers acknowledged them with respectful nods as they went about their business.

"Do you really think we can ask for more money?" Alice asked nervously.

"Of course. It's for a good cause."

"I don't want to bother him."

"Come." She took Alice's hand and led her through the maze of back hallways to Gavin's office. When his secretary saw them coming, she picked up the phone, spoke into it, and leaped to her feet. By the time they reached her, she had the door of his office open.

"He's free," his secretary said quickly.

"Thank you," she said with a smile, which she turned on Gavin as he rose from his desk.

She went to him and wasn't surprised when he drew her against him for a deep kiss. If he hadn't made it obvious he was in love with her pregnant body, she would have fallen into a depressed state weeks ago. As it was, Gavin seemed hornier than ever, and it made her feel desirable rather than repulsive. When Gavin pulled away, he noticed Alice for the first time.

"I'm here on business," she said and rounded the desk to take a seat beside Alice, who looked uneasy.

"Business? Okay. What is it?" Gavin asked.

"Well, it's the school where we volunteered yesterday," Alice said quickly. "The kids need computers, new instruments, and the air conditioning needs to be fixed."

Gavin wore an enigmatic expression. Alice's voice went up an octave as her nerves kicked in. She began to talk faster and babble about the lack of water fountains and how some classrooms needed new cubbies. Lyla crossed her legs, drawing Gavin's attention. She licked her lower lip suggestively. When his eyes narrowed, Alice's voice got louder and more urgent.

"Do it," Gavin said abruptly.

"What?" Alice asked.

"Give me a figure and we'll do it. That will make Janice happy, right?"

"Y-yes."

Alice leaped to her feet. It was clear she wanted to throw her arms around him in gratitude. Gavin's look clearly stated this was business, and he didn't want or need a hug.

"You're a great man," Alice said with a massive smile.

"Get out of here," he said. "I need to talk to my wife."

Alice gave him a thumbs-up and danced out of the office. He crooked his finger at Lyla, who tried to look innocent. She rose, stopping an arm's length away. She wasn't surprised when he reached out and brought her close, so she stood between his knees.

"Did you just bribe me into giving more money to a school?" he asked.

"Maybe."

His hands slid beneath her dress and cupped her ass. "I think I like it. You make my time at work more interesting. Kiss me."

She gave him a long, deep kiss that had his hands slipping beneath her underwear and his fingers sliding into her core. She moaned into his mouth and bucked against his fingers, which slid deeper.

"I need you," he said as he set her on his desk and freed his cock from his pants. He spit on his fingers and pushed them deep. She opened her thighs wide and lifted her ass to take him deeper.

"Holy fuck," he hissed as he withdrew his fingers and replaced it with his cock. "I can't go slow."

"I don't want you to."

He braced his hands flat on the desk and fucked her hard. She moaned and was once again grateful that his office was soundproof. He slid in to the hilt with each thrust, and she tipped her head back in ecstasy. It didn't take long for him to come. When he was finished, he went down on his knees and finished her with his mouth. Her legs were quaking, and his desk was smeared with stuff by the time they were finished.

"You should bribe me more often," he said lazily as she sprawled on his lap.

"Maybe I will."

"You should take it easy," he said and rubbed her swollen tummy. "You've been on the go for weeks. You need to cool it."

That was why she was here. She and Gavin needed alone time. "I know."

He kissed her belly. "She's going to be beautiful."

Nora already had her daddy wrapped around her finger. Gavin had been wonderful during her pregnancy. He wanted to be involved in everything, much to Carmen's surprise and grudging approval. They had a birthing class in a few weeks, and she volleyed between terror and excitement as Nora's due date approached.

She checked herself in Gavin's private bathroom to make sure she looked presentable. Her cheeks were flushed and lips a little swollen, but she could always blame it on her pregnancy. People wouldn't know the difference. She rested a hand on her belly as Nora did somersaults.

"What is it?" Gavin asked sharply when she grabbed the edge of the sink.

"She's really active."

"You should go home and rest."

"I will," she lied and kissed him before she sailed out of his office, high on her climax.

Blade fell into step beside her. He was just as protective and annoying as Gavin, and hovered around her as if she were a walking bomb. She smiled at some of the volunteers she recognized and made her way to Marcus's office. His door was open, unlike Gavin's. She had definitely come to appreciate Marcus. He was the yin to Gavin's yang. She couldn't imagine how they ever got along without him. His keen business sense and time management skills left Gavin more time than he'd ever had.

Marcus looked up when she walked in. A broad smile curved his lips. "You look gorgeous!"

She laughed while Blade made a disgusted sound. She gave Marcus a quick hug before he sat on the edge of his desk.

"What can I do for you?" he asked.

"I want Gavin to have a week off," she said.

Marcus didn't even blink. "Okay."

"It's his birthday on Monday. I thought I could steal him away and bring him back to you next week."

Marcus nodded thoughtfully. "That's fine. He doesn't have anything that can't be rescheduled. I can take some of the meetings that shouldn't be put off. Where are you going?"

"California. I rented a yacht."

He gave her a concerned look. "Have you ever been on a boat?"

"Once. I'll be fine. Maybe after the baby comes, you can go on a long vacation."

"What for?"

"To relax?"

Marcus spread his arms wide. "I've been working my ass off to get where I am today. I'm relaxed when I'm at my desk, making decisions and money."

She shook her head. "You businessmen."

Marcus brushed imaginary dirt off his shoulders. "We live for it."

"I hope someone comes along and forces you to take a break."

"You have someone you want me to try out?" Marcus asked, wagging his brows.

"I only know man eaters," she said, and he laughed.

He led her out of his office with a casual arm tossed over her shoulders. Blade looked disapproving, but he always looked that way. She let out a grunt as Nora kicked hard. Marcus's easy smile vanished as she clutched her stomach.

"Are you okay?"

"Yeah, she just—" She winced as Nora kicked again. "She's trying to break out."

"What?"

Marcus looked like he might pass out. She grinned, grabbed his hand, and placed it on her tummy. Marcus tried to pull away until he felt the kick. He froze, and his eyes went comically wide.

"Holy crap."

"I know."

She released him and wasn't surprised when his other hand joined the first. He looked almost giddy as he waited and then received another kick.

"Oh, boy, I hope you drive daddy crazy," Marcus whispered to her belly.

"What the fuck!"

They both turned to see Gavin bearing down on them. She stepped in front of Marcus and held up both hands as employees ran for cover.

"Nora's kicking," she said.

"What does that have to do with him touching you?" Gavin demanded.

She reached up to clasp his face. "Hey, Hulk, he's just feeling her kick."

"You're mine," he hissed.

She sighed. "I couldn't be more yours if you tried. Now, stop making a scene. I needed to talk to Marcus about something."

"Talk to him about what? What do you need? I can help you with everything!"

"I want to surprise you."

"You know I hate surprises."

She gave him a wounded look. "Even from me?"

He hesitated and then glared at her. "You're trying to manipulate me."

She beamed. "Is it working?"

Gavin jabbed his finger at Marcus. "I'll see you in the ring tomorrow."

"That's fine," Marcus said easily, and then compounded his sins by giving her belly another pat. "I'll see you later, gorgeous."

She grabbed handfuls of his suit when he tried to go after Marcus. "Gavin, seriously."

"He's begging me to end his life."

"Gavin, pay attention."

Feral amber eyes focused on her, and her smile widened. God, Gavin was a possessive psycho. He was a man on the edge, but he always reined it in around her. She couldn't guarantee Marcus's life, but she figured he could handle himself.

"I love you," she said, and his tension eased. "You come home to me as soon as you can."

"Why?"

"So you can make me yours again."

"WHAT THE FUCK are you doing in California?" Gavin roared.

She held the phone away from her ear. "I wanted to be near the ocean." Well, on it if he wanted to get technical. "The jet is waiting for you."

"What the fuck, Lyla?"

"This is my surprise."

"To give me a heart attack? You're in another state!"

"Well, you'd better hurry," she said and winked at Beau, who gave her a chiding look.

She stood on the deck of the yacht and looked out at the ocean. They needed to get away from Vegas and let the water soothe them just for a little while. She packed everything he needed, and the yacht was set. She was happy to note that neither she nor Beau was seasick. She had to throw a crying fit so Blade would keep his mouth shut. If she hadn't been pregnant, she never would have gotten away with it.

It took less than two hours for Gavin to board the yacht. She waited for him with a glass of champagne and sparkling water for herself. His mouth was pressed into a thin line, and although she couldn't see his eyes, she could feel the heat emanating from him.

"You made it in time to see the sunset," she said and handed him the glass.

"Lyla."

"Did you have a nice flight? Mine was a bit bumpy, but—"

"You flew?"

He smashed his champagne glass and grabbed her by the shoulders. He gave her a small shake and leaned in close. "Lyla, you don't take off without telling me."

She refused to let him intimidate her. "We needed time away, and it's your birthday next week."

"And I would have come. Just tell me. I went home, and you were gone!"

She heard the fear in his voice. "You thought I left you?"

He released her and ran both hands through his hair. "I didn't know what to think."

"Didn't you see my card on the bed?"

"No. I realized the house was empty and called your cell."

"Maybe I should have taped the card to the door or something," she mused.

He tore off his sunglasses. "No, you *tell* me, not write me a fucking card."

"Gavin." She went to him and wrapped her arms around his waist.

He glared down at her, and she felt awful. "I didn't think you'd jump to that conclusion. I mean, why would I leave you?"

He didn't answer.

"I wouldn't do that," she said and tugged off his suit jacket, so it dropped to the deck. She unbuttoned his shirt halfway, so he could feel the cool breeze. "We needed time together, so I rented the yacht for a week."

She poured him another glass of champagne and pet Beau to reassure him that neither of them was in danger. She forced him to drink champagne as she stood beside him, looking out at the horizon as the sun set. It took Gavin a half hour to chill. The night was cool but comfortable enough for them to lounge on the deck and listen to the water slosh against the side of the boat.

"Are you still mad at me?" she asked.

"You're trying to kill me."

She clucked her tongue in disgust. "We're going to have fun. Marcus will take care of the meetings that can't be rescheduled, and if there's an emergency, I have your laptop."

"Marcus?"

"Yes. We were talking about this trip when you went psycho on him yesterday."

"I think I broke his jaw."

"You what?"

"We boxed. Maybe I should see if he's all right."

"You're damn right you should! Oh, my God, you're such an ass! He's a great COO. Why would you do that?"

"He likes to push my buttons."

"So you broke his jaw?"

"I don't know whether I did or not. The ambulance came for him. I didn't have a chance to check on his status since I had to take over his meetings for the day. I got your text, asking me to come home early, and I forgot about him."

"You're ridiculous," she snapped and pulled out her cell and called Janice, who knew everything. "How's Marcus?"

"He has a concussion and several bruises, but he's fine," Janice said succinctly.

"We just wanted to make sure he's okay. Thanks." She hung up and glared at Gavin. "You gave him a concussion."

"Maybe I should teach him how to box."

"You have a problem!" She got up and walked into the cabin. "Come on, Beau."

She walked into the master bedroom and ignored the romantic meal set up for them. She took a shower and when she finished, found Gavin talking on the phone while he stood in front of a row of windows that looked out at their surroundings. She was slightly mollified when she realized he was talking to Marcus. After feeding Beau and making herself a plate, she settled on the bed.

Gavin hung up and turned to her. "I offered to go back if he's not feeling well, but he's at the office right now."

"He loves his job."

Gavin grunted. "I'm going to shower."

She watched Friends reruns. The yacht tipped from side to side, lulling her into a pleasant doze. She had bursts of energy, which quickly faded. She needed this week away from Vegas as much as Gavin did; he just didn't know it. Volunteering, fluctuating hormones, and preparation for the baby were exhausting. She drifted to sleep before Gavin joined her in the bedroom.

SHE STARED out at the crashing waves. Sea spray landed on her face in a light mist, which made her feel cool and relaxed. She shifted her feet, which sank into fine, warm sand. Someone stroked her hair. She turned her head and saw Manny sitting beside her on a white sand beach. His shirt was unbuttoned halfway down his chest. The gold chains around his neck and rings on each finger glinted in the sun, while his bare toes peeked out from his slacks.

Her heart gave a painful twist. Even as she realized this must be a dream, she reached out to touch his face.

"Manny." Her fingers touched skin marred only by age lines. She grasped his hand and buried her face against his warm palm. "I miss you so much."

"I see Gavin listened to me."

She looked up and took in every detail of his face. His chest was damp from the ocean spray and humidity.

"Listened to you about what?" she asked.

"Starting a family."

She looked down at her protruding belly covered by a thin sarong. "We're going to name her Nora."

"I know. I'm honored."

She closed her eyes as pain and loss ripped through her. "I wish you were here."

"I am."

She closed her eyes and soaked in his presence. He seemed so real and solid, but even in sleep, she knew the truth.

"I'm happy that you and Gavin finally got your act together."

She let out a choked laugh. "It's an ongoing battle."

"He needs you, Lyla. Don't give up on him."

"I won't," she vowed.

"That's my girl."

She could smell his musky scent mixed with sunblock and ocean. She saw his gold cane in the sand and smiled.

"I knew you were with me."

She looked up. "What?"

"I felt you reach me before I died."

Her breath seized. She dragged herself across the floor with a knife protruding from her chest to be near him. Images from that day began to intrude on the dream. The sound of the waves began to fade. She clutched him desperately.

"Not yet, not yet," she chanted. "I need more time."

"You're so brave, so strong." Manny's voice was a soothing balm to her soul. "No other woman would be able to handle Gavin and the trials you've been through."

"Please don't go," she whispered.

"I'm always with you."

She shook her head as tears poured down her cheeks. "It's not fair."

He cupped her chin. "I'm good, baby girl."

"I'm not." She grasped handfuls of his shirt. "I think about you every day. I miss you so much."

"You need to stay strong. There are more trials to come."

"What?"

"He's still out there, Lyla. He'll come for you and the baby. He won't stop. Keep Nora safe."

"What are you talking about?"

The warmth of the sun faded, and the sky began to darken. Over Manny's shoulder, she saw movement. A man in a black suit and mask stood at the far end of the beach. Her heart leaped into her throat. She clutched at Manny even as the monster reached into his jacket and pulled out a gun.

"Manny!"

She jolted awake, mouth open on a scream. She clapped a hand over her mouth and lay in bed, trembling. Gavin slept with his back to her. Beau padded out of the darkness and nudged her arm with his nose. She slid out of bed, sagged to her knees, wrapped her arms around Beau, and wept silently. She felt as if she had lost Manny all over again.

When she composed herself, she kissed his muzzle and went to pee. Her reflection showed haunted, bloodshot eyes, a pale complexion, and colorless lips. She pulled a jacket on over her tank top and tights before she left the cabin with Beau. It was still dark out. She settled on a deck chair with Beau between her legs, keeping her feet warm as the cool ocean breeze swirled around her.

That had been some dream. How could her mind create something so realistic? *Keep Nora safe.* She wrapped her arms around her stomach. Manny was right. The sadist who stabbed her never intended for her to live. He would come back to finish the job.

She clung to the good parts of the dream, but the bad refused to be ignored. Grief rose so strong, she could barely contain it. Like Carmen, she had lost someone she loved more than herself. There was no coping mechanism. All she could do was focus on little tasks and keep putting one foot in front of the other. Her heart and mind still couldn't accept that Manny was gone. Nora would grow up without knowing Manny or understanding Gavin's overprotectiveness. She refused to allow Nora to feel a modicum of the terror and horror she endured at the hands of the underworld.

On a sudden surge of anger, she went into the cabin and retrieved her gun from her purse. Gavin was trying to lose himself in her and the baby to calm his inner beast. It must torture him to know that the man who killed his cousin and father was still out there.

"Ma'am?"

She blinked up at a crew member.

"Do you want me to take the dog to the shore?"

"Uh, yeah, I'll come too," she said, wiping her face and sticking the gun in her pants.

She climbed into a smaller boat with the crew member and Beau. They walked along the shore as the sun came up. Beau raced along the beach before rounding back to her and then taking off again to do his business. There was no one around. The isolation soothed her. She dug her feet into the cold, wet sand and eyed the yacht that bobbed just outside a cove. After the dry desert air, the ocean breeze felt like heaven. She knotted the arms of her jacket around her neck as she strolled.

On the trip back to the yacht, she groaned when she saw Blade and Gavin waiting with their arms crossed. Gavin put his hands on her as soon as he could.

"You're not making this easy on me, are you?" Gavin asked as he hauled her aboard.

"Beau had to do his business."

"You should wake me up."

"I have my gun." She brandished it, which made the crew members scatter.

Blade snatched the gun and checked it, but the safety was already on.

"You shouldn't be handling a gun unless it's an emergency, especially in your condition," Blade said.

She ignored him and poured water into Beau's doggy bowl.

"Breakfast is ready," Gavin said and gestured to a table full of food.

Blade made himself a plate and retreated inside after shooting her a nasty look. Apparently, Gavin passed the time waiting for her return by chewing him out. She piled her plate high. Despite her unease, she was starved.

"Your eyes are swollen."

She ignored Gavin's quiet observation.

"Are you okay?"

She nodded and continued stuffing her face, hoping he would take the hint. He snatched a Danish out of her hand.

"Lyla, talk to me."

"I'm fine," she said and reached for another Danish, which he took from her as well. "Damn it, Gavin, I'm fine!"

"You're not fine. Normally, you don't carry your gun. Something spooked you. What?"

Obviously, he wasn't going to let this slide. "I had a nightmare."

He searched her eyes intently. "About Dad?"

"Yeah." The silence stretched, and she blurted, "He warned me that the crime lord wouldn't stop until he finished the job."

He eyed her for a moment before he said, "It was a dream."

"But you think that too, right? That's why you want me to go to the gun range and why you train? You think he's going to come back."

"I'm not going to let anything happen to you."

"You said you were trying to draw him out of hiding?"

"No one's willing to give him up."

A chill crept up her spine. "Which means he's powerful."

"I'm going to get him."

"You'd better."

He blinked. Her heart still felt as if it was being torn in two. It had been a blessing and a curse to have the dream about Manny. She missed him so much. Was it her overactive, PTSD subconscious making things up, or a spiritual intervention?

She leaned forward, hair whipping around her as she glared at her husband. "That fucker doesn't deserve to live. He's not allowed to. You do one more kill, Gavin. I won't feel safe until he's gone."

He was silent for so long that she wondered if she'd said something wrong. He rose, leaned across the table, and kissed her. Just when she was getting into it, he pulled back with a grin.

She scowled. "What the fuck? I tell you that fucker needs to die, and you smile at me?"

"You're a crime lord's wife, all right."

"Former crime lord," she corrected.

He shrugged. "Once a crime lord, always a crime lord. I'm hard-wired to take justice into my hands. My resources and lack of morals make it easy."

She watched the ripple of muscles beneath his tight shirt. Gavin was a beast. He'd bulked up to ridiculous proportions, and it looked fucking delicious on him. He looked like a UFC fighter. He was ready for war, she realized. He wasn't taking anything for granted. He would fight dirty to keep her and Nora. Lord have mercy on whoever was dumb enough to mess with him. After her experience with the sadist, she wouldn't hesitate to pull the trigger. She couldn't stand by and watch someone else be taken from her. No fucking way.

"What's the plan?"

"Plan?" she echoed, trying to get her mind off violence and blood.

"You said I'm free for a week?"

"Yes." She took a calming breath. "It's your birthday in a couple of days. I don't have any plans. I thought we could catch some sun, swim, eat, and chill."

"Sounds good to me." He glanced at Beau, who was getting a suntan. "I can't believe you brought that dog on a yacht."

"He'd freak if I left him home for a week." She pointed to the beach. "We can go up and down the coast, or we can go ashore if we're not into it. We can do whatever. No plans."

"No plans sound good."

She beamed. "Yay. Birthday weekend!"

<hr>

LYLA SLUMPED on the couch and moaned.

Gavin's birthday weekend was a success. They lazed in the sun, swam, fucked, slept, and ate to their heart's content. He had only picked up his laptop once, and she felt refreshed and ready to rumble when they returned to Las Vegas. She accompanied Alice to the school where they volunteered, armed with new computers, instruments and much more. Janice was there, as were several reporters. Lyla did an impromptu interview, which Janice reassured her had been perfect.

A week ago, she and Gavin attended a birthing class. It was illuminating, reassuring, and horrifying. She was nervous as hell about labor, but she told herself—and the instructor reiterated multiple times—that women had been doing it since the beginning of time. She would survive. Just when she thought she couldn't get any bigger, she did. Now, she literally couldn't touch her toes. Even putting on yoga pants was a struggle. It was the final stretch, and she was big, miserable, and horny as fuck. Gavin was delighted.

Even now, only four hours after he left, she needed him. God! She put Beau in the backyard, locked the front door, and was about to go upstairs to relieve herself when she remembered Gavin watching the live feed on his desk. What were the chances he was watching her right now? She couldn't call his office to ask him to come home and fuck her, but if he saw it for himself and wanted to join... that was on him.

She shoved a section of the couch in front of one of the cameras. Horniness gave her extra strength. She felt as if her body was on fire. Thank God the weather was cooling, and they were going into the holidays because she would have been miserable during this part of her pregnancy in the summer. As it was, she wanted the temperature in the house around sixty and broke into a sweat at night. Gavin grumbled when she shirked his body heat. Between the two of them, they generated enough heat to warm people in Russia.

With effort, she stripped off her clothes and lay naked on the couch. Gavin wouldn't fail to miss that, would he? The message was clear if he didn't have his ear glued to the phone or was in a meeting. A part of her wondered if Blade had access to the cameras, but her hormones decided it was worth the risk. Blade knew she didn't have plans today, so he had no reason to tap into the feed. She propped herself on some pillows and started slowly, just rubbing her hand over her tummy. Nora was going to be a bruiser. She had her daddy's right hook and made it known that she wanted out.

"Eight more weeks, love," she murmured to her stomach.

She felt a spurt of impatience and then fear. The nursery was ready, but she didn't know if she liked the lavender walls. Maybe she should have—. She was supposed to be tempting Gavin to come home to fuck her, not daydream about paint colors on the couch butt naked. She looked up at the camera before she spread her legs, giving him a bird's-eye view of one of his favorite places, before she touched her breast and winced. They were ridiculously large and sensitive. How did other women handle huge boobs on a daily basis? She was fine with her normal B's, thank you very much. This was a bit much for her. Speaking of which, Carmen had taken out her breast implants, which was a shocker. Carmen's look changed so drastically in the past months that she was almost unrecognizable.

Her cell rang in the kitchen. She was going to ignore it, but it could be Gavin. She scowled when she saw Carmen's name. Speak of the devil... To allow Gavin more time to stalk her, she answered the phone before she repositioned herself on the couch.

"How's it going, hot mama?" Carmen asked.

"I'm a fucking horn dog," she moaned.

A pause and then, "Are you a horny toad or fucking a hot dog?"

She snickered. "I'm a horny toad, and I hate it."

"Why? You have a man to fuck."

"Uh, he works."

"So?"

"So, he can't stay home on fucking duty. I don't think Marcus is going to accept that excuse."

"Screw Marcus!"

Distracted by the unexpected outburst, she said, "Carmen?"

"What?"

"Did something happen between you two?"

"Why the fuck would it?"

"Carmen Pyre!"

"What?"

"Tell me, you discreet slut."

A pause and then, "Something almost happened, but I stopped him."

"Why?"

"Why? Because I'm still in love with my husband!"

She closed her eyes as the sound of Carmen's ragged sobs filled the line. It had been two years since Vinny's murder, but Carmen cried as if her heart were breaking. Divorce or falling in love was one thing. Those were choices. What happened to Carmen was cruel. She didn't get a second chance. One day, Vinny was here, and the next, he wasn't.

"I'm sorry, baby. Do you want me to come over?" she asked and looked down at her naked self.

"While you're horny? I don't think Mom or I can help you," Carmen said, calming slightly.

"Bitch."

Carmen sighed. "I don't feel like myself."

"What do you mean?"

"I knew who I was with Vinny. Now, I keep changing the way I look, hoping my reflection will match how I feel."

Lyla frowned, disturbed by this conversation. "And how do you feel?"

"Dark."

Hence, the black hair and risqué outfits. "Do you want to talk to somebody?"

"I'm talking to you."

"You know what I mean. Like, a professional?"

"Fuck no."

"Then what do you need?"

Carmen hesitated. "The same thing you do, I think."

"What?"

"I need to get laid. Just... get it over with, you know?"

"If you're not feeling it, don't do it for the hell of it."

"We'll see," Carmen said. "I'll see you tomorrow? Shopping and pampering?"

"Yes."

"Okay, preggo, have an awesome fuck."

Lyla tossed the phone and then glared at the camera. For all she knew, Gavin didn't even watch her anymore. Maybe she was performing for no one. In that case... she squeezed her breast and gasped when yellow liquid spurted over her belly.

"What the fuck?"

She wrung her hands before she realized it was probably colostrum. It was normal to start leaking right before the birth. She went into the kitchen to clean herself. Could this be any less romantic? Hell, she still needed to get off. Her vagina had a mind of its own, and it wanted to be filled not with her fingers, but with Gavin. Was this what it felt like for men all the time? The inability to think past getting off? God.

She grabbed her clothes and stomped upstairs, unwilling to embarrass herself any longer. What if this was all recorded, and Blade could recall it whenever he wanted? Stupid, stupid. These pregnancy hormones clouded common sense. She went to her bathroom and had her hairbrush in hand when the front door slammed. She was torn between relief and mortification. Was it Gavin or Blade? She heard running footsteps and then her name being shouted. Gavin. She tossed the hairbrush on the counter. He walked in with his tie undone and his shirt unbuttoned. He lost his jacket at some point and was already undoing his belt.

"How much did you see?" she asked as he started toward her.

"I saw you move the couch and was going to call Blade when you started the show. I watched you on my cell as I drove here."

He pushed her against the counter before he went down on his knees, lifted her leg over his shoulder, and lapped at her pussy.

"I don't want you to eat me out," she said testily. "I'm already soaked. I want your cock. Fuck me from behind."

His response was a moan. She dug her hands into his hair and pulled until he looked up at her.

"I need to be fucked hard."

"Your wish is my command."

She allowed him to continue tongue fucking her as he stripped off his clothes. When he rose, she braced her elbows on the counter and stuck out her ass. She glared at his amused, self-satisfied expression.

"I think being pregnant suits you. I like you desperate for me."

"This is the only baby you're getting, if the last two months will be like this."

She gritted her teeth when he got down on his knees and kissed her ass. He massaged the large globes and then lapped before he rose and positioned himself behind her. Their eyes met in the mirror. He slicked the head of his cock with her juice, and when he slid it up and down teasingly, she wanted to kill him. She pushed back, taking his cock hostage, and he chuckled, obviously delighted by her aggression. How did other women handle this? If she could, she would demand he fuck her at least five times a day. Maybe more than that. She couldn't ask her mother if she'd been a horny toad when she was pregnant, and this so wasn't the time to be thinking about her mother. She reared back to urge him on.

"Fuck," Gavin growled as he powered into her. "I think we should have five kids."

"Your dick might fall off, and I might need to find another man."

She wasn't prepared for the hard slap on her ass. She jolted and then shrieked when he smacked her again, hard enough to make her skin tingle. She looked in the mirror and saw that he was pissed. Seriously?

"Gavin!"

"Don't talk to me about other men," he growled and rubbed his hand over her swollen belly. "Don't you fucking dare."

"It was a joke," she snarled.

"Two things you should never joke with me about. One, other men. Two, leaving me. Pretty simple, baby."

She moaned and moved back against him. "Okay, I won't. Please, I need this."

"Do you like my cock?" he growled as he placed his hands on her shoulders.

"It's perfect," she said with heartfelt honestly.

"Then take it."

She met his eyes in the mirror as he began to pound into her. She spread her legs as he fucked her the way she needed. She closed her eyes to absorb the feeling of Gavin claiming her, of the pleasure he evoked. It didn't take long for her to climax. When her eyes shot open, she found Gavin watching her in the mirror. His face contorted as he came. He rested his face on her spine and rubbed his hand over her belly.

"I know this isn't easy for you," he said quietly, "but for what it's worth, I'm enjoying your pregnancy."

She snorted and slid out from under him. She cleaned herself with a washcloth, aware of his heated gaze, and winced when she slid on a loosely fitted dress. Even the sensitive contact against her breasts hurt.

"I'm hungry," she announced and walked out of the bathroom.

He cursed as she headed to the kitchen, half convinced she might die if she didn't get food in her body in the next ten minutes. Beau whined by the sliding door. When she let him in, he bumped his head against her side. She grabbed celery sticks and peanut butter and was in the middle of her second when Gavin appeared in shorts and nothing else.

"You're not going back to work?" she asked with her mouth full.

"Have mercy on me. I'm beat."

She offered her half-eaten celery. He stared at it as if it were a stick of dynamite.

"No, thanks. What do you want for dinner?"

"French fries."

"What else?" he asked as he pulled out a salad and sandwich.

"A chocolate shake."

He paused in the act of forking up leafy greens. "What else?"

She considered and added, "Shrimp tempura."

He shook his head. "I'll tell one of the guys to make a food run."

She was over the celery sticks. She searched the fridge and made herself a glass of chocolate milk while Gavin watched. Satisfied for the moment, she waddled over to a chair and put her hands on her belly.

"I'm a sex and food machine!"

"You're almost done," he said, and sat at the table with her. "What are you doing tomorrow?"

"Carmen's going to pamper me."

"Good." He pulled out his phone and typed something.

She regarded him for a minute before she said, "How often do you check the cameras?"

He glanced at her and then continued to type. "Once an hour. I can watch from my phone as well."

"Is it recorded?"

"Don't worry. I'll delete it."

13

LYLA

She wiped sweat from her brow as she finished dressing and looked at Beau.

"Pregnancy isn't for pussies," she said.

Beau cocked his head to the side and then ambled over with his tail wagging. He nudged her tummy with his nose and sat. She leaned forward to scratch him under the chin. He closed his eyes in doggy ecstasy, and she covered his face in kisses. She couldn't imagine life without him. Beau seemed to sense her precarious moods and never budged from her side.

"You're such a good boy. You ready to go?"

She had a pregnancy massage scheduled and could barely contain herself. The last two months of her pregnancy had been hell. Her back ached, she was sleep-deprived, and she didn't know her body anymore. Last night, she went to the bathroom ten times. She didn't know whether she had to pee, poop, or fart. Unable to sleep, she decided to go for a swim at two in the morning. Gavin dozed on a lounge chair as she floated in the heated pool. When she was tired, they went to bed, and she finally slept.

She stood, hands outstretched for balance. She sucked in a breath at a brief flash of pain. She raised her shirt and watched her stomach shift as Nora moved. God, this kid had energy to spare. She fetched her purse and checked her pistol to make sure the safety was on and that she had an extra clip just in case. Since her dream about Manny, she had been on edge. Gavin beefed up her security, but it didn't make her feel safer. She could hear an invisible clock counting down to a showdown she wasn't privy to. Nora would be here soon. Was that what the sadist was waiting for? Fuck that.

"Come on, Beau."

She held the rail as she walked downstairs. Beau trotted by her side as she made her way to the front door. Their property was always teeming with guards, and today was no exception. Five SUVs lined the drive.

She looked at Blade. "You don't think this is overkill for a trip to the spa?"

"Gavin doesn't think so."

No, her husband wouldn't think having a security detail of twenty men was overkill. "Let's go."

She and Beau climbed into the back seat while Blade drove with his second in command, Jordy, riding shotgun. Jordy had a baby face, which was deceiving, since he had to be capable of carrying out brutal tasks if he was in Gavin's employ.

"Where to?" Blade asked.

"We have to pick up Carmen and my aunt first," she said.

Beau rested his chin on her thigh and closed his eyes as they left the property. She texted Carmen that they were on their way and stroked Beau's head. It had been eight months since Gavin showed up in Montana and married her. She rubbed a hand over her swollen stomach. Of course, he wasn't satisfied with just marrying her. He had to get her pregnant as fast as possible. The strength of his love humbled her. She wouldn't have been able to handle him in her younger years, but everything felt right now. They had been through enough trials to last them a lifetime, and they were still here.

Carmen and Aunt Isabel came out to the SUV when they pulled up. Carmen sat in the last row of seats, while Aunt Isabel sat on Beau's other side and stroked his back. Aunt Isabel chattered all the way to the spa about the benefits of the wrap she was going to get. She enjoyed spending time with her aunt and cousin. Her mother wanted in on their girl days, but Lyla refused. There would always be drama with her parents, and they would never stop hounding her for money. With her daughter on the way, she wanted all negativity out of her life, and that included her parents. She wanted to keep those who loved and cared for her close. Everyone else could go screw themselves.

She sucked in a breath as she stepped down from the SUV. Carmen rubbed her stomach as if she were a lucky Buddha.

"How's Nora?" Carmen asked.

"Really active today." She winced and arched her back as a sharp pain passed through her belly.

"I'll be in the waiting room," Blade said in a low voice. "You have your phone?"

She checked her purse, nodded, and entered the locker room. The smell of eucalyptus raised her spirits. Naked women paraded with perfect, Barbie-like bodies. Aunt Isabel, Carmen, and Lyla were the only ones without implants. She slipped into a robe, which gaped at the throat, revealing her scars. The women stared, horrified by her swollen belly and disfigured chest. She was too restless and achy to care. The unrelenting pressure in her pelvis wasn't going away and seemed to be getting heavier by the hour. Would her last two months of pregnancy be like this? She hoped not.

Her therapist was a groovy hippie around her mother's age who made her feel comfortable and safe. The therapist put her on a table with a cutout for her tummy. Lying on her stomach for the first time in months was heaven. She fell asleep ten minutes into the massage and felt like a million dollars when she waddled into her facial. The esthetician was a Thai woman who spoke little English, which suited Lyla just fine since she didn't feel like talking.

She wasn't allowed in the sauna, steam rooms, or Jacuzzi, so she sat on a heated lounger and dozed. Aunt Isabel and Carmen went from treatment to treatment like giddy schoolgirls. They finished their trip with nails and hair. Lyla got a mani and pedi with pink and white designs and a blowout.

"I'm hungry," she announced.

"For what?" Carmen asked.

"Burger and fries."

Carmen shook her head. "You have the worst munchies I've ever seen."

"Wait until it happens to you!" She caught Carmen's almost imperceptible flinch and put her arm around her cousin. "I'm sorry."

Carmen took a deep breath. "You know, Vinny wanted kids and I wanted to wait?"

She sighed. "It wasn't meant to be."

"I know."

They walked out of the locker room. Beau, who had been laying at Blade's feet in the waiting room, jerked out of his hold and ran to her. When she leaned over, he licked her face. She sputtered and laughed.

"I want a burger and fries," she announced to Blade.

"Third time this week," he said without inflection.

"Don't judge me!"

"I'm not judging, I'm making an observation."

She jabbed her finger at him. "You don't need to tell Gavin."

"He wants to know."

"He doesn't need to know everything that I put in my mouth!"

"I follow my orders."

She rolled her eyes as they piled into the SUV and drove to the nearest burger joint. When they reached Aunt Isabel's house, she stretched out on the couch and fell asleep. Two hours later, she woke to the sound of laughing. There was a heavy weight on her ankles. She didn't have to look to know it was Beau. Her lips quirked as she listened to Aunt Isabel and Carmen singing with the radio. She sat up and winced as her womb clenched. She shouldn't have ordered that second burger...

"What is it?"

She turned her head and saw her shadow, Blade, sitting in an armchair. "Did you take a nap?"

"I don't nap."

"When do you sleep?"

"When you do."

She stared at him. "You don't stalk me on the house cameras, do you?"

Before her mind could go nuts about the shit he must see, he shook his head.

"I used to, but I'm not supposed to access the cameras unless there's an emergency." He jerked his head at a diamond studded watch Gavin gave her a couple of months ago. "That watch has a heart monitor, so I know when you're sleeping or distressed. It also has a GPS."

"And neither of you thought to tell me this?"

He shrugged. "It's better than following you around the house or sleeping right outside your bedroom. I get alerts when you're asleep or awake. Gavin deactivates it when he's with you." He gave her a piercing look. "Your nightmares are becoming less frequent."

Finding out he was privy to something so private, she paled. She had known Blade just as long as Gavin. Blade had been Gavin's bodyguard before he became hers. She spent more time with Blade at her side than Gavin, but she knew next to nothing about him. The day of Manny's murder, Blade had been shot five times and managed to alert Gavin in time to save her life.

"I never thanked you," she said quietly.

He was silent for a moment, and then he said, "I did my job."

"Both of us almost died that day."

"I'm sure it won't be the last time I'll be shot."

"Why do you do it?"

"That's my job."

"But why choose this? Is it the money?"

He didn't respond immediately. The smell of fresh baked oatmeal cookies drifted into the living room, stoking her appetite, but she resisted.

"I threw my life away before I hit puberty. I was a junkie going nowhere when Manny executed everyone in my gang but decided to give me a chance since I was so young. I watched the Pyres take control. If you think they're ruthless, you should see what the gang lords did to their members. They infected them with HIV, got them hooked on drugs, or made them commit murder to prove their loyalty. If you tried to leave, they raped or killed your wife, mother, neighbor, anyone you cared for. Life means nothing to them. All they care about is territory, respect, and money. The public is fair game. The Pyres put a stop to that. They make it... civilized, if you will." His eyes gleamed. "Yeah, they kill and torture, but only if you're stupid enough to betray them. They don't cut off limbs, pluck out your eyes, or make you watch as your son is bled out in front of you."

Her skin rippled with goose bumps. She stared into fathomless black eyes and could almost hear the echoes of the horrors he had seen. In the kitchen, her aunt and cousin began to sing "Gimme More" by Britney Spears.

"I taught Gavin how to shoot and fight. He was conditioned to walk into a daily hell and be able to function under pressure. You don't know what Manny did to him to accomplish that."

As if Beau sensed her distress, he ducked under her arm and nudged her hand. She stroked his head.

"Emotion is a sign of weakness in my world. When you started dating, Gavin didn't change, so you weren't seen as a weakness to exploit, just a piece of ass."

She gave him a baleful look.

"When you left, he went cold and got heavily involved in the underworld dealings. He wasn't like Manny, who ran the show and had people carrying out orders. Gavin got his hands dirty. He dealt with everything personally. Everyone knew his face. The things he did to bring the criminal underclass to heel are legend. He became the most feared man in the state. The fact he could transition from the crime lord to the polished CEO scared the shit out of everyone. When he brought you back, his image began to crack." Blade shook his head. "The filth in the underworld can smell weakness a mile away. Vinny got gunned down, and then you and Manny were attacked."

"So, it's my fault?"

"Your effect on Gavin has caused a ripple effect through the city. The underworld is in chaos, and the man who's taken the throne is a sick fuck who encourages violence and destruction. They lace candy with drugs and hand them out to kids, they slaughter and steal... The new crime lord is good at keeping his identity a secret. So far, all we've been able to discover is that he has a fondness for leaving mutilated victims in his wake."

"So, what's the answer?"

His eyes flicked to her stomach. "Most men who have been through what Gavin has can't live normal lives, but he's managed to do so through you. He made his choice. He won't give you up. The whole city could go up in flames, and he wouldn't go back to the underworld if it meant losing you."

"What do I do?"

He didn't answer for a long minute. Their gazes held. She gripped the back of Beau's neck as something built inside her.

"I don't know," he said finally. "All we can do is hope we can bribe someone to give up the identity of the new crime lord, kill him, and hope whoever's next to take the throne isn't as sick as he is."

She moaned as a cramp dragged at her insides.

"What is it?" he asked sharply.

"I'm having these pains," she said, and Blade stiffened.

"Are you sure it's not labor?"

"It's probably that Braxton Hicks thing."

"What?"

"False labor." She let out a long breath as it faded. "Damn. It keeps coming and going."

"Like labor?"

She shot him an irritated glance. "Contractions are supposed to be consistent. This has been happening since yesterday. Sometimes I don't feel anything for three or four hours."

"We'd better head home," he said and rose.

"I'll say goodbye to Carmen and Aunt Isabel first."

She walked slowly toward the kitchen and tried to ignore the ache in her belly. Carmen and Aunt Isabel were dancing in the kitchen while they prepared a casserole. After her talk with Blade, she was glad to see her family so carefree and happy. She couldn't believe how much Aunt Isabel had come out of her shell since Uncle Louie's passing. The longer Aunt Isabel and Carmen were together, the closer they became. She wished she could have that type of relationship with her mother.

"Stay for dinner," Aunt Isabel said.

"I'm not feeling that great, and Gavin will be home soon." She kissed her aunt on the cheek and waited patiently as Aunt Isabel patted her belly.

"You're going to be such a gorgeous girl," Aunt Isabel cooed. "We can't wait for you, Nora. You're so loved."

She blinked back tears. Yes, her baby was going to be loved. Nora wouldn't have Vinny, Manny, or Uncle Louie. Instead, she had Gavin, Blade, and Marcus. It was an interesting mix, but they would dote on her.

"And I'm going to be the coolest aunt ever," Carmen said to her belly. "I'll teach you all the things your mother doesn't want you to know."

She rolled her eyes and kissed Carmen on the cheek. "Thank you for today. It's just what I needed." She caught her breath caught as another pang came and went.

She made her way to the door where Blade waited. He got into the driver's seat while Jordy opened the back door for her and Beau. She shifted restlessly on the seat, unable to find a comfortable position. If felt as if Nora was doing jumping jacks on her pelvis.

They drove out of Aunt Isabel's neighborhood, which was run down and not in the safest area. Maybe Carmen and Aunt Isabel could move closer to her once the baby was born... She spotted a crew of gang members standing on the corner, and her stomach dipped. Blade painted the underworld in a way that made it so real, she could feel it pressing in on her. She knew what Gavin was capable of. She witnessed him beat that guard to death with such methodical precision that she knew it wasn't his first time. The underworld needed a crime lord, one with a code who could control the sick perverts and sadists, but it couldn't be him. There had to be someone else...

She gripped the door handle as a cramp gripped her uterus in a vise. "Shit."

"What?" Blade called from the front.

She writhed on the seat. "C-can you pull over?"

"Why?"

"Pull over!" she shouted and put her hands on her belly, which was hard as a rock. "I need to walk. I think sitting is making the cramps worse."

He pulled off the main road and followed a small side street to an empty field. She stepped out of the SUV and began to pace. As the sun began its descent, the temperature dipped. Beau trotted after her and nudged her with his nose.

"You okay?" Blade asked.

She turned and found him beside her. The entourage of SUVs following in their wake parked. Guards got out to see what was going on.

"I'm just going to walk around a little." Beau whined in the back of his throat and stared up at her. "Go, run."

Beau hesitated.

"Go on," she said.

Beau darted across the field, running full out. She rubbed her stomach and took a deep breath. They weren't in the best part of town, so she was grateful for her security.

"You should go to the hospital and call Gavin," Blade said.

"I have eight weeks left until my due date."

"You could always have her early."

"No."

He shook his head. "You don't take your health and safety seriously."

"Why should I when I have you and Gavin?"

Although he glared at her, she thought she saw a glimmer of amusement in his eyes.

"Do you think one life is worth sacrificing to save thousands?" The question popped out of her mouth before she could hold it back.

"It depends on who cares for the life you're sacrificing."

His words hung in the air between them. He clasped his hands behind his back. His stance, as always, was military straight.

"My family was murdered in front of me when I was eight years old. I haven't felt much since then. I thought Manny was the cruelest man I'd ever met until Gavin took over. Those men... I didn't believe they had feelings until you came around. It's the craziest shit I've ever seen. I thought love was a myth made up by people who couldn't face how fucked up the world really is."

He cocked his head to the side as he considered her with a dark, intense expression she couldn't identify.

"You and Gavin have been through major shit and put your issues to the side to become a unit. Never seen anything like it in my life."

"And?"

"I thought the scariest thing in the world was a man with nothing to lose."

"It isn't?"

"No, the scariest thing in the world is a man who has everything to lose." He took a deep breath, his big chest expanding as he glared at her. "Never believed in family, loyalty, or love before I watched you and Gavin. What you two have is worth protecting."

She and Blade had never been friends. They had always maintained a professional distance. This was the first time he had opened up to her, and it made her mind reel with the knowledge that people could survive such pain and suffering. Gavin and Blade had both been raised to survive in hell and were capable of such brutality yet treated her with care and respect.

She reached out and placed her hand on his arm. She felt his muscles jump beneath her fingers. He jerked, eyes flaring as he stared at her. She opened her mouth to speak, but a strange popping sound made her turn. Before she could see what was going on, Blade threw her to the ground. She landed with enough force to knock the wind out of her and groaned as another pain clutched her stomach.

Blade pulled out his gun and fired. The sound nearly burst her eardrum. She rolled away and looked across the field and couldn't comprehend what she was seeing. Her guards were firing at... each other? There was a battle taking place, and they were using the SUVs and trees for cover.

"What the fuck is going on?" she shouted over the gunfire.

Blade didn't answer. He hauled her up, shoved her behind him, and emptied his gun. Two guards dropped. He reloaded and backed up with her behind him. She clutched fistfuls of his suit, unable to comprehend what was happening. Three guards ran forward, guns raised, with Jordy leading the pack, eyes cold and blank. Blade shot twice, wounding two but not killing them. Jordy stopped and took aim. A gray shape launched itself out of the darkness. Beau clamped Jordy's arm in his mouth and shook his head savagely. Jordy screamed, firing his gun wildly.

"Beau!" she screamed.

"Let's go!" Blade shouted.

More of her security ran forward. She panicked. She couldn't tell who was trying to defend or kill her. Blade reloaded as he shielded her with his body and killed two security guards who had been with Gavin for over a decade. He slapped the keys in her hand and shoved her.

"Get in the SUV and lock the doors. It's bulletproof."

She ran the last few feet to the SUV and ducked as a bullet hit the car less than a foot away. Blade returned fire. She yanked the driver's door open, scrambled into the seat, and slammed the door. The SUV rocked from the force of the bullets pelting its side. She dropped sideways with her hands over her head. The glass didn't shatter. She curled around her daughter, wondering if this was it. Through the terror, anger rose. She had to fight back.

She sat up and jumped as two men tried the door. Her guards stared at her as if she were something to be annihilated. They began to shoot at point-blank range. She put the keys in the ignition and fired up the SUV. Even as she slammed her foot on the gas pedal, the window was splattered with blood as another guard shot her attackers from the back.

The SUV shot forward. She could still hear the ping of bullets, but she ignored them and focused on getting out of the thick of it. When she was on the outskirts of the field, she made a U turn and braked hard. Her breathing was choppy as she flipped on the headlights and reached in the back seat for her purse. She pulled out her gun and fumbled with the controls to move the seat forward as she examined the field. She located Beau, who was wrestling with Jordy on the grass. There was a flash as Jordy fired his gun. Beau's body jerked, and her heart stopped as he flopped on the grass. Jordy got to his feet and raised his gun for a killing shot.

"No!" she screamed and slammed her foot on the gas.

The SUV kicked up dirt as it lurched forward. Men dodged out of the way as she barreled across the field toward Jordy, who swung his head around. Rage obliterated all other emotion. No. This couldn't happen to her again. She wouldn't allow it. Beau lay still and lifeless on the dirt, gray coat gleaming with blood.

Jordy fired. His bullet hit the windshield, splintering the glass in front of her, but it didn't shatter. She leaned to the right and kept her eye on her target as he fired again, inches from the last bullet. Jordy turned and fled, but he couldn't outrun her. When the bumper was inches from him, Jordy dodged, but she anticipated that. She turned sharply and hit him. There was a sickening crunch of bones and a strangled cry as she ran him over.

The SUV skidded as she turned and paused to take in the scene. Blade hid behind a tree and was being approached from two sides. She slammed her foot on the pedal and went after one of the traitors. He met the same fate as Jordy. Sweat trickled down her forehead as she turned the SUV around again and rolled the window down to take a shot. A traitor screamed as she got him in the gut. That would be a painful death. She swung her gun around when someone pounded on the passenger door and saw Blade. She unlocked the doors, and he hopped in.

"Roll up your fucking window," he snapped.

"Is it over?"

"I don't know. Let's get out of here."

"Jordy shot Beau."

"Lyla, we have to go. I don't know who we can trust—"

"I'm not leaving without him!" She drove toward Beau, who hadn't moved. When she tried to get out of the car, Blade clamped a hand on her arm.

"Keep your ass in here!" he ordered before he hopped out.

He went to Beau's body and held up his gun when two guards approached. They tossed their guns, and Blade lowered his. She heard low voices, and then the trunk opened.

"Is he alive?" she shouted. She wanted to see and touch, but she couldn't pry her hands off the steering wheel.

"He's breathing," Blade said and slammed the trunk.

The driver's door opened. She raised her gun, and a guard held his hands up.

"I'm not going to hurt you, I promise," he said, his suit splattered with blood. "I'm going to drive him to the vet."

"I can drive," she said, voice shaking.

"You need to call the boss. Are you hurt?"

"I-I..." she stammered, unable to get out a word.

"Come on."

The guard pulled her out and helped her into the back seat. When she caught a glimpse of Beau in the trunk, she dropped the seat and crawled over to him. Her hands hovered over the bullet wounds. He was breathing too hard and fast. She pressed herself against his back and willed him to live.

Fear gripped her by the throat. Beau was her companion, her friend. He couldn't die. She wouldn't allow it. She ignored the pain ripping through her stomach and hugged him close.

"You can handle this," she whispered. "You were such a brave boy. Mommy loves you so much. Stay with me, Beau. Just stay with me."

When the SUV lurched forward, she clutched Beau. Blade was shouting from the front seat, but she didn't care. The sound of her cell phone broke through her hysteria. Gavin. She scooted toward the back seat, where her purse was. She snatched her cell phone and put it up to her ear as she lay beside Beau again.

"Tell me you're okay."

Gavin's voice was guttural. She opened her mouth to speak, but a sob escaped instead. She buried her face in Beau's wet fur and tried to get a hold of herself.

"Lyla, please."

"Beau's hurt," she managed to get out.

She heard him suck in a deep breath.

"I know. Blade told me. Tell me you're okay."

She shook her head. "I-I'm not okay. Why does this keep happening?" A cramp in her belly made her moan. She panted and tried to ignore what was happening to her body. Everything had to wait until she got to the vet.

"I promise I'll get him, baby."

The SUV braked hard, making her slide a foot. The SUV doors opened and shut. Blade opened the trunk, reached for Beau, and dragged his body into his arms. Beau wasn't moving. The other guard helped her out of the trunk. She sagged to the pavement on her hands and knees and breathed through another gut-clenching cramp.

"We're at the vet," she said through gritted teeth as she forced herself up with the phone in her hand.

"Don't get out of the SUV," Gavin ordered.

"Beau needs me."

She stumbled into the reception area, which was in chaos. The other dogs present were in a frenzy over the smell of blood. Blade was in a shouting match with the receptionist, who was wringing her hands. A door opened and a man in jeans and a shirt appeared. She was about to ask if he was the vet when she felt a gush of warmth. She looked down as water pooled around her, and another cramp made her whole body shudder.

"This can't be happening," she panted.

Blade placed Beau on the counter and pointed at the guard who came in behind her. "You stay here and make sure that dog doesn't die. I need to get her to the hospital."

"No, I want to stay—" she babbled, but was cut off when Blade scooped her up in his arms and ran back to the SUV.

"What the fuck is going on?" Gavin shouted on speakerphone.

"Her water broke. She's in labor," Blade snapped as he placed her in the passenger seat and belted her in. "Sunset is the closest hospital."

"It's too early," she said hoarsely when the contraction ebbed, so she could speak. "She's not due for eight weeks."

"I'm twenty minutes away," Gavin said, voice tight.

As Blade put the car in gear, another contraction hit. The contractions were coming closer together and each one was stretching out longer.

"Get Carmen on a three-way call. She needs to be there," she said to Gavin.

Blade drove on the freeway, leaning to the right of the distorted part of the windshield, so he could see. She held on for dear life. Beau's life hung in the balance, her baby was eight weeks early, and she killed three men today. She ground her teeth together as Blade took an exit. She saw the hospital in the distance. Her bad day was far from over. Giving birth, the event she had been dreading and anticipating for months, was here.

"Gavin?" Carmen said on speakerphone.

"Lyla's in labor. She's going to be at Sunset Hospital," Gavin said.

"I'm on my way," Carmen said and hung up.

"How are you doing, baby?" Gavin asked.

"We're at the stoplight before the hospital," she said harshly as she tried to control the pain.

"Good girl."

"Did you send someone to get Jordy a-and the others? They just turned on us, Gavin. I couldn't tell who was who and—"

"Lyla, not now. We'll handle it later."

Blade circled the hospital and stopped in front of the emergency room. Another contraction hit, and she clutched the door handle and console and tried to practice the breathing technique she'd learned, which did nothing to help her focus. She didn't have her baby bag, which Carmen put oils in to help her through labor.

"Holy fuck. I don't think I can walk. Gavin, this is happening too fast. The contractions are too close. She feels like she's right there—" She screamed as another contraction snuck up on her.

When the fog of pain cleared, she saw three men waiting beside the open door with a wheelchair. Blade set her on the seat and accompanied her as they rushed through the emergency room and across the hospital to another wing. She had two more contractions before they reached the delivery room. A doctor she had never seen stuck his fingers up her vagina.

"You're seven centimeters dilated," the doctor said.

"I-I'm eight weeks early," she said.

"The baby will be here very soon."

People were throwing questions at her, but she couldn't focus on anything. The contractions were so close together that she didn't have time to rest in between. They stripped off her bloody clothes and draped her in a hospital gown. They placed her on a bed and put her feet in stirrups.

"My husband," she began and then fell back on the bed and grasped handfuls of the sheet.

"Lyla, I'm here."

Gavin appeared at her side and she reached for him. "Thank God. Gavin, she's coming. I need—"

She bore down as the contraction obliterated all thought.

"Don't push!" a nurse barked.

Gavin brushed her hair back from her face and kissed her brow. "Hold on, Lyla. Just breathe."

Fear and panic clawed at her throat. This was what she had been waiting for, but now that the moment was here, she wasn't sure she would survive. There was a confused tangle of voices and people looking under her gown and asking questions. She let Gavin handle it as she focused on her body, which felt as if it was trying to destroy itself.

She trembled like a plucked bow and stared up at Gavin as the contraction ebbed. The lethal predator that lurked just beneath the surface stared at her.

"You could have died today," he whispered.

"I didn't."

"You almost did."

She clutched his shirt. "Beau has to live. I won't let him die."

"Blade is talking to the vet."

"I want to know—" she began and clenched her teeth as another contraction hit. How did women endure two days of labor? She wasn't sure she could handle another hour. She endured pain like this only a year ago when the sadist had attacked her. The fear and horror of what occurred on the field amplified her labor pains to unbearable levels.

"Beau is still alive. He's in surgery," Blade reported.

Two nurses shouted in the hallway, and a second later, Carmen appeared with a Taser. She slammed the door and rushed over.

"I made it! How the hell can you be in labor? You left my house two hours ago. Is that blood in your hair?"

"They fucking turned on me—" she began before another contraction took hold.

The doctor came in and measured her.

"You ready to push?"

She was more than ready. She was covered in sweat and shaking like crazy. Carmen stood on one side, Gavin on the other, while Blade guarded the door. She stared at the ceiling and tried to get into the headspace that would allow her to focus past the pain. Today had been a day full of death, fear, and desperation. Tears leaked out of the corner of her eyes as she squeezed two of her best friend's hands.

"Lyla, when the next contraction comes, you have to push," the doctor said.

She nodded and took deep breaths. Her womb tightened, and she leaned forward and bore down. She stared at the doctor positioned between her legs. She listened to him count and fell back on the raised bed when the contraction passed.

"You're doing great, Lyla," the doctor praised.

"Holy shit," Carmen said and rubbed her arm. "You're almost there."

Gavin's face was closed off. There was a battle taking place in him. She knew all too well what it was. Of course, the underworld chose today to rise up and make a mark against them. Nora's birth would forever be tainted by Gavin's old life and nemesis.

"Here we go," the doctor warned.

She felt the contraction coming and met Gavin's gaze. On a day like today, they needed something like this to remind them that life would go on. She bore down and pushed for all she was worth. She felt as if her vagina was ripping in half... and then it was done.

Her ears rang as the doctor placed a small bundle on her chest. The baby began to change color right before her eyes. Nora clawed the empty air and burrowed close for warmth, screaming at the top of her lungs.

The nurses took Nora briefly to clean and weigh her, and then placed the baby on Lyla's chest. Despite being eight weeks early, Nora was a healthy six pounds, four ounces. She had a head full of black hair, and when her eyes opened, they all saw the flash of bright blue. Gavin placed his hand on Nora's back. His daughter could fit on his palm. Something elemental moved through her as she registered that she was now a mother.

When the medical personnel cleared out, leaving them alone, there was a strained silence.

"What the fuck happened?" she whispered hoarsely. She felt numb from today's events and couldn't stop shaking.

Blade widened his stance and clasped his hands behind his back. "The men were bribed by the new crime lord. The mission was to kill Lyla. Eight switched sides. We lost two men. All the traitors are dead."

"Identity of the new crime lord?" Gavin asked, his voice as calm as could be, but the air around him sizzled with rage.

Blade shook his head. Carmen looked between them with wide eyes.

Her throat burned with the need to rage. She buried her face against Nora's soft skin and absorbed the feel of her. Nora was so small and defenseless and had been so close to dying today. There was so much hate and evil in the world. She and Gavin were Nora's only defense against the darkness waiting for her.

Tears streamed down her face as she listened to Nora's quick breaths. Tiny hands gripped her hair as Nora nuzzled close. This was her child to protect, and she would do so. She rested Nora on her shoulder and looked at Gavin, who was watching her, waiting.

Tears trickled down her face, but her voice was steady as she said, "You go back into the underworld, you find him, and you kill that fucker slowly."

ONCE A CRIME LORD

DEDICATION

To my fans who made this possible—I appreciate you so much!

1

LYLA

Lyla Pyre rocked her four-month-old daughter as she ran her fingers through the full head of jet-black hair Nora inherited from her father. Nora's eyelashes fluttered as she nursed, revealing silver blue eyes identical to her own. Nora was perfect from the top of her head to her tiny, pudgy toes. She couldn't imagine life without her, yet she had come so close to never experiencing this. She held a miracle in the crook of her arm.

Something that sounded like a snorting pig interrupted Lyla's thought. She glanced down at Beau, a gray pit bull who was fast asleep at her feet. She saved Beau from a dog shelter after volunteering there for several months, and he had become a loyal companion. She ran her foot down his back and felt the ridges from bullet wounds. Beau was shot trying to protect her when a handful of bodyguards turned on her. It had been a long recovery for Beau, but he was alive, and that's all she cared about. He spent most of his time in Nora's nursery, keeping guard.

She switched Nora to her other breast so she wouldn't have to pump. She wasn't proud of many things, but creating a human being was a pretty big deal. Having a baby with Gavin Pyre, the man she loved, was a blessing. She wanted to offer Nora the world, but first, her daddy had a few things to take care of. Gavin's mission was to track down the man who bribed her guards to kill her while she was seven months pregnant and who brutally murdered his father, Manny Pyre, two years ago.

Nora fell asleep with her mouth open. She dabbed her mouth with a bib and rested the baby on her shoulder, rubbing her back lightly. She closed her eyes as she rocked, taking comfort in the quiet. The nursery had become her sanctuary in the past four months; a peaceful room untouched by the horrors of the outside world. Here, they were safe.

Beau's head rose suddenly, which caused his dog tags to clink together. A man stood in the doorway. Even as her heart jumped into her throat, she recognized her husband. She'd only seen him a handful of times over the past four months. His scruff made him look even more dark and dangerous than normal. The air around him simmered with a coiled tension that made people get out of his way.

Beau trotted over and sat in front of him. Gavin looked down at the dog for a moment before he patted him on the head and then scratched him under the chin. Sometime during Beau's recovery, Gavin had finally accepted him as part of the family.

Gavin strode forward, hazel eyes glinting in the dim light. He set his hands on the arms of the rocking chair and stared at her. Her heart stuttered.

"Gavin?" she whispered.

His eyes moved to Nora. He reached for her, gently lifting the baby from her shoulder. He cradled Nora's head in one hand and her body in the other. He scanned his daughter, taking in every detail he'd missed in the three weeks he hadn't seen her. Nora frowned, hands reaching out for an anchor. He kissed her forehead and then placed her on his chest with her little face tucked against his neck. Nora relaxed instantly and let out a shuddering breath as she drifted back to sleep.

"Everything okay?" she asked.

It was hard to determine his mood. When Gavin came home, he was capable of anything. The aggression and brutality he exerted in the underworld clung to him. Most of her communication with him was over the phone, and that was infrequent. He spent ninety percent of his time in the underworld and the rest in the business world where he was CEO of Pyre Casinos, a chain on the notorious Las Vegas Strip. When he could carve out time, he spent a handful of hours at home before he was gone again. It had been hard on them, but she reassured herself this was temporary.

He stared intently at her. "Did you have a good day?"

She rose from the chair. "What are you talking about? What's going on?"

He cupped the back of her neck, and hauled her against his side. "Gavin—"

He kissed her, a deep and carnal kiss that made her body go up in flames. She clutched his arm and dug her nails into his chest, very aware of Nora's weight against her arm. Apparently, he was capable of kissing her mindless and holding Nora without a problem because he did so until she forgot her own name. When he pulled back, she stared at him with her body throbbing.

"I watched you in our bedroom this afternoon," he said.

"What are you—?" Her voice died out, and her face went up in flames. "Oh, my God."

She tried to push away, but he kept her banded against him. He kissed her forehead, cheek, and then jaw.

"You had your checkup with the doctor, but you didn't say we could have sex," he said against her temple.

"I..." she fumbled and then swallowed. "You've been busy." She couldn't ask her husband to come home to have sex when he was trying to find a serial killer.

"I'm never too busy to make you come."

"Gavin!"

"What?" He captured her lips again and squeezed her ass. "You're ready, right?"

She still had her pregnancy weight, and her body definitely wasn't something most men would call beautiful since her chest and abdomen were marred by gruesome scars. It should have been impossible for her to feel sexy in sweatpants and a loose top, but the way Gavin was looking at her made her feel like the most desirable woman in the world. She winced as her breasts began to leak. That was definitely not sexy.

"I'm, um—" she stammered.

"I'll make you ready," he said and moved toward the crib.

Deprived of his support, she swayed before she found her balance. Gavin nuzzled Nora and kissed her on the mouth.

"Sleep, baby girl," he murmured before he placed her in the crib. He turned and strode back to Lyla. "Bedroom."

"Gavin, you haven't—" She bit back a shriek when he picked her up and strode to the master suite.

"You don't want to fuck, then I'll go down on you and you go down on me."

He kicked the bedroom door shut, dumped her on the bed, and braced himself over her. His face was hard and drawn with lust. He definitely didn't look like a sweet lover.

He had always possessed a dark side, but now that he was back in the underworld, the feral part of him was close to the surface. There was a storm inside him, fighting for release. Desire warred with insecurity. Her body tingled with the knowledge that if she let him, she could be thoroughly fucked tonight.

"What's it gonna be?" he asked.

"Gavin—"

He straightened and yanked her sweatpants off. In the next second, her legs were being spread. Her body convulsed at the first lash of his tongue. He went deep, gorging on her while she sank her hands into his hair and closed her eyes against the lash of pleasure. His fingers intruded as he lapped at her clit, driving her crazy.

"Gavin."

His fingers curled, and she erupted beneath him. He growled and did it again.

"Gavin," she panted.

He didn't speak, didn't stop.

Her hands slid from his hair to the back of his neck, dragging him into her heat, raising her legs high. His eyes flashed up to hers. Those mesmerizing lion eyes commanded she give herself to him. He sucked and curled his fingers again. Her heels slammed on his shoulders as she arched. He cupped her ass and ground her against his mouth. She collapsed on the bed as the orgasm passed. He didn't move his mouth from between her legs. He continued to feed from her. She tried to squirm away, but his hands flexed on her hips, keeping her in place.

"Gavin," she moaned.

She jerked, shuddered, and ran her hands through his silky hair. When he stopped, she opened heavy eyes and saw that his were dark and hungry.

"What do you want?" she whispered.

He yanked, and she slid off the bed onto his lap. His hand sank into her hair, gripped, and held her still for his kiss. He drank from her as if she was life itself. She ran her hands down his chest and felt him shudder. He clutched her tight as if he wanted to absorb her.

When he pulled back, her lips were swollen and pulsing. He rose and left her on her knees in front of him.

"Suck me," he ordered.

Her mouth quirked. She traced the hard length of him through his slacks and tempted the beast by nuzzling him. He stood with his legs braced apart, arms clasped behind him like a soldier. He said nothing, but a muscle in his jaw locked.

She took her time exploring him through his clothes, even reaching down to cup his balls and give them a gentle squeeze before his control snapped. He gripped her hair and gave her a punishing kiss.

"I'm not in the mood to be teased," he said against her mouth.

"I am," she said as she traced his jawline.

He resumed his pose. "You know the consequences."

She sure did. She was getting wet just thinking about it. She undid the buckle, slowly dragging the belt free, and unhooked his slacks. She dragged the zipper down, the sound magnified in the hushed quiet. His cock, unencumbered by boxers, fell into her hand before the zipper was all the way down. She ignored his erect dick and reached up to unbutton his shirt. A low growl of impatience filled the room. She ducked her head to hide her smile.

She wrapped her hand around the base of his cock and stroked him. A drop of precum formed at the tip of his penis. She captured it, and he bit back a groan. Her body began to heat again, and milk leaked from her breasts. She ignored the sensation and tugged his pants down so she could cup his balls. Gavin rocked forward, imbedding half his length in her mouth. She groaned and heard him swear as the sound vibrated along his sensitive cock. She leaned back and swirled her tongue around the tip and then traveled along the length of his shaft to his balls. She licked delicately.

"That's it," he hissed.

He yanked her up. Even as she braced her hands against the wall, he sank his cock into her. He gripped her hips and didn't stop until he was fully imbedded inside her. Her body stretched and yielded. She panted as Gavin dropped his face in her hair.

"I need this," he growled before he pulled out and slammed home with such force that she cried out.

He moved, deep thrusts that made her teeth clench. He was a man possessed. She took everything he gave and asked for more by arching into his thrusts. He brushed her hair to the side and bit her neck, hard enough to shock her.

"You'll never be free of me." He collared her throat as he continued to plunge home. "I'll never get enough of you."

"Gavin!"

His hand moved to her chest. She panicked and shoved his hand away before he could feel her damp bra. His rhythm faltered. Without warning, he pulled out, whirled her around, and slammed her back against the wall. Gavin was a carnal beast and not about to be denied anything. He looked half savage, half warrior in his unbuttoned starch white shirt, suit jacket, and nothing else.

"You don't push me away," he ordered and went for her breasts again.

When she knocked his hand away again, he bared his teeth.

"What the fuck did I just say?"

"I-I'm leaking," she muttered, mortified and turned on at the same time.

She wasn't prepared when he ripped her loose top in half. She wore a nursing bra, which wasn't even close to cute. Why the hell did he have to see everything? She raised her hands to cover herself, but that didn't deter him. He deftly undid the hooks on her bra, and it fell away. She tried to escape, hands clamped over her damp breasts, but he boxed her in.

"When I get aroused, I start leaking. It's embarrassing—" she began.

He gripped her wrists, spread her arms, and examined her breasts, which definitely weren't as perky as they'd been before she gave birth. Sex was about fantasy, and her post pregnancy bod, scars, and leaking breasts dimmed her libido significantly.

When his head ducked down, she collided with the wall. She sucked in her breath, which did nothing to prevent Gavin from capturing her nipple in his mouth. He suckled. She screeched and tried to stomp his foot. He dragged her up so her breasts were at the perfect height for him to feast. She shoved his head, but he didn't budge.

"Gavin, stop!" she shrieked.

He ignored her. As he sucked, more milk gathered heavy in her tits. Gavin switched to the other breast, and she fought the sexual pull, but he was relentless. Knowing there was no escape, she stared down at him as he fed. Her lactating didn't turn him off. On the contrary, he seemed hungrier than ever. As she watched, the place between her legs went liquid. When she couldn't take anymore, she yanked his head up and covered his wet mouth with hers.

He let her drop low enough for him to slide back inside. He fucked her hard, raising one thigh to go even deeper. He wouldn't allow distance between them and accepted everything about her, even the things she didn't like about herself. How could she not love him?

His unrelenting thrusts pushed her over the edge. As her body milked him, he came, gripping her ass and mashing their bodies together until he stopped pulsing inside her. She panted against his naked, heaving chest and waited for her body to calm down.

"Okay?" he murmured.

"Yeah," she said lazily.

When he finally disengaged, he carried her into the bathroom. He filled the bathtub and shrugged off his clothes. He settled her in front of him. She leaned back against his broad chest. They sat there with the occasional slosh of water echoing in the massive bathroom.

The charged energy around him had dimmed somewhat, but it would never vanish completely. It was a part of him.

Outside these walls, the world wasn't a beautiful place. It was dark, brutal, and grim. The underworld was a place filled with untold horrors and people with no souls. Gavin had been taught not only how to survive in darkness but how to control it.

It had taken her being nearly gunned down while seven months pregnant to come to terms with the fact that the underworld needed a ruthless dictator at the top... and that man was her husband. He spent the past four months reclaiming his territory. It was clear from his cold fury that he hadn't been able to locate Sadist, the crime lord who took the title when he murdered Manny Pyre. Sadist haunted her nightmares, which were amplified with fear now that she had Nora.

"I miss having you beside me at night," he said as he rested his face in her hair and inhaled. "It's been hell, baby."

"I miss you too."

"Nora's getting so big."

She smiled without opening her eyes. "She is."

His arms tightened around her. "You haven't been sleeping much."

She dropped her head back to see his face. "What do you mean?"

He tapped the watch on her wrist. "It has a heart monitor. You barely get five hours a night, and it's not because of Nora."

"Don't worry about it, Gavin."

"Why aren't you sleeping?"

She didn't answer. He cupped her cheek and ran his thumb over her bottom lip.

"Your panic attacks are becoming more frequent."

She scowled. "Blame Blade. He keeps springing surprise attacks on me throughout the day to see how I'll respond."

"It's a precaution."

In case she had to fight for her life. Again. "I know."

"You're becoming better than a decent shot."

His voice was warm with approval. She tilted her chin proudly.

"Yup and I can kick ass."

His mouth twitched. "You're cute."

She surveyed Gavin who was all muscle. "Well, I can't kick ass like you, but I put two of your men down."

"Because you did a crotch shot."

Of course, he knew that. "How often do you watch me on the surveillance cameras?"

"Enough."

She narrowed her eyes. "How much?"

He kissed her forehead. "A lot."

"I can't believe you watched me this afternoon," she grouched.

"You should be happy I watched, or I wouldn't be here right now." He cupped her breast and thumbed her nipple, making her jolt. "Why didn't you give me the green light if we could have sex?"

"You're busy."

"So?"

"You have better things to do."

His hand tightened on her sensitive breast. "Lyla, you're my number one priority."

"Giving me orgasms isn't a priority."

"It is to me." He dropped his forehead on hers. "I've been waiting to have you again. I jerked off watching you in my car, took care of business, and came to you as soon as I could."

"That's romantic," she said dryly.

"You want romance?"

She made a face. Their relationship had never been about flamboyant gestures or sweet words. "I don't need romance."

He looked offended. "I can give you romance."

She imagined him on his knees with a rose clamped between his teeth and began to laugh. He didn't have a romantic bone in his body. When she ran from him, he blackmailed her into coming back. A year and a half later, he gained her marriage vows by threatening to harm her cousin, Carmen. He was no Prince Charming. The thought of him trying to be romantic was ludicrous. It wasn't until she glanced at his face that she realized he was far from amused.

"Gavin, it's not a big deal," she said, patting his arm. He was a crime lord, not Romeo. "I never asked for romance."

He grasped her chin and glared down at her. "Was your ex romantic?"

"Jonathan?"

God, she hadn't thought of him in months. Jonathan, the IT consultant she'd left behind in Maine, had been the definition of a gentleman. He was the sweetest man she had ever met, and it wasn't an act. He wooed her with long drives along the coast, picnics on the beach, and conversation. The memories slipping through her mind seemed like they were from another lifetime.

A growl made her focus on her husband. "What?"

"You're smiling."

"Oh."

"You're still smiling."

She couldn't straighten her lips, not when he was giving her such a disgruntled look.

"Was he romantic?"

She shrugged.

"What does that mean?"

She threw her hands in the air. "Who cares if Jonathan was romantic?"

"I do."

"Well, it doesn't matter now, does it?"

"It does."

She rolled her eyes. "You are seriously one of the most primitive men I've ever met." She held up left hand and wriggled her ring finger where the blue diamond sparkled. "We're married and have a kid together."

"Was he romantic?"

He was such a bullheaded ass. "Yes, he was."

He tensed, and she realized she should have lied.

"Gavin, romance is nothing compared to—"

"I'll give you fucking romance."

He got out of the tub, and she grit her teeth.

"Gavin, this is stupid."

He hauled her up and toweled her dry.

"You don't have to—"

He picked her up like a bride and carried her into the bedroom. He dropped her on the bed and braced himself on all fours over her.

"I want to be the one to give you everything," he stated.

She clasped his face between her hands. "You do give me everything."

"Except romance."

She jerked his head down and kissed him. He tried to pull away, but she wouldn't let him. She licked his bottom lip until he opened his mouth and slid her tongue inside. Her emotions, which had always been volatile whenever it revolved around him, flared. She poured her love into him so he could feel it.

Gavin shuddered and kissed her back. He kissed her with such force that she sank into the mattress. His hands moved over her body, reclaiming every inch for himself. She smiled against his mouth as he slid inside her. He rocked himself deep, and they both groaned.

"I live for you," he said.

Her heart thudded against her rib cage. "I know. You're risking your life for me."

"Since my life means nothing without you, it's not a hardship." His eyes bored into hers. "What do you want, Lyla?"

"I want to feel safe." It was the one thing he couldn't give her, not until Sadist was dead. It was the reason she couldn't sleep. When she slept, she had nightmares of the knife-wielding psycho. Her paranoia even leaked into her waking hours. A slamming door or tone of voice could send her into the past where she drowned in bloody memories.

"I'm going to get him," he said.

If there was one man who would find the fucker who haunted her nightmares, it was Gavin. "I know."

"I'm going to bring his head to you on a platter," he vowed.

She grinned. "Is that your idea of romance?"

When he grimaced, she laughed and wrapped herself around him.

"Anyone can give me romance, but no one can give me what you do."

The monster inside him that made him the most feared man in the underworld watched her with starving eyes.

"And what's that?"

"Real love."

He stopped moving.

"Any man handing out roses on the street can charm a woman. Any man can plan an elaborate proposal with jet planes spelling out the big question, but no one can promise to love you forever. No one can promise that they won't get divorced or be there for each other through thick and thin." She gave him a mock glare. "Do you promise to love me forever?"

"Yes."

No hesitation. Her heart warmed. She smiled as she clasped his face.

"What about a divorce?"

"Fuck no."

"You promise never to leave me?"

He leaned down and said against her lips, "Once this is over, you won't be able to get rid of me."

She didn't have to ask the last question because they had been through more than most couples went through in several lifetimes.

He made love to her with a gentleness that brought tears to her eyes. He adored her. It was in every touch, every look. He teased her until she clawed his back and cursed at him. He brought her to an orgasm so good that she cried. She held him tight, absorbing the fact he was strong, warm, and alive. Sending him back into the underworld made her sick with worry, but they had no other choice.

"I love you," he whispered.

She smiled with her eyes closed. Maybe Gavin wasn't what most people would call romantic, but he was her type of romantic, and that's all that mattered.

He shifted to get out of bed, and she clung to him, not wanting to end this moment.

"Not yet. Ten more minutes," she mumbled sleepily. She couldn't remember the last time she slept through the night. If he just lay with her for an hour...

"I'm not leaving."

One eye opened. "You aren't?"

"You think I can leave you now that I had you again?"

She beamed. "You're spending the night?" It was a night for romance and miracles.

"Yeah. I just need to check my phone."

She flopped onto the pillows and listened to his voice as he spoke to someone in Spanish. She let the sound of his voice lull her and slipped into the first peaceful sleep she had in months.

2

LYLA

SHE WOKE TO THE MOST BEAUTIFUL SIGHT IN THE WORLD. GAVIN SAT ON the bed with Nora on his lap. He spoke to his daughter who bounced excitedly, bright blue eyes shining as she responded to him. It made her stomach feel warm and squishy. This is what she always wanted. Seeing them together was her version of utopia. Gavin had been the one who insisted on kids, and she was so happy he had.

He nuzzled Nora, who made a happy shrieking sound and wrapped her arms around his head. Beau pranced, wanting to play, but knew that Gavin wouldn't allow him on the bed. Beau ran to her so she could smother him with kisses while he growled low in his throat in appreciation.

"Nora's trying to sit up," she said.

Gavin gave his daughter an admonishing look. "Stop trying to grow up so fast!"

Nora wasn't intimidated by her father. She let out a happy gurgle and drooled. Lyla sat up, clutching the sheet to her bare chest.

"Da da da," Nora chanted as she bounced.

"Yes, I'm your daddy," he said and brushed kisses over her face, "and he loves you so much."

Her heart clenched. During the short stretches of time that Gavin was home, he doted on Nora. Carmen warned him that he would spoil her. The last time she said this, Gavin gave her a cool look. "She deserves to be spoiled. She's mine." Carmen threw up her hands, but Lyla saw her hiding a smirk. Carmen couldn't resist giving Gavin shit. They had an odd relationship, but it worked for them, so she didn't interfere.

"She's hungry," he said.

She reached for the baby. He watched as Nora found her breast and latched on. She flushed when she caught his heated gaze. She wasn't used to having him around for feedings.

"You shouldn't feel insecure about your body, especially about something natural like lactating. It made me hot to see you pregnant. Why would it be any different to see this?"

"I didn't think men would—"

His eyes narrowed. "You don't need to think about what other men want. You only need to think about me."

She rolled her eyes. "Obviously, I'm not thinking of anyone else. How could I?"

"Make sure it stays that way." He ran a hand down her face. "You slept deep?"

"Like the dead."

"Feel good?"

She nodded. He ruffled Nora's hair. In the bright morning light, she saw a fresh cut on the back of his hand. She grabbed his hand to examine it and felt her stomach dip.

"Is this from a knife?" she asked.

"It's nothing."

Fear cascaded through her. "What happened?"

"It was nothing."

"I can't lose you," she whispered.

"You won't."

"What if you're shot or—"

"I've survived much worse."

She bit her lip. "If you can't find him, maybe—"

His expression tightened. "Don't, Lyla."

"It's been four months. Maybe you killed him already and don't know it," she said even though she didn't believe it.

"He'll surface. He always does."

Guilt and worry dogged her every waking moment. She had become a paranoid recluse, only leaving the house to go to doctor's appointments. Thank God Carmen was here. Carmen didn't ask if she could move in. After Nora was born, she arrived with two suitcases and claimed a room. Surprisingly, Gavin didn't make a fuss about it. Carmen made her house arrest bearable.

"I know what I'm doing, Lyla. Don't worry about me."

"How can I not worry about you?" she snapped.

"I was raised in the underworld. I'm getting close."

She tightened her hold on Nora. "You are?"

"I'm making people nervous. That's good." His eyes glittered. "I'm going to get him."

"I just want this to be over." It had been over two years since the attack that claimed Manny's life and left her scarred.

"It will be." He sucked on her neck. "Coming home to you keeps me human."

She elbowed him. "Sex isn't the answer to everything!"

"Yes, it is. It reminds me how much I have to lose, and that isn't fucking happening."

She waved a hand in his face before dropping her eyes to Nora. "Watch your language."

He grinned. "She's four months old."

"So?"

He shook his head. "I'm heading into the office. Janice and Alice have been asking about you and the baby. Do you want to come?"

Effectively distracted by the offer, she felt her heart soar with excitement even as her belly iced with fear. "Is it safe to go out?"

"You're in my casino. Your security detail will be with you, and you won't be left alone."

She hesitated only a moment before she said, "I'd like that."

"We'll leave in two hours," he said and headed for the bathroom.

Even while she felt safe in Gavin's fortress, she was beginning to feel the first stages of cabin fever. Before, she went out three to four times a week. Now, she left the house once a month. She and Carmen kept busy by training four times a week with a self-defense/mixed martial arts instructor. And Blade made sure to keep their tactical skills up to par by taking them regularly to the gun range on property. Carmen, who had been raised with an enforcer father and married into the Pyre clan, understood the measures that needed to be taken for their protection.

She texted Carmen who responded immediately, saying she was down for the 'excursion.' She scanned her messages and saw a text from her mother: *Please call. Really need to talk to you.* She ignored the text. The last time she spoke to her mother was the day Nora was born. Her mother asked for money, of course. Traumatized by the attack at the field and Nora's birth, she hung up on her mother and ignored all messages since then. Her father, a gambling addict, had fucked up again. It was nothing new, and she was tired of cleaning up his shit.

Just as Nora finished eating, Gavin emerged from the shower. He took Nora so she could get ready. This felt so normal and domesticated. She had an extra spring in her step as she applied makeup for the first time in months and donned a navy-blue wrap dress. She added a white scarf to cover her scarred chest and as a cover in case she had to nurse. She draped a coat over her arm and added stiletto boots.

She found Carmen in the nursery packing a bulging baby bag.

Carmen gave her a lascivious grin. "Did you get any sleep last night?"

She smiled. "A little."

Carmen no longer looked like the Playboy bunny she had been when her husband Vinny was alive. The crying spells had waned in the passing years and Carmen seemed to be adjusting to her new lot in life. She took out her breast implants, dyed her hair black, and still managed to hook every man within a ten-foot radius. After wearing sweatpants for four months, it was a shock to see Carmen looking like her old self. Today's ensemble was a nude skirt that hugged every curve of her body from waist to ankle and a white lace blouse. Carmen completed the look with white heels and large diamond stud earrings. The look was deceivingly demure, but an outright challenge to any man.

"You're asking for trouble," she said with a grin.

Carmen beamed and posed with her hands on the stroller, looking like a seductive MILF. "I love trouble."

Carmen ruined her image by twerking in her tight skirt. Apparently, Carmen had been feeling the effects of cabin fever and had finally cracked.

"Okay, so you're dying for trouble. I get it. You packed Nora's things?"

Carmen gave a mock salute. "Yes, ma'am, and I dressed Nora too. Let's get the hell out of here!"

She laughed as Carmen wheeled everything toward the hallway. Blade, Lyla's bodyguard, efficiently folded the stroller and shouldered the bag.

"You're getting good at that, Blade. When are you going to become a daddy?" Carmen asked as she sashayed past.

"When hell freezes over." He glanced at Lyla who had her arms crossed. "No offense. Babies aren't my thing."

"But Nora loves you," she said.

"I like her well enough since she's my goddaughter," he said with a straight face, "but she needs a lot of everything, and I don't have time for that."

She patted his chest. There was a time when Blade scared the living daylights out of her, but those days were long gone. Blade took a bullet for her and was fast becoming part of the family, something he didn't seem thrilled with.

"Maybe when things calm down, you can have your own life," she said.

His dubious expression clearly stated that he didn't believe there would ever be a time they wouldn't need his services. When they walked into the kitchen, they found the cook finishing up fresh omelets.

"I miss coffee," she said.

"You can have some, can't you?" Carmen asked as she ate a banana.

"Not much and I want to load it with creamer, so it's best not to."

Her weird pregnancy cravings were gone, thank God, but she was still eating more than she used to. The workouts with her instructors and breastfeeding were burning off calories, but her body still needed more to produce milk. She was a bit self-conscious with the extra weight, but if Gavin didn't mind, then why should she? She was a mother, after all, not a supermodel. She jolted when Beau flopped at her feet. She glanced down and received a baleful look from the dog who realized they were leaving him behind.

"I don't think Daddy's going to let you in his casino," she said to him.

"I've been texting Alice," Carmen said.

"About what?"

"Some of her volunteer projects."

Alice, the Community Outreach Coordinator for the Pyre Foundation, was in charge of charitable events for the Pyre Foundation and making a positive impact on the community. She and Carmen had volunteered at several events, but after the last attack, she retreated completely.

"Next week, Alice has a volunteer day at a hospital. Gavin gave a generous donation to add a new wing."

Gavin walked in with Nora cradled in one arm. She was momentarily sidetracked by his slick appearance. He wore a crisp gray suit with a light blue shirt and silver tie. There was nothing hotter than a man with a baby.

He raised a brow. "Ready?"

"Uh, yeah." She ignored the pool of desire in her belly. He took her twice last night. How the hell could she still be horny? She thought once they had Nora their libidos would slack off. Not so, apparently. "You didn't tell me you donated money to a hospital."

Nora's pacifier bounced as she yanked on her daddy's tie. Gavin didn't bother to snatch it from her chubby hands.

"It's a good cause." He shifted his sleeve to glance at his watch. "Let's go."

She bent down to kiss Beau and promised she would be back as soon as possible. On the way to the door, she made sure to check the safety on her gun. Carrying a weapon saved her life, so she wouldn't be caught without one. She was sure Carmen was packing as well. The world they live in forced them to take extreme precautions.

They walked into the crisp morning air. She automatically glanced around to take in her guards. She didn't know what Gavin did to test the loyalty of his men, but she was aware that a quarter of them mysteriously disappeared after he conducted some interviews.

Gavin placed Nora in the car seat and rode shotgun while Blade drove. She scooted in beside Nora with Carmen on her other side.

"This is going to be the first time everyone sees her. You like her outfit?" Carmen asked.

Nora was dressed in black leggings, a knit sweater with a cute heart design, and matching boots and cap. She brushed the back of her hand against Nora's cheek, which was toasty warm.

"She looks adorable."

"Of course, she does. I bought her that," Carmen said proudly.

She made faces at Nora, who giggled and reached for her. She allowed Nora to mess up her hair before she pulled back and left her hand on her daughter's lap to play with. She couldn't resist turning in her seat to look at the entourage of SUVs following them. It was normal to feel paranoid after what she had been through, right? Her eyes touched on the trunk. She had a vivid memory of lying back there holding Beau, willing him to live after he had been shot.

She took a deep breath and faced forward. She willed away the flashbacks, but they refused to be ignored. She could still hear the pop of gunfire as her guards turned on one another. Adrenaline flooded her body, urging her to go into fight or flight mode. She sat back, closed her eyes, and tried to calm down. She had done every-thing in her power to avoid situations that would cause her anxiety to skyrocket, such as leaving the house. When she felt steady enough, she opened her eyes and saw Blade watching her in the rearview mirror. She looked away.

Gavin's fortress lay on the outskirts of the city, far from the prying eyes of society. The desert was an unforgiving place, much like the people who occupied it. She had come to appreciate its starkness and take comfort in the isolation of their home.

Las Vegas was an oasis in the middle of the Mojave Desert. The lure of money and sex had enticed millions to The Strip to try their luck since the 1930s. She resisted the urge to cover Nora's eyes as they cruised down The Strip. Women with pasties on their nipples and skirts too short to cover their asses tried to make a quick buck by posing with nerdy tourists or preteen boys. Others dressed as popular characters while street performers tried to entertain the crowds.

Blade stopped in front of one of the Pyre Casinos. Gavin unbuckled Nora from her car seat and carried her inside. She shouldered the baby bag while Blade followed with the stroller. Despite her excitement about leaving the house, she was on edge. People were everywhere, and the noise was overwhelming. The smell of smoke was heavy in the air, and even though it wasn't even ten o'clock, cocktail waitresses held trays laden with liquor. There were no kids in sight, of course. Las Vegas wasn't child friendly, a point she tried to impress upon Manny when she was young and naïve. However, Manny had allowed her to create a black stallion statue instead of another naked figure for the gamblers to touch for luck.

They made their way through the casino to the executive offices. Gavin's employees stopped and stared at the sight of him with a baby. Several of the braver souls stepped forward to greet Nora, who was fascinated by all the new faces. Gavin didn't offer Nora to any of the cooing women gathered around him. He was a possessive bastard and didn't want to give up his daughter for a second.

"Lyla!"

She smiled as Marcus approached. Before Gavin could interfere, his good-looking COO kissed her on the cheek and wrapped her in a tight hug. Marcus had become dear to her in the brief time she'd known him. Not only did he shoulder Gavin's workload, he was also unfailingly loyal. Marcus acted as if he was a Pyre himself and pushed to expand the business and leave behind a legacy for the next generation.

"How are you?" Marcus asked as he cupped her cheek.

She loved that about Marcus. He could be cutthroat in business, but he was affectionate and treated her like a long-lost sister. He didn't follow the rules of propriety where she was concerned, which drove Gavin insane.

"I'm good," she said.

He stood back and beamed. "You look great!"

Her anxiety fell away. "Thank you."

"Where's my goddaughter?"

Gavin scowled as he broke through the ring of female employees around him. "I never made you Nora's godfather."

"You should," Marcus said, unperturbed by his surly attitude. He bent to catch Nora's attention. "Hi, baby, I'm Uncle Marcus." He held his hands out to her.

Gavin began to smirk, but that vanished when Nora reached for Marcus, a complete stranger. Gavin started to turn away, but Marcus snatched Nora from her father who flushed with rage. Lyla wrapped her arm around Gavin's waist so he wouldn't harm Marcus.

"Cool it," she said and tried to hide her smile.

"I don't like him touching you," Gavin growled.

How many times had she heard that since she met Marcus? It was obvious there was nothing romantic between them, but Gavin never failed to comment on it.

"He's like my brother."

They watched Marcus talk to Nora who was taken by his smooth voice and All-American good looks.

"We should make him her godfather," she said.

Gavin stiffened. "Hell no."

"Why not? Look at him with her. I trust Marcus with Nora."

He grunted. "I don't want him to think he's family."

"You trust him with your business and money, why not your family?"

Gavin didn't answer.

Marcus settled Nora on his hip and raked Carmen from head to heels while the nightclub manager she spoke to grinned like a fool. Marcus's normally expressive face revealed nothing of what he was thinking.

"Oh my gosh! You're here!"

Alice, wearing purple slacks and an unflattering blouse with large flowers, embraced Lyla and then backed away, clapping her hands. "You look great! Where's the baby?"

Before she could answer, Alice spotted Nora in Marcus's arms. She rushed over and talked to Nora who flapped her arms and smiled so wide that her pacifier dropped. Like Gavin, Marcus didn't relinquish his hold on Nora. Alice was disappointed, but she wasn't about to play tug of war with a baby or snap at her boss.

"He's hogging her," Alice complained and then bounced on her toes, eyes lighting up as she remembered something. "Are you able to volunteer at the hospital next week? Carmen said she'd talk to you about it."

"I'm not sure," she said as Gavin gripped the back of her coat.

"I'm on my way to a meeting with Janice to discuss the event. It's going to be our largest to date!" Alice eyed Gavin uncertainly, clearly uneasy about addressing him directly. "Are you coming, Mr. Pyre?"

"No," he said shortly.

Alice didn't bother to hide her relief. It was clear she wasn't comfortable around her boss. She turned back to Lyla. "You want to come to the meeting?"

She looked up at Gavin. His jaw was locked. Clearly, he didn't want her out of his sight, but she was curious about the event and felt bad for not participating. Before Nora was born, she had been extremely active in the Pyre Foundation and enjoyed volunteering.

"Lyla?" Alice prompted.

She went on tiptoe and kissed Gavin's bristly jaw. "I'll be back."

She glanced at Marcus who presented Nora to the casino workers as if she were his. "You'll keep an eye on Nora?"

"Of course. Blade," Gavin bit out, and Blade materialized by her side. "Bring her right back to me."

"Yes, sir," Blade said.

She slipped away from Gavin to kiss Nora on the cheek. She looked around for Carmen, but she was gone. She tamped down her alarm. Carmen could take care of herself. Alice waved tentatively at Blade who regarded her impassively. Four guards joined him.

"Did I miss something?" Alice asked out of the side of her mouth. "I thought we haven't seen you because of Nora. Is something else going on?"

"That's just Gavin being Gavin," she said dismissively.

Revealing anything about the attacks wasn't an option. Alice might keel over from the shock. Alice was a Utah native, a state known for its strict religion and conservative views. She never asked Alice what prompted her to come to Las Vegas, but was glad to have her as a friend. Alice was a beam of light in an otherwise dark city filled with greed and lust.

"You look great," Alice said admiringly as they walked through the casino.

"Thank you. I'm starting to feel... better."

Seeing Nora being fawned over by Marcus and the other employees made her feel as if she was a part of a community rather than a lone ranger. For the first time in months, she wasn't worrying about Gavin in the underworld or Nora's future. She could live in the moment as she walked arm in arm with Alice through a casino teeming with people.

"What are your plans today?" Alice asked.

"I'm not sure. Gavin said you and Janice have been asking about Nora, so I thought we'd visit. Carmen came too, but I don't know where she's gone off to."

"Oh, I should have invited her to the meeting." Alice waved her hand. "Well, she's been involved from the beginning, so she knows everything anyway."

Carmen had been in on the plans for the hospital event? How? She hadn't left the house.

Alice steered her into a conference room where Janice was holding court. Gavin's Public Relations Coordinator was a force to be reckoned with. Janice single-handedly pulled Gavin's tattered image out of the trash after Gavin went to jail for money laundering and Manny's grisly murder was splashed across the news. Between Alice and Janice, the Pyre name had become a beacon of hope in the communities that badly needed a benefactor.

"You're back!" Janice exclaimed, running forward in spiked heels and a tailored suit. She gave Lyla a fierce hug and then looked at Blade, the only guard who entered the room. "Where's the baby?"

"With Gavin and Marcus," Lyla said.

Janice's eyes bugged. "You trust them with a baby?"

"I don't think I could pry her away from them. Gavin's obsessed and Marcus has elected himself her godfather."

"Blade, make yourself comfortable," Janice said, ever courteous, and led Lyla to the table.

Janice introduced her to six women who were managing this event and immediately began to outline the festivities. Gavin helped repair two wings of the hospital, which had been destroyed during a fire, and made a sizable donation to build a new one. The hospital was celebrating the completion of the new wing, which Alice saw as an opportunity for the Pyre Foundation to reach out.

Alice spoke enthusiastically about the itinerary. It was clear this had taken months to plan, and the amount of people involved was staggering. Over one hundred Pyre employees were volunteering their time to pass out goodie bags and care baskets. Thanks to Carmen's connections, they had an impressive list of celebrities attending the event to draw the press. Her brows shot up when she heard Kody Singer agreed to make a little girl's dying wish come true. Carmen was talking to her past fling?

Every person in the room possessed an abundance of love, caring, and hope. It made the underworld seem like an alternate universe. How could there be people with no souls on the same planet with someone like Alice who believed in the good in every human being? Just being in this room filled with compassionate people soothed her fear and worry. The best way to combat the darkness was to get involved and be around those trying to make a positive difference in the world.

As the meeting concluded, the staff and volunteers hugged her. She had been alone for so long that the simple show of affection and camaraderie made her eyes sting with tears. Alice and Janice stayed behind to ask about Nora and how she was doing as a new mother. She hadn't been this relaxed in months and found herself wishing everything could stay just as it was at this moment.

"So, are you coming to the event?" Alice asked.

"Yes."

"Yay! I'm so glad. I've missed having you around."

"Is Gavin coming?" Janice asked archly.

"No. He has other things to see to," she said.

Janice didn't push. She wasn't sure how much Janice knew about the truth behind the rumors surrounding Gavin's involvement in criminal activities.

"Gavin lets his money speak for him, which is what matters," Janice said briskly. "He's done wonders for the community through the Pyre Foundation."

"We should have a girls' day," Alice said.

"Yes," Janice agreed. "Carmen and the three of us... and Nora, of course. I gotta run."

"Me too," Alice said after a harried glance at her Minnie Mouse watch.

"Love you, see you soon," Janice said and kissed Lyla on the cheek.

Alice copied her, and both women disappeared at a fast trot. She glanced at Blade who stood by the door during the meeting.

"Not a good idea," he said bluntly.

"It's a good cause. I want to help."

"Too many variables. Gavin won't allow it."

Cold, hard reality smothered her good mood. She glared at Blade.

"I can't lock myself in the house for the rest of my life. People need help."

"You can't help anyone if you're dead."

She stepped up to Blade and pressed her gun against his middle. He didn't flinch. He just stared at her with dark, fathomless eyes.

"I am so sick of hiding from that bastard. If he comes for me, I'll be ready this time."

"You can't be prepared for everything."

He disarmed her so quickly she didn't have a chance to hang onto the gun. Her pistol thudded to the ground several feet away. He grabbed her arm and yanked hard. She whirled and found herself in a chokehold. Even as panic tried to grab her by the throat, the lesson her self-defense instructor drilled into her took over. She kicked her stiletto boot up hard and fast as if she would kick her own ass and felt it connect with her target. Blade released her instantly and sank to his knees, hands over his crotch. He didn't make a sound as he knelt on the floor as if he was praying.

It had become a weekly ritual for Blade to surprise her at inopportune moments. The skirmishes were unexpected and tested her delicate nerves, but her response time kept getting better. It wasn't easy to endure these attacks. It triggered memories of the past. She shuddered and tried to shake off the chill.

"Are you okay?" she asked.

Blade growled but didn't look up. She fetched her pistol and put it in her purse. She brushed a hand over her scarf to make sure it covered her chest and felt tip of a raised, ragged scar. She knew each mark by heart and could vividly recall the agony as Sadist inflicted the wounds, staring down at her with soulless black eyes. She paced as she tried to suppress the memories. She turned on Blade who still hadn't moved.

"I guess that really works," she said.

If looks could kill, she would have perished. Blade's jaw flexed as he restrained himself. He rose slowly and took an experimental step before he waved his hand.

"Let's go," he said in a husky voice.

She didn't need to be told twice. She walked out of the conference room and was confronted by the rest of her security detail. Two guards took the lead and two fell behind while Blade kept pace beside her. They walked on the outskirts of the casino.

"I'm ready, don't you think?" she asked.

"Gavin won't let you attend. The enemy could shoot you from a distance. Maybe I'll let them," he said, clearly still agitated over her crotch shot.

"But this guy likes to play." Her stomach pitched as flashbacks began to wash out her surroundings. "He could have shot Manny and I the first time, but he didn't. He drew it out. He wanted to teach us a lesson and use his knife..."

Everything around her faded into nothingness. Memories of the day Manny was killed slammed into her. The elegant casino disappeared, and she was once again in Manny's mansion, hands pinned behind her as she watched Manny being beat to death. Her body broke out in a cold sweat, and terror flooded her. Someone grabbed her arm and she wrenched away.

"Don't touch me!" She backed up and tried to shake the visions away as the sound of bones breaking and the cruel laughter of the monster who systematically tore Manny to pieces echoed in her ears.

"Lyla, it's okay. It's me."

She came up against a wall, braced her hands on her knees, and tried to catch her breath. She clenched her teeth against the need to scream. She felt exposed and vulnerable with the guards watching, waiting for her to get a grip. She wished Alice or Janice was here to chase away her nightmares.

"Lyla, it's me," Blade said.

"G-give me a minute," she wheezed and placed a hand over her racing heart.

"It's all in your head."

She raised her head and glared. "You think I don't know that?"

"This isn't the place to have a panic attack," he snapped impatiently.

She was considering the pros of shooting him when she heard one of her guards say, "Can I help you?"

"Morgan?"

She straightened abruptly. Something about that voice snapped her out of her nightmare and into the present. It couldn't be... She looked around Blade and came face to face with her past. Her body went cold with shock. Jonathan, the ex she left in Maine, was standing less than eight feet from her.

3

LYLA

"Jonathan," she whispered.

Jonathan was just shy of six feet with light brown hair and eyes. He was clean-cut and approachable in khaki pants and a purple button up shirt. He had the softness of a man who didn't go to the gym, and the paleness of someone who worked in front of a computer twelve hours a day. He hadn't changed a bit. Seeing him sent a spear of something sharp and painful zinging through her. It was as if Gavin's questions about romance had conjured him out of thin air.

Memories of their first meeting tickled the back of her mind.

"Can I take you out to dinner?" he'd asked the first time he stepped up to her window at the bank.

"Sorry, no," she said and tried to steer their conversation back to a professional level. "Do you want to deposit this into your checking account?"

"Boyfriend?" he persisted.

She finally met his gaze head on. "I'm not looking for a relationship."

"Are you looking for a friend?"

She took in his awkward smile and nerdy appearance. It wasn't the first time she had been asked out, but it was the first time that line had been used, and it hit her in the gut. She had been alone for so long, and this guy exuded quiet strength and goodness. It was the lack of artifice in his clothing and smile that tempted her to drop her shields.

Even though she wanted to say yes, she replied with, "Maybe some other time."

Jonathan didn't give up. For the next two months, he came in at least once a week and wait until she was free, even if it was to withdraw ten dollars. Despite his persistence, he always kept the conversation light and never failed to make her smile. He always ended with a request to go out, and she finally accepted. It was one of the best things she had ever done.

Her first everything had been Gavin. She didn't know anything else. Jonathan was a breath of fresh air. He lived modestly and had a normal nine to five. He filled her life with innocent movie dates and weekends exploring lighthouses along the coast. Their relationship morphed naturally. She kept waiting for something fucked up to surface, but it never had. Being with Jonathan restored her faith in humanity until Blade arrived and shattered her world.

"Morgan," Jonathan said and stepped forward.

He stopped when her guards blocked his way. Lyla drank him in. It was like seeing a ghost. She mourned the simple life she'd had in Maine, and now it was in her face, rousing memories that made her feel as if she was in free fall.

"Morgan, are you all right?" Jonathan asked urgently.

"I'm..." She couldn't think. Her past life and lover was here. She had been happy with him and now... She was suddenly very aware of the layer of cold sweat on her skin, her scarred chest, and the gun in her purse. What happened to the bank teller who dated Jonathan Huskin and lived an ordinary life on the East Coast?

"We need to go," Blade said abruptly and grasped her arm.

When Blade fetched her from Maine, Jonathan had been on a business trip. That was a lucky coincidence since Blade had orders to kill him. Blade had never met Jonathan, but he wasn't slow on the uptake. Blade knew exactly who he was.

"What are you doing in Las Vegas? Who are these men?" Jonathan asked.

Her stomach rocked with regret and guilt. Jonathan was a great guy. She hadn't let herself think of him after she returned to Gavin, but it was all coming back. Jonathan had been gentle, caring, and dependable. He coaxed her out of her fear and paranoia and into a healthy relationship that left her cautiously hopeful until Gavin ruthlessly took over.

"Why did you leave, Morgan?"

The ache in his voice made her eyes sting with tears. After all this time, he still cared. She opened her mouth, but no sound came out. Blade propelled her forward.

"Morgan!" Jonathan kept his distance so the guards didn't get physical with him. "What's going on? Who are these people?"

"We're her security detail," Blade said. "I'd back off if I were you."

"Why do you need security?"

She closed her eyes against the sound of his voice, which roused nostalgia and happy memories that clashed with her recent panic attack. Her insides were a mishmash of emotion and turbulence.

"Morgan, tell me why you left," he begged.

Morgan. That name belonged to a woman who didn't exist. Seeing Jonathan was just too much on top of everything else. "What are you doing here?"

"I'm here for a conference. Why do you need security? Did something happen? Are you all right?"

"She's married to the casino owner, Gavin Pyre," Blade said abruptly. "I'd watch my step if I were you."

Jonathan stopped in his tracks and disappeared from sight as Blade marched her along.

When she discovered who Gavin was beneath the tailored suits, she left him. She got as far away from him as possible and met Jonathan, who could offer her the normal life she craved. Jonathan loved her out of her trust issues and many hang-ups. He became her rock and talked about moving to the suburbs, starting his own company, and having her be a stay-at-home mom. That felt like a lifetime ago.

"There's no going back."

She glanced at Blade. "I know that."

"Then why do you look so devastated?"

He led her to Gavin's office and gave a perfunctory knock before he opened the door. Nora stood on Gavin's desk, hands braced against her father's chest as he conducted a business call on speakerphone. Blade closed the door behind her. She stood there for a moment, trying to get herself together. Nora bounced excitedly and held out her hands.

"Hold," Gavin said and pressed the mute button on the phone.

With one arm wrapped around their daughter, he grasped her by the chin and kissed her. She was too rattled by Jonathan's appearance to respond. Gavin pulled back. She felt the heat of his gaze on her face but didn't meet his gaze.

"Okay?" he asked.

"Yes."

She settled on the couch with Nora and shifted her scarf so she could breastfeed. Gavin resumed his call and paced as he talked.

Seeing Jonathan had shaken her to the core. Cozy memories of a life she forced herself to forget drifted through her mind. Jonathan had been the first person to make her feel safe after she left Gavin. If she had stayed, would they be married by now? Life with him would have been smooth sailing. She definitely wouldn't be scarred, responsible for killing at least two men, or dogged by panic attacks.

She focused on Gavin as he paced. Jonathan and Gavin couldn't be more different from one another. Gavin was dominant and possessed a palpable aura of power and danger. His role as the crime lord fed his natural tendency to control and manipulate things to his liking. Even as a teenager, she sensed something wild inside Gavin and ignored it to her own cost. He was borderline psychotic, possessive, and domineering, but he loved her, and she loved him.

Gavin caught her staring and raised a brow. She immediately

shifted her gaze to Nora. She leaned down to draw in the baby's sweet scent and wasn't prepared for the onslaught of sorrow. She had lost so many people—Manny, Vinny, her parents. Jonathan was a man she would trust with her life, but if he knew the real her, he would run and never look back. Her heart squeezed painfully over things that could never be.

That note of hurt in his voice when he asked why she left made her feel like crap. The day Blade came for her was the first time Jonathan had gone on a business trip since they moved in together. Did Jonathan think she had been waiting for him to travel so she could leave him?

"Lyla?"

She jerked and saw Gavin watching her. Apparently, he had finished his call.

He frowned. "What's wrong?"

She cleared her throat and adjusted Nora in her arms. "Nothing's wrong."

There was a long silence. She clenched her teeth and hoped she appeared serene rather than deeply troubled.

She mentally bitch slapped herself. Jonathan was her past. There was no sense in wondering what could have been. This was her reality. She was married to Gavin Pyre and had a child with him. Her life would never be normal. She would have security guards, a gun, and night terrors for the rest of her life. She couldn't get rid of her scars or change the fact that Gavin blackmailed her into leaving Jonathan and then coerced her into marriage. Gavin was who he was and she... She was now a part of him, good and bad.

"How did the meeting with Alice go?" he asked.

She placed Nora on her shoulder and rubbed her back. "It went well. Your donation for the hospital was very generous."

"It's a good cause." He paused and then said, "I don't want you going to the event."

"I'm going," she said with more heat than she intended.

His brows drew together.

She tried to soften her tone. "Like you said, it's a good cause, and they need as many hands as they can get. I want to be a part of it."

"There will be other events."

She tensed. "I want to go to this one."

"I said no, Lyla."

After the effort Alice, Janice, and the employees had put in, the least she could do was show up. Besides, she needed to do something to remind herself of the good still happening in the world. Why spend another day pacing the house, waiting for bad news when she could make a positive impact in her community?

"I'm going," she said firmly.

There was a loaded silence in the soundproof office.

"You haven't left the house for months, and now you want to volunteer at a hospital event to give him another shot?"

She didn't need Gavin to clarify who he was referring to. "I'm not going to the mall. I'm going to an event being hosted by your foundation."

"No."

No discussion, no elaboration. Just, *no*. The dictator telling her what she could and couldn't do. She ground her teeth.

"Blade will come with me. So will the other guards. I've been training—"

"You train in case of an emergency, not so you can attend parties."

"It's not a party!"

He slashed a hand through the air. "This isn't up for debate. My answer's no."

"I already told Janice and Alice I would be there."

"I'll talk to them."

She glared at him. "So, I'm supposed to stay cooped up in the house forever?"

"Not forever, just until I find him."

"And when will that be?"

His eyes narrowed into slits. "What's gotten into you?"

"I need something to look forward to."

Her bottled-up emotions churned inside her. Jonathan's appearance reminded her of a simpler time. She needed to be around good people and do something normal even if her life was far from perfect. Nora fussed, making her feel awful for raising her voice.

"You haven't complained about being confined," Gavin pointed out. "This morning, you were scared to leave the house, and now you want to attend a large public event?"

She closed her eyes and tried to rein in her temper. She didn't want to fight. "This is important to me."

"Like I said, there will be other events you can attend in future. I'm through discussing this."

There was a short knock before Carmen poked her head in the office. "There you are."

She welcomed the interruption. She got to her feet and slung the baby bag over her shoulder. "I want to go for a walk."

Carmen looked back and forth between her and Gavin. "Sure."

Gavin didn't say a thing as she walked out of the office. Blade eyed her suspiciously as she made her way through the employee hallways. She placed Nora in the stroller and grit her teeth when Blade and the rest of her security detail surrounded them. Seeing Jonathan made her realize how fucked up her life was. Security guards, guns, and the constant threat of violence—that was her reality.

"What's going on?" Carmen asked.

She gripped the handles of the stroller and attempted to smile at the employees she recognized. "I just saw Jonathan."

"Who?" Carmen asked.

"My ex."

"What ex?"

She gave her a baleful look.

Carmen's mouth sagged a little. "Here? Did he see you?"

"Oh, yeah, he saw me."

"Does Gavin know?"

"No."

"What is he doing here?"

"He's here for a conference."

"You *talked* to him?" Carmen asked in a scandalized whisper.

"I was having a panic attack, and he noticed me. Maybe that got his attention, I don't know." She grimaced and shook her head. "He wanted to know why I left him."

"It's been, what, over two years since you left? I can't believe he spoke to you. Most guys would have flipped you off."

"Jonathan's not like that."

"He's an IT consultant, right?"

"Right."

"What is that, by the way?"

"I don't know. He's obsessed with computers."

Carmen shook her head. "I can't imagine you with anyone besides Gavin."

When they turned toward the casino, Blade materialized at her side.

"What are you doing?" he asked.

"I want to go home."

Blade pulled out his phone. She had no doubt who he was calling. She resisted the urge to slap the phone out of his hand and decided her energy was put to better use by keeping an eye out for Jonathan.

"Lyla wants to go home," Blade reported and then handed the phone to her.

She didn't want to talk to him, but knew she wouldn't be able to leave without his consent, which grated on her nerves. Coming out today had definitely been a mistake. The measures Gavin took to ensure her safety now felt like a noose around her neck.

She took the phone. "Yes?"

"What's wrong with you?" Gavin growled.

"Nothing's wrong with me. I want to go home."

"You fight to go to the hospital event, and when I tell you no for your own good, you want to leave?"

"I'm tired." It was the truth. The past two hours had put her through the wringer.

"You weren't tired before you went to that meeting with Alice, and you weren't tired a minute ago when you argued with me."

God, he was such a bulldog. "I don't want to argue. I just want to go home."

"We'll talk when I come home."

That surprised her. "You're coming home tonight?"

"Yes." He sounded as if he was speaking through clenched teeth. "You welcomed me home last night, and you're going to do the same tonight. If this meeting couldn't be put off, I'd force you to come back to the office and settle this now."

"There's nothing to settle. You said no, and I'm supposed to do what you say, right?" She wasn't sure where the words were coming from, but her tone was full of attitude.

Out of the corner of her eye, she saw Carmen make a clawing motion. Clearly, she approved, but Blade shook his head in warning.

"You're going to pay for that," he promised. "Give the phone to Blade."

Her mouth was a tad bit dry as she handed the phone to Blade who listened for a moment and then pocketed it. He led the way into the casino, which meant Gavin had given his permission for her to leave.

"Holy shit, Lyla. You're baiting him. I hope you can take the heat," Carmen said.

She wasn't trying to bait him. The last huge fight they had was when he forced her to marry him. To date, she had never won a fight, but she was too pissed off to care.

"Are you doing this purposely so he'll punish you?" Carmen drawled.

She glared at her cousin.

"Don't knock it till you've tried it."

Blade and the rest of her guards stopped just outside the lobby. She listened with half an ear as Blade told the driver to bring the SUV around. She took the time to scan the milling crowd.

"Do you see him?" Carmen asked in a low undertone.

Was she that obvious? "No."

"Was he good in bed?"

After being dominated by Gavin in her teens, Jonathan's gentle lovemaking made her feel cherished and empowered. He let her lead, and their time together had been filled with affection and laughter. She couldn't begin to compare fucking Gavin to making love with Jonathan. The experiences couldn't be more different.

Carmen clearly picked up on her reticence because she tried to make it easier.

"Fine. Rate him on a scale of one through five."

"Four."

"Really? Impressive."

"He was..." She fumbled for words. "He was great. If you met him—"

Carmen gripped her arm. "You know that's not an option, right?"

Her words were an echo of Blade's. She bristled and looked pointedly down at Nora. "I know that."

"Okay. Because you sound like you're thinking... I don't know."

"I wasn't expecting to see him, and then he was just *there*. It was like seeing Manny again." She waved her hands. "It's the shock. Seeing him reminded me of my other life."

"Let's go," Blade interrupted.

They walked outside. Blade placed Nora in her car seat. He fumbled with the buckles and swore fluidly under his breath. When Lyla offered to help, he gave her a look that made her sit back with a shrug. Nora chattered excitedly and touched his face when Blade leaned forward to examine the tiny mechanisms. He froze, gave Nora a reproving glare that made no impact on the baby, and checked the straps before he slammed the door.

As the SUV left The Strip behind, she let out a long breath. God, she felt as if she'd spent all day away from home instead of a couple of hours. She forgot how fast life moved. For four months, she'd taken a time-out to learn how to be a mother and refine her fighting skills, so she could act accordingly in case of an emergency. One day out of the house and her equilibrium disappeared and she became emotionally shipwrecked.

She glanced at her cousin who had gotten all dolled up for today. "Sorry we didn't stay out long."

Carmen shrugged. "Don't worry about it. Today was a bust for me too."

"Where did you go?"

"I gambled a bit, won a thousand dollars, and got hit on a lot."

"And?"

"Nothing."

"So why was today a bust?"

Carmen didn't reply and her intuition pinged.

"What happened with Marcus?" she asked.

"Nothing happened with him."

"Do you want something to happen with him?"

Carmen examined her nails. "No."

"Carmen."

"What?"

"You're gunning for him, aren't you?" She was relieved to focus on another topic. "Wait. So, he wanted you, you turned him down, and now you're trying to get him to make a move again?"

Carmen looked irritated. "I never said that, and I can get any man I want, thank you very much."

"And you want Marcus."

"I didn't say that."

"You don't have to. You won money, got hit on, and still aren't happy."

Carmen tapped her nails together, a nervous habit she didn't exhibit often. "I don't know what I want."

"You don't have to figure it out today."

"I have to figure it out sometime. I can't live with you forever."

"Yes, you can."

Carmen snickered. "I'm sure that'll go over great with Gavin."

"He doesn't get a say," she said sharply.

Carmen's brows rose. "Wow. You really did love your ex, didn't you? He's got you all riled up."

How could she explain what Jonathan had been to her? She had been struggling to survive when he came along. He coaxed her out of the dark and just... loved her.

"He was good to me. I never wanted to hurt him. I walked out with just a note."

"You love Gavin," Carmen said.

"I know that, but…"

"But what?"

"Seeing him reminded me how fucked up my life is."

"It isn't fucked up. You have a baby and a man who loves you."

She jerked her thumb at the line of SUVs behind them carrying the rest of her security.

Carmen shrugged. "You have security, so what? You're rich."

"So are you. I don't see you with an entourage of hired guns."

"You're high profile."

"I killed at least two men," she whispered.

"They deserved it."

"Well, yes, but still."

Carmen slapped her thigh. "I can't believe you ran them over with a car. That is totally badass."

"It wasn't badass. I was desperate."

"I wish I could kill somebody."

"Carmen!"

"What?"

"You can't *want* to kill somebody!"

"I mean, kill somebody who *deserves* it, duh."

"You're crazy."

"No, I'm not. I grew up in the business and know how it works. Some people deserve to live and some don't. If you don't put the wild dogs in their place, they spread rabies, so we contain or eliminate it. Simple."

Carmen's father had been an enforcer, so she grew up knowing what happened in the underworld. Lyla hadn't. Everyone around her had a crooked view of the world, which was why she latched onto Jonathan. She didn't have to turn a blind eye or twist her morals to be with him.

"You were born to be a crime lord's wife," Lyla observed quietly.

It made more sense for Carmen and Gavin to be together, but

there was no attraction between them. Maybe it was true that opposites attract since Carmen had been with Vinny who was even-tempered and steady while Carmen was restless, manic, and hyper.

"I was a crime lord's wife for less than a week."

She saw the sheen of tears in her cousin's eyes and leaned into her. "Vinny was a good man."

"He was. No one can replace him."

"No," she agreed, "but hopefully you have room in your heart to give a part of yourself to someone else."

"I don't think I have anything to give. I'm just horny."

The driver shifted restlessly. She was glad they were pulling up to the fortress. She didn't need security guards offering to relieve Carmen's needs. Carmen deserved better than a quick fuck.

They walked into the house and collapsed in the living room. Nora laughed delightedly when Beau rushed to greet them and sniffed her madly.

"So, are you going to help at the hospital?" Carmen asked.

"Gavin said no."

"He's right," Carmen said as she slipped off her heels and lounged on the couch like Cleopatra.

Lyla scowled. "I can't stay in this house forever, and this event sounds amazing. It's the largest effort yet. How come you didn't tell me you were rounding up celebrities to help with this?"

"I knew you'd want to help, and Gavin would kill me for suggesting it. But since Alice got you fired up that's not my fault."

"I want to be a part of this. I want to be around normal people for a day."

"I'm normal!"

"No, you aren't. You're as crooked as they come."

Carmen waved her hand. "Don't flatter me when I'm so horny."

She sank onto a couch across from her. "I want to help."

"Gavin hasn't found a lead?"

"No. How long is this going to last? One day, I'm going to want to take Nora to a park to meet other kids. I might want to go shopping or visit your mom instead of making her drive here."

"Mom doesn't mind."

"That's not the point! We're here twenty-four seven. I keep waiting for another attack or a phone call telling me Gavin's hurt." Her hands clenched into fists. "I want to do something. I need to help, and I want some kind of normal in my life. This isn't what I want for Nora."

"It won't always be this way, and Gavin can handle himself."

"I know that, but he's still human. He bleeds and can be killed just as easily as someone else."

"I think of him as The Terminator," Carmen said. "He can go into any situation and come home without a scratch."

She thought of the knife wound on the back of his hand. "He's human."

Carmen gave Nora big, smacking kisses. "I used to be so focused on going to the clubs. Now, this is my whole day, and I'm good with it."

"We're getting old."

Carmen sniffed. "You're getting old. I'm just getting more fabulous."

"Whatever you say."

Carmen settled Nora on a blanket, turned on her belly, and propped her chin on her hand. "Tell me about him."

"Who?"

"Your ex, hello!"

She pictured him in her mind. "He's cute."

Carmen scrunched up her face.

"Jonathan's an average guy in every way. He's cute, polite, stable."

"Gavin would kick his ass," Carmen predicted.

"Of course he would. I don't think Jonathan knows how to throw a punch."

"If Gavin finds out about him, mention that. Maybe Gavin will let him live."

"Gavin can't get mad about Jonathan. We have a baby together."

"So?"

"So, I'm taken."

"That hasn't stopped Gavin from being a jealous psycho."

True. "He won't find out about Jonathan."

"You'd better hope not."

She played with Nora and Beau while Carmen watched TV. When Nora and Carmen drifted off, she carried the baby upstairs with Beau on her heels. She activated the baby monitor, which gave her a view of the crib from her phone, and walked outside. She wrapped her arms around herself as she paced around the pool.

Of course, she didn't regret Nora or her marriage to Gavin. Despite the rocky dips in their relationship, they were meant for each other. She knew it in her bones, but that didn't stop her from realizing how much she changed since she left Jonathan. With Jonathan, she could be herself. With Gavin, she had to stand her ground against his much stronger personality and her moral compass no longer had a needle.

She changed after witnessing Manny's demise at the hands of the sadistic crime lord. Seeing Jonathan made her realize how far off the path she'd traveled. It forced her to look at her life, and it was uncomfortable. She'd seen and experienced things Jonathan never would and that colored her world in shades of gray. She hoped once they discovered Sadist's identity, she and Gavin could settle into some kind of normal. Until then, she would live under the suffocating security blanket Gavin provided.

She went inside and stretched out on the couch across from Carmen. Even in sleep, her cousin looked photo-shoot ready. She inwardly snorted and checked on Nora from her phone. Her daughter was sucking her thumb. She listened to her daughter's quick breaths and shut her eyes.

4

LYLA

"Lyla."

She opened her eyes. It took her a moment to realize she was stretched out on the couch in the living room. Gavin sat beside her, hand on her hip while he held Nora in the crook of his arm.

"She's hungry, and there aren't any bottles in the fridge," he said.

She sat up and smiled at Nora who drooled over his pristine slacks. She glanced at the couch where Carmen had been and found it empty. She yawned as she shifted her dress aside to nurse Nora.

"What time is it?"

"Four," he said.

"That was a long nap."

When he didn't reply, she looked up and found him watching her closely.

"What?" she asked.

"We argued today."

"I know."

"I'm doing this to keep you safe."

He wouldn't let up. She hadn't even been up for five minutes, and he was already drilling her. No, she would never have a restful life with Gavin.

"You're donating so much money to a good cause, and I want to help."

"There will be other events."

"I want to go, Gavin."

A muscle clenched in his jaw. "You're pissing me off."

"Why?"

"You're being distant and bitchy."

She said nothing.

"You're still doing it."

"I'm a human being. I have emotions. I can't ditch them as easily as you do."

He tensed. "There it is again. What the hell happened at that meeting with Alice?"

"This has nothing to do with Alice."

"Then what is it about?"

Nora made an urgent sound, clearly uneasy about their heated tones. Lyla made comforting sounds and angled her body away from Gavin.

"We'll discuss this later," she said pointedly.

For several seconds, he didn't move. She wondered if he would push the issue, which he was fully capable of doing. He never backed down from a fight.

"This isn't over," he said.

She watched him stride to his office and shut the door. At the meeting with Alice and Janice, the fear and worry lifted, giving her a glimpse of life outside the underworld. She wanted to be a part of it so badly that her eyes burned with tears. Couldn't she tiptoe into the light for a couple of hours without being shot at? They needed to live in spite of the dark cloud hovering over them. How long would she have to live in isolation?

She took a deep breath and tried to smile at Nora who was watching her with rapt attention. "Why is life so complicated, baby?"

Nora splayed her tiny hand on Lyla's cheek and regarded her mother seriously. She kissed her daughter and burped her before she headed upstairs. Carmen ambled in during Nora's bath.

"How's my goddaughter doing?" Carmen asked Nora who flapped her arms excitedly.

"I'm going to freak out when she starts walking and talking," she said as Nora sat in the tub with only a hand braced against her back for balance. Babies were amazing. They were intuitive, intelligent, and observant. She loved watching Nora respond to her surroundings. She wanted Nora to be around people like Janice, Marcus, and Alice, not locked up in this house.

"She's growing up fast, isn't she?" Carmen sighed. "I can't believe we were babies once." Her eyes widened. "I can't imagine Gavin as a baby."

Lyla snickered as she imagined Gavin as a stern-faced baby. Carmen chattered to Nora who listened to every word with large eyes. Carmen carried Nora to the nursery to change her. She started to follow, but came face to face with Gavin who blocked the doorway.

"Can you watch Nora?" Gavin called.

"Sure," Carmen said from the nursery.

"I need to talk to Lyla."

He closed the door. She stared at him for a moment before she turned away and went back into the bathroom. She drained the tub and hung the damp towels.

"I watched the surveillance videos," he said from behind her. "Blade said you had a panic attack, but he didn't mention that a man came up to you."

She stilled. Gavin was too damn thorough.

"Did you know him? He followed you through the casino."

With dread coating her stomach, she turned to face him. "He's an old acquaintance."

He regarded her with an inscrutable expression. "Who is he?"

"Someone I used to know."

"Who?"

She realized with a sinking heart that he wasn't going to let it go. "It doesn't matter."

"If it doesn't matter, why won't you tell me?"

"Because I don't want you to freak out."

He folded his arms across his broad chest. "I don't freak out."

She threw up her hands, completely over this fucked up day. "Fine, Hulk out, but I don't want to deal with it."

"Tell me."

"It was Jonathan."

His expression didn't change. "Jonathan?"

She could see it didn't register. "My ex."

She saw his body lock and his eyes took on a dangerous cast. "What the fuck is he doing here?"

"He's attending a conference."

He cocked his head. "You spoke to him?"

"He recognized me."

"And you spoke to him?"

"Yes."

"And you weren't going to tell me?"

"Nothing happened."

"Nothing happened," he repeated, and the way he said it sent a ripple of alarm down her spine. "After you saw him, you picked a fight with me."

"I picked a fight because I want to volunteer at the hospital event. That has nothing to do with Jonathan."

"Don't say that weak fuck's name in this house."

She took a step back. "Are you serious?"

He prowled toward her.

"Am I serious about hearing that the man you lived with and gave you romance saw you today?" He leaned down so their faces were inches apart. "Am I serious about the fact that you weren't going to tell me? Fuck yes, I'm serious, Lyla. Deadly serious."

"What do you want me to say?"

"I want to know how you felt when you saw him."

She blinked. "Felt?"

"Yes. Felt."

"I was shocked. I never expected to see him again," she said.

"And?" he pressed.

"I felt... sad."

"Why?"

"He's a good man."

"A good man," he repeated without inflection.

"Will you stop that? Geez." She ducked under his arm and paced away so she could breathe. "He asked why I left him, and I..." She wrung her hands, looked up, and realized she'd made a massive mistake.

"You don't owe him shit," he snapped.

"You don't know him!"

"I don't need to. He's nothing."

"He isn't nothing. Jonathan took care of me. He was my friend. I disappeared, but when he saw me today, the first thing he asked was if I was okay. If a woman left you high and dry, would you bother saying anything to her if you saw her again?"

"What the fuck are you talking about? I did that. You left me and I looked for you for three years! Yes, I fucking know how it feels, and I brought you back twice because you belong with me."

She rubbed her throbbing temples. "This is pointless." He would never understand what Jonathan had done for her. She had been broken and lost after she left Las Vegas. Gavin's betrayal had shattered her, and she had spent years alone because she was terrified to let anyone in. Jonathan healed her with his steadfast patience. He was a good man and an even better friend, one she had left behind.

"Do you love him?"

He was watching her with a predatory stillness that screamed danger.

Gavin stirred her emotions into a tangled, seething frenzy. The love she had for him had the power to destroy her and it had in the past. What she felt for Jonathan paled in comparison. It was sweet, gentle, and caring. Safe. That was how Jonathan made her feel. With Gavin, she had to go to war. Was it no wonder she clung to Jonathan? Gavin scared the shit out of her.

She shook her head. "No, I don't love him."

He stared at her for a long minute, almost as if he was weighing the truth in her answer before he held out a hand.

"Come here."

She saw the beast getting riled and couldn't find it in herself to care. It had been a shock to see Jonathan. It was normal to wonder about a different path. If Gavin had given her some fucking space, she would have worked this out on her own. But of course, Gavin didn't give her time and was determined to prod her open wound.

"Come here, Lyla."

"No. I want to shower."

"I need you," he said, his tone forceful and threatening instead of comforting and lover like.

"Later."

She turned from him and slipped out of her clothes. There was no sound from him as she stepped into the shower. When she glanced back, she saw he was gone and breathed a sigh of relief. How the hell had this day gone so wrong? She got ready for the day with a spring in her step, and now she wished she'd never left the bed.

It wasn't until she was wringing out her hair that a disturbing thought crossed her mind.

"Gavin!"

No answer. She slipped into her robe and dashed into the bedroom, which was empty. With a growing sense of panic, she rushed downstairs and burst through the doors of his office. He sat behind the desk, a phone to his ear.

"Don't hurt him!" She rounded the desk and didn't stop until she was pressed against him. "Don't, Gavin!"

He stared at her for what seemed like an eternity before he said, "I'll call you back."

He set the phone on the desk, folded his hands across his middle, and gave her his full attention. Every instinct she possessed told her to back away, but she stayed put.

"Who were you talking to?" she asked.

"I don't see why I should tell you since you clearly don't volunteer such information yourself," he said softly.

She felt the hit, but didn't acknowledge it. "Were you giving orders about Jonathan?"

He didn't answer, which confirmed her fears.

"Gavin, you can't—"

"I can do whatever I want," he interrupted silkily.

"But he didn't do anything—"

"He touched you."

"What?"

He rose from his seat. She couldn't stop herself from taking a step back. His control slipped enough for her to get a glimpse of his icy rage before his expression smoothed back into placid lines.

"He knows what it feels like to be inside you," he said quietly as he stalked her. "He knows what you taste like. That's why he ran after you today. He thought there was a chance to get you back even though you left him. He knows who you are now. He won't stop."

"Jonathan isn't like you," she said. "He's not going to blackmail me. He's a—"

"Good man?" he broke in sharply. "Yes, we know I'm not that."

"This is ridiculous! You can't go after Jonathan because we used to be together."

It was clear from his expression that he didn't agree.

"How can you be so mad at him when you cheated on me with hundreds of women? I saw you fuck other women, yet you threaten the one man I've been with? How dare you!"

He came at her in a rush. He pinned her against the wall and raised her so they were eye to eye.

"I told you about the other women. I didn't want my shit to touch you."

"It doesn't matter why you did it. You did, and I have to live with those memories!"

"Why are you bringing this up?"

"You hate Jonathan enough to hurt him, but don't think I should feel the same way over the women you've taken?"

"Those women meant nothing to me," he said through clenched teeth. "I got off and didn't give a shit if they did. I never slept with them, never talked to them. I didn't use the same woman twice—"

She slapped him across the face, shocking them both. The awful silence made her heart race. She lowered her stinging hand and pushed against his chest.

"Let me go."

He didn't move or speak.

"Back off, Gavin!"

He didn't move, and she lost her temper. She struck out again, but this time he caught her hand. He hauled her over his shoulder and carried her to the couch. He dropped and mounted her in a nanosecond and pinned both her hands above her head with one of his.

He collared her throat. "That part of your life is over."

"I know that."

"But it made you think about what you'll never have, which is why you argued with me. You know I'm not a good man. I've done horrible things and will do more in the future."

His insight was scarily on point. Gavin was successful in business because he had a keen intuition that kept him one step ahead of everyone else. He had never practiced this talent on her before, and it left her quiet and wary.

"You've paid a price for being mine." His hand brushed over the scars on her chest. He undid her robe and stroked her stomach. "I should have let you choose, but I couldn't. You belong with me."

"I'm not trying to get away from you, Gavin."

"You're holding back from me because of him," he said.

"I'm not! Listen to me! It was a shock to see him. I just needed time to think."

He leaned down so their faces were less than six inches apart. "You don't need to think about him. You don't owe him anything. All you need to think about is me." He was poised over her like a beast ready to pounce. Dangerous emotions flickered through his eyes. "I need you."

"Gavin—" She let out a shriek as his fingers tunneled inside her. She tried to scoot away, but it was impossible with his heavy weight on top of her. He still had her wrists pinned above her head, leaving her body completely open to him.

"You feel this? This is all that matters," he said as she gasped and bucked beneath him. "Even if you begged me, I wouldn't let you go."

"I'm not going anywhere. Don't hurt Jona—"

"Don't say his name," he growled against her cheek as his fingers played her expertly.

"Promise you won't hurt him," she demanded and closed her eyes to block out the pleasure so she could focus.

His fingers stopped moving, and she opened her eyes. If she didn't trust him not to hurt her, she would have shrunk away in fear.

"You're thinking of him while I'm making love to you?"

"You're trying to distract me with sex!"

He kissed her with a desperation that ignited her. She arched into his hand, and when he released her wrists, she clasped his face and kissed him back.

"I have to have you," he growled as his hand went to the front of his pants. "I have to make sure you're with me."

"I am with you."

"I won't stand for another man in your mind." He wedged his cock between her thighs, which were clamped together. "I can't have you questioning what we have."

"I don't, Gavin! Let me—"

She tried to spread her thighs, but he wouldn't allow it. She grasped handfuls of his shirt as he forged through her tight folds. They both moaned as he sank in to the hilt. He braced his hands on either side of her head as he thrust.

"Who do you belong to?" he growled.

"You."

"Who do you love?"

"You."

"Say my name."

"Gavin Pyre."

He moved faster, and she held on tight.

"You wear my ring," he said through clenched teeth, eyes alight with possessiveness. "You bear my name and had my child. You'll never be his again."

She moved with him. "No, I won't. I'm yours."

He planted himself deep, and she moaned.

"You won't speak to him again."

"Gavin, it was a freak thing—"

He cupped her chin. "Ever. You don't ever talk to him." He gave her a gentle kiss. "I love you too much. I need to know you love me back."

"I do," she said and moved with him. "I've given you everything."

"I need more," he said, burying his face in her hair. "I need everything. He can't have even a splinter of you. He's lucky he has fucking memories of you. If I could take that from him, I would."

"Gavin." She dug her nails into his ass. "Make me come."

He fucked her hard until she exploded beneath him, breaking a nail as she clawed his back.

"Fuck, Lyla," he groaned as he ground himself deep and came.

She quivered as he rolled them on their sides. He tucked her against the back of the couch with his arm and leg tossed over hers. She brushed kisses over his face and ran her hand through his hair to soothe his beast. She suspected he would be upset if he found out about her run-in with Jonathan, but she never anticipated that he would be upset enough to do the other man bodily harm.

"I love you," she said against his mouth.

He cupped her jaw and opened his eyes. Despite their recent passion, his face was still hard and implacable.

"You have nothing to worry about," she said. "It was nothing. I'll never see him again."

He brushed his thumb over her lips.

"The girl he loved doesn't exist. He doesn't even know my real name."

"You don't love him," he said.

"No."

"You'll never leave me."

It wasn't a question; it was a demand.

"I promised you that before we had Nora."

"I need to hear it again. You didn't have a reason to leave me before."

"Gavin, I promise."

He pressed against her as if he couldn't get close enough. His cock, which was still buried inside her, slid deeper.

"You know I'd do anything for you, right?" he murmured.

"I want to attend the hospital event," she said swiftly.

He cursed. "Lyla—"

"Seeing Jonathan," she began and squeezed him when she felt him stiffen, "made me realize how controlled my life is."

"There's a reason for that."

"I know, but for how long?"

"I can't allow you to put yourself in danger."

"Then come with me."

"I'm working."

"Just a few hours, Gavin. You can be there and so will Blade." She wanted him to feel the sense of community she had in the meeting today. He gave generously but didn't witness the difference he made in the world. He needed to step into the light so the underworld didn't consume him.

"I said no."

"Please."

She tried to lighten his mood by pouting outrageously. His eyes warmed fractionally. She lunged at him, kissing the hell out of him, and pushing until he ended up beneath her. She rocked against him just because it felt so fucking good.

"Just let me go to this event and I swear I won't ask for anything else for the next six months," she begged.

"Lyla."

"I love Alice and the Make-A-Wish people are gonna be there. There's gonna be singing, games, dancing. Please, Gavin?"

He smacked her ass, and she stopped moving.

A muscle jumped in his jaw. "You're a pain in my ass."

"Please."

"What about Nora?"

"I'll ask Aunt Isabel to watch her."

"I shouldn't let you go."

She sensed his capitulation and kissed the hell out of him to celebrate. She had finally won a fight! "You're the best husband!"

She rolled off him and retied her robe. He sat up and glared at her.

"What?"

"Did you just manipulate me with your pussy?"

"Yes," she said smugly.

He tucked himself away and towered over her. She wasn't intimidated.

"You manipulate me with your cock, so we're even," she said.

He brought her against him and kissed her long and slow.

"I want you to be happy," he said.

"I am happy. I just wish Sadist was dead and you were here with us. I don't like you being gone and..." Her hand brushed over the cut on his hand. "I worry all the time."

"Don't."

Oh, like it was that easy. "This hospital event is a day of joy," she explained. "It's about hope. I need that. That's why I want to go."

He grunted. "Let's shower."

They walked out of the office and didn't run into anyone on their way upstairs. They showered together, both quiet and thoughtful. Gavin dressed in another suit, which meant he wouldn't be spending the night.

When they entered the dining room, they found Carmen with Nora and Beau. Carmen went into great detail about her gambling experience today, which Lyla was grateful for since Gavin didn't say a word. Carmen shot her a loaded glance, and she shook her head in warning.

When he rose from the table, Nora reached for him. He picked her up and headed to his office with Beau on his heels and closed the door.

"What was that about?" Carmen demanded.

"He found out about Jonathan."

Carmen's eyes bugged. "And you're still alive?"

"He didn't take it well."

"Of course, he didn't. He's Gavin."

"I realize that."

Carmen glanced at the closed office doors. "He's not happy."

She sighed. "No, he isn't, but we'll get past this. Maybe the hospital event will cheer him up."

Carmen's eyes popped. "He's going to let you go?"

"Yup."

"Damn, girl, you must be amazing in bed."

5

GAVIN

Gavin settled Nora on his lap as he typed on the computer. He was grateful for her presence because she stopped him from losing his shit. Claiming Lyla on the couch did nothing to purge the dark, tangled emotions pulsing in his chest.

The troubled, wistful expression on Lyla's face as she breastfed in his office at the casino had bothered him all day. She hadn't been quick enough to smooth it off her face when she realized he was watching. He assumed Alice or Janice had said something to upset her until he questioned Blade who mentioned that she had an episode in the casino.

He watched Lyla's panic attack on the surveillance cameras earlier, but now that he knew the full context of what occurred, he had to watch it again. He accessed the casino security cameras and enlarged the video. There was no way to isolate the audio, which pissed him off.

He watched Lyla stumble to a stop. He had to switch to a different camera angle to witness a startling blankness settle over her face. When Blade touched her arm, she recoiled as if she had been shot. Fear and loss claimed her features. His heartbeat accelerated with the need to react. Lyla backed up against the wall and braced her hands on her knees as she tried to catch her breath. Blade stood in front of her, obstructing his view.

A man stopped on the outskirts of Lyla's security detail. One of the guards noticed him before the others and held up a hand to stop his approach. He would get a raise. Gavin changed camera angles again as Lyla straightened and recognized the man. She looked as if she'd seen a ghost. He leaned toward the screen so he could capture every nuance of her expression—shock, pain, regret. Her lips moved, forming the bastard's name.

He stopped the video. He focused on Nora who smiled at him. He rubbed his face against her soft skin and blew raspberries against her neck. She squealed delightedly and wrapped her arms around his head. He inhaled her innocence, and it calmed the savage beast inside him. He didn't care that she yanked on his hair or drooled all over him. He would take whatever she gave him. Nora wasn't identical to the little girl in his dream; she was even better. He loved that she had her mother's silver blue eyes and couldn't deny that he was pleased she'd inherited his black hair. He didn't question his need to brand Lyla and Nora. They were his.

When he felt fortified enough, he watched the rest of the video. It didn't matter that her ex wasn't handsome or a bodybuilder. Lyla wasn't a superficial person. She cared more about the substance of the person, which was why she left him the first time. His money, looks, and lifestyle hadn't been enough to make her stay. It was obvious that the sight of this guy gutted her. She couldn't conceal her feelings, which is why the ex followed. He was trying to speak to her, believing he had a chance. Did he?

He cradled Nora in one arm as he watched Blade propel Lyla through the casino. Blade hadn't told him about the ex because he wasn't a stupid man. Blade said Lyla had a panic attack and suggested Gavin talk to her. Blade left it up to her to tell the truth.

The first time he watched the video he assumed the guy had mistaken Lyla for someone else. He hadn't been paying attention to Lyla's reaction since he assumed she was shaken by the panic attack, not the man. Now, he catalogued everything about the encounter.

Lyla was clearly shaken, and when the guy finally stopped his pursuit, he looked heartbroken. Welcome to the club, fucker. That was how he felt the first time Lyla left... and the second time. What had Blade said to make the ex stop dead in his tracks? He wanted to know every word spoken, but it wouldn't cool his rage. He was already dangerously close to hunting the bastard down and making sure he didn't see the next sunrise. He could already imagine the warm, slow drip of the worthless bastard's blood on his hands. He should have sent Blade back to Maine to finish the job years ago.

Nora rubbed her face against his shoulder, bringing him back to the present. Lyla wouldn't leave him, but that look of remorse on her face made his soul feel as if it was being shredded. He had done everything possible to redeem himself for past sins. In the past, his only competition had been himself and now... Now, the only man on the planet she had feelings for had surfaced and caused her to feel... what? What if she tried to leave him for the normal guy? She was crazy enough to do it. She was gnawing at the bit, trying to get out of the house. She wanted to volunteer at the hospital. Just the thought of her in a crowd made his palms sweaty, but if he prevented her from going, it would be another strike against him, and he had enough of those already.

He opened up the report on Jonathan Huskin. Huskin was five-foot-ten, one hundred eighty pounds with brown hair and eyes. Graduated from Boston University with degrees in Computer Science, Business, and Computer Engineering. He made eighty-five thousand a year, paid his taxes, and spent a lot of time traveling for work. He was the only child of Mark and Jackie Huskin who lived in Boston and were retired college professors. Had Lyla met his parents? He sneered at the screen. This guy didn't even have a parking ticket. Huskin had never been in a car accident, arrested for public intoxication, or been late on his fucking rent. He had no debt and made some investments that were doing fucking splendid.

"Da, da, da," Nora chanted.

If he killed the crime lord, he could give Lyla the life she wanted. Every time he came home, he dreaded the inevitable questions: *Any leads? Did you find him?* There was no trace of the fucker he called Phantom. Why would this man scale an all-out attack on his family, mutilate Rafael Vega, and put twisted leaders in positions of power only to disappear when he showed up to reclaim his title? It didn't make sense. He wanted to believe the crime lord was dead, but life never handed anything to him gift wrapped. The Phantom was out there, biding his time. For what? Another chance at Lyla? Fuck that.

He kissed his daughter's forehead and walked out of the office. He could hear the distant murmurs of Lyla and Carmen talking in the dining room. They spent every day with one another and still managed to find shit to talk about. What the fuck?

He headed to the nursery with Beau on his heels. He sat in a rocking chair and settled Nora against his chest. She rubbed her face against his shirt and fussed a little. When he put his hand on her back, she calmed instantly. As he rocked back and forth, he stared straight ahead.

Having Lyla order him to go back into the underworld lifted a weight from his shoulders. It saved him from breaking his promise to her. She knew he was a killer and still welcomed him home with open arms even though his hands were still wet from washing off the blood.

He stroked a hand down Nora's small back. They were a family. They were happy, right? Uncertainty gnawed at him. The urge to dominate and control warred with his need to give her what she desired.

When Nora was asleep, he settled her in the crib. Beau got to his feet to greet someone. He didn't have to turn to know who entered the room.

Lyla came up beside him. "You have the magic touch."

His chest tightened. Sometimes, he wondered if God designed him just for her. She made his life light up in color. Every smile, every touch made him crave more. He loved everything about her and couldn't imagine being without her. He wanted to ask about Huskin, but he didn't want to hear her answers. It didn't matter anyway. Lyla was his.

"I have to go," he said.

She took a deep breath and let it out. "I know."

He wanted to brand her again until he was certain no other man was on her mind, but he had shit to do. He shouldn't have stayed last night or come home this evening, but settling things with her was more important than the shit going down in the underworld.

She wrapped her arms around him. "So, the next time I need to get laid, should I call or text?"

"Both. Immediately."

She laughed as he leaned down to kiss her. He stroked her tongue with his and absorbed her taste, hoping it would tide him over until he could make time to come home again. When he raised his head, he was pleased when she rose on tiptoe to prolong the kiss.

"I love you," he said.

"Love you too. Hurry home to us," she said.

He gave her one last kiss before he walked out of the nursery with the feel of her imprinted on his body.

When he walked out of the house, there was a car waiting for him. He glanced over the small number of guards. With so many of his men turning traitor, he had to rebuild his army from the ground up and even brought in some retired talent from his father's time.

He nodded to Barrett, a man in his late sixties built like a tank. Barrett knew the score and had been an excellent asset in the past months as Gavin made his way through the underworld. Barrett stood by his side, cracking heads as if he hadn't retired fifteen years ago when he found out he fathered a child with a prostitute. Barrett hadn't lost his edge.

On their way to The Strip, he made phone calls and checked his email. Marcus was the most efficient, annoying bastard on the planet. He kept Gavin apprised of every little detail that was going on in his casinos. He sifted through the information and made a mental note to talk to Marcus when his door opened. He nodded to the bellboys, valets, and other staff. Three of his guards accompanied him. His head of security for the casino waited just inside the door.

"Lance," Gavin said and inclined his head.

Lance handed over a room key. "Here it is, sir. Room forty-two twenty-one."

Gavin walked toward the elevator with his men on his heels. The doors opened to reveal Marcus who looked as perky and alert as he had this morning. He smiled at them.

"Twice in one day? This must be a record," Marcus said cheerfully and made no move to exit the elevator.

He glared at his COO. How Marcus was aware of every move he made, he would never know. He pressed the button for the forty-second floor and examined Marcus who wore his suit as if he had been born in it.

"What are you doing here, Marcus? It's almost midnight."

"I've taken up residence in one of the suites since there's always an emergency." Marcus messed with the handkerchief in his suit pocket. "Word around town is you're dead, so I make sure I'm always around to squash the rumors."

He couldn't care less about the rumors surrounding his absence. He had a mission, and he wouldn't stop until it was completed. He had to admit that if it wasn't for Marcus's cooperation, there was no way he could spend as much time in the underworld as he did.

"When you're burned out, let me know," he said.

"Burned out? I live for this," Marcus said, rocking on his heels with his hands in pockets.

"One day, business won't be enough." He felt ancient and craggy beside Marcus's boundless optimism and energy.

"I can't imagine that."

"Do you need my signature for something?" he growled as the elevator doors opened.

"No. I learned to forge that months ago."

Gavin sent him a sharp glance before he exited the elevator. A year ago, a comment like that would have gotten Marcus a beating, but now he had bigger problems on his hands. Lyla was right. He trusted Marcus with his life and business, so why not trust him with Nora? If someone had the dogged determination to see things through, it was Marcus.

"You want to be Nora's godfather?" he ground out.

"What are you talking about? I am her godfather."

He stopped in his tracks and fisted his hands so they wouldn't go around Marcus's throat. "You aren't."

"Of course, I am."

He stalked down the hallway with his guards and Marcus, who seemed determined to tag along. If Marcus wasn't so intelligent, he would have killed him months ago. He was a fucking know-it-all.

"Lyla looked amazing today, by the way," Marcus said casually.

He tensed. "Don't."

"And my goddaughter knew who I was. Remember, she even reached for me even though you were holding her—"

He stepped into Marcus's personal space. "I haven't gone into the boxing ring for months, and I'm due. You want to schedule an appointment?"

Marcus grinned at him. "Nah, I'm good."

"Motherfucker." He continued down the hallway and ground his teeth when Marcus strolled by his side, whistling. "What do you want?"

"Nothing."

"I thought you had an endless list of shit to do."

"I took care of it."

"I can give you another list."

"No problem."

Too bad Marcus had the Pyre Casinos organized to a T. He dumped all his duties on Marcus four months ago, and aside from a few excellent questions, Marcus handled his workload with little effort and hadn't made a peep of protest.

"Remind me to give you a raise," he muttered.

"Already gave myself one."

He would have taken exception to this, but he arrived at the room he was looking for. He swiped the key card and walked in. The guards stayed outside, but Marcus followed him inside. Gavin surveyed the hotel room, which was tidy aside from a blazer tossed over the chair and the rumpled bedsheets.

He slipped on gloves and glanced in the bathroom, which showed a toiletry kit hanging from the towel rack. A sleek suitcase rested on the luggage rack. He opened it and quickly rifled through the contents. Either this guy was boring as hell, or he was an undercover agent who had the most mundane set of props to bore anyone hoping to find anything interesting.

"You want to tell me why we're in a guest's room?" Marcus asked.

"No."

His tone didn't dissuade Marcus from remarking, "There doesn't appear to be anything out of the ordinary. Looks like a standard businessman." He nodded to the crisp shirts hanging in the closet. "He's probably here for a conference. Why are you interested in him?"

Gavin didn't answer. He opened the laptop and stuck a USB flash drive into it before pulling out his phone and pressing speed dial five. Z, his tech genius, answered halfway through the first ring.

"Boss," Z said without preamble.

"Can you hack it?"

"Give me five minutes."

The laptop screen flickered as Z did his thing. Dozens of screens opened and closed at a rapid pace. Gavin turned from the laptop to find Marcus watching him closely.

"Business," he said.

"Is that so?" Marcus didn't look convinced.

Perceptive motherfucker. He wasn't going to tell Marcus why he was hacking Huskin's laptop. To distract them both, he said, "The Monk deal?"

Marcus's focus shifted instantly. "What about it?"

"Up the stakes by fifteen percent. He's a slimy bastard. Monk loves to back out at the last minute. Make him put his money where his mouth is."

"Anything else?"

"I'm hoping to wrap up my business soon so don't penalize the construction company for the delays. It's normal, and we're not in a hurry. As for the guy who slapped us with a penalty from the Nevada

Gaming Control Board you mentioned in an email last week, I'll deal with him."

"Terry? I can handle him."

"He's dirty, and he's gunning for us. I'll have a chat with him and find out who his employer is."

"He was appointed to his position by the governor."

He raised a brow. "Then I'll pay him a visit as well."

How the Phantom managed to do so much damage in so little time he would never know. What did the Phantom offer to recruit such powerful, high profile people? For the past four months, he worked his ass off and was no closer to discovering the Phantom's identity than he had been a year ago. His days were filled with paranoia, blood, and violence. Uncovering the deals Phantom made with the filth of the underworld made him sick. He thought he knew what evil was, but it was nothing compared to the twisted fucks he was currently dealing with.

"Anything else I should know?" Marcus asked.

He glanced at the laptop and saw computer codes flashing across the screen. "The amenities for the homeowners are generous and well worth the fees. And Falkner designed the floor plans, so I know it's the best use of style while still maintaining our signature and keeping it classy. Good job."

"Wow. You really do read my emails."

"They do the trick when I need a nap. In the future, don't write that formal shit. Get to the point. I don't have time to rifle through fifty emails a day."

Marcus nodded. "Got it."

His phone rang, and he picked up. "Yeah?"

"There's a lot of security on this laptop. I'm going to need more time," Z said.

"Have you found anything interesting?"

"Am I looking for something in particular?"

"No."

There was a pause on the other end. He could feel Marcus watching him, probably trying to figure out what the hell was going on. The sane, civilized part of him knew that he had a dozen other things to do besides rifling through Huskin's shit, but he couldn't help himself. He had to know everything there was to know about this guy.

"It looks like the laptop owner likes to write programs," Z reported.

He frowned. "What type?"

"I'm not sure yet, sir."

"How much time do you need?"

"I don't know."

He hung up and called one of his men. "Where is he?"

"At the Bellagio fountains."

"I'm on my way. Let me know if he makes a move." He headed to the door and over his shoulder said, "When the files are uploaded to that drive, hand it to the guards outside."

"Where are you going?" Marcus called.

"Hunting."

He strode to the elevators and made his way through his casino. He inhaled clouds of cigarette smoke, cheap perfume, and alcohol. A drunk stumbled into his path. Knowing that the man was making him richer allowed him to shove the man out of his way instead of killing him. His skin felt too tight for his body. The beast inside him demanded blood. It took every ounce of control he possessed to walk calmly through the crowd, a demon amongst lambs.

The lights and noise along The Strip were as familiar to him as his own home. He made his way to the Bellagio fountains where tourists congregated to watch a water show. He spotted one of his men who turned his head to the left. Gavin followed his line of sight to a lone figure leaning against the stone wall, watching the show.

He made his way to a spot adjacent to Huskin so he could examine the man who seduced Lyla into believing he was a good guy. Huskin looked like a nerd who played video games in his spare time. He was ordinary in every way from his brown hair and eyes to his facial features and build. He wasn't tall or short, fat or skinny. He was just... average. Huskin didn't seem aware of the crowd or the change in songs. He stared blindly at the water. The possibility that Huskin was remembering his time with Lyla made his hand edge toward his weapon. Only the fact he could still taste her kept him from losing his shit.

The show ended, and the crowd began to disperse. A man tapped Huskin on the shoulder. Clearly, the man didn't speak English, but anyone could tell from his exaggerated hand motions, that he was asking Huskin to take photos of his family. Huskin obliged, patiently capturing memories as the family switched positions multiple times. When the German thanked him profusely, Huskin smiled and waved as they walked away. Huskin appeared to be a nice guy, but everyone had a dark side.

He followed Huskin through the crowd. Huskin didn't look around at the distractions Las Vegas had to offer. He was too deep in thought. Gavin stalked him for a block before he spied an alley. He grabbed his switchblade and sped up to get closer to Huskin. Lyla reassured him that he had nothing to worry about, but he wouldn't take chances when it came to her. He would keep fucking up. It was inevitable. If she decided to leave him, he wouldn't allow her to have someone to run to. Fuck that.

Three men on the sidewalk created a rhythmic racket on tin buckets that was drawing a crowd. Huskin slowed, allowing Gavin to close the distance between them. He extended his hand to propel Huskin into the alley and paused when he saw it was already occupied. Two Mexicans stood in the entrance and they were both staring boldly at him. His instincts pinged a moment before one of them reached into his jacket. Fuck. He didn't hesitate. He threw the switchblade and saw the man's head kick back. His partner's eyes bulged, and he too reached into his jacket, but it was too late. Gavin barreled into him, shoving him out of the neon lights and into darkness. The man shot wildly, narrowly missing Gavin's leg, which pissed him off.

The street performers banged away, drowning out the gunshot. Gavin slammed the gangster's head into the wall with all his strength. The man crumpled to the ground several feet from his partner who had Gavin's switchblade sticking out of his face. He peered down at the bodies and noted the tattoos on their neck.

The underworld was calling.

He texted his men about the bodies and strolled out of the alley. He paused a moment to scan the crowd for Huskin, but he was gone. Fuck. An SUV pulled up to the curb. Gavin climbed in and glanced at his man.

"We're going for Santana," he said.

"You got it, boss."

Santana didn't know who he was messing with. He thought his drug operation was too big for anyone to touch him, but he was wrong. The Phantom let Santana into the city, and his filth was spreading deep and fast. He informed Santana that he had taken back the throne, and this was Santana's response—two men. What an insult. Santana had a reputation for being brutal in his home country, but Gavin had a reputation as well. He didn't care that he didn't have the manpower that Santana did. He would gut him... and tend to Huskin later.

6

LYLA

Lyla took aim and fired. The pistol bucked in her hand. The shock reverberated up her arm, but she held firm. She emptied the gun, reloaded, and walked forward, firing with steady, focused precision. The ping of metal rang in her ears. She imagined that the metal plates were the scum of the underworld.

"Halt!"

She flipped the safety on and holstered the gun in her shoulder holster. Blade walked up to her targets to check her accuracy. They had been at this for an hour, and her shoulders were beginning to ache.

"You're improving," he said after examining her targets.

She raised a brow. "That's all you have to say?"

"I don't need you to turn into an assassin. I just need you to be accurate enough to stay alive."

"Are we done?" she asked.

"We have one more exercise."

Even though she knew what was coming, her stomach iced with dread. Blade and two other guards donned helmets with tinted face guards.

"You ready?" Blade asked in a muffled voice.

She nodded.

"Fight for your life," he said.

There was a moment of silence, and then they lunged. She whirled and ran as fast as she could across the massive backyard enclosed by a high wall. She wouldn't win in a physical altercation, so running should always be her first option. The pool sparkled in the distance. Safety. If she reached the fortress, the game would end. She ignored the sound of heavy footfalls behind her and focused on the prize.

Arms wrapped around her middle and lifted her off her feet. She grabbed his finger and wrenched it back savagely. The man shouted and began to teeter to the side. She tossed her elbow back into his face. If he wasn't wearing the helmet, she would have broken his nose. The guard released her, and she sprinted for safety. The second guard tackled and then pinned her by sitting on her abdomen. She thrust her hips up with all her strength and felt her heart skip when she barely budged her opponent. She improvised by grabbing him by the balls and squeezing. The man yelped and dropped to the side. She rolled, gained her feet, and pulled her gun on the last man who held his hands up in surrender.

"Do you have to keep going for my balls?" the man on the ground wheezed.

"My instructor said I could yank them off," she said and holstered her weapon. "You got off easy."

"You may not always be able to use your gun," Blade warned, taking off his helmet and revealing that he had been her last opponent.

"I know," she said and holstered the weapon.

She put her hands on her hips and tried to catch her breath. No matter how much she trained or what moves she mastered, she was very aware that a man would always be stronger. She had to fight dirty; there was no getting around it. This was always a sobering exercise because she knew how real the danger was.

She looked at the guard who had his hands over his crotch. "Sorry."

"Maybe we should wear padded suits if you're going to keep going for the goods," Blade said.

"You do that," she said before she jogged back to the house.

She entered through the kitchen and found Carmen at the table with Nora.

"That was wicked," Carmen said and high fived her.

She gulped down water and kissed Nora on the cheek.

"What did Blade say?" Carmen asked.

"I'm getting better."

"That's it?"

"I know," she said as she plopped on a seat. "He's a hard ass."

"He always hangs back and watches how the guards attack, so he can try something different on us," Carmen said.

"I swear, I keep looking around every corner because he keeps jumping me. Serves him right if I break something," she muttered.

"Are you ready for tomorrow?"

"Yes!" She clapped her hands, beyond excited for the hospital event. "Your mom is excited to babysit."

"She loves babies and Nora in particular."

"How's she doing without you in the house? I know she was uneasy the first month you were here."

"She's getting along just fine. She sees her friends all the time and even asked if I'm moving out."

"Wow. Are you?"

"I don't know. It doesn't make sense to buy a house and I don't want to live in a condo. I think I'll stay with you or Mom until I figure out what I want to do with my life." Carmen stared at Nora while she played with Carmen's necklace. "I feel like I've been wandering around since Vinny died. Helping Alice with these events keeps me busy. My connections have finally come in handy."

"That's good."

"My schedule revolved around Vinny, and now I don't know what to do." She drummed her nails on the table and bit her lip. "I feel like I can't move on with that fuck still on the loose."

Vinny had been Sadist's first victim. Sadist wasn't the one who pulled the trigger, but he called the hit. It had been a domino effect after that.

"That's understandable," she said quietly.

Carmen rested her cheek on Nora's head and hugged her tight. "Maybe I'll have a munchkin myself. I want our kids to be close in age."

"Uh, I think you need a man for that."

"There's men everywhere."

"I mean, a good man."

Carmen shrugged. "I'm loaded. I don't need a man."

"Carmen."

"What?"

"What about your wild hairs?"

"What?"

"You always get a hair up your ass and take off to Africa on safari or some shit."

"You can take kids on safari."

She held up a hand. "Please tell me you're kidding."

"Who wants to go on a trip?" Carmen waved Nora's hands in the air. "I do! I do!"

"I don't think so."

"I still have the RV," Carmen said and bobbed her brows.

"I enjoyed our time on the road."

"I did too. It was a good time out."

And now they were back in Las Vegas. She shook her head as she remembered the shotgun wedding and Gavin's bullying tactics to make her say her vows. He really was a psycho.

"Is Gavin coming to the event?"

"I hope so. Let me call him."

She paced the living room as she dialed his number. On the fourth ring, he answered.

"Lyla."

The sound of his voice felt like a caress. One thing was for sure. Her marriage would never be dull. Gavin was a lot to handle, and his sexual appetite would always keep things interesting.

"Hi, baby. I wanted to ask about tomorrow."

"Tomorrow?" He sounded distracted.

Her heart sank. "The hospital event?" She tried to keep her voice light and airy.

There was a short pause. "You still want to go?"

"Yes." When he didn't respond, she tacked on, "Please, Gavin."

He didn't speak.

"I want you to come," she said, and then realized she had absolutely no idea what he was doing at that moment. He could be in a boardroom or standing over a body. "I mean, if you can make it, I'd like that."

Still no response. She stopped pacing and closed her eyes.

"I can't go?" she murmured.

"I'll be there in time."

She tossed her fist in the air and did a little jig. "Yay! You're the best. I'll call Alice."

"Okay."

She put a hand on her hip. "By the way, if you have time after the hospital, I'm due."

"Due for what?"

"For you."

A pause. "Then I'll be in you after the event."

She beamed and did another little jig. "I love you."

"The next time I'm home, do that dance for me," he said.

"What dance?"

"The one you're doing right now," he said and hung up.

She looked up at the camera in the living room and shook her head. Damn Gavin. Had he been watching her before she called or tapped in after he answered? He would always keep her on her toes.

Her phone rang and she almost answered before she saw her mother's name. She declined the call and skipped into the kitchen.

"I'm going!" she crowed.

"Awesome. I'll text Mom about Nora."

"And I'll call Alice," she said gleefully and stopped when her phone chimed from a voicemail.

"Who's that?"

"My mom."

Carmen cocked her head. "You think she wants to see Nora?"

She sighed. "That's what I want to think, but I don't think so."

Carmen shook her head. "Your dad is an ass."

"Yeah." She wished her mother would leave him. She would happily take her mother in, but that would never happen. Her mother would rather suffer with her father than get out of the toxic, hopeless marriage. She couldn't be a part of it anymore. She had enough shit on her plate.

Lyla spun her phone on the table. "Am I being selfish by asking Gavin to go to this event?"

Deep down, she knew Gavin was right. The smart, safe thing to do was hide in the fortress until he killed Sadist, but how long would that take? It had been four months of silence, and she was ready to do something. She couldn't let another opportunity pass her by. Since her trip to the casino, she had been more restless than ever. She was nervous about leaving Nora, but that time would have come eventually.

"Wanting to attend an event that will help others isn't selfish," Carmen said. "Not every outing will end in blood. It's going to be okay, Lyla."

7

LYLA

LYLA TOOK A DEEP BREATH AS THE SUV PULLED UP TO THE HOSPITAL, which was teeming with press, celebrities, volunteers, patients, and medical staff. Gavin stood on the sidewalk and opened her door. He looked as polished as always in a navy suit and matching tie. He wore aviator glasses that concealed his mood. He helped her out of the car and turned to help Carmen as well. Carmen ran a hand over a blush-colored gown that made her look deceptively sweet. She had turned into British royalty for the day. Lyla wore an army green dress she'd been wanting to wear for a while with a black trench coat.

"The Pyre family is here!" Janice exclaimed, making her way through the crowd. "This is great! Gavin, do you want to give a speech?"

"No."

Janice didn't look surprised by his abrupt answer. "No problem. Alice is prepared. I'm so glad you decided to come."

Janice led them through a group of celebrities talking to reporters. Carmen had definitely pulled together an eclectic and high-profile group of celebrities. Up front was Bridgette Mackee, an actress who starred in a summer blockbuster, and the brilliant and eccentric film director, Phoenix, along with The Punisher, a UFC fighter.

Kody Singer spotted Carmen and abruptly left his interview to greet her. He smiled and grasped both of her hands as he talked. As Gavin pulled Lyla through the crowd, Kody caught sight of him and took a hasty step back. Clearly, Kody hadn't forgiven Gavin for putting him in a headlock during the opening night of Incognito.

When she waved at Kody, he averted his face. She inwardly shrugged and squeezed Gavin's hand. "Okay?"

"Yeah," he said without looking at her.

She ignored his clipped tone and focused on her hectic surroundings. Gavin shook hands with the celebrities, all of whom were staying at one of the Pyre Casinos. He introduced her to those she didn't know and grudgingly obliged the press when they asked for pictures of them.

Gavin stepped away from her to take a call. From his body language, she suspected something serious happened. His mouth was tight when he returned to her side. Everyone around her took a step back. She didn't ask what happened because he wouldn't tell her anyway.

Janice and the hospital director led the way to the new wing of the hospital, which was marked off with a bright red ribbon. Alice faced the crowd and beamed with pride.

"Thanks to the Pyre Foundation, we were able to build a new wing and restore two damaged by a fire. Let's give a round of applause to Gavin Pyre!" Alice announced.

Cheers sounded around them. Lyla smiled while Gavin acknowledged the crowd with a curt nod.

"Mr. Pyre, will you do the honors?" Alice asked, holding out a massive pair of scissors.

She felt him stiffen. Clearly, he didn't want to be in the limelight. Nevertheless, he stepped forward. He didn't pause for effect or look at the clicking cameras as he cut the ribbon. As applause rang out, he handed the scissors back to Alice and resumed his position beside her. She wanted to elbow him, but was wary of provoking him further. Gavin was making it clear he wasn't happy about being here and had other things to do.

"You can go," she said just loud enough for him to hear.

He looked down at her. She didn't have to see his eyes to know that he was pissed. He had been tense from the moment she arrived. He cupped the back of her neck and squeezed. A warning. She grit her teeth. This was the first time she had left Nora to go on an outing. It was a big day for her, and she wouldn't let him ruin it.

"Come on, there are so many people to meet!" Alice exclaimed.

She slipped out of Gavin's hold and went with Alice. She felt someone breathing down her neck and glanced back to see Blade on her heels. At the end of the corridor, Gavin paced as he talked on the phone. Good riddance.

Volunteers handed out gift baskets and goodie bags to patients. On the basketball court, NBA star Michael Heatton helped patients shoot baskets. The celebrities were out in full force, taking group photos or sitting at the bedside of the recovering, sick, or dying.

She spotted Kody and Carmen in a little girl's room. Lyla knew from the meeting that meeting Kody was the cancer patient's dying wish. The wan girl perched on Kody's lap and beamed at the camera while her parents stood against the wall with tears in their eyes.

Alice grabbed two bouquets of sunflowers and handed one to Lyla.

"Let's go spread some sunshine," Alice said so enthusiastically that Lyla couldn't help but smile in response.

Alice fearlessly walked into rooms to talk to patients young and old. Blade scanned the occupants before he waited in the hallway. Alice made everyone feel special. Something about her spirit lit up the room and made everyone believe that everything would be okay. These people were going through the worst time in their life. The Pyre Foundation was here to offer support, hope, and let them know they weren't alone. Even as she handed out sunflowers, the patients showered her with gratitude and love. She was overcome with emotion as she listened to their hardships and tried to offer words of comfort.

She didn't know how to respond when a patient clasped her hand and said, "You and your husband are doing God's work."

Alice was bursting with light. "She sure is, Maggie. I'll see you next week."

"Yes, child!" the old woman called as they walked out of her room.

"Next week?" she murmured.

"I visit the hospitals in my spare time," Alice said as she marched her down the hallway, stopping to direct several volunteers before she continued.

"What spare time?" Lyla muttered.

"I know, right? It's important for me to remember that there are people much less fortunate than me. Hospitals are one of the loneliest places on earth."

Alice stopped to talk to some volunteers and directed Lyla to continue visiting patients. Lyla paused in front of a room and faced Blade

"Where's Gavin?"

"Attending to business."

She narrowed her eyes. "What's going on?"

"Nothing you need to worry about."

"He needs to meet these people."

"There are millions of people like this," Blade said. "Gavin's helping in his own way."

Blade's phone rang. She sighed as she walked into the room by herself and spied an old man sitting up in bed reading a newspaper.

"Hello. How are you?" she asked with a smile.

The man dropped his newspaper and surveyed her through narrow eyes. "You aren't a nurse. What are you doing in here?"

She was a bit taken aback by his rude tone, but reminded herself that he was in pain and probably going through a lot. "Today, we opened up a new wing of the hospital, and we're spreading a little joy."

She offered the flower.

"If you want to spread joy, there's something else you can do for me." He looked pointedly at his lap.

She retracted the flower and gave him a tight smile. "I don't think anyone can help you with that."

He cackled. "You got some spunk. Maybe you're not a blonde bimbo after all."

It was a good thing she was the one who entered this room and not Alice. Alice would have blushed, encouraging the asshole to be even more inappropriate. Remembering Alice's boundless optimism, she decided to ignore his awful first impression.

"How is your recovery going so far?" she asked.

"Lousy. It's one fucking thing after another."

"What brought you here in the first place?"

"A run-in with an old acquaintance."

She frowned. "Meeting with an old friend made you sick?"

"I never said he was a friend."

The bathroom door opened. She turned and saw a strange looking man with angular features, sunken cheekbones, and protruding eyes. They widened comically when he spotted her. He was leaning heavily on a cane, which slipped, causing him to topple face first to the floor.

"Oh, my gosh!"

She placed the flowers on the old man's bed and leaned down to help the man to his feet. It was an easy feat since he was emaciated. Something tickled the back of her memory and then it hit her.

"You're Rafael's brother," she said. "We met at Lux."

Rafael's brother was dressed much the same as he had been the first time they met at a bar. That felt like a lifetime ago. He wore a button up shirt tucked into slacks. A thin belt circled his tiny waist. She picked up his black cane and held it out to him.

"Are you okay?" she asked and noticed that his hands were trembling. Too much coffee or nerves?

"You know my sons?" the old man asked.

"Sons?" she echoed and turned to face him. "Rafael's your son?"

"Was," the man said sourly. "He's dead."

She put a hand against her chest. "Oh, I'm sorry."

She didn't know much about Rafael other than the fact that he was good looking, Gavin loathed him, and he ran a prostitution ring. She glanced at Rafael's brother who still had yet to say a thing. He didn't look like Rafael or his perverted father.

"Who are you?" the old man asked sharply.

"I'm Lyla. The Pyre Foundation is putting on an event today. I'm helping."

"Pyre?" the old man asked sharply.

"Yes, Pyre."

"What's your name?"

She had been trying to avoid that tidbit. She lifted her chin. "Lyla Pyre."

The old man's expression became chillingly hostile. "You're Gavin's wife?"

Something about the way he said it made her hand inch toward the pocket in her purse holding her gun.

"You know Gavin?" she asked cautiously.

"He's the acquaintance who put me in here in the first place," the old man said. "He shot me in the shoulder and wrist." He held up his arm so she could see an angry red scar on his otherwise pasty skin. "He doesn't care that I'm old, that sadistic fuck."

It was hard to feel sympathetic after his perverted welcome. "Why'd Gavin shoot you?"

"Because he was pissed."

"So, he shot you?"

"I pulled a gun on him, he dodged the bullet, and I hit Steven instead." He nodded at his mute son with the cane.

She reached into her purse and closed her hand around her pistol. This bastard could have killed Gavin. Of course, the one room Blade didn't check had to be occupied by Gavin's enemies. Did Steven and his father run the prostitution ring? Steven looked like a nerdy professor, not a part of the underworld. Steven didn't fit in with his family. No wonder he was so... odd.

"Who are you?" she asked.

"I'm Paul Vega." He waited for a reaction, and when he didn't get one, he said, "I'm offended your husband didn't think to warn you away from us. Is he here?"

"Yes, he's on his way," she lied.

"That bastard has ice running through his veins." Paul shook his head and leaned back against his pillows. "He kills Santana two hours ago and then comes to an event his charity puts on. Fucking genius."

Her hand tightened on the gun.

"He poked the hornet's nest on this one." Paul's eyes gleamed. "Santana's the biggest drug lord in Mexico. He set up shop here a couple months ago."

And Gavin killed him two hours ago? Her stomached clenched.

Paul tried to look innocent but didn't manage to pull it off. "I thought as his wife, you'd know such things."

"I don't need to know what's happening in the underworld," she said.

"You're missing out." He inclined his head at Steven who was doing a great imitation of a statue. "He just started talking again."

"Excuse me?"

"Your husband broke Steven's jaw and shattered his kneecap. He's had two surgeries and still has a fucking cane."

She couldn't care less about Paul, but she didn't understand why Gavin would attack Steven. She turned to him. "Are you okay?"

Steven didn't answer. His face was still as a lake. When they met at Lux, Steven made a friendly attempt to buy her a drink, but now he was just blank.

"Why did Gavin attack you?" she asked.

"Steven walked in after Pyre tried to choke me," Paul answered for his son.

Reluctantly, she turned back to Paul.

"Steven tried to defend me and this is what Pyre thinks is fitting punishment" Paul snorted. "Look at him. He's no match for your husband."

"When did this happen?"

"Six months ago, give or take." Paul winced as he shifted his thigh. "He still hasn't tracked down the new crime lord, huh?"

That surprised her. "You want to track down the crime lord who killed Manny?"

"I don't give a fuck about Manny," Paul spat. "I tried to kill him myself, but he had a sixth sense for a setup. Wily fucker."

She wanted to beat him with her purse. "If that's so, then why are you looking for the other crime lord?"

"He killed my son."

"The crime lord killed Rafael?" That rocked her world. She didn't know Sadist had made hits on anyone but the Pyres.

"Rafael was killed a couple of days before Manny."

"What makes you think it was the crime lord?"

"He likes knives," Paul said, eyes gleaming. "I hear you know something about that."

Her chest scars tingled. "And Gavin knows this?"

"Pyre thought Rafael had taken over. That's why he showed up in my office," Paul said.

"He shot you in your office?"

"That's Pyre for you."

Gavin did this when she was pregnant with Nora, she realized. "Did the crime lord kill anyone else besides Rafael and Manny?"

"A bunch of mutilated bodies turned up around the city, but no one of note. I think he got a taste of blood and liked it," Paul said.

"What the fuck are you doing here, Vega?"

Blade walked into the room, pocketing his phone. His hand was on the butt of his gun. Steven held up one hand in surrender while Paul sneered.

"If it isn't the mighty Blade, Pyre's sidekick," Paul said.

"I'm Lyla's bodyguard now." Blade's eyes shifted back and forth between the two men, and a glint of amusement lit his eyes. "Looks like you two had a run-in with some sort of criminal. Someone I know?"

Paul bared his teeth. "I hope someone guts him."

Blade focused on her. "Let's go."

She didn't argue. She didn't say a thing to Paul or Steven as she walked out.

"What the hell were you doing?" Blade snapped.

She jolted. "What?"

"The Vega's are sick fucks."

"I didn't know that."

He shook his head. "If Gavin finds out they're here, he might finish them off. He isn't in a good mood."

"Is it because he killed that drug lord?"

He glanced back at the hospital room. "Fuck."

"Did Gavin really kill him?"

Blade clasped his hands behind his back. "You should talk to him about this."

"Paul said Gavin is responsible for their injuries."

"That's also something you should discuss with him."

She opened her mouth to argue when Alice ran toward her.

"Do you hear that?" Alice exclaimed.

Alice grasped her arm and raced down the corridor as enthusiastically as a five-year-old. She was glad she hadn't worn ridiculous heels like Carmen so she could keep up. On the lawn, Mariah Gearthart sang acapella. Patients, visitors, and medical staff opened windows or made their way outside so they could listen to her angelic voice. Alice led her to the front of the crowd and put her arm around an older woman and began to sway. Alice got the whole crowd going. Mariah sang several songs before she bowed. Everyone clapped and rushed forward to take pictures with her.

Somehow, she ended up on the basketball court with the NBA star and was obliged to take a shot at the basket in front of a crowd of onlookers. Thankfully, she made the shot and settled on a bench to watch the festivities with a smile on her face. She wished Nora were here. How would she be in a crowd? Would she cry or be fascinated by all the activity?

"Lyla."

When she glanced behind her, her smile vanished. Jonathan wore a cap, sunglasses, and high collared jacket. She glanced around for Blade who was ten feet away, talking to another member of her security team. She gripped the edge of the stone bench as it hit her. Jonathan called her Lyla. He knew her real name.

"You shouldn't be here," she said, staring straight ahead.

"Because your husband is a mob boss?"

She stiffened. Apparently, Jonathan had done his homework. But if he believed the rumors about Gavin, why was here? "You don't know anything about my husband."

"Is your real name Morgan or Lyla?"

She silently willed him to walk away. She promised Gavin that she wouldn't talk to him, but she owed him her name at least. "Lyla."

"And you created a new identity when you left him? Is that it? Is that why you tried to warn me off?"

He was too perceptive for his own good. She wanted to turn, but didn't dare. She felt Blade's gaze on her. Jonathan stood back far enough that he was coasting beneath the radar. "What are you doing here?"

"I needed to see you."

"Why?"

"Because I need to know the truth."

"About what?"

"Why you called yourself Morgan, why you left."

"I can't discuss it. You should go." The answers to those questions didn't matter anymore.

"Are you afraid of him?"

"I'm not afraid of my husband, but you should be. If he sees you, he'll—" She broke off as Blade started toward her. "Get out of here."

"Problem?" Blade asked.

She turned casually and saw that Jonathan had faded into the crowd. She shook her head and got to her feet. "I'm hungry."

"There's a spread in the lobby."

Like her trip to the casino, her day wasn't turning out exactly the way she imagined it. First the Vega's and now Jonathan. She grabbed a sandwich and bowl of fruit and settled on a seat in the lobby. Her guards settled around her. When Janice joined them, Blade moved to accommodate her.

"This is fantastic!" Janice said as she pocketed her phone.

"You and Alice have done an amazing job," she agreed.

"I think she's trying to outwork me, but I won't let her." Janice stole some fruit from her plate. "Who's watching the princess?"

"Carmen's mom."

"I still haven't seen her yet. When are we going to get together?"

"When are you and Alice free? You work around the clock."

"We'll figure out a day," Janice said and took a sip from her drink.

"Can I get you something?" Blade asked.

"No, thank you," Janice said as she continued to pick at Lyla's food.

She didn't have friends aside from Carmen because it was too dangerous, but as employees of Pyre Casinos, Janice and Alice fell into a different category. Janice and Alice threw her a baby gender party and baby shower. She wished she could spend more time with them. Also, Nora needed aunts to dote on her.

When Janice's phone rang, she rose. "We'll talk later, okay?" She said as she answered and hurried away.

She searched for Jonathan, but it was impossible to pick him out of the crowd. What did he hope to accomplish by researching her? Appearing at the event today was out of character for him. He wasn't one to pursue or obsess over something, but then again, he probably couldn't resist the mystery. If he really suspected that Gavin was a mob boss, he should have the sense to steer clear of her.

"Hey." Carmen took the seat Janice vacated and ate the rest of her food.

"Where's Kody?"

"Restroom."

She gave Carmen a sharp glance, but she was too busy munching to notice. "You didn't go to the restroom with him, did you?"

Carmen gave her a very catlike stare. "Why would I do it in a bathroom when there are beds everywhere?"

She blanched. "Please tell me you didn't."

Carmen crossed her legs. "Then I won't."

"Having fun?"

Carmen nodded and then got to her feet. "There's Kody. We're going to head out, okay?"

She watched Carmen rush across the lobby toward Kody, who had a foolish grin on his face. She watched them leave with a heavy heart and continued to watch the crowd before she pulled out her phone to check in with Carmen's mom.

"Hey, honey!" Aunt Isabel said.

She relaxed. "Hey, Aunty. How's it going?"

"We're having so much fun! She's adorable. I can't wait for all my friends to meet her. She's so much cuter than some of the babies I've seen."

She laughed. "That's mean, Aunty."

"Telling the truth is a necessary evil, baby. Everything going good at the event?"

"It's great. So many people volunteered to help."

"That's good to hear. There's so little good to report these days."

"Yes. How's Nora? Did she cry?" She bobbed her foot nervously. It was the first time she had ever left Nora with someone, and she couldn't enjoy herself fully. Of course, after all she had been through, it was a miracle she had the courage to leave Nora at all.

"No, she's such a good baby. She's very loving. You're doing an excellent job, Lyla."

That warmed her heart. Aunt Isabel filled the space left by her own mother. All her parents cared about was each other. Nora didn't rank on their priorities as anything other than a way to get back into her inner circle so they could ask for money. Aunt Isabel and Carmen were all she needed.

"I'll be home in an hour or two," she said.

"Take your time. We're doing just fine."

"I love you. Thank you."

"No problem."

She hung up and took a fortifying breath. Nora was safe and being smothered with love. She looked around the lobby and watched celebrities mingling with patients and their families. Spirits were high. Alice flitted from group to group to make sure everyone was having a great time. It was clear that she was in her element.

Gavin walked toward her. People gave him wary or curious looks as he passed. Despite the fact that Gavin killed a drug lord less than five hours ago, his suit didn't have any suspicious splotches and he was perfectly groomed. He didn't appear to be worried, guilty, or anxious about his recent activities. On the contrary, the only thing he was agitated about was her. When he stopped in front of her, she got a whiff of his cologne. He smelled delicious. How the hell could he walk into the underworld smelling and looking like a million dollars? That would irritate the hell out of the criminal underclass for sure. Maybe he used his polished appearance to his advantage. No one who looked the way he did should possess the skills of an assassin.

"Time to go," he said.

"After lunch, we're supposed to take a group shot on the lawn," she countered.

"You've been here long enough."

The director of the hospital approached, beaming. He inclined his head respectfully to Gavin. "Mr. Pyre, you've done so much for our hospital. I hope you know how much we appreciate your contribution and all that you've done today."

The director held out his hand. Gavin hesitated a second before he took it.

"We're happy to help."

"And you," the director reached for her hand and gave it a gentle squeeze, "you are a godsend."

She raised her brows at Gavin before she smiled at the director. "You're so kind to remind my husband of that."

The director laughed and waved his hand. "Would you like a tour of the new wing?"

Gavin opened his mouth, but before he could answer, she linked her arm through the director's.

"Yes, I would," she said and ignored Gavin's low growl.

The director blinked when Blade and four guards rose. She patted the director's arm.

"Precautions," she said.

The director nodded hastily. "Yes, yes. I understand."

Gavin followed them to the elevator. The director kept up a steady stream of polite conversation, but Gavin didn't engage. The director tossed him worried glances, probably worried that Gavin wasn't impressed by how they used his money. The director went into great detail about the state-of-the-art equipment and innovative floor plan. It was interesting to walk through the corridors and peek into unused, pristine rooms. She enjoyed the behind-the-scenes tour. The director pointed out the paintings on the wall donated by a local artist and led her into a hospital room. The aqua accent wall made the room inviting and soothing rather than clinical and detached. She walked to the window and locked out at the shopping center across the street and the red mountains in the distance.

"This is beautiful," she said.

The director pointed out the bed sheets, which were a higher thread count than they had ever been able to afford.

"The Pyre wing is going to be many people's home away from home."

"Pyre wing?"

"You didn't know it was being named after your family?"

Her family... "No, I didn't."

"We couldn't call it anything else," the director said jovially.

Gavin stood with his arms crossed in the middle of the corridor. She went to him and gave him a hug.

"Let's go," Gavin said abruptly.

"But—" the director began.

"I have business to attend to," Gavin said shortly and propelled her down the corridor.

She was dimly aware of the director talking to Blade and the other guards as they trailed behind them.

"Rude," she muttered.

"I have a lot to do today."

"Like what?"

"Don't worry about it."

What did he have to do after he killed a drug lord? What was the next step? She opened her mouth and then closed it. Did she really want to know? Not really. If she knew what his agenda was for the day, she would get even less sleep than she already did.

Before they reached the elevator, the doors opened, revealing eight Mexicans. They were dressed in heavy jackets, jeans, and too long shirts. Tattoos covered what she could see of their skin.

Gavin halted, pulling her to an abrupt stop. The man standing in front of the group smiled, showing a mouth full of silver teeth. Even as he reached into his jacket, a deafening bang sounded from beside her. The man's smile vanished as a hole appeared in the middle of his forehead. He staggered backward into two men who fell with him.

Gavin released her and squeezed off two more shots. A man clutched his chest. It looked as if a ripe tomato had been hurled at him. One of the men raised his gun and shot wildly. An agonized screamed sounded behind her. Even as she turned, Gavin ran forward.

8

LYLA

"GAVIN!" SHE TOOK A STEP AFTER HIM, ONLY TO STOP IN HER TRACKS AS she got a firsthand glimpse of Gavin in combat mode.

He disarmed the man with the gun with a brutal chopping motion. She heard something break, and the man dropped to his knees with a scream. Gavin kicked him savagely in the face before he turned to the next man and executed an uppercut punch. There was a sickening crunch as the man collided into the wall. He crumpled to the ground, leaving a gruesome red smear in his wake. One of the gangbangers tried to run out of the elevator. Gavin hauled him back in just as the elevator dinged and the doors closed, locking him into the enclosed space with three armed men.

"No!" she screamed.

"Lyla."

She turned and saw Blade on his knees beside the hospital director who lay in a pool of blood.

"No, no," she whispered, shaking her head. "What's going on? Who are they?"

"Santana's men." Blade rose, hand dripping with the director's blood. "He's gone."

"He's dead?" She couldn't comprehend it. Everything had

happened so fucking fast. Not even two minutes ago, the director had been talking passionately about the new wing of the hospital and now he was a lifeless heap on the floor. "This can't be happening."

"It is." Blade pulled out his phone and speed dialed a number. "Z, access the hospital cameras. We're gonna need some interference." He hung up and looked at the other guards. "Two of you clean this up. The other two, follow me."

Blade grabbed her arm and led her back through the new wing. A ding stopped them in their tracks. The elevator doors opened and Gavin appeared with bodies in disturbing positions at his feet. Even as she took a step toward him, his head turned sharply to the left. The guards standing over the director went down on one knee and cleared their guns even as distant shots rang out.

"Fuck, let's go," Blade snapped.

Gavin pulled the fire alarm. Lights flashed and a deafening blare echoed down the corridor. Her guards threw open the door that led to the emergency exit stairs. As Blade propelled her into the stairwell, she looked back and saw Gavin cut a man's throat with a knife and then toss it into another man's face. Men were converging on him like ants. None of the gang members seemed to care that she and her guards were getting away. They were here for Gavin.

"We can—" she began, not wanting to leave him.

"Gavin can take care of himself. He can't focus with you around. We gotta get you out of here," Blade said.

People filled the stairwell, so Blade and the guards were forced to holster their weapons. As they climbed down three flights, she focused on putting one foot in front of the other. She wanted to fight by Gavin's side, but Blade was right. Her combat skills were sloppy and amateur at best. Gavin could hold his own.

The confusion and panic of the crowd around her amplified her own. The edges of her vision darkened with memories just waiting to latch onto her and send her spiraling into waking nightmares. It was happening again. Another battle, another tragedy, another scene with bodies in her wake.

Blade grabbed her arm in a painful grip as they entered the lobby, which was a hubbub of chaos. Patients in hospital beds and wheel-chairs were everywhere. Medical personnel struggled to be heard over the blaring alarm. They yelled for help to get the patients onto the front lawn. Alice and Janice were in the midst of the fray, directing people outside.

When she took a step toward them, Blade hauled her back. "We have to get out of here."

"But I can—"

"No. My job is to keep you safe. We don't know how many more there are."

She could barely keep up with his long stride. The guards pressed in close, and she struggled to keep her shit together. Of course, the day of the hospital event had to be the same day Gavin killed a drug lord.

They walked through the deserted emergency room and left the hospital behind as they crossed to the parking garage. Blade pulled out his phone and called the drivers.

"Lyla!"

Jonathan jogged toward them. She was torn between hugging him in relief or screaming at him to stay away from her.

"Are you all right? What's going on?" Jonathan asked.

"Jonathan, you should leave," she said as they entered the ground level of the parking garage.

"Is there a fire?"

One of her guards reached into his jacket.

She grabbed the guard's arm to stop him from removing his weapon. "No!"

"We don't have time for this," Blade hissed.

"Go, Jonathan!" she snapped.

Squealing tires sounded as two SUVs whipped around a corner and stopped in front of them. Blade reached for her arm and then shoved her to the ground. Bullets ricocheted against the bulletproof car. She pulled her gun out of her purse and rolled, knocking Jonathan off his feet.

"Get down!" she yelled as she took in her surroundings.

Gang members used parked cars for cover. Her guards scrambled to do the same.

"Get in the fucking car!" Blade shouted at her.

She army crawled toward the SUV and tried to block out the noise. One of her guards dropped with an agonized yell. She stopped and raised her gun.

"Lyla, go!" Blade barked with such urgency that she resumed her slow progress to the SUV.

She made it to the back door and reached for the handle. A bullet sparked against metal less than six inches from her hand. She dropped, and the driver's door opened.

"Get in!" the guard shouted as he covered her.

She dove onto the back seat. As she slammed the door, she heard the ping of bullets bouncing off metal. She sat up, tossed her purse, and flipped the safety off her gun. Men were everywhere. Her guards were pinned and they were in an enclosed space with lots of hiding spots. Her eyes fell on Jonathan who was on the ground, hands over his head. He was a sitting duck.

She cracked open the door and shouted his name. Jonathan dropped one hand and looked in her direction. He couldn't see her through the tinted window so she stuck her hand out and gestured for him to come. To her relief, he began to crawl toward her. She couldn't watch him bleed out in front of her. When Jonathan was right below the door, she tossed it open and covered him. Jonathan leaped in and slammed the door.

"What's happening?" he shouted and ducked as bullets bounced off the window.

"Get her out of here!" Blade roared at her driver.

Even as the guard backed into his seat, a man rushed out from behind a car. She heard the click of an empty chamber as her guard ran out of bullets. The man shot him at point blank range and stuck his ugly face in the SUV. She pulled the trigger. The man staggered back, face a bloody mess. She crawled over the console and slammed the driver's door before she fumbled with the seat settings and locked the doors.

"What's going on?" Jonathan shouted from the back seat.

"Didn't I tell you to stay away from me?" she shouted back.

She looked in the rearview mirror and breathed a sigh of relief as Blade and the three remaining guards got into the SUV behind her. Blade honked and jabbed his finger at her. She didn't hesitate. She jammed her foot on the gas pedal and careened toward the exit. She caught a glimpse of the front lawn of the hospital flooded with people before she whipped onto the highway and passed a squad of police cars.

She set the gun in the cup holder and clutched the steering wheel with shaking hands. A perfect day ruined by the underworld and its fucking politics. The hospital director, a good man, was dead. Hundreds of sick and terrified people were now milling on the hospital grounds, waiting for word on an imaginary fire. Had the gunfight between Gavin and those men spilled into the rest of the hospital?

"Lyla."

She glanced at Jonathan in the rearview mirror. His hair was disheveled, and he was pale with shock.

"What's going on?" he whispered.

"You should have gone on with your life and forgotten about me."

"You have a gun." His voice was faint with shock. "And you know how to use it."

Damn right she did. She trained to know how to kill, and that was what she'd done. Her hands flexed on the wheel. Just like the last time, she didn't feel an ounce of remorse. If anything, she wanted to turn around and do more damage. Her chest burned with rage. Those fuckers. They didn't care about innocent bystanders. They opened fire anytime, anywhere.

The sound of her phone ringing filled the car. "Pass my purse!"

He tossed it on the console. She dug in her bag as she navigated the freeway and kept an eye out for cops.

"Are you hurt?" Blade asked when she answered.

"No."

"Good. Drive home."

"Okay. Any word from Gavin?"

"No. I have men driving from the compound to you. I'm going back to help. Are you going to be okay?"

Her heart clenched. "You think he's...?"

"Don't borrow trouble. Get home, you hear me?"

"Yes," she said and hung up.

"This has to do with your husband being a crime boss, doesn't it?" Jonathan asked.

She glanced at her ex who had no idea how close he came to death today. "Where are you staying?"

"Lyla, talk to me."

"About what?" she demanded.

"About what's happening."

"It's safer if you don't know. You can't tell anyone what you saw today. I have to drop you off somewhere safe. Where should I take you?"

"I'm staying at one of the Pyre Casinos."

She wanted to strangle him. "You need to leave as soon as possible."

"Why?"

"My husband will freak when he finds out you were at the event today. How could you be so foolish?"

"I heard your husband's foundation was putting it on and thought you might be here. I extended my stay, hoping we could talk."

"About what?" she shouted, pounding the wheel with her fist. "What you saw today? That's my life now, Jonathan."

"How can you say that and think I won't ask more questions?"

"I can't take you to The Strip," she said to herself and took the next exit off the freeway.

"Where are you taking me?"

"Check out of your room by phone and don't go back for anything. You might be on someone's radar now..." She cruised down the highway, searching for a nondescript accommodation for him. Her phone rang, and she saw Blade's name again. "Yes?"

"Where the fuck are you going?" Blade snapped. "I told you to go home. You're veering off course."

"I need to get him somewhere safe."

There was a sharp silence. "You have him in the car with you? I was hoping he'd been shot, so I wouldn't have to do it."

"Dammit, Blade. He doesn't know!"

"Fuck, Lyla. You're putting yourself at risk for him. I can't let you do that."

"I'll check him into a hotel and leave, I promise."

"I'm turning around."

"No! Help Gavin!"

"You're my first responsibility. Gavin would have my head if anything happened to you."

"I'll do this and go home."

Blade hung up. She cursed and turned into a motel. She put the gun in her purse and looked at Jonathan. "Let's go."

He slid out of the back seat and walked beside her. "What's going on?"

"They're coming for me. You need to check in and lay low."

"But—"

"I need a single room," she told the bored front desk clerk.

"How many nights?" the girl asked without looking up from her cell phone.

"One," she said and glared Jonathan into silence.

He had to leave tomorrow. If Gavin didn't come for him, Santana's gang might. She had to impress upon him how fucking serious this was.

She checked him in under a false name and paid with cash. She grabbed the key and rode the elevator to the second floor.

"Lyla, I don't understand what—"

"You don't need to understand." She located his room, unlocked the door, and pushed him inside. She jabbed a finger in his face. "I'm not the girl you knew. You can never see me again, got it?"

She turned away and wasn't prepared when he gripped her arm and dragged her into the room. He slammed the door, which bounced open from the force he used. Her mouth dropped. Jonathan manhandling her was just as shocking as a gun battle in a hospital.

He braced his hands on her shoulders. "I spent the past two years wondering what happened to you. Now that I've found you again, you think I can walk away, knowing you're in danger?"

She opened her mouth, but no sound emerged.

"It's me," he whispered.

She swallowed hard. "I know."

The familiar scent of his cologne surrounded her. She gripped handfuls of his shirt as reaction set in. Another battle, another time pulling the trigger. Fuck. Her eyes filled with tears.

He clasped her face between trembling hands. "Talk to me, Lyla."

"I have to go. You have to forget what you saw today. My husband will kill you if he finds out about this. Use your computer skills to disappear."

"Did you leave me because of him?"

"Jonathan, don't."

"Did he do something to make you leave? I reported you missing. I was obsessed with the thought that you'd been kidnapped, but the cops couldn't find anything. I've been going crazy, and then I see you in the casino, and... You think I can just move on with my life without knowing what happened? You knew I loved you. I would do anything for you."

As she stared into his tortured eyes, her heart twisted with regret. "I'm so sorry, Jonathan. I never meant to hurt you. I'm not that woman anymore. You should forget we ever knew each other. It's over."

"Who are you?"

"I need to go."

He didn't release her. "Please, give me something."

She saw the confusion and frustration bubbling beneath the surface. She never should have gotten involved with him. She'd known there was a possibility Gavin would find her, and she moved in with him anyway. He didn't belong in her world. Her world was dark, dirty, and perilous. He had a future and the possibility of a happily ever after.

"I love my husband," she said.

He closed his eyes as if her words physically hurt him. She felt a resounding pang in her breast. She had been trying to spare him this, but there was no getting around it.

"I can't tell you about his business because I don't know much about it. You need to let me go, Jonathan, for your own good."

He stared at her. "You've changed."

She tilted her chin. She wasn't going to apologize for that.

"You killed a man today, but you're still the girl I knew. I don't care what you call yourself. You still feel something for me. I can see it in your eyes. You saved my life today."

"You saved mine," she said and felt the prick of tears.

He gripped her arms. "Are you in trouble? Do you need to get away from your husband? I can make you disappear."

"I should have made sure Blade took care of you after I located her in Maine."

She whirled and saw Gavin standing in the doorway. His suit was splattered with blood, but he was standing without assistance, which meant the blood wasn't his. Her burst of happiness and relief disappeared as he raised a gun.

"Time to rectify my mistake," Gavin said in a quiet voice that scared the crap out of her.

She stepped in front of Jonathan and spread her arms wide so he wouldn't get a clear shot. "Gavin, don't!"

"Get out of my way or I'll prolong his death," he said softly.

She set her teeth. She had been through a bloodbath today and wouldn't allow him to create another. "Jonathan's going to leave. I'll never see him again."

"You promised you wouldn't talk to him."

"I didn't ask him to come!"

"Move, Lyla."

He shifted to get a clear shot, and she went on tiptoes to cover Jonathan, "Gavin, stop!"

He holstered the gun and pulled out a knife already stained with red. He advanced with lethal intent. She knew what he was capable of. Jonathan didn't have a chance in hell. Her heart threatened to beat out of her chest. This was spiraling out of control.

"He's done nothing wrong," she said.

"He touched what's mine, and he's trying to take you from me."

She took two steps forward with a hand up. "I'm not going to leave with him. I told him I love you."

Gavin shoved her to the side. She pivoted as he raised the knife for a killing strike.

"Gavin, *no!*"

Fear gave her the speed she needed. She launched herself at Jonathan, causing him to stagger back as she wrapped herself around him, shielding him with her body. She closed her eyes and waited for the blow, but nothing happened. She raised her head and looked behind her. Her skin prickled as she looked into Gavin's eyes, which were incandescent with rage.

"Release him," he said.

"Gavin, please!"

"Blade," Gavin bit out.

Blade advanced into the room and ripped her away from Jonathan. She clutched at Jonathan with desperate hands, pulling him with her. Blade squeezed her wrists, causing her fingers to contract and release him.

"No, Gavin, don't!" The scream came from her gut. "Please don't! He hasn't done anything wrong!"

"Get her out of here," Gavin said.

Blade lifted her into the air, and she fought savagely, all to no avail. She caught a glimpse of Gavin advancing toward Jonathan who wasn't going to raise a hand to defend himself. She couldn't let Gavin wipe Jonathan off the face of the earth. The only crime Jonathan committed was befriending a woman who belonged to Gavin Pyre.

"Gavin, you kill him, I'll leave you!"

Blade froze. For a moment, she wasn't sure if Gavin heard her, and then he turned slowly. His face had been wiped of all emotion. Blood dripped from the knife that had already seen unspeakable horrors today. The room was so quiet, she swore she could hear the drops hit the carpet.

"You're choosing him over me?" Gavin asked.

"He's done nothing wrong," she repeated. She shoved against Blade who dropped her. She walked up to Gavin, eyes never leaving his for a second. He was capable of taking on six men at once. One move and Jonathan would be lost to her forever. "Don't do it."

His stillness scared the shit out of her. She stopped a foot away and tentatively reached out. Her fingertips wrapped around the hand that held the knife. His skin felt like warm iron beneath her fingertips.

"Please," she whispered, "don't."

Gold eyes bored into hers. His energy pulsed in the air, raising the hair on the nape of her neck. The promise of violence swirled around him.

"He'll leave, and we'll never see him again," she promised. "I'm not going to run away with him."

"You promised you would never leave me," he said.

"I can't let you kill him."

"Because you love him?"

"No, because this isn't right."

His hand flashed out and gripped her chin. "He wants you. He loves you. I can't allow him to live."

"You can," she insisted as terrified tears coursed down her cheeks. "You have to."

Her hand trembled as she cupped his face. When he didn't move, she stroked. She was very aware of their audience and how precarious the situation was. Anything could incite him to attack.

"Please." She took a risk and moved in closer. The breast of his suit was stiff with blood, but she didn't care. She wrapped herself around him, silently pleading with him not to do this.

He touched her hair and a moment later, he picked her up. She collapsed against him and shuddered in relief.

"Thank you," she whispered.

He carried her out of the room. Over his shoulder, she saw Jonathan sag to his hands and knees. Now, he knew all his suspicions about her husband were correct. Gavin wasn't civilized or rational. He was a crime lord who did whatever he pleased. Jonathan was lucky to be breathing. She lost sight of him as Gavin strode down the corridor. Blade and two guards followed.

"You won't kill him?" she whispered.

When he didn't answer, she stiffened. He would come back and finish the job later.

"Promise me!"

No response.

She shoved against his shoulders. "Gavin, you can't—"

He slammed her against the wall, knocking the breath out of her. He raised the knife she didn't realize he was still holding and pressed the slick blade against her cheek. She stopped breathing.

"Do you want me to bleed him dry in front of you?" he hissed.

Her heart stopped. "No."

"Then don't fight me."

The monster that lurked inside him was in control now. Her husband was nowhere in sight. She was very aware of cold steel against her cheek and his charged body caging her in.

"You betrayed me," Gavin hissed.

He tipped his head back and let out an angry roar before he brought the knife down. She screamed and raised her hands to protect herself as the knife sank into the wall six inches from her head.

She felt a whoosh of air as Gavin's body disappeared. She lowered her arms and saw Blade standing in front of her, facing off with Gavin.

"Get out of my way," Gavin demanded.

"I'll take her home and give you some time," Blade said calmly.

He bared his teeth. "Get the fuck out of my way."

Blade reached into his pocket and pulled out a syringe. Blade had sedated Gavin several times after Manny was murdered. It was clear Blade thought he needed another dose.

He stepped up to his second in command. "Are you threatening me?"

The guards took a reflexive step back, but Blade didn't budge.

"It's my job to keep her safe, even from you."

Blade was putting his life on the line by defying his employer. She opened her mouth to intervene, but she was too late. Gavin snatched the needle and plunged it into Blade's neck. Blade flinched, but didn't try to protect himself. He emptied the syringe, and Blade dropped to the floor.

"No one comes between us," Gavin said.

He stalked toward her. She tensed to make a run for it and blinked when Blade shot to his feet and put Gavin in a chokehold from behind. He produced another syringe and deployed it into his neck. Instantly, Gavin swayed.

"You fucker," he wheezed.

"I have to save you from yourself," Blade said grimly as Gavin dropped face first on the carpet and didn't move.

She and Blade stared at one another.

"Call the elevator," he ordered.

She stumbled toward the button and pressed it as Blade pulled the knife out of the wall, handed it to one of the wary guards and hefted Gavin over one shoulder. The elevator arrived with a merry ding, and they all got in.

9

LYLA

SHE STOOD IN THE CORNER OF THE ELEVATOR, STARING AT GAVIN draped over Blade's shoulder. How Blade was able to handle his weight was a mystery. The guards stood as far away from Blade as possible, as if they expected Gavin to wake and kill them.

She shook from head to toe. He almost killed her. He was inches from—

The elevator opened on the ground floor. Blade dug in Gavin's pocket and tossed one of the guards a set of keys. The guard jogged toward Gavin's Aston Martin while Blade dropped Gavin in the trunk of the SUV as if he was a piece of luggage. He closed the back and pointed at her.

"Get in," he barked as he rode shotgun.

The driver floored it. She hastily belted herself in as the SUV careened out of the lot. She glanced in the trunk as Gavin rolled from his back to his front.

"Marcus, it's Blade. Expect some visitors," Blade said into his phone. "Yeah, Gavin and Lyla are fine. We're taking them home. Expect Gavin to be absent from work for a while. Who? Carmen? Yeah, she left before the shooting. I don't know who with. Some fucking actor or some shit. I gotta go."

She closed her eyes and willed this day away. She was physically and emotionally maxed out. All she wanted was to lie in a quiet, dark room with her baby and pretend the outside world didn't exist. No matter which way she turned, disaster was inevitable.

Blade spoke rapid, furious Spanish on the phone. She understood enough to realize he was filling in for Gavin, speaking to his men who were in cleanup and contain mode. They would erase or disturb surveillance cameras at the hospital, parking garage, and even the hotel where Jonathan was. Gavin had the power to erase a person's identity and could kill in plain sight without being caught.

She looked back at his large, lifeless body and shivered. When he woke, there would be hell to pay. Not only would she have to answer for Jonathan, but she was the reason he had to be sedated. Didn't he realize the difference between justice, self-defense, and outright murder? She clutched the door handle because she needed something to hold onto. How could her life go so wrong in so little time?

When they pulled up to the mansion, she opened the front door and was greeted by Beau who barked and licked her hand. She smoothed a hand over his head and then looked past him to Aunt Isabel who had Nora on her lap. Nora babbled excitedly when she saw her.

"How was your day, dear?" Aunt Isabel asked.

Before she could think of a response, the guards walked in with Gavin. Aunt Isabel's face went ashen with fear. She leaped to her feet.

"Is he hurt?" Aunt Isabel asked.

"Sedated," she said as she took Nora from her.

Aunt Isabel opened her mouth and then shut it. As the widow of an enforcer, she knew not to ask.

"Where's Carmen?" Aunt Isabel asked.

"She went out with Kody Singer."

"The actor?"

"Yes."

She kissed Nora on the forehead. The smell of baby powder clashed horribly with the stench of cold sweat and dried blood.

"Here." She handed Nora back to her aunt. "I need to see to

Gavin." She looked up the stairs, but the guards were nowhere to be found. "Where'd they go?"

Aunt Isabel pointed, and her stomach clenched. She headed toward the basement. She had been here twice in her life. The first was to witness Gavin beat a traitor to death, and the second was to find her father in a similar condition. She felt a sense of déjà vu as her damp hands slid over the iron railings. Unforgiving fluorescent lights revealed a concrete room with suspicious splotches on the floor and Gavin sprawled on a cot with a thin mattress. The guards nodded to her as they passed.

Blade stripped off Gavin's bloody jacket, revealing his double shoulder gun holster and guns in his waistband. Blade lifted Gavin's pants leg to reveal two more guns and his empty knife sheath. He removed Gavin's shoes and socks and investigated them thoroughly.

"In his shoe?" she asked skeptically.

Blade held up a thin switchblade. "Gavin's always prepared."

"No kidding." She wrapped her arms around herself as she watched Blade systematically disarm Gavin, even taking his belt. "What was in the first syringe?"

"Water."

"You knew he would use it on you."

"I suspected."

"You know him well," she said and swallowed. "Do you think he would have...?" She couldn't finish her sentence.

"I don't know."

"You don't know and sedated him anyway?"

"All I know is you can make him do anything." He fixed her with a piercing expression. "You should have let Gavin kill him."

"I can't—"

"He's a dead man walking. Gavin will kill him. There's no getting around that."

"I can't let him kill Jonathan. He didn't do anything wrong."

Blade shook his head. "You're not in Kansas, Dorothy. You're in the underworld where men mark their women by carving or tattooing their initials on her face. I'm surprised Gavin hasn't pressed you to do it."

She stared at him. "Tattoo my face?"

He shrugged. "Tattoo something. It doesn't have to be your face."

"Gavin's not a thug."

"Don't kid yourself. Gavin survives in the underworld because he's as ruthless and cruel as they are. He understands them because he *is* them. He just has money, power, and a legit company to run."

She ran a finger down Gavin's rigid, menacing face. "What are you going to do when he wakes up?"

"See how he reacts."

"You know he's going to be pissed."

"Yes."

"Locking him up is going to make it worse, don't you think?"

He flipped the switchblade with one hand. "You didn't see him after Manny died."

She watched the switchblade tumble through the air before Blade caught it and wove it through his fingers. He never took his eyes off Gavin.

"Gavin hasn't been himself since Vinny and Manny were killed. He's on a hair trigger. He calmed down once he got a ring on your finger and got you pregnant, but what you did today..." He shook his head. "It would push any man over the edge."

"I can't let him kill Jonathan!" she shouted.

Her outburst didn't impress him. "Gavin demands unwavering loyalty from everyone he does business with. Why should you be the exception?"

Her mouth dropped. "I am loyal to him! What are you talking about?"

"You chose your ex over Gavin."

"Not letting him kill isn't choosing Jonathan over him! That doesn't make sense!"

Blade shrugged. "When he wakes, you're the one who has to face him. You have about four hours to figure out how you want to handle it."

He walked out of the basement, leaving Gavin barefoot in slacks and a shirt. She knelt beside the bed and looked at her husband. Even unconscious and unarmed, he was a scary bastard. They had been through too much for this to break them. How could she make him understand that she wasn't in love with Jonathan? She had feelings for him, of course, but she wasn't going to leave Gavin for him. Killing Jonathan because of his insecurities was crossing the line. She accepted that he killed, but she couldn't let him do this.

"I love you," she whispered before she left the basement. She had four hours before he woke and all hell broke loose.

Aunt Isabel stood in front of the TV, which played live footage of the chaos at the hospital. She paused behind her aunt as a reporter spoke.

"The fire alarm activated. No one is quite sure why. Some witnesses say they heard gunshots, but so far, the police have not been available to confirm or deny that there was a shooting incident. It's going to take a while for everyone to be accounted for, but right now, all seems to be well. The Pyre Foundation was here today with several celebrities spreading a little joy and hope." The reporter turned to Janice who stepped forward with her million-dollar smile. "Janice here is one of the organizers for this event. Can you tell us what happened here today, Janice?"

"I didn't hear any shots fired or see anything suspicious," Janice said. "When the fire alarm went off, we all pitched in to make sure everyone got out safely."

The reporter nodded. "And can you tell us about this event you had today?"

"Of course," Janice said.

Despite the events of the past hour, her lips curved. Janice always managed to spin everything into a positive light for the Pyre Foundation's image. Her faint smile faded. When would they find the hospital coordinator's body? He was dead, along with some of her security and a bunch of gang members. Did Gavin have cops in his employ who would cover up the incident? The parking garage was far enough from the hospital that the isolated incident had gone unnoticed, but what happened when everyone found their cars decorated by bullets?

"Lyla, are you okay?" Aunt Isabel asked.

She let out a long breath. "Yes."

Aunt Isabel hugged her tight. Her eyes filled with tears, but she refused to let them fall. When her aunt pulled back, she hoped she didn't look as scared as she felt.

"You've been through so much, honey," Aunt Isabel said quietly. "Trust Gavin to take care of it."

Her stomach clenched. "I'll try."

"That's my girl."

The front door burst open, and Carmen rushed in with her shoes in hand, hair a mess. She skidded to a stop when she spotted them.

"Why the fuck aren't you answering your phone?" Carmen bellowed.

She pulled her phone out of her pocket and saw that it had a blank screen. "Oh, it's dead."

Carmen pressed a hand against her chest and sagged against the back of the couch. "You bitch. I hate you."

She hugged her cousin who dropped her shoes and hugged her tight. Beau butted his head against Carmen in welcome. Carmen pet him but didn't release her.

"Where's Gavin?" Carmen asked in a muffled voice.

"In the basement."

"What? Why?"

She moved her eyes to Aunt Isabel who was watching the news. Carmen noticed the direction of her glance and nodded before she released her.

"We were at a restaurant, and they had the news on. I got in touch with Alice and Janice, but neither of them knew what happened to you, and I..." Carmen blinked back tears. "I fucking hate this. Every time I leave you alone, shit goes down." She lowered her voice. "Was there a shooting?"

"Yes." She picked up Nora before remembering that she was covered in God knew what. "I'm going to give Nora a bath."

Aunt Isabel nodded. "We'll be here if you need us."

Carmen collapsed on the couch and cuddled against her mother, who pulled her close. She was glad Aunt Isabel was here but wished she could get a hug from her own mother after a day like today.

She paused in the doorway of the master suite and tiptoed to the bed. She reached beneath the nightstand and quietly pulled the gun from its hiding place. She methodically checked the room with Nora on her hip and relaxed when she found that they were alone. She attended the event to restore her faith in humanity, but all she had gained was another dose of paranoia and fear.

She bathed with Nora and then settled on the bed to breastfeed. God, she had nearly been gunned down again. Would this ever stop? She plugged her dead phone in to charge. The screen flickered to life. A series of beeps, rings, and chirps sounded. She thumbed through her phone and saw several texts from Janice, Alice, and Carmen. She listened to two frantic voicemails from Carmen and deleted one from her mother before she could hear the first word.

The bedroom door opened. She reached for her gun, only to stop short when she saw Carmen who changed out of her tailored dress. Face bare of makeup and dressed in yoga pants, Carmen crawled on the bed and sat cross-legged in front of her.

"Spill," Carmen demanded.

"Where's your mom?"

"She went home. She got out of this life and doesn't want to be around for whatever happens next."

"She's a smart woman."

"The news obviously doesn't know what the fuck went down."

She draped Nora on her shoulder to burp her. "The hospital director gave Gavin and I a tour of the new wing. We were about to leave when a gang came out of the elevator. Gavin started blasting away and pulled the fire alarm when he realized there were more of them than he thought. Gavin killed a drug lord this morning and then came to the hospital event. Those were his men."

Carmen made a rolling motion with her hand. "Go on."

"They were gunning for Gavin, so Blade got me out of there. In the parking garage, we got jumped. Jonathan was there."

"Who?"

She ignored the spurt of annoyance. "Jonathan, my ex."

Carmen frowned. "What was he doing there?"

"He wanted to talk to me."

Carmen held up a hand. "Oh, hell no! You talked to him?"

"He followed us to the parking garage and nearly got shot. I drove him to a hotel when I found out he was staying in a Pyre Casino. I told him to forget he ever knew me. He was worried about me. He said he could help me disappear, and that's when Gavin showed up." Nora burped, and she settled her daughter on her lap. "Gavin tried to kill him. I stopped him."

Carmen's mouth dropped open.

"Blade sedated Gavin because he..." She swallowed hard as she remembered Gavin's murderous expression. "He was out of control. He slammed his knife into the wall this close to my face." She held up a hand to show her and shivered.

Carmen put both hands over her face and groaned. "Shit."

"Yeah."

She dropped her hands. "You have to let that guy go."

"I have."

She leaned forward. "No. I mean let him go, as in, let Gavin do what he's gonna do."

"What?"

"Lyla, Gavin's a psycho."

"No, he isn't," she said hastily.

Carmen gave her a put-upon look. She remembered the look on Gavin's face as he approached Jonathan and sighed.

"He's... not normal."

"He's fucking unhinged, okay? Jesus, you're acting like Gavin's a pussycat. He isn't. He's a straight-up killer, and he'll do whatever it takes to get what he wants, comprende?"

"Why are you telling me this?"

"Because you don't get who Gavin is. He's going to kill your little ex, and he's going to make him suffer."

"Jonathan didn't do anything wrong!" she said for what felt like the tenth time.

"In your eyes. Gavin won't let you feel an iota of affection for any other man. Gavin's the most possessive psycho I know, and that's saying something!"

"Carmen, he can't kill Jonathan."

"He will."

"I won't let him," she said fiercely.

Carmen stared at her for a pregnant moment and then sighed. "There she is."

"Who?"

"My cousin from California."

"What?"

"You can take the girl from the beaches, but you can't take the idealism out of the woman."

"You think trying to save an innocent man is idealistic?"

"It's unrealistic when your husband is Gavin Pyre. This guy isn't innocent. He showed up at this event. Why? Because he wants you. That makes him guilty as fuck, and that's why Gavin's going to take him out. If your ex knew who Gavin was, he should have stayed away."

"He thought I was in danger. He was worried about me."

Carmen made the sound of a buzzer when you answered wrong on a game show. "Two strikes. Now, he's out."

She glared at her cousin. This was why she needed to get out of the house. Carmen and Blade believed it was perfectly acceptable for Gavin to kill anyone he wanted. "Gavin can let him live."

"He can?"

"After what happened, I can guarantee I'll never see Jonathan again."

Carmen shook her head. "You don't get it. Gavin won't let you have split loyalties."

There it was again. Loyalties. "I am loyal to Gavin. Jealousy and possessiveness aren't justifications for committing murder!"

"Lyla, you live in the underworld! Gavin doesn't need justifications; he just needs cause. He's blown guys heads off for not responding fast enough to a question. Having you defend another man made him lose his motherfucking mind! Can't you see that?"

"I won't let him do this. We've been through so much." She brushed a hand through Nora's hair. "This is small in comparison."

"You being with another man in a hotel room doesn't sound small."

"It wasn't like that!"

Carmen rolled her eyes. "How the hell could you get yourself in so much trouble in so little time?"

She threw her hands up. "I've been with only two men in my life, and I have to stop one from killing the other. My life is fucked up."

"That's your fault. You chose Gavin, knowing what kind of man he is."

She wanted to argue but decided it was a moot point. "The hospital director was killed. Was that on the news?"

Carmen sobered. "No."

Her head throbbed, so she stretched out on the bed. Beau jumped up, circled twice, and settled with his eyes on her.

"How'd it go with Kody?" she asked, desperate for mundane conversation.

"He asked me to go to Europe with him."

Panic flooded her. She didn't want to be alone, but Carmen deserved to have a life. "What did you say?"

"I told him I'd think about it." Carmen gave her a shrewd look. "But you know I'm not looking for commitment."

She tried to hide her relief. "I know."

"And how can I even think about going when you're neck deep in this shit?"

She rubbed her face against the pillow and cuddled Nora close. "It's a mess."

"When is Gavin going to wake up?"

"In two or three hours."

"And what are you going to do?"

"Make him promise not to touch Jonathan."

Carmen stared at her. "You can't be serious."

"What else can I do?"

"Let Gavin do what he's gonna do and hope it's over quickly."

"I can't do that."

"Lyla, Gavin grew up in the underworld. He doesn't have morals."

"I can't let him kill Jonathan."

Carmen sighed. "Let me take Nora and let you catch some z's."

"Are you sure?" she asked as her eyes closed.

"Yeah. You're going to need your strength to face Gavin after he's been sedated."

Carmen bounced Nora on her hip as she walked to the door. "Your mama's crazy, baby girl. This world isn't for the faint of heart. Did I tell you about the time I watched my dad blow this guy's brains out? I think I was seven."

"Carmen!" she groaned.

"Nora needs to know these things."

"At four months?"

"The earlier, the better. Her dad's Gavin fucking Pyre. She's going to know how to shoot a gun before she's six years old."

She burrowed under the covers and moaned when her phone rang, but after a quick look at the screen, she answered, "Hey, Alice."

"Oh, my God! Are you okay?"

"I'm fine. Are you?"

"Yes. Did you leave before the shooting?"

"During. Blade got me out."

"And he's okay as well?"

"Yes."

Alice let out a breath. "Janice and I have been worried sick. It's madness here."

"Has anyone been hurt?" she asked, clutching the phone, waiting for the inevitable discovery of the hospital director.

"I'm not sure. We're still trying to account for everyone. I wanted to make sure you were okay. Your phone was off earlier."

"I know. My battery died. I'm sorry." She hesitated. "Is there anything I can do?"

"No. You coming today was great. I just hate that something like this had to ruin it. I have to go. Thanks for everything you did. It meant a lot to me."

Before she could respond, Alice hung up. She dropped her face on the pillow and moaned. If she hadn't come, none of this would've happened.

10

LYLA

"Lyla."

A hand shook her shoulder. She grunted and blinked at Blade.

"What?" She felt drugged. Her mind was suspended in no man's land.

"Gavin's awake."

That brought her back to reality with an unpleasant jolt. Images of the director covered in blood, shooting a man in the face, and Gavin swinging a knife at her slid through her mind in rapid succession. She sat up and grabbed the lapels of her robe, which were gaping open. Blade was too busy typing on his phone to notice.

"How long has he been up?" she asked.

"Half an hour."

"He's been up that long, and you only woke me up now?" She scooted off the bed and headed to the closet.

"He stopped trying to break down the door ten minutes ago."

She paused. "He tried to break down an iron door?"

"Yeah. He nearly fucking did it. You calling him the Hulk isn't far off the mark. I've seen him do crazy shit when he puts his mind to it."

"Is he asking for me?"

"He hasn't said a thing since he woke up."

She grabbed the first set of clothes she got her hands on—a pair of sweatpants and a shirt with a big heart on the front. Blade headed to the door the moment she emerged from the closet.

"Wait. I want to know what's going on," she said.

"With what?"

She stared at him. "The hospital incident."

"What about it?"

Was he being deliberately obtuse? "The hospital director was killed. You're not going to be able to cover that up, are you?"

"The cops suspect gang activity, but it's hard for them to get confirmation since the surveillance cameras were damaged. We took care of our bodies, left the gang members there, and made it look like they turned on each other." Blade jerked his head at the door. "Come, let's get you to Gavin."

Her hands became damp with sweat as she followed. It had been a while since she had to handle an out of control Gavin, and she wasn't sure she was up to the challenge.

"I'll be watching on the surveillance camera in case you need help," Blade said when they reached the basement.

She glared at him. "You're making me more nervous."

"Just prepping you, Dorothy."

"Asshole," she muttered.

When she didn't reach for the handle, he leaned against the wall and put his hands in his pockets.

"Do you really think he'd kill me?" she whispered.

"No," Blade said. "Hurt you, yes. You're his weak spot, his Achilles' heel. No matter how you look at it, you chose another man over Gavin today. After taking care of business at the hospital, he tracked you to the hotel and found you with another man who offered to make you disappear. Of course, Gavin's going to kill him. Then you made matters worse by touching him and pleading for his life. Gavin won't share you."

"I'm not asking him to!"

He shrugged. "Gavin has his own set of rules. You live in his world, you live by them. Period."

He was her husband, and she should be able to talk to him. She could make him understand, right?

"The longer you make him wait, the worse it will be," Blade said.

"You're the one who drugged him!"

"You weren't in any state to handle him."

"I know," she muttered. "Thanks." But now she had to deal with Gavin's wrath, which she could only imagine was worse than it had been at the hotel. She made no move to open the door.

"I'll come with you," Blade decided.

She couldn't hide her relief. "Okay."

She eased the heavy door open and examined the dented side of it before she stepped onto the landing. She peered down the stairs but couldn't see the rest of the room from this angle. Her heart pounded in her ears as she waited for Gavin to appear, but he didn't. Fuck.

She started down. She felt as if she were walking to her doom rather than to talk to her husband. Of course, in most American households, husbands weren't sedated or locked in basements to stop them from going on killing sprees. She allowed Gavin to go back into the underworld to destroy Sadist, not kill anyone he felt like. They had so much bigger problems than her ex who was in love with a woman who didn't exist.

Halfway down the steps, she saw Gavin in front of the cot. He stood just beyond the circle of fluorescent lights. His eyes were a burning copper that didn't bode well for her. He looked as if he had been shipwrecked. His shirt was unbuttoned and splattered with blood and his slacks were shredded at the knee, probably from trying to break the door down. She made it to the bottom and stopped with her hand on the rail.

"Are you okay?" she asked.

He didn't move or speak. She was dimly aware of Blade standing behind her. On the surface, he looked composed, but the air crackled with his energy, which was dark and vicious.

"Changed loyalties, have you, Blade?" he asked softly.

"My loyalty is to both of you. I did what I thought was best."

"If you hadn't already bled for her, I'd shoot you." A muscle jumped in his jaw. "Get the fuck out of here, Blade, and turn off the cameras."

She stiffened, and turned to see Blade assessing him closely. Blade caught her nervous glance, nodded, and then left. She listened to the sound of him climbing the stairs and flinched when she heard the door shut, locking her in the basement with her husband.

"Did you come here to plead for his life?" he asked.

"Yes."

"Don't bother." He prowled in the shadows. "Why were you with him in the hotel room?"

"He got caught in the crossfire when we were ambushed in the parking garage. I couldn't leave him there, so I dropped him off at the hotel."

"You promised not to talk to him."

His unemotional voice made her skin prickle with alarm.

"I didn't know he would be there," she said.

"You saw him before the attack, didn't you?"

Her heart sank. "Yes."

"What did he want?"

There was only one reason for Jonathan's appearance, and they both knew it. In her eyes, it didn't matter why. Jonathan wanted nothing to do with her now, so what he said prior to the attack didn't matter. "He wanted closure."

"Is that right? And how did he think he would accomplish that?"

"He just wanted to know the truth."

"And what did you tell him?"

"To move on and forget he ever met me."

"Didn't you warn him what I'd do?"

She shivered. "Yes."

"And he still took the risk. He knew the consequences for trespassing, Lyla."

"He doesn't understand your world—"

"Our world."

He closed in on her, and her body locked against the need to run. He was a natural predator. Fleeing would only make things worse.

"You fucked up today," he said.

"So did you." The feeling of being hunted pissed her off. She shouldn't be afraid of her husband, but she was. The polished veneer was what most people saw, but she knew about the beast beneath the pretty exterior. "You could have killed me."

"If I didn't love you so much, I would."

Her breath whooshed out of her. "What?"

"I told you why I never committed fully the first time," he said as he backed her against the wall and planted both hands on either side of her head. "I didn't want anyone to have such power over me."

His will was so strong that she could feel it pressing in on her, demanding her submission.

"You have the power to save me," he said quietly and rubbed his thumb over her bottom lip. "And destroy me." His eyes met hers. "Today, you destroyed me. You threatened to leave me for him."

"Gavin, I couldn't let you—"

His thumb slid into her mouth. Her lips closed reflexively before she tried to turn her head away.

"Gavin," she garbled as his thumb slid deeper. What the fuck was he doing?

"Suck," he ordered.

"We have to—"

He leaned down so their faces were inches apart. "Do it, Lyla."

Her mouth watered as she held his feral gaze. He was on the precipice. One wrong move and he would lose it. Since his hand was in her face, she saw that his knuckles were swollen and ripped from God knew what. She raised her hands and felt him tense until she gripped his wrist. She brushed her finger over the cuts and then did as he asked. She sucked.

"I was so desperate to keep you safe, to get you away from those fuckers. I tracked you to that hotel, unsure why you were there, and I hear him say he can make you disappear." The fingers resting against her jaw tensed. "There's something you don't understand about me, something you never did. When it comes to you, I'll do whatever it takes to have you with me. I'll steal you from another man, blackmail your father, or threaten someone's life to bind you to me." His eyes met hers. "Or kill a man for coveting what has always been mine."

She pulled back. "Gavin—"

He replaced his thumb with his pointer and middle finger and sank them deep so she stopped trying to talk. His fingers skittered over her tongue and thrust slowly in and out of her mouth. She shifted restlessly. Why the fuck was this turning her on? And how could she be turned on when she should be pleading for Jonathan's life?

"I'm not the kind of man you want to fall in love with you," he said quietly, eyes fixed on her lips. "Men like me, when we find a reason to live, we hang on too tight. I know men who have killed their wives because they can't handle how she makes them feel."

She dug her nails into his chest and felt his muscles tense in reaction.

"I never understood that feeling until today," he said.

"Gavin—"

He wrapped one hand around her neck and pulled her away from the wall. He walked her backward until the back of her knees hit the cot. The narrowing of his eyes gave her a split second of warning before he whirled her around and bent her over. Her hands landed on the thin mattress. He yanked her sweatpants down and trailed rough, calloused fingers over her bare ass. Goose bumps rose over her body.

"What are you doing?" she demanded and tried to wriggle away.

"Don't move," he ordered.

"Gavin—"

"Don't talk."

He placed his hips firmly against her ass and rocked as he bent over her. She could feel his cock pressed firmly between her cheeks. When he lapped the back of her neck with his tongue, she shifted restlessly.

"This isn't right," she said through clenched teeth.

He worked the two fingers she had been sucking into her damp heat. Her mouth dropped open at the pleasure and pain. When his fingers curled, her back arched, and she went on tiptoes, calves burning.

"If this is wrong, then why are you wet?"

He rested his slick thumb against her asshole, and she jerked, but that fucking mammoth hand on her back kept her bent over and at his mercy. She sucked in a breath as his thumb penetrated. She wriggled her ass to dislodge him, but he wasn't deterred. He withdrew his thumb to replace it with the slick fingers from her pussy.

"Gavin, we need to talk."

She bucked forward as he laved the dimples above her ass.

"We're done talking."

She felt the head of his cock. Alarmed, she reached back to splay her hand on his rock-hard stomach to slow him down. He gripped her waist and impaled her on him. She let out a strangled shriek.

"That's it, baby girl. Let me in."

"I-I don't think I can take—"

"You don't have a choice."

He pulled back before imbedding himself fully. She screamed. He collared her throat with one hand and her breast with the other and bowed her upwards.

"Gavin," she gasped.

"You bring out the best and worst in me." His bristly jaw scraped her soft cheek. "A man like me can't have a weakness like you, but I do. Some think because I'm married and have a kid that it's made me soft, but being with you has made me more dangerous than ever."

She dug her nails into his arm as he began to fuck her ass.

"I've already thought of ten ways to kill him," he said through gritted teeth.

She tried to pull away. "Gavin!"

He didn't miss a beat as he kept thrusting nice and slow. "Strangling him would make me happiest. Up close and personal."

"Please—"

"I'm going to kill him. Nothing will stop me. I'm going to bathe in his blood until it's cold, so I know he's really fucking gone."

He pumped his hips hard enough to make her scream, and then he bent her over again. His hand kneaded her breast before it skated down her abdomen to her clit. He grabbed her hair and wrenched her head to the side so he could kiss her. When he pulled back, she saw his eyes were filled with rage and lust.

"You think you've tamed me? You're not even close. You can't control me."

There were no inhibitions, no rules. It was just her and him, and nothing else mattered. His hand sank into her hair and pulled as he thrust home. He fucked her ass as if he owned it, which he did. She climaxed, screaming and clawing at the mattress. He made her feel like a savage. He growled like a wild animal as he came, grinding himself against her before he pulled out abruptly.

She collapsed on the mattress, panting. He zipped up his pants and turned to her. His climax hadn't cooled his temper. If anything, he looked angrier. Her heart sank.

"If I didn't love you so much, I never would have stepped down from my position, and my father and Vinny would still be alive."

She felt as if he punched her in the stomach.

"If we didn't have Nora, I'd lock you in here," he continued.

The pleasure he evoked from her body was replaced with despair. She wanted to curl up in a ball. Instead, she whispered, "I gave up a normal life to be with you."

He said nothing. He stared at her as if she were something distasteful.

"You force me into your world, but I'm not a part of it, and I won't bow down to it." She lifted her chin. "I had to change. I understand that, sometimes, people need to die. I don't have to agree with what you do or how you do it, but I trust you'll know what's required, but in this... There's a difference between killing a thug in the underworld and murdering a man who thinks he's in love with a woman who doesn't love him back."

Tears burned her eyes. She rose, very aware of her throbbing behind, his seed leaking out of her and the way he tensed as she took a step toward him. She searched for the right words and willed him to understand.

"I trust you to do what needs to be done in the underworld. I trust that you won't lose yourself, that you won't cheat on me. I trust that you'll find that fucker and avenge Manny and Vinny. I've changed since I watched Manny die, but I haven't changed so much that I can ignore the fact you want to kill an innocent man." She held up a hand when he opened his mouth. "He. Is. Innocent. He dated a woman he thought was single. He was nice to a woman who had no one, and there are too few people like him in the world. What I felt for him can't compare to what I feel for you." She searched his eyes, looking for recognition or acceptance. "You married me and told me that you would do whatever it took to make me love you again. I love you, but if you do this, you'll break me, break us."

She reached out, and even as fear coursed through her, she stroked a hand down his imposing face.

"I love you," she said.

No reaction. The predator weighed every word out of her mouth.

"You can't erase my memories by killing him. We've been through too much to let Jonathan rip us apart. If you do this, you'll destroy us."

She waited for a full minute for him to say something, but he remained silent. He was a living, breathing statue of a man who wouldn't yield. As the silence stretched, she realized his silence was her answer. She dropped her hand as a tear coursed down her cheek.

"Nothing I say will make a difference, will it?" she whispered.

"No."

She averted her eyes and walked toward the stairs. When she reached the door, she banged on it hard enough to make her hand ache. A guard opened the door, and she walked out with him on her heels.

She walked toward the kitchen and let herself into the backyard. She welcomed the hard slap of cold air and paced across the cold tiles to a lounge chair. The last hint of light faded from the sky. She settled on a chair and stared blindly into the pool lit by underwater lights as tears gathered in her eyes.

Nothing had changed. Gavin would do whatever he wanted despite how she felt. She was as scared, pissed, and helpless as she had been when Gavin went back into the underworld when Vinny was killed.

She looked up at the blanket of black sky above her. There was no bird flying overhead or shooting star to signal that all would be well. This was the real world where good didn't always overcome evil.

The back door opened. She wiped her eyes and saw Blade coming toward her with a trench coat. She accepted the coat and wrapped it around her to ward off the cold.

"You're in one piece," Blade observed.

"Doesn't feel like it," she mumbled.

"You'll get past this."

"Why is it always me that has to get over it and not him?"

"Because he's a badass motherfucker."

"So?"

"So no one can stop him when he wants something."

"My life is always going to be like this, isn't it?"

"Like what?"

"There's always going to be an attack, and I'll have to make decisions that will tear me up inside."

"You'll get used to it."

She wiped away a tear. "And if I don't want to?"

"You already know the answer to that," Blade said and went back inside.

She blew out a shaky breath and wrapped her arms around herself. Life was hard. Life as a crime lord's wife was even harder. She wished Manny was here. A tear she couldn't stop slipped down her cheek. *If I didn't love you so much, I never would have stepped down from my position, and my father and Vinny would still be alive.* That fucking killed her, but what was worse was he was right. If he hadn't stepped down for her, Sadist wouldn't have made a play to become the crime lord. Vinny wouldn't have volunteered to take his place, and Manny would be traveling the world or browsing through antique shops if it wasn't for her. The cost of her and Gavin being together was astronomical... and they were still paying.

She turned her head when she saw movement out of the corner of her eye. Gavin stood in the shadows. He came forward, the clip of his shoes loud in the hushed silence. He looked every inch the wealthy businessman and not a man with murder on his mind. He looked as flawless and untouchable as James Bond in his tailored suit, hands in pockets, expression nonchalant. In contrast, she felt as if she was on the verge of falling into an endless chasm from which there would be no return.

He stopped in front of her. She couldn't meet his eyes, not when he looked at her as if he hated her. There was nothing more to say. He would do what he wanted, and there was nothing she could do to stop him. She felt so goddamn helpless. She thought the days of not being in control of her destiny were a thing of the past. Apparently not. Everyone sided with Gavin and thought it was his right to take Jonathan's life. She didn't agree. If he killed Jonathan, would she leave him?

The silence stretched. What did he want? His presence fanned the throbbing pain in her chest. He was tearing her apart, but that was nothing new. She was always the one who had to conform, not him. No matter what she said or did, he wouldn't change, so where did that leave her? Was this the beginning of the end for them?

She jolted when a calloused hand cupped her chin. He tilted her face up. She kept her eyes closed. A tear leaked out of her left eye. She hoped it was too dark for him to see, but his thumb brushed it away before it could travel halfway down her face. Her breath hitched as another tear escaped. She wasn't prepared for the gentle kiss he pressed against her lips.

She opened her eyes, but he was already on his way back to the house. "Gavin."

He didn't stop. He walked back into the house and disappeared from sight.

11

GAVIN

Santana's brother trembled like a plucked bow as Gavin held his head at an angle guaranteed to end his miserable existence. Santana's men scattered after he executed their leader. He thought he bought enough time to attend the hospital function and come back to finish gutting Santana's operation. Seeing those gang members in the elevator with Santana's brand on their neck sent a spear of ice-cold terror through his body when he realized he had put Lyla at risk.

"How did you know to send men to the hospital? Are you tracking me?" he bit out.

Santana's brother's mouth flopped open and closed like a fish. He bent his head a fraction more, and he squealed like a stuck pig.

"How did you know?" he bellowed.

"I-I got a call."

"From who?"

"Stark."

Everything in him went on high alert. "Eli Stark?"

"Si. He's an informant, sells information. He gave the location of hospital."

"What else?" he asked.

"That's it, I swear."

Gavin broke his neck, rose, and stared down at the body without really seeing it. Eli Stark. This wasn't the first time he heard whispers of Stark, but it would be the last. Once, he considered Stark a loyal associate, but that changed after Stark's mother had been brutally attacked. Stark blamed him for not protecting her, which gave him motive to turn traitor. Selling information to a Mexican drug lord? It didn't sound like Stark, but people changed. After his mother's attack, Stark quit his position as detective and went on a bloody rampage to avenge his mother before he fell off the map. It was time to draw him out of hiding.

He dug through the dead man's pockets and found condoms, drugs, and a cell phone. He used the dead man's thumb to unlock the phone, debated whether to cut it off for future use, but decided to change the passcode instead. He scrolled through recent calls, most of which were unavailable.

He dialed his tech genius. "Z, it's me. I need you to tap into this phone and unblock some numbers."

Z didn't ask questions. "Give me ten minutes."

"And locate Eli Stark's mother."

A pause. "Sir?"

"I don't know her name. She's been in a coma for two years."

"I'll find out," Z said.

He pocketed the phone and glanced around the room. The blood-splattered walls reflected how he felt on the inside. Bodies littered the ground around him. It took him less than two hours to track Santana's brother to a set of cabins on the outskirts of the city.

Santana was a sick fuck. He had made sure to clear out the child prostitutes they discovered earlier this morning. He didn't feel a lick of remorse for drawing out Santana's death since he found the fucker molesting a baby. If he let the justice system do their thing, Santana would get several life sentences and live off taxpayer's money, reading books and educating himself about the legal system to see how he could get out. Or he would join one of the gangs in prison and claim the lives of too many prison guards who were just trying to make an honest living. Fuck that. He knew Santana's brother would retaliate, but he hadn't expected them to stage a public attack that cost four of his men's lives and put Lyla and too many others at risk. Stupid fucker.

He was high on rage and feeling especially savage. The lethal fury racing through his veins hadn't dissipated as he slayed anyone who crossed his path. The fight with Lyla made him crazed. He couldn't fault Blade for drugging him today. What he felt this afternoon when he walked into that hotel room was inexplicable. Blade had done his job and prevented him from doing something unforgivable to his wife. In the basement, he had lost control. He wanted to hurt, to punish her. Lyla would lie to protect this guy, which showed how deep her feelings for Huskin ran. He wouldn't allow it. She was supposed to heal him, not break him. Hearing her cry and plead for another man's life made him homicidal.

He reloaded his gun and walked outside to see if there was more work to do. Unfortunately, his men had already taken care of everything. Those who thought they were safe in these cabins were now strewn across the sand. His men knew the drill and were already loading the bodies into the SUV to bury them in the desert where they would never be found.

A man at his feet moaned. He looked down and saw that the man had been shot twice in the gut, a painful way to die. When he saw Gavin, his eyes bulged, and he made urgent, terrified noises. He crouched beside the man who tried to edge away. He pulled out his knife and yanked the man's head to the side to examine Santana's brand—a skull tattoo with the number twenty-four in roman numerals on his throat.

"I'm gonna need this," he said, tapping the tattoo with the tip of his knife.

The man tried to push his hand away. Gavin restrained him with ease and got to work. By the time his phone rang, the man was dead and he held a dripping slice of skin with Santana's brand. He grabbed a switchblade and pinned the piece of skin on the door. If more men tried to take refuge in these cabins, they would know he wasn't far behind.

"Yeah?" he said into the phone.

"I unscrambled the numbers. What are you looking for?" Z asked.

"An incoming call that came in around nine or ten this morning." An hour or two before the attack.

"There was a call at ten oh one. It's a prepaid phone, not registered to anyone."

"Give me the number." As Z rattled off the number, he wrote on the wall in the only ink he had in abundance—blood. "Got it."

"The caller was at the hospital when he made the call."

He tried to rein in his beast. "And which hospital is Stark's mother at?" He waited, but already had a sneaking suspicion that he knew the answer.

"Same hospital. She's on the fourth floor."

Was it chance that Stark had been visiting his mother at the same hospital where the Pyre Foundation was having an event? "I'm gonna call the number. Try to pinpoint his location."

"Will do, sir."

"How is everything with the surveillance tapes?"

"Scrambled."

"Good work."

He hung up with Z and glanced at the bloody numbers as he plugged them into his phone. As the phone began to ring, he walked into the silent cabin so the caller wouldn't hear the groans of the dying.

The line picked up, but no one spoke. The silence stretched.

"This is Gavin Pyre," he said.

He thought he heard an indrawn breath on the other end but couldn't be sure.

"You fucked up today. I'm coming for you."

The line went dead. He stood in the middle of the cabin for a moment to get himself under control. There was a fine trembling in the hand holding the phone. He needed blood so badly, he could taste it.

He dialed Z again. "Did you get his location?"

"He's at the hospital."

Adrenaline fizzled in his veins. The monster inside him roared with the need to end this fucker. He swallowed his need to mutilate the dead bodies and washed his hands before he walked outside. He slid into his car and didn't have to signal for a group of men to follow. Six men stopped what they were doing and loaded into an SUV.

He headed back to the city. There was a firestorm taking place inside him. Fury burned a hole in his gut. When he was gutting Santana this morning, the man claimed he didn't know the identity of the Phantom. He figured Santana was telling the truth since he cut off his fingers one by one. Either Eli Stark was the Phantom or was working with him. Either way, this was going to end.

He strode into the hospital with his men following at a discreet distance. The lobby was filled with cops, reporters, medical staff, and concerned family members who were still trying to figure out what had happened this morning.

He took the elevator to the fourth floor. As he strode through the corridor, he approached two cops. Their hands edged toward their weapons. Every officer in the state recognized his face. The dirty ones knew exactly what he was capable of while the other half suspected and dreamed of being the one to bag him. Too bad they had never been able to pin shit on him until the money laundering charge. He had been at such a low point that he hadn't acted swiftly enough and had to serve time or let them dig deeper and possibly find evidence of other, more grievous transgressions. He eyed the cops boldly, daring them to do something. They didn't make a move.

He glanced into rooms as he passed. Most patients were asleep. Hospital staff rushed through the halls despite the late hour. He opened a door without knocking and leaned in, expecting to see a sleeping patient. Paul Vega sat up in bed, papers scattered over his sheets and a laptop on his tray table. Paul peered over the top of his glasses at him. The light from the screen illuminated the hatred in his eyes.

Gavin stared at him. What the fuck? The fact that his lifelong enemy was a patient at this hospital was too convenient. Was this the only fucking hospital in the city?

"Fuck off, Pyre," Paul growled.

He glanced at his men. "Find Stark's mother. Two of you stay with her. The other two sweep the hospital floors and see if you can locate Stark."

He stepped into Paul's room and closed the door. "What are you doing here, Paul?"

"What the fuck does it look like? I have pneumonia." Paul took off his glasses and glared as he advanced across the room. "You're not allowed in here."

"I'm allowed anywhere. No place is off limits. I thought after I fucked you up in your office, you'd realize that."

It was true that Vega looked like shit, but his frail appearance didn't mean he wasn't dangerous.

"I have a lot of work to do, Pyre."

He stopped beside the bed. "Restful day?"

"No thanks to you," he said sourly. "You must have a death wish to kill Santana. You stirred up a hornet's nest and don't have the manpower you need to overcome the hell you unleashed."

In his youth, he witnessed Paul's futile attempts to wrench the title from his father. Despite the fact he had thrashed Paul soundly, Vega still didn't respect his authority, which made his fingers itch for his knife.

"You're losing your hold on the city, Pyre," Paul said quietly. "Why don't you just give it up?"

"Give it up to who?"

Paul gathered his papers and began to stack them, rapping them on the tray table to straighten them out. He was nervous. Gavin eased closer and saw him tense.

"You know something you aren't telling me, Paul?" he asked, voice light and pleasant.

Paul studied his papers as if the information on it were more important than their conversation. "I'm too busy running my practice to delve into the underworld."

"Yet you knew I got Santana. How?"

"I have my sources."

"You're lying to me, Vega."

"I don't owe you shit. You told me you'd find the crime lord who murdered Rafael, and you haven't."

"I will."

"He's too powerful. You're in over your head. He's giving us—"

Paul stopped, but it was too late.

"You're joining forces with the man who murdered your son?" he asked.

Paul bared his teeth in a snarl. "I either join or end up like Manny. He's rewarded me, offered me more than you fuckers ever did." Spit flew as his emotions got the better of him. "How many can you kill? You think your name will protect you? You have nowhere to turn. Manny and Vinny are gone, and he's already carved up that pretty wife of yours. Who's next?"

He wasn't aware that he moved. He didn't hear the laptop crash to the floor when he wrapped his hand around Paul's throat or notice Paul's hand scrabbling over his suit. He wasn't aware of anything until he saw Paul's glazed eyes staring back at him. He was dead. The fact that he didn't remember strangling Paul should have alarmed him. It didn't. One less enemy was a plus in his book.

The door opened. He raised his head as Steven Vega paused on the threshold, leaning on a cane. Before Steven could do more than register that there was a man standing beside his father's bed, Gavin had him pinned to the wall. Steven's eyes were wild with panic as Gavin squeezed his skinny neck. Steven wriggled like a fish on a hook with tears in his eyes. He was so pathetic that Gavin's beast retreated in disgust. He tossed Steven on the ground who landed on all fours and cowered.

"Your father's dead," he announced.

For a moment, Steven didn't react and then his head snapped up. He watched Steven limp toward the bed and reach for his father, only to let his hands hover over Paul's face.

"He sided with the man who took my place," he stated. "You know anything about that?"

Steven shook his head without looking away from his father. His hands dropped as a tear slid down his cheek.

"I should kill you," he said quietly.

Steven's thin body went rigid.

"If you're smart, you'll stick to the courtrooms and not get involved in the underworld like Rafael and your father." He paused and added, "If you don't, you'll meet the same fate. You understand me?"

Steven didn't move.

"Yes or no?"

"Y-yes," Steven whispered.

He left the hospital room without another word. He scanned the hallway and saw his men standing in front of a room. He approached and told them about Paul Vega. They immediately set off to take care of the paperwork and whatever else was needed.

He walked into Maureen Stark's hospital room. A lone sunflower perched in a vase on the table. He gripped the bedrail and leaned down to examine her. She had a shock of white hair, was on the heavy side, and bore no resemblance to Eli.

It had been over two years since Eli's mother went into a coma, yet he hadn't pulled the plug. The bloody trail he left in the wake of her attack was proof he had feelings for her, but his unwillingness to let her go revealed his devotion. The hospital bills were hefty and stacking up fast. Was that why Stark betrayed him?

Images of his own mother passed through his mind. She was soft-spoken, gentle, and affectionate. He thought of Lyla and Nora and turned away from the bed. His guards were watching him, waiting for orders.

A crime lord couldn't afford to have a heart.

"Get rid of her," he said as he walked past them and left Maureen Stark behind.

12

LYLA

She sat on the floor with Nora who lay on her back and played with her toys. Beau sat beside her. She absently scratched his back as she glanced at her watch and then reached for her phone. Jonathan could have changed his number in the past two years, but... The phone rang four times. She wasn't sure whether to be relieved or worried and then...

"Hello?"

"Jonathan?"

"Lyla? Are you okay?" he asked immediately.

She dropped her face in her hand. She wasn't sure what she was. "Yes, I'm okay. Are you?"

"I'm back in Maine."

"You still live in the same place?"

"Of course."

She bit her lip. "Jonathan, you can't stay there. I tried to talk to him, but..."

"No one can control him. That's why that guy sedated him."

She stiffened. "You saw?"

"Yes. You're in danger, Lyla."

He had no idea. "So are you. I'm so sorry—"

"I shouldn't have interfered in your life. You left me for my own good. I realize that now."

"I don't know what he's going to do, Jonathan."

"Did he hurt you?" he asked sharply.

"No."

"Don't worry about me. I can take care of myself."

"How?" Her spine snapped as she sat up straight. "You're not going to go to the cops, are you?"

"Would that do any good?"

"Probably not."

"Then I'll handle it."

Her gut clenched. "I want you to keep in touch with me. I have to make sure..."

"Make sure I'm breathing?"

She wasn't going to answer that. "Call me every day, morning and night."

"I don't think that's a good idea."

"I don't care!"

"Lyla, calm down."

"How can you be so cavalier about this? You saw him yesterday."

"I did." A pause and then, "I'm worried about you."

"You should be more worried about yourself."

"I never imagined you were hiding something like this." He sighed. "That's life. Sometimes you're stupid enough to fall for a girl who used to date a crime boss. That's the luck of the draw."

"This isn't a joke."

"I know," he said, sounding more sober. "I'll be in touch."

"Call me when you go to work and when you come home."

"Isn't he monitoring your phone?"

He had in the past. It was why she hesitated to call Jonathan, but she couldn't handle the suspense of not knowing whether he was alive or not. "He has more important things to do."

"If you say so."

"Call me when you get off work," she ordered.

"Yes, ma'am. Stay safe."

"You too."

She hung up and dropped her face between her knees. Jonathan was still alive. She hadn't been able to sleep after Gavin left. How could she after the things he said in the basement?

When the front door opened, her head rose. She blinked when Marcus strode into the living room. She rose, alarmed.

"Is something wrong?" she asked as he came toward her.

He didn't stop until he wrapped his arms around her. She was startled for a moment before she hugged him back.

"Marcus, you're scaring me."

He pulled back and set his hands on her shoulders. His eyes were troubled.

"I know what happened at the hospital yesterday," he said.

"Oh."

Of course, he did. How could Gavin be MIA at Pyre Casinos without Marcus's cooperation? It surprised her, though. Marcus seemed too straitlaced to know everything that Gavin did on the side. Apparently, even Marcus wasn't what he seemed.

"Are you all right?" he asked as he scanned her.

"Yes, I'm fine. Is that why you came?"

"Yes. Blade briefed me. I wanted to make sure you're okay."

That was thoughtful. After what happened yesterday, his concern was like a balm to her raw nerves. Fighting for her life had become a regular occurrence, but Marcus treated her like a fragile flower, and she liked it.

"I'm okay. You're so sweet for coming out here."

"Of course," he said simply, as if his arrival was nothing out of the ordinary. "Blade said Carmen left the hospital before the shooting started?"

"Yes."

"And she's safe?"

"Uh, yeah. Did you want to...?" She pointed upstairs, but he shook his head.

"No, I just wanted to make sure everyone was fine."

He looked down at Nora who screamed in delight at nothing in particular. He knelt beside the baby in his flawless suit and grinned at her.

"You're a happy girl, aren't you?" he asked as Nora's eyes lit up. "You're going to drive your daddy crazy, right? I'll teach you how."

The front door opened again, and she tensed, expecting to see Gavin, but was stunned when Alice and Janice rushed in.

"Oh, my gosh!" Alice shouted and gave her a bone crushing hug while she babbled fervent apologies.

"I'm so sorry! What are the chances that some gangsters would choose to come into that hospital to battle during our event? I'm sure Mr. Pyre is furious. I'm scared to check my emails. He can't fire me over this, can he? I heard the authorities still don't know why the gang members were there, but there were two incidents, one in the new Pyre wing and one in the parking garage." Alice pulled back and examined her. "Are you hurt? Are you okay? Do you need to talk to someone?"

"No, I'm okay." Their arrival was like a breath of fresh air, clearing out the doom and gloom hanging over the fortress.

"Are you sure?" Alice pushed. "Sometimes people can be traumatized by the sound of gunshots or what could have happened."

If only she knew... "I'm fine."

Alice stepped back and noticed Marcus holding Nora. Her expression cleared of all worry. She hopped and clapped her hands.

"I never got to hold her the other day. Oh, my God, she's adorable! Give her to me, Marcus!"

Janice came forward and also gave her a hug. "I'm so sorry about yesterday. Although it was truly unfortunate, we got even more positive publicity for the Pyre Foundation so..." Janice juggled her hands as if they were scales. "No one was seriously injured except for the hospital director. Did you hear?"

Lyla suppressed a vivid image of the director lying in a pool of his own blood. "Yes, I did." She felt as if there was a hole burning in her chest. Knowing the cause of the shooting and playing dumb was absolute hell.

"From the amount of damage done, the cops are shocked that only one innocent was killed in the crossfire."

How many of Gavin's men had been killed? Nora shrieked in delight as Alice blew raspberries on her neck. Beau decided the crowd was too much for him and trotted out to the backyard.

She surveyed the small group in her living room. "Coffee?"

"Yes!" all three of them said at once.

Happy for the company, she headed to the kitchen, and they all trailed after her.

"When did you leave the hospital?" she asked.

"Around ten last night. We stopped here on our way to work," Janice said.

Their level of commitment was unheard of. "You stayed there until ten? Didn't you get there at six in the morning?"

"Yes, but the hospital staff and patients were all frazzled," Alice said. "Everyone's scared and confused. We couldn't leave."

She swallowed her guilt as she handed out cups of steaming coffee. Janice and Marcus talked about some business function coming up while Alice bobbed around the kitchen with an ecstatic Nora. Alice looked paler than normal but still happy. How the heck could she look this awake after dealing with a crisis?

"What's your next project?" she asked.

Alice's eyes lit up. "I'm teaming up with a dog shelter and a school to have a play day."

Her heart lightened. "That sounds fun. I want to help."

Out of the corner of her eye, she saw Marcus's head turn in her direction, but she ignored him. Marcus had never been one to hover around her like Blade, but it seemed this shooting had shaken him.

"It's going to be great," Alice said. "We're inviting parents to join as well. We're hoping to get a bunch of adoptions out of this."

An image of kids running with dogs in a field lightened the heavy weight on her chest. She would like nothing more than to be a part of it, but once again, she would have to sit out not only for her own safety, but for others as well.

Beau came through the doggy door and planted himself at Alice's feet, staring up at Nora.

"I see Beau's bonded with Nora," Alice said.

"He's obsessed with her."

"Why shouldn't he be? She's adorable!"

Alice baby talked to Beau who wasn't impressed. His ears twitched in her direction, but his tail didn't wag. Alice didn't seem to mind Beau's subtle rejection.

"I'm so happy Beau found a home with you and Mr. Pyre. If I didn't work so much, I'd get a pet myself. One day I will."

"Well, good morning," Janice drawled.

She turned and saw Carmen dressed in a red silk robe and Hello Kitty slippers. Her eyes were bleary from sleep, and she appeared to be confused by the company. She didn't blame her. The last time they had this much people in the house was during Nora's baby shower. It had been a hollow tomb ever since.

"What's going on?" Carmen asked and made a beeline for the coffee pot.

"We stopped by to make sure you and Lyla are okay after yesterday," Janice said and then examined her red nails. "Although I thought I saw you leave with Kody Singer before everything went haywire."

"Yeah." Carmen yawned and noticed Marcus for the first time. "What are you doing here?"

"Good morning, Carmen," Marcus said politely.

"She's not a morning person," she said and shot Carmen a chiding look.

"Well, I'm off." Marcus set his cup in the sink and kissed her temple. "Let me know if you need anything."

"Thanks, Marcus," she said as he stopped by Nora and then headed out.

"You made Marcus her godfather?" Alice asked.

"Yes. Marcus and Blade."

"And I'm her godmother," Carmen said as she hopped up on the counter to drink her coffee.

"Your bodyguard is her godfather?" Alice asked.

"He'd take a bullet for her."

"Anything happen with Kody?" Janice asked Carmen as she glanced at her watch. "Usually celebrities are difficult, but he was really sweet and prompt. You add gorgeous on top of that, and I couldn't ask for more."

"I want something a little more than looks and the ability to be on time," Carmen said. "We were at a restaurant when we saw the news. I came right home."

"Are you gonna see him again?" Alice asked.

"I don't know." Carmen looked extremely bored with the conversation.

"I think she should date Marcus," she blurted.

Carmen jolted, nearly spilling coffee on herself. "Lyla!"

"You and Marcus?" Alice asked excitedly.

Carmen glared. "Marcus and I are nothing."

"Do you want to be something?" Janice asked with a raised brow.

Carmen hesitated, and Janice pulled out her phone.

"What are you doing?" Carmen demanded.

"I'm checking his schedule."

"I don't want him!"

Janice narrowed her eyes at Carmen. "I think thou doth protest too much."

Carmen scowled at them.

"I love Marcus," Lyla said.

"He's a fair boss," Alice said earnestly. "Mr. Pyre is..." She flushed and then shook her head wildly. "I mean, Marcus is great."

"Gavin's not mean to you, is he?" she asked.

Alice threaded her fingers together. "No. He's just..."

"What?"

"Scary." She waved her hands. "I mean, he's intimidating."

"He is," she agreed with a nod.

Alice blinked. "He's your husband, and you think he's intimidating?"

"He can be." Alice only knew Gavin in the civilized business world. If she knew how Gavin was at home or in the underworld, she would faint.

"Marcus needs a woman in his life," Janice said to Carmen who had her lips compressed into a straight line. "He works too much, and if I'm saying that, it's pretty bad."

"I don't need you guys to hook me up with Marcus. If I want him, I'll have him," Carmen growled.

Janice glanced at her watch again. "Alice, we have to roll."

Alice nuzzled Nora. "I'll see you soon, pretty girl."

There were hugs and kisses all around, and then they were gone.

"What was that?" Carmen asked.

"What normal feels like," she said as she settled on a chair to feed Nora.

"No, I mean about Marcus."

She eyed her frazzled cousin. "There's something between you two."

"There isn't," Carmen grouched and peered into the cupboard closest to her. "Why are you up so early anyway?"

"Couldn't sleep."

Carmen found a box of graham crackers and munched. "What's the latest drama?"

She glanced around but saw no sign of Blade. "I called Jonathan."

"You didn't!"

"I needed to make sure he's alive!"

"Not for long."

"Don't say that."

"Fine." Carmen demolished a square and reached for another. "But you know I'm right."

Blade walked into the kitchen. "After Nora goes down for her nap, I'll meet you two in the weight room."

Carmen gave him a baleful glare. "Go away, Satan."

"Your trainer isn't coming today, so I'm filling in," Blade went on as if she hadn't said anything.

"Don't you think we deserve a day off?" Carmen snapped, waving her graham cracker.

"No," Blade said and walked out.

"When we spar, I'm going for his balls," Carmen said.

13

GAVIN

HE WALKED THROUGH THE APARTMENT LYLA ONCE LIVED IN WITH Huskin. The apartment was a fusion of traditional and modern. He didn't see the appeal. He looked out the window at Portland, Maine. It was just after midnight, and there was no movement in the neighborhood. A private car waited across the street for him while other guards kept an eye out for Huskin. What was the nerd doing out so late at night? If he were smart, he would heed Lyla's advice and run.

He turned from the uninspiring view and paced through the apartment, shoes clicking on the hardwood floors. Huskin's office was predictably geeky with comic books and Star Wars posters on the wall. He had a three-screen computer set up and gadgets Gavin couldn't begin to identify. He couldn't imagine Lyla in the environment. He couldn't imagine her anywhere but where she was—with him, where she belonged.

He hesitated in front of the bedroom but forced himself to enter. There was nothing out of the ordinary. Like Huskin's hotel room, it verged on boring. He was grateful since any hint of Lyla's sex life with this guy was only going to make him draw out his death.

A photograph on the nightstand caught his eye. A Lyla he didn't recognize smiled shyly at the camera. She looked incredibly young in a hoodie with Huskin wrapped around her. There was a lighthouse in the background along with the choppy sea. She was the one who'd taken the photograph since Huskin's arms were around her waist. He closed his eyes as a deluge of pain cascaded through him. Only Lyla could do this to him. No other person on the planet had this much power over him. He remembered her indignation about the women he'd been with. What she didn't understand is he fucked those women without emotion. She had loved another man. No comparison. He put the picture down and walked out of the bedroom. He didn't look around for any more photographs because he couldn't take it. He settled in an armchair facing the door and waited.

How did men handle seeing their women with someone else? He sat forward with his elbows resting on his knees and his hands folded as if he was praying. He took a deep breath and tried to control the impulse to destroy this tidy apartment and turn it into the mess he was becoming. Did Huskin have more photographs of her? Naked photographs? His chest expanded with the need to roar, but he choked his demon and tried to stuff it back into the dark depths. Wrecking Huskin's apartment would do nothing to assuage his need for retribution. He needed Huskin to accomplish that feat.

He closed his eyes as his head throbbed. He couldn't afford to sleep longer than two or three hours at a time, not with Santana's men on the loose and the underworld revolting. The longest stretch he had been unconscious in months is when Blade sedated him. Fuck. There were people to hunt, question, and possibly torture for information, yet here he was in Maine, waiting for Huskin to walk through that door so he could rip out the invisible dagger twisting in his heart.

An image of Lyla's silver-blue eyes filled with tears flashed in front of him. *I love you, but if you do this, you'll break me, break us.* He wasn't noble. He wasn't the idiot in the movies who let the woman walk away with the better guy. Fuck that. He would murder any man she thought could make her happy or give her a better life. Even after all these years, she underestimated what he was capable of. He had always known he didn't deserve her, but he wasn't going to give her the opportunity to find the right guy. He couldn't believe she fucking found him—Mr. Boring with his nine to five and safe little life. What did Huskin say to her before the attack at the hospital? What was said in the hotel room before he overheard Huskin saying he could make her disappear? Lyla had done an excellent job evading him for three years. He didn't need her to have a connection with a man who could make her disappear forever. Just the thought of coming home to an empty house without Lyla and Nora made him insane.

He thought they were through being on opposing sides of an issue where neither of them would compromise. First, it had been his position as crime lord, which she had changed her stance on. Now, she was asking him not to kill a man who wanted to save her from him. A normal man would feel jealousy, ignore it, and be satisfied with the fact she wore his ring, bore his child, and said she loved him. He wasn't that rational or evolved. Lyla had left him twice and for very good reasons. Even now, any psychologist or sane friend (thank God Carmen grew up in his world and didn't encourage Lyla to leave him again) would tell her to take Nora and run. He wouldn't allow it. Lyla would get past this. She had to because he wasn't going to deviate from his course. Huskin had to die.

Huskin lived a safe existence free of the evil he walked through every day. Z sent him a recording of Lyla's conversation with Huskin this morning. She didn't think he had time to monitor her? Was she fucking crazy? She couldn't comprehend the depth of his obsession. She tried her damnedest to warn Huskin that his life was in danger, but Huskin wasn't concerned. Even through the recording, Gavin sensed the tension between them of things left unsaid. Hearing the easiness between Lyla and her ex made his insides feel as if acid was eating away at his organs. She dared call her ex. He didn't know how to handle her rebellion. His first instinct was to lock her in the basement. An echo of his father's voice slipped through his mind. *The way to make a woman stay isn't by abusing her. It's by loving her so much she can't imagine being without you.* Fuck. He couldn't love Lyla any more than he already did. They didn't have the same relationship as his parents. He couldn't control her. She'd left him twice. His mother never left his father; she supported him no matter what.

His phone buzzed in his pocket. He pulled it out and read the text. Finally. He couldn't bear to sit here any longer with his thoughts. He was a man of quick decisions and actions—except when it came to her. She turned him into an indecisive, raving lunatic. If he didn't love her so much, he'd hate her for her influence over him.

He heard approaching footsteps, the jingle of keys, and then the door opened. Jonathan flipped the light switch, placed his messenger bag on the stand beside the door, and turned. There was no surprise or fear on his face, just weary acceptance.

When Gavin had entered the apartment, he searched for a security system and found none, which he thought was odd at the time, but he was too focused on his mission to ponder it. How could Huskin possibly know he was here? Or had he been expecting him?

His demon began to salivate, eager for the kill. He could shoot Huskin, but that would be too quick. He could break his neck—no, he could start their session by breaking his fingers, digit by digit since those hands knew what Lyla's skin felt like. On that thought, he should slice off his dick for daring to trespass. Maybe he could—

"No gun?" Huskin asked.

He shifted his jacket so Huskin could see a real gun, not the ones he saw on video games. "You aren't surprised to see me."

Huskin shrugged. "You would have killed me in that hotel room if Lyla hadn't made such a scene. I knew sooner or later you'd finish the job."

Huskin's phone rang. He waited to see what he would do. Huskin eyed him for a moment before he slowly reached into his pocket.

"It's Lyla," Huskin said.

Every muscle in his body tensed, but he kept his face expressionless. Fuck it. He would lock her up in the basement, blister her ass, and then fuck her until she came to her senses. He didn't care what Dad said. Calling another man? No. *Fuck* no. The tips of his fingers twitched with the need to grab his gun and finish this guy. He was a nobody, yet Lyla's loyalty to him made Huskin his worst nightmare.

As Huskin's hand moved toward the phone his moved to his gun. Huskin pressed a button, and Lyla's voice filled the room.

"Jonathan, you nearly gave me a heart attack! You got off work hours ago! Why've you been ignoring my calls?"

"Sorry, I was working late," Huskin answered.

"Oh, my God. Why aren't you taking me seriously?" Lyla snapped.

"I am," Huskin said, eyes fixed on Gavin.

"You aren't. You don't know what he'll do to you."

"I think I do," Huskin replied.

The sound of a baby crying filled the room, short-circuiting Gavin's killing haze. Nora. Fuck, he missed his baby girl. Why was she crying? He hated that sound with a passion. He would never be able to ignore her cries if he was in the vicinity. Thank fuck she wasn't a fussy baby. The sound of his daughter in distress ripped at him.

Huskin nabbed his attention when he staggered as if he had been shot. He leaned against the closed apartment door with an anguished expression.

"You have a child with him?" Huskin whispered.

There was a long pause on the other end. "Yes. A daughter."

Huskin dropped his face into his hand and didn't speak.

"I thought I told you," Lyla said.

"No, you didn't."

Huskin knew having a child changed everything. It was the reason he impregnated Lyla as quickly as possible. He wasn't just Lyla's husband; he was the father of her child, and that made them a family. Huskin clearly grasped that Lyla would have to leave her husband and child to be with him, which wouldn't happen. *That's right, motherfucker, she's all mine.*

"I told you, I love my husband. I'm married, and I have a daughter."

Her desolate tone made his gut tighten. He hurt her, but he couldn't stop, not when she was focused on keeping Huskin alive.

"I have to go," Huskin said hoarsely.

"I'm sorry, Jonathan."

"Bye, Lyla."

Huskin hung up and looked at Gavin with a suspicious sheen to his eyes.

"What are you doing here?" Huskin said abruptly.

Gavin blinked. He couldn't believe this little shit. He had thirteen weapons on his person, not counting his bare hands, which could do more damage than people believed.

"What?" he asked, daring Huskin to speak to him in that tone again.

"You have her. What the hell do you care about me for?"

The killing rage shattered as Huskin's words penetrated. Lyla was his, and she wouldn't leave him for Huskin. He didn't like loose ends or the fact that Lyla had history with another man, but that couldn't be helped. The only thing that would alter her love would be to hurt a man who clearly had no chance with her.

Huskin pushed himself away off the door, set his phone on the counter, and slumped on a kitchen stool. "You want to kill me on principle, don't you?"

Perceptive bastard.

Huskin met his gaze boldly. "I've read a lot about you. From what I saw in the hotel room, it must be true."

He said nothing.

"The media insinuated you're involved in organized crime. I know you've been to jail, and your father was murdered." Huskin paused for input, but continued when Gavin merely watched him. "When I met Lyla, I couldn't understand why such a beautiful woman couldn't look me in the eye."

He stirred but forced himself to stillness. He had been trained to control his heartbeat to fool lie detectors and could lay in wait for his prey for days. Huskin was clearly suicidal. He'd be damned if he showed Huskin that the bastard hit a nerve.

"I figured she had been abused by her family or," Huskin inclined his head, "by a boyfriend."

He leaned forward. Huskin's tone was cool and clinical, but the insults were anything but.

"It took me months to gain her trust, but she never told me who she was running from. It was you. That's why she got a new identity and started a new life."

Gavin rose. If Huskin wanted to die, he would do it up close and personal as he had been fantasizing about. Huskin was calm personified, as if he was fine with meeting his maker right here and now. It was unnatural. Even those who worshipped the devil didn't want to be in hell with him.

"She's changed," Huskin stated and ran his hand over the countertop. "The way she walks and talks... The woman I knew wasn't capable of telling someone off, much less killing a man."

Blade had recounted Lyla's latest kill to him. Knowing that she could handle herself in an emergency allowed him to focus on his shit. He was damn proud of his wife.

"What have you done to her?" Huskin asked.

He advanced slowly. "The world we live in demands that we adapt, so we do."

"Your world? Meaning the criminal world?"

He stopped a few paces away from Huskin. "You're better off not knowing."

They eyed one another in silence. The air pulsed with accusations and charged emotions.

Huskin shrugged. "I guess I should warn you that you're being recorded."

He raised a brow. "Why are you warning me?"

"Because you have to tell someone they're being recorded before the evidence can be used in a court of law."

Fuck. The nerd pulled a fast one on him.

"I'm glad you didn't destroy that picture on my nightstand. It's the only copy I have," Huskin said.

He was impressed and intrigued despite himself. He was always informed about the latest technology, and whatever Jonathan was using was something he had never heard of. "You knew I was here. Why didn't you call the cops?"

"Curiosity. You didn't wreck the place, and you didn't have the gun pointing at the door when I came upstairs. Besides, if I don't counter my command in the system, whatever the cameras record in the next three hours will be sent to the police. Lyla would be free to live her life while you rot in prison for first-degree murder." Huskin tapped the screen of his cell phone. "Even if you look like you're in control, I know differently. The system is picking up your vitals. Your heart rate has stabilized, but it's still elevated."

Huskin was too straitlaced to make up stories, which could only mean that he had access to an extremely sophisticated surveillance system. He reflected on Huskin's office of tech gadgets and made the mental leap.

"You created it, didn't you?"

Huskin hesitated and then admitted, "After Morg—I mean, Lyla, disappeared, I couldn't stand not knowing what happened. It didn't make sense for her to leave. I thought she had been kidnapped. I called the cops but had no proof. Creating a sophisticated, undetectable surveillance system has become a hobby of mine."

He didn't like that Lyla was the inspiration for Huskin's creation, but he was a businessman and a paranoid one as well. "How many cameras do you have?"

"Enough."

Huskin may be naïve, but he had a backbone. This shouldn't have pleased him, but it did. "Quit your day job. I'll be your investor, but I get first dibs."

Huskin blinked. "You're kidding."

"I run casinos, among other things. You don't want to be an IT consultant for the rest of your life, do you?"

"You're not going to kill me?"

"Who said I was going to kill you?"

"You're armed."

"You can never be too careful."

"I'm not going to be part of the mafia," Huskin said staunchly.

His mouth curved despite himself. Huskin was a self-righteous little thing, but he appreciated his candor. It wasn't often that he met someone with morals and standards. Meeting someone like Huskin reminded him there was a world beyond the criminal underworld and Las Vegas. To balance out the evil he faced every day, there had to be light in the world. For him, that was Lyla. Jonathan was also a representative of the good that very few possessed. He could almost understand Huskin's appeal for Lyla. Huskin was his antithesis. Gavin had to comfort himself with the fact that Huskin would never again have the pleasure of being buried inside his wife.

He pulled his vibrating phone out of his pocket. Lyla. He couldn't afford to speak to her in Huskin's presence. Huskin hadn't betrayed his presence, but he didn't want to push Huskin more than he had already. It was clear Huskin loved Lyla, enough to sacrifice his life so she could be free. It was romantic and idiotic. How would Lyla respond if she found out that her nerd was willing to put it all on the line for her? Did she already know, and that was why she fought so hard to save Huskin? He couldn't match Gavin physically, so he fought in his own way—with intelligence and technology. Little surprised him, but Huskin managed to do the impossible.

Huskin regarded him steadily as he tapped his fingers on the countertop. "You're going to hurt her."

He said nothing.

"You're out of control."

"You're alive, aren't you?"

Huskin shook his head. "What does she see in you? It can't be your money or looks."

"Lyla and I have history."

"I always knew she was too good for me." Even as Gavin nodded, Huskin added, "And for you too."

Fuck. He resisted the urge to laugh. "She is, but I'm not letting her go."

"You live in a dangerous world. You could get her killed."

He didn't need a fucking lecture from Lyla's ex, but he could see that the guy was genuinely worried. Heartbreak was written all over his face. He decided to do something nice for the first time in his life and give the poor schmuck some reassurance. "I have something important to take care of before I get out."

Huskin gave him a derisive look. "How do I know that's true?"

"Because it's Lyla's ultimatum."

Huskin examined him keenly. "That's why you're letting me live. She said she'd leave you if you killed me."

Fucking smart bastard. "Lyla wouldn't leave me."

"Are you sure?"

The desire to be nice fled as quickly as it came. "Don't push me, Huskin."

"I'm not going to let you get your hands on my surveillance system."

"You need an investor, especially since your mother has pancreatic cancer and you're thinking about moving back to Boston to help."

Huskin stiffened. "How do you know that?"

"I have a tech guy named Z. He'll contact you."

"I won't be forced into this!" Huskin got to his feet, jaw set.

He raised a brow. "You know I run casinos. My investment will be legitimate with papers and lawyers involved."

"I can handle this myself."

"How can you when you have a full-time job and a mother who doesn't have much time?" He paused for emphasis and twisted the knife. "Lyla's in danger."

Huskin's brows bunched together. "I know that. Because of you!"

"You know my father was murdered."

"Yes."

"Lyla was with him that day."

Something flickered in Huskin's eyes.

"She was stabbed eight times. I nearly lost her."

Huskin sank back on his stool as if his legs were too weak to hold him up.

"The killer is still on the loose. That's why I'm in the underworld, to finish this. He attacked Lyla for the second time four months ago when she was seven months pregnant."

"What the hell are you doing here?" Huskin snapped. "You need to catch him."

"He's smart and careful and sends out troops while he cowers in the dark."

"Maybe I can…" Huskin's voice died out, and he glared. "I'm not doing this for you, Pyre, I'm doing it for Lyla!"

He nodded gravely. "I know. Your surveillance system could be handy not only in my casinos but also in our home."

Huskin didn't speak for several minutes. He waited patiently.

Huskin sighed. "I'll give notice tomorrow."

"I'll have my lawyer contact you."

"I won't be a part of the mafia."

He started toward the door. "Who said I was part of the mafia?"

Huskin cursed under his breath and then stood. "Why aren't you asking me to destroy the tape of what we just talked about? Aren't you afraid I'll call the cops?"

"No."

"How can you be so sure?"

He paused with his hand on the door. "Because I know what kind of man you are."

Huskin frowned.

"I know why Lyla trusts you." The knowledge still felt like someone was carving up his insides, but he understood why she fought for Huskin's life. He was a good person, and there were too few in the world. "You're an honorable man. You'd never do anything to hurt her."

Huskin said nothing. His pain filled the room. Gavin opened the door so he could take a breath of fresh air. He knew what Huskin was going through. They were in love with the same woman, and they'd both lost her at some point. Unluckily for Huskin, he wasn't an honorable man. He would fight and kill to keep Lyla by his side. This time, he didn't have to.

"Move to Boston to be with your mother," he ordered and then softened the blow by adding, "I lost my dad. I know what it feels like. You should be there when it happens."

Huskin took a deep breath and nodded.

"I'll have Z contact you," he said and closed the door.

He walked out of the building and approached his private car. A guard got out of the passenger seat.

"Cleanup, sir?"

"No," he said as he got into the back seat.

"No?"

Gavin met his startled gaze. "No cleanup."

The guard inclined his head. "Yes, sir."

As the car left Huskin's apartment behind, he called Z.

"Sir?" Z asked wearily.

"A man named Jonathan Huskin has developed a sophisticated surveillance system I want you to look at."

Z sounded a bit more awake as he answered, "Sure."

"Let me know what you think of his program and assess his skills. If he's good, you may have a partner."

"I'll get right on it, sir."

He made a few phone calls before they reached the runway. He boarded the jet, accepted a glass of water, and popped aspirin as his men took their seats. His phone began to ring. He glanced at the unavailable number on the screen and answered, "Pyre."

"Where's my mother?"

He hadn't talked to Eli Stark in years, but he still recognized his voice. It took less than a day for Stark to realize his mother was MIA.

"So, you finally decided to return my call," Gavin said.

"You called me?"

"I did the talking while you played possum last night. I told you that you fucked up."

"What are you talking about? I haven't talked to you in years. I'm a free agent."

"Cut the crap, Stark. Santana's brother ratted you out. I know you were feeding Santana information."

His men fell silent once they heard Stark's name. They all knew Gavin wanted his head.

"I don't know jack shit about this," Stark said.

"This isn't the first time your name's come up."

"I'm not involved in anything to do with Santana."

"How are you paying for your mother's medical bills?"

A pause. "That's none of your fucking business. Give her back to me."

"Who's the crime lord?"

"I don't know. I'm not working with him."

"How much does it cost to make you talk?"

"I don't know who he is."

Eli sounded as if he was speaking through clenched teeth.

"Call me when you determine a price." Maybe Stark would be good for something before he gutted him.

"Did you—?" Eli's voice was thick with rage. "If you killed my mother, Gavin, I'll end you."

"Not if I end you first," he said as he hung up.

His men waited for orders, but dispersed when he didn't give any.

Once upon a time, he would have trusted Stark with his life, and now, very soon, he would kill a man he once considered a friend. It wasn't the first time, and it wouldn't be the last.

He eyed his men as the engines revved. He was ninety percent certain the men in his employ were loyal, but there was always a chance he had a rat in the bunch. He couldn't get Paul Vega's words out of his head. *How many can you kill? You think your name will protect you? You have nowhere to turn.* Like Paul, people were hedging their bets on him or Phantom. The fact that Phantom was still alive and had made successful hits on his family hurt his reputation and made him look weak. Men like Stark would sell him out in a heartbeat. He didn't know who he could trust. Aside from torturing and killing every man in the underworld, the only way to solidify his claim to the title was to execute Phantom publicly.

The Phantom had to be someone he knew. No outsider could roll into Las Vegas and take the underworld from him. The Phantom slipped into the underworld too easily. It had to be someone who was already established. When he bowed out and Vinny took his place, the Phantom saw his chance and took it by calling the hit on his cousin before going after his father to win over the bloodthirsty underworld. He couldn't trust any of his former contacts. Like Paul, they had been bribed in some way. Fuck, Paul joined up with the man who carved up his own son. It was unbelievable. He had no backup and no one to turn to...

"Tell the pilot to head to New York," he ordered.

"You got it, boss."

He pulled out his phone and tapped into the security cameras at home. Their master suite was dark. He could barely make out Lyla beneath the covers. He still wasn't sure how he wanted to deal with her. He switched to another camera and saw Blade prowl through the hallway. He paused in front of Lyla's closed door before he went into the nursery to check on Nora. He stood over the crib for a minute before he pet Beau and then went downstairs. Blade was the only man he trusted implicitly, which was why he was Lyla's shadow. He wasn't sure how Blade would react if he tried to give him another job.

All was quiet at home. He was too close to New York not to stop by for a short visit. His battles in Las Vegas could be delayed a few hours.

14

GAVIN

Two hours later, Gavin stepped out of a taxi in front of a townhouse. Memories of his childhood and teenage years skipped through his mind. He was dimly aware of slamming doors as his men joined him. He started toward the townhouse that belonged to the Romans, one of four families who ran New York's underworld. It had been a second home to him as a child. Before he touched the front gate, three men in suits and trench coats stepped onto the front steps. As he opened the gate, a guard raised his hand in warning.

"Hold it right there."

"Mr. Pyre?" An older guard pushed the younger man aside and gave him a respectful nod. "It's been a long time."

"Yes, it has," Gavin said. "Are they here?"

"They are, sir. Are they expecting you?"

"No."

"Let me escort you."

"Thank you." He passed the younger guard who took a step back now that he knew his identity.

Gavin stepped into the townhouse, which was warm and smelled of fresh cookies. A gleaming wooden staircase led to upper and lower floors. The townhouse was five stories tall. A grand chandelier lit the entrance hall. There was a hushed quality to the richly furnished home despite the fact it was milling with security.

A large painting framed in gold caught his attention. He walked toward it as the older guard requested that his men wait in the formal sitting room. Gavin gave his permission with an absent nod and surveyed the family portrait of the Romans. A severe Italian-Spanish man in unrelieved black sat beside an English woman with a sunny smile and brilliant green eyes. A little girl with dark brown curls and her mother's eyes perched on her father's lap. Three boys stood behind their parents and sister. Roque, the oldest, looked to be in his early twenties and took after his father with broad shoulders, black hair, and his mother's eyes. The second brother, Raul, was in his late teens and had a lean figure and keen hazel eyes. The third brother, Angel, had pale blue eyes and olive toned skin.

The last time he was here he attended Marco and Margaret Romans' funeral. His father stayed in New York for months to console the siblings and help Roque establish himself with the four families.

"This way, Mr. Pyre."

The guard led him downstairs. He glimpsed New York's skyline from the large windows on the second floor. Guards in flawless suits were openly armed and eyed him suspiciously but didn't stop their progress. Two guards stood in front of the basement door. The guard accompanying him spoke to them in a low voice. They pounded their fist three times on the door before they inclined their heads and backed away.

Hip-hop music assaulted his ears as he stepped into the basement, which had the look of a high-end club. There was a bar against one wall along with a round table for poker. His shoes sank into the lush black carpet. Strippers who danced without a care in the world occupied two silver poles. Raul, the middle Roman brother, sat on a black leather couch in a three-piece suit. He ignored the strippers and stared intently at his laptop screen while he sipped wine. Raul turned his head, and when he saw Gavin, shot to his feet, startling one of the strippers who slid a foot down the pole before she caught herself.

"Jesus Christ!"

Raul set his glass down and spread his arms wide. Even as he embraced Gavin hard enough to make him grunt, there was a thump and shriek behind one of two closed doors. Over Raul's shoulder, Gavin saw Angel appear, wearing nothing but a pair of black boxers with a gun in his hand. The man before him was far from the teenager in the portrait. When Angel spotted Gavin, a broad smile spread over his face.

"Son of a bitch!"

Raul stepped back and Angel took his place. Angel hugged Gavin and then kissed him on both cheeks. Gavin raised a brow at his cousins who couldn't be more different if they tried. Raul was the businessman in the Roman family. His tailored suit, slick hair, and glass of wine encapsulated who he was—cultured, sophisticated, controlled. Angel in his boxers with lipstick smears on his body was just as telling. Angel was the rebellious youngest brother, a party animal and playboy. He saw movement in the room Angel vacated. Four naked women slipped on lingerie.

"Why didn't you tell us you were coming?" Raul asked.

"Impulse trip. I had business in Maine."

"Come, come," Raul said and waved a hand at Angel. "Make him something, would you?"

"What do you want to drink, Gavin?" Angel walked to the bar and stuffed the gun in the back of his boxers.

"Whiskey. Neat."

Raul sat and grabbed his glass of wine. "How long has it been, cousin?"

"Too long." He took the glass Angel handed him. "A lot has changed."

Angel settled on the couch with a glass of clear liquid and didn't acknowledge the woman who settled on his lap. "No kidding."

"Your basements changed," he said as the women vacated the room they occupied with Angel and sauntered forward. He sized them up and wasn't surprised to see that they all possessed perfect bodies, flawless features, and greedy eyes.

"I persuaded Raul and Roque to let me liven up the place." Angel waved a hand to encompass the decadent man cave. "We come here to unwind and try the talent." He nodded approvingly at the prostitute grinding on his crotch. "You game, Gavin?"

"No, I'm married," he said and ignored the woman who sat beside him, so close he could feel her body heat and the fragrance of her perfume, which was tainted by Angel's cologne.

"I heard that," Raul said. "We didn't get an invitation."

"Shotgun wedding." He glanced at the prostitute who placed a hand on his upper thigh. "I'm married."

"Your wifey isn't here," the woman purred and arched her back to show off her fake breasts covered in pink glitter, which she pressed against his arm. Her hand sank into his hair as she leaned into him, hooking one leg over his. "What she doesn't know can't hurt her, can it?"

She grabbed his cock, and he lost it. He grabbed her hand and flipped it back. The prostitute fell off the couch and dropped to her knees so he wouldn't break her wrist. The strippers on the poles stopped twirling while the other women edged back slowly.

"I'm married, you understand now?"

The prostitute nodded fervently, eyes wide and terrified. She looked toward Angel whose total focus was on Gavin. Her whimpers of pain filled the room as the music paused between tracks. He forced her to stay on her knees for a full minute before he let her go. She collapsed face first on the carpet and then scooted away, cradling her sprained wrist.

Angel smacked the ass of the frozen prostitute on his lap. "Looks like my cousin's not in the mood. Why don't you all clear out?"

The women didn't hesitate. In their haste to vacate the room, they forgot to saunter. Angel grabbed a remote and turned off the music.

"I'm glad you didn't break her hand," Angel said, spreading his legs wide as he downed the rest of his drink. "She's talented. Of course, she doesn't need her hand to do her work, but it speeds up the process so she can take more men in one night."

Before Gavin could respond to that, Raul interjected, "So there's married and married. I'm guessing you're the latter."

Gavin nodded. "My wife is everything to me."

Angel stared at him. "You're a fucking legend. I can't believe you're monogamous. You fucked around more than all of us combined."

"Lyla's different."

"I gotta meet her," Angel said and then eyed him. "You never returned our calls."

Gavin inclined his head. "I know. I couldn't handle them at the time."

"We couldn't make it to the funerals because of business," Raul said.

"I got your cards."

"What did you do to the fucker who did in Uncle Manny?" Angel asked.

It always came back to that. Gavin felt the familiar slap of rage and sipped his whiskey to cool down. Denying himself the pleasure of ripping Huskin limb from limb, his recent interaction with Eli Stark and the fact he had no leads on the Phantom left him feeling edgy and violent. Whiskey traveled through his body and settled in his gut, taking away the unrelenting burn.

"That's why I'm here."

"Why?"

"I haven't caught him yet."

There was a sharp silence. His cousins stared at him as if he materialized out of thin air.

Raul scooted to the edge of his seat and raised a hand. "What do you mean, you haven't caught him yet?"

"This guy is a fucking ghost."

He couldn't sit still. He rose and refilled his glass. Retribution in their world was brutal, swift and done back tenfold. All of them would rip the world apart in the name of vengeance, but in the end, Lyla had been more important to him. He hunted her when he got out of prison instead of the man who claimed the title. That cost him.

Now, he was trying to reclaim an underworld that was in chaos and run by a faceless, sadistic killer.

"This guy took over the underworld long enough to fuck up the whole city. It's going to take years to clean up the filth he unleashed. He's too smart to reveal his identity to anyone."

"What do you need?" Raul asked.

The pressure on his chest lifted. Ever since Vinny died, he'd felt something missing. Vinny had always been at his side. Gavin didn't question his loyalty as he'd had to question every other person in his life. There was no replacement for family. This feud with the Phantom had been going on long enough. It had been an impulse to visit his cousins, and his intuition hadn't steered him wrong. Even though they hadn't seen each other in nearly a decade, family was family, and they would aid him in whatever he needed.

"I need a man I can trust at my back until this is over."

Raul and Angel looked at one another for a heartbeat and then Angel inclined his head.

"Angel will go with you," Raul said.

He nodded. "And after I kill this Phantom, I want out."

Once more, the Roman brothers looked at one another and then back at him.

"Out?" Angel echoed.

"My wife's suffered enough. I promised her I would kill this guy and get out."

Silence reigned.

"After I kill Phantom, I want to hand over the underworld to a replacement I can teach to see if he can hack it."

Angel leaned forward. All signs of the ladies' man vanished. His pale blue eyes were narrow and intense. "You want to give up your title?"

"Yes."

"And you need someone to take over?"

"It's not that easy. The city is in turmoil, and the fuckers I've kept under lock and key are causing public shootings and kidnappings when they feel like it."

Angel leaned back and rested his arms along the back of the couch. "I'll do it."

"Angel," Raul said sharply.

"You have everything under control here," Angel said. "Roque's coming out of the joint soon and then what? I'll be third in command, and with you two at the top, I'll never see any action. What's happening in Vegas sounds like my kind of party."

Gavin considered Angel, who was several years younger than he was. The three Roman brothers had grown up in the family business as he had. Angel was the youngest and most reckless. He wasn't sure what his cousin had been up to in the past decade, but if he would hand the city to someone, there was no one better than family.

"Roque will have my head if I let you go off to Vegas and become a crime lord on your own without backup," Raul said.

"I'll be there," Gavin said, and his throat tightened. "I tried to hand the underworld over to Vinny, and they gunned him down. It won't be easy. They're like wild animals. One mistake and you're dead."

Angel's eyes gleamed. "Now you're trying to turn me on."

"Are you sure you want to do this?"

Angel smiled as innocently as a toddler. "You can't stop me now that you've issued a challenge like that. When do we leave?"

"Whenever. My plane is on standby."

"Your own plane. Fuck." Angel strolled toward a phone in the corner of the room and spoke quickly in Italian.

"Can he handle it?" Gavin asked Raul in low tones.

"Yes," Raul said succinctly. "I'm the accountant; Angel's the enforcer. I keep the books clean, and Angel makes sure we don't get fucked over. We had trouble when Roque went to prison, but Angel put a stop to that, and he was just out of high school. Don't underestimate him. We haven't had any trouble for a while now, and he's getting restless. I have to drown him in women and find things to keep him busy. I was worried he would take off before Roque got out and try to take over another city."

"Take over?" Walking into another crime lord's territory was suicidal.

"Angel wouldn't hesitate to kill anyone if it meant having some action." Raul sighed and drained his glass. "If we didn't already have control of the largest city in the United States, Angel would have gone there and tried to conquer it."

"Sounds like he needs a hobby," he said mildly and wondered how his cousin would react to the mayhem going down in Sin City.

"People underestimate Angel because he's young and too pretty for his own good. Your city sounds like Angel's type of playground."

Angel hung up the phone and settled on the couch with his legs crossed. "Viva Las Vegas. Fuck yes. This is turning out to be an interesting night."

"I need to kill this fucker. He's been playing me for years, and it's going to stop. I have a family now, and I can't put them at risk. Besides, I have enough on my plate with my partner wanting to expand Pyre Casinos."

Angel shook his head. "I can't imagine you married with a kid."

"Believe it."

"Family is everything. If you want out, you need someone to take over who knows how to run it and who won't lose themselves in the filth." Raul looked at Angel, who was grinning like a maniac. "Don't think I'm not going to keep tabs on you."

"You do that." Angel got to his feet. "Gav, you have to say hi to Luci. She'll kill you if she finds out you were here and didn't see her."

"I don't want to wake her," he said and glanced at his watch. It was three in the morning.

"Tonight's family night so I came over. She was messing around in the kitchen an hour ago," Raul said.

As they left the basement, he noticed the guards looked to Angel and not Raul for guidance. Raul had always been more reserved than Roque and Angel. He was the steadfast brother and the voice of reason. As Angel spoke to the guards in low tones, Gavin walked alongside Raul.

"How's Roque doing?"

"He's alive," Raul said with a shrug. "He gets out of prison next year."

"I was in for a year. I don't know how Roque's handled being in for seven."

"I don't either. Once he's out, I'm going to the Bahamas."

"You've shouldered the load for a long time."

"Same as you." Raul shook his head. "I don't know how you and Roque do it. If it wasn't for Angel, I would have let the underworld go a long time ago."

"It's in our blood, just as it was in our father's."

The Roman family had their fair share of heartaches and betrayal. It went hand in hand with being a part of the underworld. They all paid a price for being crime lords. He couldn't imagine Roque being imprisoned for nearly eight years. Every criminal in prison would be gunning for him. How many men did Roque murder to stay alive? If Roque was a force to be reckoned with before, New York would shudder in terror when he was released.

They reached the third floor. Angel slammed open the door that led into a massive kitchen, which had all the latest appliances. A beautiful woman with dreamy green eyes and waist-length dark brown curls stood in front of the kitchen island scraping cookies onto a large platter.

"You can't be done already!" she complained. "There were six women. I should have another hour at least! You need to work on your stamina, Angel."

Angel grabbed a cookie and tapped her nose. "I'm going to Sin City, princess!"

Luciana frowned at her brother and didn't seem bothered by the fact that he wore only his underwear and had hickeys, bite marks, and lipstick on his skin.

"What are you talking about? Are those girls still here? I want them to try my almond cookies."

"I'll take one of those," Gavin said as he stepped into the kitchen.

Angel ducked as his sister tossed the metal spatula and hurled herself at Gavin as if she were eight years old.

"Gavin!" she screamed.

He couldn't stop himself from smiling as he caught Luciana and whirled her around as if she were still a kid instead of a full-grown adult. Luciana shrieked in delight and kissed him on both cheeks.

"What are you doing here? Do you want some cookies?"

"Yes, I would," he said and set her down.

Luciana rushed to the platter and used tongs to put two cookies on a dainty plate that felt as sturdy as construction paper in his hand.

"Would you like a cup of tea?" she asked.

He suppressed a flinch. "No, thank you."

Luciana pushed him onto a stool and propped her chin on her fists. "What are you doing here, Gavin?"

"I need help." He took a bite of the warm cookie and felt his eyes flutter as the taste awakened a sweet tooth he didn't know he possessed. "Fuck me."

"You need help?" Luciana sounded shocked.

"I'm human," he said with a shrug.

"Which is *why*," Angel said dramatically to get his sister's attention, "I'm going with him."

Luciana's eyes bounced from Gavin to Angel and then to Raul who poured himself a cup of tea.

"You're going to Las Vegas? I want to go too!"

"The situation isn't good, Luci," he said as he reached for more cookies.

"You're going to leave me with Raul?" Luciana said indignantly.

Raul scowled. "What's wrong with that?"

"You never come home, and you don't let me do anything! At least Angel takes me dancing once a week."

Angel grinned at her. "I'm sure Raul will take you to the office to show you his accounting skills."

Her eyes widened in horror. Gavin stiffened when she focused those hypnotizing green eyes on him.

"Can I come too?"

Raul and Angel tensed, but they didn't try to interfere. He was leery of accepting Angel's help after what had happened to Vinny, but he trusted Raul's judgment. If Raul said Angel could do it, he believed him. But there was no way in hell he would toss Luciana into the mix.

"It's too dangerous," he said and took another cookie.

"But Angel's going!"

He wasn't used to having anyone argue with him aside from Lyla. Emotional outbursts weren't his scene.

"I have a gun, and I know how to use it," Angel said loftily and leaned against the wall, looking like a Hispanic version of James Dean.

Luciana grabbed a knife from the chopping block and hurled it at Angel. The knife imbedded into the wall three inches above his head. Angel raised a brow while Raul glared at his sister.

"What did I tell you two about playing with knives?" Raul snapped.

"I'm an excellent shot," she said hotly. "I can take care of myself. And don't you dare lecture me about guns. You know I'm just as good as both of you."

No one who knew the Roman's reputation would be able to imagine them gathered in a kitchen at three in the morning arguing while drinking tea and eating warm almond cookies like a normal family. The appliances in the kitchen changed, but the feeling of belonging and warmth hadn't. Gavin rummaged in the fridge for milk as Raul and Luciana began to shout at one another.

"Gavin's searching for Uncle Manny and Vinny's killer, Luci. This is serious shit. And after, he's going to step down," Raul said.

Her eyes popped. "Step down? And who's going to take—Angel? You? No!"

Angel's expression softened. "You know I've been wanting to do my own thing for a while now."

"But..." Her eyes filled with tears. "It's so sudden! When are you leaving?"

"Tonight."

As a tear slipped down her cheek, Angel pushed off the wall and hugged her. He whispered in her ear as she cried. If anyone paid a high price for being a Roman besides Roque, it was Luciana. She had been twelve when her parents were murdered and had witnessed the whole thing. Her brothers were understandably overprotective, and her life was much more restricted than Lyla's.

He was forcefully reminded of Nora as he watched Angel console his sister. How would he react when Nora wanted to go off on her own? Would he refuse or accompany her? What if she wanted to go to college in another city? It sent a chill down his spine. He shook away the disturbing thought. He would deal with it when the time came... or lock Nora in the basement until she saw things his way.

"When can I visit?" Luciana asked as she wiped away her tears.

"As soon as it's over," he assured her.

"You promise?"

"Yes. I'll send for you and then you can meet my wife and daughter."

"You have a daughter?" She thumped his chest with surprising force. "And you haven't sent me pictures? What the hell is wrong with you?"

He didn't know how to react, but he noticed Raul hiding a grin behind his teacup. Dainty bastard.

"I've been busy killing people," he said.

"That's not a good excuse," she said, not cowed by in the least. She put her hands on her hips. "Your daughter's the first of the new generation. She needs to know her extended family."

Her words warmed him. This is why he came. For too long he had gone without family, without support. He isolated himself after Vinny and his father's death instead of reaching out. Reuniting with his cousins made him feel as if he had an army around him. Their support gave him hope that this nightmare would be over soon.

A maid wearing a uniform that looked as if she worked in a high-end resort walked into the kitchen and inclined her head.

"Your bags are ready, Mr. Roman," she said.

"Thank you."

Angel went to his suitcase and opened it up to reveal an impeccable packing job. Angel ruined it by rummaging around until he found jeans, a white shirt, and leather jacket. While he changed, Gavin answered Luciana's questions about Lyla and Nora.

His phone rang. When he saw Z's name, he picked up immediately. "News?"

"Boss," Z hesitated and then finished in a rush, "something went down at your place."

Icy dread doused the warm feelings in his chest.

"I noticed a disturbance on the surveillance cameras and tried to call Blade, but his phone had a busy signal. I tried several guards and no one picked up. I just got the cameras back online. I think there was an attack at the front gate. Looks like something rammed into it, and there's a fire on the south side of the property the men are putting out. I don't see any dead bodies. I can see men on the property, but I can't get through to anyone. I can only watch the live feed and try to figure out what's going on," Z said in a rush.

Even as he opened his mouth to ask about Lyla, Z launched into another hurried explanation.

"I checked the house cameras. The rooms are empty. I don't see your wife, Blade, the baby, nothing. I tried to review the footage, but it's been fucked with. I don't know what happened. All phones are out of order. Your wife's watch isn't working either. I can't track her. I'm trying to get in touch with the guys and bring everything back online."

"Let me know what you got as soon as you have it," he rapped out and hung up.

He pulled up the security feed on his phone and flipped from angle to angle, his heart accelerating with every empty room he saw. If there was a hit on the house, Blade would have gotten Lyla out. There were emergency procedures in place that Blade would act on immediately if there was an attack. They wouldn't take chances, not after his father's house had been infiltrated. Blade would take them to a safe house and stay until he made contact.

He called Lyla's phone and received a busy signal. Same with Blade. Knowing he left her open to another attack made him feel like a worthless bastard. If he hadn't left to kill Huskin, he would be there right now, not on the other side of the country.

"Gavin?" Luciana asked tentatively.

He looked up and saw his cousins watching. "There was a hit at the house. Someone fucked with the cameras and no one can call in or out. Blade and my wife are gone."

Luci shoved Angel. "Go on. Get out of here." She launched herself at Gavin and gave him a fierce hug before she pulled back, green eyes narrowed. "Make this motherfucker pay."

He kissed her and turned to Raul, who clapped him on the back.

"Anything you need, Gavin, you call," Raul said and hugged Angel. "Give the Vegas underworld our love, brother."

Angel showed his teeth. "Of course."

"And let us know when this fucker's buried. We'll pull out our best wine and toast Uncle Manny and Vinny."

Gavin walked out of the townhouse, chilled to the bone. He was thousands of miles away while his wife once again went through hell. She had to be alive. He wouldn't allow himself to think of any other outcome.

15

LYLA

SHE SAT UP, MOUTH OPEN ON A SOUNDLESS SCREAM AND THRASHED wildly. Something heavy crashed to the floor, jolting her out of her nightmare. The only sound in the room was her harsh breathing. There was enough moonlight coming through the window to see that she was safe in her bedroom at home. It was just a dream.

She flopped back on the pillows and bit back a sob. The nightmare was a mix of new and old horrors. She relived Manny being tortured by Sadist and felt the knife dig into her skin at the same time that she heard Nora scream, which jolted her awake.

She fumbled for the lamp and realized that's what she knocked to the floor. She slipped her gun into the back of her leggings and tiptoed into the nursery. The sound of Nora's even breathing made her weak with relief. She stood there for several minutes before she went down the hall to Carmen's room. She slipped beneath the covers, took a deep breath and tried to calm herself.

"Lyla?" Carmen rolled over, tossed an arm over her waist, and felt the gun. "You okay?"

"Nightmare."

Carmen grunted. "Must have been a bad one."

Even now, she could recall the sound of crunching bone and the ominous silence when Manny stopped screaming. She shuddered. "It was."

Carmen squeezed her. "It'll be okay."

How many times had Carmen said that since Manny's murder? When would it be okay? She was so tired of being afraid. Sadist dominated her dreams and waking moments. It was unbearable. If she ever got the chance to face Sadist, she wouldn't hesitate. She would do whatever she could to kill that fucker. No matter how much she built him up in her mind, he could bleed and therefore die. She had to remember that.

Her body begged for sleep, but her mind wouldn't cooperate. She tried the breathing technique, but after fifteen minutes, she gave into her body's compulsion to move. When she threw back the covers, Carmen moaned.

"What are you doing?"

"Sorry. I'm going to get something from the kitchen."

"What time is it?" Carmen asked hoarsely.

She glanced at the clock. "Midnight."

"I'll come too."

"You don't have to."

"I know, bitch, but you need me."

Carmen slipped into a silk Chinese robe with a dragon on each breast. She belted it with a yawn and slipped into two fluffy pink clouds that masqueraded as house slippers. Carmen carried her phone and checked on Nora through the video monitor as they passed.

"What was the dream about?" Carmen asked as they started downstairs.

"Same old."

"Sadist?"

"Yeah."

"The only way you can exorcise that fuck is to watch him die. Maybe Gavin can mount his head on the wall after. Then you can throw darts at him anytime you want."

Lyla paused in the entrance of the kitchen, dumbstruck by the imagery. "That does hold some appeal. Damn, I'm going to the dark side."

"You never had a choice. Besides, it's better on the dark side. You do what you want and don't have to spend your time feeling guilty. You want something? Go get it. No if, ands, or buts. Besides, knowing Sadist is dead would make me feel better." Carmen dug around in the cupboards and came up with cocoa packets and a bag of colorful marshmallows. "Maybe after he's dead I'll know what to do next."

Lyla tossed a kettle popcorn packet in the microwave and tried to shrug off the images that clung to her memory. How did her mind conjure up Sadist's voice so perfectly? That mocking, sweet voice that should have belonged to a nice man, but instead belonged to a monster.

Carmen handed her a mug with a mound of heart and star marshmallows.

"I think I need some cocoa with my marshmallows," she said dryly.

"You have to eat the marshmallows to get to the cocoa," Carmen said and popped one into her mouth. "Come on, they're good for you."

"I'm going to tell Nora not to believe a thing you say."

She ate a green marshmallow. She felt as if she were thirteen again. Who knew that she would be married to a crime lord, have a child with him, and still be eating popcorn and marshmallows with Carmen as if they were still innocent preteens?

"It's good, right?" Carmen asked.

"Yes. This is how I should end all shitty days." She poured popcorn into a bowl. "I'm so sick of this. I want this to be over. I want Gavin home, I want Sadist dead, and I want Jonathan alive."

"Two out of three isn't bad."

Lyla glared at her. "I need all three."

"You can handle two out of three."

"Jonathan has to live."

"Girl," Carmen drawled, "just take what you can get. Before you saw Jonathan at the casino, you forgot he existed."

"Yes, but I believed he was in Maine, doing his thing. It's a different story if my psycho husband murders him!"

"I can't believe you didn't tell him you had a kid."

She flinched. Carmen had been there when she made her last call to Jonathan. Hearing the devastation in his voice made her chest ache. She kept hurting him and didn't know how to stop. "I thought I told him!"

"Well, you didn't," Carmen said heartlessly.

"Every time I see him, I'm in a state of shock. Fucking give me a break. I didn't do it on purpose."

Carmen munched on marshmallows. "Who knew your life would become a soap opera? A love triangle with a nerd and a possessive, psychotic husband who worships the ground you walk on."

"Gavin doesn't worship the ground I walk on." *If I didn't love you so much, I'd kill you.* She hadn't been able to get his words out of her head.

"Gavin would do anything for you." When she opened her mouth, Carmen waved her hands. "If Jonathan was an asshole, Gavin killing him would be romantic!"

"But he's *not* an asshole!"

Carmen sighed and ate a pink marshmallow. "I know. So sad."

"Every time I think Gavin and I are on the same page, he does something to make me question if our lives will always be like this."

"Sorry to break it to you, babe, but once a crime lord, always a crime lord. Even if Gavin gets out of the underworld, which is debatable, he'll never really be out. You know that."

Blade walked into the kitchen and glared at them. "What are you two doing up?"

"You want some popcorn?" Carmen extended the bowl, which had popcorn mixed with more marshmallows.

Blade's lip curled. "No."

"Your loss," Carmen said and munched away.

"Have you heard from Gavin?" Lyla asked.

"No."

She called Gavin after she spoke to Jonathan. Even if he was mad, she still wanted to hear his voice. He didn't pick up. What had she expected?

"Do you know if he's in Las Vegas?" she asked.

Blade gave her a direct look. "I don't keep tabs on the boss."

"Would you tell me if he went to Maine?"

"No."

She scowled. "If Gavin told you to kill Jonathan, would you?"

"Yes."

No hesitation.

"Why?" she demanded.

"Because whatever it takes for Gavin to do his job is worth it," Blade said.

"What the hell does that mean?"

Blade's phone rang before he could answer. He glanced at the screen, frowned, and said, "What?" He listened for a moment and then glanced at Lyla.

Her heart skipped. "What?"

"Your dad's here," he said.

It took her a second to register. "Now?"

"Yes. He's at the gate. He's been beaten pretty badly."

She didn't give a fuck. "I don't want to see him." Whoever beat him had a good reason, she was sure. The last time she saw her father was the day of Uncle Louie's funeral. She threatened to shoot her father if she heard him slander Manny again. Seeing her father so wasn't what she needed right now.

"He says he needs to talk to you. It's urgent," Blade said.

"You know how I feel about him," she snapped. She had been avoiding her parents for months. How dare her father show up here out of the blue? Of course, Gavin wasn't here to kick his ass.

"I know he's a bastard, but he says it's an emergency."

"A money emergency," she sneered.

"I want to be sure," Blade said and gave orders to allow her father on property.

She should have taken sleeping pills. Blade would have had a hell of a time trying to wake her up for this awful confrontation. Just the thought of having to face her father made her stomach churn with anger, hurt, and dread. For most of her life, she had played the obedient daughter. Even after she moved out of her family home, she gave a large portion of her allowance to her father, but it was never enough for him. Gavin used her father's gambling debts to blackmail her into leaving Jonathan. Sacrificing her life for her father's made no difference to him. It wasn't until she had been nearly killed and witnessed Manny's murder that she finally saw her father for who he really was. Life was too short to spend it around someone who didn't love or respect you.

Blade left the kitchen with Carmen on his heels with the popcorn bowl in the crook of one arm. Lyla made herself busy to buy time.

"Where is she?"

Her father's shout stoked her maelstrom of emotions. This was her house, not his. He didn't think she might be asleep at midnight, or that she might be exhausted because she had a four-month-old? No, he arrived in the middle of the night, beaten up and shouting. Yes, that was Pat Dalton.

She stalked out of the kitchen. Her father had, indeed, been thoroughly thrashed. It wasn't the first time she'd seen him in this state. Gavin had the honor of dealing out a much-deserved punishment, which made no impact on her father. She didn't feel an iota of sympathy since she was sure this was a warning from a loan shark.

Pat Dalton looked as if he walked through a slaughterhouse. His clothes, which she belatedly realized were originally a beige pajama set, had been tie dyed with blood splatters. His face was swollen and battered, but his injuries didn't match the amount of blood saturating his clothes since he was standing without assistance. His crucifix, which he shouldn't be allowed to wear, was covered in crusty red flakes. She stopped several feet away and caught a whiff of the metallic stench that clung to him.

"What do you want?" she asked, not in the mood for his shit.

His muddy brown eyes, normally filled with disdain or jealousy, now held an enraged terror that got her attention more effectively than a shout. A premonition caused her to glance around the room, but her mother was nowhere to be found.

A sense of urgency grabbed her by the throat. "What happened? Where's Mom?"

"She's gone."

"What do you mean, gone?" Panic slammed into her with the force of a freight train. "Where is she? Whose blood is this?"

Hands encrusted with rivulets of dried blood flexed at his sides. "They took her."

Her world rocked on its axis.

"Who took her?" Blade barked in a no-nonsense tone that made Pat jerk.

He ran trembling hands over his chest as if to make sure he was still intact. "I-I was sleeping. I woke up when these men pulled me out of bed. They were wearing masks and began to beat me. I could hear Beatrice screaming. I think there were four of them. One of them hit me here." He touched his temple where he had a lump the size of a golf ball. "I must have passed out. When I woke up, the house was ransacked and she was gone."

"You owe someone?" Blade asked.

Before Pat could answer, Lyla lunged for him. Blade yanked her backward and wrapped an arm around her.

"Lyla, get a hold of yourself!"

"What did you do now?" she shouted at her father.

Pat took a step toward her, the cords on his neck sticking out as he roared, "What have *I* done? What have *you* done?"

That penetrated enough for her to go very still. "What?"

"I have a real job. We're barely making ends meet. I don't have the money to gamble. My nose is clean. There's no reason for someone to take your mother unless it has to do with you." Pat jabbed his burgundy-colored finger at her. "You and Pyre are up to God knows what."

She couldn't be responsible for her mother's disappearance, could she? "Why has she been calling me?"

"She wants to meet your kid. Why else?"

Guilt threatened to choke her. "W-when I had Nora, she asked for money."

"We had a rough patch, but we pulled through, no thanks to you."

The way Pat looked at her as if he would love nothing more than to squeeze the life out of her made her body erupt with goose bumps.

"All your mother wanted was to meet her grandkid, and now she's... she's—"

"Why didn't you call 911?" Blade asked her father.

Pat's hands fisted at his sides. For a second, she thought he wasn't going to answer. Before she could scream at him, Blade released her and backhanded her father with a casual ruthlessness that told everyone without words that he would get answers by any means necessary. It happened so fast that no one had time to react. Her father's mouth sagged as he stared at Blade with a hand pressed against his face.

"If you want your wife to be found alive, stop fucking with us and answer the question. This isn't a pissing contest," Blade rumbled. "What makes you think Gavin has anything to do with the break-in and your wife's abduction?"

Her father reached into his pocket and pulled out a Post-it note splattered with blood. In beautiful, elegant scrawl, the note said, *Tell Lyla I'll see her soon.*

There was a loud roaring in her ears. That sick fuck had her mother... No, this couldn't be happening.

"Gavin will get her back, Lyla," Carmen said.

She opened her mouth, but no sound came out. All the calls and texts from her mother she ignored since Nora's birth came back to haunt her. The thought of her mother in Sadist's hands made her ill.

"You'd better not be lying, Uncle Pat," Carmen spat. "If Gavin doesn't kill you, I will."

"Why would I lie about this? Beatrice is missing!" Pat shouted.

There was a crushing weight on her chest. Sadist was still fucking with them. Now he branched out from the Pyres to her family. Why? What was the point? The fact that Sadist had taken her mother and not her father scared her shitless. Sadist knew her mother was her weak spot. How could he know that?

Carmen smacked the screen of her phone. "What the fuck?"

"What?" Lyla asked numbly.

"My phone doesn't have service."

Blade pulled out his own phone. He jabbed his finger at the screen, held it to his ear, and cursed. "Fuck."

Lyla walked to the landline and picked it up. There was no dial tone. She stared at Blade and Carmen who watched her expectantly. She shook her head. A muscle jumped in Blade's jaw. He opened his mouth just as a faint popping sound came from outside.

16

LYLA

"Get away from the window!" Blade shouted and shoved Carmen to the ground.

"What is it?" she asked, hoping it wasn't what she thought it was.

"Gunfire."

"It's him." Sadist was here to finish it. She pulled out her gun and rose.

"Get Nora," Blade ordered. "We don't have enough men to hold them off."

Her daughter's name snapped her out of the red haze. Blade shoved her toward the stairs and pulled out his gun.

"Hurry!"

Carmen barreled toward her. "Come on, Lyla."

She whirled and ran upstairs with Carmen. There was a loud boom that made the windows shudder. What the fuck? Did they bring bombs? It was happening all over again. Her worst nightmare was coming true. Sadist was launching an all-out attack. He was here to finish them off. Where the fuck was Gavin?

Beau stood in front of the crib, tail standing at attention, growling low in his throat.

"I'll get Nora. You have a leash for Beau?" Carmen asked, digging through the drawers and coming up with a baby carrier.

"Yeah. Come, boy," she said and dashed into her bedroom.

She snatched Beau's leash and a bag of guns and ammo before stuffing her bare feet into a pair of sneakers. She clipped the leash to Beau and went down on her knees. His ears flicked from side to side as he listened to the commotion outside. She gripped his face and looked into his alert eyes.

"Stay with me, okay? Stay with Mommy. You're going to be okay."

She dashed into the hallway and saw Carmen had Nora strapped to her chest with a baby bag slung over one shoulder. Their eyes met for a moment before they moved toward the stairs.

"Let's go!" Blade bellowed.

They rushed downstairs as Pat tried to scuttle under the couch. Blade hauled him up and shoved him toward the wine cellar.

"Where are you taking me?" Pat demanded.

"We're getting out of here," Blade said.

"What? How—?"

Blade pointed a gun in her father's face. "Do what I say or die. I don't have time for this shit."

Pat glanced at her before he held his hands up and allowed Blade to propel him forward. Blade punched in the code for the wine cellar, and they rushed down the wide steps. Blade closed the door. The sudden silence put them all on edge.

"What the fuck is going on?" Pat asked again.

No one answered because they all knew what was happening. Carmen swayed as she cradled Nora's neck. Her baby was still blissfully asleep. Thank God Nora could sleep through a gun battle.

The cellar was a small room with three walls full of wine bottles. She had been here a handful of times, but she knew what to do. She went to the third shelf and pulled off eight bottles before she saw the square panel. She tapped it and typed in her code before she realized Gavin might have changed it since she went on the run the first time. The panel flashed green and swung inward. She was so relieved, her eyes stung with tears. She shot to her feet and pushed the wall open.

"There's a way out?" Pat sounded stunned.

He tried to go first, but Blade hauled him back and nodded to Carmen and Lyla. Lyla stepped forward. Two lights at ground level lit up as Beau edged forward, sniffing madly. A dark tunnel stretched out in front of them. The darkness was so dense that she took a step back and bumped into Carmen. Blade and Pat forced her forward. More lights flared.

"Lyla, lead the way," Blade ordered.

Beau eagerly started forward and pulled Lyla after him.

"Still no phone service," Blade reported from the rear. "Let's roll."

Lights welcomed them into the hollow tunnel made of rock and stone and faded once they passed. Nora fussed, but they couldn't stop. She focused on putting one step in front of the other and felt naked without her phone, a flashlight, or adequate clothing. The cold penetrated easily through the large weave of her oversized sweater and leggings. Carmen hadn't changed out of her robe or house slippers and had to be freezing.

The tunnel seemed endless, and the feeling of being safe began to wane. Where the hell were they going? The sound of her father wheezing came from behind her. It felt like a half hour passed before the tunnel opened into a cave with a dirt floor. Four ATVs waited for them. By mutual accord, Blade and her father climbed onto one. Lyla forced Beau onto the floor in front of her and took Nora from Carmen who got into the driver's seat.

"Gavin doesn't leave anything to chance, does he?" Carmen asked as she turned the key in the ignition.

"No." She only wished he could have foreseen that Sadist would strike again. Fuck, four months of radio silence and now this.

Blade took off on a narrow dirt path with only the headlights of the ATV for light. It was like an awful Disneyland ride. They hit ruts that made Lyla clamp her legs around Beau and hang onto Nora for dear life. They climbed steep inclines and then rushed down slopes. Dirt gave way to sand and they continued. The fact that Gavin had carved an escape route through the mountains was unbelievable. The sheer planning and work that must have gone into this was mind-blowing.

Blade braked in front of a small fleet of SUVs in a cave. Beau scrambled out of the ATV while Lyla stepped out with Nora. The SUVs pointed at a wall that seemed to be made of solid rock. Blade pulled out his phone.

"Any luck?" Carmen asked.

"No service, but that's not surprising since we're in the middle of nowhere." Blade jerked his chin at Lyla. "Gavin should be able to track her through her watch."

"Where are we going?" Carmen asked.

"Safe house in Arizona."

"Can't we stay here?" Pat asked.

"No. The protocol is to head to a safe house so that's where we'll go. Get in the car."

Blade got into the driver's seat, and her father took shotgun. Carmen lifted the back so Beau could jump in. Lyla slid onto the back seat and huddled in the corner to breastfeed Nora who calmed instantly. She stroked her daughter's face as the fake wall of rock lifted, showing an endless expanse of desert highlighted by a half moon.

Blade messed with the GPS, which showed a snowy screen.

"Fuck," Blade swore.

"Do you know where you're going without directions?" she asked.

"Yeah."

Blade navigated through the desert without lights. They were in the middle of nowhere without a road in sight. Her teeth rattled as the SUV handled the off-road terrain with ease. How could Blade possibly know where they were? She swallowed her questions. She trusted Blade with her life, so she'd let him take the lead.

She felt nothing. She was past fear or anger. Sadist would never stop. She looked down at Nora and could see just a hint of her face from the moonlight streaming through the window. Nora's eyes were open and moving around the dark interior of the car. Nora clutched at her as the SUV dipped into holes. She held her close and noticed that Carmen managed to put a cap and socks on her daughter despite the chaos.

Carmen leaned between the two front seats, face tight with exhaustion and worry. Lyla looked down and saw that her once pink house slippers were now brown and filthy.

"What's going on?" Pat asked.

The tension in the car ratcheted up to a screaming pitch. This war had been going on under her father's nose for years. Despite the fact that Manny had been murdered, Gavin went to jail, and she had gone missing, her father hadn't asked questions until now. She thought of her mother and squeezed her eyes shut. She would get her back.

"Someone has it out for the Pyres," Blade said finally. "It's the same guy who killed Manny."

"So, it is your fault!" Pat shouted and tried to turn in his seat.

Lyla clenched her teeth as guilt raked her insides.

Carmen got in his face. "You've never been a father to Lyla. As far as I'm concerned, you should be happy we didn't leave you there to die."

"You've always been a disrespectful bitch—"

Blade's fist flashed out and Pat slammed into the window. The sound startled Nora who began to cry. She cuddled the baby close and murmured to her as Blade spoke.

"I don't like you." Blade's voice held no inflection, which made his delivery all the more effective. "You're a lazy, shady fuck who has no respect for anyone. You're all mouth and can't back up your shit. You were all for Lyla being with Gavin as long as she gave you money. Far as I'm concerned, Gavin should have killed you when he caught you stealing. That's the price you pay for taking what isn't yours. The only reason you're still breathing is because Gavin loves your daughter, yet you treat her like trash."

They all jerked to the left as the tire dipped into a hole.

"I don't like you," Blade said again. "And I don't care who you think you are. Right now, you're not in control, you don't call the shots, and you have no rights. I hear anything I don't like coming out of your mouth, I'll put us all out of our misery and put a bullet through your head before I dump your body in the middle of the desert. Shut your trap or I do it for you. We clear?"

Not a peep from her father. Lyla dropped her head back as it throbbed with the beginning pangs of a tension headache. Holy fuck. One innocent trip to the casino started a chain of events that couldn't be stopped. Where was Gavin? Hopefully, he already knew what happened and was able to track her through the GPS imbedded in her watch. What if he was in trouble too? No, she couldn't think that way. It would drive her crazy, and she had to keep her head.

She peered out of the window, waiting for a car to appear out of the darkness. She hoped Sadist's men didn't get through the guards to the house. What if they touched Manny's urn? She closed her eyes and fought tears. She should have taken him.

She lurched forward as the SUV slid onto pavement. Blade spun sharply and slammed on the gas.

"How long will it take to get to this safe house?" Carmen asked.

"Two hours," Blade said.

"I know about the one in Utah," Lyla ventured, desperate to discuss anything but the cloud of doom hanging over them. "How many safe houses does he have?"

"Half a dozen. The one in Arizona is one of the closest, and I know how to get there." He tapped the unresponsive GPS. "I don't know what the fuck is going on with this shit."

Carmen pulled out her phone. "Still no service."

Nora sat on her lap and burped loudly. Beau leaned over to make sure she was all right and waffled in Lyla's hair. She reached back and scratched him under his chin.

"You're such a good boy," she praised.

"Yes, you are," Carmen agreed and kissed his cheek.

"Get some sleep," Blade advised.

"How?" Lyla asked as she bounced Nora on her lap.

"We don't know what else that fucker has in store for us tonight. You should rest while you can."

She dropped her face on Nora's chest and inhaled. Sadist wouldn't get her baby. She dropped the seat and crawled in the back of the SUV with Beau and found some blankets. She placed Nora on her back and watched her baby kick and wave her arms. Beau lay beside her with his head on his paws.

Thoughts of her mom in Sadist's hands chilled her to the core. Sadist didn't keep his victims. She squeezed her eyes shut. She watched Manny die. God wouldn't be cruel enough to take her mother too, could he? Helpless despair filled her chest, drowning her. Why did Sadist hate her so much? It was a coincidence that Sadist caught her at Manny's house that day, but now he was striking out at her family. This was personal.

She tucked Nora against her body and breathed in her scent. The world could fall around her, but she would do whatever she had to for her daughter. She fought to bring Nora into this world, and she would pay whatever cost to keep her here. Her thoughts turned to Gavin, and her chest burned with fury. If he was in Maine on a personal vendetta, leaving them vulnerable to an attack, she would never forgive him.

***

"Lyla."

She opened her eyes and found she was curled protectively around Nora who was sound asleep. Beau was gone, and there was a harsh chill coming through the open doors of the SUV. Carmen reached for the baby and hustled into the darkness.

She felt worse than she had before she slept. Her mind was sluggish and unfocused. She scooted out of the back of the SUV and landed on coarse sand. A small cabin sat at the base of a canyon in the shape of a horseshoe. Jagged peaks seemed to touch the starry sky. She walked around the SUV and saw that the safe house was at the top of a steep incline. On the horizon was the faint glow of city lights. She wished they were in the city, not in the middle of nowhere with no one around for miles.

She walked toward the cabin, which was set deep enough into the canyon that no one would see the lights. She stepped onto the worn, creaking porch and heard Blade cursing.

"What is it?" she asked.

"Still no reception. I've been checking every fifteen minutes since we got on the road," Blade snapped and stuffed his phone in his pocket. "Did they bug our phones? What the fuck?"

The house had one bedroom and was sparsely furnished with wooden chairs and not much else. Carmen came out of the bedroom with a blanket wrapped around her and Nora. Pat sat at a small dining table, face buried in his hands.

She used the facilities and splashed water on her face to wash away the grogginess and grime. The bathroom had one set of towels and toilet paper, but nothing else. She looked at herself in the dingy mirror. The woman looking back at her possessed dull, defeated eyes.

She trudged into the kitchen and opened the cupboards, which were empty. The house had electricity, but no rations, not even drinking water. She was thirsty enough to drink from the rusty tap. Carmen huddled on a twin bed with Nora in the only bedroom.

"I changed her diaper and put on the warmest clothes she has," Carmen said through chattering teeth.

Beau trotted through the house, sniffing the floor excitedly.

"I'm going to talk to Blade," she said.

Her father sat at the table, staring intently at his phone. Blade's punch gave him a fresh set of bruises on his cheek. He looked like a walking dead person. She wished he would wash up. Knowing he was covered in her mother's blood made her feel sick.

She walked outside and found Blade standing at the top of the hill, looking out over the desert.

"What are we going to do?" she asked.

"Most of the safe houses are near cities where we can pick up supplies." He jerked his head at the distant city lights. "How do you want to do this?"

She blinked. Blade was asking for her advice? "What do you mean?"

"I'm not going to leave you here if you're not comfortable."

She wasn't 'comfortable' with any of this, but they had no choice.

"I need you all to stay calm. My instinct says you should be safe here. I need to get to a phone to call Gavin. He needs to know where we are. We could have gone to any safe house. This is one of the oldest." He glanced back at the house. "I would take Pat with me, but he doesn't have extra clothes, and I can't afford to have him draw attention since he's covered in blood. Can you handle him?"

"Yes. Carmen will stay too."

"I'll take Beau, so he won't distract you if your dad acts up."

Blade whistled, and Beau came out on the front porch. When Blade opened the car, Beau hopped into the passenger seat. She fetched the bag of ammo she brought along and slung it over one shoulder. She and Blade faced one another.

"Thanks for getting us out of there," she said.

"It's my job to keep you safe."

She went with her gut and wrapped her arms around him. Life was too fucking short. She was exhausted, terrified, and hovered on the verge of despair. Blade was one of her people, and she wanted him to know that. He didn't hug her back. That didn't stop her from giving him a hard squeeze before she drew away.

"Tell Gavin that I'm going to kick his ass when I see him again." She would do worse than that if she survived.

Blade glanced at the bag slung over her shoulder. "Are you sure you can handle Pat?"

"Yes."

"I'll be back as soon as I can."

Blade got into the car. She caught a glimpse of Beau's doggy face as they drove away. Blade was indestructible like Gavin and her biggest defense... and he was leaving them to contact Gavin. She took her phone for granted. She also took Gavin for granted and now... Now everything was up in the air. She had no idea if her mother was dead or alive, the fate of the guards at her home, or what horrors the sunrise would bring. Her life had become a series of tragedies and trials. Where was her happily ever after?

"Lyla?"

She turned to see her father on the steps.

"Where's Blade?"

"He went into the city to contact Gavin."

"He left us here?" he shouted.

She tightened her hold on the bag of bullets. She wasn't in the mood for her father's belligerent attitude, which returned as soon as Blade left. Her father's face went purple with rage. After looking into the masked eyes of a killer and facing certain death numerous times, her father's tantrums were a walk in the park. She eyed him objectively as he huffed and puffed as if he had the ability to turn into the Hulk.

"Where is your husband?" he demanded as if he had every right to know.

She walked up the steps and had every intention of ignoring him until he jerked her to a halt.

"Where is he?"

She wrenched her arm out of his grasp. "Don't touch me."

"So, he's back to his old tricks, huh?" He sneered. "He gets you pregnant and then takes off and lets you deal with his mess?"

"You don't know anything about my life. Shut up and stay put."

She walked into the house. Carmen was trying to entertain Nora who was awake and extremely fussy.

"Blade went into the city to call Gavin," she reported as she sat on the bed and took Nora to breastfeed again.

Carmen stretched out with her head pillowed on her arm. "Smart."

"So, it's just us for now."

All her training was to prepare her for this moment—a moment she hoped wouldn't come again. The fact that she had company this time around made it worse, somehow, because there was more at stake. Carmen and Nora were here, and they were both integral to her life. If she lost either of them... Where the fuck was Gavin? If he was in Maine—

"This is awful," Carmen said.

Lyla focused on her. "What do you mean?"

Carmen tugged the blanket around her. "The waiting to see what happens next."

She brushed her finger over Nora's cheek and was relieved to find it warm to the touch. "It's a game to him."

"Sick fucker. What's the most painful way to die? That's how he should go."

She thought of her mother and squeezed her eyes shut as a flood of emotion filled her. Why take her mother? What did he want with her?

"Lyla, she's going to be okay."

She blinked rapidly.

"She'll pull through, just like you did," Carmen said.

"I hope so."

The sound of rapid footsteps made her stand. She looked through the open doorway as her father paced from one end of the room to the other, twisting his hands together and muttering to himself. Of course, he didn't bother to keep guard. He was probably thinking of more shit to heap on her shoulders.

She sat quietly and tried to calm her whirling, chaotic thoughts. When Nora drifted off, she lay her beside Carmen who tucked her close. She cleaned up in the bathroom and splashed her face once more. She was so weary that she felt sick, but she couldn't rest until Blade came back.

When she exited the bathroom, her father's muttering seemed even more frenzied. He didn't seem to be aware of her. Was he finally reacting to Mom's kidnapping? She tried to catch what he was saying, but it was too low and jumbled for her to understand.

She cracked open the front door and listened. There was absolutely no sound aside from her father's faint footfalls. She held her gun at her side as she walked out on the porch and then down the steps. She had another gun in her bag. She thought of tucking both into her leggings, but that was stupid. Maybe she should get a belt with a double gun holster. She would look like a woman from the Wild West with a gun on each hip. That was how she felt. She was part of a world where there were no rules and no safe place.

The faint glow of the city was a beacon in the distance. The desert stretched out before her, covered in cacti, shrubs, and trees. There was no road, which would make Blade's progress slow and arduous. She wrapped her arms around herself as the cold penetrated. She closed her eyes and focused on calming herself. She was alive, and Nora was safe. She couldn't do anything for her mother at the moment. All she could do was stand here and wait for something to happen. Her fighter instincts were elevated. Even when her hand went numb, she refused to tuck the gun away. Everything in her screamed out a warning. Sadist was always one step ahead. How many times would she escape before she ran out of luck?

When her face was numb from the cold and there was no sign of a car, she walked into the cabin, which was only fractionally warmer. She walked into the kitchen and was debating whether to drink from the tap again when she realized her father wasn't in the living room. The bathroom was empty, and the bedroom door was partially closed. She swung it open and had a split second to take in the scene. Her father stood over a sleeping Carmen and Nora. The bag of ammo was open and her father had her second gun in his hand.

A loud blast ripped through the room, startling Carmen and Nora awake. She wasn't aware of the fact that she still held her gun or that she pulled the trigger. Her father's body jerked like a puppet on a string as a bullet sliced through him. The gun he held fell with a dull thud. Nora began to cry and kick frantically as her grandfather fell to his knees beside the bed with his blood staining the wooden floor.

17

LYLA

"Lyla, what—?" Carmen began, eyes wide with horror.

She braced herself against the doorjamb as her legs buckled. She just shot her father who intended to kill his granddaughter in cold blood.

"Lyla?"

Carmen's voice roused her from her horrified stupor. She stood on the opposite side of the bed, Nora clasped to her chest, face ghost white.

"Get her out of here," she whispered.

"What happened? Why would he—?"

"Carmen, go."

Her mind was a blank slate of rage and denial. She vowed that Nora wouldn't be exposed to this lifestyle, yet her grandfather had been shot less than a foot from her at four months old. She had questions for him, and she couldn't do it with Carmen and Nora present.

Carmen's eyes locked on hers before she nodded and left with Nora. The sound of Nora's screams faded as Carmen moved into the kitchen, leaving her with Pat. She forced herself to move forward until she stood in front of him. He pressed a hand to the wound in the middle of his chest.

"Why?" she whispered.

"I had to," he said through clenched teeth.

"You had to kill your granddaughter?"

She felt as if she were having an out-of-body experience. Surely, this wasn't real. Maybe she was having a waking nightmare. She watched blood gush through his fingers with detached fascination.

"Tell me why."

He glared at her. "Fuck you."

His phone flashed in the pocket of his bloody pajamas, catching her attention. Even as her father tried to reach for it, she knocked his hand away and held it up.

A text from a blocked number flashed across the screen: *Fifteen minutes out.*

His phone had service. She stared at her father as everything coalesced in her mind, and the blood in her veins turned to ice. "You're working with him?"

"I don't know what you're talking about," he puffed.

Something erupted inside her. She kicked her father right over his bullet wound. He fell flat on his back with a tortured yell she didn't hear over the roar in her head. The taste of betrayal permeated her mouth. She raised the gun as she stood over him.

"Tell me the truth about Mom." When he didn't answer fast enough, she pulled the trigger. He writhed beneath her, clearly in agony, but she felt nothing. "Talk." She didn't have time.

Fifteen minutes.

"They have her."

"Why should I believe you?"

Although his eyes were dilated with pain, hatred gave him the strength to spit, "They raped her in front of me. One right after the other."

The hand holding the gun wavered. She felt as if she had been kicked in the stomach.

"They told me if I wanted to see my wife again that I would go to your house." His body shook as if he were receiving tiny electrical shocks. "It was supposed to end there. They didn't know there was an escape route. There's a bug in my phone that disrupts electronics, which is why the phones don't have service."

"You should have told me this from the beginning! We could have done something."

Her father's sneer was a weak imitation of his normal disdain. "Why? You think Gavin can solve this? He can't. His shit has leaked into my life, and now your mom's... Now she's..."

"Why kill Nora?" she asked, but there was no reply. He was gone.

Lyla jumped when the phone chimed, a reminder of the unread text. She pulled up the exchange of messages from the blocked number.

We're tracking you. Any sign of Pyre?

No, her father replied.

Where are they traveling to?

A safe house in Arizona.

Are they able to use their phones?

No.

There was a long lag and then her father said, *Blade left to go to the city.*

Good. Save us time. Take care of the brat. Don't kill your daughter. He wants her.

There were no more other messages from her father, but that last text made her heart race.

Fifteen minutes out.

She swallowed bile and knelt beside the bag of ammo in the corner. She grabbed her second gun and stuffed bullets and magazines into her pockets. She didn't look at her father as she walked out of the bedroom. Carmen stood in the kitchen with Nora strapped to her chest.

"Lyla?"

"They're coming." She stared at her daughter who cried pitifully. Like them, Nora was overtired, scared, and confused. They were in the middle of nowhere with no backup and Sadist's men on the way. Terror threatened to obliterate her icy composure. This was it. She could feel the walls closing in around them.

"Sadist?" Carmen whispered his name. "He's coming?"

She held up the phone. "They've been tracking us."

"Is Uncle Pat...?"

"He's dead. We have to get out of here."

"And go where?"

"We can't be in the house when they get here. We have to make a run for it."

Carmen opened her mouth to argue and then closed it. "Okay."

They ran onto the porch and down the steps. She cautiously approached the incline and searched the desert landscape. She didn't see the headlights of an approaching vehicle, but she knew they were out there. Fifteen minutes. Fuck.

She rounded the house and started after Carmen and Nora. The canyon loomed around them, protecting and trapping them. Was there a way through? A cave they could hide in? They wove around cactus that towered six feet high, waist-high shrubs, and creepy looking trees without canopies. There were scorpions, snakes, and God knew what else out here, but they had no choice. The moon cast enough light for them to avoid being impaled by the spines of the wild cactus.

She skidded to a halt as the phone vibrated in her pocket.

Why are you on the move?

She held the phone away from her as if it turned into a snake. How could she be so stupid? Of course, they were tracking the phone. Her first instinct was to toss it as far as she could. The other part of her knew the key to finding her mother and possibly the identity of Sadist was in this piece of evidence.

"Hold up," she called. "I'm going to call Blade."

"Run and call him!" Carmen retorted.

"They're tracking the phone."

Carmen stopped in her tracks. "Call him and toss it, Lyla."

She dialed Blade's number and silently promised she would thank him for forcing her to memorize it. Her heart thudded in her ears as the phone began to ring. She glanced back the way they had come and was surprised at how much ground they covered, but they were nowhere near the base of the canyon, their only hope for cover. Just when she feared the call would go to voicemail, he picked up.

"Who is this?"

"Blade, it's me." She clutched the phone with both hands.

"Lyla? Whose phone is this?"

Her throat closed up.

"Lyla?"

"He's dead."

"What? Who?"

"My dad. I shot him. He was going to kill Nora."

"Fuck."

"You need to come back, Blade. They're coming. They should be here any minute. My dad's phone was interfering with the signal. They've been tracking us the whole time."

"Get out of the house."

"I am. We're heading toward the canyon."

"I spoke to Gavin. He's in New York. I'm on my way back."

The ice in her veins spread to her heart. Gavin was miles away. By the time he got here, it would all be over. She was truly alone with Carmen and her daughter in the middle of nowhere with a team of trained killers about to arrive any minute.

"He said they gang raped my mom in front of him."

The words burst out of her mouth before she realized she said anything. She ignored Carmen's horrified gasp.

"He has her, Blade, and he wants me too. They told my dad to kill Nora and take me."

"Lyla, run."

"What about Mom?"

"You're my first priority. You find a place to hide. I'll find you."

"But the phone—"

"Get rid of it. Hide. Stay alive until I get there."

He hung up. She stared at the screen as another text appeared: *Did you take care of the kid?*

She gripped the phone so hard, she was surprised it didn't shatter in her grasp. She turned off the phone, put it in her pocket, and stared at the edge of the ridge.

"Come on, Lyla," Carmen said, her voice sharp and urgent. "Go."

Carmen stomped back to her with a mewling Nora. "What the hell are you doing? We're sitting ducks out here."

"We should split up. They're going to find Pat's body and realize we're on foot. They won't kill me, but they have orders to kill both of you. You have to go."

"Don't do this to me."

"Promise me you'll take care of her."

"*No.*"

"Promise me!"

Carmen grabbed her arm and tried to pull her along. "We're going to stay together!"

She twisted out of Carmen's hold and pressed kisses over her daughter's face. Nora wailed pitifully and gripped her clothing. The placid remoteness that allowed her to think began to fracture as she gently unfurled Nora's tiny fingers and stepped back.

"Go, Carmen."

"I'm not going without you!"

"They're going to find us quick, especially with Nora crying," she said above her daughter's howls.

Carmen's terror was easy to read even in the dim light.

"You run and don't stop."

"Please," Carmen whispered, shaking her head as tears streamed down her face. "Please don't leave me."

"I'll hold them off until Blade comes and distract them if I have to. Here." She tucked the second gun into the pocket of Carmen's robe. "Go."

"Lyla, you can't do this to me."

"I love you. Now, go!"

They stared at one another. For a moment, she thought Carmen wouldn't leave.

"If you get one fucking scratch on you, I'll kill you," Carmen hissed before she whirled and ran as fast as she could toward the mountains. The blanket from the house streamed behind her like a cape.

She circled around the house so she would see them arrive. She replaced the bullets in her magazine. Eight bullets. Eight tries to defend herself before she had to reload. She crouched behind a mesquite tree. Most of the landscape had only spotty coverage so they lucked out in this location.

She found a spot about thirty feet from the house. From this angle, she could see the front porch and the ridge where they would appear. She went on tiptoes to search for Carmen, but there was no discernible movement and the only audible sound was her own ragged breaths.

She took a deep breath and let it out. She could do this. She had to. No Gavin, Blade, security guards, or Beau. It was just her, a gun, and her wits.

Sadist had her mother gang raped. The walls around her heart shuddered under the weight of guilt, sorrow, and rage that savaged her insides. Sadist killed Manny, kidnapped her mother, and manipulated her father into murdering his grandchild. She refused to look at the house, as if that would erase what she'd done. This had to be a dream. If this were real, she would be scared out of her mind. Instead, she felt nothing but the bite of fury and an icy coldness that obliterated all thought. She welcomed it because whatever came next, she couldn't afford to have a conscience. The need to retaliate was a drum beat in her blood. For the first time in her life, she understood what drove Gavin when Vinny and his father were murdered. She didn't feel like a person, more like a machine with a mission and purpose—survive, protect, and kill if necessary.

Time passed. She didn't feel the cold. She didn't feel anything. The environment was unforgiving—just like her. These men belonged to Sadist. They were monsters who carried out orders to murder children. She wouldn't go with them. She would die before she allowed them to take her to Sadist. Did he personally want to dismember her while she was still alive? Fuck that. If anyone was spilling blood, it would be her. What morals she had shriveled up and died in the house along with her father. No matter what the cost, she would protect her own. Neither Carmen nor Nora would die here. She wouldn't allow it.

She scanned the landscape once more and then dropped into a crouch when she heard an approaching vehicle. She was eerily calm. Headlights pierced the darkness, and a minute later, two SUVs pulled up in front of the house. Doors opened and men stepped out, guns drawn. She slowed her breathing as if that would conceal her better. She was too far away to hear what they were saying, but the rumble of their voices carried in the quiet.

Two men from each SUV approached the house. She watched as they kicked the door open and walked in. Within seconds, they reappeared. They walked to the SUV and reported their findings to their comrades. Two more men exited the SUV, guns drawn. Eight men. They wore some kind of black-on-black ensemble. In short order, the SUVs rounded the house with four men flanking them on foot. They headed toward the canyon, which sent a spear of unease through her until she saw that the SUVs were going to have a hell of a time finding a path between the massive cactus, mesquite trees, and prickly shrubs.

She focused on the two men who stayed behind. Lookouts. They knew Blade would make his way back at some point and would alert the others if he approached. She couldn't let that happen.

"You think the daughter did it?" one man asked the other.

"Her or the smoking hot cousin."

There was a pause. Her muscles ached as she moved in a half crouch and closed the distance between them. She was about twenty feet away, close enough to see that the men were Hispanic and in good shape. She didn't dare go any closer since there wasn't anything higher than waist-high shrubs to hide behind.

"Must have been the daughter. Pyre married her for a reason. Word is she's building up quite a tally. She killed some boys during the last two runs." He elbowed his comrade. "You think he'll let us try the daughter?"

The other man shrugged. "Sounds like he wants her for something special."

He grabbed his crotch. "I'll bet. The mother wasn't bad. Took her twice before she passed out."

She stopped breathing. He had a nice smile, couldn't be over thirty, and looked like a decent guy, but the words coming out of his mouth told the real story. This man raped her mother?

"You think she's still alive?"

"If she is, she won't be for long," the other said as he pulled out a cigarette.

"If she's still at the compound, I'll do her again before he buries her. I can't believe these mental bitches went on foot."

She raised her gun, but froze when he walked in her direction to look around the house to watch the progress of the search party. Headlights pierced the darkness while the men yelled to one another as they spread out. She took her eyes off her quarry as worry pierced through the dull roaring in her head. She prayed Carmen found a good hiding spot and managed to calm Nora. She should be following the search party to create a diversion to give Carmen time, but she wouldn't last long without backup. Blade was their only hope of getting out of this alive, and these two men were going to prevent that.

"They couldn't have gone far." The cigarette bobbed in his mouth. "You got a light?"

"No."

"You think the dead guy has one?"

"He's in his fucking pajamas."

"You think there's something in the kitchen?"

"No."

"One sec."

The man abandoned his post and jogged toward the house, leaving her alone with the man who raped her mother. He was less than ten feet away and had no idea of her presence. She glanced at the search party. Would they hear the gunshot? The rapist jerked his head around, and she heard it, the sound of an approaching vehicle.

He reached into his pocket for his phone. When she sprang up, his head snapped around. Their eyes met for one heart stopping moment before she pulled the trigger. His head kicked back, black droplets spraying everywhere before his body dropped.

"What the—?"

She swung the gun around and shot the second man in the doorway. He staggered back as she got him in the chest. Blade crested over the ridge and barreled around the house. The search party fired at the SUV.

With their attention on Blade, she ran toward the canyon to find Carmen and Nora. There was a pained scream as Blade took a leaf out of her book and ran over a man. Three down, five to go. The enemy vehicles were trying to turn around to face the threat and not having much luck since the wild vegetation boxed them in.

"Hey, there she is!"

A man spotted her, and she dropped on all fours. Car engines roared, men shouted, and bullets flew. She heard a bark. She lifted her head in time to see Beau leap out of a window and launch himself at a man who fell backward with an agonized cry. Fuck it. She focused on the bigmouth who noticed her and pulled the trigger. The first shot nicked his shoulder, but the second put him down.

"What the fuck?" someone shouted.

She focused on an enemy vehicle battling a cactus. The driver seemed to have given in for the moment. He had a high-powered rifle balanced on his open window and was blasting Blade's windshield, which wouldn't hold up for long. She used her last three bullets and the deafening blasts ceased. She pulled a full magazine out of her pocket and slammed it in before she followed the sound of Beau's growls. She put the bastard out of his misery and nudged Beau away from the body.

"Beau, come," she ordered.

Blade rammed into the driver's side of the second SUV with enough force to tip the vehicle on its side. Blade ran to the upended vehicle. Three shots and silence descended.

Seven down. One left. Where was he?

Blade rounded the SUV, chest heaving. "You all right?"

"Yes. I split up with Carmen and Nora."

"Where?"

She pointed in the general direction she saw Carmen run. "There's one guy left."

"Fuck." Blade raced back to his SUV and whistled for Beau.

She went to the SUV with the driver slumped out of the open window. She made sure there were no surprises in the back seat before she took the wheel and followed Blade as he flattened shrubs. She ignored the blood on the steering wheel and seat. Her entire being focused on any movement over the still desert landscape.

Out of the corner of her eye, she saw a flash accompanied by a popping sound. Her heart dropped to her toes. She wrenched the steering wheel to the left and plowed over everything in her path. Branches reached into the open window and scratched her arm and cheek. She didn't notice. She slammed the SUV to a halt when it couldn't go any farther and ran as fast as could, dodging through the monstrous cactus.

She rounded a tree and tripped over a body. "No!"

"Lyla."

She raised her head and saw Carmen with Nora strapped to her chest, gun in hand. She squeezed her eyes shut as relief cascaded through her in a heady wave that left her lightheaded.

"Are you hurt?" Blade asked.

Carmen walked forward as if she were sleepwalking and didn't answer. Blade took a bawling Nora from Carmen who did nothing to stop him.

"She's freezing. Come on, we don't have much time," Blade said and rushed back to the car with Nora.

Carmen helped Lyla to her feet. They stared at one another for a long moment.

"Okay?" she asked.

Carmen nodded.

"Stupid bitches."

She looked down at the man at their feet. How he could be

bleeding to death and smirking at them was beyond her. She had been close to death herself, and it wasn't anything to joke about.

"He won't stop coming," the man said through clenched teeth. "He's going to destroy Pyre."

"Who is he?" she demanded.

His eyelids fluttered as he tried to stay conscious. "No one knows who he is. He isn't stupid."

"Where's the compound where they're holding my mom?"

He raised his dirty finger, stuck it in his mouth and hummed. Her stomach turned over.

"She was great, by the way."

She slammed her foot on his chest and heard something break. "Where is she?"

Blood trickled out of his mouth as he convulsed. She dropped to her knees, grabbed handfuls of his jacket, and shook him.

"Where?"

"You're too late," he said before his body went lax.

She dropped him and covered her face with her hands as emotion consumed her.

"Lyla?" Carmen whispered.

She rose, took the gun from her cousin, and started back to the cars. Her mind was a blank slate as she got into the enemy SUV and slammed her foot on the gas. She heard Blade yell her name as she wrenched the vehicle around and started back toward the cabin.

She slapped her hand on the GPS built into the dashboard. A map of their routes appeared on the screen. There was one location the SUV kept returning to, a large red dot in the middle of Las Vegas. She set the course as she passed the safe house and started down the ridge. Her rearview mirror showed Blade's flashing headlights far behind her. She didn't stop. She couldn't.

When the SUV skidded onto the highway, the first hint of light brightened the sky. She stared blearily at the bloody sunrise, which seemed appropriate after the night she'd had. Her body was coiled so tightly, she felt as if she might shatter.

She drove with such single-minded intensity that she didn't

realize Blade had caught up to her until he tried to run her off the road. She jerked the wheel to avoid him. Blade's window was down, and he was more furious than she had ever seen him. He shouted at her, which was pointless since her windows were rolled up. He jabbed his finger at her and held up his cell phone.

She slammed her foot on the gas even as she reached in her pocket for the forgotten cell phone she picked off her father. She turned it on and immediately saw Blade's number on the screen. Apparently, there was enough distance between them for him to have a signal. She had less than twenty minutes between her current location and this fucking compound. She wouldn't let anyone stop her.

"Pull over," Blade ordered.

The lump of rock in her chest where her heart used to be weighed a ton. "No."

"What the fuck are you doing?"

"They have my mom."

"We have men working on it."

"They have her at the compound."

"I don't give a fuck where they have her. Pull over, Lyla."

"Fuck you, Blade. I'm getting her. The GPS tracks all their routes. There's one place they keep going back to. It's their compound. I know it. You want this to stop? Send as many men to this address." She rattled it off and merged onto a freeway. "I'll be there in nineteen minutes, with or without backup."

"Gavin said—"

Her control shattered.

"Fuck Gavin!" she shrieked and slammed her hand on the steering wheel. Emotions threatened to break her in half. She clenched her teeth to stuff it back in. She didn't have time for a breakdown. That would come later when her mother was safe. "I'm tired of waiting for other people to take care of me. I can do that my fucking self. This is my mom. I got her into this; I'm getting her out. You want to help? Call the guys, get them there."

"Lyla," Blade's voice turned soft and coaxing. "Let me—"

"Get them there, Blade."

She hung up. She was done playing this game. It had to end now. Sadist wasn't allowed to claim the one parent she had left.

The phone rang. Gavin's number showed up on the screen. She barely resisted the urge to toss it out the window. She turned the phone off instead. Fuck him. Blade mentioned that he was in New York, which was too close to Maine for her peace of mind. If he went after Jonathan, therefore leaving her to deal with this shit on her own, she would never forgive him.

The GPS led her past downtown Las Vegas. At a stoplight, a pedestrian passing in front did a double take. She couldn't begin to imagine what she looked like. For the first time, she looked at her hands, which were rust colored with dried blood. She didn't have to look down at her sweater and tights to know they hadn't fared much better.

When the light turned green, she slammed her foot on the accelerator. The compound was in the middle of a block of abandoned warehouses. Her senses prickled with an odd sense of déjà vu. Two thugs kidnapped and held her in a warehouse years ago. She had been unconscious when they brought her in and too distraught to notice when she left. Everything in her screamed that this was the same place. A glimpse of Blade's SUV in the rearview mirror stabbed at her icy determination. Nora and Carmen couldn't be here.

The sight of a group of vehicles made her heart slam into her throat until one of the doors opened and she saw Barrett, an older guard who Gavin had put in charge of security at home. He was alive. She lowered the window as he came to her door. She couldn't read anything from his implacable expression. He took in her bloody appearance without batting an eye.

"We'll take it from here," Barrett said.

She tightened her hands on the wheel. "No. I'm going in."

Blade appeared at her window and brushed Barrett aside. The vehicle with Carmen, Beau, and Nora sped away. Her grip on the steering wheel eased slightly. At least they were safe.

"Lyla—" Blade began.

"We're wasting time," she said impatiently. "I'm not leaving until I see her alive."

"You don't want to see this."

"Yes, I do." It couldn't be worse than killing her own father. She didn't need anyone to shield her from Sadist's work. She had first-hand experience, and it was her mother. It was her duty to be here. When she caught up to Sadist, she would pay him back tenfold.

"Gavin's gonna—"

"Gavin isn't here," she snapped. "We're wasting time."

She could feel him debating whether he should get physical with her. She looked straight into his merciless black eyes. "Don't."

Blade shook his head. "Fuck. You don't move from my side, got it?" He turned to Barrett. "How many men do you have?"

"Thirty. More on the way."

"It'll be too late by then."

"Blade, Gavin's gonna—" Barrett began.

"I got her. She can hold her own. You focus on directing the men." Blade slid into the passenger seat. "Let's roll."

Barrett didn't look happy about the situation, but he jogged back to his SUV. She started through the maze of warehouses.

"I have to do this," she said.

"I know."

He reloaded their guns and watched the screen as she navigated around car piles and garbage. When she was a block away, he told her to stop. She obediently parked. He slid out and spoke to the men who armed up and put on earpieces.

The past six hours began to hit her all at once. She rested her face on the steering wheel, took a deep breath, and gagged when she smelled the stink of the driver's dried blood and guts. She sat back, rolled down the window, and took deep breaths of fresh air. Exhaustion threatened to drag her under.

"Lyla?"

She opened her eyes and saw Blade standing at her window.

"Okay?" he asked.

"Yes." It was almost over.

"Here."

He held up a man's jacket with a zipper in the front. She stepped out of the car and nearly crumpled. She grit her teeth as she forced her quaking legs to support her. She couldn't lose her head now, not when she was so close. Blade stared at the warehouse as she stripped off her stiff, filthy sweater and slipped into the jacket. Her shredded leggings showed nasty scrapes from her run in the desert. She zipped the jacket and wrapped her arms around herself for warmth.

The echo of gunfire reached her. She started toward the sound, but Blade caught her arm, pulling her to a halt.

"They're clearing the way," he said and tapped his earpiece.

"I need to—"

"Lyla, we could be outnumbered ten to one. Just wait. You're not invincible. You're no help to your mom if you're dead."

She grabbed her gun and stuffed two magazines in her pocket. Her mind was a spinning whirlpool of fragmented thoughts and images. The sounds of the battle taking place in the warehouse beckoned to her. Violence and death—they were becoming her constant companions. An image of her father's body flashed through her mind. She closed her eyes and waited for the stabbing pain in her chest to recede.

"I guess target practice came in handy."

She opened her eyes to find Blade watching her.

"You did well," he said.

The price of admission into the underworld was blood, and she had spilled more than her fair share. No matter what she did, the underworld kept dragging her back.

"Look at me."

She focused on Blade who looked disgustingly capable. His hand rested on the butt of his gun, and his clothes, while soiled, weren't ripped and covered in blood as hers was. His eyes, while bloodshot, were alert and clear.

"Carmen told me everything. You did what you had to," he said.

She couldn't take a full breath. She felt as if there were glass shards in her chest.

"You were everything I could have hoped," Blade continued as she tried to hold herself together. "You were cool under pressure and executed with the precision of a professional. You didn't let emotions get in the way. You did well."

Her fingernails bit into her palms.

"It was either you or them. I'm damn glad it was them." He stepped close and cupped her chin in his hand. "You hear me? You did the right thing."

"I did the right thing by killing my father?"

"It was either that or have Nora and Carmen dead before sunrise."

Her throat swelled. She dropped her face forward until it hit his chest. She tried desperately to contain the maelstrom inside her. If she let loose, she wasn't sure she could put herself back together again. He slid his hand into her tangled hair and said nothing. She grabbed a fistful of his jacket and clenched her teeth against the need to scream.

When Blade stiffened, she looked up and saw that he had one hand cupped over his earpiece. A muscle leaped in his jaw.

"Copy," he said and looked down at her. "Let us take care of this."

"Is she alive?"

He hesitated, and her heart stopped.

"It isn't pretty. She needs to go to the hospital. Let them bring her—"

She ran toward the warehouse with her gun in hand. One of Gavin's men was manning the door. He held up a hand as she approached, but after a glance behind her, he stepped aside.

Although the exterior of the warehouse looked like a rust bucket, the interior was brand new. The warehouse towered three stories high. High windows let in light from every angle. On the first floor were three rooms with the doors wide open. She glimpsed drugs in one room and money in another, but her eyes were on the second floor where a group of men gathered in front of a set of rooms.

"Lyla, you don't want to see this," Blade said from behind her.

"She's up there?"

"Lyla—"

She ran toward the iron staircase and ignored the bodies littered over the steps. Nothing penetrated the urgency rushing through her. She needed to see her mother to make sure she was okay. When she reached the second landing, Barrett stepped forward, face grave.

"Mrs. Pyre, you don't want to—"

"Let me pass," she ordered.

The men didn't move, so she shoved her way through their ranks and stopped in the doorway. She took one look into the room and felt her world disintegrate. She screamed, a sound filled with rage and despair. No. No. This had to be a nightmare.

"Lyla."

Blade gripped her shoulder and tried to pull her backward.

"No!" She ripped free and passed three naked dead men to reach her mother who was bound by wrist and ankles to the four posts of a bed. The mattress was saturated with her mother's blood. Her mother had been whipped and beaten so severely that the only feature she recognized was her mom's platinum locks. Her shaking hands hovered a foot over her mother. No part of her had been left untouched. It looked as if a wild animal had mauled her. There were deep slashes across her face and abdomen. Her hanging skin glistened with cum and blood.

"Mom?" Her stomach lurched as she used the sleeve of the jacket to wipe slime from her mother's face. "Mom?" She tugged on the restraints. "Get these off her."

No one moved.

"Get them off her!"

Four men rushed forward and quickly cut the restraints. One guard shrugged out of his jacket and tossed it over her body.

"Mom? Can you hear me?" She placed one hand over her mother's lips and one on her chest. Her chest moved a tiny fraction at the same time that Lyla felt a small puff of air on her palm.

"She's alive!"

Blade picked her mother up as gently as possible. Her mother didn't make a peep as Blade started toward the door, rapping out orders. She turned to follow, but stopped when she tripped over one of the naked men sprawled on the floor. Her mother had been in this state and they—. She pulled out her gun and emptied the magazine into his body, which shuddered from the impact. She reloaded, walked to the next man, and repeated the process until all three men were bullet filled piñatas. She wasn't sure she had a heart anymore. She didn't feel anything.

She started toward the door, but a flash of red caught her eye. She looked up and saw a camera with a red light over the doorway. She didn't ask for permission. She snatched the gun from the nearest man's belt. The guards backed up as she aimed at the camera and shattered it with one shot. She slapped the gun against the guard's chest and walked out of the room. Gavin's men gave way as she walked down the staircase like an automaton.

Blade had her mother in the back seat of the SUV. She cradled her mother's head on her lap and stroked her hair, which was caked with blood and other stuff she wouldn't let herself examine.

"I'm sorry, Mom," she whispered. "I'm so sorry."

18

LYLA

Lyla stared at her mother who lay in a hospital bed in the ICU. Her body was wrapped in bandages, and a machine was helping her breathe.

Their entrance into the emergency room caused a sensation. Her mother was whisked away, and she had been treated as well. They cleaned the wounds on her legs, arms, and face while asking questions about her mother and why she was covered in blood. Blade said something about a camping accident, and she nodded since the doctor seemed to need some kind of confirmation from her. As for her mother, Blade concocted a story about hiring a private investigator that was looking into her disappearance and located her in this state. The doctors said the police would have to be contacted. This should have scared her, but she felt nothing. After her latest near-death experience, being questioned by cops didn't rouse a hint of anxiety.

The doctor's litany of her mother's injuries played over and over in her mind.

"Your mother's injuries are traumatic. She's lost a lot of blood. She's had several strokes due to someone choking her. She has multiple head fractures as well as a broken ankle, broken shoulder..."

The doctor continued, but she couldn't hear over the white noise. Seeing her mother in the warehouse had been bad enough, but knowing the extent of the physical trauma made her entire being recoil.

"She's in a coma," the doctor said clinically. "It's amazing she survived such a brutal attack. I hope the cops can find the monster who did this."

Lyla dropped onto a chair beside the hospital bed. She reached for her mother's hand, which had chunks of flesh missing from it. Three of five fingers were in braces. They hadn't left an inch of her untouched. She kissed her mother's palm, right over a deep gash.

"I'm sorry." Her voice sounded as dead as she felt.

Their history faded into nothingness. This woman was her mother, her flesh and blood. She couldn't bear to look at her face because it was so gruesome. Her mother didn't deserve this. The dam that kept her from losing her mind since the attack crumbled. She rested her mother's hand on the bed, buried her face in the sheets and sobbed her heart out.

There was no getting around it. This was her fault. Because of her connection to Gavin, her parents had been dragged into the underworld with her. She would have paid any price to save her mother from this.

The only sound in the room was the heart monitor, which increased her anxiety. Any moment now, she expected to hear her mother's heart flatline. She trembled with the need to retaliate, to lash out at someone. She felt as if she were balancing on the edge of a cliff. A gust of wind could tip her into a black hole from which she'd never emerge. She felt this way when Manny was murdered—helpless, horrified, and enraged. A scream built in her throat. The doctor said they had to 'work' on her mother as if she was a car they had to put together.

"Lyla."

She lifted her head as Gavin walked into the room. He looked as slick and untouched as always. In comparison, she felt as if she had been skinned alive—raw, violated, and vicious. She stood and backed away as he approached.

"Stay back," she said hoarsely.

He didn't stop.

"Don't you dare touch me." She pointed at her mother. "Look at her!"

His eyes flicked to the hospital bed. His expression hardened before it swung back to her.

"I'll never forgive you for this," she whispered.

When he reached for her, she knocked his hand away. That didn't deter him.

"I don't want you touching me!" She didn't want anyone touching her, not when her soul felt so savaged. "You said you would protect us! I told you not to go, and you *left*—"

He hauled her into his arms. She fought him as if he was Sadist. She completely lost it— scratching, biting, and screaming. Her breath whooshed out of her as he pinned her to the floor. Tears of grief and rage blinded her. She trusted him to take care of her, and he betrayed her.

"I hate you!" she screamed. "I'll never forgive you!"

She was dimly aware of shouting medical staff and then Blade was there, shoving Gavin aside. She lurched up and latched onto her bodyguard. She was splintering into a million pieces. She couldn't stop shaking, and she needed to hold onto someone who had never let her down.

"Lyla."

Blade smoothed her hair back as he rose with her in his arms. He moved swiftly. She buried her face against his chest, screwed her eyes shut and tried to hold onto her violent emotions.

"Drug me," she whispered.

His step faltered. "What?"

"Sedate me."

"You sure?"

"Do it. I-I can't take anymore."

"Lyla."

She clutched him like a child in desperate need of reassurance and comfort. She let out a stifled shriek as the tears came. The horror of the past seven hours barreled into her, leaving her devastated.

She felt a pinch in her neck as Blade injected her. A blessed numbness spread over her shattered soul, swept away her sorrow, and replaced it with nothingness.

———

SHE OPENED HER EYES. She was flat on her back in a soft bed and didn't have the strength to move her limbs. Every inch of her ached. She felt as if she had been run over by a truck. Her mind was a complete blank. There was no sense of time or space, and she wasn't concerned. Sleep threatened to pull her back under. She closed her eyes and bent her foot in a mini stretch. The stab of pain caught her off guard. She shifted her legs, which scratched against the fine sheets like sandpaper and then it all came flooding back.

She shot up in bed and couldn't stop her gut-wrenching scream. It didn't take longer than ten seconds for a door to her right to burst open. Blade appeared in the doorway with his gun. She was home in the master suite she shared with Gavin. After the safehouse in the middle of the desert and the grisly warehouse, the rich cream colors and luxurious setting seemed all wrong.

"Is it safe?" she asked.

"Yes. They attacked the front gate and tossed an explosive on property, but they didn't penetrate when they realized we escaped," Blade said.

"How long have I been out?" She tried to throw back the duvet, but it seemed like an impossible feat at the moment.

"Six hours. You should sleep longer."

"I need to see my mother."

"There's nothing you can do for her, Lyla."

Her heart stopped. "She's...?"

"Your mother's alive, but her state hasn't improved."

"I should be there."

"We have men guarding her. They'll let us know if any changes."

She opened her mouth to argue, but stopped when Carmen appeared with Nora on her hip. Carmen rushed forward and set Nora on her lap before she buried her face in Lyla's hair. Beau leaped on the bed, nudged her with his wet nose, and settled beside her with a huff.

"I thought I was going to lose you," Carmen whispered, voice thick with tears. "Don't you ever scare me like that again."

Nora smiled up at her, unfazed by her near-death experience. Lyla's hand trembled as she ran the back of her knuckles down Nora's soft cheek. The baby nuzzled her chest, clearly seeking a meal. She recoiled.

"What is it?" Carmen asked, raising her head.

She glanced at Blade who was already closing the door. She raised Nora away from her chest and kissed her on the cheek.

"Did Nora eat?"

"Yes, I gave her cereal. Why?"

"She's acting hungry."

"She probably wants to bond with you. She's been a little stressy. Besides, your boobs must be full."

The moment Nora nuzzled her, her breasts filled with milk, but her heart was racing. Last night, she turned a corner. Her father was the first of five men to die by her hand. Every kill pushed her closer to a precipice from where there would be no return. What she witnessed in the warehouse shoved her over the edge into a straight-up killer with no conscience or morals. Even now, something dark and twisted inside her demanded retribution.

Nora grinned at her, making her heart squeeze with a wild rush of emotions. She wanted to cuddle her daughter, but memories of what she'd done kept her from holding Nora too close. She didn't want to infect her baby with... her. Having Nora breastfeed suddenly felt abhorrent. A normal person would be horrified that they killed their own parent, but she felt nothing. Was it because she was in shock or really felt nothing? Maybe she was morphing into a sociopath.

"Lyla? What's going on?"

She hugged Nora close. "Thank you for taking care of her when I was..." Going off the rails, killing people, and shooting the dead bodies of her mother's rapists. Her throat closed up. "Thank you."

Carmen shot to her feet and smacked her head. "Don't you ever do that to me again, bitch!"

She blinked. "What?"

"You tell me to take Nora and run while you sacrifice yourself? Do you know what that did to me? I could hear gunshots going off and I thought... I thought..." Carmen paced and waved both hands in front of her face as tears poured down her cheeks. "I didn't know what was happening. I was trying to keep Nora quiet, and that guy found us."

Carmen paused to savagely kick Beau's doggy bed before she resumed her frantic pacing. Beau, Lyla, and Nora watched avidly. Carmen planted her feet and did a Peter Pan pose.

"I shot him." Carmen sounded half defiant, half proud of herself.

"Yes, you did."

Carmen sniffed. "He was my first."

"I know."

Carmen let out a gut-wrenching scream and punched her fist in the air. A second later, she bizarrely stomped the ground with one foot as if she were trying to put out a fire.

"I got him! That should teach him to mess with a woman with a baby! That motherfucker! He was calling me like a dog. 'Here slutty, slutty.'" Carmen made a gun with her thumb and pointer finger. "I got him, Lyla. I did it."

"You did good."

Carmen took a deep, fortifying breath. Her bravado faded to reveal the vulnerability and terror she tried to conceal. She fell to her knees beside the bed.

"How did you do it?" she whispered.

"Do what?"

"How did you have the," Carmen made fists with both hands and shook them in Lyla's face, "*cojones* to tell us to run? To go back and face those men by yourself..." Carmen covered her face with both hands and moaned. "I can't do that ever again. I can't."

"I'm sorry."

Carmen grasped her hand and squeezed as her eyes shimmered with tears. "Aunt Beatrice?"

Her throat closed up. Carmen rose and hugged her. She took a deep, shuddering breath as the tears spilled over.

"I think there's something wrong with me," she whispered as Carmen's cotton candy scent engulfed her.

"Why?"

"My mind went blank and I just... I just..."

Carmen pulled back to give her a fierce look. "You became a fucking badass." She splayed one hand on her chest and waved the other in the air as if she was in church. "I mean, Lyla, you took out five professionals. I heard about what they did to your mom at that warehouse... and what you did too."

She couldn't breathe. She set Nora on the bed, went to the window, and threw back the curtains. Guards milled on the property. There was no sign of the attack that sent them fleeing through the underground tunnels. If she hadn't heard the sound of gunfire taking place or the bomb, she wouldn't believe there'd been an attack on the fortress.

"Lyla?"

She turned and saw Carmen watching her with Nora on her hip. She ran her hands over her face and saw that although she wore a clean nightgown, she was still covered in... stuff.

"I need a shower," she said and headed toward the bathroom.

"What are you going to do?" Carmen asked as she settled on the vanity bench with Nora.

"What do you mean?" she called as she stepped under the spray and vigorously began to scrub herself. She wondered how many people's blood she had on her skin.

"Blade told me you saw Gavin at the hospital."

She didn't want to discuss Gavin. She was so fucking angry with him. He risked their relationship because he couldn't stand that she had been with another man. Gavin's blind jealousy resulted in this— a fuck up of epic proportions. Had Sadist known that Gavin wasn't in

Las Vegas and that's why he scaled this attack? If Jonathan was dead, how would she handle Gavin?

"Gavin must have gone through hell, trying to come home when all this crap was going down," Carmen continued.

She stepped out of the shower and examined her reflection. She didn't look any different, but her eyes seemed a shade darker. Was that possible? Her skin was paler than normal, which was expected. The woman looking back at her had bloodshot eyes and an impassive expression that concealed the turmoil going on inside her.

"This has to end," she whispered.

"Yes," Carmen agreed and kissed Nora. "Gavin is probably slaying everyone in his path, trying to find out who Sadist is."

"Did you undress me?" she asked suddenly.

"Of course. Blade isn't going to do it. He wants to keep his head on his shoulders."

"The phone was in my pocket—"

"Blade gave it to Gavin."

She blew out a breath. Sadist didn't trust anyone, which was how he survived this long, but he was human and could make a mistake. She hoped they found something on the phone that would identify him. He wore a mask the day he killed Manny even though he never intended to leave behind a witness. Sadist was intelligent, cautious, and cruel—a dangerous combination.

"What are you doing?" Carmen asked as she slipped on jeans.

"I have to see Mom."

"You're going out again? It's not safe!"

"You don't know what they did to her, Carmen. I can't leave her there alone. I owe her more than that." She focused on Nora who was chewing on Carmen's shirt. "Can you stay here and watch her?"

"Lyla, you took on those guys at the cabin, your dad, and then went on a rampage to find your mom. You need to eat and chill."

"I don't have time to chill." She slipped on a shoulder holster and put her leather jacket over it. She slipped ammo and a magazine into her purse and went into the bathroom to fix her hair, which was wet, limp, and in her face.

"Let Gavin do what he does best. You're putting yourself at risk—"

She slashed her hand through the air. "Mom's in the hospital because of me. If I wasn't with Gavin, this wouldn't have happened in the first place. If it was your mother, would you leave her there alone?"

Carmen sighed. "You're running on fumes."

"I'll sleep when I'm dead."

"Not funny."

She grasped Carmen's face between both hands and rested her forehead against her cousin's. "I need you here with Nora. You're the only one I trust to carry this out. I could do what I had to at the cabin because I knew you would protect Nora with your last breath. I need you to do this for me."

Carmen sniffled. "I'm supposed to be the protector, not you."

Her lips twitched into a small smile. "Once all this is over, I'll let you take the lead again." She kissed Carmen and then Nora. "I'll be back."

She yanked the bedroom door open and came face to face with Blade. His eyes flicked over her.

"You're armed," he said.

"I'm going back to the hospital."

"Lyla, you're exhausted. Maybe you should…"

She ignored him and marched downstairs and out the front door. Her attention fixed on Gavin's silver Bugatti, which rounded the drive. Her heart slammed against her chest. She had only a fuzzy memory of what went down between her and Gavin in the ICU, but it hadn't been pretty. The sight of him made her lightheaded with rage. He not only sacrificed the future of their relationship by going after Jonathan, he had put all of them at risk and this was the result. She would never forgive him.

Before she could decide what to do, the Bugatti stopped and a man unfolded from the driver's seat. It wasn't Gavin. He was gorgeous and looked fresh off the cover of Bad Boy magazine. He was tall and lean and wore a black tee with jeans and a thick leather belt riding low on his waist. He gave her a brilliant smile as he strode toward her.

She glanced at the guards who were watching their interaction closely. Nobody made a move to stop him.

Before she could move back, he grasped her shoulders and kissed her on both cheeks. She had been treated to this gesture in the past by Manny, but she was nonplussed by this greeting coming from a stranger.

"I'm Angel," he announced as if that was supposed to mean something to her.

An apt name for a man with a face like that. "Who are you?"

"I'm family."

"Excuse me?"

He looked her over. "Where are you going?"

"Who are you?"

"Where are you going?" he repeated.

"To the hospital."

He nodded. "Your mother?"

She stepped away from him. "Seriously, who are you?"

"Angel Roman."

She froze. Everyone knew about the notorious Roman family from New York. She knew the Pyres were related to the Romans but had never met any of them until now. "You're visiting?"

"Something like that," he said with a smile she didn't trust.

The door behind her opened and Blade appeared.

"Angel," Blade said, voice tight.

"Old man," Angel acknowledged and jerked his thumb at the Bugatti. "Want a ride? I'm testing out Gavin's car to see what I want to buy."

"I'll take her," Blade interjected and gestured to the guards to bring a car around.

"We'll meet you there," Angel said and draped an arm across her shoulders.

"Angel—" Blade began.

Angel turned his head. All signs of the affable bad boy vanished. His eyes were cold and sinister.

"I know who she is. You think I'd let anything happen to her?"

Blade said nothing.

"We'll meet you there," Angel said firmly and led her to the Bugatti.

She glanced at Angel as he climbed into the driver's seat and revved the engine.

"We always have drivers," Angel said conversationally as he peeled out of the driveway and barreled toward the gates. "This car is nice. What car do you drive?"

"Blade usually drives," she said faintly as they passed through the gates with inches to spare.

"Maybe when this is over you can drive yourself," Angel said easily as he shifted gears and put on mirrored shades.

Silence fell. She didn't feel like talking, especially to someone she didn't know. She looked out at the desert, which passed in a blur thanks to Angel. He might not drive often, but he handled the car with the efficiency of a race car driver.

"Gavin's going to fix this."

She tensed but didn't look at him.

"He came to New York, said he wanted to step down because you've paid too high a price for his role. We heard what happened to Uncle Manny and Vinny, but we weren't able to come out for the funerals. Shit's been tense in the city. We thought everything here was taken care of until Gavin showed up and told us about this fucker."

Something clicked in her brain. "You're taking his spot?"

"Yeah."

"You don't know what you're taking on."

"You know who I am."

"Yes."

"Then you know I was born and bred for this."

"Gavin was too."

"Gavin would do it for the rest of his life, but you want out, so he'll give you that. He's fully capable of doing this until the end of time." He shifted gears and then said, "You didn't grow up in the life. I get it, and hearing what you went through, what you're still going through, I don't blame you."

"You said Gavin went to New York?" she asked quietly.

"Yes."

"Do you know if he went anywhere else?"

Out of the corner of her eye, she saw him glance at her.

"What do you mean?"

"Do you know if he stopped anywhere else besides New York?"

"He mentioned something about Maine, I think. Why?"

Confirmation, even though she hadn't needed any. Her heart felt as if it weighed ten pounds.

"Gavin's checking on the leads from the warehouse, phone, and GPS on the vehicle you drove. He asked me to watch over you," Angel said.

"I didn't ask where Gavin is."

"I know. I'm telling you."

She fisted her hands in her lap.

"Heard you yell at him this morning." When she said nothing, he added, "Saw Blade bring you out, drug you. Heard the state your mom's in, don't fucking blame you."

The city loomed in the distance. She wanted to tell Angel to shut the fuck up but had a feeling he would ignore her order.

"Heard your dad swung the other way, and you killed him... and a bunch of others."

She closed her eyes to stop herself from attacking him.

"You may not have grown up in our world, Lyla, but you're handling yourself just fine."

"Shut up," she whispered.

"You did what you had to. Life sucks, and you're still here, protecting what's yours. There's no shame in that."

Silence descended, and she thanked her lucky stars. She focused on keeping her mind blank as Angel navigated through the city to the hospital. He parked the Bugatti. Before he could turn off the car, Blade slid into the slot beside them. She started toward the hospital and was brought to a halt by Angel who snatched her hand and laced their fingers together.

"What the hell are you doing?" she snapped and tried to pull away.

"You're shaking."

She hadn't noticed until he pointed it out. "That doesn't mean you need to hold my hand."

"Doesn't hurt." He eyed her disgruntled face and grinned. "You're cute."

"I'm not used to strange men holding my hand."

"We're family."

"How, exactly?"

"Gavin and I are first cousins."

Oh, shit. That was a little too close for comfort. "I don't need you to hold my hand. I'm fine."

He squeezed. "You're not fine. Let me take care of you."

"Why do you care?" She didn't expect a bloodthirsty Roman to be the handholding type.

"When something happens to one of us, it happens to all of us."

"I'm not family."

"You are now. You're Gavin's, which means you're mine too."

She blinked. "Excuse me?"

"You're mine," he stated boldly. "Someone fucks with you, they fuck with me. You and Gavin have been without family for too long."

She was so distracted by Angel's primitive views that it almost distracted her from what she was about to walk into. She went to the ICU desk, and when she gave her mother's name, she received a wary glance. She wasn't sure if it was because of the nature of her mother's injuries, because the nurse heard about her freak out, or because of the host of men surrounding her.

"We're limiting Beatrice Dalton's visitors," the nurse said, eyeing her group.

"We'll wait here," Angel said and kissed her cheek.

She didn't know what to make of him. He was blunt, affectionate, and annoying. She glanced at Blade before she followed the nurse to her mother's room.

"No changes," the nurse said.

Even though she knew what to expect, the sight of her mother's bandaged body with tubes coming out of her still hit her like a ton of bricks. She stopped in the doorway, unable to get her legs to move.

When she composed herself, she sat by her mother's side and cradled her hand. She stared at her mother's swollen eyelids and willed them to twitch or, better yet, open. Nothing. She rested her aching head on the edge of the bed and breathed. Her mother was all she had left. She had to live.

The beeping monitor and the sound of all the machines got on her nerves. She tried to ignore them, but the longer she sat there, the worse it got. She hated seeing all the tubes and needles and found herself reaching for the IV to rip it out of her mother's arm before she jerked away. She was turning into a fucking psycho. Was she trying to kill her own mother? She forced herself to leave.

When she left the ICU, she found Blade, Angel, and the rest of the guards in the hallway. Angel moved forward and took her hand again.

"Good. I'm starving," he said. "You hungry?"

"Hungry?"

"Let's see what they have in the cafeteria. How's your mom?"

"Same," she said numbly as she stared at their clasped hands. She was holding hands with a member of the Roman family, one of the most ruthless and notorious crime families in America.

Angel noticed her glance and shrugged.

"It's a habit you'll have to get used to. I'm always taking Luci out, and you have to keep a hold on her or she'll disappear."

"Luci?"

"My sister."

"How old is she?" she asked, trying to imagine Angel escorting a young girl around New York City.

"Twenty-five."

She was outraged. "You have to hold your twenty-five-year-old sister's hand?"

"You don't know Luci. She could get into trouble at a library."

"Do you hold your brother's hands too?" she asked snidely, offended on Luci's behalf.

"Only when they're drunk," Angel said without missing a beat.

"Do you always hold women's hands?"

"Only the ones I don't want to lose track of."

"And you're not married?"

"I have wild oats to sow, baby."

"You just said family means everything, blah, blah."

"Yeah, but that doesn't mean I have to get married. I'm sure I'll have nieces and nephews one day... and cousins. Lots of cousins. I'm built to protect; that's my job."

She wasn't hungry, but she took the tray Angel handed her. She frowned when he put a salad and sandwich on it. Blade and the other guards piled mounds of food on their trays and took up a section of the cafeteria.

"Eat," Angel said before he bit into his pizza.

When she made no move to eat, he grabbed her fork and stabbed greens and a piece of chicken. When he brought it toward her face, she snatched the fork from him. Clearly, he intended to feed her. She chewed and when she didn't go back for more, he took the fork and repeated the process.

"I can feed myself!" she snapped.

"Then do so."

"No wonder you've never married. No woman would put up with your bullshit," she muttered.

"It's not bullshit. I'm taking care of you."

"It's not your job to take care of me."

"Of course, it is."

She looked at Blade. "I can't pass on these genes. I'm not having any more kids."

"Don't count on it," Angel muttered.

She didn't realize she'd reached for her sandwich until she swallowed the first bite. She glared at Angel when he snickered. "You're annoying."

"So, I've heard. By the way, Luci wants to visit after Gavin guts this motherfucker."

"Luci?" Blade echoed.

"Yeah."

"She's coming to Las Vegas?" Blade asked sharply.

"When it's safe."

She raised her brows. "You know her?"

"Met her a long time ago," Blade said.

Angel's expression tightened. "Yes, a very long time ago."

She looked back and forth between them. "When?"

Blade glanced at Angel and then her food. "Eat and I'll tell you."

Angel held Blade's gaze for a long moment before he demolished his hospital food. Apparently, Blade had history with the Romans. Not surprising, really, but she had the feeling it wasn't going to be a happy story. Nevertheless, she wanted to hear it. When she finished, Blade dumped her tray and signaled to the other guards who were already on their feet.

As they left the cafeteria, she asked, "So, what's the story?"

When Blade didn't speak, she glanced up and saw him looking down the corridor. She followed his gaze and halted when she saw Gavin striding toward her. He wore a black suit and crimson tie. Her stomach rebelled at the sight of him.

$$19$$

LYLA

She whirled but found her way blocked by Angel and the other guards.

"Get out of my way!" she bellowed.

No one moved. She reached into her jacket for her gun. Blade disarmed her and took the second gun for good measure. Before she could snatch a weapon from one of them, a hand whirled her around. The next thing she knew, she was dangling over Gavin's shoulder.

"Let me go!" she shouted.

She wasn't up to a confrontation, and she had nothing to say to him. She pounded his back and cursed when her hand hit one of his guns. That would leave a bruise.

She heard Angel laughing and braced her hands on Gavin's back to give him a dirty look. Blade watched them with his arms crossed over his chest.

"Do something!" she snapped.

Blade shook his head before Gavin turned a corner and she lost sight of them. She was about to scream her head off when Gavin slammed into an empty hospital room. The only light came through tiny slats in the blinds.

"Gavin, don't you dare—" she began, but lost her breath when he dropped her on the bed with enough force to stun her.

He straddled her and yanked off his tie.

"What the fuck do you think you're—" she began, but was silenced by a hand over her mouth.

She tried to bite and claw, but he easily overpowered her. His tie replaced his hand. He pinned her arms to her sides using his thighs. She had never been more enraged in her life. She surged beneath him and silently vowed to make his life a living hell.

The second she could wriggle a hand free, she did so and went for his eyes. He grabbed her hand and lifted it over her head. Something cold and hard wrapped around her wrist. She tugged, realized she was handcuffed to the bedrail, and shrieked into his tie. He bound her other hand just as quickly.

"You motherfucker!" she seethed through the gag.

He splayed his body over hers, subduing her kicking legs easily. He gripped her jaw when she tried to head butt him and leaned down, close enough to see the determination burning in his eyes.

"You aren't allowed to hate me," he said quietly.

She glared at him. She could do whatever the fuck she wanted. He couldn't control her emotions.

He surveyed her rebellious face and then kissed her over the gag. She jerked back. He wasn't perturbed. He kissed the curve of her jaw, the line of her throat and then slid down to her chest. She stiffened as he unbuttoned her shirt.

"I really like the bras with these front clasps," he said conversationally as he undid hers.

She grit her teeth as he licked her nipple and then sucked one into his mouth. She yanked on her cuffs, which fucking hurt. She tried to twist away without success. His hand stroked her belly as he played with her breasts as if they were in their bedroom at home and he had all the time in the world. She saw a shadow pass by the window and began to struggle again.

When he flicked her nipple with his tongue, she jumped. He released one breast and moved to the other. She hung onto the bedrails as she tried to curb her body's reaction to his ministrations. He thought he could distract her with sex? He was sorely mistaken.

Minutes passed and her toes curled in her boots. Fucking Gavin. The sound of his suckling filled the room. She vibrated beneath him. The fucker knew every sweet spot she had and was trying to drive her crazy.

He suddenly buried his face between her breasts and clutched her to him. He took a deep breath and then another before his grip eased. He looked up and caught her gaze.

"Blade told me what happened," he said gravely. "I'm sorry."

She didn't want to hear that from him. Sorry wouldn't erase the fresh blood on her hands or her mother lying comatose in the ICU.

"I know you blame me for what happened with your parents."

She erupted beneath him. He straddled her middle and gripped her face with both hands. She had no choice but to meet his gaze. Any semblance of cool control was gone. His eyes were seething, and he was breathing hard, as if he was trying to hold something back.

"I'll take the blame for your mom, but I refuse to feel guilty about your father. If you hadn't killed him, I would," he hissed. "And nothing you said could stop me from making him suffer for even thinking of betraying you. Thank fuck you had the courage to do it, baby girl, or I'd be kneeling by your grave right now. I wouldn't survive that."

She closed her eyes against a surge of tears.

"I know you want time." A pause and then, "But when have I ever given you that?"

She opened her eyes and glared through the tears.

"You don't need time. You need me, Lyla." He shook his head, kissed both breasts, and then slid down her body to her belly. "And I need you."

He unzipped her jeans and began to peel them off. She spread her thighs in a vain attempt to keep her jeans on. Gavin cupped her pussy, and she automatically clamped her thighs together, allowing him to yank them off. Fucker. A group of nurses paused outside the room, and she panicked. She kicked him in the shoulder and jerked her head at the silhouettes. He barely spared them a glance, caught her ankle during the next kick, and bent her leg up and wide.

"Gavin, don't!" she garbled through the gag.

He settled between her thighs and kissed her over her black lace underwear. She jerked and tried to jam her heel into the back of his head with no luck. He rested his face against her inner thigh and laughed softly, which made her renew her efforts to kill her husband.

"You should know, you fighting me is only making me want you more," he said softly.

She yanked hard on the cuffs, which clanged loudly.

"I like your bite." He nipped her sensitive skin. "And you like mine."

Arrogant motherfucker. She wished she was bone dry... but she wasn't. Her stupid body was ready for him.

"Blade told me you took out trained guards and then used dead men for target practice in the warehouse. I never imagined you like this, but I like it." He ripped off her underwear and ignored her muffled swearing. "No, I love it. You protect what's yours at any cost. You're my equal, baby girl, my badass. Mine."

He put his mouth on her. She tried not to react, but it was impossible. He went deep and ate her out as if she was the rarest delicacy on the planet. She panted through the gag and didn't even have the option of trying to brain him by clamping his head between her thighs since he had them splayed wide.

It took her less than five minutes not to give a fuck about the crowd in the hallway. She forgot why she was in the hospital, how Gavin fucked up, and about her desert hunt. All that mattered was what he could give her—sweet oblivion.

"Gavin," she moaned.

His finger dipped into her pussy and then trailed to her ass. His finger explored and then circled teasingly. She didn't hesitate. She rocked back on his finger and took it up her ass. He groaned as if he was the one being tortured and raised his head.

"I can't," he hissed.

He sat up, unzipped his slacks, and planted himself deep with one thrust. There was no finesse or teasing now. He was breathing hard, and his hands cupped her ass so he could go as deep as possible. Her hands strained against the cuffs while her body undulated against him.

"I need this," he said hoarsely and buried his face in her hair. "I need to make sure you're with me."

She was with him, all right. She was so with him that if she wasn't cuffed, she would be clawing the hell out of his back and commanding him to fuck her hard.

"I can't do this again, Lyla. My heart can't take it," he said as he rocked inside her. "This needs to end. Now."

She couldn't agree more.

He lifted her legs over his shoulder, and he was hitting that spot —but not hard enough!

"Gavin!" she shouted and found him watching her.

"You're beautiful."

She milked his shaft with her inner muscles. His eyes narrowed, and he stopped his teasing, soft rhythm that wasn't taking her over the edge.

"You want me?" he growled.

She nodded and then glared for good measure.

"Then that's what you'll get," he said and slammed home.

She hung onto the handrails as Gavin did what he did best. She was glad for the gag since it muffled her moans. He hit that spot, and she erupted. He rode her through it, and then tucked his head beside hers on the pillow as he pounded her into the bed until he came with her name on his lips.

She floated. She didn't have a care in the world. She was cock drunk and liking it. Nothing existed outside this room.

Gavin lifted his head. His expression was too severe for her liking.

"Now, you're going to listen," he said.

She stared at him. Couldn't this wait?

"I went to Maine to kill Huskin."

She stiffened. Cold, hard reality replaced her drowsy weightlessness. Gavin, who was still inside her, rocked, sending pleasurable zaps through her still sensitive body.

"You know what kind of man I am," he said as his eyes bored into hers. "I'm not the schmuck who will stand aside while another man who has history with my wife makes a play. No man is allowed to touch you. No man is allowed to come between us. You don't protect another man from me. Huskin overstepped. He knows the rumors about me and still made a play for you, one he knew could mean his life. He made that decision."

Gavin brushed his hand down her cheek. He was watching her closely.

"You understand?" he asked.

Grudgingly, she nodded and felt him relax a little. He kissed her brow and continued to shift inside her as if he wanted to keep her ready for another round.

"You don't choose another man over me, Lyla."

She wasn't! As if he could read her thoughts, he leaned in closer.

"You did. I'm your first priority, not some ex you haven't seen in years, even if he has a heart of gold," he sneered. "I was raised to take what I want and destroy anybody in my way." His hands smoothed down her sides. "I don't take chances with you."

"But—"

Gavin clamped his hand over the gag. "Hush, baby girl."

She glared at him.

"I get it," he said.

Get what?

"I get why you were with him." He burrowed deeper inside her so that her mouth fell open on a gasp. "You wanted sweet and normal, baby girl, but you aren't. You never were. You were pretending. What you had with him, not real. You feel this?"

He rocked inside her. Her toes curled, and her moan filled the room.

"This is what I'm fighting for, what I'll die for. You were made for me. Maybe I'm not what you wanted, but I'm what you need." He kissed away a tear at the corner of her eye. "You should have told him about Nora from the start."

She jerked. How could he know that?

"Knowing you had a kid made a difference to him. Why do you think I insisted on getting you pregnant? It matters, having a baby together. It binds you irrevocably to me. Even he gets that." He tugged on her earlobe with his teeth. "You think I don't have time to listen to your phone calls? You're wrong. Everything that concerns you is my top priority. Don't ever make the mistake of thinking you come second to anything."

He began to move with more purpose.

"Huskin's resourceful and now an employee of mine."

She couldn't believe it.

"He created a sophisticated surveillance system designed to send evidence to another source within hours of my crime." He tucked his head beside hers and muttered, "Fucker's too smart for his own good."

"Gavin," she huffed.

He nuzzled her sweetly while his body drove her nuts.

"Being thousands of miles away when you needed me..." His voice changed, became rougher. "Worst feeling in the world knowing I left you open for that sadistic fuck to—"

There was an anguished note in his voice. She raised her hand to touch him, but it was still bound.

"I fucked up. I'll take whatever you want to throw at me. You shouldn't have been put in a position to do the things you had to do." He raised his head and looked at her. "But thank fuck you did. I'm going to make the Phantom suffer. I'm going to bring you his head so you know it's really over." He brushed his thumb over her bottom lip. "Do you hate me, baby?"

Of course, she didn't hate him, but she wasn't happy about being gagged, handcuffed, and fucked in a hospital room. He was insane. He didn't give a fuck what anyone thought, and there was no stopping him when he wanted something. She glared at him and gave him nothing.

He squeezed her breast before he reached into his jacket pocket and pulled out a key.

"I like seeing you cuffed and gagged," he mused as he released one hand. "We need to do this more often."

She yanked the gag down. "Get off, Gavin!"

He kissed her cheek when she turned her face away. "Still mad?"

"I'm going to be mad at you for eternity!"

"Eternity's a long time," he said as he released her other hand, which she immediately used to brace on his shoulders to create space between them. This was a spectacular fail since he gave her his weight and her arms collapsed.

"Fucking heavy ass brute," she huffed.

"I told you when we married to punish me." He rolled so she was on top and then manipulated the bed controls so they were in a sitting position. "Give me your best shot, Lyla." One hand went to her clit. "And I'll give you mine."

"Gavin, you can't—"

Her head kicked back as he simultaneously pinched her clit, bit her neck, and slammed balls deep into her.

"I can do anything I want," he growled against her skin. "I'm going to do whatever it takes to have you with me."

"You're such..." She panted and stopped when he did something amazing with his cock. Against her will, her arms went around him.

"Such what?" he crooned into her sweat-soaked hair as he controlled her movements with his hands on her ass.

"You're—you—you fuck..." She couldn't string a sentence together, much less think of a decent insult when he was pleasuring her.

"This is how I need you, desperate for me."

She was dimly aware of the mechanical whirr of the bed as it switched positions. She braced her hands on either side of his head as the bed flattened and caught a glimpse of his hungry expression before he sank a hand into her hair and pulled her down until their lips collided. He banded a hand around her waist to keep her in place as he fucked her. Gavin drank in her moans, pleas, and whimpers and demanded more. She ripped the sheets from the bed as she climaxed, wrapped herself around him and hung on for dear life. He planted himself deep and came while brushing kisses over her face.

"You don't play fair," she whispered.

He didn't answer as he ran his hands over her naked body while he was still fully clothed. She laid her cheek on his chest and listened to his rapid heartbeat as her tremors ebbed.

"I was so scared," she whispered.

His hands stilled.

"I told Carmen to run with Nora. All I had was one gun, eight bullets. I hid and waited." She let out a shuddering breath and his hands began to move again, stroking and soothing. "I heard them talking about fucking Mom. I killed them."

She could still feel the gun bucking in her hand and the chill of the desert.

"I went cold. I didn't care who they were. I just pulled the trigger." She let out a long breath. "All I could think about was what they were doing to her." She swallowed hard. "I shot dead bodies."

"Would it make you feel better to know I've done the same?"

"You have?"

"They're good target practice."

She raised her head. "Are you serious?"

"Lyla, no matter what you do, I've already done it."

"That shouldn't make me feel better, but it does. Do you have any leads?"

His energy, which had eased considerably after two orgasms, flooded the room. The hairs on the nape of her neck rose.

"Not yet, but I'll get him, Lyla."

"He's playing us." Cold fury poured through her. She couldn't stop it. She dug her nails into his chest and felt his muscles flex in response. "I want his head, Gavin. Whatever it takes, you do it."

He kissed her hard and deep and then drew away with his chest heaving.

"You were made for me," he murmured. "Do you still hate me?"

She thumped him on the shoulder and slid off him. Her legs weren't quite steady when they hit the floor. "I'll think about it."

She swiped up her jeans and was thankful for the connecting bathroom so she could wash up. She looked thoroughly fucked. Her cheeks were flushed, hair a tangled mess, lips swollen, and eyes glazed with satisfaction. Damn Gavin.

He came into the bathroom, looking disgustingly slick. His suit was a bit rumpled, but he appeared just as composed as he had when he brought her in here.

"I'm leaving Blade, Angel, and eight guards," Gavin said, running a hand through his hair. "I have two men watching Carmen's mother just in case."

She nodded and turned to face him. "Angel tells me he's going to take your place. He's... interesting."

"You'll get used to him."

"Can he do it?" she asked, thinking of Vinny.

"He's from New York."

"Meaning?"

"Meaning he won't let anyone fuck with him." He caged her against the sink. "You okay?"

She nodded.

He cupped her face. "I'm sorry."

She blinked back tears. "It's done. Go get him."

He kissed her and then led her out of the hospital room. Blade and Angel were talking in the hallway. They turned when the door opened.

"Did you kiss and make up?" Angel asked with a lascivious grin.

"You're annoying," she snapped.

"Lyla!"

She looked down the corridor and saw Marcus rushing toward her. When he reached for her, Angel blocked his way.

"Who are you?" he asked aggressively.

Marcus looked Angel up and down before he asked, "Who are you?"

"Angel Roman."

Marcus glanced at Gavin before he held out a hand. "Marcus. We've never met. I usually deal with Raul."

"Raul's the businessman," Angel acknowledged and shook his hand.

Marcus walked around him and engulfed her in a hug. "How are you, honey?"

"You let him touch your wife?" Angel demanded of Gavin.

"Lyla won't let me kill him, and he makes me a lot of money."

"Still, he isn't family," Angel muttered.

She rolled her eyes at the Neanderthals and pulled back to give Marcus a tremulous smile. "What are you doing here?"

"Gavin told me what happened. Are you all right?"

"I'm okay."

"Carmen?"

"Good. She's home with Nora."

Marcus cupped her face. "Be safe, dammit."

"I will."

Marcus kissed her on the cheek. "I have to get back, but I had to see you." He looked at Gavin. "Let me know when it's over."

Gavin nodded. "I will. Now, get back to the casino. The cops are all over us."

Marcus nodded and left without another word.

"He's a ballsy bastard, isn't he?" Angel muttered.

"He's great," she said defensively.

"You can't touch men like that outside the family. It's indecent."

Her mouth sagged. "What did you just say?"

"Gav, you can't let her—"

"Since when does a hug equal giving a guy head?"

"We don't let our women—" Angel began.

"Not the time." Gavin cupped her face and kissed her one last time. "I love you. Stay with Blade and Angel."

"Where are you going?" she asked.

"Hunting."

With that, he walked away, leaving her with mixed emotions.

"Can you walk?" Angel asked with false concern.

Blade elbowed Angel with enough force to make him gasp for air and sink to one knee. She tipped her nose in the air and walked back to the ICU. When she sat by her mother's side and took her hand again, she felt more human and a lot less like a ticking time bomb.

Gavin would find Sadist and kill him. She had to keep that front and center in her mind so she wouldn't go crazy. Despite the fact that Sadist always seemed to be five steps ahead, she had to remember that he was human and could bleed... and therefore die.

She looked up as two nurses walked in. She released her mother's hand and took a step back so they could do what they needed to. She watched the nurse check her mother's drip and noticed that her hand was shaking. Too much caffeine?

"Mrs. Pyre," the other nurse said, drawing her attention. "Are you doing all right?"

"As well as can be under the circumstances," she said.

"Do the police have any leads?"

She felt something tight grip her heart. "No."

The second nurse rummaged in the cart beside the bed. Obviously not finding what she was looking for, she moved toward another cart in the corner.

"I haven't seen a case this bad in years," the first nurse said and squeezed her arm. "I'm so sorry."

"Thank you," she said and was dimly aware of the second nurse moving behind her.

"We're going to do everything we can for your mother, okay?"

"Okay—" she began and hissed when something pricked her neck. She recognized the feeling since Blade sedated her only a couple of hours ago. She reached up to pull the syringe out, but before she could her legs gave out and she crashed to the floor.

"Hurry up, get her on the gurney. We'll wheel her out under a sheet and then—" the nurse said and then everything went black.

20

LYLA

She woke feeling like her arms were going to fall off. She moaned and realized several things simultaneously. She was on her knees on cold, hard stone. She was also blindfolded, gagged, and her hands were bound behind her. It took a full minute for her to think past the pounding in her head. She scooted backward to ease the tension on her shoulders. Her hands hit rough cement walls and skated down to discover that the chain shackling her wrists together behind her back were threaded through a metal circle at the base of the wall. The length of chain allowed her to rest on her knees, but it wasn't long enough to allow her to stand.

She leaned against the wall, but this did nothing to alleviate her cramping muscles. Memories of the nurses passed through her mind. She bared her teeth as rage beat back the fear. If those nurses hurt her mother, she would gut them herself.

She shifted and heard the clink of a chain, which seemed unnaturally loud in the enclosed space. Unlike the cuffs Gavin had used on her earlier, the metal shackles on her wrist were at least three inches thick and no joke. Her watch with the GPS was gone and so was her wedding ring. She was still in her jeans and button up top, but her leather jacket and shoulder holster were gone.

The sound of an agonizing scream reached her ears followed by another. Her heart leaped. Was this Sadist's torture chamber? Her mouth watered as bile rose. She struggled to swallow since the gag was so tight that her mouth couldn't close. Her lips ached. She tried to shift the gag out of her mouth by rubbing it against her shoulder. When her neck cramped, she straightened abruptly and let out an infuriated scream.

Fuck Sadist! If he was going to kill her, get it over with! Even as her emotions raged, an image of Nora appeared in her mind. She yanked savagely against the chain. Nora needed her. So did Gavin. Oh, Gavin. He would Hulk out. And Carmen would freak out too. She should have stayed at home like Carmen said, but no, she had to sit by her mother's bedside and now here she was in... wherever the fuck this was.

She wasn't sure if seconds, minutes, or hours passed. Her shoulders burned, went numb, and then came to life with a dozen needles stabbing into her, making her moan in pain. She tried to work the gag free without success. She went through every emotion possible, yanking at the chains and growling like a wild animal. When rage obliterated all thought, she finally gave into the tears of helpless rage and then despair.

She heard the jingle of keys and thought she was hallucinating. Then she heard the squeak of a doorknob and a slight gust of wind as the door swung open. Through the blindfold, she saw the faintest hint of light. She balled her hands into fists. Would he stab her to death? Beat the crap out of her or just slit her throat?

She breathed heavily through her nose as she waited. And waited. The screams she heard earlier were loud and piercing now that the door was open. Her heart pounded with dread and fear. She scooted back and then stiffened when the door closed and she was thrown back into complete darkness. What the fuck?

There was no sound in the room. Was a guard checking on her? Someone had the wrong room? She didn't hear the scrape of a key in the lock. Dizzy with fear, she waited for something to happen. Long minutes passed. She shivered and then moaned as a shaft of pain shot through her arms.

"Lyla."

The voice came out of the darkness right in front of her. She screamed and reared back so hard that she collided with the wall. It was him—Sadist. She would never forget that soft voice. Her body erupted with goose bumps, and she completely lost her shit. She fought against the chains, desperate to get away from him. Two years had passed since this monster murdered Manny and carved her up. There was no one to save her, just like last time. This was it. This was the end.

"It's been too long," Sadist crooned.

She faced the direction his voice emanated from and screamed. If she weren't bound, she would claw his eyes out and try to kill him with her teeth.

"I must say, I like seeing you like this."

Of course, he did. He was a sick fuck.

"You know, Lyla, you're quite fascinating. You have nine lives. You're my only victim who survived. The cuts I made were fatal, yet here you are."

Oh, God, he sounded closer. She imagined he had a knife held in front of him that she would impale herself on if she was stupid enough to try to attack him with her arms bound behind her. She tried to get away from him, but there was nowhere to go. She willed the wall to swallow her. She couldn't be at the mercy of this man twice. God wasn't that cruel, was he?

"Imagine my surprise when I bribe Gavin's guards to kill you and, even pregnant, you survive. What are the odds?"

The touch of a smooth hand against her cheek made her stomach revolt. She edged away, but the stupid chains kept her in place. The touch came again, a finger stroking down her cheek and then her neck.

"You're so beautiful. Everyone sees what you want them to see, but I know better."

He grabbed the front of her shirt and pulled. Buttons popped off and then rolled across the floor. She scooted back, which did nothing to deter him. He ran his hands over her raised chest scars and hummed in the back of his throat. Her stomach heaved, and she resolutely swallowed. Oh, God. What was he doing?

"You bear my mark, Lyla. What does Pyre think of that? I hope he thinks of me every time he touches you. The almighty Gavin Pyre brought to his knees by little old me."

Sadist chuckled. She was lightheaded with rage. This monster killed Manny, stabbed her, and ordered the brutal rape of her mother. He was right here, inches from her, and she could do nothing.

"I heard you killed your father." A pause and then, "That's something you and I have in common, killing a family member, but they deserved it, right? You've become quite heartless, Lyla. I like it."

His hand collared her throat and brushed over her fluttering pulse. She tried to evade his touch with no luck. She was powerless to do anything and he knew it.

"Such fire. What happened to the sweet innocent who pleaded for Manny Pyre's life?" Even as her breath caught in her throat, he continued, "You still don't know who I am, do you? I always wondered if you would figure it out, but you never noticed me. I thought you were different at first, but you turned out like every other woman. I hate women. I've never met one who wasn't focused on the bottom line. My mom sold me to my dad for two thousand bucks, and my dad abused the hell out of me, trying to turn me into a tough guy like Gavin. What Dad never realized is I don't have to be a tough guy. I can be my own type of man, and that's even more powerful. I'll never be able to kill Gavin, but I know someone who can."

She felt a thrill of fear when she heard the hiss of a zipper. One hand slid through her hair and over her bruised lips.

"I approached your father. He was in deep, of course. He was about to lose his house and was ripe for the picking since he hates Gavin. Who doesn't? He's a rich, macho asshole who thinks the world should bow at his feet. He collects more enemies than anyone I know, but too many still fear him. They're here tonight to watch the crime lord take his final bow."

His hand traced her scars with frightening familiarity.

"Your father sold you and your daughter to me for five hundred thousand. We took your mother for insurance and raped her in front of him so he knew the score. I never intended to let either of them live. First, you survive my blade and now your mother. It's quite... aggravating."

When she screamed her fury at him, he tapped her nose reprovingly.

"Tonight is my finale; the end of the Pyre Empire and the beginning of my reign. Lucifer will lure Gavin here after I'm done with you. He's the only one who can take Gavin, and he has a score to settle with him. I need Gavin's end to be public, so there's no mistaking who's in control now. Too bad you won't be able to watch, but I promised Lucifer I'd give him a show in return for ending Gavin."

He sank a hand into her hair and gripped as he pressed his cheek to hers and inhaled deeply. His skin shouldn't be soft, smooth, and warm. No human could be this evil. She tried to knock him off balance, but the fucking chain kept her anchored and harmless. Fuck!

"Are you ready to give everyone a show?" A cold finger traveled over the scar inches from her heart. His breath hitched. "Lucifer taught me how to kill, how to prolong a death, how to make people respect you. You have to do it with flair. Gavin's good at that, but then again, so am I."

His voice was uneven. Her heartbeat slowed as if his voice was poison. Her body felt heavy with dread and hopelessness. This was how she would die, with Sadist's voice in her ears.

"Unfortunately, Lucifer says I'm not allowed to touch you until everyone's present to enjoy it. Shame. I'm going to enjoy this, Lyla. I always finish what I start, which means I'm paying your daughter a visit tomorrow."

His hand gripped her hair and yanked back savagely. He groaned and then she felt a string of something wet and warm splatter over her face. She retched and tried to turn her face away, but Sadist kept her still until he was done. He panted and examined his handiwork before he shoved her so she fell on her side on the floor.

"That's for my father," he said.

There was no sound of retreating footsteps, but she felt a draft when the door opened. She saw a flash of light through the blindfold and heard torturous screams before the door closed, enclosing her in hell.

21

GAVIN

HE BLASTED THE WOMAN'S HEAD OFF AND ALLOWED THE WARM SPRAY OF blood to splash over him. He waited for a flicker of satisfaction, but he felt absolutely nothing.

The nurse who had taken Lyla did it as a favor for her crackhead boyfriend who worked for Marcel, a gangbanger he had never heard of. Both nurses, the crackhead boyfriend, and Marcel lay at his feet. None of them had shit for him, which meant they were pawns. It had to be Phantom. The thought of Lyla in his grasp made his insides contract. He held up her wedding ring and watch, which had been in the nurse's pocket.

"What now?" Angel asked.

He called on every contact he had, but everyone's phones were off. No one was at home, in their office, or on The Strip. They were just... gone. Something was going down tonight. He sensed it with every fiber of his being. He had no leads, no one to hunt. Nothing.

His phone rang. He reached into his pocket, eyed the unavailable number, and put it to his ear.

"Gavin."

It took him a moment to place the voice. When he did, something close to fear shot through his system. "Lucifer."

The man on the other end chuckled. "I'm flattered you recognize my voice."

It had been years, but no one forgot the sound of the devil's voice. Angel and Blade were watching him, but they didn't ask questions; they waited patiently.

"I have something you want," Lucifer said.

Every hair on the nape of his neck stood.

"I'll be waiting for you."

Lucifer hung up. He slowly lowered the phone and took a deep breath.

Blade's hands balled into fists at his side. "Lucifer's involved in this shit?"

"So it seems."

"Who's Lucifer?" Angel asked.

"I need to go home," he said and snatched the keys for the Bugatti out of Angel's pocket.

"What the fuck? You're going to get changed when you know where she is?" Angel asked.

"Lucifer won't start until we get there. He likes an audience." He glanced at Blade. "Burn the fucking house down."

He got into the Bugatti and tore out of the neighborhood. In his rearview mirror, he saw the flicker of flames.

Nine hours ago, Angel forced his way into the ICU and found Lyla missing. It took too fucking long for them to figure out what happened and hunt these fuckers down. When he got the call about Lyla missing, Blade had a syringe ready, but his wrath was ice cold. He couldn't afford to lose his shit.

He pulled up to his home. The guards that came toward the car froze when he emerged looking like an extra from Kill Bill. He walked in the house and took the stairs two at a time. He stripped off his suit, showered, and redressed. When he finished, he slipped on brass knuckles and strapped on a collection of knives. He walked out of the bedroom and hesitated only a moment before he entered the nursery.

Carmen sat in the rocking chair with Nora in the crook of her arm. Her face was ravaged with worry and fear. Bloodshot eyes flicked to him when he entered. She rose.

"Did you find her?" she whispered.

"I got a call from Lucifer."

He didn't need to say more. Carmen understood. The blood drained out of her face.

"Lyla's in Hell?"

He didn't answer. He didn't allow himself to wonder what they'd done to her because that would shatter his control and he couldn't go into Hell with anything but a clear head. He had to believe she was there, alive and whole. Any alternative was unacceptable. He took Nora from Carmen. His daughter blinked up at him with her mother's eyes. The edges of his control began to fray. He suppressed the killing haze and buried his face against his daughter to drink her in.

This would end tonight. If Lyla didn't return, neither would he.

"Gavin," Carmen whispered.

He clenched his teeth to hold back the rage building in his throat. His hands shook as he held his daughter. Nora kicked his chest and waved her arms. She looked up at him with such trust and innocence. *I'll bring Mom back.* He said it silently because he wasn't capable of speaking. He tipped her against his chest and took a deep breath, the first in what felt like hours.

Carmen's baby blue eyes shimmered with tears. "Bring her back."

He nodded and handed the baby over. "Take care of her."

Carmen's fear clouded the air. "Gavin."

"No matter what happens, you take care of Nora," he ordered.

Tears began to fall.

"Promise me," he snapped.

"You can't do this to me."

"Promise me, Carmen."

She grabbed a handful of his shirt and yanked. He obliged and took a step forward. He and Carmen had a long and complicated history. They loved with an abandonment one never recovered from, and they loved the same people, Vinny and Lyla. They'd both lost Vinny. He'd be fucking damned if he lost Lyla, and he saw the same fire in her eyes. If Carmen didn't have Nora to care for, she would come with him. He had no doubt Carmen would spill blood if it meant getting her cousin back.

"You bring her back," she said hoarsely. "And you make that motherfucker pay."

He nodded, and she released him.

"You got this, Gavin."

"You armed?" he asked, even though there was a host of men on property.

She lifted her sweater to show a gold gun in the waistband of her pants. He nodded and turned away from her.

"Be safe," she called after him.

He blocked out the sound of Nora fussing. Angel and Blade were waiting in the driveway. He glanced at his men who looked uneasy. It was clear Blade told them their destination.

"Good luck, boss," Barrett said, and several others echoed it.

He nodded and slid into the passenger seat. Blade floored it. No one spoke as they zoomed toward the neon lights of The Strip.

"I called Marcus, told him if this goes bad, he becomes CEO," Blade said.

He nodded and glanced at Angel in the back seat. "You don't have to come."

"Don't, Gav."

"You don't know what this is."

"Then why don't you explain it to me since Blade hasn't said shit. Who's Lucifer? You think he's the one who did in Uncle Manny?"

"No, it wasn't Lucifer." He was sure of it. Lucifer didn't wear masks. He wanted people to know about his kills.

"So, Lucifer is helping the guy who did in Uncle Manny?" Angel surmised.

"Looks that way."

"And this Lucifer is a big shot in the underworld?"

"Not in the underworld."

"Then where?"

"In Hell."

"Hell?"

"A Death Club."

"A what?"

"An underground fight club gladiator style where only one opponent lives. No guns allowed. It's also a brothel and slave trade hub."

Angel leaned between the two front seats. "And this is all under the radar?"

"Yes."

"An underground fight club, huh?"

"The brothel is for hardcore customers. It's common for the whores to die on the job," Blade said. "And who knows what else goes on there."

"Why would Lucifer want Lyla or work with the guy who did in Uncle Manny?" Angel asked.

"Because he has a score to settle," Blade said. "Gavin broke the rules and Lucifer's never forgiven him for it."

"How'd you break the rules?"

"Only one opponent survives," Gavin said. "I fought Lucifer and didn't kill him."

"Why not?"

"Because I didn't want to run Hell."

A pause and then, "So what did you do?"

"I knocked him out and left. Haven't been back since. Lyla's the only reason I'd go back and Lucifer knows it."

"You think Lucifer kidnapped Lyla so you two can duel to the death?" Angel asked.

"I don't know." He had a feeling Phantom was involved. Lucifer wasn't the kidnapping type.

"How long has it been since you beat him?"

"Five years ago." The day after Lyla left him the first time.

"Whose side is Lucifer on?"

"No one's." He rubbed his thumb against the brass knuckles, which had done damage in his youth. "In Hell, anything goes. The people who go to a place like this are killers looking for the kind of entertainment they can't get anywhere else." He thought of Lyla being in a place like that and closed his eyes. Lucifer wouldn't do anything to her yet.

"How come you never told me about Hell? Fuck. This place sounds like Disneyland."

"You might want to call Raul," Blade said.

"No need. We're all coming out of this alive," Angel said.

Blade bypassed the glittering Strip and turned onto a dingy street with broken streetlights, dirty liquor stores, and abandoned buildings. Blade pulled into the parking lot of a nude bar. The sign out front wasn't lit, and only two other cars were in the vicinity.

"No one's here," Angel said.

"There's lots of ways into Hell. This is one of them," Blade said. "There's a locked compartment under your seat. Stash your gun there."

Gavin didn't take his eyes from the shabby building, which had no windows.

"You have a knife?" Blade asked Angel.

"Of course."

"Good. You're going to need it," Blade said as they stepped into the bar.

Death and depression clung to the walls of this place. He could taste it in his mouth. The dancers moved with a sluggishness that indicated they were high on something. The men lounging in the dark corners didn't move or speak. The beat of music struck a dark chord in him. The type of people drawn to this place had no hope or souls. These men didn't care whether they lived or died. Once you entered Hell, your life was on the line. Many entered, few left breathing.

He ignored the dancers, patrons, and bartender as he weaved between the tables. He walked through an open door beside the stage. The light here wasn't much better. He walked down a hallway with rotting planks and into the dressing room where the dancers were doing drugs and completely oblivious to their presence. He turned to the walk-in closet, which was filled with the shit strippers wore before they bared it all. He pushed on the wall of hooker shoes, and it swung open.

"Holy fuck. We don't have shit like this in New York. We have to step it up," Angel murmured.

Gavin led the way down the narrow, creaking staircase and approached a group of men guarding a black metal door. They were smoking and playing poker. One man looked up and surveyed them with one eye. His empty socket was on full display.

"We got Vegas royalty here, boys," he drawled.

The men threw down their cards and started patting them down.

"You fighting?" one of the men asked.

Gavin didn't answer because it went without saying. They spied his brass knuckles and admired his knives before they moved onto Blade.

"That you, Blade? It's been a while, hasn't it?" One Eye stepped to the side so he could see Angel. "Who are you, pretty boy?"

"This is my cousin, Angel," he said.

One Eye grinned, displaying the three teeth he had left.

"We make demons out of angels here." One Eye suddenly narrowed his eyes. "Your cousin?" He eyed Angel with more interest. "You a Roman?"

Angel nodded, and One Eye elbowed his friend.

"Roque's brother."

"You know my brother?" Angel asked.

"Everyone knows your brother. He stepped into the arena several times. Those were nights to remember."

"They're clean," the other man announced.

"Lucifer expecting you?" One Eye asked Gavin.

"Yes."

"I have a feeling tonight's gonna be entertaining, boys." His eye roved over the three of them and nodded. "Very entertaining."

One Eye opened the door and gave them a mocking bow as they passed.

"Welcome to Hell, my brothers."

He walked forward and heard Angel suck in a breath. Hell was a two-story amphitheater with wide staircases that led to the sandy pit that saw more action than the Colosseum. Nearly every seat in the arena was taken. The only sound in Hell was metal clashing as the men in the pit fought with swords, rousing Gavin's beast.

He turned to the scattered tables in front of the bar where men watched the action on screens instead of the bloodthirsty crowd where their throats could be slit. He focused on a man lounging at a table with a crossword puzzle in front of him, drinking Coke. The giant man watched the TV screen as idly as if he were watching a commercial. He snorted in disgust when one of the fighters was decapitated. He twirled a pen between two fingers and scanned the crowd. When he saw Gavin, the pen stopped moving and a wide smile curved his mouth. Lucifer's Polynesian, Russian, and Swedish blood made him into a monster of a man. Despite his size and reputation, he managed to appear as unthreatening as a California surfer, but Gavin knew better. Lucifer knew every method on earth to kill a man. He resisted the compulsion to grab his knife as they approached.

"I never thought I'd see the day when you lost control of the underworld," Lucifer said in greeting.

"I want my wife."

Lucifer waved a hand with red nail polish. "I heard you were partial to your wife, but I didn't believe it. What makes her different from any other?"

He wasn't going to have this conversation with him. "Give her to me."

Lucifer ignored his order and steepled his hands in front of him, fingers touching at the tip, perfectly aligned. "A friend of mine came to me with a generous offer. He offered to share the experience of torturing your wife in the pit using his considerable skills and then summon you for the rematch I've been waiting for."

Blade and Angel crowded him, ready to restrain him if need be, but his demon was in control, and it wasn't easily baited, not with Lyla's life at stake.

"This is generous of my friend," Lucifer continued blithely, "but you and I go way back, Gavin, and I want a fair fight. I want you clear-headed, not distracted because you see your wife in pieces."

"I have no interest in ruling Hell."

Lucifer's eyes danced with excitement. "So sure you'll beat me?"

"Yes." He had no choice but to win. He wouldn't think of any other outcome.

Lucifer waved a hand. "Come now, Gavin. I think you'll come to appreciate Hell as much as I do. My friend can run the underworld and you, Hell. I'm sure you two can see eye to eye if you put your hostilities aside."

"No."

"Was what he did so bad? He set you free, Gavin."

"What the fuck are you talking about?"

"After he murdered your father, you went on a rampage. I'm impressed you managed to hide that many bodies. That's you, your true self, the one your father knew you would become. That's why he put you in the pit at twelve."

He felt Angel's sidelong glance and ignored it.

"You and I are one and the same." Lucifer licked his lips. "We need violence the way other people need sex."

"What I need is my wife."

Lucifer snorted. "Your obsession with this one woman is unhealthy."

"Is she alive?" Blade asked.

Lucifer's eyes flicked to him and narrowed. "Going soft, Blade?"

"Is she?" Angel demanded.

"You Romans, so family oriented," Lucifer mocked. "What are you doing here, Angel?"

"You know me?"

"Of course. You've built up quite a reputation in New York."

"Then you'll be happy to hear that Angel's going to take my place in the underworld," he said. "So, your friend is out of the running."

Lucifer rarely poked his head out of Hell, but if he chose to, he could make Angel's rule of the underworld hell on earth.

"A Roman in Sin City?" Lucifer mused with a cruel smile. "What about New York?"

"Raul can handle it, and Roque will be out soon. I need a challenge," Angel said.

Lucifer chuckled. "You came to the right place. These two," he jerked his head at Gavin, "have torn the underworld apart."

"I didn't start this war," he said quietly.

"Are you sure?"

"Yes."

An agonizing scream from the pit incited a cheer from the crowd.

Lucifer stacked his feet on the chair opposite and considered him. "My friend came to me because he needs you to die publicly, and he can't match you. He's been saving you for me. A gift, if you will. Tonight's the finale."

Lucifer didn't blink his soulless eyes. He was like a snake, waiting for the perfect moment to strike.

"Word on the street is that you're going soft, Gavin. You step down as crime lord for some woman, and now the city is in shambles. Every enemy you ever made is here tonight to watch you lose your throne."

"What do you want, Lucifer?"

"I told you, a fair fight."

"That isn't it." He was certain of it.

Lucifer loved games, especially one with high stakes. It was no coincidence that Lucifer called him before Lyla was brought into the pit. Lucifer wanted something bad enough to double-cross his friend.

Lucifer spread his hands. "What could I possibly want?"

He had no fucking clue what a man like Lucifer could want from him. "You tell me."

Lucifer said nothing for a long minute. In the pit, there was the sound of a cracking whip and a piercing scream.

"You and I both know there's very little in life that interests me," Lucifer drawled. "Everything is so fleeting." He gestured to the TV screen as a whip sliced a man's face open. "Tonight, I would enjoy my friend's show and I could fight you, but then it's over like that." He snapped his fingers. "And then I'm bored again."

It took every ounce of his control not to grab Lucifer by the throat and throttle him. He didn't have time for Lucifer's sociopathic ramblings, but he held all the cards. Lucifer held the key to two things Gavin needed: Lyla and the Phantom's identity. Fuck.

"I'm looking for an arrangement with more longevity," Lucifer said.

He ignored the chill that ran down his spine. "Which is?"

"I've always had a soft spot for you, Gavin. We have a lot in common. We were both raised in Hell. You part time, of course. I can't deny I'm happy to see you home. This is where you belong."

There was no point in arguing with Lucifer, so he said nothing. Angel and Blade were very still on either side of him. They were all waiting for the axe to fall.

"I call you into Hell, and you walk in as if you own the place in a fucking suit, knowing that alone is enough to make men want your head." Lucifer grinned. "Fuck. I have your wife, your Achilles' heel, and you come in stone cold. He wanted you on your knees, but you'll never give in." Lucifer shook his head. "Fuck, Gavin, I've missed sparring with you."

"What do you want, Lucifer?"

"What do you think about being my sidekick?"

His beast slipped the chain. He leaned forward. Wood crackled as he sank his brass knuckles an inch into the table. "Not gonna happen. What do you want?"

Lucifer drummed his fingers. "For starters, I want a good show."

"A good show," he repeated flatly. Lucifer's idea of a show was to watch someone dismember a body piece by piece.

"My friend and I go way back. Not as far as you and I, but still... He keeps in touch and brings me gifts, unlike you."

He couldn't imagine what kind of 'gifts' Lucifer enjoyed. Lucifer had been born in Hell and had seen and done things that made his stomach churn.

Blade stepped forward. "You want a show?"

Lucifer's eyes glinted with bloodlust. "Always."

"Then we'll give you one," Blade decreed. "All of us will fight."

Lucifer eyed them each in turn, weighing what he knew of their combat skills.

"I want more," Lucifer said, and shifted his focus back to Gavin. "Why did you stop coming to Hell?"

"What?"

"You used to come once a month. You took on as many men as you could in an hour and then left, calm as you please. Then one night you show up, challenge me, beat me, don't kill me, and never return. What changed?"

Lucifer might not have normal emotions like compassion or fear, but he possessed a healthy dose of curiosity. Although Lucifer wore an indifferent expression, his eyes were anything but.

"I found a reason to live." Like the women he used, Hell was another outlet. When Lyla left, it changed everything. He didn't realize he loved her until she disappeared. Finding out what happened to her became an obsession, a drive that overrode his destructive demon. The fight with Lucifer was the last time he'd indulged himself and then he went cold until he got her back.

Lucifer's lip curled into a sneer. "And you live for your wife?"

Blade shifted. "Lyla's special."

"There's no such thing as a special woman."

"You must have heard about her body count. It's pretty impressive."

Lucifer waved a hand. "She ran over some guys with a car and shot a couple of morons. Big deal."

"She killed her father."

Lucifer's attention sharpened. "Her father?"

His sudden interest made Gavin tense. Blade was trying to negotiate for Lyla's life by playing on Lucifer's fondness for the violently unique, but he had a feeling this could backfire in a bad way.

"Her father sold her out. Lyla found him about to murder her kid. She shot him, no hesitation."

Lucifer looked at Gavin. "You have a kid?"

"A daughter," he said grudgingly.

Lucifer's expression was thoughtful as he asked, "What else?"

"Lyla unloaded a clip each into three men who raped her mother. She has nine kills, and she just started. Who knows what she'll do in the years to come?"

Lucifer looked unduly impressed. Graphic images of what he could do to Lucifer danced through his mind. He forced himself to look away and saw Angel staring at Lucifer as if they'd uncovered the devil. He understood the feeling. Dad brought him here to teach him a lesson—about real evil and how little those in Hell cared for life.

"Can you imagine how their daughter will turn out?" Blade continued. "Between Gavin and Lyla, she's going to be a monster."

He glared at Blade. What the fuck was he doing?

"They could have more kids," Blade went on. "Do you know what havoc they'll wreak? They could be regular patrons here."

Lucifer held up a hand. "Okay, okay. Fuck." Lucifer downed the last of his Coke as if it was a shot and got to his feet. "I have conditions."

He shifted restlessly. Blade gripped his arm and squeezed.

"First, I'm coming with," Lucifer declared.

Blade nodded.

"Two, I meet them once a year."

He stiffened. "Meet who?"

"Lyla and your kid."

He started toward Lucifer, but Angel and Blade held him back.

"What for?" Angel asked.

"To hear about their kills," Lucifer said as if that should be obvious.

"What if Lyla doesn't kill anyone else?" Blade asked.

"If she's as interesting as you say, that shouldn't be a problem."

"Why do you want to see the kid?"

Lucifer had a peculiar expression on his face. "I've never been a part of a child's life."

"For good reason," Angel muttered.

Lucifer frowned. "I could teach her. With their blood in her veins, she has to be a fighter. It would be... interesting."

He lunged, but Blade and Angel hauled him back.

Lucifer frowned at him. "Don't you want your daughter to be prepared?"

"For what?" he asked through clenched teeth. Adrenaline pumped through his body. The sounds of another battle in the pit made him yearn to feel the clash of steel and give Lucifer the fight he hungered for.

"Your daughter will be hunted all her life," Lucifer said and he stilled. "Your family has generations upon generations of enemies. Even if you step down, it'll never stop. Once you're in, you can't get out." Lucifer spread his arms wide. "I can teach her how to be invincible. She's a girl, so..." Lucifer tapped his chin. "I can teach her how to use her brain and not her strength. Even if she turned into a weight lifter, she couldn't best a man that way. She has to think dirty. Pluck out eyes, rip off dicks. That kind of thing."

Lucifer was definitely insane, but something strange was going on. It was almost as if he was feeling paternal. Angel shuddered, and Gavin made up his mind.

"Fine."

Lucifer stopped listing all the ways Nora could kill with her bare hands. "Huh?"

"You can teach Nora when I think she's ready to know that shit." Hopefully Lucifer was murdered before that time came. If not, he would take care of Lucifer himself.

"What about annual visits?"

"No."

Lucifer crossed his arms. "Then the deal's off."

"Fuck. Fine. It'll be supervised."

Lucifer pointed at all of them. "You all fight tonight, right? I want three deaths per man, so nine deaths minimum. I want them bloody."

He would drop as many bodies as he had to. "Deal."

"I want *bloody*, got it?"

"The faster you give me my wife, the faster you get your fight," he snapped.

Lucifer held out a hand. Angel and Blade released him. When Gavin went to shake his hand, Lucifer withdrew.

"Maybe you and I can spar occasionally?"

"Two seconds or the deal's off," he barked.

Lucifer quickly shook his hand. "Okay, fine. *Geez.*"

"Take me to my wife."

Lucifer went to the bar and grabbed another Coke before he waved a hand, indicating they should follow. Lucifer led them down a dimly lit hallway and halted before a red elevator. He pressed the down button and turned to Gavin.

"You know, there hasn't been a kid in Hell since you and me?" Lucifer asked as he popped the top of his soda.

"For good reason," Gavin said. "Our fathers were the only ones fucked up enough to have us fight to the death before we were teenagers."

Once more, he felt Angel's glance but didn't return it.

Lucifer shrugged. "It's kept us alive."

The elevator arrived. They stood behind Lucifer with their hands on their weapons as the elevator traveled down two floors. The elevator opened to reveal a hallway with red walls and carpet. Moans, squeaking beds, screaming, and snapping whips echoed down the corridor.

Lucifer walked up to the first room and opened the door. Gavin shoved him aside, expecting to see Lyla. Instead, he found a man fucking a woman chained to the wall. There was blood everywhere. Whether it was his or hers, he didn't know or care. He slammed the door and turned on Lucifer who was opening the next door, exposing a woman stomping on a man's dick. The woman looked up.

"Carry on. Wrong room," Lucifer called and shut the door.

"What the fuck are you doing?"

"I don't know which room she's in. She's here somewhere."

When he reached for Lucifer, Blade stepped between them.

"How many rooms are there?" Blade asked Lucifer.

"Sixty-six."

"If you're fucking with me—" Gavin began.

"I'm not," Lucifer said crisply. "They should be coming for her any minute now."

Blade and Angel ran through the hallway, opening and closing doors. He slammed Lucifer against the wall and grabbed him by the throat. When he began to apply pressure, Lucifer did nothing to stop him. On the contrary, he looked delighted.

"You're trying to change your stripes, Gavin, but you can't deny what's inside you."

"What the fuck are you talking about?"

"You're a junkie like me, but it's not for drugs. No, it's for violence." Lucifer's voice was hoarse from his unrelenting grip. "By unleashing his true self, he freed yours too."

He tossed him to the side. Lucifer was too quick to fall on the floor. He pivoted with perfect balance.

"You try so hard to deny your desires, Gavin. It's a crime."

"Fucking find my wife," he snarled.

Lucifer opened another door, revealing a man with a drill about to do primitive surgery on a woman who splayed on the bed, looking blissed. Lucifer gave the fucked-up couple a thumbs up and closed the door.

"Stop!" Blade shouted.

At the end of the corridor a man held a limp woman draped over his shoulder. It took only a second for Gavin to recognize Lyla's distinctive blonde hair. He started forward even as the man turned, revealing Eli Stark's profile.

22

LYLA

The sound of the door opening roused her. The faintest hint of light penetrated through the material. Terror flooded through her. She erupted, straining at the chains. Her wrists protested, but she couldn't stop. No, she would fight to the death.

"Stop."

It wasn't Sadist's voice, but it could be one of his cronies who would take her to the 'show.' She screamed into the gag.

"I'm not going to hurt you," the gravelly voice said.

She didn't believe him for a moment.

"Stop fighting. I'm going to get you out."

That penetrated. She paused and felt the brush of fingers on her face. She jerked back, nearly braining herself on the wall in her haste to avoid the man's touch.

"That fucker," he said and then, "hold still."

The chains went taut, and she resisted the impulse to fight like an animal. When the chains loosened, she fell face first on the floor. Her arms trembled as her muscles protested being in such an awkward position for so long. She bit back a whimper and tried to lever herself up, but her arms were useless.

Two hands tucked under her armpits and pulled her into a sitting position. She had no balance and began to tip to the side. The man cursed and clamped a hand on her shoulder to keep her upright. Cramps wracked through her, and she moaned.

"Are you hurt?" he asked.

A goon fetching her for the 'show' wouldn't care that she was hurt, right? A kernel of hope flared, and she shook her head since he still hadn't taken off the gag. She desperately wanted to pull down the blindfold to see who he was, but her arms were limp noodles at her sides.

"We don't have time," he said impatiently.

A hard grip forced her to her feet. She whimpered as needles shot through her legs. A broad shoulder rammed into her stomach, and she was suddenly airborne. He gripped the back of her thighs and began to move. Her arms hung down, bouncing against his ass as he walked. She twitched her fingers and sucked in a breath. Fuck, that hurt. Her head spun as her white knight (or was it new captor) turned left and then right. The muffled sounds she'd been hearing through the door for hours were now at full blast. Screams and moans assaulted her ears. If she had the strength, she would have covered her ears. God, what was this place?

"Stop!"

Her stomach lurched as the man carrying her came to an abrupt halt and turned, making her dizzy and nauseous. He slid her off his shoulder and placed her in front of him. When her legs buckled, he banded an arm around her waist to keep her upright. She felt a flash of gratitude, which faded once she felt the tip of a knife at her throat. Seriously?

"Lyla?"

Her heart skipped. "Blade?" she screamed through the gag.

Hope blossomed. Oh, God. Oh, God. Please be Blade. She would obey his dictates for the rest of her life if it was him.

"Let her go, Stark," Blade said.

Stark? The name tickled her memory but eluded her for the moment. God, Blade was here. She was so close to getting the fuck out of here... She flexed her hands, and this time embraced the pain.

She stayed very still as the knife pressed hard enough against her throat to make her stomach flip. Ever since Sadist carved her up, she couldn't handle knives. Why couldn't these bastards just shoot her and end it quick?

"It's over, Stark," Blade continued. "Let her go."

"What are you doing, Eli?" an unfamiliar voice asked.

Unlike Blade, this guy didn't sound worried, just curious.

"Pyre has my mother," the man holding her growled.

Her mind scrambled, trying to figure out who he was and then it hit. Eli Stark, the dirty cop who approached them at Lux. The gorgeous one with turquoise eyes. His mother had been viciously attacked before he could testify in court. Gavin had his mother? Why?

"Let her go and I'll make your death quick."

Her heart nearly beat out of her chest. Gavin was here. She was going to live.

"I keep telling you, I have nothing to do with any of this shit," Eli snapped. "Someone framed me."

He was so close, his breath fanned her cheek.

"Kinda hard to feel sympathy for you when you're holding a knife to an innocent woman's throat." Angel's voice was soft but full of menace.

Her heart was so full, it felt like it would burst. They were all here. Okay, so maybe having family wasn't such a bad thing after all.

"Pyre took my mother. I have nothing else to bargain with," Eli hissed.

"You think Gavin's going to make a deal with a man who bound, gagged, and tortured his wife?" Angel barked.

"I didn't do this," Eli retorted.

"Really? Who did?"

"Fuck if I know. I found her like this."

"If you're not involved, how did you know she was here?"

"I have my contacts." Lyla grunted when the knife dug into her skin. "Stay the fuck back, Pyre!"

"Did you kill Stark's mom?" asked the cool, detached voice.

No one answered.

"That would be a damn shame if you did," the bland voice continued.

"Why's that?" Angel asked.

"Because he's telling the truth."

There was a beat of silence.

"What?"

That was Gavin's voice, flat and remote. Whoever had that dry voice was seconds away from death, he just didn't know it.

"Eli's not working for my friend. He's been too busy indulging in some vigilante justice. He's the perfect man to pin this on since he has the contacts and has been out of the spotlight, and oh yes, you two had a falling out." The man's sigh was full of admiration.

"If Lucifer's telling the truth, what did you plan to do with Lyla?" Gavin asked, voice whisper soft.

"I needed insurance since you wouldn't listen to me," Eli said.

"I want to hear it from her," Gavin said.

Eli tightened his grip and took a step back, dragging her with him. "Stay where you are, Pyre."

"If you're innocent, let her go. If not, I'll kill you. You have thirty seconds."

Gavin sounded homicidal. It was music to her ears. For a beat, Eli didn't shift. She mentally urged him to hurry the fuck up.

"You know I had nothing to do with this, right?" Eli murmured under his breath.

She nodded. The knife left her throat and the gag loosened.

"He didn't bring me here," she said immediately and began to cough.

Eli's arm dropped away, and she swayed only to be caught up against a solid chest. She didn't need to take the blindfold off to know who he was. She wrapped quivering arms around Gavin and felt her tears soak the blindfold. His hand cradled the back of her head.

"My mother, Pyre," Eli barked.

"One floor up in the hospital under the name Grace Stein," he said as he held her so tight she could barely breathe. "I don't kill old, defenseless women."

"This is touching and all, but you're running out of time," the irritating voice said.

Gavin didn't release her when she tried to raise her head and see who the fuck that guy was.

"Gaaaaavin," the man whined. "You promised."

He eased his hold on her to tug down the blindfold. She shut her eyes against the blinding light.

"Who took you? Do you know who he is?" he asked.

She opened her eyes and peered into his dangerous gold ones. He was really here. She ran her hand down his face with a trembling hand.

"I don't know," she said and began to wheeze again. "Water."

She heard a door open behind Gavin. The sound of someone being whipped made her push away, but he didn't release her.

"We have to help," she said.

He shook his head. "No, we don't. We're in a brothel."

She stilled. "Brothel?"

There was a fine hum of vicious energy around him. She wanted to burrow against him and beg him to take her home, but she knew that couldn't happen. They had unfinished business, which included killing Sadist once and for all. She tried to suppress her shit and focus.

"Here."

It took considerable effort to look away from Gavin to the man standing beside him. She surveyed the beast holding a bottle of water in his humongous hand. This guy looked like a wild mountain man with a full beard, a braid halfway down his back, and black, glittering eyes. He had to be over six-foot-five and built like a warrior from an age past. He wore baggy beige pants and a fitted tunic top, which showed every muscle beneath the fabric. She dimly registered that he wore red Crocs and nail polish, but his eyes were what distracted her. He was staring at her with a hunger she normally associated with

Gavin, but it wasn't sexual, it was something else. An eagerness for...
something.

"You need water," he said.

His voice didn't match his appearance. A man like him should
have the deep rumbling voice of a bear, not the airy lightness of a
schoolboy. Something about him put her on edge. She didn't trust his
smile or hippy attire.

She reached for the water bottle and noted that Gavin was eyeing
the stranger as if he hated him. What the fuck was going on here? She
tilted the bottle to her lips. She spilled a little on herself and Gavin, but
he didn't release her. She downed half of it before she took a breath.

"I'm Lucifer," the mountain man/hippy said.

"Lucifer?" she repeated sharply. "Gavin, he's working with Sadist.
He—"

"He's double-crossing him."

She stared at him. "Why?"

"Gavin made me a better deal."

Before she could ask what kind of fucked-up deal, Gavin asked,
"Who is he?"

Lucifer clapped his hands together. "He's so good at this! No one
suspects him. A wolf in sheep's clothing. He's been a longtime patron
of Hell. He does well up there"—Lucifer pointed up at the ceiling—
"and down here. I don't know how he does it. I admire him, actually."

"Who. Is. It?" Gavin bit out.

Lucifer gave him a sly look. "That's for you to figure out, isn't it?"

Gavin cupped her chin, forcing her to look at him. "You need to
leave."

"I don't think so," Lucifer said.

He tensed. "She isn't a part of this."

"No one's leaving until I get my show."

"Show?" She was beginning to hate that word. They were in a
brothel. What kind of show was he talking about?

"I don't want her here for this," Gavin growled.

"Why? You're afraid she'll see the real you?" Lucifer shook his head. "Besides, she has to come. She's the only one who knows who he is."

"I don't," she insisted.

"You do," Lucifer said with such certainty that her stomach lurched.

"Are you hurt?" Gavin asked.

She stared into his eyes and pushed all her inner turmoil aside. She needed this to be over. She needed to see this through. "No."

He looked at Lucifer. "Take us to him."

Lucifer eyed Eli. "You in?"

Eli looked at Gavin. "We're clear?"

Gavin glared at him. "We have things to discuss. Later."

"You in?" Lucifer pushed.

"To go into the pit? There's nothing in it for me," Eli said.

"You get a lot out of it." Lucifer held up his thumb. "First of all, you're gonna get a great show." His pointer finger popped up. "Second, fighting at Gavin's side will make him owe you." He held up his pinky. "Third, you'll please me, which may get you a favor in the future." He held up a scarred ring finger. "Fourth, tonight's going to go down in history." The middle finger joined the others. "And last but not least, you'll find out the identity of the man who called the hit on your mother."

Eli didn't move, but the corridor suddenly seemed a little smaller than it had been a second ago.

"What did you say?" Eli's voice held no inflection, but his turquoise eyes were suddenly blazing.

"You didn't think some street thug called the hit on your mom, did you?" Lucifer examined his fingernails. "I thought you knew that came from someone higher up."

Eli clenched his fists at his sides. "Who is he?"

Lucifer's smile was chilling. "That's the big mystery, isn't it?"

Eli took a step toward Lucifer and then stopped. Lucifer was nearly salivating, silently daring Eli to touch him. She didn't know who the fuck Lucifer was, but she knew enough about dangerous men not to trust a smile, a sedate wardrobe, or a man with a sweet voice. She watched Eli rein in his emotions.

"Are you in?" Lucifer asked.

Eli gave Lucifer a look that said he would love to dice this guy into pieces. Lucifer was completely unaffected. On the contrary, Lucifer looked as if Christmas came early.

"This is fantastic," Lucifer said and clapped his hands before he started down a god-awful red hallway.

Gavin took her hand. She felt him trembling. She knew it wasn't nerves. He was revved up.

"I'm okay, Gavin," she said.

He didn't look at her. "You're not."

She swallowed hard. No, she wasn't. "I will be once he's dead."

He kissed the back of her hand.

"Where are we?" she asked over the shouts of a woman with the filthiest mouth on the planet.

"This is Hell."

She looked up and was ensnared by his blistering gaze.

He jerked his head at Lucifer's back. "He runs it. He's off his rocker."

They boarded an elevator. Gavin boxed her into the corner.

"How many men does he have with him?" he asked.

"He has a board of twenty," Lucifer said.

"Twenty?" Angel echoed.

"Twenty," Lucifer confirmed with relish, "against you four."

"Fuck," Blade said.

"You got this," Lucifer said encouragingly as the elevator traveled down. "Gavin and Blade are veterans." He pointed at Angel and Eli. "As for you two, I hope you have beginner's luck or know how to use something other than a gun to defend yourselves."

Blade and Gavin were veterans of Hell?

"What about guards?" Gavin asked.

Lucifer snorted. "Their guards would wet their pants before they reached the door. You can't pay any run-of-the-mill security guard enough to come into Hell."

"Good."

The elevator doors opened. Unlike the noisy, hideous red corridor, this place was whisper quiet and opulent with gleaming white marble floors, walls, and shimmering chandeliers.

Lucifer stepped forward with his arms spread wide. "Nice, huh? I charge the rich fuckers who don't want to be in the stands a bundle to watch at ground zero. They like the gore just as much as the common folk; they just won't admit it."

Lucifer started down the wide hallway, Crocs squeaking.

Gavin's hand flexed on her. "Maybe you should stay here."

"No," she said immediately. "I need to see this."

"There's twenty of them," he growled.

"And you won't let any of them touch me. This is what we've been waiting for, and I know his voice. You need me, Gavin."

"I do need you. I need you breathing."

"And I will be."

His eyes flicked to Blade. "One scratch and I'll kill you."

Blade inclined his head. Gavin approached Lucifer who ran his finger along a gleaming table and frowned.

"Fucking dusty. Unacceptable," he muttered.

"Lucifer," Gavin clipped.

"Right. This way."

"You want the underworld? This is where you take it," Gavin said under his breath to Angel who nodded.

Lyla and Blade followed in their wake. Blade had a knife the length of her forearm in his hand. A man who looked like a pirate paused in front of closed double doors with a silver cart that had two bottles of champagne and crystal flutes. Lucifer shooed him away and knocked on the door.

"Come."

Lucifer gave them a shit-eating grin before he opened the door and rolled the cart inside. This was it. Sadist was in this room. Years of death, nightmares, and fear would be settled right here, right now. Her heart leaped into her throat as Gavin blithely walked in after Lucifer. No hesitation. She expected to hear gunshots, but there was nothing and that was worse. She moved forward, pulling against Blade's grip on her arm. She wasn't sure what she expected, but the sight that met her eyes took a few seconds to digest.

The room looked like an executive lounge with elegant furniture, a boardroom table, and a wet bar all in snowy white. But that was where normal stopped. Twenty men sat at the table, all in black suits and metal masks. Each mask was horrifying enough to induce nightmares whether it was a snarling animal or a demon. A wall of glass separated the men in suits from two men with ancient weapons fighting on a turf of sand. She caught a glimpse of an arena before the screaming tension in the room forced her to focus on the men at the table who were half standing, staring at Lucifer, Gavin, Eli, and Angel. Blade forced her to stop behind him in the doorway.

"What the fuck are you doing here, Pyre?" a man wearing a horrifying clown mask asked.

Gavin slammed his fist in the man's face. There was the ping of metal and then the crunch of bone as the mask caved in. She saw a gush of blood slither down the man's throat and heard a gasping breath as the man crashed to the ground and clawed at the mask with his legs kicking.

Another man leaped up from the table with a dagger in each hand. Blade widened his stance to conceal her. She leaned to the side, heart in her throat as Gavin eyed the man with a nonchalance that made her want to scream. He dodged the first swing and the second. On the third swipe, Gavin grabbed his wrist and reversed the knife. With a suddenness that stunned everyone, he hit the butt of the dagger, which lodged in the man's chest. The man fell, gasping and twitching.

Four men converged on Gavin. She saw Eli and Angel engage with them before Blade shoved her back. A second later, a man barreled into him. She saw the whites of his eyes through a snarling rabbit mask before she saw a flash of silver and he slid to the ground in front of Blade. She pressed against Blade's back to look into the room and saw Eli's face and neck now splattered with red.

"You all know why I'm here," Gavin said over the muted sound of the battle taking place in the sandy pit and the masked men's last rattling breaths. "And I know why you're here."

In the arena, a man wielded a weapon she had only seen in medieval movies. It was a stick with a chain and metal ball with spikes attached. She grasped the back of Blade's jacket as it imbedded into a man's skull with a sickening thud.

The scene with Gavin was just as disturbing. The steady clip of his shoes as he circled his prey gave her goose bumps. Even though Gavin was clearly outnumbered, none of the men moved. They watched his progress silently.

"Who the fuck do you think you are?" said a belligerent man wearing a wolf mask.

Gavin knocked the mask off his face and grabbed fistfuls of his suit. "I'm your fucking crime lord, bitch."

Gavin's fist flashed out and the man's head kicked back. He landed on his ass and shook his head, dazed.

"Lucifer here was kind enough to let me know where you were meeting," Gavin said with a politeness that clashed with the flashes of temper he was exhibiting. "Lucifer tells me there's some debate on whether I've lost my touch since I claimed my wife. Let's put it to the test, shall we?"

Gavin placed both hands on the table. Blood spread across white marble.

"I hear you had plans for my wife tonight."

No one spoke, no one even breathed.

"You dare to desecrate *mine*." Gavin hissed the last word, the veins in his neck popping as he tried to contain his fury. "I've been waiting two years for this moment. Two long years since my father and cousin were killed. Now, tonight, it ends."

A loud pop made everyone jump. Lucifer made a carry-on gesture as he poured glasses of champagne.

"He's sitting here, in this room."

Gavin accepted the flute of champagne Lucifer offered and took a sip. She had seen Gavin go gonzo, but right now, he was control personified. This was the crime lord. Absolute control, absolutely terrifying. She could feel the chill from across the room. This was the man who beat that man in the basement with a single-minded focus and detachment. There was no doubt in her mind that no man in this room was a match for him. Gavin wasn't a mere man. He was born for this—to make others cower and beg for mercy. Wrath seeped from his pores. His sheer will on display, and it was beautiful to behold.

"Whoever my enemy is," Gavin said as he stepped on a body in his path. Bones cracked. "He's patient. He's a great planner..." He finished his glass and set it in front of the man with an eagle mask. "And he's going to get everything coming to him. So much so that anyone half associated with him will be annihilated."

He yanked the cord holding the mask in place. It clattered on the table and revealed a familiar face that scrambled her thoughts.

"Governor," Gavin acknowledged as casually as if they were at a dinner party. "I stopped by your office a week ago."

The governor was ghost white and sweating profusely.

"You told me you didn't know the identity of the crime lord, and that you weren't working with him," Gavin said pleasantly.

"I-I came here for—" the governor began and stopped abruptly.

"For what? The show?" Gavin picked up the eagle mask and leaned in close. "Did you choose the eagle because you're a patriot?"

The governor's mouth opened and closed. "Gavin, please, I knew your father—"

"And he's dead."

Gavin smashed the beak of the metal mask into the governor's eye. The man's scream made her shudder. Gavin slammed the governor's face repeatedly against the table until the mask was flat and the older man didn't move.

"I think there's been some confusion about my title," Gavin said calmly as he resumed his stroll. The masked men edged away. "Your presence here means you don't see me as the crime lord and have hedged your bets on the other guy, which means your lives are forfeit."

Gavin braced his legs apart as he surveyed the group.

"Give him up."

There was a beat of silence and then a man at the opposite end of the table stirred. He tipped back his troll mask, revealing a face that wasn't hard on the eyes.

"What are you going to do, Gavin? Kill us all?" the man asked with an insolence that made her grip the back of Blade's jacket.

"Detective Malone," Gavin acknowledged.

Malone looked at Eli. "What are you doing here, Stark? I thought you died in a hole somewhere months ago."

"I'm looking for the guy who ordered the hit on my mom," Eli said.

Malone's eyes moved to Angel and narrowed. "You can't bring another crime family into this. What happens in our city is our business."

"Angel's taking over, so this is now his city as well," Gavin said.

There was a touch of unease in Malone's voice as he said, "Roque hasn't served his entire sentence."

"I'm flattered that you know so much about my family," Angel said with a grin. "Raul can handle himself."

"Everyone knows the Romans," Malone muttered and switched his attention back to Gavin. "You can't kill us all."

"Can't I?"

A smug smile curved Malone's mouth. "You already killed the governor. What are you gonna do? Kill a police detective, a senator, judge, and gaming commissioner?"

"Why not?"

"You'll cripple the city! Every cop and FBI agent in the country will be gunning for you!" Malone snapped.

"I think we need new people at the top," Gavin mused, almost to himself, and then glanced at Lucifer who was walking toward Lyla and Blade with champagne. "Hey, Lucifer, what do you do with the bodies in Hell?"

"I have my own crematory, of course. I'm not gonna waste time digging graves in the desert," Lucifer said.

"You hear that, Malone? No evidence. Lucifer will turn you into ash and flush you down the toilet. The fucking FBI won't find a tooth.

What happens in Hell, stays in Hell," Gavin said quietly. "That's why you should've never walked through those doors."

The masked men glanced at one another. The tension in the room rose to a screaming pitch. Someone would make a move.

Gavin tugged on the strings of a man wearing a wicked demon mask. The mask slid across the table, revealing Steven Vega who was visibly trembling. He raised his hands to cover his head as if he expected a blow.

"Steven, what are you doing here?" Gavin asked.

When Steven didn't answer, Gavin gripped him by the hair and yanked viciously. Steven yelped.

"I asked you a question."

"Y-you k-killed my father!" Steven whimpered.

"So, you joined the other side? I warned you what I'd do."

"What's the meaning of this, Lucifer?" one of the men at the table asked.

"What do you mean?" Lucifer asked as he sipped champagne.

"You brought Pyre here?"

"He arrived early, promised me a good show, and I get to play godfather to his kid."

She jerked. "What?"

No one heard her. The men were all looking at one another, trying to communicate silently.

"Masks off," Gavin ordered.

Long seconds passed. No one moved. She edged backward. In the arena, two men fought with swords. Adrenaline, anticipation, and fear stole her breath.

"Give him to me," Gavin said.

"And you'll let us go?" a man with a lizard mask asked.

"No."

"You can't take us all on," Malone said.

"You think not?" Gavin asked and all hell broke loose.

Men pulled out knives, machetes, and axes from beneath the table. Gavin narrowly dodged a ninja star that cut his cheek. He brought his hands up, brass knuckles gleaming as men rushed him.

"Gavin!" She couldn't hold back the scream, but the battle cries of the men drowned it out.

Eli and Angel were lost in the scuffle, and Blade backed her out of the room. She could feel him vibrating. The need to engage must be riding him hard. There were still too many men against Gavin, Angel, and Eli but, for some reason, no one had a gun. She heard something shatter and peeked through Blade's arm. A masked man used his chair to break into the arena. Apparently, he thought his odds were better out there.

"Look at them run," Lucifer said gleefully.

She caught a glimpse of a man on top of Gavin with a machete inches from his face. She shoved at Blade.

"Help Gavin!"

"I can't."

Blade sounded pained.

"If he dies, I'll kill you," she screamed and shoved him again.

The knife in Blade's hand trembled. The fight in the room poured into the arena. Another masked man raised his axe above Gavin's head.

"Blade!" she screamed.

Blade tossed his knife, which sank into the man's belly. He screamed and dropped his weapon too close to Gavin's head for comfort, distracting the man with the machete long enough for Gavin to gain the upper hand.

The masked men tried to leave the sandy pit, but the spectators blocked off the stairs. Thwarted, they scrambled to arm themselves from a wall of weapons, which included whips, chains, swords, spears, and other primitive weapons.

Gavin, Angel, and Eli hopped into the arena. There was a moment of silence, and then the spectators began to cheer. It was like they were at a football game. The masked men made a circle around Gavin, Angel, and Eli who were unarmed aside from Gavin's brass knuckles and Eli's knife.

"Blade," she whispered. "Go."

"I can't!"

"I'll stay right here. There's no one in the room!" she shouted, shoving at him as one of the masked men began to swing a chain above his head.

"Fuck!" Blade whirled on Lucifer and gripped his shirt. "Watch her!"

"Sure, sure," Lucifer said. "You'd better get out there."

"You won't let anyone touch her?" Blade demanded.

"You said she can take care of herself."

"You—"

"Blade!" she screamed as Eli staggered from a whiplash.

Blade snatched knives and an axe from bodies before he ran into the arena. He broke the circle surrounding Gavin by cleaving a man's head in two. It was brutal, chaotic, and gory. This was ten times worse than a gun battle.

She skirted the bodies and ran to the shattered window. Eli's dagger landed in the throat of the man wielding the whip while Gavin played with a man who was trying to cut him in half with a sword. Gavin waited for his moment, pivoting while the man swung wildly, his actions becoming more desperate. When he miscalculated and staggered forward, Gavin's hand flashed out, brass knuckles flashing in the stadium lights. His victim's head snapped to the side. Blood and teeth splashed across the sand. Gavin followed this with a punch to the temple that made her look away. Fuck.

She tapped the edge of the window anxiously but wasn't able to look away for long. There was a piercing scream followed by the roaring crowd. She looked back and saw Angel wielding a trident with the same ease that he drove the car. The crowd leaned over the rails, yelling their heads off as Angel sliced a man's stomach open.

"Isn't it beautiful?"

Lucifer came up beside her with a champagne glass and a round metal shield. She gave him a disbelieving look before Eli sliced a man's calf open and followed that up with an efficient throat slit. Blade stood back from the others, gauging and taking out the masked men with an efficiency that made her realize this wasn't his first time in the pit. Gavin claimed a sword. The sight of him in a bloody suit with a sword would be imprinted in her mind for all time. She was about to take a breath when a man wearing a wolf mask snapped the whip at Gavin's back. She let out a battle cry and would have launched herself forward, but Lucifer yanked her back.

"No women in the arena," he said.

"You—"

She whirled around to search the room for a weapon to toss and saw Steven Vega hiding beneath the table. Despite his position, something about his face riveted her. He didn't look terrified. No, he was... seething. Something vicious flashed in the dark depths of his eyes, and her world imploded.

23

LYLA

Even as she tried to come to terms with what she was seeing, Steven crawled out from under the table. He straightened and smoothed a hand over his suit.

She would recognize the malevolence in those eyes anywhere. She had been nice to this fucker. She talked to him in the bar and helped him up when he fell in his father's hospital room. This man defiled her, used her parents as pawns, and massacred Manny, the only father figure she'd ever known. He robbed Nora of the privilege of having Manny as a grandfather and Vinny as an uncle. The memory of this man tortured her every night for over two years, and he had been hiding in plain sight. He was a true wolf in sheep's clothing. She built Sadist up in her mind to be an invincible monster when he was just a sicko in a mask. No one would dream that the timid lawyer was actually a sadistic killer capable of running the underworld, not when he left a trail of mutilated bodies in his wake.

"I told you, you're always at the wrong place at the wrong time," Steven said.

No stutter. That soft, gentle voice assaulted her ears, making her stomach roil and head pound with nightmares.

"It's you," she whispered.

His eyes glittered with rage in his pale, angular face. "So, you finally see me, do you? When we met at the bar, I thought you were different until I found out you were with Pyre. You're just like the rest of the whores." He picked up his cane and pointed it at her. "Time to finish what I started."

The way he was pointing the cane made it clear that it wasn't a normal walking stick. She half turned to protect herself, even though she knew it was a futile gesture and squeezed her eyes shut. She heard a gunshot and then the sharp ping of metal.

"You know that's against the rules," Lucifer barked.

She opened her eyes and saw that Lucifer had deflected the bullet with his shield. Steven now had his cane pointed at Lucifer.

"You stay out of this," Steven ordered.

Lucifer handed the shield to Lyla who nearly dropped it. The shield felt as if it weighed fifty pounds, but it could deflect bullets so... She held it in front of her with both hands as Lucifer headed toward the madman.

"You know it's not allowed," Lucifer snapped.

Steven's expression twisted. "How could you betray me like this? You ruined everything!"

"I didn't ruin anything. I made a deal to get a better show, which is what you're interrupting. Give me the gun."

Steven jabbed the cane at him as he retreated. "Pyre made fools of both of us. You hate him."

"I don't hate him," Lucifer said. "He's the closest thing I have to a brother."

Steven's mouth sagged. "That's not what you led me to believe!"

"I find your hatred for others amusing."

"Amusing?" Steven echoed.

Lucifer was walking toward a serial killer with a gun. He had no weapon that she could see and was baiting Steven on top of that. Lucifer was obviously insane. She looked for an escape route, but with Steven by the door, the only exit was the arena and that wasn't happening. She caught a glimpse of Angel going for the death strike, raising the trident above his head before bringing it down and being sprayed in red mist.

"You find me amusing?" Steven shouted.

She raised the shield just below her eyes and prepared to duck if Steven started firing wildly.

"You've been a source of entertainment for me," Lucifer continued in a voice that was bored personified. "I gave you the skills you hungered for to work out your rage, and I was amused by your ability to manipulate and fool Gavin and the others this long, but you can't hide behind the mask forever. It's time to step into the light."

"That wasn't your call to make!" Spit flew as Steven raged. "You kept my secrets. You made me believe I could do anything. I have the underworld in my hands, and you turn against me now. Why?"

"You wanted me to give you your throne. I don't believe in giving anyone a handout. You want your throne, take it." Lucifer gestured to the pit. "You want Gavin? He's right there. Take your throne, don't use me or anyone else to do it."

"You made me who I am!" Steven screamed. "I thought you were my friend."

"I don't have friends," Lucifer said, brutally blunt. "And I let you play in the brothel, but you never got in the pit. You never step into the light because you don't have the confidence to take an enemy head-on. No crime lord can lurk in the shadows forever. There has to be more to you than the mask because one day they'll find out the truth. This was your opportunity to show everyone what you're made of." Lucifer's voice became scathing. "Yet you hide under the table and insult me by bringing a gun into my house. If you can't survive without a gun or the mask, then you're nothing. You're not worthy to claim the title. You're a coward."

There was the sharp crack of a gunshot. Lucifer jerked and a red stain spread over his right shoulder. Lucifer looked at the hole in his shirt and then back at Steven who took a wary step back even though Lucifer was unarmed.

"You always were a lousy shot," Lucifer said.

Yes, he was unhinged.

"I'll give you one more shot," Lucifer said and spread his arms wide.

She looked over her shoulder at the arena for help but all four guys were engaged in bloody battle. Gavin now had two swords and was hacking body parts to the crowd's delight.

The second gunshot made her duck. She peeked around the side of the shield, expecting to see Lucifer on the ground. Instead, she saw Lucifer rip the cane out of Steven's hands and break it over his knee before he backhanded Steven with enough force to make the smaller man spin and fall on his hands and knees.

Lucifer met her gaze from across the room. "You want your revenge? Take it."

She was so shocked that she didn't notice Steven crawl beneath the table and launch himself at her until it was too late. She saw the flash of metal and brought up the shield instinctively. His knife landed on the shield and scraped over its surface.

She backed up and shifted the shield in time to see Steven coming at her again. The impact of his blow made her stagger backward. She grasped the shield desperately, which was too fucking heavy for her to lift with one arm as it was intended to be used.

"Go on the offense," Lucifer called like a basketball coach.

She jumped back as Steven aimed below the shield to slice her legs or belly. He swung savagely. She wouldn't be able to hold the shield forever.

"I'm going to carve your heart out and shove it in Pyre's face," Steven ranted as he bashed the shield. "He'll kill me, but he'll have nothing."

His vicious, mocking tone made her stop in her tracks. Something dark unfurled inside her. No running. This would end here. Steven came at her again, and she braced for impact. As he slashed down, she rammed the shield up and into his hand. Steven screamed as the knife went flying. He cradled his hand and froze when she blocked him from retrieving his weapon.

They stared at one another. In the arena, the crowd booed. She and Steven both turned to look. Eli was sprawled on the sand. Angel stood over him, trying to keep the last of the masked men at bay. Gavin ran toward Blade who was trapped against the wall by three men who were tossing daggers at him as if he were a dartboard.

Steven glanced at her, his expression malevolent and sly. He hopped into the arena and grabbed a scythe. He would do what he did best—hit when no one was looking. She searched for his knife and then turned back to the arena. She took aim and tossed the knife as hard as she could. It sank into Steven's lower back. He staggered and howled in pain.

She wasn't aware of anything but her prey. This was it. She hefted Lucifer's shield, hopped through the window, and rushed across the sand. She used both hands and all the momentum she could get and bashed Steven in the back of the head, sending him face first into the sand. Rage obliterated all thought. She gripped the shield, raised it over her head and brought it down with every ounce of strength she possessed. For Manny, for her mother, for Vinny, for Carmen—

The shield was ripped from her hands. She whirled, teeth bared, and stared at a blood-streaked Blade, Gavin, Angel, and Eli. Beyond them, the arena was strewn with body parts and hundreds of silent spectators in the stands.

"You took the show, sweetheart," Angel said.

"You want to tell me why you're trying to dismember the Vega wimp?" Gavin asked.

"It's him," she panted.

"Who?"

"Sadist." No comprehension on his face. "The crime lord."

Gavin froze. "What?"

"It's him. He's the wolf in sheep's clothing. He doesn't have a stutter. He's the right body type, dark eyes; he's been here the whole time!"

Gavin kicked Steven onto his back. His limbs flopped at odd angles.

"I testified against your clients and caused you to lose some high-profile cases," Eli said quietly.

"And you were at the hospital before Santana's men attacked," Gavin said quietly. "You're the one I talked to on the phone the night I killed your father."

Something evil stirred to life in Steven's eyes.

"You think you're big shots," Steven hissed, blood oozing from his mouth. "You're just like Rafael. You push your weight around. You think no one will challenge you." A deranged smile curved his mouth. "I showed you. I took everything from you."

"I should have killed you the night I killed your father," Gavin said.

"I did what my dad and Rafael could never do! If you hadn't shattered my knee and I didn't get my jaw wired shut, I would have killed you sooner."

"That explains the four months of silence," Gavin said.

"I had you," Steven snarled, his face twisting into something less human. "If Lucifer hadn't interfered, I would have exterminated the Pyres and ruled—"

Gavin ran Steven through the chest with his sword. The sound of the blade sliding through muscle and grazing bone made her feel sick, but she didn't look away. Steven screamed, the sound so high pitched and tortured that her hands fisted at her sides. It took every ounce of control she possessed not to look away.

Gavin walked away and returned with another sword. The power-hungry demon retreated when Steven realized he would be impaled again.

"Please—" Steven got out before another sword joined the first.

By the time Gavin finished, no less than six swords stuck out of Steven's body. He shuddered as his blood drained out of him. No one moved, no one spoke.

Lucifer grabbed his bloody shield. There was an angry murmur when the spectators saw his bullet wound. Lucifer eyed Lyla for a long moment before he held out a fist.

"That was awesome," he said solemnly.

Did he want a fist bump? She hesitated, but he didn't lower his fist. The setting was surreal enough that she hit his massive fist with her smaller one.

"He brought a gun into Hell." Lucifer shook his head. "Doesn't he know me at all?"

With a swift savageness that took her aback, he brought his shield down. Steven's head rolled away and the spectators grunted in approval.

"I might have to revise my rules about women in the arena. That was great." Lucifer smiled at Gavin, Blade, Angel, and Eli who looked as if they walked through red rain. "How you feeling, boys?"

No one spoke. They were jacked, and Lucifer knew it. She couldn't stop shaking.

"Need to visit the whorehouse? First rounds on me," Lucifer said graciously and then eyed Lyla. "I also have men—"

Gavin's hand moved. Lucifer raised his shield. A knife sparked as it collided with metal and then toppled to the sand. Lucifer grinned unrepentantly at Gavin.

"Just a suggestion," he said with a shrug.

Gavin turned to her and cupped her face with gritty hands. "Are you hurt?"

"No."

She glanced at Lucifer who was watching them with his head tilted to the side, eyes narrowed. "Lucifer saved my life."

Gavin dropped his forehead on hers. "Fuck."

"He stopped the bullet with his shield." She smoothed her hands over his tattered shirt. "Are you hurt?"

"Nothing that'll kill me." He wrapped his arms around her. "It's over."

"You kept up your end of the agreement. That was a bloody good show," Lucifer said. "I knew Lyla would figure out it was Steven."

"All this time you knew," Gavin said.

"Yes."

"Why didn't you tell me?"

"Why should I? I don't have an investment in the underworld, and

I admired Steven for having the balls to dethrone you Pyres. You've
had it too easy for too long."

"It'll take a decade to right the wrongs Steven's done in two years,"
Gavin hissed.

"Good thing Angel's hungry for it, huh? You're not planning on
getting a hobby, are you, Roman?"

"Nope," Angel said dryly.

"You hear that? No harm, no foul."

She whirled in the circle of Gavin's arms. "No harm?"

Lucifer eyed her coolly. "You're alive, aren't you?"

She tried to take a step forward, but Gavin held her back. "He left
mutilated bodies all over the city!"

Lucifer glanced around. "You mean like this?"

She bared her teeth. "He destroyed Manny."

"Manny's an awful man."

"You didn't know him!" she shouted.

Lucifer took a step forward, eyes locked on her face. The bottom
of his shield dripped with Steven's blood and other stuff. She was
dimly aware of Blade, Angel, and Eli drawing near.

"I know Manny," Lucifer said quietly. "He wasn't a good man."

She tossed her head back. "He changed."

Lucifer's eyes narrowed before they focused on Gavin who held
her tight against him.

"Maybe," Lucifer conceded. "But the man I knew would sacrifice
his son to the underworld."

"I survived," Gavin clipped

Lucifer nodded. "So, you did." His eyes dipped to Lyla before he
said, "You lucky fuck."

She focused on the bullet wound, which was still oozing. She
couldn't resist. "You should see to that."

Lucifer snorted. "My dad used to shoot me once a week so when
the real thing came, I wouldn't go into shock. This is nothing."

She turned to Gavin. "Nora, Carmen?" she asked urgently.

"They're at the house."

"I want to call. She must be terrified. I need to hear her voice, tell her it's over."

Gavin lost his jacket at some point, and his shirt was shredded and blood soaked. He ran a hand over his pockets and then looked around.

"Here." Blade offered his phone.

She swiped her finger over the screen, leaving a streak of red in her wake. She paced away as the men talked in low tones and stopped in her tracks when she saw the body parts strewn over the arena. It had been a bloodbath. Even as her stomach roiled, she heard Carmen's breathy voice on the other end.

"Blade?"

"Carmen, it's me."

"Lyla?" Carmen sounded faint and then screamed, *"Lyla?"*

"It's me," she whispered as tears threatened. Everything was catching up to her—being hunted in the desert, her mother's attack, being chained, and witnessing a gory battle worthy of Roman times.

"Are you okay?" Carmen asked.

She nodded even as her mouth said, "No."

"Are you hurt?"

She shook her head before she realized Carmen couldn't see it. "N-no. A-are you guys okay?"

"Yes. Did Gavin get him?"

"Yes. It was Steven Vega."

"Vega? Rafael's brother?" Carmen sounded incredulous. "Are you sure?"

She looked down at Steven's head. His eyes were open and staring at her. This fucker tortured Manny, stabbed her, hunted her like some fucking dog while she was pregnant and would have killed Carmen and Nora... With a scream, she drew back her foot and kicked Steven's head, which sailed across the two-story arena into the crowd of spectators. There was a yell as men tried to dodge her missile and then a ringing silence filled the arena. For the first time, she realized there were no women in the crowd and these men looked like gangbangers... or worse. She took a step back and prepared to run when Lucifer laughed.

He tossed an arm over her shoulders. "Your hand to hand combat needs work, but you have great potential."

"Who's that?" Carmen asked.

She didn't know what to think of Lucifer. He allowed Steven to jack off on her and would have watched men torture her, but then he fucking saved her from a bullet. He really was insane. She had the simultaneous urges to kill him, hug him, or order him to see a doctor. She didn't care that he could handle the pain. She didn't want him to die... or did she? It was just her luck that she was indebted to an irritating, heartless psycho. "Fucking Lucifer."

"Lucifer?" Carmen sounded horrified. "Oh my God, Lyla. Get away from him."

"I'm trying." She shoved him, which made him laugh even harder. "Asshole."

"Lyla, he's a sociopath. He runs Hell. You have to—"

"It's fine." She got away from him and tried to ignore the hooting and catcalling from the stands. She gave the crowd the middle finger, which made them laugh uproariously. She gave up and headed toward the ruined executive lounge. "Are you okay? How's Nora?"

"You took ten years off my life, but I'm okay. Nora's asleep. Are you coming home?"

"Yes."

Carmen sighed. "Is it really over?"

She took a deep breath and glanced into the arena at the bodies of Sadist and his henchmen. "Yes."

"I love you."

She closed her eyes and clung to her love and warmth. "I love you too. I'll see you soon."

She hung up as the guys came through the shattered window. She handed the phone back to Blade and did a double take. She grabbed his chin and went on tiptoe to examine the deep gash on his cheek.

"What happened?" she snapped and spotted two deep lashes on Angel's chest. Eli was dragging his left leg and trailing blood from a wound she couldn't see. She whirled on Lucifer. "You have a doctor here?"

Lucifer stared at her. "No."

"They need stitches!"

Lucifer leaned toward her. "This is Hell, honey. They're not supposed to leave unscathed. Just be happy they're breathing and so are you." Lucifer looked toward Gavin. "You might want to wash up before you leave looking like you left a butcher shop."

Lucifer walked toward the exit, and they followed. Gavin grabbed her hand as he stomped over the fallen bodies and tracked bloody footprints over the white marble floor. Lucifer led them down a hallway and pointed at several doors before he disappeared.

Gavin led her into a room fit for royalty. Like everything else on this floor, everything was blinding white. This bothered her on so many levels.

"I don't..." she began, trying to pull back.

Gavin dragged her into a luxurious bathroom. A circular shower stall stood in the middle of the room along with a sunken bathtub. She wasn't prepared for Gavin to drag her to the ground, rip her top down the middle, and savagely yank off her jeans.

"Gavin," she whispered as he unbuttoned his slacks and pulled out his cock. "There are probably cameras..."

He dragged her into position beneath him, spread her thighs and brushed his cock over her slit. She bit back a moan and heard his growl of approval when he found her hot and slick. She tried to scoot away, but he grabbed her thighs and yanked her into place beneath him.

"They'll see!" she hissed.

"Let them watch. They'll never have what I have, the fuckers."

He wouldn't be denied. He positioned her and slid inside. His eyes closed, and he shuddered as if he couldn't handle the sensation. He didn't stop until he was in to the hilt. His hot breath fanned her face. She was pinned beneath his vibrating body. She could feel him holding back, trying to spare her whatever was going on inside him.

"Gavin."

Metallic golden eyes pierced hers. The monster that ruled the underworld stared back at her. She wasn't afraid. On the contrary, she stroked a hand down his bloody face. This man, this scary, wonderful man would die for her. He wouldn't give up, and he wouldn't back down.

"I love you," she said and blinked back tears.

His mouth slammed down on hers, and he began to move. She tasted blood but didn't fucking care. She wrapped her arms around his neck and kissed him for all she was worth. He growled into her mouth and fucked her against the unforgiving floor. After the horrors of the past hour, she needed to lose herself, and he was giving her an outlet. She dragged her nails down his back and clawed at him, begging him to push her over the edge.

He lifted her leg high and ground against her before he pulled back and then slammed home with a teeth-jarring smack. It took less than five minutes of his antics for her to climax, tipping her head back and screaming as it tore through her. He joined her, clasping her desperately close and fucking her with a force that bordered on pain. So many emotions flickered through his eyes—fear, relief, rage, and bloodlust.

He gasped her name as he came and lay on top of her, nearly suffocating her beneath his bulk. She didn't care. They survived, Sadist was gone, and they could finally move on.

"Okay?" he husked.

"Yeah." She would be.

He hauled her up and bustled her into the circular shower stall and braced her against the wall when she swayed on her feet. He tapped a button on the floor with his foot. A massive shower head rained over them and began to wash away the blood and fear.

They stared at one another. So much passed through her mind, but she didn't know what to utter out loud. His energy pulsed in the enclosed space. He cupped her chin and kissed her, hard and deep. When he pulled back, his eyes roved over her face as if memorizing every line.

"I'm so fucking proud of you."

She blinked. "What?"

"I killed the last man, turn, and see you toss the knife in Vega's back and then attack him with a fucking shield." His lips didn't move, but his eyes warmed fractionally. "You were a savage out for blood. You were magnificent. Every man in that arena would have killed to claim you."

"What?"

He brushed sweet kisses over her forehead, down her nose, and over her cheeks. His hands moved over her as if he couldn't help himself. She reached down for one of the bottles at her feet, read the label and began to bathe away the night. Neither of them said a word as they tended to one another.

When she'd bundled herself into a robe, he went into the bedroom to see if there was anything in the closet and came back with a tiny slip of fabric, which turned out to be a dress. She slipped into it and was horrified by her reflection. The dress was obviously from one of the whores. It barely covered her pussy or nipples. It was slinky, tight, and left nothing to the imagination. Her chest scars were on full display. She was debating whether she should wear the robe out of Hell when she caught sight of Gavin.

He wore an outfit identical to Lucifer's—loose beige pants and a tight Henley that showed off his muscles. He plucked at the tight shirt as if it was a rag. He saw her biting her lip to hold in her laughter. He hauled her against him with his hands on her ass.

"You think this is funny?" he murmured as he nipped her neck.

"Yes." How she could find anything funny after the night they had, she didn't know.

"Fucking Lucifer."

"What's this about godfather duty?"

His hands tightened on her. "He's going to teach Nora how to fight."

"*What?*" She shoved at him, but he didn't release her.

"He won't teach her until we're ready."

"The underworld won't touch her. You're passing the title to Angel."

"We can never let our guards down. You know that."

She moaned and rested her face against the hollow of his throat. "I don't want to think about that right now. Sadist is dead. That's all I care about. The end."

Gavin answered a knock on the door, revealing Blade who was dressed exactly like him. For some reason, he looked even more ludicrous.

"Let's get out of here," Blade said.

Gavin put his arm around her shoulders. "Let's go."

Blade led the way down the white hallway. Angel and Eli waited by the elevator dressed in the same odd outfit. Angel looked her over and didn't flinch when he took in her scarred chest.

"Nice dress," he said with a grin.

She scowled at him and glanced at Eli. "Are you okay?"

"I'll live."

The elevator doors opened, and they got in.

"What are you doing for work?" Gavin asked.

It took her a second to realize he was talking to Eli who didn't answer.

"Your hospital bills are backed up," Gavin continued.

"What's your point, Pyre?"

"You looking for a job?"

There was a beat of silence before he said, "Depends on the job."

"I hear there's a detective position open with the Nevada PD."

Angel snickered.

"Or if you're looking for something more flexible, Angel's taking my title and needs someone who knows the ins and outs of the underworld."

The elevator doors opened, revealing a dark hallway.

"I'll give you a call, Pyre," Eli said as he limped in another direction.

"We still have to talk," Gavin said in a hard voice.

"I know," Eli said without looking back.

They walked down the hallway. There were no screams of torture or pleasure, but she wouldn't relax until they were out of here. They rounded the corner and walked into what felt like a sports book betting station. Men were everywhere, and the largest TV screens she had ever seen hung on the walls. It was a circular floor with a bar and tables and chairs surrounding the top level of the arena. There was a lot of activity going on as they piled bodies on stretchers.

The noise level dimmed as they started through the crowd. No one smiled or spoke to them, but she felt their eyes on her. After the night she'd had, she wasn't feeling remotely modest. These men saw her kill a man. What were scars and tits in comparison?

Gavin led the way to a large metal door. As he swung the heavy thing open, someone called his name. He cursed under his breath before he turned to face Lucifer.

"Leaving so soon?" Lucifer asked.

"Got shit to do."

Lucifer stared openly at her scars. She resisted the urge to cover her chest or belt him across the face. Lucifer's eyes locked with hers. Something was happening in the dark depths she couldn't define.

"You should wear your scars with pride. You survived and had your revenge. Every man here knows it," Lucifer said.

She didn't know what to say to that.

"I look forward to hearing your stories in the future." Lucifer grinned. "And meeting your daughter. Are you planning on having more kids?"

"Lucifer," Gavin bit out.

"What? I want to know."

"We haven't talked about—" she began.

"Yes," Gavin growled.

Lucifer clapped his hands. "Great."

"It's been a long night," Blade said.

"Yes, yes," Lucifer said and clapped them on the back. "The city lost some prominent leaders tonight. Watch your back."

"That's a given," Gavin said.

He led her past a group of men smoking cigars and playing cards. A dark, gloomy hallway led to rickety stairs, and then Gavin pushed on a wall, which swung open. She walked into a... closet? She heard the distant pulse of stripper music and glanced at the minimal costumes. She grabbed a feather boa and draped it around her neck as Blade's phone rang.

"Lyla."

She turned from her perusal of the empty dressing room. "What?"

"That was the hospital."

Fear grabbed her by the throat. "What happened? Did someone...?"

"She's awake."

She froze. "What?"

"Your mother. She's awake."

"We have to go now. How do we get out of here?" she demanded.

Gavin took her hand. "This way."

He led her through the dressing room into a strip club with strobe lights. She didn't glance at the strippers or the patrons. She hauled ass toward the door and emerged in a deserted parking lot. Blade beeped the lock on an SUV, and they climbed in.

"They weren't sure she would wake up," she whispered.

"I know. This is good," Gavin said quietly.

"You think she remembers?" She closed her eyes. "I hope she doesn't."

"We'll see."

The SUV was silent as Blade drove to the hospital. Since this was Las Vegas, no one glanced twice at the stripper with three hippy companions as they walked through the halls.

"You should all get checked out," she said absently.

None of them responded or broke away from their group. The ICU nurse didn't miss a beat when they walked up to her counter.

"Has she spoken?" she asked urgently.

The woman's expression softened. "No. Let me take you to her." She glanced at Gavin, Blade, and Angel. "We don't want to overwhelm her."

Gavin nodded and squeezed her hand before he released her. She walked swiftly toward her mother's room. Her mother looked worse, if that was possible. As she approached, her mother's eyes opened. The color of her eyes didn't seem as vibrant as before, but she didn't care. Her mother was alive.

She took her mother's hand carefully in hers and kissed her scarred fingers. "Mom, it's me."

Her mother blinked slowly. There was no flash of recognition.

"It's Lyla," she said.

Her mother stared at her for a long moment. Her eyes were dull and lifeless.

"I'm sorry, Mom," she whispered.

Her mother closed her eyes, took a deep breath, and then opened them again. Her bruised lips formed a word. She leaned in close.

"What? What are you trying to say?"

Her mother said one word in a shaky whisper filled with pain. "Pat."

Her heart stalled in her chest. Her father. Her mother loved him more than life itself. Of course, his name would be the first one on her lips. She bowed her head and tried to think of what to say. Her mother made urgent noises as she tried to say his name again. Her insides rebelled. She couldn't look into her mother's eyes and admit what she'd done.

"Lyla."

Her mother sounded a little stronger but still racked with so much pain. Lyla raised her head. Her mother was watching her with tear-filled eyes.

"Pat," she said.

Lyla shook her head. Her mother closed her eyes and averted her face. Lyla ground her teeth against the slap of hurt. She hadn't even told her mother that she was the one that pulled the trigger.

"M-mom? Do you need water or—"

"Leave."

She opened her mouth to argue, but one glance at her mother's broken body made her obey. She kissed her mother's brow and walked out of the room.

"How is she?" Gavin asked.

She collided with his chest, and he hugged her tight. He kissed her temple.

"She's alive, Lyla. That's all that matters."

"She asked about Dad," she said against his chest.

"What did you say?"

"I just shook my head. I couldn't..."

"You did what you had to, Lyla."

"But he was my dad." She swallowed hard. "I can't tell her."

"She has a long recovery ahead of her. That's enough to deal with right now."

Gavin wrapped her securely against him. They stayed that way for a long minute. She thought of her father's last moments, the fallen men in the sandy pit, and her mother's uphill battle. The knowledge of what was to come weighed heavily on her shoulders.

"How are we going to do this?" she whispered.

"One day at a time."

She looked up at her husband and saw that despite all that occurred, he didn't look weary or uncertain. He was focused and ready to take on the world. He would never back down and would protect his own with his last breath.

"I love you," she whispered.

His eyes heated. He cupped her jaw and kissed her long and slow. She clutched at him and felt his lips curve against her mouth. He hauled her into his arms and walked out of the ICU.

"Gavin, what...?"

"We're exhausted, and I need to hold my daughter." His gaze slashed down to her. "We're spending the next week in bed. I don't give a fuck what comes up."

Angel snorted as he and Blade fell into step behind him.

"We'll do what we can for your mom, but I won't let you feel guilty for Pat's death. I would have done him in myself and made him suffer," he said as he stalked through empty hospital corridors. "We're alive, and that's all that matters. Vega's gone, along with most of those who have been conspiring against me for years. Fuck 'em."

He walked into the chilly night and deposited her into the back of the SUV while Blade and Angel slid into the front. He pulled her onto his lap so she straddled him. He looked at her, the only illumination that of passing streetlights.

He clasped her face between his hands and pressed his face to hers. "I love you." The words reverberated with fierce emotion, enough to make tears fall. "We've been through hell, baby girl. That's at an end. I'm going to give you the paradise I promised. Whatever you want, it's yours."

"And if I just want you?" she whispered.

He closed his eyes. "That goes without saying. God, you're a fucking miracle."

She brushed kisses over his face and rocked against him. She felt him harden beneath her. She didn't give a shit that Blade and Angel were less than a foot away.

Life was fleeting and fragile. She didn't want to think about tomorrow. She wanted to live in the present, and right now, her husband was staring at her as if she was his reason for being. She took that in and let it wash away the guilt, rage, and lingering fear.

It was done.

When they pulled up to the house Angel and Blade stayed outside to talk to the hovering security. Gavin led her inside. They made their way upstairs to the nursery.

Carmen was nowhere in sight, but Nora was sleeping peacefully in her crib, arms over her head as if she was rocking out at a concert. Gavin gathered Nora in his arms and carried her to their bedroom. She sprawled on the bed as he sat with his back against the headboard. She rested her head on his thigh and stared at her family. As images of the night slid through her mind, she held on tight.

"It's over," she whispered.

"Yes."

"We're safe."

"Yes."

She looked up. "And you're out of the underworld?"

"For the most part, yes. Angel's the new crime lord."

She nodded, but she didn't believe him. Once a crime lord, always a crime lord. The underworld would always be on the periphery of their lives. As Gavin stroked his finger down Nora's cheek, a shaft of warmth pushed away her dark thoughts.

Sadist was dead, her mother would live, and everyone she loved was breathing. Gavin was holding Nora, who had no idea what kind of world she had been born into. They would move on and live their happily ever after... right?

AUTHOR'S NOTE

Hi All,

I hope you enjoyed the first 3 installments of the Crime Lord Series! I originally intended for this to be a two book series and now I don't see an end in sight! A lot of people have asked if there will be a prequel for Gavin and Lyla... I'm playing around with the idea. I promise they will be featured in future books.

The next book in the series is *Awakened by Sin*, which is Carmen's story! Sneak peek at end of book!

Love,

Mia

P. S. At the end of each book, I offer a bonus scene. To have a link for all 3 scenes sent to your inbox, join my email list: https://www. subscribepage.com/CLSbundlebonus.

BOOKS BY MIA KNIGHT

Crime Lord Series:

Crime Lord's Captive

Recaptured by the Crime Lord

Once A Crime Lord

Awakened by Sin

Crime Lord's Paradise

Singed Series:

Bitter Heat

Bitter Secrets

Bitter Confessions

ABOUT THE AUTHOR

Mia Knight is the author of the Crime Lord and Singed Series. She writes dark, contemporary romances that make you question your beliefs and leave you feeling drained and emotionally bereft. If you like your men dark with questionable morals and a possessive edge, you've come to the right place.

When Mia isn't writing, she's most likely on a road trip. She loves coffee, daydreaming, and the sound of rain storms. She is constantly shadowed by her dogs who don't judge her when she laughs and cries with the voices in her head. Mia's also a notorious hermit so please be patient if she doesn't get back to you promptly.

Website: https://miaknight.com/
Newsletter: https://www.subscribepage.com/MKNewReleases

goodreads.com/authormiaknight

bookbub.com/profile/mia-knight

instagram.com/authormiaknight

facebook.com/miaknightauthor

patreon.com/MiaKnightWrites

reamstories.com/miaknightwrites

SNEAK PEEK

AWAKENED BY SIN, BOOK 4

Seven Months Ago

From her vantage point in the VIP section, Carmen Pyre took in Incognito, the newest nightclub to open on the infamous Strip. The grand sweeping staircase and elegant chandeliers gave the club an upper-class feel, but the staff's uniform of leather and lace put off any notions that this was a run-of-the-mill club. An unholy crimson light set the mood and transformed the club into a decadent hell that encouraged them to indulge in their darkest fantasies. The atmosphere reeked of mystery and carnal delights, but she felt none of it.

Her nails dug into her leather clad thighs. It felt as if someone had picked up the blueprint for the dream house she planned with her late husband and invited her to do a walk-through without warning her beforehand. Every detail was achingly familiar. She could feel it, those fucking tears just beneath the surface. The night she came up with the concept for Incognito played out in her mind in vivid detail. She'd always had a thing for costumes and role playing. One night while 'serving' Vinny as a flight attendant, she came up with the idea of a club that would take advantage of the "What happens in Vegas, stays in Vegas" slogan by helping people conceal their identities. Incognito was her husband's last project, one he never got to see completed before he was murdered.

You look beautiful, baby.

Her body locked as Vinny's familiar, reassuring voice drifted through her mind. She hung her head as memories cascaded through her. She spent a year and a half trying to outrun memories of her husband. Now that she was back in Vegas, there was no escaping him. He was stamped into every square inch of this place. His voice whispered in her ears, stirring up a flurry of pain and loss that caused her chest to contract. She had been looking forward to attending this event, to let loose and forget her troubles. The Strip was her playground, an environment she had thrived in since she was sixteen. She'd hoped to be invigorated by the manic energy from the crowd, not be reminded of everything she had lost.

A striking couple made their way in her direction, distracting her from her inner turmoil. The woman had honey blond hair, a slinky black halter dress, and a black lace mask with diamonds highlighting silver blue eyes. The man at her side was built like a linebacker and wore a dashing tux and black mask that made him seem even more dangerous than normal.

Lyla's eyes lit up as she rushed forward with a big smile. "You look great!"

She hugged her cousin like a child in desperate need of reassurance. Lyla was the sister she never had and a beacon of hope in her otherwise dreary world. It had only been a few hours since they parted ways, but she wouldn't take anything for granted, not anymore. She pulled back and felt her pain recede as she took in Lyla's sparkling eyes. Her cousin was happy. No one would guess she'd been viciously attacked by a psychotic killer or that the high-necked gown she wore covered gruesome scars. The image of Lyla lying lifelessly in a hospital bed was etched in her memory for all time.

She dredged up a smile as she gave Lyla's ass a sharp smack. "You too."

She switched her gaze to Lyla's husband, Gavin Pyre. The CEO of Pyre Casinos and former crime lord of Las Vegas glowered at her. She had known Gavin for nearly a decade, long enough to see the good, bad, and downright evil in him. He was on her shit list, despite Lyla's reassurances that her new husband wasn't abusing her. Four months ago, Gavin showed up in Montana and forced Lyla to marry him by threatening her life. She still hadn't forgiven him for that.

Vinny's murder kicked off a series of bloody events, which left Uncle Manny dead, Lyla mutilated, and Gavin in prison. She spirited Lyla out of Las Vegas during this tumultuous time and went on the road. For a year and a half, they pounded the pavement only for their adventure to end abruptly when Gavin and his goons showed up. Not only was she a witness to Lyla's forced marriage, Gavin came bearing even more bad news—her father had died from a heart attack. They returned to Las Vegas in time for the funeral. She hadn't recovered from Vinny's death and now had to cope with another staggering loss.

"Carmen," he said tersely.

She gave him a cool look. "Gavin."

"Don't get into trouble tonight."

Her temper, which had begun a slow burn the second she saw him, ignited. "Excuse me?"

"You look like—"

Lyla clapped a hand over her husband's mouth. "You look hot, and you're going to cause a commotion. He's nervous."

She flipped her hair and adjusted her boobs in her lace bustier. "He should be." There was a two-inch gap between her top and the skintight leather pants. A glance in the mirror before she left the house told her that she looked sexy, confident, and in control. No one would see beneath the slutty exterior to her shredded insides. The white mask she'd been handed when she entered the club was the perfect finishing touch for her outfit.

Gavin yanked Lyla's hand from his mouth. "I just want to get through tonight without drama. Got me?"

His orders never failed to get on her nerves. Vinny had always deferred to him. How Lyla put up with his autocratic ass, she would never know. The only way she could handle him was to view him as an overbearing big brother. And like any sibling would, she did her best to antagonize the hell out of him.

"I'm not making any promises," she said.

Available on all retailers!